THE
CURSE
AND THE
KING

CHARLENE RALPH

CLAY BRIDGES
PRESS

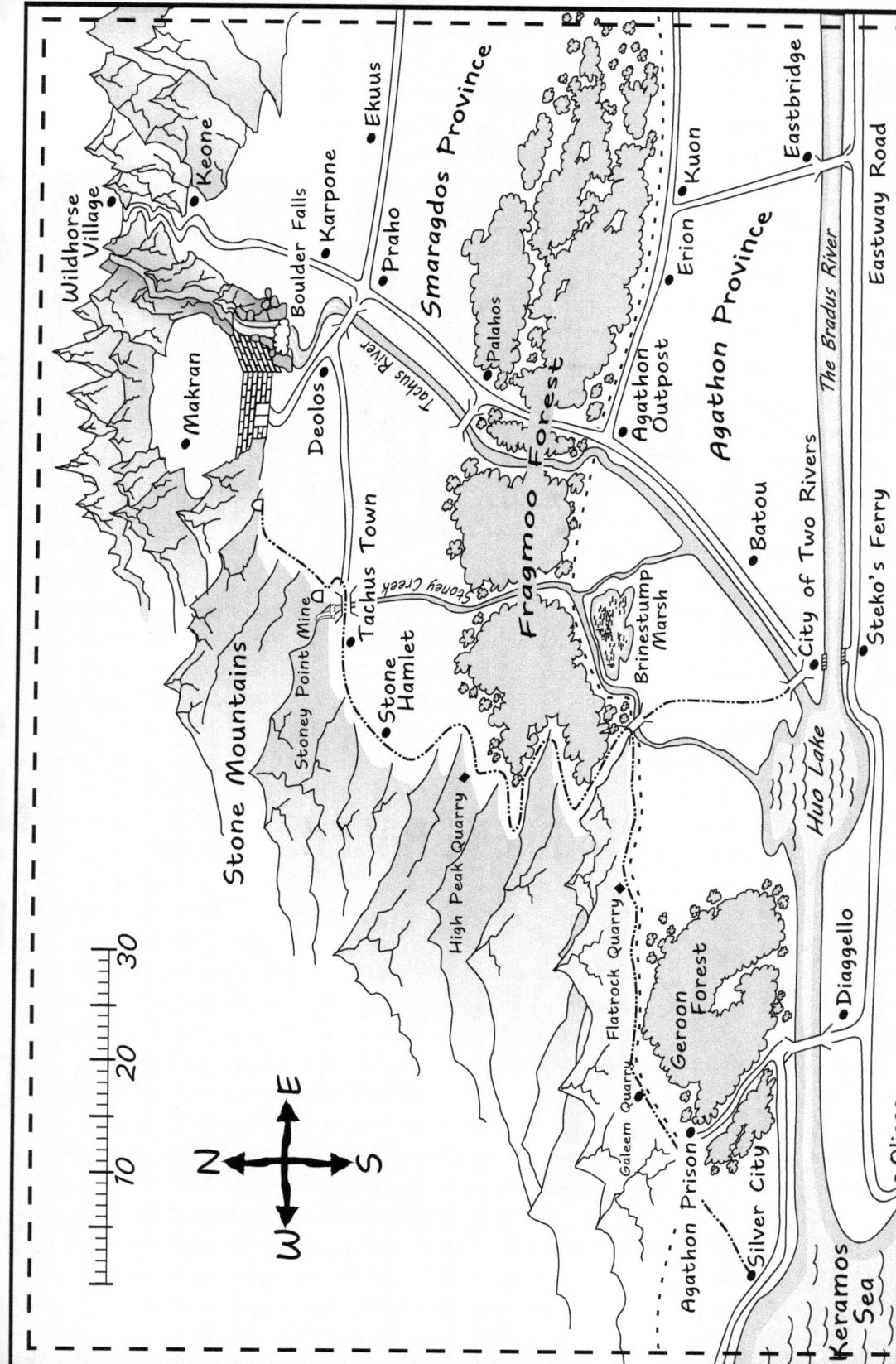

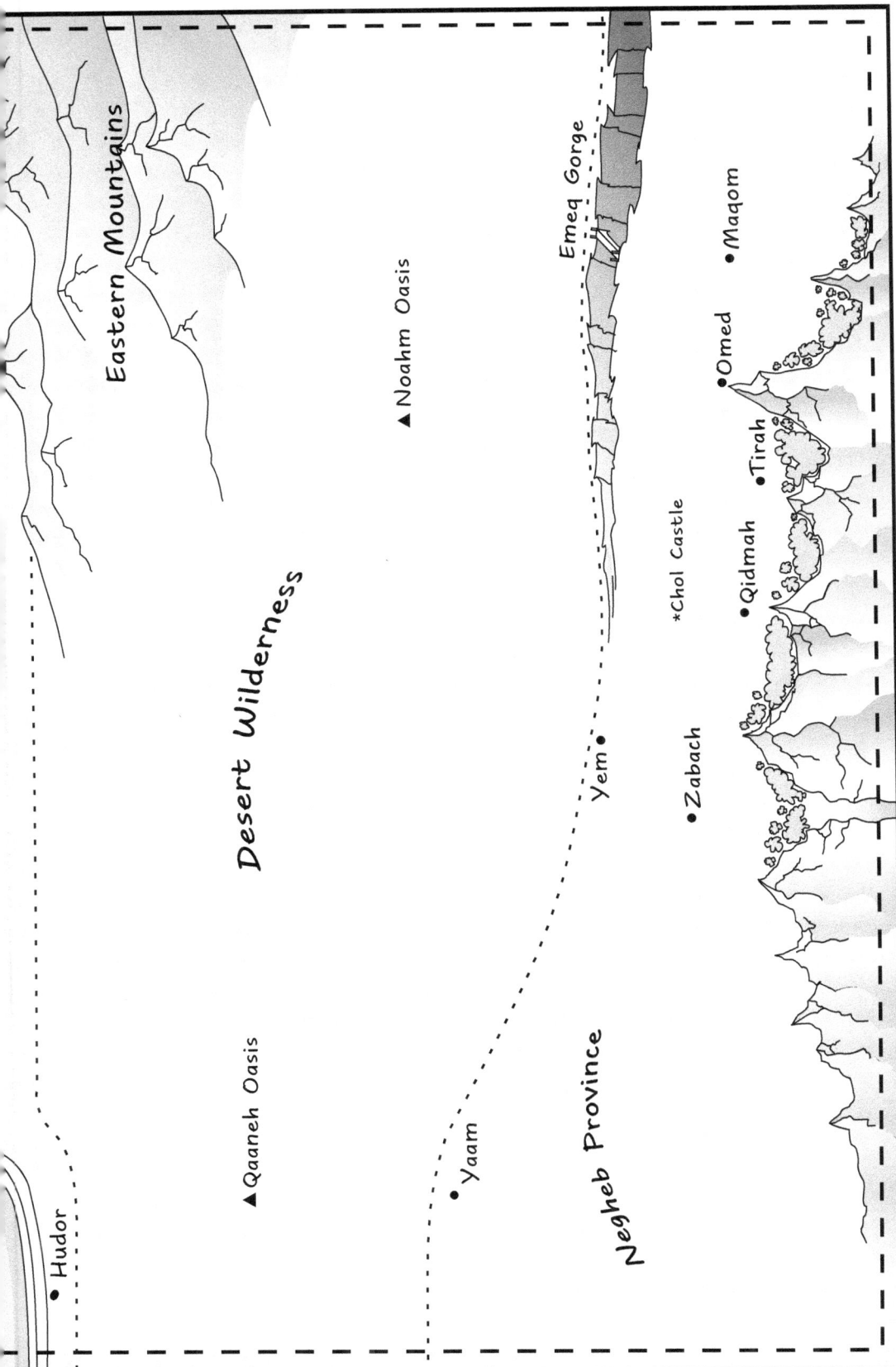

·——❦ One ❦——·

The day dawned gray and rainy, but that had been the case for what seemed like weeks to the young man who looked out a narrow prison cell window.

"At least it's no better out there," he thought, trying to feel cheerful, but as he sat down on an iron-framed bed, he hung his head gloomily. His long sandy brown hair fell down around his face, and tears formed in his eyes. He always hoped a new day would make him feel better, but the incessant rain and cold had brought him to the lowest point of his life. Years had passed in that lifeless stone and mortared cell, with the tall narrow window letting in precious little light. He kept to himself as much as he could, fearing the cold-hearted guards and the other prisoners, most of whom seemed to be looking for a fight.

1

The raucous call for breakfast came, and one by one the doors were opened, and the prisoners hustled along a dimly lit tunnel. They came to a long flight of stairs and were joined by other prisoners as they descended past the lower levels, part of an ancient military fortress that had been built into the side of the mountain.

"Come on, Crow, you vermin," growled one of the hideous guards brandishing his spear, "Step quick or yer gonna feel the butt end of this in yer back again!"

Soon they were all down in a large hall, in a line receiving bowls of sour porridge and taking their seats at various heavy wooden tables. There were about a hundred prisoners, dirty and uncouth, shoving and pushing to sit where they wanted. Crow always stood to the side until almost everyone was seated, trying to keep out of trouble, but today he was not so lucky.

"Always waitin' for everbody else!" snarled a particularly ill-tempered prisoner. "What 'er you, better'n us?" The man, who was big and bear-like with tangled hair and a thick black beard, stepped toward Crow, who kept his eyes down and shrank away.

"Answer me, boy!" bellowed the man.

Suddenly, Crow was struck with a vivid memory from long ago. He was kneeling in the sand by the sea, holding his hand flat on a rough wooden table. All he could see was the sun shining brightly on the sea and for some reason, he was terrified to move. Suddenly, a huge black shadow blocked the sun, and a horrible voice pierced through his thoughts.

"Answer me, *boy!*" As the flat of a short sword came down across his knuckles, the pain made his head reel, but the voice cut through the pain.

"Har!" yelled the man. "Now maybe you'll keep them fingers out of me money bag! Next time, I'll cut 'em off!" The boy breathed in sharply, fiercely, and screamed, "No! No! No more!" He sprang to his feet, and the man's dark face suddenly twisted into an angry mass of surprise.

The man yelled out in a drunken stupor, raised the sword and swung, but the boy ducked under it as it passed within an inch of his head. The man lunged toward him, but fell sideways, losing his grip on the sword. In an instant, the boy had the sword in his hand, but he jumped back, terrified.

The man hefted himself to his feet and let out a maniacal laugh, with his eyes fixed on the boy in a deadly stare. "Go on, boy; you keep the sword. I'll kill you with me bare hands!" The boy fixated on his cruel, calloused hands and could only stand there trembling.

"Well, come on, boy; kill me before I kill you," laughed the man, who suddenly took a step forward. The boy skittered backward in a panic, forgetting the sword as it swung limply in his hand.

"They don't pay me enough to keep puttin' up with you," yelled the man, as his eyes turned black with murder. He lunged at the boy, who stumbled backward and fell over something behind him, and then everything went black.

As he came to, he found himself half underneath the man who was lying there, unmoving, with sand stuck to one side of his ugly, sweaty face. The boy struggled out and got to his feet, trembling and weak. His thoughts and feelings were a maelstrom, and he grimaced in horror when he saw the sand staining dark with blood.

He heard voices yelling behind him, down on the beach. They had seen what happened. He turned to run, but his legs buckled. Fear choked him to silence as the angry cries rang out louder and closer behind him. Tears filled his eyes but suddenly, his horse was there, and he leaped upon him and buried his face in his mane as he sprang away and ran like the wind.

Crow was jolted out of his memory by a cuff to the side of his head, but an older man with graying hair stepped to his side, "Now, Dob, leave the boy alone, he ain't doin' no harm."

That seemed enough to dissuade the ill-tempered man, who just grumbled and took his seat at a nearby table. Crow nodded in thanks at the old man and then sat at the end of a table, staring into his bowl of food. It seemed that it had been years since he had thought of his life back then, or even of his horse, Zeo. Crow imagined him—big, black, and gleaming like an onyx stone. His memories were vivid, and tears formed in his eyes as he wondered where his horse was or if he was even still alive.

"Hey, son, you better get to eatin'," said the old man who had sat down next to him, "Or you'll be goin' without." Crow downed his food quickly, barely tasting it, though there was little good to taste in it.

The following weeks were the most painful of Crow's life, as he thought more and more about his other life and beloved horse. It seemed that things couldn't get any worse for him, but one day, the dawn did not come. He heard thunder in the distance and stayed in his bed, pulling his blanket closer around him. Suddenly, lightning split across the sky and lit up the walls like daylight. Seconds later, a tremendous crack of thunder seemed to shake the whole mountain as his cell floor quaked beneath him. Rain began pelting down in huge drops outside as the wind howled and whistled through his narrow window. Crow was unnerved, and a cold fear gripped him as the storm descended with a palpable fury. It rocked the whole mountain, sending mortar and stone crashing to the floor. The lightning cut through the pitch darkness, slashing Crow's senses as the deafening thunder pummeled him to the floor. The shrieking voice of the wind made his head reel as he clutched his ears. Everything was falling down around him, and the outer wall cracked and fell away, dragging half the floor with it. He leaped backward, against the door, but the sheer terror of it all seized his consciousness and wrenched it from him. He clawed at thin air as everything surged together into a swirling mass of destruction, and then all went black.

Crow came to with a start and found himself on the floor. His head hurt as he sat up, squinting and bewildered. He wondered how the sun could be so bright and hot in his cell. As his senses cleared, he opened his eyes wide in horror and saw a terrible scene of destruction. The whole prison was just a mass of rubble, broken up and fallen like a landslide down to the foot of the mountain. All that was left of Crow's cell was part of the floor, jutting out like a shelf, with a precipitous fall on three sides. His precarious position caused him to panic, but a greater fear of falling over the edge cemented him to his place. As he sat there gathering himself, Crow's thoughts came together; he was trapped on the edge of the mountain, high above the land below.

But the wooden door to his cell still stood, and he hoped with all his might that it would be a way out. He carefully got to his feet and stepped to the door, but a twinge of vertigo made him stumble and fall against it. He grabbed onto the handle to steady himself and found that the door moved freely, but it creaked so loudly that he nearly jumped out of his skin as he realized how eerily silent the whole place was. He pulled the door open, but as he looked into the passageway, he became shackled by a terrible fear of the dark. He wondered about the other prisoners and imagined that there were other things hiding in the darkness as well.

"Is someone there?" he whispered, but his voice was too low for anyone or anything to hear him. Anxiety held him fast, and he slowly sat down in the comfort of the sunlight. Tears came and as time wore on, he began to feel hunger and thirst. Eventually, the sun began to descend, and it suddenly struck him that he would not want to be where he was when night fell. Desperation unceremoniously pushed him into the passageway. He stood silent and still for a few minutes and then began to carefully feel his way along, fearing there would be a sheer drop-off or that the tunnel would cave in at any moment. This sent his mind racing as he panicked, overwhelmed with the desire to get out.

His head reeled, but he suddenly saw a thin strip of dull red light down below. He continued carefully down, having to climb over fallen bricks and stones and piles of rubble. As he reached the bottom, he gasped for breath, realizing that he had stopped breathing at some point. Crow crept silently to the door, listening carefully, but all was silent. As he tried the handle, it made a horribly loud clank, and he froze, listening breathlessly, but there was still only silence.

He felt that the door would open and when he pushed it just enough to peek out, he saw a large guard room with a table and chairs, a few cots, and a fire pit. He thought it strange that it wasn't all destroyed. The unnatural silence was broken only by the sound of buzzing flies. Crow stepped into the room to see a half-eaten meal on the table. He left the meat to the flies, but wolfed down the cheese and the bread, which seemed a few days old. He disliked ale, but that was all there was to drink, so he gulped down a half-empty flagon, trying not to taste it, and finished with a grimace. He stepped to the side of the doorway that opened into the yard and looked out warily. There was not a soul in sight, nor a sound to be heard, but he still moved quickly to the cover of what was left of the warden's building. The prison wall continued from it unbroken to the front gate, which still stood and was open. Crow crept along and came to it, looking out past the huge stone and mortar column that anchored it.

The grass was lush and green beyond it, giving way to a golden field of taller grass gently moving with the breeze. Crow's fear was suddenly displaced with a realization that he was on the verge of freedom. Hope filled him more sweetly than a full-course meal would have at that moment. As he looked out past the gate, he saw that the road from the prison went across an open field and then into a dense forest. Feeling like he was taking his life in his hands and trembling with fear, he started quickly down the road. He glanced this way and that, but quickly broke into a run until he was in the cover of the forest. It was damp and cool. Most of the trees were pine, interspersed with yellow poplar and hedge-apple trees. There was little underbrush as most of the ground was covered with pine needles. As he looked back at the mountains, painted orange and red with the fading light of the sun, a smile spread across his face, something that was as foreign to him as feeling the earth beneath his feet. A rumble of thunder turned him back toward the forest, and it suddenly seemed much less safe than it had only a few minutes before.

Crow started quickly down the road, which was smooth and hard-packed from the passage of many wagons. He went on for a little while, but his hunger and thirst had returned, and he began looking for water or the sound of a stream.

Suddenly, his thoughts were shattered by the sound of hooves on the road ahead of him. He froze but could only see for a hundred feet or so before the road gradually bent left into the trees. Another crash of thunder shook him as he bounded into the forest and found nowhere to hide except up in the trees. It was the beginning of the summer season, and the trees were full of leaves, so he climbed up into the thick foliage and waited, listening breathlessly. The horse was coming closer, but Crow was startled by something moving in the sparse underbrush behind him. He turned but couldn't see anything. The horse had stopped. He listened harder. Nothing. He breathed out slowly but stopped short as he heard a short whistle behind him on the road. He started and nearly fell, causing a few bits of branch and bark to fall to the ground with a deafening crash. He sat like a stone as he heard something creeping slowly toward the tree, and fear struck him like an icy knife in his stomach. He looked down and saw glowing eyes, glinting with deadly intent. It stood stock-still, a low growl deep within it. It was a wolf, black as night and bigger than any Crow had ever seen. Suddenly, a woman appeared behind it and followed its gaze right up to Crow. He felt like he'd been pierced through as he caught his breath.

"Who are you, and why do you hide?" she asked in a loud, commanding voice. It sounded like a thunderclap after all the silence. Fear still gripped Crow, and he could not speak.

"What say you?" asked the woman who had long black wavy hair and a dark complexion. She was slim and shapely, wearing a white linen shirt, brown breeches, and black boots. A short sword in an ornate red scabbard hung at her side.

"Hi ho! Is there something amiss with you, man?" she yelled.

Crow blurted out, "Uh . . . no."

"Why do you hide?"

"I . . . uh" was all that Crow could muster. It seemed like he hardly knew how to talk anymore.

Perturbed, the woman said to the wolf, "He seems a harmless fool. Come."

And she started back toward the road.

As she passed out of sight into the trees, Crow called out, "Wait!"

She stopped and said, "And what, my kind sir, shall I wait for?"

"Well, uh . . . do you have anything to drink?" he blurted.

Frustrated, she came back, looked up at him and said, "What, indeed, is wrong with you?"

"Uh, nothing . . . I, well . . . I am very thirsty," he said.

She paused and then asked, "Where are you from?"

"I . . . uh . . ." was all he could say, not wanting to make known to her that he was an escaped prisoner.

She shook her head and said, "Look at you. Your clothes are rags; you have no provisions or weapon of any sort. I have never seen anyone more unprepared to be where they are. I should love to hear how you have got yourself into this predicament, but I must find a place to camp before the rain comes."

She turned to walk away, but his question stopped her, "What about that . . . wolf?"

She called the wolf's name and said something he could not hear. "It is safe now," she said and started toward the road.

He sat remembering those glowing eyes, but his thirst jolted him into action and after looking around for the wolf, he dropped to the ground. He stood still listening for big, black wolf paw sounds, but heard none. The horse whinnied softly, and the saddle creaked as the woman started riding away. Crow came out to the road, but the wolf was nowhere in sight.

He caught up to the woman, who turned toward him and asked, "Do you know of a suitable place to camp?"

"Well, no," he said, glancing about for the wolf again.

"I am not surprised. You seem to know little of anything. I only ventured to ask because I have not traveled this way before. I suppose you have no knowledge of the land toward the north either."

"Well, that is true. I have . . . I have not seen the lands that way, except from . . . high up and far away."

She knitted her brow and pursed her lips and then asked, "Have you just fallen out of the sky, or have you been flying with the eagles?"

He did not know how to reply, and as thunder again rumbled in the distance, she abruptly said, "I have no more time for this."

She spurred her horse forward, and Crow trotted to keep up. "This road .

. . it leads up to a prison," he said.

She suddenly checked her horse to a stop, and Crow stumbled past a few paces. She crossed her arms and sat back in her saddle, staring straight at him causing him to quickly look away.

"A prison? I thought you did not know anything?"

"Well, I . . . I came from there," he said without thinking.

The woman, becoming annoyed, asked, "What do you mean, 'You came from there'?"

He began to speak, but she interrupted, "From Agathon Prison?"

"It . . . the prison is just rubble . . . now."

Her agitation increased as she asked, "How is that possible?"

Meanwhile, a breeze had kicked up bringing much cooler air and the smell of rain. "I must be on my way," she said curtly. "I expected to be where I was going by now and do not wish to get wet."

Suddenly, her demeanor softened, and she said, "I am sorry. I am a bit weary and hungry." She looked at Crow and shook her head slightly and asked, "Where are you going?"

He just shook his head and said, "The prison could give you shelter."

He stood there looking at a loss, and the woman said, "But you said that it is destroyed."

"Not all."

"How far is it?" she asked. "Quickly. The rain is coming behind us."

"A few miles—" began Crow, but she said, "Come, you must ride with me, or we shall get wet." Crow froze, speechless and unable to comprehend even the thought of being so near her.

Time seemed to stop, and the next thing he heard was, "Well, do as you will."

Crow stood there, wondering what to do, but as the woman passed out of sight, he suddenly felt more alone than he ever had in his life. He was like a statue in the middle of the road, immobilized with doubt and shame.

When the rain started coming down in big pelting drops, it jolted Crow out of his muddled indecision. By the time he arrived back at the prison, he was soaking wet and shivering in the cool night air. He stopped at the gate post and saw a warm light flickering in the guard house, but again, indecision rooted him to the ground. As the rain came down harder and the wind began gusting, the thought of a warm fire and maybe something to eat finally prodded him across the yard. The door was slightly ajar, and he knocked on it and then pushed it inward.

"Oh," said the woman as she turned toward him, "I had nearly given up on you."

Many thoughts flooded Crow's mind, but he could not put any of them into words and only moved over to the fire.

"You must be cold . . . and still hungry," said the woman, motioning to the table. "I found all of this in the other building out there."

Crow took a loaf and some cheese and returned to standing near the fire. The woman was unpacking some of her belongings and asked, "What is your name?"

He began to speak, but then stopped, and the woman smirked, "I suppose, since you are an escaped prisoner that you should not tell a stranger your real name." She looked at him, but he stood unspeaking.

"Well, *my* real name is Makarios," she said with a laugh.

Tears came to his eyes as thoughts of his childhood washed over him. "When I was young, the other children . . . ," he said trying to compose himself, ". . . they mocked because I was thin, calling me scarecrow . . . and then just Crow."

He winced and stared into the fire, "But Nikos is my true name." He hadn't thought of it in as long as he could remember, and it sounded foreign to him.

She sat looking into the fire as he ate, and after a while she said, "This is all so strange here, with the prison destroyed like this. Were there no others who survived?"

Nikos told her all he knew and as he finished, she said in a serious tone, "Some say that the storm was an omen—"

Nikos looked at her quickly and asked timidly, "Of . . . what?"

"Well, I do not believe in such things," she said abruptly and began stoking the fire. He stood there thinking about omens and began to feel uneasy but kept his thoughts to himself.

Makarios said, "Your clothes . . . they look like you have worn them for years . . . and no shoes. You were in prison a long time?"

Nikos suddenly thought of how he used to live by the sea and that he was almost always in the sand and never even had any shoes. His thoughts carried him so far away that he didn't even reply to her.

Makarios, who was somewhat annoyed by his lack of response, continued, "So, I am wondering, why were you in prison . . . what was your crime?"

Immediately, he felt an agonizing pain of guilt and then the shame and horror of what had happened. He put his face in his hands and only hissed through his teeth as his hands tightened into fists. He sat down heavily in the chair at the table, and eventually he spoke, but in a voice that did not seem his own, "I killed a man."

Makarios sat unmoving, but also unbelieving, "You are no murderer."

"I should have just run away!" he cried as tears filled his eyes.

"Nikos, you are not a criminal. Tell me what happened if you are able."

But he just shook his head and sat in silence. After a good long while, he began to feel that it would be a relief to talk about it and said in a subdued tone, "I never knew my mother or father. I do not know what happened to them. I lived with a man named Kakos who was not even a relative. He was cruel to me and drank too much wine."

He recounted the story until the fire had died down to embers and it was nearly dark in the room. He was exhausted and as he lay down on one of the cots.

Makarios moved to the other and then spoke into the dark, "You must give up blaming yourself," she said quietly. "You were defending your life."

Since that day, Nikos had thought of himself as a murderer, and the weight of the guilt was so heavy on him that he couldn't think of himself any other way.

"You should never have been imprisoned," she continued. "But now you are free, so it is as it should be."

Nikos's mind filled with conflicting thoughts and feelings, but he could put none of them into words. Sleep came slowly to him.

Nikos awoke midmorning and saw that the door was open and Makarios's belongings were gone. He jumped up, desperately hoping that she had not left, but stopped short at the door, suddenly filled with feelings he had never felt before. He saw Makarios across the yard saddling her horse, and his heart welled up in a way that really frightened him. In a panic, he looked away, with his eyes landing on her horse. He was big, thick and chestnut brown with a black mane and tail, white blaze, and four white socks with long, fluffy hair around his lower legs.

Suddenly, he thought: *"My horse! I must find him! Is Zeo truly out there somewhere? Where could he be? Does someone own him? Or is he living free and wild?"*

He was shaken out of his thoughts by a voice, "Will you stand in the doorway all day?" His attention jerked toward Makarios, but the wolf, who was lying near the wall, caught his eye. He was not as big as he had looked the night before, nor was his fur black, but a dark gray with silver tips. His gaze was riveted on Nikos.

"You need not fear him," said Makarios as she finished cinching up her saddle.

Nikos stepped out and came toward her, but the wolf only watched him and did not move.

Makarios took her horse's big head in her hands, kissed his nose and then turned to Nikos. "Well, I must be on my way," she said smiling and swung up into the saddle.

Nikos stood there feeling useless and wondered what was going to happen. He wanted to stay with her more than he had ever wanted anything in his life, though he was uselessly trying to ignore it.

"What will you do?" she asked, but he only shook his head and looked distraught. Makarios felt a twinge of annoyance and reined her horse around, causing her wolf to leap up and come to her side.

Nikos stepped back and in a fit of desperation blurted out, "I . . . I . . . don't know. Until yesterday, I had not talked to anyone in what seems like a whole lifetime, and well, when you . . ."

He trailed off suddenly feeling quite self-conscious. As she sat waiting for him to finish, he felt trapped, which scared him more than just telling her what he was thinking, so he said, "When you smiled before, I thought to myself that I had never seen anything more beautiful in my whole life."

Makarios was quite taken aback and unprepared for his directness and blurted out, "You think I am beautiful?" She unexpectedly felt awkward, her eyes stinging with emotion.

And Nikos stood there stiffly, wishing that the earth would swallow him up.

"It matters not," she said regaining her composure. "I must be on my way!"

But a courage came into Nikos, and he said zealously, "What do you mean, 'It matters not'? It does matter. *You* matter!"

Makarios reined her horse back a few steps as the wolf circled about, his eyes locked on Nikos as she said stiffly, "I . . . I must be on my way. Follow the road through the forest, and you will come to an inn. It is many miles. Farewell."

She pulled a small bag from her pack and tossed it to him and then spoke to her horse, who bounded away across the yard in a moment and then turned north, disappearing over a hill. Nikos again stood in her wake like a statue, but this time he felt like one as his emotion set like stone. After a while, he walked to the gate and stood there looking after Makarios, but all he saw was an empty world. Soon his attention turned to the small bag she had given him, and he found in it a fair number of silver coins. He felt immense gratitude as he thought about how no one had ever given him anything that he hadn't worked hard for and even then, he never got all that he deserved. He pondered that for a good long while and again began to feel something he had never felt before—something he couldn't understand.

He longed after Makarios, but the cruel voice of his foster father shattered his thoughts, *"Wishin' don't make it come true!"*

Discouragement suddenly took hold of Nikos, and he quickly turned away toward the forest road. After a few moments he scowled and thought fiercely, *"Someday, it will!"*

As the sun rose higher, the forest began to lighten, but the cooler temperature within the shade of the trees remained. Nikos thought about finding his horse, and this brought him a sense of hope. He walked for a good while and began to get thirsty; soon, he began hearing the trickle of running water. It was away on his left and didn't sound too far away, but the forest got darker the farther in he looked. He hesitated for a bit, but his thirst moved him as he thought, *"I can keep the road in sight."*

The underbrush was sparse, and the going was easy and with the ascending sun, the light was good. Nikos breathed in deeply and, except for wishing that he was still with Makarios, he felt happier than he ever had in his life.

It wasn't long before the terrain of the forest changed from flat ground and pine needles to darker earth with mossy boulders. There began to be more logs and a thorny kind of underbrush with the ground sloping down underneath trees that were bigger and older looking. Nikos looked back and could still see the line of the road, and although the stream beckoned as if it was just over the next rise, it didn't seem to be getting any closer. He stopped, undecided about continuing, but he suddenly felt a strange sense of adventure run through him and thought, *"No matter, I will eventually get somewhere."* He began descending a slope, leaving the road behind.

Not much was alive in the forest, except the trees, so it was very quiet. After he had walked a good long way, he still had not come to the stream, and he started wondering if it was real. The ground was falling away more steeply on his right, and he had to watch his footing among slippery rotting logs and rocks that were slick with moisture. The going became more difficult, with the rocks becoming more numerous and sometimes jumbled together, gripped in the roots of huge trees. Nikos's sense of adventure was fading into apprehension as he looked about himself, listening for the sound of the stream, but there was only silence. The trees were strange looking and seemed dead except for the canopy of gray-green leaves far overhead. Nikos looked deeper into the forest and felt that there were things in there that he did not want to meet. As he was wondering what to do, he suddenly had the overwhelming sense that something was right behind him, and he stiffened in horror. He spun around, but there was nothing there. Looking closer at his surroundings, his attention was taken by a very odd-looking boulder with strange- looking moss on top of it. Suddenly, it moved, and a cry of fear rose in Nikos's throat, but utter terror choked it into silence.

He stumbled backward in a panic and fell, incredulous of what he was seeing. The boulder uncurled somehow and rose up. It had what looked like arms and legs and a face with moss that hung down around it like hair. It towered over him, at least nine feet tall. He stared in disbelief as its eyes opened, and its great stony face spoke, "What are ya doon here?"

Its voice was gravelly and booming. Nikos was speechless; all he could do was stare at the thing, shaking in terror. It took a step toward him, and the ground shook. Nikos thought it was going to crush him into the ground. But suddenly, it squatted down in front of him and put its hands on its knees, looking right at him with its forehead all jumbled up in a questioning sort of way.

"Can ya talk?" It leaned closer, peering at Nikos, and then it raised one of its huge arms. Nikos was frozen with fear as its thick finger came within inches of him, but it only gave him a light poke in the side.

"What's the matter wit ya?" It poked him again, a little harder, but Nikos only sputtered. It sat back with its palms on the top of its knees and elbows sticking out with its head cocked to one side.

Nikos's fear was subsiding as he could see that this thing did not intend to hurt him. Its childlikeness made it seem harmless, but it was very thickly muscled and possessed tremendous strength. Nikos could also see that his fear had exaggerated the thing's appearance. As he looked more closely, it was somewhat like a man and not nine feet tall, but only about seven. He took a deep breath and hitched his way up to a sitting position against a tree behind him.

The thing just kept looking at him as Nikos spoke in a weak voice, "Have you not seen a human being before?"

Its forehead piled up into a giant question, "What's a yoomin bean?" it asked.

"Well, people . . . uh . . . men."

It raised its eyebrows in recognition and said, "Men, yes, mmm hmm, yer a man,"

Its face cracked into a big smile, but then tumbled down into a big frown as it looked away and said, "But not like other men, bad men,"

It turned its gaze back to him and said, "Why are ya different?"

Nikos felt that he had the upper hand somehow and was less afraid. "Well, what do you mean, different?" he asked.

"Yer were nice to Polus." It seemed to remember some pain, but its attention quickly focused on him again.

"Is Polus your name?"

"Polus is Polus" he said. "What's yer name?"

"I am Nikos."

A silence followed, and after a few moments Nikos said, "Are you a . . . a . . . man?"

Polus got a sad, faraway look in his eyes and said, "Polus is all wrong. He's not right. He grew all wrong."

Nikos got up to his knees and peered up at him. "You are a human being?" he asked skeptically.

Polus looked at him, and a great tear welled up in his eye and cascaded down his face. "Polus is all wrong; they made him go away . . ."

Another tear fell, dropping to the ground. He turned half away from him and hid his face; his great shoulders were shaking, but he made no sound. After a few minutes, he took a big sniffly breath and wiped his huge arm roughly across his face. He paused and took another breath before turning back around.

Nikos sat still just looking at him, feeling sad for the creature.

Polus stared vacantly at his feet for a while and then rolled his big eyes up to meet Nikos's eyes.

"Why is yer differnt?" He seemed truly in a quandary as if a human being couldn't be anything but bad. His eyes opened just a little wider as he looked at Nikos expectantly.

Nikos pressed his lips together and very slightly shook his head, "Hmm, well, I don't know . . ."

"Why dint yer want Polus to go away from you, like all men?"

He thought a moment, "Well, I kind of like you . . . ," said Nikos.

But Polus suddenly froze, his mouth agape; his eyebrows rose, and his eyes opened wider. Nikos could see his mind working furiously.

"But . . ." he said and seemed to work hard to get his thoughts in order. When he spoke, it sounded as if he were reciting something. "But Polus is dumb and ugly and worthless. Polus should go away and never come back . . ."

His face twisted into such a display of rage that Nikos pressed back against the tree in mortal fear. Polus's hands clenched into fists, but Nikos saw that he was looking past him, as if at some unseen person that he was remembering.

Nikos sat up again and at his movement, Polus quickly looked down at him. Immediately, the anger on his big face dissolved into a plaintive kind of hope, and he said, "Yer dint want Polus ta go away?"

Nikos spoke emphatically, "No."

Polus sat back heavily on the ground so that it shook. He was dumbfounded as his mind worked back and forth, trying to make sense of things. As he sat there, Nikos wondered what kind of a being Polus was, since there was much about him that didn't seem to be human. He had a low, thick forehead; long arms; and a grayish hue to his skin and was heavily muscled. He wore no shoes or shirt, only a pair of old pants.

Polus shook his head back and forth, and his face looked pained as he squinted his eyes and then opened them wide saying, "Polus isn't dumb or ugly or worthless?" He looked like he was listening to what he had just said and then he repeated it, more matter-of-factly, "Polus *isn't* dumb or ugly or worthless!"

He leaped up and clapped his hands together, "Ha!" he exclaimed. Suddenly, he stopped and looked down at Nikos and asked, "Is Polus weak?" He clenched his teeth together and frowned and then said, "They said Polus was weak."

Nikos thought a moment before he responded, thinking it a good thing that Polus thought he was weak, but the truth was that he was immensely strong. Nikos had to be honest, so he said, "You are not weak, but strong."

Rage came over Polus's face again. Nikos wondered who he was thinking about and was glad that he was apparently on Polus's side.

"They *lied* to Polus," he said seething through gritted teeth, his eyes narrowed to slits. His breathing increased and all in an instant, he smacked his big, knotted fist into his palm like a thunder crack.

"Lied!" he yelled and then even louder so that Nikos instinctively covered his ears. "They *lied!*" His eyes looked black. He drew his lips back in a grimace and again breathed hard through clenched teeth.

Nikos was glad that he had not lied since it seemed to be a particularly sore point for him.

Polus started pacing back and forth and began methodically pounding his fist into his palm while chanting "Lied, lied" at the same cadence. He seemed in a world of his own.

Nikos stood up and noticed his thirst again. It seemed like it had been hours since he had met Polus.

Suddenly, Polus stopped and looked directly at Nikos with his eyes still lit with fury. He asked, "Should liars be punished? How does yer punish liars?" He had a murderous look in his eyes, and Nikos knew without a doubt that if whoever he was thinking of was standing right there, he would have crushed their head like a melon. The rage Nikos saw in him seemed to have welled up and collected itself from years and years of dormancy. He thought he had better do something before Polus stomped off and killed someone.

"Polus, I am very thirsty . . . and I am lost . . ."

Polus immediately stopped his raving, and as he looked at Nikos, the fire in him went out like a candle in the wind. His forehead knotted together in a myriad of emotions, and he took a big, deep breath.

"Lost?" he said in a detached way.

"Yes, and I am thirsty . . ."

"Yer wants water?" he asked, seeming very eager to please. He raised his jutting eyebrows in anticipation.

"Um, yes . . ." Nikos said slowly, considering the condition of any water that could be found in the area.

"Polus knows where there is water, good water!" Nikos hoped that what he said indicated that he thought there was such a thing as bad water. He turned and motioned with his arm and called out, "Foller Polus!"

He lumbered off down the slope, moving very quickly, and it was all Nikos could do to keep up with him. After going a couple hundred feet, Nikos nearly lost sight of him in the increasing gloom of the forest. The terrain was worse than before, and Nikos was slipping and stumbling along, falling behind; he was about to call out for Polus to wait when he stopped and pointed.

"There!" he said triumphantly. Nikos came staggering up, breathing hard

and looked in the direction Polus was pointing. He expected some kind of mucky pool, but he saw two big stones standing with a stream flowing out from between them into a big hollowed-out boulder, forming a crystal-clear pool about three feet wide and two handbreadths deep. The water overflowed onto a big flat rock and then away down the slope.

Polus looked like he was just bursting to say something, but all he did was motion for Nikos to drink. The water was amazingly cool, sweet tasting, and unusually satisfying. Nikos stood up and noticed that the stone had a fine, carved edge of a beautiful floral pattern.

Polus bent down and looked him in the face and said, "Polus made it!" He seemed immensely proud and added, "Keeps the water clean!"

There was ornate scrollwork carved into it that continued down the front of it as well. "You made this?" asked Nikos.

Polus's face broke into a big smile, and he nodded his head emphatically. Polus's smile continued as he motioned Nikos to follow him as he lumbered away through the forest again.

A large clearing opened ahead and as Nikos came to the edge, he blinked his eyes in the brightness of the sun. Polus had gone to the right and disappeared over a steep slope near the edge of the clearing and soon reappeared with a rusty old hammer and pick.

"Tools," he said, "Polus's tools." Polus stood next to Nikos, hunched over watching his face.

"You carved that with *these*?" Nikos asked skeptically.

He nodded excitedly.

"How did you learn to do that?"

Polus started answering, but he stopped for a moment, looking sad, but then continued, "Before they made Polus go away, he watched old man Semmy make things out of wood or stone with tools, but then he died, and then they made Polus go away . . ."

He trailed off, and his eyes took on a vacant look as if he was seeing another time and place. Suddenly, his great face piled up into a rage, and he gritted his teeth.

"They lied to Polus! They *lied*! Polus *hates* liars!" He yelled so loudly that Nikos covered his ears again. Polus's whole body began to quake with fury as he looked away toward the south.

Nikos was frozen with fear when suddenly, Polus spun around to face him, his huge body taut and menacing and his eyes black with murder. He did not seem to recognize Nikos as he took a step toward him. Nikos jumped backward falling over a tree root, but something suddenly leaped over him and landed square on Polus's chest, causing him to fall backward down the steep slope. Nikos heard a voice that sent sparks of emotion flooding through his whole body.

"Nikos!"

He felt a hand upon his shoulder and cried out, "Makarios!"

Nikos ran to the edge of the slope and saw that Polus had the wolf subdued with his hands around his neck. He looked up startled, and he stopped squeezing but didn't move as his eyes jerked to Makarios and then back to Nikos.

"Let the wolf go!" said Makarios. "He is mine."

Polus looked down at Lukos and asked, "Yers?" He squinted his eyes and looked to the side and then back at Makarios. Lukos whimpered but wasn't struggling.

"Is he yer *friend?*"

"Yes, since he was a pup," she answered.

Polus suddenly looked back at the wolf and seemed horrified. He grimaced and pushed Lukos away as he scrambled backward, feeling anxious and sorry and sick all in one moment.

"Polus is sorry . . ." he said with his eyes downcast as the wolf slunk away and came somberly back to Makarios, eyeing Polus with a low growl.

Nikos turned to look at her, unbelieving that she was there right in front of him.

"What was going on here?" she asked. "It looked like you were about to be killed." Nikos looked down at Polus who was still sitting there, now with his knees drawn up to his chin and his arms wrapped around them.

Makarios looked questioningly at Nikos. "So . . .?"

"Uh . . . well . . . he was in a rage."

"About what?"

"Some folks treating him bad, away that way," said Nikos pointing south. "But why are you here?"

She looked away and crossed her arms. "I had a real feeling that you were going to get yourself into trouble. It seems I found you just in time."

Nikos was wholly overcome with seeing her again, but she turned her attention quickly to Polus.

"Look, what about him? What is his name?"

"Polus."

"What was he so angry about?"

"In the town where he used to live, they told him he was stupid and ugly and worthless, and they made him leave. When I said he wasn't any of those things, he got enraged about being lied to."

Makarios looked thoughtful and then asked, "Why are you so far off the road?"

"I was thirsty and —"

At that moment they were startled by a movement to their left, and Lukos leaped up growling. Polus emerged from the trees walking slowly toward them, and they both were amazed at how silently he had moved through the forest. He looked dejected as he stopped squarely in front of Makarios. Lukos growled more fiercely and edged a little closer, but Polus fell to his knees before her and bowed his head.

"Polus is very sorry," he said, utterly consumed by guilt. He just knelt there with his arms hanging limp and his head down. She reached toward him, and he flinched as if he were going to be struck.

Nikos stood transfixed as Makarios took a hold of his big, gnarled hand and said, "I forgive you, Polus."

His eyes were filled with tears, and he tucked his head down even further. She held tight to his hand as his tears fell and after a moment, he raised his head slightly, but kept his eyes on the ground.

"What is 'forgive'?"

"That means that I will not punish you for what you did." His face knotted into a tremendous look of puzzlement. He brushed his tears away and looked up at her.

"But Polus was bad."

"That is right; you were bad, but I shall not punish you. It will be as if you were not bad." He shook his head slowly and looked at her hand holding his. He squeezed his eyes closed and gently pulled his hand back, moving away from her.

"Polus dern't know what ta do." He was confused and slowly walked away as if in a daze. He glanced partially back in Makarios's direction, but not far enough to look at her, and kept walking.

She looked after him for a moment and then turned to Nikos, who had never seen such compassion in another human being before and was amazed. The beauty he had seen in her smile earlier in the day paled in comparison.

She disregarded the look on his face and said, "I should be on my way . . . I can take you back to the road."

Nikos could not get his thoughts in order as he felt terribly guilty for having caused all that was happening. He sat down dejectedly on a boulder and Makarios, after taking a deep breath, remained silent. Polus was sitting on a big log about thirty feet away with his elbows on his knees and his chin in his great, gnarled hands staring at the ground.

"I am afraid he will seek revenge," said Nikos quietly.

Makarios sat down next to him, and his heart welled up like he had never felt in his life before. He turned to her, but Polus approached them and stood in front of Makarios, averting his eyes. He clasped his hands together and worked them around nervously. It seemed all he could do to keep from looking at her while at the same time finding it impossible to not look at her.

Suddenly, he stood stock-still, took a breath, darted a look at Makarios, and whispered, "Polus is sorry."

"You need not be sorry any longer," she answered gently as she stood up; "I have forgiven you."

His whole face knotted up into great puzzlement again. It seemed like he didn't know which way to turn. He looked to the left and then the right and rubbed his head.

With his hand still on his head, he looked directly at Nikos and said, "Do you know forgive?"

Nikos was startled and had only a vague idea of what it meant, but before he could answer, Polus turned back to Makarios who said, "Forgive means you won't get punished."

Polus' face jumbled up again in confusion. "It dernt seem right," he mumbled and began to retreat into his own little world.

Makarios said, "Well, it is true; it isn't right or what you *deserve*, but forgiveness is what I choose to give. Now come, tell us about this meadow. It seems strange that it is here in such a thick, gloomy forest."

Polus's face immediately brightened as he said, "It is not strange. It is Polus's home. Before, it wernt home, but were all sad and dark like the rest."

He looked up and motioned around the clearing and to the forest beyond, "Polus could'na stay in happy places where she smiles," he continued and pointed toward the sun, "because bad men chase Polus away."

His face suddenly changed, and Nikos felt a sudden, cold fear, but Makarios pulled on Polus's hand and called his name, which snapped him out of his thoughts. He looked at her, and his face softened, and he became wholly absorbed with her presence. Nikos felt a twinge of jealousy, not only because of how he was looking at her, but because of the tremendous effect she seemed to have on him.

She spoke quickly, wanting to keep his attention from turning to the thoughts he had had, but it seemed to Nikos that there was no danger of his thoughts being anywhere but on her.

"Tell us how this became your home," she said.

His face brightened again, and as he looked around, he explained, "Polus did it. Polus made room fer her to come in."

He started to motion with the hand Makarios was holding, but stopped and used his other to point to the sun again. "You mean you took down all the trees that were here?" Makarios asked incredulously.

Polus nodded his head excitedly and said, "Come and see what Polus made with them." He took a step but stopped and looked down at his hand, which Makarios was still holding. She let go, and he paused a moment. "Polus never had no one here before . . ."

His voice trailed off and a sudden pang of loneliness turned his face into the saddest thing either of them had ever seen. He began to choke up, but it passed quickly as Makarios came nearer to him. His eyes locked onto her, and he watched her expectantly as they went down the hill.

"This is Polus's home," he said as he grasped the handle of a huge wooden door that stood in the side of the steep hill. As the door swung in, they were surprised to see light within.

Polus said, "It's her," and he motioned upward. "Polus made a way fer her ta come in here too. Come and see."

The floor was packed dirt, cool and damp, and the walls and ceiling were smooth logs. It was a large rectangular space and high enough for Polus to stand up in. Immediately to the left was an alcove about four feet high dug back into the wall. Dried meat and smoked fish were hanging there along with some baskets of potatoes and carrots and other roots and herbs. At the far end of the room, there was a window up at ceiling level. Except for a bed piled high with furry hides, there was little else but an odd assortment of tools in one corner and some cooking pots near a fire pit.

"It is very nice," said Makarios.

Polus looked as proud as could be with her response and led them back up to the field.

"Everything you have here is beautiful!" said Makarios.

His face popped into a big smile, and he beamed at her with years' worth of happiness all expressed in one moment, but then he looked confused, and his lip began quivering. Tears welled up and then seemingly not knowing what he was doing, he scooped Makarios up into his big, knotted arms and hugged her and said, "You make Polus happy and sad all together . . ."

And just as quickly as he had picked her up, he gently put her down. He took a step back with teary downcast eyes, looking pained and confused as he clutched his chest.

"Polus feels . . . something . . . he dern't know . . . about yer . . . in here," he said as he gave his chest a thump with his fist.

Nikos looked back and forth between them, transfixed.

Polus bent forward and looked directly into Makarios's eyes and very earnestly said, "Polus feels so strong something." He continued looking directly at her, anxiously waiting for an answer as if his life depended on it.

Makarios was at a loss for words, and Polus shifted his gaze to Nikos and asked, "Does yer know?"

He was becoming unsettled and agitated, and Nikos, who was already uncomfortable, became even more so.

"Polus," began Makarios trying to break the tension, "some may call it love . . ." she trailed off as Polus relaxed a little, but then looked away puzzled.

He stared off for a while trying to organize his thoughts and then raised his big eyebrows and said in wonderment, "Love is *good*. Polus never wants yer to go away."

He knelt on one knee in front of her, taking her hand. He was looking down at the ground, but he raised his eyes as he said, "Polus *love* Makarios."

Then he leaned forward and hugged her very gently and leaned back again, looking at her expectantly. He seemed a bit more confident and less ashamed of himself.

Nikos looked at Makarios and saw that she was very uncomfortable when Polus suddenly blurted out, "Does Makarios love *Polus*?" He looked at her excitedly, imperceptibly nodding his head.

She was searching for the right words, but Polus's countenance began to fall, and he said slowly, "Yer doesn't love Polus?"

"Well, it is not as simple as that," she said.

Polus's agitation began escalating, so she quickly added, "Let us not worry about that, but I will stay with you for now."

Polus's face immediately split into a huge mischievous grin as he leaped up and threw his hands in the air. He was spinning around, whooping and hollering until he was halfway across the clearing.

Nikos found himself admiring Makarios even more for her courage to just speak her mind and how she knew the right things to say.

"I wonder how this is all going to work out," she said, seeming a bit worried. They both fell silent as they watched Polus, who was still across the clearing jumping around and joyously throwing handfuls of leaves and grass into the air.

After a few minutes, Makarios called out in a loud, strong voice, "Polus!"

He froze like a statue as leaves and grass fluttered down around him. He looked slowly in her direction and then bounded toward her, and as he got closer, Nikos was struck anew with how big he was. He came to a stop in front of her, bent forward with his hands on his knees, every muscle taut with expectation.

She said to him, "Polus, it is almost supper time, and we are hungry. Would you mind if Nikos and I stayed in your house?"

Polus's face brightened and he said, "Polus would be very happy to have yers stay with him." His face leaped to another level of happiness, but then he looked away, and his face fell into sadness.

Tears welled up in his eyes and he said, "Polus never had anyone stay here; Polus has always been . . . alone," He slowly sank down onto the ground until he was just sitting there staring off. He began to sob, burying his face in his hands.

Makarios immediately went to him and amid his sobbing, she could hear him saying, "alone, so alone . . ." He seemed not to notice Makarios, and he just cried and cried.

Nikos stepped closer to Makarios, and they looked at each other. Tears welled in her eyes and as Polus's sobs began to lessen, she said, "Polus, you are not alone now."

He wiped his tears away, and Makarios moved slightly back from him as he drew a big, trembling breath and said, "Polus isn't alone, is he?" He raised his eyebrows and looked at Makarios and then at Nikos and said, "Is yer Polus' . . . *friends*?"

Makarios and Nikos looked at each other and then at Polus who was looking back and forth between them. "Yes, Polus, we are your friends," said Makarios with a sense of commitment to the situation.

Nikos felt a twinge of jealousy, but then he thought, how foolish; Polus is not much more than a child.

"So, you will let us stay with you then?" asked Makarios.

Polus raised his eyebrows and pursed his lips together and then said, "Polus would . . . he would . . . *love* that." His face split into a wide grin, and he stood up and looked around as if he was seeing things for the first time. He was happier than he had ever been and said to Makarios, "Polus will make his house ready fer yer . . ." and then he looked at Nikos adding, "And fer yer." Then he bounded off, disappearing down the slope.

"It is sad that he has been all alone here," said Makarios. "Do you know how long?"

Nikos shook his head and after a moment said, "But each time he got mad, he looked away south."

"The only town that way is Diaggello," she replied.

Soon Polus reappeared and said, "Polus's house is now house for three!" He came over to them and tentatively reached for Makarios's hand and gently took hold of it. They went down into his house and saw that he had arranged two more places to sleep, one near to his own bed and the other against the opposite wall.

He seemed wholly focused on Makarios as he gestured and said, "Fer yer." Turning to Nikos, he pointed to the bed next to his and said, "And fer yer," patting him on the back, which was more of a thumping that caused him to lurch forward a step.

"You are very kind," said Makarios.

"Polus will make a fire now and cook some food fer yers."

He immediately set to work on that, and Makarios said, "Polus, I am going out to take care of my horse, alright?"

He stopped immediately and turned to her. "Does yer *love* yer horse?"

Makarios seemed taken aback. "Well, . . . I suppose I do." Polus looked puzzled but returned to his work.

Up in the clearing, Makarios gave a short whistle, and her horse came quickly across the field, nuzzling her in the chest. She stroked his neck and after removing his tack gave him a good brushing down. Nikos stood there feeling useless and thought back to when he had met Makarios, and all that had happened. It seemed like weeks ago. Makarios finished up with her horse and then turned him out into the field, and they returned to Polus.

"What is that delicious smell?" Makarios exclaimed as she set her saddle and bridle down.

Polus turned and said, "Tato stew! Polus learned ta make it from old woman he knew."

There was no table, so they sat on their beds with very large bowls that Polus was not stingy with filling. As they ate, there was little talking, except the occasional, "Oh, this is so good," or "What vegetable is that?"

The stew was better than anything Nikos had ever eaten, and the feeling of fullness was more satisfying than anything he had felt in a long time. As they finished, Polus put some more wood on the fire and collected the dirty pots and bowls and went out the door. The fire sparked and crackled to new life and brought a brighter glow to the room.

Makarios looked up at Nikos briefly with a slight smile and asked, "So, do you want to tell me how beautiful I am again?"

He was quite startled by her question but saw that she seemed to be even more so as her face flushed red.

"I am sorry," she said and covered her face with her hands, having become quite flustered, but she continued, "It's just that, well, ever since this morning, I have hardly stopped thinking about what you said."

Nikos raised his eyebrows in surprise and took a breath to speak, but he had nothing to say. He couldn't believe that she thought that much about what he thought of her.

She moved toward the fire and crossed her arms, looking into it and said softly, "No one has ever said anything like that to me before . . ."

But she did not finish as a tear rolled down her face. Nikos was surprised at her sudden show of emotion and jumped off the bed. She turned toward him, but at that moment, Polus came back in whistling and clanking his pots. He stopped dead when he saw Makarios and then looked back and forth between her and Nikos.

Nikos stopped breathing and felt a cold fear, but Makarios quickly said, "Oh, Polus! Here you are!" as she turned to the fire and pulled her sleeve across her face. "I was just enjoying the fire. It is so nice with it getting a little cold outside."

But Polus came forward and peered into her face. "Is yers sad?" he asked softly and then glanced back at Nikos with a look that made him quite uncomfortable.

"Oh, no, no. I'm fine."

Polus looked thoughtful and then puzzled. Then he hung the pots up on pegs in the wall and said, "Polus is so happy that yers is here."

Evening had come on and the sun was nearly down as they climbed into their beds. Polus was asleep in minutes, and Makarios soon followed, but Nikos lay there, bone-tired and sore. All his time in prison hadn't done him any good, and he was exhausted. In spite of that, he lay there a long time, watching the fire die down. Soon, there were just hot coals that looked like they were moving as they glowed brighter in one spot and then another. Left alone with his thoughts, tears welled up as he thought back over the last few days. Everything about his life was so different, and the world seemed so big and unknown. He wondered about all there was out there—so many things that he didn't know and so many things that were bigger and grander than he could even imagine. What is his place in this world? What is his purpose? What if he was recognized as an escaped prisoner and sent back to prison? Would he have to hide for the rest of his life? The questions began coming faster and tumbling over one another as he fell into a fitful sleep.

Nikos awoke with a start and wondered where he was. He rubbed his eyes and as sleep cleared from his head, he remembered the night before. Makarios and Polus were not there, so he hopped out of bed and headed for the door, but his aching body brought him up short. He winced and groaned and stood still, slowly stretching his limbs and then went out, squinting in the bright sun. He heard some talking and laughter away to his left just within the forest, and he started down a well-worn path toward the sounds. Makarios and Polus were in front of a log shed that was built amongst some big pine trees. The sun shone brightly, casting sharp shadows on the ground.

Makarios called out, "Nikos, look at all these things that Polus has made!" She held out a small wooden bowl that was smooth and round and made of dark wood with a very fine leafy pattern carved around the top edge.

"That is good!" he said.

"Polus loves to make things!"

"He has made a lot of things," said Makarios. She showed Nikos that the shed was full of many carved things such as bowls, tool handles, and some statues of bears and birds and other animals. Some were made of stone and others of wood. Nikos was again amazed at the quality of the work.

"What do you do with these things that you've made?" asked Makarios.

Polus looked down at the ground and said somberly, "Polus just keeps them mostly, but sometimes he goes to the city by the sea and trades fer soap or salted fishes." Nikos wondered if he received as much as his things were worth in trade, but somehow, he expected that he got taken advantage of.

Polus continued, "But Polus dern't go there very much. It is far away, and men are bad to Polus." His brow knit together in an angry scowl.

Makarios quickly broke his attention and asked, "You have soap? I think Nikos could do with a good washing up."

Polus looked up from the ground, and his scowl was instantly replaced with a bright grin. "Yer wants to take a bath? Polus loves to wash up too!" Then as quickly as his face had changed to a smile, it crumbled back into a scowl.

He looked away to the south again and said, "They never let Polus take a bath or give him soap or anything!"

His anger increased, and his eyes lit up with rage. He gritted his teeth and seethed, "Always work, work, *work*! They never gave Polus *anything*! Then they sent him away with *nothing*!" He pounded his fist into his palm and took a step forward, as if he were going somewhere.

Nikos stood there, frozen in fear. Lukos appeared almost instantly and stood at Makarios's side growling, back hairs bristling. Nikos started to feel panic when suddenly, Makarios stepped into Polus's path, thumped him on the chest, and yelled, "*Polus!*"

He stopped dead in his tracks with his huge arm reared back poised to strike with a granite-like fist. His eyes locked onto Makarios, and he started to swing.

Nikos couldn't move, and Lukos was about to spring when Makarios hit Polus again and yelled his name. This time he heard her, and he seemed to solidify into a statue, his arm still in the air. He blinked a few times, and then his eyes slowly rolled down to Makarios, who tried to divert his attention from the whole situation.

"How about the soap?" she asked.

Polus's raised hand fell limp at his side, and he dropped his gaze to the ground at Makarios's feet and said, as if to himself, "Polus is bad. Polus is very, very bad." He started to look up, but when he got to the level of Makarios's knees, tears welled up, and he squeezed his eyes shut.

Makarios took a step toward him and was about to say something, when Polus said, "Bad, Polus is bad," and started trembling and crying.

Makarios started to say his name, but he took a step back and through spluttering tears, he cried out, "No! Polus is too bad fer forgive!"

Makarios tried again to speak, but Polus yelled, "*No! No forgive!*" His emotion intensified, and he sobbed, "Polus *is* dumb and ugly and worthless! Polus *deserve* to be alone!"

He turned and ran up the hill into the clearing and by the time Makarios and Nikos got to the top of the hill, Polus was already crashing into the woods on the north side. He was crying out in an angry, disconsolate voice, "No forgive!"

Tears filled Makarios's eyes as she said, "Nikos, what have we done? We've stirred up so much pain and anger in him."

Nikos stood there, again feeling useless, but after a few moments said, "We've wakened good feelings in him too, or at least you have . . ."

She paused a moment and then went up the hill into the clearing and sat down on a large boulder, looking toward where Polus had gone. She was quickly joined by her wolf, whom she hugged and petted as he lay down next to her.

"I wish to be on my way," she said, "but I cannot leave like this. I hope he comes back soon."

Nikos stood there, not knowing what to say or do. His mind was trying to formulate something when Makarios said, "I suppose you ought to get washed up. Take that path down to the pond. I shall wait here for Polus."

─── Two ───

Nikos started off, suddenly feeling very tired from all that had happened. Not only did his body hurt, but his heart and mind were overwhelmed as well. He wished for no more adventure and glanced about as he entered the forest. It was mostly pine, and the smell and cooler air were quite refreshing, which set him somewhat at ease. He thought about Polus again and kept hoping he would see him or that he would come out of the woods and be feeling better. But all the way to the pond, all he heard was the murmuring of the stream and the occasional bird fluttering away and small animals scurrying through the underbrush. The path ended at some large flat rocks that angled down into the water. A few frogs leaped away with a plunk into their watery hiding places as he approached. With the sun hot and blazing and the sapphire blue sky dotted with big, puffy white clouds, it felt like paradise.

Across the pond, the tops of the trees were swaying in a gentle breeze. He raised his hands to the sky and to everything around him and wanted to hug it all. A smile spread across his face as he ran full tilt and launched himself into the pond. As he came up to the surface, he realized that his swimming skills were still in order, even though it had been so long since he had been in the water. It felt glorious. He paddled over to the waterfall and climbed up on some rocks that were beneath it and sat there, enjoying the cool water coming down on him.

Nikos felt like the whole world was before him as he looked to the far end of the pond and up the left-hand shore. The trees on that side seemed cut back from the pond, with a few saplings here and there dotting underbrush and field grass. Then he noticed what seemed like a path or a road running next to the pond. He dove in and swam over and came up onto a gravelly shore. To the left there was indeed a path or the remnants of an old road that had once been wide and well used, and to the right, it continued along the pond and disappeared into the forest. Nikos felt oddly drawn to go down it a ways and found it overgrown; he wondered why it had been abandoned. As he passed into the forest, the path seemed to disappear into beds of pine needles and sparse undergrowth. He looked this way and that and noticed that some of the trees seemed to be standing in lines, arrow straight through the forest.

Presently, he came upon the stream cutting across in front of him and the remnants of an old wooden bridge. Its timbers were broken and rotted, and some had fallen into the stream. It had been built for a much wider crossing than the one that now existed. But suddenly, Nikos noticed a huge footprint in the mud at the edge of the stream and more footprints on the other side.

"Polus!" thought Nikos, and he remembered what Makarios had said about a town being that way. He raced back up the path, dove headlong into the pond, swam quickly across it and took to the path on the far side. As he neared Polus's house, he started calling out Makarios's name. He ran past the shed and was turning up the hill to the clearing when she met him coming down it.

"What is it?" she exclaimed.

"Polus . . . footprints . . . I saw . . . in the mud." He panted as he pointed down the path toward the pond. Suddenly, a look of recognition and fear spread across her face as she said,

"Surely, he's gone to Diaggello! And here we have been sitting the whole time!" She looked quickly about and whistled for her horse. She had him saddled in no time and swung up onto him.

Suddenly, Nikos's thoughts flashed back to how they had parted that morning at the prison, but this time, she held her hand out to him and shouted, "Quickly!"

Before he knew it, he was up behind her, and they were thundering off down the path. They passed the pond, jumped the creek and raced down the track between the towering pine trees. Soon, the forest closed in a bit, and they had to slow down.

"I am not sure of the way," said Makarios, "but it looks like this track continues straight south."

They rode on for a while and then Makarios said, full of concern, "I expect that it was the chief who put Polus out. He is the marshal of Diaggello and has been in charge since I was very young. Unfortunately, he is quite cruel and cares not a whit for anyone but himself."

She paused, in disgust and then continued, "He has only gotten fatter and richer and more conceited and has come to fancy himself king of the world!"

Finally, they came to the edge of the forest. The sun was nearly overhead as they came into a grassy field that slopped gently down to a very wide and slow-moving river. They arrived at the river's edge, and Makarios found what she expected to see.

"He crossed the river here," she said. "I am not surprised that he could swim that far, but I will not ask Samos to do the same." Again, they were off at a gallop and headed west down the bank of the river for a few miles.

"I hope we are not too late," said Makarios as they approached the road that led to the bridge. There were a few people traveling on it—some on horseback, others walking, some riding on a wagon or two. Nikos felt nervous and avoided eye contact as Samos clattered up onto the wooden bridge.

Makarios turned to him slightly and said, "Do not fear; no one will know you. You are in disguise with that beard of yours." She finished with a wink and a smirk. He wasn't sure how to take her remark but had to admit that what he had wasn't much of a beard at all. But he grinned and felt gratitude for her making him feel a bit easier.

"I have a foreboding feeling that Polus has surely gotten himself into trouble," said Makarios. "But it may be the other way around."

"What do you mean?" asked Nikos.

"Well, the chief isn't much of a marshal, and his deputies are not much more capable of dealing with trouble, especially trouble as big and angry as Polus."

Makarios shook her head and continued, "The chief would deserve nearly anything he gets from Polus, but for Polus's sake, I hope he calmed down and never even came here."

They turned left off the bridge and moved up into a gallop, passing many outlying farms and soon came into Diaggello. It was a lazy, peaceful town, full of shopkeepers and tradesmen, and at present, seemingly undisturbed.

"I am surprised . . ." began Makarios as they rode past shops, people sitting on porches, others loading wagons or just walking along on their way somewhere.

Nikos looked a fair way down the road and saw some people much more animated than the people he had seen thus far. "Look there!" he whispered.

"I see . . ." said Makarios slowly. "Keep your ears open. I am going to ride past." The group was mostly men and young boys and a few women near the marshal's office talking among themselves.

"Never saw anything of the like . . . huge 'e was!" exclaimed an older man as a young boy kept jumping up as high as he could with his arm above his head yelling, "An' 'ee was this tall. Taller'n two people!"

A middle-aged woman said, "Almost broke the marshal's whole building in pieces. Sure could use a strong lad like that on my farm; he'd do the work of three men!"

A few of the boys started reenacting what they had seen by pretending to bang on the marshal's building, while another made some movements that Makarios lost sight of behind the people.

She continued a bit and then stopped at a hitching rail and said, "I am going to see the chief."

Nikos followed at a distance but stopped short of the crowd. The heavy wooden door was twisted on its hinges with stones and bits of mortar laying on the ground. Inside, a skinny, scraggly looking man was sitting at a desk strewn with papers, an ink bottle, and some ledger books.

He looked up from his writing in a disinterested way. "Help you, ma'am?"

"I'm looking for the chief."

"Not here, ma'am. Went home cuz he don't put up with commotion."

Makarios looked around, expecting to see Polus in one of the cells at the far end of the room, but they were empty. "What commotion?" she asked.

The man slowly leaned back in his chair, crossed his arms, and chuckled. "Now, ma'am, what'd you do, just ride into town or something?"

"As a matter of fact, I have," she said, trying to maintain her composure, but the man seemed to relish his position.

"Well," he said slowly, "don't suppose it's any of your business . . ."

Makarios's anger was quickly rising when a young man stepped through the open doorway. "Hey, Spoggos, what harm is there in tellin' 'er?"

The man behind the desk looked sharply at him and said angrily, "That's *Deputy* Spoggos to you! This is my jail, and I'll run it the way I say! Now shut up and git out!"

The young man seemed to have no respect for the deputy. "Your jail, ha! You ain't the chief!"

The deputy pushed his chair back and stood up saying, "You're gonna land in one of those cells if you don't git out, Graffo!"

The young man seemed to know just how far to push the deputy and ducked back out the door, saying to Makarios, "I can tell you what happened ma'am . . . saw the whole thing."

Without even another glance at the deputy, Makarios went out, making her way through the noisy crowd as the young man motioned her to follow. He was about twenty years old, with long blonde curly hair that fell to his shoulders; he was clean-shaven and well-muscled. They went across the town square and down to a shop on the left as Nikos made his way over to them.

When they got to the shop, the young man turned, nodded, and said, "I am Graffo, son of Karasso. I have seen you many times in Diaggello."

"Yes," she said. "I have a farm some miles east of here. I am Makarios, and this is my friend Nikos."

The shop had a wooden porch with some chairs and a table under an overhanging roof, and Graffo motioned for them to sit down. He began, "Well, I was here in the shop working when suddenly I hear a big ruckus. A giant of a man came stomping into town, in a rage, yelling for the chief. He kept yelling, 'Liar, liar!' Everyone in town came out of their shops and businesses, but many ran back in just as quick. The big man . . . he was a funny color . . . well, he finds the chief's office, but the chief had barred the door. So, then I start to recognize him . . . Polus, that's his name, I think—"

Makarios interrupted. "You know him?"

"I think it was him. I haven't seen him in a long time, but he's not the kind you forget. Well, anyway, he worked with my grandfather in our shop doing carving and inscribing. He had to stay in the back though, out of sight. Even when he was young, he was very big and strong and . . . his temper wasn't good for business."

Makarios said, "I think we are indeed talking of the same person. Go on."

"Well, as I said, he comes stomping into town and starts banging on the marshal's building, shouting, 'Liars must die!' Spoggos and a few other deputies come running, but they were too afraid to do anything and ran into the marshal's building from the back and barred the door. Soon after that, some soldiers from the barracks came charging up on horseback and tried roping Polus, but he pulled one of them off his horse as easy as anything. By then there was a crowd of people yelling and jeering, and the horses were getting spooked, and there was all kind of confusion. Dust was in the air, and Polus kept banging on the marshal's building, and it started to get broken up. That's when three soldiers from Smaragdos province showed up. One of them had these strange looking knives and says, 'How about we try one out on something that's alive?' I couldn't believe it, but he threw it right at Polus, and it went end over end and stuck right in his side as he was raising his arm to pound the building again."

Makarios asked anxiously, "Is Polus alright?"

"Well, I don't know. As soon as the knife struck, he froze like a statue. Then he grabbed at the knife and pulled it out and fell to his knees and started crying. He just knelt there with his head down and shoulders heaving. At first no one moved, but then the soldiers from the barracks rushed at him and got the ropes on him and tied him up. He didn't even resist but kept saying something about how bad he was."

"We must see if he is alright," said Makarios. "Where did the soldiers take him?"

"Well, after he was tied up, they put a strangle chain on him and took him around back, and then the chief came out, all red-faced and very angry. He called for his carriage and headed out of town. I suppose he went home for the day. He hates trouble."

"He *is* a selfish beast," said Makarios. "But we must find out about Polus." They went back to the marshal's office.

As they entered, Deputy Spoggos threw up his hands in mock exasperation and said, "Can a man get nothing done?! What do you want now? It's not as if this noisy crowd outside my door hasn't been enough of a distraction!"

Makarios calmly answered, "We should like to know what has happened to Polus, the man who caused all the commotion earlier."

"Oh, is that his name? Thank you very much. I *am* trying to write a report of this incident."

He put his pen down and said abruptly, "Fine. I'll tell you what happened to this Polus person if it will keep you away from here. The soldiers took him to the barracks. Chief said he wanted him out of here and wanted nothing more to do with him, except that he wants him executed."

Spoggos grinned ever so slightly and looked at Graffo, who looked at Makarios and shook his head. "Do not worry; he will not be executed."

He scowled at Spoggos who said rudely, "Well, go on, get out!"

They all went out, and Makarios said to Graffo, "Would you be so kind as to provide some water for my Samos here that is a bit better than these public troughs?"

"More than happy to, ma'am, and a drink for you and your friend as well!"

Graffo turned toward his shop and called out, "Roos!" A small skinny boy appeared as Graffo continued, "Fetch a bucket for this horse and a drink for this fine lady and her friend."

He immediately turned and went back into the shop. As they passed quickly through the town square, Nikos noticed a statue that stood in the middle of a fountain.

"Who is that?" he asked. "He looks to be a fine, honorable sort."

The other two scoffed and Makarios said, "It is supposed to be the chief, but he imagines himself much differently than he is." They reached Graffo's shop and had a cool drink. The small boy, Roos, stood by, waiting for further instruction.

Makarios took a liking to him and, as she smiled at him, asked Graffo, "Whose boy is this?"

"He is an orphan from Oligos."

"You are a fine young man. Thank you for the water," she said.

Roos kept his eyes on the ground and said, "Welcome, ma'am."

Makarios turned to Graffo and said, "Thank you very much for your hospitality."

They trotted off across the square and as they passed the statue of the chief again, Nikos asked, "Is the chief in charge of the whole province or—"

Makarios quickly said, "No, no; he is only the marshal of Diaggello, but he is very corrupt. He receives bribes and payments from many of the shop-keepers here. He shows favor to some, and others who abide by the law get treated unfairly. It has made him very rich."

"He just does whatever he wants?" asked Nikos.

"Well, within a certain reason. Master Hegomai is the ruler of Diaggello, but he leaves everything up to the chief, as does Krino the magistrate. I don't doubt that the chief fills their purses so they will go along with him. Even Stagos, the captain of the guard, won't stand up to him. I suppose he is on the chief's payroll as well."

They rode in silence for a while and then seeing the barracks up ahead, Makarios said, "Let's hope Captain Stagos is agreeable today, but I expect he will be in a very bad temper. I can't remember the last time there was trouble in Diaggello."

Nikos thought about his imprisonment again and was silent as a wave of anxiety came over him.

The barracks was a large stone building, with a big yard and room to house two hundred soldiers. It was enclosed by a tall stone wall with a guardhouse built into it next to an iron gate. Two soldiers were sitting at a table outside, one younger and the other older with gray hair, long beard, a big stomach and an unkempt uniform. They were playing some kind of card game and as Makarios rode up, they paused.

The older one leaned back in his chair and said, "What's yer business?"

"We would like to see a prisoner who was brought in today. He has been wounded with a knife—"

"Oh *him*! He's in the hole. No one can get near 'im. Haven't been able to do a thing for him. One thing's sure, being in the hole will be like nuthin' after the chief gets through with him."

They dismounted and Makarios continued, "I would like to tend to him."

The older guard, whose name was Baga, laughed incredulously and said, "I'd like to see that!"

But glancing at Makarios, the younger one said, "But, Baga, he could . . . *kill* 'er."

"Be quiet you! I'm teachin' you how to do soldiering, and prisoners are allowed to have visitors!"

He stood up and banged on the gate, "Kah! Open up! That brute has a visitor!"

The gate was unbarred with a loud clang and swung open. The guard inside looked at Makarios with surprise as Baga grabbed his arm, pulled him toward the table, and yelled, "Watch over this young'un here; I'm takin' 'er myself!"

Makarios and Nikos quickly followed Baga, whose short, stocky legs carried him faster than they expected.

As they were a little bit behind Baga, Nikos asked in a hushed voice, "These are soldiers? They are nothing like the ones up at Agathon Prison."

Makarios nodded and added, "I suppose the years of peacefulness in Diaggello have led to a decline in regulations, or else the chief's influence—"

At that moment, Baga turned around and yelled, "Come on you two; hoof it!"

They passed a long row of two-story bunk houses with a few soldiers here and there, and some of them called out after Makarios.

"Shut yer mouths!" yelled Baga. "And git back to yer duties!" They came to the end of the soldiers' quarters and arrived at the prison. Baga barged in and startled the guard, who sprang to his feet and grabbed for his sword, which clattered to the floor. He stood up straight and offered some kind of a salute, but Baga ignored him and grabbed a ring of keys from a hook on the wall.

He stomped over to a grated door and with a barely perceptible softening of his attitude, he said, "Now you sure you want to see that brute?"

"Yes, I am, Sir Baga."

He paused, surprised at the respect she showed him and then said, "Well, come on then; yer life is yer own."

He led them past some cells, most of which were empty. Tall narrow windows let in a fair amount of sunlight, but there was still a sense of gloominess to the place. They came to a heavily reinforced cell at the end of the cellblock that had nothing in it but a ladder and a trapdoor in the floor. Baga let them in and relocked the door as Makarios and Nikos looked at each other, their faces full of concern. They stepped to the trapdoor and listened, but no sounds came from the hole.

Makarios knelt down and quietly called out, "Polus?"

Only silence followed. She knocked on the trapdoor lightly and said, "Polus, it's Makarios and Nikos; we want to help you."

There was a slight sound of snuffling and movement and then silence.

As Nikos was about to speak, Polus said, in a voice full of pain, "Polus is bad."

"But Polus," said Makarios, "you are hurt; we want to take care of you." All they heard was some painful groaning, and a tear fell down Makarios's face.

As she reached for the latch, Baga said, "Now, missy, I don't know as I'd do that." He unexpectedly seemed to have genuine concern for her.

"Polus, I am going to open the door," she said and waited for a reply.

Just when it seemed there would be none, Polus said tearfully, "Polus is bad. Polus is shamed."

Makarios opened the latch, and Nikos took hold of the door and pulled it over. The hole was pitch dark, and he said, "Polus dernt want to come out."

Makarios asked Baga, "Can we have him come out of there? I can't see anything, but I know he has a wound that needs tending."

Baga was sincerely moved and almost without even knowing it, he said, "Yes of course, missy," and he called to the soldier at the front, "Hi! Meno! Bring some clean cloths and soap and warm water."

Makarios turned and said, "Why, Sir Baga, you prove yourself to be more of a gentleman than one would think you capable of."

He was about to respond when Makarios's attention was brought quickly back to the hole by Polus's voice, "Polus hurt. You can help Polus."

There followed some labored movements, and Polus came to the opening, his face dirty and streaked with tears.

Wincing in pain, he reached an arm up toward Makarios, who took his hand in hers and said, "Oh, Polus, I am so glad to see you."

Baga motioned to Nikos to get the ladder and with much painful effort, Polus climbed up out of the hole. His side was swollen and red; the wound encrusted with dirt and blood.

"Oh, Polus, I am so sorry," said Makarios as she hugged him gently.

"Polus was bad, but you forgive?" he asked.

"It is the chief who must forgive you, Polus. He is the one that you were bad to, but let's not think of that now. Let's take care of where you hurt." By that time Meno had brought the things Baga had asked for.

He looked warily at Polus as he unlocked the door warning, "Now, don't you try nuthin'! qu He quickly put the bucket inside the cell and then blurted out.

"Now, missy," said Baga, full of anxiety, "Mightn't he get all in a rage? That gash looks mighty bad."

"Well, Sir Baga, that's a chance I shall have to take," she answered as she addressed Polus.

"Now, this is going to hurt, but I want you to be brave and hold still."

Polus slowly nodded and grimaced as he raised his arm. He had bled quite a bit, so Makarios focused on just getting the wound clean.

"Polus hurt!" he cried.

"Yes, yes," said Makarios, "but it is better already. See, it is all clean now."

She bandaged him up as best she could and said, "You will be alright, Polus."

His eyes dropped to the floor, and he just stood there, but as Makarios was turning to speak to Baga, he said softly, "Polus love Makarios."

He hugged her, and Makarios said unexpectedly, "I love you too, Polus."

His face split into a huge grin as he stood back and beamed at her. "Polus is glad you came," he said, "And yer too," looking at Nikos.

Makarios sighed and said, "Now we must see what the chief is going to do with you." She and Nikos went to the cell door with Polus right behind them.

"Polus, I am sorry, but you must stay here," said Makarios. "This is where people who have done bad things have to stay, until they are forgiven."

Polus looked troubled and said, "No, Polus go with you!"

Makarios gestured to Baga to open the door, which he did, and she and Nikos quickly slipped out. Baga locked it behind them.

Polus took hold of the bars and said, "Polus go with you!" He began to get agitated, so Makarios reached through the bars and took his hands in hers. She looked straight into his eyes, but he looked quickly to the floor.

"Polus," she said softly, "we will come back, but for now you must stay here." His temper was quieted, and Makarios continued, "You see, people cannot just do whatever they please. No one is allowed to break up the chief's building. It is wrong to do that, and if someone does wrong, they must be—"

But Polus, listening very intently, interrupted, bringing his eyes up to meet hers asked,

"But what about forgive?"

"Well, not everyone forgives," she replied slowly.

Polus looked away, puzzled. He began to look angry again, and Makarios gave a little pull on his hands and said, "We will go see the chief and ask if he will forgive you. But for now, you must stay here." He seemed to accept this as his face twisted up in sadness.

He looked at the opening to the hole and asked plaintively, "Does Polus have to stay in there again?"

Makarios looked at Baga, who was transfixed by the whole scene. He blurted out, "Now, missy, I'm under orders." But he paused looking undecided and then said to Polus, "Do you promise to be good?"

Polus nodded emphatically, and Baga continued, "Then so be it; but I better not hear even a squeak from you, or it'll be the hole again!"

Makarios turned quickly away, and Baga took them back to the front gate.

"Hope you fare well with the chief, missy," he said. "But he's gonna want that big fella locked up in the hole forever or dead . . . or worse."

Soon, they were back in the town square and Nikos, though concerned about Polus's fate, suddenly thought about finding his horse. He looked about, especially scrutinizing the stables as they rode past, but a careful look left him disappointed. With the chief gone for the day, they headed east out of town.

After a while Makarios said, "I must stop by my father's house and see about my brother Moros. My father sent him to a quarry north of here a few weeks ago to work, and he should have been back in time for hay harvest. I was on my way to fetch him when I came upon you."

Soon, they turned off the road and into a field of tall brown grass and after an hour or so, came to a farm. There were many men in a field baling hay and as they approached, an older man who was tall and lean with graying hair called out, "Ah, my daughter!"

A wide smile spread across his weathered face as he strode toward them saying, "This is not your brother!"

Nikos cast his eyes on the ground as Makarios's father looked at him carefully and said, "Well, I think that you will do as well as Moros to help with this hay."

Makarios was about to speak when her father said, "Now it is almost suppertime; Dorea ought to have things nearly ready."

He quickly turned back to his work and called over his shoulder, "At supper you can tell me how you went out for your brother and came back with a stranger."

Resigned, Makarios went to the barn, gave Samos a good rub down and turned him out into the pasture.

"I suppose we shall stay here for the night, rather than go to my farm. It will make for a shorter ride back to see the chief tomorrow."

They headed toward the house, and Nikos said, "I will help with the hay. . ."

"My father says many things to test others, to read their character. He will expect you to work, though, if he feeds you and gives you lodging."

She scowled thinking of how ungracious her father could be. The smell of stewing meat came suddenly to them, and Nikos took a deep breath.

"Your mother is a fine cook."

"She is not my mother," said Makarios. "She is a widow from Huo Lake. She sold her land many, many years ago and now lives here doing the cooking and washing and helping with the animals. My mother died when I was only seven years old."

"I am sorry—" began Nikos.

Makarios said quickly, "Do not be sorry. My father is a good man, and Dorea has been as a mother to me."

As they came into the house, Dorea exclaimed, "Makarios! It is good to see you!"

She hugged Makarios and then turned to Nikos, "And who is this?"

Makarios smiled and said, "He is my friend Nikos." Dorea was a short, stocky, and comfortable looking old woman with a kind face.

"Did your brother not come back with you? He is sorely missed with the hay harvest going on."

"No, he is not with me, but I shall tell you and Father more at supper."

"Well, it is good to see you again and to meet your friend Nikos." She nodded at Nikos and turned back to her preparations.

Soon, Makarios's father came in followed by four young men who had been helping him in the field. Nikos was feeling overwhelmed and wished he could be somewhere else, but they all sat down at the table and began to eat.

"So where is your fool brother?" asked Makarios's father. "You could not find him?"

"I did not get up to the quarry to look for him," she began and seeing Nikos's uneasiness said, "Father, we have been through much in the last number of days . . ."

Her father immediately looked at Nikos and said, "So, you are the reason that my daughter did not get her brother back here for the hay harvest?" Baros laughed in a gruff sort of way, and Nikos swallowed hard keeping his eyes down. Suddenly, thoughts of his foster father, Kakos, flooded his mind.

Makarios said heatedly to her father, "I am sorry for not finding Moros. Nikos and I came across each other by chance, and he needed help."

"She saved my life," said Nikos, stealing a glance at Baros who leaned back, crossed his arms, and let out a laugh.

"Ha! Well, what about that! Sounds like you had an adventure!"

"Now, Master Baros," interjected Dorea, "you don't need to go making light of things. You can see the boy is all shaken up."

She stood up and tugged on Nikos and said softly, "Come on with me."

Makarios stood up with them and said crossly to her father, "We both will help with the hay tomorrow since I did not bring Moros home, and you were kind enough to feed us." She turned sharply and followed Dorea and Nikos into the kitchen.

"Now, sonny, it's alright," said Dorea as she seated them at a small table. She gave Nikos a pat as Baros called for her to bring them some ale; she closed the door as she went out.

"I am sorry for my father being so harsh," said Makarios, "That is his way."

"He just reminded me of . . . the past," said Nikos as he continued eating.

Dorea came back in and exclaimed, "Oh, sonny, I'm glad to see you've finished the stew. Anyone can see that you've had a few less meals than is good for you."

"It was very good, ma'am, thank you," said Nikos.

"Well, you're very welcome. Now you two best be off," she said.

Then looking at Makarios, she added, "You know how your father's temper can get up when he starts with the ale."

Makarios gave a nod, and she and Nikos went through the pantry and back to the barn. "We shall avoid my father if we sleep here," said Makarios. "There are a few bunks where the hired men used to stay."

The sun was getting lower in the sky, and it was dim in the barn as they settled down on some straw mattresses. Makarios fell asleep quickly, but the unfamiliar surroundings and the raucous outbursts of laughter that came faintly down from the house kept Nikos awake well into the night.

Nikos awoke with a start to Makarios's voice. "The sun is up, and breakfast is waiting," she called from the doorway.

A southerly breeze brought the smell of griddle cakes and bacon to him, and he arose quickly. He followed her sleepily up the hill, and they found Baros and the four hired men around the table in the main room waiting to be served. Makarios looked warily at her father.

"My daughter, I am sorry for my manner last night. I should like to hear of what happened on your way to find your brother."

"Thank you for your kindness, Father."

Dorea came in with plates piled high, and as they ate, Makarios told her father the story of coming upon Nikos and then of finding Polus but left out anything about Agathon Prison.

Her father, amid mouthfuls of food, said heartily, "So, this big brute of a man needs the help of my only daughter, does he? Well, then you have my leave to go immediately."

He gestured toward his hired men and said, "We shall get the hay in and if ever that wayward brother of yours returns, he shall earn his keep twice over!"

Makarios smiled and said, "Thank you, Father."

Breakfast was finished quickly, and Baros said, "Let's get at it, boys!"

He nodded at Nikos and went out as Dorea came back into the room and said, "He does always surprise me. Just when I think his heart is made of stone . . ."

Makarios and Nikos were about to go out when Dorea said, "Oh, sonny, I have some clothes for you that will do better than the rags you're wearing. Moros won't miss them, and they seem about your size." She went to the pantry and emerged with some trousers and a shirt and a pair of short, worn leather boots and handed them all to Nikos.

"Thank you, ma'am," he said.

She gave him a quick hug and said, "Now you two be careful with that chief."

They went out, and Makarios said, "I am going to the bathhouse, but you'll find the pond wonderful for washing up in . . ."

She left him, and he went down to the pond and after a quick wash, he tried the boots on and found that he quite liked them. Soon they met back at the barn, and Makarios called Samos in from the pasture.

"My father has agreed to let you ride Dusko, but you will have to go without a saddle; she will be unmanageable otherwise," said Makarios. She pointed to a black horse that was somewhat small but compact with long legs and gray and white speckles along her back.

"Take that bridle there, and go get her," she said with a grin, "if you can." Nikos turned and with some apprehension, hopped the fence and walked toward the mare. As he got nearer, her head came up quickly, and he could see that she was young. She pawed with her front hoof and shook her head.

Nikos stopped and called out, "Come on, Dusko!" She pranced sideways and then galloped off a bit.

Nikos called out again, "Hi, Dusko!" and then unexpectedly sat down on the ground, which intrigued the horse and caused her to come toward him. When she got close to him, he jumped up and ran away from her. She pursued him and after running some way, Nikos suddenly turned around and started at her.

The mare skidded to a halt and was about to veer away when Nikos turned away again and shouted over his shoulder, "Catch me if you can!" and ran toward the fence. Dusko half reared and kicked her back feet out and charged after Nikos. The game was on as they chased each other about, and soon Nikos had made a friend. She accepted the bridle easily, and Nikos jumped lightly to her back. He took a tight grip on her mane as she reared up and bucked a bit, as he expected, but she calmed down quickly.

He rode her back to the fence and saw Makarios standing there with a look of incredulity. She exclaimed, "Truly, I am amazed. She has never suffered a rider like this. My father tried to break her but gave up and has only kept her for breeding. I thought I would fool you a bit with her, but I am the one fooled!"

"She is the same breed as my Zeo," said Nikos as Dusko moved about excitedly. "I haven't seen another one like him until now."

"She is an Askonian," said Makarios, "which means stardust. They raise this breed for racing in Ekuus, a town way up north in Smaragdos Province."

Nikos looked at Dusko with renewed interest and said, "How does your father come to have her?"

"From the stables in Diaggello, though I don't know how she came to be there. Those who raise this breed keep their horses quite to themselves."

Makarios looked at the young mare and smiled as she continued, "My father bought her last summer at a very good price, though she has turned out to be quite a nuisance."

"How old is she?"

"Almost three; my father plans to breed her later this summer."

They set out for Diaggello, but Dusko was a bit rambunctious, and Nikos had to keep talking to her and rubbing her neck to keep her calm.

"She is really listening to you," said Makarios. "I am still amazed that you are able to ride her so easily."

Nikos said, "She really wants to run."

"Once we get out of the field and onto the road, we'll let these two stretch their legs a bit."

They came out onto the road and Dusko pranced sideways excitedly. Nikos held her in check, but she seemed to sense the road ahead. Her ears flicked back and forth, as she listened to Nikos, who was speaking softly to her.

Makarios looked at Nikos and said, "Well, we've got a straight road ahead; keep up if you can!"

At a word from Makarios, Samos leaped into a gallop, but before he even took a moment to think, Nikos tightened his knees on the mare, grabbed a handful of mane, leaned forward, and shouted, "Go, Dusko!" and she was off like a shot.

Nikos hooted with delight and reveled at the wind in his hair and the freedom he felt. He was surprised at how fast Dusko was as she easily caught Samos and swept past him.

"Keep up if you can!" he called out merrily as they left Makarios and Samos far behind, galloping on until Dusko was out of wind.

Nikos reined her in and hopped off when he realized she had worked herself into a lather; he walked along beside her, "You're not used to running like that are you?" She pushed her nose into his arm and whinnied softly.

Soon, Makarios caught up and said, "She truly is full of surprises! How fast she is!"

"With a bit of training, she could be even faster," said Nikos, taking some pride in the mare. After a while, Nikos remounted as they came near to Diaggello.

"I hope the chief is in a fair mood," said Makarios. "I think we shall have only this one chance to persuade him to be fair with Polus."

Nikos silently agreed. As they entered the town, it was already bustling with merchants and tradesmen. They made their way along and came to the marshal's building, finding Deputy Spoggos within.

He shouted, "You again! Do I not have enough to do? What is it now?"

Makarios's face tightened into a scowl, but she said pleasantly, "We shall be happy to accommodate you, Deputy Spoggos, and give you nothing to do. We are here to see the chief."

"Well, thank you very kindly, *ma'am*!" he said callously. "But he ain't here; he's on holiday."

Makarios started to ask when he would be back, but Spoggos interrupted, "Nope! Don't know when he'll be back. *I'm* in charge," he said jubilantly and then barked, "Don't ask about that Polus fellow either! He's stayin' in the hole until I say so!" He sat back and crossed his arms in a defiant way.

Makarios knew she would get no further help from him and curtly said, "Thank you, Deputy Spoggos. Good day." She turned sharply and went out.

"We shall go and see Polus," she said to Nikos, "and then ride up to the quarry and see about my brother." They passed through the crowds quickly and were soon at the barracks, seeing only the young man at the guardhouse.

He stood up quickly and said tentatively, though trying to sound tough, "What's your business?" But meeting Makarios's determined gaze, he quickly added, "Ma'am."

"We are here to see Polus."

His pretense of sternness was gone as he said, "Yes, ma'am," and banged on the gate, "Kah! Open up!"

The gate clanged and creaked open, and the young man said, "Take them to see that big bloke."

He nodded at Makarios as she rode past and then said to Nikos, as he gestured at Dusko, "Hey, she's a beaut! Ain't never seen one like her."

"She's an Askonian—from up north," said Nikos proudly, feeling much surer of himself aboard the mare. The young man, whose name was Hemoth looked with wonder at Dusko as the gate closed.

"Keep an eye on her," said Nikos. "She spooks easy." Hemoth nodded in reply, and then a soldier escorted them back. Soon, they were standing before

Polus, who was slow to wake up from a mattress in the corner.

"Polus, I am glad to see you," said Makarios. "How is your side feeling?"

But his gaze was riveted on her as he said, "Polus love Makarios." She smiled at him and inspected his wound, which looked good.

"Polus go with you?" he asked.

Makarios took a deep breath and said, "We were not able to talk to the chief." His face twisted into a look of anguish, and Makarios quickly said, "But as soon as we do, you will probably be able to come out."

Polus became agitated and grabbed the bars.

"Go with you!" he said angrily.

"We will come back as soon as we can," she said.

"No! Go with you!" shouted Polus and shook the bars.

"We will come back soon," she said as they turned to leave.

But Polus shouted louder, "No! *Go with you!*"

He shook and pulled on the bars with all his might, but they held fast. Polus's ranting grew louder and angrier, and as they emerged from the prison building, Makarios broke down in tears.

Baga came rushing up from somewhere else in the barracks shouting, "What in blazes!" When he saw Makarios and Nikos, he pulled up short and came to them.

The soldier said, "Master Baga! That Polus fellow is all in a fit, but everything is secure, sir!"

Baga ignored him as he said to Makarios, "Now, missy, what is it?"

She composed herself and said, "Sir Baga, we are sorry to have caused a disturbance. Polus should calm down soon."

Baga's face was still full of concern as Makarios continued, "We could not talk to the chief today. I am sure you will see to it that Polus gets treated well until we return."

He still seemed struck with Makarios's emotional state, but said, "Why, yes, missy; I'll see to it . . ."

"Thank you, Sir Baga," she said and immediately turned and headed for the front gate.

She spurred Samos out onto the road and as the gate clanged closed behind them, she said, "I wish none of this had happened. . . . It's terrible to see him like that."

Nikos, surprised by her rush of emotion, was at a loss for words, but she soon composed herself and said abruptly, "Well, we can do nothing more. I trust Baga to do the right thing and expect that the chief will not be back in town for a good many days. For now, I must find my brother."

They rode back through town and over the Bradus Bridge coming into Geroon Forest as the day was passing into midafternoon.

"How far is the quarry?" asked Nikos.

"Fifteen miles or so, but we can make quick time on this road," said Makarios as she looked at Dusko. "I am sure this little one would love to run again."

Nikos grinned and patted her neck, and they both broke into a fast gallop. The road cut sharply through the forest, with towering pines on either side. They galloped for a mile or so and then slowed their mounts to a trot, covering the next few miles swiftly.

Soon, they came out of the forest into the grassy field around the remains of Agathon Prison, and the warmth of the sun hit them. Nikos's heart was greatly stirred for Makarios again as he remembered how they had parted there only a few days before. They turned northeast and began following a mine cart line that came down from the quarry. The Stone Mountains towered up on their left, and it wasn't long before they heard the noise of pickaxes and hammers and carts being loaded.

They made their way to the foreman's building where Makarios found a grizzled old man seated at a table and holding a quill in his hand.

"What can I do for ya, my lady?" he said as he hastily stood up and nodded.

"I am looking for Moros, son of Baros."

The man sat back down and pulled a ledger from a shelf behind him; he began humming as he ran his finger down a list of names. Not finding Moros, he began again and stopped suddenly at the top of the list, tapping the page, "Ah, *this one*," he said and frowned. "This fool of a boy was here for less than a day. When a rumor came down the line that gold was discovered up at Stoney Point, he hightailed it up there with a few others."

He shook his head and then looked up at Makarios who said, "Thank you, sir."

Outside, she said to Nikos, "He went up to Stoney Point looking for gold."

"How far is that?"

"It is more than two days' ride north. We shall not go after him. I am more concerned for Polus. Moros will have to answer to his father."

They mounted up and rode back the way they had come, passing a few carts on the rail line loaded with stone. Soon, they passed by the ruins of the prison again but continued following the rail line rather than turning back onto the forest road.

As the sun dropped closer to the horizon, Makarios said with a smile, "There is an inn this way at Agathon village and a stable that will keep your unruly mount securely confined."

They arrived by nightfall and had a meal and then a good night's sleep. The morning dawned cloudy, and rain threatened them all the way back to Diaggello, but as they arrived, the sun shone through the clouds. They rode directly to the marshal's building, only to find a sign on the door that read, "As regards legal matters, see Captain Stagos at the barracks."

Makarios sat back in her saddle and took a big, frustrated breath. "I suppose Spoggos has gone on holiday himself," she said crossly. She reined Samos around, and they trotted off to the barracks finding Baga at the guardhouse again with Hemoth.

"Good day, Master Baga! We are here to see Captain Stagos."

"Oh, the captain has taken a bit ill. What may it be that you need to see him about?"

Annoyed, Makarios said, "The chief is on holiday, and now Deputy Spoggos is gone as well. It is not right for Polus to be jailed indefinitely without a proper trial."

"Why, yes, missy; you are quite right, but naught can be done without the chief giving the word," said Baga apologetically. "But you are free to visit that big fellow—"

"It is best not to get him stirred up again. He is well?"

Baga nodded, and as they rode away, Makarios said, "If only *I* was commanding that army, things would be set right!"

They went back to her father's farm to return Dusko, but Nikos had become quite attached to her and wished he could keep her for his own.

As they approached the hayfield, Baros looked up and called out, "Ah, I see we still have no help from that fool brother of yours! Where has he got to?"

The other men also paused in their work, leaning on their pitchforks as the two came down between the rows of hay.

"He went far up north to Stoney Point, looking for gold," said Makarios. Baros only shook his head and then turned back to the hay.

He turned and looked incredulously at Dusko, exclaiming, "Why, it's a miracle that you're riding her, boy!" The mare became nervous at his raucous voice and danced sideways into one of the rows of hay, scattering it.

"Now, watch it, boy!" said Baros a little louder.

Nikos was able to calm Dusko down and said, "Sorry, sir. I will help with the rest."

Baros's tone softened some, and he said, "Well, I sure won't turn down the offer." But as he looked at Makarios, he continued, "No, go on. Me and the boys will have this done soon. I'm sure you both have business to attend to."

"Thank you, Father; indeed, we do," said Makarios.

"Now are you done needin' her?" Baros asked, gesturing to the mare.

"Well, we are headed to my farm," said Makarios.

Baros looked at Nikos with a slight grin and said, "Seem like you two get on real well. She isn't doing anything in that pasture all day except eatin' up my grass. Take good care of her and bring her back when you may."

Nikos's face exploded into a grin as he profusely thanked Baros, who quickly turned back to his work.

They rode across the field, up past the barn, and out onto the road, going east at an easy pace. Soon, they turned off the road onto a cart path and after a mile or so came to Makarios's farm. There was a barn with a few outbuildings, a herd of about twenty beef cattle, three milk cows, some horses, and a few mules.

As they rode to the barn, Nikos was startled by a high-pitched whinny coming from one of the fields. He looked to see a big bay horse galloping toward the fence. Dusko became nervous and reared up and then came down, dancing sideways, but Nikos stayed with her and calmed her down. The bay horse came to the fence and stopped, pawing the ground and throwing his head around.

"Sar! It is good to see you as well," called Makarios, who turned to Nikos and said, "That is Sar; he is yet a stallion and is very protective of his mares." She motioned to three horses in the field behind him. Dusko was still nervous, but quite interested in getting nearer to Sar.

Makarios said, "Come behind the barn, out of his sight, and they will both calm down. They can meet each other across the fence from the other field after we take care of them."

They dismounted and as they rounded the corner of the barn, they almost ran into one of Makarios's workers, who exclaimed, "Oh! Miss Makah! Hey you ah! It is good to seh you."

Nikos had never seen anyone like her. She was short and round, with a big, long mop of wiry, brown hair and dark eyes. She was hardy and strong, about fifty years old, with very large hands and feet.

Makarios replied, "Oh, Menka! Yes, it is good to be home. This is Nikos."

Menka nodded and kept her eyes on the ground for a moment and then said, "Good to met you, Nehkos."

Nikos was puzzled at her speech, but said, "Yes, ma'am," and nodded back in the same way.

Menka, anxious to continue, said, "Miss Makah, the ahmy in Two Wivahs, wants fiftah pounds of salted met, and Daggo and I ah behind in makin' it, and weh ah out of salt." She held up a small bag that was in her hand and said, "This is the last of it."

"Thank you, Menka," said Makarios. "I will take care of getting more salt tomorrow."

"Daggo is just makin' suppah; I will have him make foh two moh." She nodded and went off at a quick pace toward one of the outbuildings, which was more like a small house.

Makarios said, "Menka and her husband, Daggo, live here and work for me on the farm. They are from a foreign land in the south and have trouble with our language. Daggo doesn't speak it at all."

Makarios provided a good feed of grain for both horses as they rubbed them down and then released them into a pasture adjacent to Sar, who quickly came over to investigate Dusko.

Makarios smiled and said, "Let's go have some supper; I am famished."

They entered Daggo and Menka's little house and were greeted by a very welcoming aroma of baking pork and sweet root. Daggo was very similar in appearance to Menka, although he had a full, long beard like his mop of hair. He nodded and smiled but said nothing.

The meal went with little conversation, and Nikos and Makarios thanked them for the meal and went up to her house. As they came onto the porch, Nikos was filled with feelings for her again and in the light of the setting sun, he said, "I am very grateful for all you have done for me."

"Come now," she said, quickly going in, "I have a room that I keep for travelers and visitors. I am sure that you will find it to your liking."

The next day, Nikos awoke to the sun shining in the window from high overhead. He promptly got up and dressed, finding himself alone in the house. He went out and saw smoke rising from the chimney of one of the outbuildings and found Makarios, Daggo, and Menka inside.

"Good morning, Nikos," said Makarios, "or should I say good day? I trust that you are well rested?" She smiled and continued in response to Nikos's quizzical look at what they were doing, "We are making dried meat. The army barracks in Two Rivers has asked for a large quantity."

Seeing that there were two big bags of salt, Nikos said, "So, you have been to Diaggello this morning. Was the chief there?"

"Unfortunately, no, but I think even if we do find him in the marshal's office, we shall not get a fair hearing. I am going to appeal to the master of Silver City as soon as I may, but this work must come first." She handed Nikos a knife and he began helping them cut the meat.

"So, this is your business?" asked Nikos.

"Yes, for many years now. I sell to the merchants in Diaggello and at Steko's Ferry," answered Makarios as she hung strips of salted meat on a thin pole.

Nikos asked, "Where is Steko's Ferry?"

"It is about fifteen miles east. Steko is my older brother. He began a business running a ferry across the Bradus River to the city of Two Rivers. A small town has arisen there and came to be called Steko's Ferry," said Makarios proudly.

She took ahold of the pole with meat on it and motioned Menka to open the door of the smoke box. Soon they had the box full and then went onto other chores, working the rest of the day.

The next day Nikos worked all day with Menka and Daggo and then went for a long ride on Dusko, arriving back at the farm near nightfall. As he came into the house, he found Makarios at a table in the main room writing in a parchment book by the light of an oil lamp.

She looked up and said, "Ah, Nikos, I was getting a bit concerned." As his eyes met hers, his feelings welled up, but she quickly said, "Nikos, I know . . ."

They both fell silent, and after a few moments, she finished, "I do not feel as you do."

He nodded and slowly acknowledged what he already knew to be true.

Nikos awoke early the next morning and found Makarios cooking griddle cakes. "Sit down; these are almost ready," she said.

After a few minutes, she brought two plates of cakes to the table and sat down. "What do you think?"

Nikos nodded, as if in approval, but Makarios added, "No, you are thinking . . ."

Nikos took a while to form his thoughts into words, but eventually said, "I don't know what I am going to do now, or even where I belong."

Makarios continued looking at her plate and said, "You can stay here as long as you need to."

An uncomfortable pause began so Makarios said, "I am going to Silver City today to appeal to the master of the city for Polus. I would not mind some company."

Nikos felt a great deal of apprehension about going into a big city but agreed to go. Soon, they were on their way and passed through Diaggello, finding that the chief still had not returned. They continued and arrived at Silver City by midday. It was a large city on the coast of the Keramos Sea, which served as the capital of Agathon Province. A high stone wall surrounded it with gates at the east and west sides, with the road passing straight through.

It was a very old city and had long ago served as a stronghold against invading forces attacking from the sea. As they rode through the gate, Nikos looked in wonder at the huge stone buildings. The city was very crowded with people going to and fro, loaded wagons creaking along, and merchants calling out and selling their goods. They worked their way through the crowds, coming nearer to the city square. The buildings were large and ornate, towering above them, but there were many newer structures that were smaller and more suited to merchants and shopkeepers.

Nikos was startled out of marveling at the buildings, as a man's voice called out, "Earn a stonecutter's wage! All who can work, come to the duty office!"

Being unfamiliar with the city, Makarios, followed by Nikos, rode over to the man who looked to be a ruffian, with long tangled black hair and a wispy beard. "Good day, sir!" Makarios shouted. He stopped in mid-cry and turned to her.

As he looked her up and down, an ugly grin spread across his face. "Ha, wench! What do you want?" he bellowed as he walked toward her.

Nikos rode up next to her, and the man scowled and said, "Well, what is it, wench?"

Makarios held herself in check and said kindly, "Can you direct me to the master of the city?"

The man pointed to what looked like a castle across the city square and said, "Over there; that's the magistrate's building."

He began to say something else to Makarios, but they abruptly rode away. At the building, Nikos said, "I'll stay here with Dusko; she's really nervous."

Makarios climbed a set of old marble steps that led into the building and pulled open a heavy wooden door.

As Nikos stood close to Dusko, keeping her quiet, he looked at the throngs of people and all the activity and didn't feel as he had expected. He felt lost among it all, like he was invisible; he felt less and less concerned that he would be recognized and more interested in everyone and everything around him.

Soon, Makarios emerged from the building, but Nikos could see that she didn't have good news.

"Master Metago is away," she said irately. "Do these officials ever do the work our taxes pay for? The marshal said he would send a deputy to Diaggello when he could spare one!"

There were many things to see and do in Silver City and much to Nikos's enjoyment, they spent the rest of the day there. By the evening, they found themselves in a comfortable little tavern enjoying a good meal. The next morning, they headed back through the city and again heard a town crier calling out for stonecutters.

"I want to see about that work," said Nikos, who was feeling oddly adventurous. "I have been thinking about it since last night."

"Oh," replied Makarios, a bit surprised. "Very well." They soon found their way to the duty office and learned that the city was hiring men to rebuild Agathon Prison. Nikos went in and quickly signed on, feeling a bit mischievous at the thought of going back there. He unexpectedly felt carefree and proud of taking responsibility for himself.

As he came to Makarios, he said, "There is a wagon leaving soon with those who have been hired."

She was taken aback and suddenly realized that she felt more for him than she had been willing to admit and said, "You are going . . . now?"

"Yes," he answered, missing everything about how she was feeling. "I was only just in time."

She immediately turned to her horse and began unpacking some things.

"Here," she said turning back, "you ought at least to have a blanket and some provisions."

"Thank you," he said, but his focus was on Dusko. "I suppose she will go back to your father."

"Yes, she will," said Makarios, who hastily dismissed her feelings for him and continued. "Corn harvest is next month, and I usually hire a few temporary workers."

Nikos nodded and said, "I would be glad to come and help."

Makarios smiled and said, "Good. Then I will see you next month, and I will bring your favorite mare."

Nikos turned and climbed up onto a big wooden wagon occupied by a dozen or so other men. The driver reined the big draft horses, and the wagon lurched forward.

Makarios turned to Dusko, put a halter and lead rope on her, and headed out of the city.

She had not gotten far when the black-haired ruffian of a town crier accosted her, grabbing her horse's reins, "Yer a sweet lookin' woman, wench! Surely you don't want to keep all that sweetness to yerself!"

Samos threw his head up, and Dusko reared up and tried to bolt. Makarios had all she could do to control them when suddenly the ruffian was struck to the ground by a man passing by on horseback.

Just as quickly, the man was off his horse, with a short sword pressed to the ruffian's neck. "You shall wish you never awoke this morn if you do not immediately give this fine lady your regrets for your ill-treatment of her!"

The man, who was tall with short black hair, a thin mustache, and a pointy goatee pressed the sword a bit harder against the ruffian's neck, as he spluttered, "Forgive me, my lady!"

Seeing his contrition, feigned as it was, the man sheathed his sword, and the ruffian scrambled away.

"I trust you are unharmed," said the man, taking a hold of Dusko's halter and patting her neck to calm her. "I am Kafar and pleased to be of service to you."

Makarios collected herself and nodded, "Thank you, sir," and then Kafar motioned to two men on horses behind him.

"These are my friends, Barah and Arak." They both nodded and said, "At your service, ma'am." Barah was big and brawny with curly brown hair and a full beard, while Arak was slimmer with lighter colored shoulder-length hair and a clean-shaven face.

Makarios, impressed with their deportment, nodded at them and said, "And quite fortunate I am to have you at my service; thank you again."

Kafar swung up onto his horse, and Makarios continued, "You are on a journey, I see," as she looked at their baggage and packs.

"Ah, yes, we are my lady," said Kafar. "Are you traveling as well?"

"Yes, I am, and I must be on my way. Thank you again." She reined Samos

around and headed east out of the city.

The three men sat there watching her ride away. Barah, being a gruff, but jovial and sensitive sort, said through his thick beard, "Now there's a fine woman if ever I saw one!"

Kafar, after a pause, said in a wistful way, "Indeed."

As Makarios passed out of sight into the mass of people, Arak, being the only one who did not seem to have fallen under Makarios's spell said, "Shall we be off, fellows? We have done all we can here."

"Quite right," said Barah clearing his throat. They spurred their mounts and headed east out of the city.

Three

Nikos was the last one onto the wagon; he sat in the back, holding his belongings close to him. The other men were of all different sorts and none of them looked too happy, except for one older, skinny man with wiry gray hair and beard, who was looking at Nikos.

"Where ya from, sonny?" asked the man.

"Uh, well, I'm not really from anywhere. I am an orphan, but I used to live in Oligos."

"Ah, lived there myself for a while," said the man and then fell silent.

Though Oligos was a small village, Nikos didn't recognize the man and was glad of it, as he thought of what had happened with his foster father. He stared at the rough wooden floor of the wagon, letting out a big heavy breath with all his carefree, adventurous spirit going with it. He suddenly wished with all his might that he was with Makarios again but felt ashamed to even look back.

"Are ya alright, boy?" asked the old man.

"Yes, I . . ." started Nikos, but at that moment the wagon came to a halt. They had passed north out of the city and had stopped at a gate that spanned the road.

"Got to pay the toll," said the old man cynically. "Seems there's a fee for everything nowadays. Comes from up north, ya know."

Two uniformed men were at the gate and as they rolled through, Nikos felt very uncomfortable as the men looked everyone over.

After they had passed on a ways, Nikos stole a look back and asked the old man, "Who are they?"

"The overseer of Smaragdos Province, Sideros-Khirah, I think his name is; they're his men, his soldiers. They collect the toll because the rail line is under his charge, since he built it."

The wagon rumbled on up the road next to the rail line and by midday had arrived at the remains of Agathon Prison. There was much activity with heavy wagons rolling here and there and some men calling out and hefting rocks, while others were digging long trenches. There was a central cluster of tents with a rough wooden building near the road, from which a man emerged and came toward the wagon.

"All of you, report to the foreman!" he called out, motioning toward the building.

The old man was gesturing toward the ruins of the prison and saying, "Can you believe how that just crumbled all to bits? It's unnatural, a portent of evil, they say. It ain't a wonder that no one survived."

"*No one?*" asked Nikos.

"Not a one. I'd hate to see what they find in that rubble as they haul away them stones."

He shook his head as they came to a stop at the foreman's building. As they waited their turn, the old man looked around at the activity and continued, "Looks like they're rebuildin' the prison out away from the mountain."

Nikos felt very strange being there, like he had come back from the dead; he was shaken out of his memories by the old man nudging him and saying, "It's your turn, sonny! You sure do more thinkin' than talkin' *or* listenin'."

Soon, Nikos was registered and shown to his quarters and then immediately put to work digging trenches for the foundation. The work was hard and hot and by the end of the day, Nikos was exhausted. He returned to his tent and flopped down onto his cot, falling asleep almost instantly.

He was awakened the next morning, soon after dawn by the sounding of a loud horn and someone yelling outside his tent, "Come on you scallywags! Get moving! Everyone out!"

Nikos sat up quickly and grimaced in pain as he felt his whole body aching. Nikos reached under his cot for his bag of provisions but found that it was gone. Anger suddenly surged through him as he realized that it had been stolen. He sat there for a few moments and looked around at the others, wondering if one of them was the thief. His anger subsided as he realized how naïve he had been to leave his possessions unattended among so many who seemed no better than vagrants and scoundrels. He went out and found himself in a crowd of men all moving in one direction. They went down the row of tents and entered a large tent at the end and formed somewhat of a line. As they moved ahead, they were given bowls of food, which they took to various make-shift tables and sat down to eat.

Nikos didn't much like whatever it was, but in spite of that, he had less than he wanted and had only just finished, when a foreman called out, "Come on, get to work now! Everybody out!"

As Nikos emerged from the tent, there was no further direction, so he went back to what he had been doing the day before. Work continued all day, stopping only for the midday meal and again for supper. Nikos returned to his tent immediately after the work ceased and again flopped down on his cot. He was hot and dirty, but he had no energy to go for a wash. He was the only one there and soon nodded off but was awakened suddenly with angry yelling.

He came to and saw that there were many more men in the tent with two who were at odds over a cot.

"That's mine!" yelled one man.

"Well, there isn't no more," the other man shouted, "and I was here first!"

On and on, the exchange went until they came to blows. Nikos was glad that in the midst of fighting, they fell out the doorway of the tent. There was more yelling, but by this time, the camp's guards had arrived. Neither man returned to the tent that night. As Nikos settled back down, another man came into the tent, carrying a pack and a blanket. He was big and brawny with curly brown hair and a full beard. He looked around and seeing no empty cots, went to a corner of the tent and rolled out his blanket on the ground. Nikos watched him and thought that there was a finer quality to him than most of the others, and he immediately felt at ease.

His loneliness prodded him to say, "I am Nikos."

"I am Barah. Have you been here long?"

"Only since yesterday; it is hard work," said Nikos.

Barah chuckled and said, "Ah yes, but only to those who think work is hard!"

Before Nikos could respond, Barah continued, "Well, it looks like my bed shall be the ground tonight. See you in the morning."

Nikos awoke to someone gently shaking him.

"Wake up! They've called for us to get up."

Nikos, still groggy with sleep, saw that it was the man he had met the night before. He got up quickly, thanking Barah for waking him, and soon they were in the meal tent.

Nikos looked disdainfully at his ration of food, but Barah had already begun eating and said, "I have had worse."

They ate for a few minutes and then Nikos ventured, "You seem a different sort than most of these fellows. What brings you here?"

Barah smiled and said, "Well, I thought the same of you. Do you live far from here?"

"I don't really live anywhere—"

He was interrupted as a camp guard called out, "Everyone out! Get to work!"

Nikos quickly downed the rest of his food, and they went out. He didn't see Barah for the rest of the day, except briefly at the midday meal. When evening came, Nikos went to the lake for a good wash and afterward, feeling quite refreshed; he sat down on an old log away by himself to watch the sun set. Far down the shore to his left, there were other men in the lake, some washing and others laughing and enjoying the refreshment of the cool water.

Nikos had turned back to watching the sun when a man called out to him.

"Barah!" said Nikos with a grin. "Did you think the work to be hard today?"

"It is good work," he answered. And as he sat down next to Nikos, he added, "So will you work here until the prison is finished?"

"I suppose I will. I do not know what else to do," said Nikos. "And what about you?"

"Well, I am on a journey from the south with my friends. We have been gone much longer than we expected and have no more money. They have gone to a town south of here to look for work."

They talked on; the sun had long since set, and the stars were twinkling in the summer sky by the time they went back to the tent. The next day passed and in the late afternoon, Nikos found Barah down at the lake fishing.

He hastily went down the slope and across the sandy shoreline and asked, "Is that allowed?"

Barah shrugged and said, "I have not heard to the contrary. Besides, would you not enjoy a fresh broiled fish?"

Nikos agreed that it would be a welcome addition to their usual tasteless rations.

He sat down and looked off across the lake as Barah said, "It is good to have more time to talk. I have been wondering about your childhood. Do you have brother or sisters? And your father and mother, are they well?"

"Well, I am an orphan," said Nikos. "I never knew my father or my mother. I do not know if I have any brothers or sisters."

Barah looked at him and patted his shoulder, "I am sorry, my friend."

Nikos nodded and continued, "I lived with a cruel man who had been charged with taking care of me."

Barah listened with much compassion as Nikos recounted his days by the lake and the cruel treatment he had endured. He told him about his horse Zeo and also of how Kakos had died. He finished by saying, "I tried to run away, but a few days later they found me. I had ridden all the way to the village of Hudor but got caught stealing foo0d. It wasn't long before I found myself in prison."

Barah said quickly, "But how are you now free?"

"Well," began Nikos, hesitating, "It was *this* prison or what is left of it."

"You were in *this* prison?" exclaimed Barah. "But I have heard that no one survived, none of the guards or even the warden."

"Yes. It was very fortunate for me," said Nikos and went on to describe what had happened.

Barah slowly shook his head. "Surely, your life was spared and in a very strange way."

After a few moments, Barah said triumphantly, "Well, you should never have been imprisoned, so it is justice that you are free." Again, he patted Nikos on the back.

Nikos fell silent as he remembered Makarios saying the same thing. Soon the sun began to set, and Barah put his fishing pole down. The lake glittered red and orange and the tattered clouds that hung low in the sky seemed to have a light of their own.

Over the next few weeks, they settled into the routine of the camp. Every tenth day was a respite from the hard labor, and all work at the camp ceased. On these days, most of the men when to Agathon village or Silver City to the taverns and pubs. Nikos and Barah, however, stayed in the vicinity of the camp preferring the calmness and peace afforded by a nearly empty camp. On these days, they spent time talking and were becoming fast friends. Nikos's vague sense that Barah was somehow different from everyone else continued to puzzle him, and though he had come to trust Barah without reservation, he still felt uncomfortable to ask about it.

Early one evening, Nikos asked Barah, "Where are you and your friends journeying to?"

Barah did not answer immediately, but after a few moments he took a deep breath and said slowly, "We are looking for something."

Nikos sensed Barah's reluctance to say much more, but after a minute or two, he continued, "Nikos, it is a very serious matter that my friends and I are about. We have told *no one* of our purpose."

Nikos was intrigued and waited eagerly for him to continue.

"You are in my confidence, my friend," said Barah steadily, "and I believe it is not by chance that we have come to know each other."

Nikos became apprehensive, feeling he was on the edge of something that he didn't necessarily want to be a part of.

In spite of that, he asked, "What is it that you are looking for?"

"Something that was stolen from us," began Barah, but then hesitated, falling into a very sober mood.

As the last bits of red clouds disappeared, he looked high up into the night sky and said, "We must speak no more tonight and had best get to sleep, or we will see the sun again sooner than we like."

Nikos had a fitful night and awoke early, feeling as if he had not slept at all. As he sat up, he was suddenly struck with a dream he had had. He saw himself walking across endless sand dunes under a mercilessly hot sun. It seemed he had walked farther than was humanly possible, but he had kept going. Soon, he became thirsty and wanted water more than he had ever wanted anything in his life. But there was only sand as far as he could see. As he came to the top of another dune, he saw in the distance what looked like a gigantic castle, gleaming white in the sun. He bounded down the slope of the dune, feeling a great hope, but suddenly fell and rolled and cartwheeled until he came to a stop at the bottom. He was covered with burning, gritty sand and coughing it out of his mouth. He looked expectantly toward the castle, but it was gone. There was nothing but endless miles of sand ahead. He felt a great dread that he would die of thirst as he stood looking hopelessly in all directions. And then, the dream was over.

Nikos rarely dreamed and was quite disturbed. He felt unusually thirsty as he dragged himself from the tent and went to the well nearby. His thirst intensified as he turned the wheel, but the bucket seemed to be getting no nearer to the top, and he began to panic as if his life depended on it. Finally, the bucket appeared from the darkness of the well.

Just as he was about to reach for it, a voice came from behind him, "Sonny, are you alright?"

Nikos jumped and spun around startled. It was the old man whom he had ridden with up to the prison.

He took hold of Nikos's arm and said, "Why, you're shakin', boy."

"I . . . uh, well, I'm very thirsty," began Nikos.

The old man pulled the bucket onto the edge of the well, and Nikos drank deeply. It tasted better than anything he had ever had.

After a moment, he turned to the old man and said a quick thank you as water dripped from his chin. "I had a bad dream last night."

"Well, you be careful now, sonny," said the old man as he poured water into a large bucket that he had brought.

Nikos, in his haste to get to the well, had not even noticed the gray sky and the damp chill in the air. He shivered and felt gloomy as he made his way to the meal tent. Soon Barah joined him; as always, he was in good spirits. As they walked toward the tent along with the other workers, Nikos's mind was filled with questions about their conversation of the night before.

As they ate, they made small talk and, on their way out, Barah said, "We will talk again soon."

The day started slowly for Nikos as he wondered about Barah and his friends and about the dream he had had. But he was soon distracted as the gray morning cleared into a hot July day. The work digging the foundation was finished, and Nikos was tasked with preparing the stones left from the old prison by chipping mortar off them. He joined many others doing the same thing and by the end of the day, he was very weary and only interested in his cot.

The following days were busier than usual as work on the outer wall was beginning, and more workers were arriving. There was little opportunity to talk alone with Barah, so Nikos contented his curiosity with waiting for the next rest day, which arrived with Barah prodding him awake.

"The day is half gone, my friend," Barah said, "and they are serving the midday meal. You know they make less on rest days. I have told the cook that we will be there shortly."

There were fewer men that usual at the meal, so Nikos and Barah had as much as they wanted.

As they left the tent, Barah said, "I could go for some apple mead; too bad they don't allow any kind of ale or mead in the camp."

"There is a tavern in Agathon Village called the Eagles Nest," offered Nikos.

"You have been there?"

"Yes, once,"

"Ah, it sounds like a fine idea. Is the village far?"

"Five miles or so west; we can follow the mine cart line."

They made for the pasture where the horses were kept and found that the old man Nikos had talked with a few times had charge of it.

"Ah, sonny! Goin' for a ride today? It's a fine day for it."

"Well, I'm hoping you can lend me a horse," said Nikos. "My friend here has his own, but I am without."

As he finished speaking, he thought of his horse Zeo and wondered again where he was. As Barah went to get his horse, the old man said to Nikos, "I suppose you can take my old girl here. She's not much for runnin', but she'll go all day."

"We're only going to the Village."

"Well, take good care of 'er, and she don't mind an apple or two if she can get 'em." The horse was an old dappled gray mare with a big barrel of a stomach and a shaggy mane.

"I'll go without a saddle if you don't mind," said Nikos.

"Well, I know *she* won't mind," the old man replied. "More and more, she gets all in a fuss when I pull the cinch tight."

Soon they were on their way, and the old mare set a slow plodding pace. Nikos felt quite happy and breathed deeply in the warm summer breeze. He looked at Barah who seemed similarly joyous and was again reminded of how he always seemed to be happy in some way. They left the camp behind and were soon alone on the road.

Nikos was about to ask Barah about his friends and what they were looking for when Barah said, "I have been eager to finish our conversation that began down by the lake. I know now that you are meant to hear of our mission. Your life was indeed spared for a purpose."

Nikos looked at Barah, feeling an unwelcome suspicion and replied, "What do you mean, 'You know'?"

"A few nights ago, I had a dream—" began Barah.

Nikos interrupted, "A dream! I had a dream the same night we talked by the lake. I was alone, walking and walking and walking in a vast, unbearably hot and seemingly endless desert . . ."

He trailed off and looked expectantly at Barah as if he could explain it.

"What else happened in the dream?"

"Well, after I had walked farther than it would seem possible, I was losing all hope when I saw a white castle off in the distance," continued Nikos.

A look of recognition came upon Barah, and Nikos, suddenly feeling fearful and overwhelmed, asked, "Do you know about this castle?"

Before Barah could answer, Nikos pulled his horse to a stop and said, "Barah, I have sensed from our first meeting that there was something different about you, and now you're saying you *know* things. And what about this secret business of yours, and how you know about part of my dream . . .?"

Nikos stopped short, suddenly running out of things to say, but he looked intently at Barah, waiting for an explanation. A few horsemen were approaching and nodded amiably as they went past.

More people were coming and going on the road, and Barah said, "Let us get off the road," and he spurred his mount into the field.

They came to a very large oak tree that stood by itself and dismounted, turning their horses out to graze. The sun had climbed high into the sky, and the two men took refuge in the shade of the tree.

Barah began, "Ah, my young friend, I had wished to explain everything to you, but until now, I have been unsure what I should tell you. You are right in saying that there is something different about me and as for *knowing* things, I had a dream last night that I believe showed me something in the future."

Nikos said apologetically, "I am sorry. What about your dream?"

"It was last night, and all I saw was that you and I were riding across a desert. Your horse was a breed I had never seen before, black with dusky white spots down the back and across the hindquarters."

Nikos started, "Was it a mare?"

"Yes, very young."

"I have ridden a horse just like that! My friend borrowed it from her father."

Barah remained silent for a moment and as his mind began filling with questions, Nikos asked, "In the dream, where are we going?"

"I do not know any more than I saw, nor do I know when it happens, only that it will," said Barah.

"But how do you know?" asked Nikos. "I've had dreams that seem to mean something, but never come to anything."

Barah did not answer immediately as Nikos was lost in thought, trying to make sense of things.

"Dreams are a small part of the story, Nikos," said Barah. He continued in a more serious tone, "I believe that you are fated to join us."

Nikos snapped out of his thoughts, and a wave of fear passed over him, but Barah put a hand to his shoulder and continued, "My friend, I know it is difficult, but I must tell you of our mission. My friends, Kafar and Arak, and I have come from the south, hundreds of miles away. We are looking for a book that was stolen from us."

Now more curious than fearful, Nikos said, "A book? You have come so far for just a book?"

"It is very important to us," replied Barah solemnly.

Nikos asked slowly and more quietly, "What kind of book is it?"

Barah looked at him gravely and said, "It is very old and sacred; it is called the Book of Chayaah-Mawveth."

Nikos's eyes widened, and he asked, "What does that mean?"

"In my language, 'Chayaah' means life, and 'Mawveth' means death."

Nikos began to feel uneasy again and hesitantly asked, "What is it about?"

Barah grinned slightly and said, "It is about life and death, my friend."

"But what *about* life and death?"

Barah took a deep breath and let it out slowly explaining, "There is much more to life than death, and there is much more to death than life."

Puzzled, Nikos asked, "What does that mean?"

"It is from the Book," answered Barah. "It means that there is more to this life than we can fully understand. Great forces are at work in this world."

He paused as Nikos began shaking his head and asked, "What forces? There is no more than this," he added as he gestured around.

"Ah," said Barah, grinning. "If you do not see it, then it is not there? Tell me, have you ever seen anything you cannot explain?"

Nikos thought for a moment and shook his head, but then thought of how he survived the prison collapse and looked sharply up at Barah.

"But that was just good fortune," began Nikos, but Barah's questioning expression prompted a more honest response. "Maybe you are right, Barah. I did feel protected somehow and like I had been purposefully set free . . ." Nikos trailed off and then said, in a distant kind of way, "But for what?"

He looked to Barah as if he could answer, but he only said, "I do not know."

They sat in silence for a few minutes as they watched people passing by on the road.

"How did the Book get stolen?" asked Nikos.

"By deceit," replied Barah as he stood up. "But we must speak no more of that for now." It was late afternoon as they mounted their horses and headed toward the road.

"You must tell no one of the things I have told you," said Barah earnestly. "I trust you will not. There is great power in the Book for good, but also much power in it for evil."

They turned onto the road and brought their steeds up to a trot and were soon at the village. There were few people at the village inn since it was still early evening. Barah and Nikos ordered supper with their mead and spent a good long time in quiet conversation before heading back to the prison site.

Work resumed as usual the next day and as Nikos worked with the stones, he kept thinking about what Barah had said about the Book, that there was great power in it. He wondered about that, but with no opportunities to speak to Barah, all he could do was wait for the next rest day. He also wondered when Makarios would come to get him to help with the harvest and hoped it would be later rather than sooner. The days passed uncomfortably in the July heat, but soon the rest day came, and Nikos arose to find Barah.

"Ah, Nikos, always the last one up, but earlier than usual today!" called Barah as Nikos emerged from the tent. "You have just missed breakfast, but I saved some for you." He gave Nikos a small loaf and some large pieces of jerky.

"They have put a floating pier in the lake, so I am going fishing," continued Barah. "I hope I have better luck than fishing from the shore."

They headed to the lake and as was usual on a rest day, they had the camp mostly to themselves. The pier was about one hundred feet out, and they found the water cooler than they liked in the misty morning air.

"I wonder what this is for?" asked Nikos as they clambered up onto it.

"I do not know, nor do I care," replied Barah as he arranged his fishing pole and bait and then sat down, letting his legs dangle over the edge. "I only hope I will catch a nice big fish!"

The pier was built of old, used boards, nailed to heavy logs and was about ten feet square. A heavy chain that disappeared into the depths of the water was attached to it.

"My friend, Makarios, will likely come before the next rest day to take me back to her farm for corn harvest," said Nikos as he sat down next to Barah. "So, I am anxious to hear more about the Book today." Without waiting for a reply, Nikos continued, "Especially about the power that you say it contains. How can a book have power? Where did it come from? Who wrote it?"

"My friend, I can only answer one question at a time," chuckled Barah. "Which will it be?"

"Well, just tell me of the Book," said Nikos, "because I have never heard of such things as you have been telling me. It all seems so . . . fanciful . . ."

"Believe me, I do not believe in someone's fancy, nor would I risk my life for it," said Barah, who paused and looked far across the lake, gathering his thoughts.

"The Book is unlike any other. It is unusually beautiful and ornate, bound in a deep red leather with beautiful inlaid gold scrollwork at its corners. 'Kathab Chayaah-Mawveth' is embossed on the front, and the edges of the pages are gilded a brilliant gold. It was written thousands of years ago with an unknown kind of ink on paper that seems not to be made by human hands."

Nikos's eyes widened as Barah continued, "It is as new as the day it was created and is indestructible, not even fire can touch it."

"That is amazing!" exclaimed Nikos, "A book that cannot be burned!" After an incredulous shake of his head, he continued, "But what is its meaning, what is it about, why does it exist?"

"To tell us about the curse of Kah-Taw," said Barah.

A wave of anxiety hit Nikos, and Barah said, "Do you wish me to go on?"

Nikos nodded slowly as Barah continued, "I am glad you are with us; but do not fear, my friend. Adventures are bigger than those who have them."

Nikos looked quizzical.

"Yes, again that saying is from the Book," added Barah. "There are many such sayings as that, but I must finish telling you of Kah-Taw. As I said, it is a curse. It is hard to describe in the common tongue, but it is the thing in all men that makes them do evil."

"But not all men are evil," said Nikos. "You have heard me speak of Makarios; she is not evil."

"It may seem she is not, but that depends on how a man sees things."

Nikos's thoughts suddenly turned inward as he thought of the innumerable things he felt guilty about.

"Kah-Taw is much more of a curse in some men than in others," continued Barah. "Many men feel no conscience at all when they lie or steal or even when they kill."

Nikos absentmindedly put his hand to his chest, feeling a strange stirring in his heart. He looked off across the lake as Polus came to his mind and the deadly rage he had seen in him. He thought of the prison guards and how some of them really delighted in causing pain. He remembered Kakos and how unexplainably cruel he was. He believed what Barah was saying and felt a certain doom come over him. But even in the midst of that, he suddenly thought that the idea of Kah-Taw was foolish and imaginary.

He said, "Barah, I have never heard of this, and it is hard to believe."

"It is indeed hard to believe because it is not something to be seen or held in your hands." He turned to Nikos and said, "But I see that you know in your heart it is true."

Nikos was conflicted and silent for a while, but he asked, "How did Kah-Taw come to be?"

"Men were not always evil. Long before this present age, an evil being called the Ra-Tsalem arose in the world and caused men to be cursed with Kah-Taw."

"But why . . . how?" asked Nikos.

"Some questions cannot be answered, but we must deal with what is," said Barah matter-of-factly.

Nikos felt at a loss and said uneasily, "What is this Ra- . . . uh, how do you say it?"

"He is called the Evil One in the common tongue. He is a very powerful and wicked being who wants to rule over all men—to make us his slaves who do his bidding. But most do not even know that they serve his purposes. He is devious in his ways, and his insidious voice is always whispering in their hearts and minds, goading them to do evil."

Nikos cowered as if something was descending upon him and said fearfully, "Where is this Evil One?"

"He is not of flesh and bone, but a phantom and cannot be seen, although he will sometimes assume the physical form of someone or something," said Barah with a hint of fear.

"Surely, you are not his pawn as well, since you know these things?"

"No," said Barah slowly. "I am not, but I once was, as all men are from the moment they first open their eyes in this world."

"That is what is different about you?"

Barah nodded as Nikos continued, "How did you free yourself from this evil being?"

"Oh, I did not free myself," said Barah after a deep breath. "It is the Tsadaq who breaks the curse of Kah-Taw. He is called the Great One and is a supreme being who exerts his power in this world. It is he who wrote the Book by dictating his words to a mystic named Saphar."

Nikos nodded slowly as Barah continued, "The Great One is more powerful that the evil Ra-Tsalem but is in a constant battle with him."

"But why?" asked Nikos with dismay. "Why does this Great One allow *any* evil if he is stronger?"

"That is not a question that can be answered, but the Book instructs us to fight evil."

Nikos again felt all of this to be far-fetched and fanciful; nevertheless, he found himself believing.

"What must I do?"

"You must seek the King," said Barah.

"What king?" asked Nikos, feeling very stirred.

"He is *the* King."

"Where is he?"

"There is a castle, far, far to the south," said Barah, "near my hometown."

Nikos, almost irrationally, was ready to go at that very moment and said quickly, "Will you show me the way?"

"You are already on the way," finished Barah with a grin.

Four

Makarios made a swift trip back to Diaggello from Silver City and decided she ought to see Polus. As she approached the barracks, she saw only Hemoth at the guardhouse, and he hurriedly stood up and came toward her.

"Good day, ma'am!" he said nervously. "I suppose you are here to see that big fellow. Well, he's . . . I mean, well . . . they took him out in the prison wagon. I don't know where . . the chief ordered it."

"Let me speak with Baga!" said Makarios abruptly.

The young man stepped back a few paces and said anxiously, "Sorry, ma'am; he's not here. He went with the wagon."

He added in a more hopeful tone, "But I expect that the chief is back in his office."

Makarios gave a quick thank you and headed off, trying to control the fury she was feeling. Within minutes she had arrived at the marshal's building to find the chief, a very fat, red-cheeked man sitting at the table talking with Deputy Spoggos.

"You!" she exclaimed. "Where have you sent Polus?"

But the chief, with a thoroughly arrogant expression, said evenly to Spoggos, "Who is this woman? What business does she have here?"

He continued to look at Spoggos, who answered uneasily, "She . . . uh seems to have something to do with that big fellow, sir, the one you sent away yesterday."

Makarios stared steadily at the chief, saying very sharply, "Where have you sent him?"

The chief took a very deliberate deep breath as he rolled his eyes slowly onto Makarios, "And what business is it of yours, my *lady*?" he asked caustically.

She roughly crossed her arms and looked at him piercingly, "Where have you sent him? He deserves a fair hearing. You cannot imprison him indefinitely!"

The chief slowly shook his head and as he leaned forward onto his desk, said in a leisurely way, "Oh, my dear, *dear* lady. Do you not understand that I can do anything I wish to, *hmm?*"

He raised his big, bushy eyebrows at her and then sat back heavily in his chair.

His demeanor was about to send Makarios into a rage, but Spoggos quickly said, "Now, ma'am, I am sure that justice will be served; after all, the chief *is* fair."

She turned her anger on Spoggos and said, "Where is Polus?!"

He did not dare to answer, but looked to the chief, who said in a dispassionate, almost bored way, "Move along now; I am tired of this."

With that, he picked up a pen and began ruffling through some papers. Makarios's rage was so fixed on the chief, that when Spoggos took her by the arm and moved her out the door, she was hardly aware of it.

Spoggos, wanting to avoid any more difficulty, said in a hushed tone, "Chief sent that Polus beast up to the prison at the Outpost yesterday. Now you best get along."

With that he disappeared back into the office and closed the door.

Makarios stood there feeling at a loss. Her anger soon subsided, and then a man's voice called from across the square, "Makarios!" She looked up to see Graffo coming toward her.

"The chief," he said excitedly, "sent Polus somewhere. He paraded the prison wagon right out of town!"

"Yes, Spoggos says he went to the Outpost," she answered. "Maybe he will get fairer treatment there."

Makarios departed and returned home discouraged. She sat on her porch and watched the sun go down, wondering what she should do. She suddenly felt very small and alone, and a tear rolled down her cheek. As she brushed it away, her wolf, Lukos, seemed to appear out of nowhere and bounded up onto the porch.

"Ah, my friend!" exclaimed Makarios as she got down next him hugging and rubbing him. He was very affectionate, and she felt greatly comforted.

As she leaned back against the wall with Lukos next to her, the men she had met in Silver City came to her mind, especially the dark-haired man named Kafar. There was something different about him, she thought, and the other two as well, but her thoughts of them faded as weariness overtook her.

In the morning, she went out and found Menka feeding the pigs. "Good morning, Menka!"

"Ah, Miss Makah! Good monin!"

"We shall take the dried beef to the army in Two Rivers today, but I have some business to attend to and will go on from there to Agathon Outpost. I will be gone a few days," she said.

"Yes, Miss. I will get Daggo and load the wagon," said Menka as she finished with the pigs.

As Makarios packed her bags onto Samos, Daggo was hitching up their two mules, Tuk and Bit, to the wagon. Soon, they were bumping down the cart path with Makarios following behind aboard Samos. When they got to the main road, they turned right and headed east. The going was easy since the road was a main thoroughfare and well-traveled, but it was still past midday when they arrived at Steko's Ferry. It was a small village, with little activity except for the two ferries, one for horses and those on foot and a much larger one for horse-drawn wagons and the like. Rummie's Tavern provided drink and lodging for travelers and did a good business.

As they approached the ferry docks, a tall, lanky man with dark, curly hair came toward them and called out, "Ah, my sister, it is good to see you!"

"And you as well, my brother!" replied Makarios. Daggo pulled his mules to a stop at the dock, and Makarios quickly dismounted and met the man with a hug.

"We are going to Two Rivers with provisions for the army," Makarios explained.

"Business is good, then?" asked Steko.

"Yes, quite . . . as much as we can manage. I see you are doing as well," said Makarios, observing the busy docks.

"Yes, indeed. There will be a bit of a wait. Come over here and water your mules and this fine one here," said Steko as he gave Samos a good rub on the neck.

As they went, Makarios asked Steko, "Did a prison wagon from Diaggello come through here in the last few days?"

"Day before yesterday. There was one prisoner, a big brute of a man."

Makarios said, "I will tell you more later; we must get across to Two Rivers. Daggo and Menka will drive back to the farm tonight and should like to arrive before nightfall."

After making their delivery, they came back, and Makarios went to Rummie's Tavern for supper. She was soon joined by her brother as he sat down with a flagon of apple mead and poured them each a mug.

"Ah, you still remember my favorite drink, my brother. Thank you."

As she took a sip, Steko said, "So, tell me, what is your interest in that prisoner?"

After a deep breath, Makarios recounted the whole story about Nikos and Polus. Her brother looked surprised at certain points and even astonished at others.

When she had finished, he said, "I never thought you to be such an adventurous sort, but I know it is your heart leading you on."

He smiled and looked at Makarios with adoration. "You are a lot like mother was."

She smiled at him and said, "Thank you; now I must be off to bed."

As she stood, she drained her mug of apple mead and said, "The Outpost is a day's ride, is it not?"

"Yes," said Steko as they went toward the rooms in the tavern.

He spoke to the tavern keeper, "Rummie, give her your best room," and then he put down a few silver coins.

Makarios looked at him with gratitude as he went out. In the morning Makarios awoke to the sound of rain outside and pulled on her oilskin coat as she went out to the stable. She saddled up Samos, fastened her pack on, and rode out to the docks. The rain was pouring down, and there was no one there except one ferry operator, who was huddled inside a small building. He was not at all happy about having to leave his shelter; he kept his head down and went about his job resolutely.

Across the river it was quiet in Two Rivers as she passed through and was soon on the road north. The day passed slowly and drearily as the rain continued. About midday, Makarios came to a small village and thought it a good place to rest a little while and get a meal. There were no taverns or inns, but only a few shops. She sought shelter under the front porch of a clothier's shop and was just about to get some provisions from her saddle bag when a voice came from behind her. Makarios turned to see a plump, middle-aged woman standing in the open doorway, the woman kindly invited her to join her husband and two workers for a meal.

"We were just about to sit down," she said.

The woman directed one of her workers to provide some hay for Makarios's horse as well.

When the meal was over Makarios said to the woman, "Thank you, ma'am; you have been very kind."

"Delighted to make your day a bit brighter, dearie," said the woman. "Good day."

With that, Makarios climbed aboard Samos and rode out of town. Farther on, the rain eased up and then stopped altogether, lightening Makarios's mood. She soon covered the rest of the distance to the Outpost, seeing only a few other travelers. The town was smaller than she expected, hardly a town at all, so she easily found her way to the marshal's building.

As she entered, Makarios was met by a tall, rugged, broad-shouldered man, who stood up from behind a desk and said, "Help you, ma'am?"

He had shoulder-length brown hair, flecked with gray, a strong jawline and a few days growth of beard. Makarios was about to answer when her eyes met his. They were piercing and green, intent and sincere and unexpectedly cut right to her heart.

"Ma'am?" he repeated.

Makarios said quickly, "Yes, you are the marshal?"

"Indeed, I am—as well as the magistrate and town master, though there is little to be master of. My name is Pike."

"I am Makarios," she said and nodded slightly. "I am here to see a prisoner named Polus who was just brought in."

"He is a friend?"

"Yes, by chance," she answered.

"Have you known him long?"

Makarios felt a twinge of annoyance and said curtly, "I wish to see him, not answer a list of questions."

Pike chuckled, which increased her annoyance, and said, "I am sorry, but he did not arrive here—"

Makarios interrupted, "But the chief sent him here, did he not?"

Pike motioned her to sit down in a nearby chair, and he returned to his seat behind the desk. "Yes, but it seems he escaped. The drivers from Diaggello rode in on one of the horses that had been pulling the wagon," he began. He paused as he saw how troubled Makarios became.

"Where is he?" she said.

"The drivers reported that he ran away to the north, into Fragmoo Forest.

He had broken the bonds on his feet and was far too fast for them to catch, though his hands were still shackled."

Makarios shook her head. "How did he escape?"

"He somehow overturned the wagon and unfortunately, it went down an embankment where the road passes close to the river, severely damaging it. One of the drivers said that the Polus fellow was limping badly and howling in a rage as he disappeared into the forest."

Makarios stood up, feeling quite at a loss.

Pike came around the desk and said, "My deputy and I searched for him but found nothing. Our hounds tracked him for only a short while and then could not pick up the scent again. We went up to the small village of Palahos, on the other side of the forest and left word with the marshal there about the escape and asked him to send word if this fellow is found."

Makarios paced a bit, thinking how hopeless it would be to try to find Polus.

At that moment, a young man came into the building and said "Hello, Pike," and nodded at Makarios, "Ma'am."

"Evening, Dero," said Pike, who gathered up some papers and a bag and then pulled his coat on while the young man hung his up.

"Perhaps tomorrow, there will be good news from Palahos. There are no taverns here in Agathon Outpost," said Pike and then with a grin, "but you may stay here in one of the day cells if you wish; we will not lock you in."

Being in no temper for jests and wanting to be alone, Makarios said curtly, "Thank you, sir, for your offer of hospitality, but I shall be on my way."

With that she went out and rode north out of town until she came to the edge of Fragmoo Forest. She went into it a short distance, and in the fading light, came upon an old stone wall and set up camp.

Five

Polus ran blindly on, deep into Fragmoo Forest, howling in anger and pain. He had gone quite a distance and was winded when he came to the ruins of an old stone building. It no longer had a roof, and half its walls had deteriorated into piles of stone, but it afforded some cover, so he entered and crouched down, listening. After a few minutes, he was convinced he had gotten away and then his attention turned to the pain he was in. His leg had been injured and as he sat down with difficulty, he began to whimper. Soon his tears were falling and as he looked at the shackles on his wrists, he suddenly struggled violently against them, and his tears burned hot with anger. He began to smash them on a large rock, only increasing his pain, but eventually one of the shackles split open and soon the other, and they both clattered to the ground. He collapsed against the wall, sobbing and exhausted.

In the morning, Polus was roused by pain and lay still for quite a while, but eventually, with labored groans, he sat up. He thought of Makarios, which suddenly brought forth a great gush of tears, and when thoughts of his house came to mind, he blubbered.

"Polus want to go home . . ."

But in all the confusion of escape, he had no idea where home was. After a good long while, his tears ran out, and he took a deep breath and said with unusual resolve, "Polus must help himself now."

He carefully peered out of the ruins, but all was dense forest. He listened carefully and heard the sound of a swiftly flowing river, but he did not have the sense to know how that could help him find his way. Without any reasoning at all, and with only an odd sense that he should go in a certain direction, he headed north, which was quite the wrong direction. He went very cautiously, pausing often to listen as he made his way slowly and painfully along. Eventually, his fear eased as he kept hearing only the natural sounds of the forest. Tears came down again as he trudged along and again thought about home, but this time he angrily squeezed his eyes shut.

"Polus help himself!" he commanded out loud.

After a good long while, he began to see that the forest was thinning out and ahead, the sun was much brighter. He unconsciously began to veer to the right, where the forest remained thick, and walked for half of the day. Eventually, the trees began to peter out in every direction. There was a road far to his right, and he heard the sound of a wagon and men laughing, causing him to suddenly crouch down. He crept away to his right and had a strange feeling that that was the way he ought to go.

Unfortunately, what lay ahead of him past the trees was open countryside. His fear of being seen kept him within the forest until evening fell. When he ventured out, the veil of darkness brought a great sense of safety, and his acute sense of hearing and ability to see well in the dark left him far from blind to his surroundings. The open ground ahead were fields of lush, green grass, and though Polus crossed many fence lines, he did not encounter any livestock, nor did he come near any dwelling.

Soon, he came to a road that ran east and west; some miles to the left were the dim lights of a small village. Polus slunk across the road and turned to the right, sensing he would find cover that way. It wasn't long before the ground began to get rough and sloped upward and then a cold rain began to fall. He came into some sparse trees and underbrush, which soon gave way to uneven ground strewn with rocks and boulders. Eventually, he came to a stop, but wanting to find some shelter, he picked his way along and happened upon the entrance to a cave, somewhat shrouded by trees and underbrush. He gladly went in, but suddenly realized that he was not alone. He stood stock-still in the darkness, not breathing, and listening intently. The only thing he heard was the shallow breathing of some very large creature. Polus moved over to the wall of the cave and crouched down, sniffing the air.

"Not animal," he thought as he sat down. Whatever it was did not stir, and Polus relaxed a bit, glad to be out of the rain, as weariness overtook him.

The morning sun was flooding the cave entrance as Polus woke with a start and jumped to his feet, finding himself face to face with what had been in the back of the cave and was now trying to slip past him.

"Ho!" it yelled and stumbled backward into the dark, cringing in fear. Polus was incredulous and couldn't believe what he was seeing.

"You are like . . . Polus," he said slowly. "Polus thought he was all alone in the world."

He stared at the ground and then back to the creature, who indeed, was of the same race. It remained hunkered down in fear as Polus furiously tried to make sense of things.

Eventually, he asked, "There are more like you . . . like us? The other only nodded as Polus tried to work out how it could be.

"You are afraid?" asked Polus in a very gentle tone, and the other only nodded as Polus added, "But why? We are the same."

Finally, the other spoke, "I am lost," he said plaintively.

"Lost?" answered Polus, suddenly remembering his own situation. "I am lost too . . ."

He trailed off, and the other who was nearly nine feet tall, stood up, though having to remain bent over beneath the roof of the cave.

"I am Uke," he said and as his fear subsided, he added, "You are hurt. I am too," and showed Polus a gash on his arm and a lot of bruising.

"How?" asked Polus.

"I fell into the river and then went over the falls . . ." he trailed off as the horror of the experience came back to him.

"You were afraid," said Polus matter-of-factly.

"I want to go home," said Uke sadly, which hit a nerve in Polus, and a tear came to his eye.

"So does Polus."

"But we are lost," said Uke.

They both were suddenly at a loss as to what to do, and each one looked to the other for direction. They came out of the cave and as Polus looked around and then up past the cave, he saw that they were at the foot of an immense mountain range. For some reason, he felt drawn to it, but both were quite indecisive and just stood there. Neither had the sensibilities to feel awkward and then, without even a real thought, Polus started up the mountain, and Uke began following.

They hiked up for a while until Polus stopped and said to no one in particular, "Polus is very hungry . . . and thirsty."

"Maybe we will come to a stream," said Uke. "I am hungry too."

The terrain was rocky with pine trees interspersed among large rock formations, which made the going difficult. As they progressed, the terrain became steeper, and they had to make detours around sheer rock faces. Their hunger and thirst began to get the better of them and coupled with the day beginning to heat up and their being lost, they both became ill-tempered. They continued on and came to a place that was not so steep and where there was more vegetation and trees other than pine. Suddenly, they heard some kind of distressed squawking away to their right, and they crouched down, peering carefully past the trees. Without a word to each other, they both slowly advanced and eventually, they saw a very large bird struggling on the ground. They made their way closer and realized that its wing was broken. It screeched and squawked as they came upon it, but all it could do was try to hop away. Polus felt a tremendous amount of compassion for the poor thing as it struggled, breathless and exhausted.

Uke said, "We can eat it."

But Polus, suddenly feeling like its protector said, "No!"

"Then I will eat it!" shouted Uke. "I am very hungry!"

"Must help it!" yelled Polus as their tempers flared.

"Eat it!" countered Uke, who tried to step around Polus who pushed him back.

"No!"

Unfortunately for Polus, Uke was a good two feet taller and much stronger, so Uke sent him sprawling. Uke grabbed up the bird, which renewed its terror-filled screeching, and in turn triggered a rage in Polus. The action that followed was furious and earth-shattering as Polus, in an impassioned and blind rage wrestled Uke to the ground and locked his arms around his neck like a vise. It wasn't long before Uke started whimpering and as Polus's emotions subsided, he let go and began to apologize.

"Polus is bad!" he said as tears stung his eyes. "Bad!"

But Uke sat up and said, "No, I am bad! Fighting is bad!"

They each tried to be sorrier than the other, but eventually their efforts petered out, and they noticed that the bird was dead.

"Now, we eat it!" said Uke eagerly, seeming to have forgotten all that had just happened.

Seeing that it was dead, and even though he still felt sorry for it, Polus could not disagree and as his hunger was severe, they both started plucking the feathers off. The scene that followed is best left undescribed, but the small amount of food that the bird afforded them lifted their spirits, and their moods improved.

They were soon on their way again, but the going was even more difficult, and though the trees were thinning out, the terrain had gotten much steeper. Neither of them had the sense to turn back or try a different route, and so they kept going. Their hunger soon returned, and again their dispositions worsened, but each was somewhat absorbed with his own thoughts as they mechanically clambered and climbed up the mountain. They crested another large rock structure and suddenly found themselves, not at the top of the mountain range, but at a false peak, from which they could see the lands below them for miles and miles.

"There is the river!" exclaimed Uke, pointing to the west.

Nothing was familiar to Polus, but Uke continued, "And the road! It goes to my home."

He had a huge grin, which seemed to fall off his face as soon as he looked at Polus, who said, "Polus is still lost . . ."

His sadness was severe, magnified by the accumulated difficulty of the last few days. Uke suddenly felt nearly as sad and patted Polus on the shoulder.

"We can find your home, maybe," he said hopefully. "But first we will go to mine and get helped."

Uke felt quite encouraged. Having seen the way home, he took the lead. They went down wherever they could, but soon the daylight began to fade, and they had to spend the night on the mountain. The morning dawned gray and damp, and there was a thick fog below them. Each of them ached with the previous day's hiking and fighting, and they did not want to move. Eventually, Uke, who now had a clear goal, got to his feet, but Polus remained where he was.

"Polus tired," he said, "and hungry, very hungry."

"I am hungry too," said Uke, "but we can get food at my home."

Being quite passive and acquiescent, he did not try to coerce Polus at all, but his offer of food still achieved the same result as Polus sat up.

"Food at your house?" he asked eagerly.

"Lots," answered Uke enthusiastically. "Mum will cook it!"

This brought Polus to his feet, amid groans and assorted grimaces, and they started off. They quickly made their way down, but soon they had descended into the fog and keeping to the right direction became impossible. Their pace slowed, and then Uke came to a stop.

"We should wait for the sun," he said. "Then we will see the way."

"Keep going," said Polus with a bit of an edge.

"Wait," answered Uke.

"Keep going!"

"Wait?"

"Keep going!"

As Uke had become afraid of Polus since their titanic scuffle the day before, this outburst jolted him forward, but in which direction he didn't know. At least they were down off the mountain, and the land had a gentle slope to it. Uke went a bit slowly, hoping for the fog to clear, but Polus was still in a temper and commanded him to go faster. After a good long trek, the ground began to rise and soon they sensed that there were mountains ahead of them.

"Polus hungry!" he yelled, somehow having made Uke responsible. "Uke lost us!" he continued. "We are at the mountain again!"

Uke's fear was rising, but amazingly, he thought about how sorry Polus could be for his temper and hoped to quell it by using Polus's own words.

"Polus is bad," he began, "for being angry."

But the tension only increased as Polus's temper rose higher.

"Polus bad?" he asked in a malicious tone. "Uke is bad for losing us! Very bad!"

Uke was surprised that his strategy didn't work and began to slowly back away, but Polus advanced on him and yelled, "Uke must be punished for being bad!"

Polus picked up a large rock and hurled it at him, but he ducked out of the way.

"Punish Uke!" bellowed Polus as he bolted at him.

Uke spun around and began running as fast as he could, going down the slope and eventually coming upon a road. Mercifully for him, his height advantage over Polus made him a faster runner, and Polus quickly found himself alone in the fog. His temper faded as quickly as the sense of aloneness overtook him. He stood forlorn in the misty air, which seemed to grow thicker and close in around him.

"Polus *is* bad!" he shouted and slapped the side of his leg, but the pain of it, coupled with his hunger and thirst, brought tears as he continued in a much sadder tone, "And lost his friend . . ."

He stood there for some time, but as the sun broke through the fog, Polus looked up squinting.

"But you are always with me," he said with a slight smile.

The road that he stood on stretched away north and south for a good long way in either direction, but he chose north, the way Uke had gone.

"Maybe Polus find him," he thought, and suddenly the scene with Makarios in the forest by his home engulfed his mind.

"Forgive!" he thought excitedly. "Maybe Uke *forgive* Polus!"

He set off quickly, nearly forgetting his hunger in favor of the idea of being forgiven.

"Forgive," he said out loud as he hurried along. "Uke will forgive. Uke is Polus's *friend.*"

Polus went along for miles and miles and by midday, the road began sweeping upward toward a range of mountains that dwarfed the one he had been on the previous days. Suddenly, Polus heard voices and sounds on the road ahead, though he could not see because it swept around some trees to the right. He darted off the road and into the cover of some vegetation. He had to lie nearly flat so that he would remain unseen, and peered through the grass as he watched men on a wagon loaded with slatted wooden boxes go by. After they had gone, Polus saw that the road snaked back and forth and ascended to a pass with mountainous ridges rising steeply on either side of it. Still fearful of being seen, Polus headed back up into the mountains, but only as far as needed to remain out of sight. His travel was slow and his hunger gnawing, but he felt sure that he would find Uke somewhere up near the pass or beyond.

"He must forgive," thought Polus trying to console the self-pity his hunger was causing. But the pass was farther than it appeared, and soon the sun began to go down. Though Polus was tired and queasy from hunger, he took advantage of the dark and went back down to the road. It wasn't long before he had come nearly to the pass and found a small village to his right. Lights were twinkling in some of the windows, but what Polus noticed immediately was the smell of food, and his acute sense of smell made it seem that it was coming from everywhere. His fear of being caught was still very great and that restrained him quite a bit as he slunk along in the dark toward the village. He smelled so many good things, but when he came upon a pen with some sheep in it, somewhat away from the village, he took his opportunity, which was not half as quiet as he wished. He had spied out a lamb near the fence by itself, but his presence instantly had all the sheep bleating as if their lives depended on it. Suddenly, a dog began barking, and the cries of some men rang out, accompanied by dancing torchlight. Polus fled empty-handed and spent the night hiding out in the mountains again.

He awoke at dawn tired and weak from hunger, so it wasn't long before desperation made him begin to forget his fear of being seen or caught. He quickly made his way down to the village, though wobbly legs had him stumbling here and there. As the sun rose, there began to be activity in the outlying farms. Mostly there were men, but some of the land was farmed by a race of beings from which Polus was from. He crouched in the shadows, still not believing that there were others like him.

As the sun rose, he skirted around the village and found many more of his kind on the north side. A feeling struck him that he had never felt before—a sense of belonging, which greatly puzzled him, but which also made him feel safe. Suddenly, he saw Uke, who was working very hard at pulling a heavy wagon full of hay. Polus felt very sorry all over again and without even realizing it, he had come out into the open toward Uke, who froze when he saw him. But Polus's countenance and obviously weakened condition eased his alarm, though as Polus approached, he gripped the wagon handle a bit tighter.

"Polus is sorry," he said and hung his head in front of Uke, who let the wagon handle clunk to the ground and stepped toward him.

"Forgive Polus?" he continued.

But Uke asked, "What does forgive mean?"

Polus thought a few moments and then said, "That means that you will not punish Polus for what he did. Even though Polus was bad, it will be as if he wasn't."

Uke puzzled it out and then asked, "Do you promise to be good?"

Polus nodded eagerly, and Uke continued, "Then I forgive!" Without a moment's hesitation, Polus grabbed ahold of Uke and hugged him tight and then let him go.

"Uke is Polus's friend!"

"Help me with the hay?" asked Uke.

But Polus frowned in a painful way and said, "Polus is terrible hungry."

"Here," said Uke, pointing to a basket in the wagon. "Old apples for the pigs, but you can have them."

Polus wasted no time and though the apples were nigh on going bad, he ate at least a dozen. He revived immediately and fell in with helping Uke with his chores.

"Mum was real glad to see me when I came home," said Uke, "and she fixed me a real big meal. She'll make us breakfast when we're done."

It came none too soon for Polus, as the apples wore off quickly. Polus felt very much at home with Uke, and all thoughts of being found by those from whom he had escaped vanished from his mind. Uke's mother indeed gladly fixed them a big meal and seemed to quite enjoy Polus's many thank yous. Afterward, Polus's adventures of the last few days caught up with him and all he did was sleep the rest of the day and through the night.

In the early morning, he was awakened by Uke, "Wake up! There is work to do!"

Polus, still very thankful for all he had received, was eager to help. They worked hard for a few hours and again came to a very ample breakfast, which to Polus tasted better than anything he had ever eaten.

"Your mum cooks good!" he said.

Uke responded, "Since you are like my brother, mum is *our* mum!"

Polus stiffened and then said slowly, "Like a *family*?"

"We are," exclaimed Uke. "You can live with us!"

Uke's mother and many brothers who were seated around the table, all nodded with big smiles. Polus was filled with such a sense of belonging that he hardly knew how to respond, nor could he understand quite what he was feeling.

His puzzled look caused Uke to ask in a somewhat disappointed tone, "You don't want to be in our family?"

Polus took a few minutes to work things out and then said, with a grin as wide as all the others, "Polus would *love* to!"

— Six —

Makarios awoke early and Marshal Pike came immediately to her mind. She felt more than she liked and, for the most part, wished to avoid him. After breaking camp, she moved out quickly, looking for a way to skirt around the Outpost.

A voice called out, "Ma'am!" Startled, she saw the young boy Dero waving for her to come toward him.

"Ma'am," said the boy again as she came nearer, "Marshal Pike would like to speak to you."

It was all she could do to mask her displeasure and give a courteous thank you. As she entered the marshal's building, Pike arose and greeted her.

"Ah, good morning, I am glad that Dero found you. I trust that you slept well."

"I did not, but it is kind of you to ask," she said brusquely.

He paused, seeing that she was unsettled, but said, "A messenger came from Palahos late last night to report that your friend had been seen, but they could not catch him. He was no longer shackled and escaped into the mountains to the north."

"Thank you for the news," said Makarios quickly. "I shall be on my way."

As she turned to leave, Pike came around the desk. "Can I offer you some breakfast?"

"Thank you, no—"

Pike stepped in front of her and looked into her eyes but was at a loss for words.

"I must be on my way," she said and went out.

Pike stopped in the doorway and asked, "Where can I send news of your friend if he is found?"

Makarios, already aboard her horse and still very stirred, said, "It is very unlikely that he will be found."

She turned to go, but conflicting feelings turned her back. She said, "I have a farm near Diaggello, off the Eastway Road."

She quickly turned and galloped off, riding hard all the way back to Two Rivers. She crossed the river at Steko's Ferry and was met by her brother.

He called out cheerfully, "Sister! How is the adventure?"

She strode over to him saying, "It has been bad and good."

Steko was puzzled, but said, "You shall tell me all about it at supper." Then he turned and called a young boy who took Makarios's horse to the stable. Soon, they settled in Rummies Tavern again, enjoying beef and potato pie.

Steko was in a jovial mood, but when Makarios described Polus's escape, he became very somber and said, "I am sorry, my sister; he sounds like a very tricky sort and unlikely to be captured."

"You are right, and that is good and bad. It is good because he did not deserve to remain in prison, and now he is free, but bad because he will have to keep hiding."

Her eyes glistened with tears, and Steko reached across the table and squeezed her hand as she continued, "I am sure he will be alright, somehow." With a forced smile, he added, "Besides the marshal at Agathon Outpost is a man of honor and will treat Polus fairly if he is caught."

Her whole countenance changed, and Steko sat back in his chair with a grin, "And this marshal seems to be the good part of your adventure, eh?"

Makarios blushed and quickly looked away saying, "You suppose more than I wish."

"Ah, my sister, it is good. He must indeed be a noble and principled man; for you would not feel such for a scoundrel," said Steko.

They talked over mugs of apple mead for some time before Makarios retired to her room. She left early in the morning, but thoughts of Pike spurred her to return home promptly.

One day in the middle of July with corn harvest approaching, Makarios saddled up Samos and said to Menka, "I am going up to the prison site to get Nikos and also hire some workers in Diaggello. I will be gone a few days."

"Yes, Miss, weh will beh weddah when you come back." With that Makarios rode to her father's farm and borrowed Dusko; she arrived at the prison early in the evening.

As she was headed to the foreman's office, a voice called out behind her, "Makarios!"

She turned to see Nikos coming toward her, so she dismounted and said, "Ah, Nikos, it is good to see you!"

He came to her and immediately hugged her saying, "I have missed you."

"You have taken on color from the sun I see," she said as she stepped back from him.

Nikos held out his arm and looked at it. "Well, we have been working long, hard days, and the July sun has been hot," he said as he gestured to a man who had come with him.

"I have met you before, have I not?" asked Makarios looking at the man, who replied, "Yes, my lady" as he bowed slightly.

Nikos looked back and forth between them and said to Makarios, "So, you have met my friend, Barah, before?"

"Yes, in Silver City, the day we were there," she said.

"He is a fine fellow," said Nikos, giving him a slap on the back. "And did you meet his two friends as well?"

"Yes, quite," she said, remembering Kafar especially. Nikos went to Dusko, and she nickered as he gave her a hug around the neck.

"So how is our friend Polus?" Nikos continued. "Barah and I have talked about many things, and he knows much about me."

Makarios was taken aback with the change in Nikos as he had become much more confident, but before she could answer, Barah said, "Would you like a drink and some water for your horses?"

Barah led the way to the corral and after Samos and Dusko were taken care of, he said, "I am sorry I can offer no refreshing ale or mead; it is not permitted here. Perhaps you are hungry, there may be something to be had at the meal tent; supper has just ended, though the fare is very poor."

"Thank you for your hospitality, I have eaten," said Makarios.

Then she said to Nikos, "I am saddened to tell you that the chief sent Polus up to the Agathon Outpost prison. But as they were traveling there, Polus somehow escaped and has not been found."

"Well, that is surprising news, but at least he is free."

"But now he is a fugitive," she said, "and injured."

Barah was thoughtful and offered, "It is unfortunate that he escaped, but I have heard about this chief; he sounds like a man who is content to be rid of

Polus and cares nothing for justice or the law."

Makarios nodded and then said in a lighter tone, "I suppose you are right. I have done all I can and, in the meantime, there is work to be done at the farm."

Nikos said, "I certainly am ready for a change in scenery and work. It has only been digging trenches and hauling stones since I arrived."

"If you can use another pair of strong hands," said Barah, "I would be happy to come along."

"I would be happy to have you, Barah," said Makarios.

The sun was descending toward the horizon as Barah said, "I can see to your horses, though there is no housing for ladies, but there is a village a short ride east of here."

In the morning, Nikos and Barah signed out at the foreman's office and awaited Makarios.

"I am anxious to go to the King," said Nikos quietly. "I have thought much about this Kah-Taw that plagues every man. I can see that many times I have done what I knew I should not do. May Kah-Taw itself be cursed!" he whispered fiercely.

"Indeed, the Great One has cursed it, and the King has defeated it, but only for those who believe," said Barah. They paused in their conversation as some men walked by and saw Makarios beyond them.

"Good morning to you, my lady!" called Barah. "I trust that you have slept well?" She pulled her horse to a stop in front of them.

"Yes, kind sir, I have," she said with a smile. "And the cold apple mead seemed especially good!"

As Barah swung up onto his horse he said, "Ah, you know where to hurt a man!"

"Well, then may I soothe the hurt with a pint of the best apple mead in the land? We shall stop at the Inn at Bradus Bridge on the way!"

She laughed as they headed down the road. They soon entered the forest and took up a steady pace on the hard-packed road.

"It is so good to be aboard this young little mare again," said Nikos happily.

They rode along for quite a while and were glad to be in the shade of the forest as the sun rose higher and the day started to get hot. Dusko began to be unruly and took to prancing sideways.

"I think she would like to go for a good hard gallop," said Makarios.

Nikos only grinned and then said to Barah, stroking Dusko's neck, "She loves to run, and she is *fast*. How about it?"

But Barah said, "I don't know; my old boy here is not the racing sort."

"Why don't you go ahead and wait for us at the bridge?" said Makarios.

With another grin, but wider this time, Nikos let Dusko go, and she was off like a shot. Nikos whooped with delight but was soon lost to sight as he disappeared down the road and around a left-hand bend.

Makarios and Barah rode on in silence for a brief while and then she asked, "You and your friends are from the south?"

"Yes," answered Barah quickly.

Sensing that he was suddenly uncomfortable, Makarios asked, "So, you have been working with Nikos at the prison?"

"Yes, he is a fine young man, and I am honored to know him."

Makarios didn't want to press but wondered about Barah's two friends. She asked, "The men who were with you in Silver City, have you parted ways?"

"For a time. They are working in a town called Diaggello. We are on a journey that is longer than we expected."

After an hour or so, they came to Bradus Bridge to find Nikos down at the river skipping stones into it.

"Hi! Nikos!" called Makarios.

He quickly rode up to meet them, and they saw that he was soaking wet. "It is a hot day, and the river is good for more than drinking," he said smirking.

They rode across the bridge and stopped at the inn. Two big windows let in much of the sun, which was now high overhead. There were few people inside, and it was quiet and peaceful as they sat down at a big wooden table. After a meal and good conversation followed by refreshingly cool mead, they left the inn.

A young, lanky blonde-haired man followed them out and addressed Makarios, "Ma'am?" he said courteously. "I heard you speak of the corn harvest . . ."

She turned to him and said, "Yes, indeed."

She paused and seeing his horse, which was old and tired looking and loaded with a fair amount of baggage, she continued, "You are traveling, I see."

He seemed a bit shy and answered, "Yes, I am Nuwa . . . from the south."

"Your horse could use a few weeks of rest in a good pasture," continued Makarios, "and she shall have it if you would be pleased to join us."

Nuwa replied with a thankful nod, and then they mounted up and rode into Diaggello.

As they entered, Barah said to Makarios, "I should like to find my friends."

She nodded, and after some asking around, they found Kafar at a carriage shop near the square.

Barah quickly had him in a bear hug after their customary greeting, "My brother, it is good to see you!"

"And you as well," said Kafar clapping him on the back. "Arak has been working at the horse stable."

There were greetings and introductions, and then Kafar said to Makarios, "I am glad to see you again, my lady."

She nodded and said, "And you as well."

Kafar nodded and they rode off, stopping to see Arak before heading to the farm.

Corn harvest began the next day. It was hard, hot work, so by the end of the day, Nikos, Barah, and Nuwa took a refreshing swim in the pond. Over the next few days, that became their habit, and they all came to know each other better, though Nuwa was a bit timid and offered little about himself.

After many days of work and another swim with Barah and Nikos, Nuwa was feeling homesick and stayed down by the pond after the other two had gone up to the barn for the night. He sat there until the stars came out and then headed up to the barn, but as he approached, he heard Nikos and Barah talking in hushed, earnest tones. Nuwa was an honest boy, but at this moment, his youth stirred a curiosity in him that made him stop and listen.

"But the Book could be anywhere, could it not?" asked Nikos. "How can you hope to find it?"

"We trust in the Great One to guide us," said Barah. "Besides, there is no other book like it. It is sacred, and the words on the cover would be a foreign script in the north. One would not forget it if they had seen it."

They paused a moment and Nuwa held his breath, not moving. Then Barah said in a lighter manner, "But first we must finish with this corn harvest, and then you must go to the King."

Nikos smiled broadly and said, "I am longing to be freed from Kah-Taw. I have been feeling more and more the grip of it."

Barah smiled knowingly, and Nikos continued, "How far is it to the King's Castle?"

"Oh, you may not have to go all the way to the castle," said Barah. "The King may meet you on the way."

"I don't understand," said Nikos.

Barah took a deep breath and said, "Nor do I. There is much about the King and the Tsadaq that are beyond all of us. Strange things can happen. He may appear to you as if you are in his presence, but then you will suddenly find yourself right where you were."

"Did that happen to you?" asked Nikos, intrigued.

Barah looked pained as he remembered the past; "It is hard to express in words. I was a terrible man before the power of Kah-Taw was broken in me. My desire for women was great, and I did not restrain any of my yearnings."

Tears welled in his eyes, but he brushed them away, "In my land, I had heard of the Tsadaq and his enemy, the Ra-Tsalem, since childhood. Many had spoken to me about what the Book taught, but I would hear none of it. One night, I tried to lay with a beautiful woman by force. I do not know if it was real or just a vision, but she suddenly appeared to change into a terrible, evil hag."

Barah grimaced at the thought, "And her face became gruesome and dreadful. I threw her from me, horrified and tried to run out, but the door was gone. The floor clattered beneath my feet, and I looked down to see it was covered with dead men's bones and human skulls. I cried out in terror, and then everything went black. I couldn't feel or see anything, but slowly a light was growing and as it got brighter, I saw the silhouette of a man standing before me. I knew he was the King, though he didn't speak. I confessed my evil and asked him to break Kah-Taw in me, and he took it away."

Nikos was transfixed. "I can hardly believe that you used to be such a man," said Nikos incredulously.

Barah looked somewhat unbelieving as well, but said, "It is nonetheless true."

Nuwa was wholly absorbed by what he was hearing, and when he went in, he did his best to act like he had heard nothing, but the look on his face caught Barah's attention. Nuwa went to his bedroll and sat down with his eyes on the ground, but his guilt overwhelmed him. "I am sorry," he blurted out. "I heard you talking, and I stopped outside to listen."

Barah had a sinking feeling, but then felt angry. "How much did you hear?"

"You are looking for a book, and I heard you speak of the Tsadaq." Nuwa stopped and looked like he expected a flogging.

"You must tell no one of the Book," said Barah.

There was silence, and Nuwa seemed to become absorbed in his own thoughts, and then he said, "I grew up in Yem, in the Negheb Province, and there were many, many times that I heard those men teaching and telling about the Tsadaq and the Book, but it was foolishness to me. I didn't believe the curse of Kah-Taw, but now I know it is true. I have found nothing of what I hoped for by coming back to the North."

He looked as if he wanted to say more, and Barah prodded him, "Speak."

"I have seen the Book," Nuwa answered in a hushed voice. "I *had* the Book. Surely there can be no other one like it. I heard you describe it."

"What do you mean you *had* it?" asked Barah. "And how did you come to have it at all?"

"I was in a village called Hudor looking for work and went into a small shop," explained Nuwa. "There were many interesting things there, and I began looking at them. When I saw the Book, I thought it strange that something so important looking from my own land would be that far to the north. I wondered what it was about and felt that I had to buy it, though it cost me almost all my silver."

He paused and looked tentatively at them, but they were eager for him to continue. "That book was not an ordinary book. I sensed there was a power in it somehow. I began to have a very strong desire to know what was written in it, but I cannot read. I had made up my mind to go all the way home to Yem when the Book was taken from me."

"Who?" asked Barah urgently, "and when?"

"Some soldiers, I think. I was at the inn by the bridge about two months ago. It was late in the evening and as I came out, three men in uniforms followed me. They robbed me and took all the valuable things that I had."

Barah could see how terrified he had been and said, "At least they didn't harm you, my boy."

Nuwa pondered a moment and then said, "But the Book—"

Nikos interrupted, "What did they look like?"

Nuwa turned to him, "They were rough looking, but clean-shaven with long dark hair. There was a blue and green emblem with a white horse's head on their uniforms, but that's all I remember."

They talked on into the night, and in the morning, they arose to another day's work in the cornfield and by midday, they had finished the harvest. Makarios had them load the wagon, and they went to the market. Nikos and

Nuwa stayed with her to help unload and sell the corn, while Barah went to see Kafar. He stopped at the stables first for Arak, and then they went to the carriage shop and found Kafar in the back working with some other men.

"Kafar, I must speak with you," said Barah. They moved away from the other men, and Barah told them about Nuwa and the Book.

"We must find out where those soldiers were from as soon as we can," said Barah.

"I shall ask Meros, the one in charge of this shop," said Kafar. "Go out to the town square and wait for me there."

He soon emerged, "Meros thinks that the soldiers were from Smaragdos Province to the north. We must go to a ferry thirty miles east of here to cross the river; then it is a day's ride north to the border," said Kafar. "We must leave as soon as we can. Let us meet early tomorrow on this road, well east of town."

"But what about this boy, Nuwa?" asked Arak. "We cannot leave him wandering about."

"He truly seeks the King," said Barah. "And Nikos as well. They are trustworthy. I will speak with them tonight."

It was nearing suppertime when Nikos, Barah, and Nuwa arrived back at the farm. After a good meal, they sat back with tall flagons of apple mead.

"Well, all the work is done," said Makarios, "until barley harvest at the end of the summer."

She asked Nikos and Barah, "Will you be going back up to the prison to work?"

There was a pause and Barah said, "My friends and I will be continuing our journey."

"The work at the prison is hard, but the pay is good," began Nikos. Then he said to Nuwa, "Perhaps you would come up there with me?" Nuwa nodded, unsure of what to say.

"Well then," said Makarios, "I must pay you your wages." She took a small wooden box from a shelf and returned to the table with it.

"The harvest was very good this year and for the first of many years, I sold all the corn."

She counted out an equal amount of gold and silver coins to each of them. But Nuwa was amazed and very grateful for the amount, hardly able to accept it. They all sat and talked for a while until they finished their mead, and then they retired for the evening.

SIX

On the way down to the barn, Nikos said to Barah, "I cannot let Makarios think that I have gone back to the prison . . ."

"Yes, my heart does not sit well either."

"And I want her to know of the curse of Kah-Taw, though we need say nothing of the Book."

Barah took a deep breath and nodded.

As they settled down in their bunks, Nikos said, "So, how will we find our way to the King's castle?"

"These days, all who seek the King find him in a mystical way, as if in a vision," began Barah.

"But where is the King's castle?" continued Nikos.

"It is very far to the south, in my country, but . . . it has been many, many generations since anyone actuallyarrived there," said Barah.

"Should I still not know the way?" insisted Nikos.

"You must go directly south, but the great Desert Wilderness will bar your way, so you must go far to the west, following the edge of the Western Mountains around the end of it. The King's castle is in a valley near Zabach."

"Is there not a shorter way?" asked Nikos.

Barah shook his head and said, "My friend, you are very near to the King; I doubt you will need to go very far at all."

At breakfast the next morning, Makarios said, "You three are awful quiet."

They looked back and forth among themselves, and then Barah said, "Makarios, I know you have wondered about my friends and me, about where we are from and why we are on a journey. We are all from Zabach, a city in the Negheb Province more than one hundred fifty miles to the south. Something very important was stolen from us, and we have been looking for it. We are also messengers of the Great One, known as the Tsadaq in our language."

He went on to tell her about the curse of Kah-Taw and its remedy and the King.

Makarios listened patiently up to a point and then said, "I think you all have had too much sun these last few days."

Nikos felt a hardness in her that pained him, and he said, "I believe in the curse and am going south to—"

"I am sorry that you believe such silliness," she said and stood up abruptly, "but do as you will."

With that, she went out, and the three sat in silence for a few moments.

It was Nuwa who spoke first. "It is too bad she does not believe."

"I suppose she has not seen enough evil or felt it in herself," said Barah slowly.

They went out and down to the barn where they were met by Menka who said, "Miss Maka has told meh to give you whatevah you ned foh the joneh."

"Thank you," said Nikos.

"Sheh has offed Dusko to you," finished Menka.

"Thank you again," said Nikos. "I shall return her as soon as I can."

Nikos wished to speak to Makarios before he left, as her response had left him feeling bad, but she was not to be found.

By midmorning, they had their horses packed with provisions, and Barah said to Nikos, "It has been good to know you."

"And you as well," he replied.

"I do not doubt that we will meet again," said Barah as they mounted up. "Farewell, my friends, and may you find what you seek."

— Seven —

Makarios watched Nikos and Nuwa ride away and all at once, she was remorseful for her hard attitude and wondered why she had felt so. She turned away, feeling quite lonely, but she went to work on some chores around the farm. By the evening, she was worn out and took a slow walk down to the pond to watch the sun set. As she sat down on the small dock, she wished for her wolf to be with her, but he was not to be found. Suddenly, she was stirred with thoughts about Pike, the Marshal at Agathon Outpost, and she quickly brushed away a tear.

Makarios awoke very early after a poor night's sleep still feeling lonely and a bit aimless. She called for her wolf, but there was no response.

Over the next few days, her restlessness increased and finding Menka, she said, "Have you seen Lukos anywhere about?"

"No, Miss Maka, but I have hood wolves howlin at night fah away."

Makarios shook her head and continued, "I am going to visit Steko and spend some time at Huo Lake."

"You ah well, Miss Makah?" asked Menka, concerned about her.

"Well, in need of a bit of a holiday, I suppose. I will be back for barley harvest. Please keep an eye out for Lukos."

Menka nodded and gave her a pat on the shoulder before turning away and heading toward the barn. Makarios packed quickly and called one last time for Lukos before heading down the road, but he did not appear. She arrived at Steko's Ferry by midafternoon and was surprised to find it very, very busy and full of people coming and going. As she came closer to the docks, she saw that another large ferry had been added.

"My sister!" called out Steko, "Welcome!" as he continued working the ferry.

She dismounted and walked over to him, working her way through the crowd.

Steko gave her a quick hug and said, "I am sorry, we are so busy. Give me a few minutes."

Makarios led Samos to a watering trough as Steko called out to a pair of young men coming up to the ferry, "Hi! You two, give me a hand here!"

They came and took up Steko's work, and he immediately came to Makarios saying, "It is good to see you again. Come away from this clamor and clatter."

He led her down the road to his small cottage and as they sat down on the porch, he said with a grin, "It is always so good to see you, my sister. What brings you here?"

She was slow to speak, and Steko became a little less jovial. "You are alright?" he asked.

She nodded unconvincingly.

"Is it about this man you met?" he asked gesturing to the north, but his grin faded quickly.

"Yes and no," she said becoming angry.

Steko took her hand, and she continued, "I am sorry. I am just feeling troubled and do not understand why."

Steko remained silent and after a moment, she said, "I should like to stay with you a while . . ."

"Assuredly you shall; all that is mine is yours," he said brightening up. "Come, you must be hungry. I have not had a moment to eat . . ."

He arose as Makarios said in a lighter mood, "I will put Samos up and then join you."

Soon, they were seated inside the cottage with a meal of venison pie and mead.

"You are very busy with the ferries," said Makarios, "and you have added a third one. Business is good, then?"

"Better than good! You see how busy—"

"Why is it so?" interjected Makarios.

"At the beginning of May, Smaragdos Province got rid of that old Sideros-Khirah fellow. Rightly was he called the Iron Hand. They elected a new overseer in his place named Rhaka. The people love him. He has lowered taxes and stopped charging for many things. Business is good everywhere."

Makarios thought a moment and then said, "I did sell all my corn this year, and at a very good price."

"Many people have moved to the towns in Smaragdos, so the demand for goods is high. The new overseer also eliminated tariffs; so, much is going into and out of the province, and great profit is being made."

He took a long draught of his mead and then said, "Oh, it had slipped my mind, but our headstrong younger brother came through here from Two Rivers a few days ago. You have not seen him?"

Makarios shook her head.

"It seems he has somehow made a small fortune in his travels, but he would not speak of how," said Steko shaking his head. "He intended to go pay Father for his keep, rather than work."

"Well, I only hope he got home safely although facing Father will be the worst of his troubles," said Makarios with a smirk.

Steko nodded with a grin, and as he stood to clear the plates, Makarios said, "I will take care of these. You must get back to the ferry."

Steko paused and then said, "Thank you, my sister," and went out.

After cleaning up, Makarios was back on the porch with a tall flagon of mead. Steko's house was a small stone cottage on the shores of Huo Lake, just off the main road. There were many people to watch as they passed by, but Makarios's thoughts were on Nikos and Barah. She wondered about what they had said about how people were cursed and about a King who could cure them; she felt a great conflict within herself. She knew Barah to be a sincere man of understanding who wholly believed in all that he had told her. But in the end, she thought him to be misled and felt pity for him, and she thought that Nikos was chasing after fantasies as well. She sat for the rest of the afternoon, sipping more than a few pints of mead while her thoughts turned from Barah and his fairy tales toward Pike.

Makarios awoke late in the morning to a gloriously sunny, warm day and found some biscuits and ham that had been left on the table for her. She smiled as she thought of her brother's kindness and generosity and poured herself some black tea that was still hot on the stove. After breakfast, she walked down to the ferry, feeling refreshed and at peace. It was quite busy again, and she worked with Steko all day and for the next few weeks. They spent some time fishing in Huo Lake and enjoyed quite a few meals of fresh, broiled gray trout.

Then one morning, at the end of the week she said, "Well, it has been a delight to have been with you, but I am missing home now and —"

Steko interjected with a grin, "Why do you fight it? Go and see Marshal

Pike."

Makarios blushed, feeling uncomfortable, but then countered, "I see no woman in *your* house, my brother!"

But he responded, "I only wish to find one as fine as you!"

Goaded by her brother and hoping for some news about Polus, Makarios packed up and departed for Agathon Outpost, arriving at dusk. She found that a new tavern had been constructed as well as a few more buildings—one from which a merchant was selling feed and grain and another offering harnesses and saddles. She went to the tavern and took a room for the night. Waking early the next morning, she sat sipping tea in the main room, feeling apprehensive about seeing Pike and began to wonder why she had even come.

She scowled to herself, trying to ignore the strong feelings she was having. "You do not even know the man," she said quietly to herself. "He is a stranger to you." She went back and forth and had just decided to go back home when a man came to the table.

"It is quite a conversation you are having with yourself," he began. Makarios looked up to see a big, barrel-chested man in overalls with a red kerchief around his head controlling a prodigious amount of jet black, yet graying hair.

"Name's Tack," said the man. "I was just finishing a bite for breakfast and looked as if you was having a talk with someone who wasn't there. It looked a mite strange."

Makarios was taken aback at his directness. "I . . . I am fine," she stammered, feeling a bit annoyed.

She stood up abruptly. He nodded and looked questioningly at her. As she turned to leave, the man said, "Well, now you take care . . ."

Makarios went out quickly, hardly looking where she was going and ran into a man who was just coming in. She nearly fell, and he caught her in his arms.

"Whoa, what is your hurry?"

She pushed roughly away, but then exclaimed, "Oh! Pike . . . I am sorry."

"You are alright?"

"Yes . . . yes," she said, composing herself.

He continued, "I saw your horse in the corral . . . I am glad to see you." She blushed but had no words.

"Naught has been found of your big friend. I am sorry," said Pike. "Come, have you had breakfast?" he asked as he gestured toward the marshal's building. "I am only just getting in. Dero would be happy to make some griddle cakes and hash . . ."

But they entered the marshal's building before she answered, and Dero greeted them. "Pike, sir. Ma'am."

"I trust you remember Makarios?" Pike said to Dero, who nodded.

Pike continued, "Would you kindly make some griddle cakes and hash?"

"Yes, sir," he answered and went into the back.

Soon, Pike and Makarios sat down to breakfast, and Dero said, "I'll be getting on now if there is nothing else. Our cow, Soo, should have her calf at any time, and I hope to be there."

Pike waved him on, and he went out.

"So, you have business up this way?" asked Pike.

Makarios flushed with emotion but had no words.

He smiled to himself and continued, "I have thought much about you," but he suddenly fell silent as well.

After a few minutes, the mood lightened and Makarios said, "I see the Outpost may succeed in becoming an actual town," she continued with a smirk, "with these new businesses here as they are."

"Quite," chuckled Pike. "Business has been good with the new overseer up north."

"Yes, and your jail has a few more occupants as well."

"I have been busy . . . indeed. I must go up to Palahos in Smaragdos Province today for a tribunal. They are holding a prisoner who is a citizen there, but who tried stealing from the feed store here." Pike shook his head. "He is young too, not much older than Dero."

As they finished breakfast, Pike said, "I am sorry I must go, but I would welcome your company."

Makarios agreed, and they were soon on their way. Agathon Outpost was situated just below Smaragdos Province, with the great Fragmoo Forest between them, stretching east and west along the border. They had ridden only a few minutes when they came to it and passed by a guardhouse with a fence and an open gate.

"There is no one here?" she asked.

"No, there are no more tolls. The new overseer ceased charging them," said Pike happily.

They entered the forest, and most of their trip was spent passing through it. The day was uneventful, but they talked all the way to Palahos and back. They arrived back at the Outpost by suppertime and were met at the marshal's building by Deputy Zuegos.

"Did that hooligan get his due?" he asked.

Pike nodded, but looked pained. "He was sent to the prison in Makran. I am sorry for him; it is a hard place."

Pike and Makarios went in, and Deputy Zuegos said, "I'll be here tonight; Dero is all caught up with a new calf. Strange too, the creature is all white and not a spot of brown on it. He has named it Too-Loo."

Zuegos went off into the prison area shaking his head as Pike turned to Makarios, but she said with a smirk, "Would you again offer me one of your day cells to sleep in?"

He laughed. "Whatever your pleasure, my lady . . . but, please, I have room in my lodge."

Pike had a small one-room house made of heavy logs with a big fireplace at one end. He had a small barn, a garden, and a dozen chickens roaming about, but no livestock. As Makarios came into his house, she saw many animal pelts strewn about and a gigantic bear pelt up on the wall.

"We called him Odus Kratos," said Pike. "He had gone mad somehow and was a savage brute, killing for the sport of it. He killed many, many sheep in Erion, leaving their carcasses to rot. He attacked men as well. We hunted him for months, and he became more and more bold, until one day, he showed himself in the light of the sun."

Makarios was incredulous as Pike continued, "We sought to trap him, and as we were checking one of the traps, he came upon us. The first spear did little to slow him down, but there were four of us, and two other spears found their mark. He was weakened as he bore down on me, and I set my spear into the ground and the beast ran himself upon it, falling dead on top of me."

Genuine fear spread across his face as he told the story. Makarios went to the wall and took the bear's paw into her hand, finding the claws to be longer than her fingers. She became lost in thought and felt a flood of emotion thinking that Pike had almost been killed by it. Her attention was brought back to Pike as he stoked the fire, and she looked at him with increased emotion.

He prepared a meal, and after they had eaten, Makarios said, "Do you have any mead?"

Pike shook his head. "No, it is not my way; I am sorry."

With the sun nearly set, Pike lit a lamp and sat down at the table.

"You may have the bed there. I am sorry there is no privacy, but I will put the lamp out when I am finished with my journal."

Makarios came to the table and said, "I have a journal too, but it is in my pack in the barn."

She quickly headed toward the door as Pike started to get up, "Can you find your way?"

"Yes, yes," she answered and went out.

He sat back down and suddenly felt how silent it was, and an unexpected and unaccustomed wave of aloneness swept over him.

Makarios returned and sat down near the fireplace on a thick fur, absorbed with her own thoughts. She wrote for quite a while, and Pike gazed at her for some time before going back to his own writing. Soon, the fire began to burn low, and Pike wondered if Makarios still had enough light. He looked over toward the fireplace only to see that she had fallen asleep.

——— Eight ———

Barah arrived on the Eastway Road where he was to meet Kafar and Arak but did not see them anywhere.

"I suppose we shall have to wait a bit, old fellow," he said to his horse as he dismounted and sat down on a stump near the road. After some time, he saw Kafar and Arak among those traveling east.

"My brothers!" he exclaimed.

They greeted one another as was their custom and then headed off east. Once they were alone on the road, Kafar said, "We have found out more about the soldiers who stole the Book from Nuwa. They were from a city called Makran in the province to the north and under the authority of a man named Rhaka, the new overseer of that province."

"Ah, that is good news," said Barah.

"We must ride a few hours to a ferry to get across the river," said Kafar.

They set off down road and arrived at Steko's Ferry by late afternoon, crossing over to Two Rivers. It was big and prosperous, situated on the edge of Huo Lake at the convergence of the Tachus and Bradus rivers.

"Let us pass through here quickly," said Kafar wanting to avoid any difficulty.

They soon left the commotion of the city behind them and continued on the road, which followed closely along the bank of the Tachus River to their left. On their right, the land opened up to a broad, grassy plain, and they soon came to the village of Batou. Though it was late in the evening, they rode on under the stars until they came to Agathon Outpost, taking a room in the tavern there. They awoke early and went into the main room of the tavern for breakfast, finding no one else there.

In the morning, they got on their way quickly and came to the border of the northern province of Smaragdos, marked by the edge of the vast Fragmoo Forest. There was a small guardhouse and a gate, which was open. But as the three approached, they saw no one there and so passed through.

Arak looked back and said, "Strange . . ."

"And the gate has not been used in quite some time, said Barah."

A sense of apprehension took hold of them as they entered the forest. The trees were thick and seemed to close in around them the further they rode. The cool, damp air and dimmer light didn't help their mood, and they again rode in silence. By midday the forest began to thin out, and they emerged to see a massive expanse of lush green grass, stretching away as far as they could see. There was a village up ahead and as they neared it, they saw a gate and guardhouse similar to the other, but it too was unattended. A small sign standing just past the gate identified the name of the town as Palahos. It was busy and thriving, and so they rode quickly through, stopping at the edge of the river to water their horses.

"This land seems very prosperous and peaceful," said Arak feeling a bit more optimistic.

They rode on and were beginning to see mountains in the distance, and by early evening they came to the village of Praho.

"I could use a draught of ale," said Barah, seeing the busy taverns.

"Yes, indeed," added Arak.

They brought their horses to a stop at a particularly large tavern and went in. It was brightly lit and full of men drinking and laughing and playing card games. The three blended in unnoticed among the raucous and loud patrons who appeared to be from many different lands.

"What'll be, my lads?" asked the keeper of the tavern.

"Ale if you've got it," said Barah as they all took seats on stools along the wall.

"Yes, sir, indeed!" he said and soon returned with three large flagons.

He was small in stature and clean-shaven with very short curly hair. "So where you travelin' to?"

"Makran," answered Kafar.

"Ah, a fine city," said the man, "One of the finest, now that the Iron Hand is gone. Well, enjoy my fellows!" and off he went.

The men sipped their ale, wondering what he meant, but did not want to ask any questions. They sat and observed the others in the tavern, but it was mostly good-natured jesting and light-hearted talk.

"It seems quite carefree in these parts," said Barah.

They talked quietly with each other for a while and as they finished their ale, the tavern keeper approached them.

"Can I offer you an excellent room at a discounted rate?" he asked. "It's the finest in the Province . . . though you'll have a mighty hard time sleepin' if that's what you're needin' to do," he finished apologetically. They got the sense that the man had a difficult time renting a room to anyone, and they declined as well.

"You could make it up to Makran by dark if you go quick," he suggested and then turned to his other customers.

Outside, Barah said, in a much more jovial mood, "Shall we go on, my brothers?"

"It is still light enough, and the road looks good," said Arak.

They silently agreed and left the village, clattering west across a bridge that spanned the Tachus river far below in a steep ravine. On the other side, the ground began to rise and after a few miles, the road took a turn to the north. It didn't take long before they were traversing low foothills as the mountains beyond loomed nearer. They went on for a while, farther than they had expected to and as they topped another rise, the failing light allowed very little view of the land beyond.

"I think our beasts have had enough travel for one day," said Kafar. "Let us get off the road and make camp. In the morning, we shall see where we are."

The day dawned bright and sunny, and they saw a mountain range far off to their left which ran north and south. After riding for an hour, the mountains bent around and loomed directly in front of them. Ahead, they could see a small building on the road and as they drew nearer, they saw an open gate.

As they began to ride through, a soldier emerged from the building.

"Now, what's yer business so early in the morning?" he said as if he had just awaken.

Without waiting for an answer, he continued, "That'll be three silver dahmas to pass up to Makran." They paid quickly, and the man returned to the guardhouse without another word.

They rode on, and Arak said, "The emblem on his uniform is what Nuwa described."

The other two nodded, but as they looked farther down the road, they saw a very high stone wall built into the arms of the mountains, which came down close on either side.

"It is like a fortress," said Arak.

As they neared it, they saw a huge iron gate standing open in the wall, which loomed thirty feet above their heads. As they went through, a few soldiers who seemed to be stationed there looked them over but said nothing. The mountains rose steeply all around the city shrouding it in the duskiness of early morning. The stone buildings crowded together with many alleys and lanes that seemed to have no purposeful arrangement, though the main road was wide and straight. There was little activity with only a few shops open and some undesirable looking men loitering about. As they came to the other side of the city, they saw that the mountains completely encircled it, falling in sheer cliffs.

"A fortress, indeed," remarked Kafar. "That gate is the only way in or out of the city."

Some distance ahead of them, there was a huge military fortress with imposing turrets at its four corners and walls about thirty feet high. It was surrounded by short green turf and precisely trimmed hedges. Its grandeur and well-manicured grounds seemed out of place with the rest of the city. It was intimidating and caused the men to pull their mounts to a stop.

"That must be where the overseer is," said Arak.

"It would be if he was 'ere," came a voice from behind them.

They turned quickly to see a small man leaning in the shadow of a building. As the man shuffled out into the light, they saw that his face was disfigured with a terrible scar on one side, leaving his eye blinded. His left arm was emaciated and missing all the fingers on his hand; he held it close to his body. He made his way around in front of them, eyeing them with curiosity from under bushy white eyebrows. He didn't speak, but the men were taken aback and had nothing to say.

"Yer lookin' fer sumthin'," he said with an unexpected, nearly toothless grin, which was contorted by his scar. "Yeh, you are."

He seemed fearless and stood leaning on his staff, waiting for a reply. The silence that followed was uncomfortably long, and eventually the little man sniggered, "Heh, you're a long way lookin' fer it."

Finally, Kafar said, "We are looking for the overseer."

The man squinted his eye at them quizzically, "Which one?"

"There is more than one?" asked Arak.

But Kafar asked, "Is not Sideros-Khira the overseer of this province?"

"No more. He finally got his due," said the man becoming very serious.

"He was evil as they come . . . and did this to me," he said, holding up his hand. "And to many others. They called 'im the Iron Hand, 'cause of how he ruled, but now there is Overseer Rhaka. He is a prince of a man . . . stopped charging tolls on the roads and tariffs; there is less tax, and 'e 'elps us folks out who's bin 'urt by the Iron Hand. He's a right fair man."

He fell silent and looked away for a moment before saying, with another foolish grin, "Name is Fadzo."

Barah dismounted and approached the little man and bowed slightly. "I am Barah," he said, "And these are my friends, Kafar and Arak. You say the overseer is not here?"

"Well, 'e's been away. Marshal Sigao is in charge. That there is where you can find him," said Fadzo pointing toward the fortress. "That's the army barracks, but it's also where Overseer Rhaka lives—in that tower there."

"Well, thank you, my kind sir," said Barah returning to his horse.

Fadzo was taken aback by Barah's respectful demeanor and only nodded in reply. He shuffled off a fair distance and then turned to watch them.

They were encouraged, but as Kafar spurred his mount, Arak said, "Wait, my brothers. I do not think all is as fair as it seems. Shall we simply go and ask for what we seek?"

They paused and then Kafar said, "You are right, Arak. We must find out more, and it may be best if we wait for the overseer to return rather than talk to the marshal."

"Well then, what about a little breakfast?" asked Barah in a lighthearted manner.

The city was waking up, and there were more shops open and a few street peddlers, one of which they found selling potato cakes and sausage. Soon, the city was bustling with people, and the three men became part of the crowd. By the afternoon, they had learned more about Makran and the new overseer, who had been in office for almost three months. He was young and industrious and had greatly improved living conditions throughout the province. Crime was very low, so he had reduced the size of the army by half.

"The new overseer is very cunning," said Arak shaking his head. "Do these people not see that?"

"What do you mean?" asked Barah.

"This Rhaka quickly gained the admiration of the people by cutting taxes and tolls, but I do not think that he is what he seems."

"Yes," said Kafar thoughtfully. "It would behoove us to take our time." The men found work in different quarters of the city and spent a week or so finding out all they could.

One morning, as they met together on the north side of the city near an old unused building, Barah said, "I have discovered that Overseer Rhaka is a great lover of books. He has a library full of them. It is no wonder his soldiers robbed Nuwa of the Book."

Kafar shook his head. "If this overseer is as fair and reasonable as he would have the people believe, then let us put him to the test. I will go and ask for the Book. If he is a just man, he will return it to us. Indeed, what else can we do?"

The other two fell silent but agreed with Kafar.

"I will go alone," he continued. "We must not all become known to him."

None of them liked the plan but thought it best. At once, Kafar rode off toward the fortress while Barah and Arak waited in the lee of the building. The gate was open during the day, and as Kafar approached, a soldier emerged from a guardhouse situated in the wall and after some words, directed him to pass through.

The minutes passed slowly for them as Arak said, "We can only hope that it goes this easily."

Barah nodded, but after some time, they began to get concerned and wondered what they ought to do. They kept their eyes on the gate, as people occasionally came and went, but Kafar did not emerge.

As their anxiety increased, the little man Fadzo approached them and shuffled to a stop. "Yer friend is inside?" he said shaking his head. "Overseer Rhaka stopped the dole to us who been wronged by the Iron Hand. We got the news of it this mornin'."

He scowled angrily and looked toward the fortress. "My friend said, 'e was too good to be true . . . guess 'e was right."

The men looked at him in surprise, but Fadzo seemed lost in his own thoughts as he punched his fist into the palm of his fingerless hand.

"Ee'll git his!" he exclaimed and then addressed Barah and Arak. "I could 'elp ya. Since you boys don't want to become known to Rhaka, I could go up to the gate and find out what happened . . . 'specially if you drop a few silver coins into this here pocket o' mine."

He held open his pocket and eyed them carefully, but they were cautious to say anything as Barah gave him two coins.

"I won't say nuthin' 'bout your book though," he grinned and immediately set off toward the fortress.

Barah and Arak looked sharply at each other as they moved out of sight of the guardhouse.

"How does he know of the Book?" whispered Arak.

"He is a sly one, but honorable," answered Barah, seeming less concerned than he ought to have been. "But whatever he knows, it is out of our hands now."

Fadzo soon returned but walked right past them and around the corner of the building and down the alley, disappearing into a doorway.

It was an old, abandoned factory of some sort and as Barah and Arak entered, Fadzo said, "This city has ears. You got to be more careful 'bout things if you want to keep a secret."

"What about Kafar?" asked Barah in a hushed tone, but the old man shook his head.

"There's sumthin' afoot with Overseer Rhaka. I wouldn't 'a thought it'd be like 'im to throw someone in the jail, but that's where yer friend is."

Barah, suddenly filled with anger, turned to the door, but Fadzo said, "Now don't git all hasty, or you'll end up there yerself."

"But Kafar has done nothing wrong!"

"Well, now we don't know what happened; maybe it was one of Overseer Rhaka's deputies. Some of them are none too nice I'm findin' out."

"But all Kafar asked for was—" began Barah.

Fadzo interjected, "Yer book, and a mighty important one at that I can see. But Rhaka, he collects 'em. Maybe he's tryin' to git yer friend to tell him why he wants it back so much." He stuck his big, bushy eyebrows out at Barah in a questioning manner.

"This is our own business," said Arak.

"Well, not since I started helpin' ya with it," grinned Fadzo. "But whatever the secret is, it's safe with me."

Barah and Arak looked at each other and were again at a loss, but Fadzo said, "Now look, I don't know about this Overseer Rhaka anymore; he's goin' bad, like an apple that's been settin' on the ground too long, so we got to be careful. Ought not *any* of us to expect fair treatment from him now, but Marshal Sigao. . . 'e might be reasonable."

Barah was feeling very impatient and said to Arak, "We should go see this marshal immediately."

But Fadzo began, "It'd be best to get a sense of things—"

Barah looked at him so sharply that he became silent.

"Barah, we are strangers here," said Arak. "But Fadzo knows the ways of this city and of these people. We must listen to him."

Barah calmed down, but his anger was still simmering as he nodded.

Fadzo grinned triumphantly as Arak addressed him, "You know this Marshal Sigao?"

"Yep, seems a nice enough sort," but then he scowled. "Course, so did Overseer Rhaka . . . until today that is."

"You will talk to Sigao then?" asked Arak.

Fadzo nodded. "Tomorrow though. Don't want to seem insistent or anything 'bout yer friend. In the meantime, all this helpin' you both is gettin' me hungry . . ."

He trailed off and looked expectantly at them. As he was poor and had very little, they followed him to a small inn and sat down to a meal.

The next day Fadzo went to the fortress, but he wasn't even permitted to pass through the gate. He came back quickly shaking his head. He again went down the alley way and into the abandoned building, climbing some stairs to the second floor. They came into a room that was apparently where Fadzo was living.

"It's no good," he said. "Things seem all stirred up over there; the soldiers are all busy, and no one is allowed in, except on important business. Sumpthin' is really changin', and I got a bad feelin' about it."

Barah and Arak looked at each other full of concern as Fadzo continued, "I'm sorry for yer friend and you both, but I guess I want to let yer business be yer own now . . ." he trailed off and looked at them apologetically, sitting down on a thin mattress on an old rusted bedframe.

"What are we to do, my brother?" said Arak to Barah, who only shook his head and asked Fadzo, "Is there no one else to appeal to?"

"Nope, but there are overseers in other provinces, maybe they could 'elp. There's a province just north of 'ere, but I don't know nuthin' 'bout it."

"Thank you for your help," said Barah.

Fadzo only nodded as the two men went out. They mounted their horses and sat for a long while looking at the fortress, but it stood impenetrable. Eventually, they reined their mounts around and went out of the city, riding slowly along the road.

"Fadzo is right about something changing," said Arak, looking gravely at Barah. "I feel an evil at work."

They fell silent as a great sense of foreboding overtook them. Once they were well away from the city, they pulled their mounts to a stop.

"We passed through a small village on our way here," said Barah. "Perhaps the marshal there could help us."

Arak, who had become quite dispirited, shrugged his shoulders.

"Well, we must do something," said Barah in a positive tone.

They quickly arrived at the village of Deolos, which was only five miles down the road. As they approached the gate and guardhouse, they found that it was no longer empty. A soldier stepped into the road in front of the gate.

"One silver damah to pass through," he commanded.

Barah said, "We only wish to see the marshal."

"No passin' the gate without payin'."

Arak quickly handed him a coin, and he opened the gate giving them no further attention. Ahead, there was some kind of fracas, and the men approached slowly.

"There ain't no tax on that anymore!" yelled a big burly man.

Another man said, "Well, there is now, orders of Rhaka, and as marshal of this town, I got to enforce it!"

"But it ain't fair!" retorted the man.

"Well, I can't help it! That's what Rhaka says, and I ain't gonna go against him!"

The argument continued and as Barah and Arak rode past, they silently agreed that the marshal could be of no help to them. The quarrel faded behind them at they rode back the way they had come.

"We *must* get into the fortress," said Barah.

"We could try to join this overseer's army," suggested Arak.

"Yes . . ." began Barah, "and we would be that much closer to the Book as well."

They returned to Makran by midday and approached the fortress. The gate was closed, but a soldier came out of the guardhouse.

"What's yer business?"

"We are seeking to join Overseer Rhaka's army," said Barah, but the soldier shook his head.

"Ain't takin' anyone new, just recalling them that have already been in. What's yer name?"

He hardly waited for a reply and said curtly, "Ain't been in? Out!"

He returned to the guardhouse, slamming the door, and they rode away, beginning to feel desperation.

"Perhaps we should see if the overseer in the province to the north could help us." Even as he said it, they both knew that it would be futile. Back in the city, they were at a loss.

"Perhaps Rhaka will eventually take new men into his army," offered Arak.

Barah nodded silently as Arak finished, "We must wait for an opportunity."

After more than a week, nothing had presented itself, and the men were desperate. They again stood on the north side of the city, in the lee of a building, looking at the fortress.

"Maybe we could get in over the wall somehow," said Arak very quietly, "and feign being soldiers."

Barah nodded in agreement. They waited until long after the moon had risen and left their horses in the city while they crept along at the foot of the mountains, which rose sharply on their left. The night was eerily quiet, and every sound they made seemed to echo off everything around them. The mountains came down in cliffs behind the fortress, and there was much fallen debris and stones. The men explored the length of the wall and eventually found a place where a large fragment of the mountain had fallen and lodged up against it. They climbed up but found that the large mass of stone was quite short of the top of the wall.

"We must build this a bit higher," whispered Barah.

Arak nodded as they remained still for a moment, listening, but the whole of the fortress was quiet. As they climbed down, they were fortunate to find some old timbers. With difficulty, and making more noise than they wished, they soon got them set and climbed up, peering over the top of the wall. Immediately, they felt the imposing presence of the center citadel as it towered ominously above them, but thankfully it was dark and as silent as was the rest of the fortress.

The two men slipped over the wall and onto the narrow stone battlement, stealing toward the northwest corner. They cautiously entered the turret and silently descended to the ground below. They looked out the door and then moved out behind a bunkhouse, ducking past the windows, but there was no one inside. They soon found that there were far fewer soldiers than they had expected and that only one bunkhouse was occupied. Even the prison building was dark and silent.

They went behind one of the empty bunkhouses, and Barah whispered, "We cannot hope to blend in with the soldiers. There are too few."

"And this citadel . . . ," began Arak shaking his head and looking up at it.

"We know nothing of who is in there, whether there are soldiers or where the books may be . . . perhaps we could at least find where Kafar is."

They made their way around to the prison at the east end of the fortress, which was a long, low building with very narrow windows. They crept up to each one, and Barah made a low trilling sound like a bird. They were getting no responses and began to fear that they would be heard by the guards when they heard an answering call within one of the cells and then a whispered voice.

"Ah, my brothers."

"Kafar, are you well?" asked Arak.

"I am," he said with difficulty. "But Rhaka has beaten me mercilessly to get me to tell him the meaning of the Book."

"I am sorry for you my brother," said Barah as quietly as he could. "But we can do nothing to get you out."

"Yes, yes," continued Kafar. "But the Book . . . Rhaka has it locked up within the citadel—"

Suddenly, there was the sound of voices from across the courtyard and the light of a torch.

"Hoi there!" yelled one of the soldiers as Barah and Arak bolted around the end of the building. They raced for the turret they had come down, but a soldier came around the back of the prison with his sword drawn.

"Stop! Who are you?" he shouted, but Barah ran straight at him and barged him to the ground. They made for the turret and bounded up it as they heard the other soldier sounding the alarm.

As they ran across the top of the wall, the soldier called out, "Hi, you there! Stop!"

But Barah and Arak made a quick escape back over the wall and were soon running across the green turf back to the city. They leaped aboard their horses just as the front gate of the fortress opened, and mounted soldiers galloped out.

"There!" yelled one of them as Barah and Arak raced down the main road through the city.

As they came to the other side, they were very glad to find that the gate open as usual. They flew down the road with the soldiers' cries behind them. Barah led the way and turned his horse to the right, off the road and into the field. They rode hard and fast over the foothills and soon came to some trees and had to slow their pace, but they realized that they had escaped the soldiers' pursuit. They pulled their horses to a stop and listened, but all they could hear was the blowing of their mounts. They had come some distance south and decided to keep going that way.

Soon, they were hearing the Tachus River on their left and began to follow it, riding for some miles. "We must get out of this province," said Barah. "We cannot risk getting caught."

As the night wore on, they came to an old unused bridge that spanned the river near the northern border of the Fragmoo Forest and made camp under it. They seemed hardly to have closed their eyes before the sun began to rise. They quickly saddled up and crossed the old bridge, which was quite rickety and unstable, but they passed over safely and headed south down the forest road. Coming to the southern border, they warily approached the guardhouse, but as they neared it, they could see that it remained unused.

By midmorning, they came to Agathon Outpost and quickly found the marshal's building. They went in and were unexpectedly greeted by a familiar voice, "Well, Barah!"

"Makarios!" he exclaimed. "It is good to see you, my lady!" She was seated at a small table and rose to greet them as Pike came from the back room.

"Will there be two more for breakfast?" he asked.

"I think yes," said Makarios eyeing them. "You have had a hard few days."

But then she said a bit slowly, "Kafar, is he not with you?"

Arak was grim and only shook his head, while Barah said, "That is why we have come. You are the marshal here?" he asked Pike, who nodded.

"The overseer in the province to the north has put our friend, Kafar, into prison unlawfully."

"I have heard that this overseer has proved himself to be a fair and generous man. It is not so?" asked Pike.

"It may have seemed so," said Barah. "But he, or his marshal or deputies have imprisoned our friend unjustly, and we can do nothing to help him."

"Please sit down," said Pike. As they crowded around the small table, Pike brought in more griddle cakes and ham, and the men thanked him for his hospitality.

"Tell me . . . ," began Pike, "what led to your friend being taken into the jail?"

When Barah and Arak paused and looked at each other, Makarios said, "Pike is an honorable and trustworthy man."

Barah, still with a look of concern, said, "Something very important was stolen from us, and we have found it to be with this overseer, Rhaka. When our friend Kafar went to the fortress in Makran to get it back, he was imprisoned."

"It is not right," said Pike, quite incensed. "But I do not know what I can do. My authority ends at the border of this province. Still, something must be done."

They finished breakfast, and Pike put one of his deputies in charge and called Deputy Zeugos to join them. They were all quickly on their way and as they came into Praho, a soldier was passing through on horseback calling out for those who had been in the army to report to the fortress immediately.

Marshal Pike and the others arrived at Makran in the early evening and went directly to the fortress.

"We must see the marshal of this city," commanded Pike to the soldier at the gate.

He was young and startled by Pike's directness and immediately sent for the marshal, who took an inordinate amount of time to appear. Eventually, the gate opened and a plain looking man with light brown hair and a short, trimmed beard approached them. He did not wear a uniform and was accompanied by three extremely large soldiers.

"I am Marshal Sigao," he said curtly. "What's your business?"

"I am Marshal Pike from Agathon Province. You have a man unjustly imprisoned, and I am requesting his release," said Pike.

"You have no authority here!" scowled Sigao.

Pike was just as quick to answer. "Neither do you have authority to confine a man without cause."

"I can do as I please!" Sigao yelled angrily. "And if you press this further, I will have you thrown in with him!"

Pike was about to respond, but Makarios stayed him with her hand on his arm.

Sigao scoffed and said, "Now maybe you could get somewhere if you had your fine woman here speak for you."

One of the soldiers snickered and as Pike took a step forward, Barah said, "We do not want trouble, just what is fair."

"No trouble!? Well, we already had trouble!" Sigao yelled and suddenly eyed Barah and Arak suspiciously.

"Now be off, or there'll be more than one confined without cause!" he shouted.

The gate clanged shut, and they were again without recourse. But Arak, who had been absorbed with the size of the soldiers said, "Were they men?"

"They are the same as Polus," said Makarios.

Pike said vehemently, "This cannot stand!"

"What can we do?" asked Barah.

As Pike calmed himself, he said, "I have a friend who may be of some help. He is in Tachus Town, some miles west of here. We can make it there by nightfall."

Nine

Meanwhile, Nikos and Nuwa had begun their journey south to find the King.

"I know the lands round about," said Nuwa. "We need not follow the road since it will take us out of the way."

Nikos nodded, and they struck off due west across the fields. They rode all day; it was fairly easygoing as they skirted around many farms and fields. As evening approached, they saw in the distance a small village situated on the edge of the sea.

"That must be Oligos," said Nikos. "Maybe I will find my horse Zeo there."

They entered a stand of red alder trees and made camp in a thicker part of the grove. In the morning, they made an early start and came to the road that passed through Oligos, on the shore of the Keramos Sea. Nikos began looking about for horses but saw few. As they left the village, they began to see a great, flat expanse in the distance.

"That must be the great Desert Wilderness Barah spoke of," said Nikos somewhat to himself.

Soon, the road turned more westerly as it ran along the edge of the sea. The sun stood high overhead as they came to the town of Hudor, a busy fishing village, with many piers and boats. Flocks of gulls were overhead, and the air was filled with their forlorn cries and the briny smell of fish. They stopped for a meal at a tavern and refreshed themselves.

As they came out, Nikos looked far down the road that went west out of Hudor, and Nuwa asked, "What is it?"

Nikos frowned a bit and said, "It seems we have come farther than Barah expected us to have to go. I am anxious to meet the King. This curse of Kah-Taw has been weighing heavier upon me the further we have come."

He was pained as he looked away to the south where the green landscape gave way to the sandy hues of the desert.

"I wonder if there is a shorter way?"

Nuwa said anxiously, "We must not venture into the desert."

"It is miles and miles to the west!" said Nikos, suddenly becoming angry. He turned to a man passing by and asked, "Do you know of a way across the desert?"

The man shook his head and hurried on. Nikos asked another man and another, becoming increasingly agitated. He turned back to Nuwa and asked, "How far is it if we go straight south from here?"

Nuwa didn't answer because he did not want to go into the desert, but Nikos's attitude frightened him. He said reluctantly, "Uh . . . two days' ride, but—"

Suddenly, Nikos swung up onto Dusko, seemingly relieved and said, "Then let us go!"

Nuwa hesitated and shook his head. "It is dangerous. There is an oasis . . . but if we miss it, . . . well, it is too far for the horses without water, and us as well."

An unusual wave of anger passed over Nikos and he insisted, "We must go! The other way is too far too long!"

His whole countenance had changed, and Nuwa quickly clambered up onto his horse. After taking a few minutes to fill their waterskins at the public well, they headed off.

Nikos's mood lightened, and Nuwa said, "We must be careful to go directly south if we are to find the oasis."

"Have you come this way before?" asked Nikos, seeming to be himself again.

"Yes, with a band of tradesmen, but coming up from the south. They seemed to know the way, but there is no path, and the dunes are always changing with the wind."

They rode on for a while longer, with Nuwa trailing behind, but fear overcame his timidity, and he pulled his horse to a stop.

"I do not have a good feeling about going this way," he said gravely.

"Do you not wish to see the King as well?" asked Nikos turning around sharply. He did not wait for a response but continued on. After an hour, the ground became sandy and began to rise as the desert opened up before them. Soon, they were traversing low dunes, and the sun beat down on them.

"Nuwa!" said Nikos suddenly. "This is what I saw in a dream I had! Only I was alone . . . and on foot, walking across endless hills of sand, and I saw a white castle in the distance."

After a moment, he added a bit anxiously, "What do you think it means?"

"I have heard that the King's castle is made of white marble. But you say you were walking alone?"

Nikos nodded as they rode on, each of them feeling a sense of foreboding. The day dragged on, and the scenery became monotonous. Long, low dunes stretched out before them, and they became discouraged. The horses labored in the sand until both man and beast were hot, tired, and thirsty. They watered their horses and drank themselves as the sun fell lower in the sky. A cool breeze began to blow, lifting their spirits a little. The land continued to be very much like Nikos had seen in his dream, and it gave him a bad feeling.

He began to wonder how he might wind up alone and on foot, but immediately dismissed the thought, deciding that dreams didn't mean anything. They rode on, and their anxiety began to rise as their thirst increased. Terrible thoughts assailed each of them as they began to think that they had missed the oasis, which could only lead to one fate.

The sun was near the horizon when they came to the top of another dune, and Nuwa called out, "The Oasis!"

With relief they rode down the slope toward the cluster of trees and lush foliage. "I am sorry for my insistence about coming into the desert," said Nikos. "But thankfully, we are here."

The oasis was not as near as it looked, but as they drew closer, Nikos stared up at the trees, such as he had never seen before.

"They are tamar trees," said Nuwa. "They will have fruit on them."

Nikos was amazed to see such lush greenery sprouting up right in the middle of a place that was so dry.

"You have never seen an oasis!" laughed Nuwa.

The light was dim as they entered into the thick vegetation on a narrow path. Within, the vegetation thinned out giving way to wide patches of grass and some smaller tamar trees. There was a pool in the center, about ten feet wide, obscured by broad leaf plants and a stream flowing out of it, running away to the south. They drank deeply as did their horses and found the water to be cool and sweet.

"Ah! That is good!" exclaimed Nuwa.

Across the clearing there was a wooden shelter built of thick logs, about four feet high and open at the front. Bunks were built into the walls at either end; a good supply of firewood was stacked inside, and there was a fire pit outside.

"Does someone live here?" asked Nikos as Nuwa unsaddled his horse.

"We do, for now, I suppose. I think it is only used by travelers."

The shadows were long across the clearing as darkness settled, and the chilled night air moved in.

As Nuwa was busy getting a fire going, he tossed a small pan to Nikos and said, "We will need that full of water."

"You can cook?"

"From necessity," grinned Nuwa. As the night grew colder, Nikos liked the idea of a hot meal. The moon was rising, and light filtered into the clearing through the towering tamar trees, enough for him to see where he was going. At the spring, as he bent to fill the pot. As he did so, a cold chill swept over him, and the hair on the back of his neck stood up. He froze, feeling a sudden fear in the pit of his stomach. He listened intently but heard only the crackling of the fire across the clearing. He slowly dipped the pot in the water and drew it out, deciding that he was imagining things when he felt an icy waft of air that seemed to pass right through him. He heard a hissing sound, followed by a barely audible growl that made the ground vibrate under his feet. Nikos had never felt such a mortal fear and couldn't move or speak.

"Nikos, the water!" called Nuwa.

He was shaken out of his state enough to move, and he ran back to Nuwa, who took the water and poured it into the pot. Nikos stood there, still shaken, staring into the flames.

"Did you see a ghost over there?" asked Nuwa lightheartedly. Nikos looked up sharply and the look on his face brought a seriousness to Nuwa.

Nikos found it very difficult to speak, but he said, "I did not see anything, but I felt something terrible." Seeing Nuwa's expression, Nikos continued, "What is it?"

"Well, there is the legend of the Kahee-Nawb," Nuwa started out slowly, shaking his head. "But it has been many generations since anyone has even heard a report of it." Nuwa paused and swallowed hard as Nikos moved closer to the fire, shaking in fear.

"What is it?"

"Some kind of beast that haunts this wilderness. No one knows if it is real or a phantom, but . . . it can kill."

"It felt as big as a barn," said Nikos terrified.

The sky was black above them, and the moon had suddenly become obscured by dark clouds.

"What does it want with us?" whispered Nikos, stiff with fear. Even before he finished speaking, a thunderous noise split across the sky. Nikos and Nuwa ducked and threw up their hands as if to ward off a blow and looked up to see the black clouds ripped away from the moon as if huge claws were tearing them apart.

The moon was unusually bright, and suddenly sharp shadows were cast on the ground. A huge black shape passed over as they bolted for the shelter, but the beast swooped down and struck them both to the ground. Then it wheeled about and landed about twenty feet away. It was terrible looking with black leathery skin and dragon-like wings drawn up above itself, standing at least fifteen feet tall. It had a body like a troll, with thick, knotted legs and arms that ended in cruel looking claw-like hands. It had two horns on its head; fangs that protruded from its mouth; and piercing, fiery red eyes. It squatted on all fours, heaving and breathing with steam rising from its clammy, black skin. It suddenly let out a shrieking laugh, so that Nikos and Nuwa covered their ears. They scrambled to their feet and stood trembling, in helpless fear.

"Now you shall die . . . slowly," it wheezed and then chuckled to itself and leaned forward with its wings aloft and began to advance.

Suddenly, a shriek of panic came from Nuwa as he bolted into the thick vegetation. The Kahee-Nawb moved almost faster than they could see and with a violent sweep of its wing, it dashed Nuwa to the ground. He fell unconscious as Nikos grabbed a burning brand from the fire and rushed at the beast, but it was too fast and leaped back.

"You shall learn of the master's power!" it screeched and with a powerful stroke of its wings, it rose into the air and climbed higher into the sky.

A terrible unearthly cackle echoed among the treetops as Nikos ran toward Nuwa yelling, "We must get into the cover of the trees!"

At that moment, the evil creature descended upon them again. Nikos swung the firebrand, causing the beast to veer away, and then he pulled Nuwa into the trees.

As he dragged him further in, Nuwa regained his senses and said, "What happened?"

But Nikos urged him to keep silent. They could no longer see out into the clearing, and it was eerily silent. Suddenly, the Kahee-Nawb crashed into the tops of the trees with a horrible screech and rent them asunder. The two cowered in abject horror as the creature landed heavily in the clearing with its horrid stench wafting over them. As its heavy footfalls came toward them, they could hear its wings rasping over the sand.

"You cannot hide in the dark," it hissed. "*I* am the dark."

The two felt every part of their being prodding them to run, but they were unable to move. The beast crashed into the undergrowth and was advancing upon them when it was suddenly struck from the side by something that was about half as big and blindingly white. There followed a terrible fight, and then only silence. Both men sat in the cover of the trees for a long while, but Nikos finally ventured to look out, with Nuwa close behind. They saw a huge black form lying motionless in the clearing.

"It . . . it looks dead," whispered Nuwa.

Nikos nodded and approached it slowly. The beast was indeed dead but showed no wounds.

"I wonder . . . what killed it?" said Nikos.

Nuwa shook his head and said, "I remember strange tales from my grandfather about this creature. We must not stay the night here."

"But is it not dead?" asked Nikos.

"It would seem so, but we must go."

"We have traveled all day," began Nikos. "Our horses will need—"

With a sudden sense of urgency, Nuwa interrupted, "Quickly now!" and ran across the clearing to the shelter, glancing back at the steaming carcass of the beast.

To their dismay, they found that the horses had broken free and were nowhere to be found. They packed up as much as they could and, after filling their waterskins, they found a path that went south out of the oasis. They followed it to the edge and felt a renewed fear as they stepped out into the exposed plain of the desert. The moon was bright and easily lit their way, so they took up a quick pace.

After a while Nikos asked, "Do you think it will come alive?"

"I do not know—only it seems there is something about it that can never really be killed."

He shook his head again and quickened his pace. Fatigue was beginning to overtake them, but fear drove them on. They listened constantly for any sounds as the dunes began to rise and fall again, getting steeper and taller. They went on into the night, but they slowed down as the moon became obscured by clouds.

Nuwa stopped suddenly and said in a fearful and hushed tone, "I am unsure of our direction."

They stood there until Nikos said, "Maybe we should wait until morning. It would be better than getting lost."

"Yes," said Nuwa slowly. "It seems the only way."

They went down the face of the dune and took cover near a jumble of rocks and gnarled, stunted trees. They were exhausted and though filled with fear, both fell asleep in minutes.

Nikos awoke early in the morning and tugged at Nuwa to wake him up, but he didn't stir. Nikos sat up and saw blood on the sand. Dismayed, he rolled Nuwa onto his side and saw a wound on the back of his head. It did not look fresh; it looked like a wound that had reopened during the night. Nikos suddenly thought back to when the Kahee-Nawb had struck Nuwa to the ground. He began to get worried and shook Nuwa again, and very gradually, he responded.

"Nuwa!" said Nikos worriedly. "Are you all right?"

He sat up slowly and reached for the back of his head, but it seemed he didn't hear Nikos.

"Nuwa," repeated Nikos, moving into his line of sight.

"Where are we?" said Nuwa in a very vague way. "Where is the King?"

"We must go to him," said Nikos, but Nuwa held his head in pain and said, "The evil is upon me."

Nikos was about to question him when he continued, "But the King is here."

Suddenly, Nuwa slumped forward and as he fell, he said, "The King, the King."

Nikos sat shocked, staring blankly at Nuwa's lifeless body.

"No!" he yelled.

But his cry was swallowed up by the utter silence and stillness of the desert. He was numb and overwhelmed with grief as the tears streamed down his face. Suddenly, thoughts of the beastly Kahee-Nawb jolted him to sober fear. He dug a shallow grave as best he could and then stood in silence for a moment, not believing that he was utterly alone.

With the sun directly to his left, Nikos shouldered his pack and struck off south, feeling an intense anger toward the beast that had taken his friend's life. It seemed so senseless and wicked. He glanced into the sky, wishing the beast was right in front of him. His temper set him at a very quick pace, and by the middle of the day, the dunes had begun to flatten again. He hoped this meant that he was nearing the edge of the desert. The sun had risen to its height and was mercilessly hot. Nikos drained the last of his water and felt a sense of guilt knowing he would have to drink Nuwa's water as well.

He looked about and unexpectedly, saw a structure off to the left. It took longer than he expected to get to it, but he was glad to find that it provided some shade. It was a column rising out of the sand about ten feet high and about ten feet in diameter. It was made of stone and mortar, but it looked very, very old; much of the mortar had been worn away. Nikos walked around it, but there was no door or window. It afforded enough shade, and he sat down with his back against the stones. It reminded him of some of the old buildings he had seen in Silver City. He leaned his head back and closed his eyes, thankful for the relief from the sun.

Nikos was jolted awake by a loud and raucous cawing sound. He scrambled to his feet and looked wildly about, his eyes focusing quickly on the only thing there was to see—a big black bird standing about twenty feet away. Nikos also noticed, to his dismay, that the sun had fallen close to the horizon. He did not want to be another night in the desert and didn't feel half so brave as he had earlier in the day when he had wanted to meet the Kahee-Nawb face to face.

The bird cawed again and hopped a few steps away. Nikos pulled his pack on and as he headed south, the bird rose up into the air and seemed to fly ahead of him. It kept itself about twenty feet ahead of him by flying and then landing and waiting. It was definitely leading him south and cawed every so often as it looked back at him. Nikos wondered about the bird and why it was out in the desert. He began to be suspicious of it, thinking that it looked evil. In spite of that, he cautiously followed it. The sun had set, and the evening sky was coming on. Nikos was anxious about how much farther it was to the edge of the desert and if they were even headed that way. He began to be discouraged. He was hungry and thirsty and very weary, but the slower he went, the more the bird squawked at him. As the wind began to blow and clouds rolled in, he picked up his pace, but began to find it difficult to see where he was going.

Suddenly, he stopped dead in his tracks, listening intently and heard what he had been fearing the whole day. Ever so faintly, he heard on the wind the screech of the Kahee-Nawb. The skies were black, and Nikos could not see where he was going, but the bird was cawing almost constantly. The screech of the Nawb came again and was much nearer. Nikos ran like a blind man, following the sound of the bird.

Suddenly, he came over a dune and saw the lights of a village ahead. He plunged down the face of the dune as the creature swept over him, its claws just missing their mark. Nikos coughed in the horrible reek it left as he raced for the village. He ran faster than he ought to have been able as he heard the Kahee Nawb screaming behind him. The sand gave way to hard packed dirt, and Nikos ran faster, seeing a big barn ahead.

He felt the heat of the Nawb as it bore down on him, but at that moment he tripped and fell headlong, falling just below the creature's terrible claws. It shrieked in horrible frustration as it wheeled up into the air. Nikos leaped up and ran toward the barn, diving through the doorway and scrambling up against the wall. He huddled breathless and terrified, but suddenly realized the creature was gone. As he listened, he again heard its maddened screams, but they were farther away and then farther away still. As Nikos regained his breath and his heart slowed, he began to calm down and think more rationally. He wondered about the black bird and where it had come from and why it had come. Was it even real?

Nikos awoke to a pain in his foot and the sound of clucking. As the sleep cleared from his eyes, he looked down to see a chicken pecking at his boot. When he stirred, it cocked its head on one side and stared at him with its beady little eye. Nikos laughed to himself and thought, *"silly chicken,"* but suddenly the night before flooded into his mind, and he quickly sat up. The chicken clucked its way out of the barn as Nikos got to his feet, still feeling tired and extremely thirsty.

"Dusko!" he thought and suddenly felt a great sense of loss. Was she still alive? Had that evil creature killed her? A tear slid down his face followed by many more as he stood there for quite some time. Eventually, he went to the door of the barn and saw that the land was much different from his own. Everything looked odd, except for the chickens; the terrain was dry and arid and filled with strange plants and trees. But it seemed a peaceful land, so he made his way into the town to find the market and merchants who were just beginning their day. He received many strange looks; some scowled because he was so different from the people of the land, whose dark complexion and black hair contrasted sharply with his own. He kept his eyes down and walked on until he came to what he thought was a public well. He took a long drink and filled his waterskin.

As an old man approached, Nikos plucked up his courage and asked, "Can you tell me the way to Zabach?"

But the old man frowned and muttered something in a strange language. Nikos tried speaking to someone else, but they didn't understand him either. He was having no luck and began to be discouraged, so he sat down on a low stone wall in front of a shop. He felt wholly alone as he watched the people going about their business. Suddenly, a voice spoke behind him,

"To know where Zabach is, you wish?" Nikos started and turned around to see a young man leaning on a broom.

"Yes," said Nikos with relief. "You know my language then?"

"My best I do, but most of the older folk . . . no," said the man as he looked Nikos over. "From where are you traveling?"

Nikos was about to answer and then paused, wondering what he ought to tell the man, who raised his eyebrows questioningly.

"I came from Hudor, in the north," said Nikos, which was true enough.

The man knit his brows together a bit and said, "To Zabach you are going, and all this way you have come; yet you know not where it is?"

Nikos was beginning to feel uncomfortable when the man chuckled and said, "Your business is your own, but strange it is. Zabach is sixty miles south and east, but that is far for one who looks ready for his journey to be over."

Nikos had no reply and felt at a loss.

The man paused a moment and then said, "To Zabach every week merchants go. In the caravan with them, you could travel."

Nikos nodded and said, "When will they go?"

"Two days, but until then stay with me. Esam is my name."

Nikos introduced himself and gratefully agreed to the man's offer. Nikos spent the next two days working with him in his basket shop, learning how to weave.

As the third day dawned, Nikos awoke feeling refreshed and encouraged, and Esam said, "To my friend, Isram, I have spoken, and he is willing for you to ride in his wagon to Zabach. He is a short-tempered man, but to Zabach he will take you."

Nikos nodded and paused, feeling anxious about how he would find the King.

"Something else?" asked Esam.

Nikos hesitated, but he had come to trust Esam, so he said, "Have you heard of the King?"

"Yes, yes. All have heard of the King and this one called Tsadaq," said Esam. "How do you say . . . big fairy tales, but each to his own."

"Do you know where the King's castle is?"

Esam shook his head. "If such a thing is, but there are in Zabach many who speak the common tongue. It is a big city; you will find someone to help."

The town began to get busy as merchants were loading wagons and coming together to form a caravan.

Esam said, "Come, my friend; I take you to Isram."

Nikos took up his pack, and Esam handed him a bag. "Tamahs, dried fruit from the tamar tree. Good they are."

Nikos nodded in thanks and followed Esam to one of the wagons. It was drawn by two camels, which Nikos was still getting used to the look of. A gruff looking old man heaved one last bag up onto the wagon and climbed into the driver's seat. He nodded at Esam, who nodded back and then looked harshly at Nikos.

"Now quickly," said Esam. "Get up. A long ride to Yem today, and tomorrow you get to Zabach."

Nikos had hardly gotten into the wagon before Isram cracked a whip over the heads of the camels to get them moving.

"Thank you for the fruit and your hospitality!" called Nikos to Esam, who gave an exaggerated bow and then turned away with a wave.

Nikos quickly discovered that the ride to Yem would not be a comfortable one. The wagon was mounded with bags of some kind of hard grain, though he found a place at the back to get his feet on the floor to help cushion the ride. Nonetheless, it was a miserable trip, and he almost wished he had decided to walk, but it was far too long of a trip on foot. By midday the road began angling north toward the desert, and soon Nikos saw what he now knew to be an oasis. As they approached, he was surprised to see a stone wall around it with only a small opening in it. Two men seemed to guard it, and as Isram stopped his camels, one came forward and accepted some coins from him. The other man stepped aside, and Isram passed through, going to the spring to water his camels.

Nikos apprehensively filled his waterskin, but Isram acted as if he were not even there. There were other travelers coming and going, some with camels and others with donkeys. Then Nikos saw a beautiful dark-haired young woman with a dozen or so goats on the other side of the spring. She held the reins of a large black mule and in her other hand, she held a staff for guiding the goats.

Nikos stood transfixed when she suddenly called out, "Your wagon is leaving."

Startled, Nikos spun around to see Isram almost out of the gate. He ran to catch up and jumped into the back but turned around to look at the woman. She was on her mule and guiding the goats away from the spring. He hoped she was traveling the same way; he watched from the back of the wagon, but eventually, they passed out of sight of the oasis. Nikos pictured her in his mind, beautiful dark skin and short black hair, much shorter than most of the women he has seen. He was struck with the fact that she had spoken in the common tongue and wondered about her all the way to Yem.

They arrived by nightfall, and Isram stopped his wagon at a large house on the western edge of the town. He was warmly greeted by the occupant and went in with him amidst jovial greetings and slaps on the back. Soon, two servants came to care for the camels, and Nikos jumped off the wagon as they led the camels to a large barn behind the house. The servants glanced back at him as they went and then spoke to each other in the language of the region. The house was on a rather large estate, and Nikos was left on the road by himself. He was a foreigner in a foreign land and suddenly that fact descended on him hard. *"What am I even doing here?"* he thought to himself. *"Maybe Esam was right, that it's all just a great fairy tale."*

Nikos became angry and insulted at being left in the dark on the road like a sack of grain. He ventured over to the barn and found what seemed like servants' quarters next to it. There were lamps inside, and he could hear talking and laughing. Slowly, he opened the door, and a sudden silence descended as they all turned to look at him. Four young men were seated around a table; they held small glasses in their hands filled with a thick dark brown liquid. Two of the men nodded to Nikos and happily motioned him to come and sit.

They began talking and laughing again, and one of them pushed a glass of the stuff they were drinking toward him and said, "Tamahish!"

Nikos smelled it, and they all laughed, but he was appreciative that they had welcomed him in. He thought the smell familiar and thought of the dried fruit he had.

He reached in his bag and pulled some out and asked, "Tamahs?"

"Ah! Tamahs," said one of them pointing to the fruit and then immediately to the drink, "Tamah-eesh!"

Nikos tried some and found it sickeningly sweet, but with a strong flavor that he quite liked.

"Good!" he exclaimed, but the men just looked puzzled and then laughed some more.

Nikos awoke the next morning feeling very hot and with his head hurting. He heard the sound of sheep bleating in the distance and as he sat up, he squeezed his eyes shut against the sun that came stabbing in from high in the sky. He was alone and couldn't think where he was, but then it all came back to him. He leaped up and grabbed his pack but stopped as his head spun and then throbbed in pain. Grimacing, he ran outside to the barn, but Isram was gone. Nikos slowly walked to the front of the house and looked down the road. *"Long gone,"* he thought.

The sun beat down, and he wondered what to do. He began walking and soon came into the village of Yem. There was little activity during the heat of the day, and Nikos wandered through, filling his waterskin again. No one took any notice of him and as he came to the other side of the village, he saw that the road split, the left fork going east and the right going more to the south.

Nikos asked a man who was riding past, "Zabach?" and motioned to either road.

The man pointed to the right and continued on his way. Nikos followed the right-hand road and ate some of the dried fruit as he went along. Many people were coming and going on the road, and he often coughed in the dust kicked up by the wagons. He received many a strange glance, and no one offered him a ride. As the afternoon wore on, the heat grew less as he went south, away from the desert. All the way from Yem, the road had been rising slightly, but now it began to descend. There was more greenery, and he could see in the distance even more and also what he hoped was the city of Zabach. His spirits lifted, and he began walking faster, but the city was farther away than it looked, and it was late evening by the time he arrived. There were many establishments that were akin to the taverns he knew at home, so he approached one of the larger ones. As he was about to enter, a woman stepped from the shadows and smiled at him. She was impossibly beautiful, and Nikos was dumbfounded.

"Ma . . . Makarios? How—"

She quickly said, "I know you have desired me."

Nikos' gaze fell to her deep red lips, and he was filled with an overpowering lust for her.

Almost as if in a daze he reached for her when suddenly, a strong hand clamped down upon his wrist, and he was jarred back to his senses as a voice spoke: "Do you take so lightly the invitation of the King? Do you so easily turn back from seeking him? Do not turn aside!"

Nikos quickly turned, but there was no one there, and the woman was gone as well. He began to think that he had imagined it all, except that he still felt his wrist where he had been grabbed.

Nikos heard the stout man's words again, "Do not turn aside!" and he paused before entering the tavern.

He was shaken, but soon a satisfying meal and more of the tamahish drink had his full attention. He paid with coins he had recovered from Nuwa and suddenly missed him very much.

As he paid the tavern owner, he asked, "Do you know the way to the King's castle?"

He grinned and said, "Oh-ho, do you wish to meet the King, my friend?"

Nikos wondered if he were sincere as the man continued, "You must go south until you come to the mountains and then turn west. But you do not meet the King just by walking there, if indeed you should be so fortunate to meet him at all."

Nikos tentatively asked, "You have met the King?"

The man smiled broadly. "Yes, but in a mystical way. No one has met the King face to face for many, many generations, but it seems you have traveled far already."

"From the north, across the desert."

The man's eyes widened. "You have come that far? It is said that a man must travel farther than he possibly can to meet the King, but for you it seems to be true."

He looked with wonder at Nikos and without waiting for a reply, he said, "Since your journey has brought you here, you will stay in one of my best rooms tonight."

Nikos was thankful for his hospitality as he showed him first to the bathhouse.

"I will have one of my maids wash your clothes as well; they have more dust in them than the ground itself!" he laughed.

The man left him, and Nikos enjoyed a good bath followed by a very comfortable night's sleep. In the morning, he awoke early and went into the main room of the tavern, where he was met by a maid who brought him a hearty breakfast.

As he finished, the maid approached and said, "The master of the tavern bids you farewell."

After bowing, she handed Nikos a bag. He bowed in return and thanked her, and she went back to her duties. Nikos went out and squinted in the sunshine and as he looked in the bag, he found it contained dried meat and cheese and a loaf of bread. He was especially glad to find a small bottle of tamahish and was surprised that the money he had paid for his meal the night before was in the bag as well. He wondered at the generosity of the tavern owner and was very grateful.

The city was still quiet with only the odd traveler or merchant here and there as Nikos made his way south. It was quite a walk to the edge of the city, and he passed many large, ancient stone buildings. On the outskirts, there were ruins of buildings, some half buried and looking older than he could imagine. Great mountains rose in the distance.

It did not take Nikos long to reach the forested foothills, but soon they grew steeper, and the mountains rose behind them. He walked for a while longer and wondered if he was going the right way when he came over a rise and saw a farm of some sort. It was at the base of a steep part of the mountain topped by a cliff of rock that jutted out. He felt nervous as he approached and kept to his left, staying amongst the trees.

Fenced pastures containing goats, mules, and cows butted up to the cliff. He went a bit deeper into the forest, but as he drew nearer, he could see that he would have to go all the way around the farm, out into the open field, or else go through the pastures. It seemed a very secluded place, and he felt that he was already intruding, but his desire to meet the King spurred him on. He went a fair distance out onto the plain and took on a very purposeful stride. He kept glancing to his left and saw that there were many barns, small houses, and low buildings; a stone fence ran around the whole place. A road passed through it all and led to the mountain where it ascended steeply, winding back and forth.

Without realizing it, Nikos had stopped and was staring up at a very distinguished gate at the top. The gate had tall spires beyond it that he supposed belonged to a castle. *"A castle?"* he thought to himself. *"The King's castle?"*

Nikos became uneasy and looked more intently but was suddenly startled by a voice asking, "What do you look for?"

Nikos was so shaken that he stumbled backward, looking about, but he saw no one.

"Here!" called a beautiful young woman standing inside the stone wall of one of the pastures. He was relieved that there was someone who belonged to the voice.

"I am sorry; I am looking for the King," he said with little more than a thought, forgetting that most had animosity toward even the idea of the King.

"Well, you will not find him up there," the woman said laughing. At once, Nikos recognized her as the woman he had seen at the oasis between Yaam and Yem.

His eyes fastened on her, and she said, "Yes, I remember you as well. I am Chayel."

"I am Nikos," he said nervously, walking toward her.

"You have come to the Sacred House of the Book," she said, and a look of recognition came upon Nikos's face.

"You have heard of this House?" Chayel asked.

But Nikos, not wanting to speak of the Book or Nuwa said quickly, "Yes, but I must get to the King's castle."

Sensing his hesitancy, Chayel pointed southwest and said, "You must continue on that way. The mountains fall steeply down from the east and west forming a deep valley, but . . ." she paused looking questioningly at Nikos.

He quickly asked, "How far is it?"

"Farther than any man can travel," she began, "but you have already come a long way. You are from the north?"

"Yes. I have come across the desert."

She wondered at him again and continued, "It has been generations since it was heard that anyone looked upon the King with their own eyes."

"I must go," said Nikos abruptly as a wave of anxiety hit him. He left her without looking back, suddenly wishing he had never come, but still wanting to continue.

Chayel called out after him, "Please return when you can!"

But his thoughts were jumbled as he passed out of earshot. He soon rounded the tall shoulder of the mountain and saw the valley Chayel had spoken of. It was thickly forested, with no apparent way through. He had expected a lane or a road, but had to push his way in, picking through the dense vegetation. Thorn bushes were numerous, and it was impossible for him to avoid them all. After a while Nikos was hot, scratched, and discouraged, and he began to feel the way the forest around him looked—dark and ominous. He wondered if there was any way through at all; doubt filled him, and all at once he felt that it was all ridiculous. *Why should I even believe it?* he thought. *This curse of Kah-Taw and some 'king'" that no one has even seen for hundreds of years? Or for that matter, he probably doesn't even exist at all!*

Suddenly, he was attacked from behind. He shrieked in fear and realized that it was the evil Kahee-Nawb beast that had him. It seemed to come out of nowhere and sought to drag him back the way he had come. The trees and underbrush cracked and crashed with thunderous noise as branches fell around him. Nikos struggled violently and got free of the beast's crushing claws and lurched forward. He spun around, gasping for air and stared in disbelief. There was nothing there. The trees were undisturbed, and he didn't have a scratch on him. He looked into the forest roundabout, but it was dim, eerily silent, and still. Shaking in fear, he continued on his way as quickly as he could; he was anxious and wished to be out of such a gloomy and foreboding place. Suddenly, he stumbled into the bright sunlight and found himself on a narrow path of short green turf in a valley of rocky cliffs and outcroppings. The forest behind him had disappeared, and the path stretched arrow straight in both directions as far as he could see.

Doubts filled Nikos's mind again, and he wished that he had never heard of the curse of Kah-Taw. Why had he come so far? *"What am I even doing here?"* he thought. *"This just can't even be real."* He turned to go back, but the grassy path stretched on for what looked like a hundred miles. *"How can this be?"* he thought angrily as he began to run, now wanting more than ever to go back home.

He raced madly down the greenway but seemed to get nowhere. He went faster, but suddenly tripped and tumbled headlong. He sat up slowly, and after his senses cleared, he got to his feet and realized he didn't know which way was which. He looked carefully at the valley walls and craggy cliffs, but from where he stood it looked like a mirror image in both directions. He stood at a loss, wondering how he was supposed to choose which way to go. Suddenly, he heard the sound of wind, though the air around him was dead still. He couldn't really tell where the sound was coming from or where it was going, but as he listened, he felt drawn after it somehow and felt compelled about which way to go.

After he had walked for a while, he saw something glinting in the distance and as he came closer, he saw that there was a wall with a gate in it across the valley. His pace slowed as he came near enough to see two tall, armor-clad figures standing on either side of the gate. Wondering if they were alive or statues, he approached cautiously. The figures were stocky, with circlets of gold on their heads and breastplates of silver, trimmed in gold, with similar greaves on their legs and gauntlets on their forearms. Their hair was long and braided, and they wore purple linen shirts and kilts beneath their armor. Nikos felt an ominous reverence for them and as he came nearer, he could see that they were living beings. They stood stone-still and solemn, facing each other, and Nikos felt that he should not take another step closer or dare even to look at them; he wondered what he should do. Immediately, he remembered the man who had spoken to him outside the tavern in Zabach and thought that these beings were just like him. Nikos began to feel uncomfortable and fearful and looked back the way he had come and as he did so, one of the beings spoke.

"Would you turn back now after coming so far?"

The suddenness of a sound alarmed Nikos, and he jumped in fright.

"Do not fear," continued the being. "I am Adar, Captain of the Elyone. You are welcome to pass through the gate."

As it opened by itself, the other being said, "I am Rapha, Messenger of the King. He welcomes you."

Nikos, being quite shaken, found it impossible to speak, and he dared not look at the beings, who nodded as he passed by them. The grassy way continued, and there were hundreds more beings. They stood at attention in perfect lines on either side facing each other across the grassy way. Their presence was disturbing at first, but Nikos noticed that as he walked past, they turned slightly in his direction. He felt a strange anticipation and quickened his pace and soon saw a gigantic white castle in the distance. Finally, he came to the foot of a long, broad set of steps, which were shallow and fanned out in a circular shape. Everything was made of white marble, polished as smooth as glass and beautiful beyond description. He was awed by it and wholly unconscious of himself as he started up the steps. At the top was a wide paved area and a porch beyond it with huge columns and another set of steps leading to the castle doors. On either side of the doors were huge white statues that looked somewhat like lions, but with longer, stouter faces and paws that were more like hands. Nikos had never seen lions before, only cats, so he was intrigued to see these creatures. He came to the porch, ascended the steps and saw that these statues were exquisitely carved.

He was just reaching to feel how smooth the marble was when a great, furry voice spoke, "Do you dare to touch one who lives in the presence of the King?"

Nikos nearly jumped out of his skin as he leaped back, but the creature, quick as a cat, reached out and caught him before he fell. In the creature's huge paws, Nikos was stunned to realize how very much alive it was as its fierce blue eyes met his. Its fur was a dazzling white, and its mane glittered brilliantly in the sun, causing Nikos to squeeze his eyes shut. The creature set Nikos back on his feet and returned to where it had been sitting by the door, sweeping its great tail around its paws.

Nikos stood trembling in fear and slowly opened his eyes as the creature said, "The King does not call many to his throne, but do not fear, those whom he calls are certainly welcome."

Nikos glanced at the other creature as the doors swung in, and he stepped inside. The hall was dimly lit with large rows of marble columns on either side, but the far end was darkened. Silence roared in Nikos's mind, and the whole place overwhelmed him with fear and a great sense of awe. He glanced back at the doors, fighting the desire to flee.

"Do not fear," said a deep, strong voice that seemed to come from everywhere in the hall all at once. Nikos snapped back around, nearly jumping out of his skin and stood trembling. Soon, a figure came forward through the darkness and as he came nearer to Nikos, the whole hall became brighter as the light seemed to emanate from the being.

Nikos stood gazing in wonder and unexpectedly heard himself say, "You are the King?"

"It is as you say," said the man, who was wearing simple sandals and a white linen robe tied about the waist with a red cord. He wore no crown and though his hair and beard were white, he was young. *"How could this be the King—dressed like a peasant and alone in the castle? Where were all his courtiers and lords and ladies?"* thought Nikos. He began to doubt whether it was all real but greatly feared to speak again. The King came forward and stood before Nikos, who cast his eyes to the floor, his mind racing with fear.

Suddenly, he blurted out, "You are really the king? You have no royal robes, no attendants; you are alone here . . ."

The King stood silent for quite a while, but then said, "I have been alone once, but it is not so now, nor shall ever be again."

His words carried such a great sense of pain that Nikos felt the sting of his own tears.

"That is all over now," said the King with an unexpected smile. "It is finished."

Nikos stood silently for some minutes and then began to weep. "I am sorry," he said. "I am unworthy . . . this curse . . . I can bear it no longer . . . can you . . . will you take it from me?"

"*Can* I?" said the King in a voice that made Nikos tremble.

"I . . . I believe . . .," said Nikos weakly, "you are the only one who can."

"You have received what you seek," said the King. "Now much is required of you. Go and accomplish your purpose."

Nikos was immediately overcome with a sense of freedom and happiness such as he had never known. Questions flooded his mind, but as he looked up, he found that he was far from the castle, at the end of the valley he had come through. The sun was high in the sky, and a warm breeze wafted by him. At his feet he saw his pack, which he hadn't even realized he had left there.

As he slung it around his shoulders, he looked down the valley, still overwhelmed and wishing with all his might that he was still with King. How long he stood there wishing and wondering and thinking, he knew not, but suddenly, he realized that the sun was going down. Exhausted and hungry, he thought about the woman at the farmstead and of going back there but feared going through the forest. The stars were beginning to come out and as he looked up at them, he noticed that he didn't feel totally insignificant as he always had beneath the vastness of the night sky. *"I am still one among millions,"* he thought. *"But now I am . . . not unknown . . ."*

Nikos awoke near midday and couldn't make sense of where he was, but then everything came flooding back to him. As he thought of the King's last words to him, he leaped up, but at a loss as to what to do. He felt an urgency to get somewhere and do something, but he asked himself, *"What is my purpose? How can I accomplish what I do not know?"*

He made his way through the forest and was soon looking out upon the plain; the city of Zabach was far off in the distance. He felt like a stranger in a strange land as self-pity and loneliness overtook him.

The events of the day before faded from his mind, and all he could think of was to go back home, *"Wherever that is,"* he thought forlornly. He hoped to get past the farmstead without seeing anyone, but it was all open country and the only way back to the city. He started off, feeling somber, sober, and confused as he stared down at the dry, rocky ground.

After a while, the woman he had met at the farm called out and came quickly to meet him, "Did you see the King?" she asked excitedly.

Nikos's mood slowed her down a bit as he remained silent and nodded slowly.

After a few moments she said, "Come. You must be hungry." The farm was busy with people doing various chores, but he accepted her invitation. She led him into the house where it was quiet and soon set some beef stew before him.

"Thank you . . . I am sorry," he said. "I forget your name."

"Chayel," she said smiling, and she sat across from him, remaining silent as he ate.

"Thank you again," he said as he finished.

"You do not seem as I expected," she said quickly, seeing that he was going to stand up.

"What do you mean?"

"Well, it is a very joyous thing to be set free from the curse of Kah-Taw . . ."

"Yes . . . it was . . ., " he began. "But it doesn't seem real now . . ."

"But you saw the King?" asked Chayel, a bit distressed as Nikos stood up.

"Thank you for your hospitality . . . ," he began, but then fell silent, lost in thought.

"Please," she said coming around the table. "I am sorry to press you, but it was so different for me when the curse was lifted—"

She cut herself short as Nikos became agitated and said angrily, "I don't even know what's real!"

He sat down again and continued in a quieter tone, "I feel like I do not even know myself anymore. I don't know you, and I hardly know how I got here or how all of this came to be or what has even happened to me."

Chayel was silent and somber, seemingly at a loss as to what to say as she sat next to him. "Well, there is this," she began and revealed some strange red lettering in her skin over her heart.

"What is it?" he asked, startled.

"It says, 'The Tsadaq Ahm, or the people of the Great One. All receive the mark when the curse of Kah-Taw is removed."

"How?"

"It just appears somehow."

Nikos immediately pulled his shirt open and saw that he had the same mark.

"It is true then," marveled Chayel. "You truly have seen the King."

"Yes," began Nikos as the whole scene was renewed in his mind. "Yes, I have." He went on to describe it all and finished with the King's last words to him. "He said that I must go and accomplish my purpose, but what is it?"

"We will go up and see Biyn," she said.

Nikos hesitated and was distressed as he said, "I had a friend named Nuwa; he was with me on this journey. We were in the desert at an oasis when an evil creature called the Kahee-Nawb attacked us."

Chayel's eyes widened in horror as she said, "The Kahee-Nawb? The Book speaks of it, but it has not been heard of in generations."

Nikos clenched his jaw and said, "It was terrible. We tried to hide and just as it came at us, something attacked it and killed it. We couldn't see because of the trees," said Nikos as his eyes filled with tears.

"Our horses ran into the wilderness. Nuwa was wounded, and the next day he died, but he saw the King . . ."

Chayel took his hand in hers as tears fell down her face. "Do not be grieved," she said compassionately. "I am sorry for the horses, but Nuwa has passed out of this world into the Ayar-Samach. In the common tongue, it is called the City of Delight. It is where the Tsadaq and the King are and is a place of supreme happiness. All of us who are of the Great One go there after we die in this world."

"So, Nuwa is alive there?"

"Yes, his death in this world is not a cause for sadness, but of gladness, though I am sure you miss him."

Nikos thought a moment, trying to make sense of things. "But how is the King in the City of Delight when I saw him in this world? I was with him. He was as real as you are."

"There is much to learn about the Tsadaq," said Chayel. "Let us go and see Biyn; he is the venerated Master here and the Keeper of the Book."

Soon, they headed up to the House of the Book, situated on a cliff that rose up behind the farm.

As Chayel led Nikos up the mountain, she said, "So how did you come to know of the curse of Kah-Taw and of the King?"

Nikos didn't answer immediately and wondered what he ought to say, but then saw no reason to say anything other than the plain truth.

"I met a man named Barah, and later his friends, Kafar and Arak—"

Chayel's response stopped him short, but he added, "You know them?"

She nodded as Nikos continued, "It is Barah who told me of the curse and the King, and. . . ." He paused and then said, "I know of the Book, that it was stolen and that they are looking for it."

She became very serious and said, "You must tell Biyn what you know."

They arrived at a high gate wrought of solid iron with a small window at eye level. Chayel called through it, and after a minute or two, a man called from inside, "Chayel, I am coming."

Soon the gate opened, and they were greeted by a tall, broad-shouldered older man with long dark hair and a precisely trimmed, graying beard.

"Welcome. I am Yasad."

Nikos nodded back to him and said, "I am Nikos."

They came into a small courtyard that had short, mown grass and a stone paved way leading to a circular pool with ornate masonry and trees in a circle around it. A stream flowed into it from the mountain behind and flowed out across the courtyard. Square stone buildings were on either side, and a large, ancient, important-looking building stood at the far end.

"Nikos has been freed from the curse," Chayel said to Yasad, "and he has seen the King."

Yasad looked quickly at him in wonder. "Welcome, brother!" he said in astonishment.

As they passed through the courtyard, Nikos looked at the high walls and the sheer cliffs beyond and asked Chayel, "How could anyone have stolen the Book from such an impenetrable place?"

"It was not by force," she answered, "but by deceit. Back in the spring, a young man named Kehsef-Tria joined us, but he was not true."

"But the mark . . .," said Nikos. "It proves us to be so."

"We had become complacent here, and the evil one, the Ra-Tsalem, made Kehsef-Tria appear to be one of us. Even our wise master, Biyn was deceived."

The few people who were there nodded in greeting as they passed, and Nikos found the place to be more peaceful than any place he had ever been. The building they were approaching was very old; it had a large ornate wooden door and two columns on either side carved with many figures and animals and scenery. They entered a large hall with columns down the length of it, which reminded Nikos of the King's castle. There was a long stone table in the middle, and an old man was seated at the far end. He arose and came toward them.

"Ah, my child!" he said addressing Chayel, who nodded.

He had long white hair, a mustache that was long and braided, hanging down either side into a long white beard.

"This is Nikos," she said as Biyn turned to him and took both his hands into his own and looked into his eyes very intently for a moment.

"My son, truly you are," he said. "But show me the mark." Nikos was confused and looked to Chayel.

"Here," she said tapping his chest.

"Oh, yes, I am sorry," he said and revealed the mark. Biyn held his finger to it for a moment and then nodded.

"We must be careful these days," he said and turned abruptly, motioning for them to follow as he returned to where he had been sitting. Books and parchments lay on the table along with an ink bottle and a quill.

"You have come a long way," said Biyn and looked at Nikos.

But Chayel said excitedly, "He has seen the King."

Biyn's eyes widened. But Nikos, feeling unnerved and out of place said, "I wish not to speak of it. Indeed, I wish to speak of nothing."

He abruptly took a few steps away and continued, "I feel that I have become part of something that I do not want to be a part of. He shook his head and was becoming more agitated when Biyn stood and put his hand on his shoulder.

"My son, there is much for you to learn, to understand, but you must remember, you have chosen this."

Nikos eyes dropped to the floor, and he took a deep breath as Biyn continued, "I will teach you many things, but there is no going back."

After a while Nikos settled down, and Biyn said to Chayel, "Be kind enough to bring us some tea. We will be in the tower."

Nikos followed the old man up a long, steep flight of stairs that wound their way up a tall tower. At the top was a room with comfortable chairs and a table and a door leading to a small balcony. Biyn stepped out onto the balcony into the bright sunshine and looked far into the distance.

"My son, what do you see?"

Nikos could just barely make out the city of Zabach; otherwise, the scene was mostly arid plain.

"There is nothing to see but the city," he answered.

"Is there nothing else?" Nikos looked hard but shook his head.

Biyn was silent for a few minutes and then said, "There is much more to see, my son, but it is a matter of where you look. Can you not see the sheep down there and the barns? Or the forest around us, or the mountains behind? And see the clouds, and there a few birds? If we would *see*, we must truly *look*." Biyn pulled two chairs to the balcony and motioned for Nikos to sit down as he continued.

"You are now of the Great One, and so you must look to where you are to go and what you must do. Do not look so far ahead that you stumble over what is under your feet."

Nikos nodded and began to feel a bit more settled. "Thank you, Master Biyn, sir—"

Biyn interjected, "Please, my boy; we are all students. Call me only Biyn. I am no one's master."

He leaned back in his chair, closed his eyes, and turned his face toward the sun and smiled. "Ahh, you do not see the sun either?" he asked and turned to Nikos with a grin.

Nikos grinned back as Biyn continued, "So, tell me of your journey here."

At that moment Chayel arrived with some tea. Biyn stood immediately. "My dear, thank you," he said, taking the tea. "I am sure you have some chores to attend to," he said as he looked out from under his bushy eyebrows.

"Yes, well, I am sure I do," she replied.

"Nikos, I am glad you are here. Come to the house later for supper."

She smiled and started down the steps.

"Thank you for the tea," he called after her. Biyn sat back down, took a sip of tea and turned his face to the sun again.

Nikos tried the tea and found it a bit sweet. He asked, "Is there tamahish in this?"

To which Biyn replied, still with his eyes closed facing the sun, "Indeed. You have had it before?"

"More than my share once," said Nikos shaking his head. "But it is good . . . in small amounts."

Biyn sat still and seemed to be at perfect peace, but he was quiet so long that Nikos wondered if he had fallen asleep. "So, tell me of your journey. You are from the north?" he asked, startling Nikos who had been looking out from the tower trying to see more things.

"Well, Chayel thought I ought to tell you about Kafar and Barah and . . . the Book." He paused, looking at Biyn who hadn't moved or even opened an eye.

"Ah," he began. "It is no wonder you have sought the King if you have met them. I trust it was Barah who did not let you get away until you were convinced?"

"Well, yes; I knew Barah best, but the Book . . . ," continued Nikos. "I know it is very important to you . . . to those who know the Great One."

"To *us*," said Biyn. "Now that you have joined us, you will learn much about the Book and from the Book, once it is returned."

Doubting that the Book could ever be found, Nikos went on to tell him about how it had been stolen from Nuwa and that Kafar, Barah, and Arak had headed north, but with very little to go on. They talked on into the evening, with Nikos telling Biyn all about his life, how he had escaped being killed by Kakos, his being miraculously spared in the prison collapse, meeting Barah, and then coming across the desert and being saved from the evil Kahee-Nawb. The sun had descended behind the mountains to the west, lighting up the sky with intense pinks and purples as Nikos finished telling Biyn about meeting the King.

"But I am wondering . . . ," said Nikos, . "He said, 'you have received what you seek.' I felt the curse lifted, but . . ."

Biyn answered, "There are many things that we seek and wish for, and many things hidden that will become visible."

He stepped to the railing and looked high into the sky where the stars had begun to appear.

"You have heard it said that it has been many, many generations since anyone has seen the King face to face. For you to have come to him, my son, to have met with him . . ."

Biyn trailed off and stood silent for a long time. Nikos's mind filled with questions, but a sense of foreboding and the silence and surrounding darkness left him unwilling to speak.

He began to feel uneasy when Biyn spoke again, "Long ago, even before my great-grandfather's time, all who sought the King came to his castle. The way was open and the path clear, but for hundreds of years, it has been becoming more and more difficult to find the King, and fewer and fewer are those who feel the curse or seek relief from it."

Biyn shook his head and looked very grave and then a bit sad adding, "Even here, the House of the Book used to be full of those learning of the Tsadaq and discovering their purpose, but you see now, there are few . . ." He looked out into the night and said quietly, "There is a light that is going out in the world."

── Ten ──

Far to the north, Pike, his deputy Zuegos, Barah, Arak, and Makarios had made their way down from Makran to Tachus Town. It was quiet and peaceful as they rode through town, and they soon came to a farm on the other side. Pike dismounted and rapped on the door of a house, which was quickly opened by a stocky but pretty woman wearing an apron.

"Why, Pike! Have you lost your way?" exclaimed the woman as she looked past him and added, "And have brought a rabble along with you!"

She laughed and invited them all into a very comfortable and well-to-do house. An older, but robust and burly man with a long gray beard greeted them.

"Well, my young Pike," he said happily gathering more chairs to the table, "What brings you to my door at this time in the evening and unannounced? You're not one for wandering far afield and especially not with a mob of people."

Pike's mood was serious, which sobered Kainos a bit. He said, "This is my deputy, Zuegos, and my friend Makarios, and these are two of three companions." They all sat down to dinner as Barah began to tell Kainos the whole story.

"Well now," began Kainos, "I've only heard good things about this Rhaka fellow, and he sure has made things prosperous in these parts, but it sounds like he's getting a bit high on his horse."

There was a long pause before Kainos continued. "Even a small army wouldn't get your friend out of there. Once a man takes the power for himself," he said shaking his head, "and has them that are loyal to him . . ."

"Then we must appeal to Lord Arkone in Silver City," said Pike. "His authority extends over these provinces, and he has an army easily of a size to enforce his rule."

"It will take at least a week to go to Silver City and back," said Kainos. Then he addressed Barah and Arak, "Your friend, he is strong?"

"Yes," said Barah. "But we do not fear death . . . if it should come."

"Ah, yes, my lad!" replied Kainos. "That is the way. We must never let fear carry us to the grave."

They finished supper, and Kainos spoke to the young woman, "Now Ella, you and the boys go take care of the horses."

She went out, and as Barah was about to object, Kainos held up his hand. "Now don't make a fuss; Ella makes a fair wage here. She lost her husband to one of them mountain tomcats a few years back, and she and her boys have been staying here ever since. Somebody's got to teach them youngsters how to become proper men."

He grinned and then continued, "Now how about some blueberry malt?" After they had cleaned up, Kainos produced a jug and some flagons, and they went onto the porch.

In the morning, Pike, Zuegos, and Makarios packed up and left for Silver City, but as they rode away, Arak slowly shook his head.

"What is it, my brother?" asked Barah.

Before he replied, Kainos said, "Now there is always hope, my lad; be of a good heart."

Arak nodded as Kainos continued, "I've got to attend to things in town, so make yourselves at home and don't be afraid of a little hard work; there's plenty of it here." He grinned and headed off to town.

Soon, Ella had put the men to work, and the day passed quickly, especially for Arak, who had begun to feel a special bond with her two boys, one six and the other eight years old. Over the next week or so, Barah and Arak became increasingly anxious about Kafar's welfare.

Waiting for Pike, Makarios, and Zuegos to return had them quite restless. One evening, as Kainos and Barah were sitting on the porch, Kainos said, "Now, my lad, you have not offered up any more about this book of yours, but I have been quite curious."

Barah paused and looked thoughtfully at Kainos before saying, "Well, it is a sacred book about life and death and good and evil and belongs in the House where it was written. We must get it back, even at the cost of our lives."

Kainos nodded but remained silent, and so Barah continued, "There is much power in it for good and for evil. I do not doubt that Rhaka would use it for evil if he could, but thankfully, he does not know the language."

But Kainos shook his head and said, "You cannot trust to that. Many have come from distant lands of late. But tell me, what else is it about this book, about you and your friend Arak; there is something different."

Barah went on to tell him about the curse of Kah-Taw and the King, and he listened intently. But soon the moon had risen, and Kainos was feeling the effects of a hard day's work and his older age. He arose and said, "I must find some rest for my eyelids, or they will soon close of their own accord, but we must talk more of this."

Barah only grinned and nodded as Kainos went into the house. In the morning, Kainos quickly came to Barah and Arak, and they could see that he was shaken.

"Your King," he began, "I know it was him . . . he came to me in a dream last night . . . I have never felt as I do . . . and there is this," he said pulling his shirt collar down and revealing a red symbol in his skin.

Barah smiled and said, "Ah, that is from the Tsadaq. We are all marked so," he said, showing his own. "It says 'The Tsadaq Ahm' or in the common tongue, 'the people of the Great One.'"

"It is good," said Arak. "If only all would accept the truth as quickly and easily as you have."

"Oh, it was not easy, my boy," replied Kainos with a weary tone. "Not at all. The struggle between my heart and mind was great. It is one thing to assent to something being true, but to feel it, to accept it in yourself, well that is something else."

Barah nodded knowingly and said, "Yes, many cannot win that fight, and some by only the barest of margins."

Kainos began to look puzzled and very thoughtful.

"What is it my brother?" asked Arak.

"There is so much that I feel I do not know now, as if I have to learn everything all over again, or that I have never really known anything at all—at the least not what truly matters."

Barah answered, "Kah-Taw clouds men's vision, but being free of the curse opens the way to begin to see the world as it truly is."

"It is a lifelong journey," added Arak.

They talked together the whole day, telling Kainos all they knew about the Great One and the words of the Book and about their own lives.

As sunset neared, they were glad to see three familiar riders approaching. "Lord Arkone will do nothing for us," said Pike grimly.

TEN

Barah stood up, filled with indignation and shouted, "Is there no rule of law? Then Overseer Rhaka must be met sword for sword!"

Though Kainos was in hearty agreement, he said, "We cannot win by force of arms." They discussed things all through supper, but in the end, they found no answers.

In the morning, there was little talking as they sat at breakfast, until Kainos spoke. "Pike, my boy, what do you know of this Book that these fellows are seeking to get back?"

"Only that it is very important to them."

"It is important to all of us because it is the way of life," continued Kainos. He added, "Barah explained many things to me last night and—"

"No!" exclaimed Makarios suddenly. "It is only the imaginings of men, fairy tales!"

She stood up, and Pike rose beside her saying, "Makarios, it is their belief. Are they not free to believe as they choose?"

She shook her head and stepped away from the table as she said, "I have heard this before, and there is no truth in it."

She had become very agitated as the others sat in stunned silence.

"I will hear no more of it," she said and gathered up her belongings.

She headed toward the door, but then turned and addressed Arak and Barah, "I am sorry for Kafar. I do wish you well in getting him freed."

With that she went out quickly, followed by Pike who was trying to calm her down. All were quiet for a few minutes as they finished breakfast; then Arak said to Kainos, "So, Barah has spoken to you about Kah-Taw and the King?

But before he could answer, Koros, Ella's eight-year-old son interrupted, "Who is the King?" he asked full of curiosity.

"Koros! Now you know you mustn't cut in in such a fashion!" scolded Ella.

The boy apologized as Ella commanded both boys, "Come, we must clean up, and you, Koros, will do *all* the washing up."

They quickly cleared the table and then Kainos said, "Yes, the King came to me in a dream last night. I accepted that the curse of Kaw-Tah was in me as well, and now . . ." He paused recalling what he had experienced.

"And now what?" asked Zuegos, intrigued.

"I am free of it," answered Kainos with a smile. "Have you not ever felt controlled by a force that made you do things you ought not to?"

Zuegos suddenly became uncomfortable and said, "I think I ought to be getting back to the Outpost."

"But, my friend, you must—" started Kainos, but deputy Zuegos was already headed toward the door. At that moment Pike came in and said, "She is gone, back to her farm. I could not reason with her."

"I am off as well," said Zuegos, trying to sound lighthearted, but his uneasiness was plain to see.

"You are leaving?" asked Pike puzzled.

"Yes, well, it is best I get back."

He glanced quickly at Kainos before going out.

"What is this?" asked Pike looking hard at Barah. "It is unlike my deputy to behave so. And Makarios, what is this that she is calling fairy tales?"

He remained standing, but Kainos said, "My boy, please sit down. I know little more than you, but these men do not believe in fairy tales, nor was their companion willing to be imprisoned for mere imaginings."

Pike calmed himself and sat down as Barah said, "Pike, we are sorry for causing any difficulties, but we cannot help what is. The Book we are trying to retrieve is an ancient, sacred book and contains truths that many people do not want to accept. It is unlike any other Book and has great power in it that can awaken and empower evil in men. That is why it is so important for us to get it back to the House where it belongs."

Pike listened thoughtfully as Arak added, "I fear that this overseer Rhaka may have found someone who knows our language and that he is learning from the Book. His sudden change of heart in recent weeks and brazen disdain for the rule of law would seem to indicate that."

Pike saw the sense of it and silently agreed; after a few moments, he asked, "Rhaka's evilness will only increase?"

Arak nodded ominously, and Barah said, "The more he learns, the more power he will gain from the Book, and it is likely that a very powerful being called the Ra-Tsalem will come upon him, empowering and goading him to even greater evil."

Suddenly, Pike was overwhelmed with a cold fear and a sense of utter helplessness. He looked as if he could not see, and fell white as a ghost. He cried out and suddenly jumped up but fell to the floor.

"Pike!" exclaimed Kainos as they all leaped to their feet, but Pike did not move. Barah lifted him a bit, and they saw that his head was bleeding.

"What happened?" asked Kainos, filled with a fear he had never known,

TEN

but Barah and Arak did not know what to answer him.

"Pike," said Barah, cradling his head, "Pike . . ." but he did not stir.

"Is he alright?" asked Kainos full of fear.

"I do not know what happened to him," answered Barah.

"Did it not appear as if something threw him down?" asked Arak, uneasily.

Barah only nodded as Kainos called out, "Ella! Ella!"

She quickly came in and exclaimed, "Oh! what has happened?"

"Bring some cloths and warm water," commanded Kainos.

They soon had Pike bandaged up, but he still had not come to. They moved him to a couch near the fireplace as Barah and Arak looked at each other with a deep concern.

"What is it, my friends?" asked Kainos anxiously.

"We do not know," began Barah, "but there is an evil at work."

The three men gathered their chairs around Pike as Kainos, looking worriedly at Pike, asked, "Will he be alright?"

"We must believe so," said Barah. "But the only hope, for any of us, is to get the Book out of Rhaka's hands. We *must* do *something*. There's got to be some way. We must return to Makran."

After a moment, Arak said, "Pike is meant to come with us."

"How do you know this?" asked Kainos.

Barah answered, "Many of us have certain abilities, and Arak can perceive unseen realities, and sometimes the future is revealed to him."

"Why must Pike go with you?" asked Kainos.

Arak shook his head and said, "I do not know, just that he must."

Kainos felt some doubt but kept it to himself. At that moment Ella came in and went to Pike, taking his hand, but he did not stir. She was pained and turned to go back out when her youngest boy peeked out from the kitchen,

"Mama! Mama! Ask them about the King!" He ducked back into the pantry, and they heard his brother and him scuffling about and giggling.

Ella paused and then blushed; she said, "Forgive me, Kainos, but I, well . . . *we* have heard much of what you have been talking about. Koros especially wants to know who this King is."

Kainos glanced at Barah, who took a deep breath before he said, "You have heard us speak of Kah-Taw, a cursed evil that all men are born with?"

Well, our King—he is the only one who can cure us of it."

Ella nodded a bit apprehensively and in the brief silence, they noticed that the two boys had become very quiet.

"Koros! Brachus!" called Arak. "You may come and join us."

They rushed out and stood on either side of Arak, whom they had become fond of.

"Who is the King?" asked Koros excitedly. "What is his name? I have only heard of kings in stories, but sometimes they're bad, and sometimes they're good. Is your King a good king?"

As he drew a breath to continue, his mother said, "Now, Koros, be still and listen!"

He climbed onto Arak's lap, and Barah continued, "Our King is certainly a good King—"

But Koros, full of curiosity, interrupted. "Where is he? Can we meet him?"

At that moment, Pike groaned, and they all turned to him as Kainos knelt beside him, asking, "My boy! Are you alright?"

"Yes, but what happened?" he asked. As he tried to sit up, he squeezed his eyes closed in pain and lay back down.

"It is the evil one," said Arak grimly. "His ways are mysterious . . . and powerful."

"Now, he ought to rest," said Ella.

But suddenly, Pikes eyes popped wide open in horror as he said, "I . . . I saw it," he stuttered, turning pale. "It . . . it came at me and struck me to the ground. It was gruesome, sickening . . . huge and black . . . its wings . . ."

But Kainos gently took hold of him, saying, "Pike, my son, calm down, calm down; there is nothing here." Pike nodded almost imperceptibly and soon his color returned, and he opened his eyes again.

"You had best take some more rest," said Kainos. "Here, Ella, bring him something to drink."

Pike settled back down, but remained alert and after a few minutes, Ella said, "The boys and I are going out to attend to our work."

Koros, however, was not in agreement, and as they went out, he complained about wanting to hear more about the King.

"It is best the little ones are gone," said Arak. "Pike, what you saw was an evil creature called the Kahee-Nawb, and it is indeed real, but it has been a hundred years since anyone has even heard a report of it."

"This creature," asked Kainos, "He is described in the Book?"

Arak nodded as Pike said quite somberly, "If he is real, then he is a formidable foe."

"I must tell you that what you saw may also have been a look into the future. This does not bode well," said Arak.

Pike, who was unaccustomed to feeling fear, became even more uncomfortable than he was from the pain in his head. "This evil creature you saw, did it say anything?" asked Arak.

Pike was startled as he asked incredulously, "The beast can speak?"

Suddenly, Kainos, who had begun to feel indignant over the injury it had caused to Pike, asked in a fiery tone, "There is a way to kill it, is there not?"

Barah and Arak looked at each other and fell silent. "I have studied little about the Kahee-Nawb," said Barah apologetically.

Arak added, "And I know even less."

They looked at each other again, and Barah said, "Unfortunately, we would be quite ill-prepared to meet it in battle."

Both men felt ashamed of their lack of knowledge, partly owing to the fact that the beast had not been heard of in so long.

"Well, what *do* you know of it?" asked Kainos with a bit of an edge.

Neither man had much to offer, but Arak said, "My whole life I have known of the Tsadaq and have been taught from the Book, but even Master Biyn spent little time teaching about the Kahee-Nawb. All I know is that it is a manifestation of the Ra-Tsalem—"

Kainos interrupted, "My friends, my *brothers*, surely the Book teaches the ways of this creature and how to defeat it."

Arak interjected, "Yes, and it is true that victory is most easily won when the ways of the enemy are most fully known."

"That is from the Book?" queried Kainos.

As Arak nodded, Kainos continued, "At least you know that much, but I am amazed that you know so little about how to fight this evil. You spoke of an evil being called the Ra-Tsalem. What is it?"

Barah answered, "He is unseen, a phantom without physical form and has power that is far beyond any mortal man. His fury is like a messenger of death, and nothing can appease him. He can sweep through the land like the wind and fill it with the slain, and he never says, 'Enough!' His authority is from himself, and he comes only for violence. He seeks to rule and then destroy all that is good and just—"

But Kainos interrupted, "You quote these things by rote, as if this beast is a myth and poses no real threat! You saw what he did to my boy, Pike, and surely that is but the littlest of his power."

He was furious and began to pace back and forth.

"But we are the People of the Great One," said Arak in a less than compelling manner.

"Kainos," began Barah, "you are right. Though we have come far and have sacrificed much in our quest for the Book and would even give our lives, we have not taken things as earnestly as we ought."

He fell silent, and soon Kainos calmed down and, looking at Arak, he said, "Yes, we *are* of the Great One, though I know little of him as yet, but the King, last night in the vision it was so real, like no dream I had ever had. I sensed a power in him that was also far beyond mortal man."

"Yes," said Barah, "The Book proclaims, 'As the Great one, so the King,' but it is hard to understand."

"My friends," began Pike and all turned to him. "All of this that you are talking about sounds absurd, and I would think it nothing more than a fable but for what happened to me. What is the Great One, and who is this King?"

Barah explained everything, and then Pike addressed Kainos, "So, you have become one of them, the Tsadaq Ahm?"

Kainos nodded and revealed the red symbol on his chest, which immediately intrigued Pike, and he put his hand upon it, but quickly drew it back saying, "It has a heat of its own. I have never seen such a thing!"

He was genuinely alarmed and looked back and forth between the three men.

"Pike, my boy," began Kainos, "this is disturbing to me as well, but there is no denying its truth, and that it is good. For surely there is good and evil in this world, and to not be on one side is to be on the other. You must make a *choice* for good because the curse births all men into evil."

But Pike shook his head and seemed in a quandary saying, "I believe there is truth in this, but I cannot accept that there is this evil in me. I cannot see it to be so."

Kainos was about to speak, but Arak stopped him, "All must come of their own accord. For now, we must turn our attention to getting the Book."

The three looked to Pike, and Barah said, "Are you still with us?"

Pike nodded and said, "If the words of this Book contain the power you say, we must get it back with no delay, for is there not great danger in it being copied? Its power would be multiplied—"

But Barah said, "The Book cannot be copied. If one were even to begin to write down the words of the Book, the paper on which they were written would ignite into flame."

But Pike was incredulous and said skeptically, "Have you seen this happen?"

Barah shook his head as Arak said, "The Book proclaims it to be so."

Pike raised an eyebrow and as he was about to object, Kainos interposed, "We may debate these things, but we all agree that the Book must be retrieved. Let us focus ourselves on that and leave the rest for now."

"Indeed," said Barah. "The truth can stand alone, but falsehood needs many allies."

"You quote from the Book again," said Kainos grinning.

And Arak added, "Its words are power . . . for good or ill."

By the next afternoon, Pike was well enough for them to talk over what they might do.

"Though Arak and I found a way into the fortress by climbing up some fallen rocks," said Barah, "I am sure Rhaka will have set things in order behind the wall."

"And we cannot break in," said Arak.

"I have written an order that Rhaka must release Kafar to me on the ground that he committed a crime in my town and that he must be tried in my court," said Kainos.

The other three remained silent until Arak shrugged his shoulders and said, "Let us hope for success." But none of them felt very hopeful.

They arrived at Makran by midday and as they approached the north side of the city, Barah said, "We will stay here, since we are known by Marshal Sigao."

Kainos nodded and rode off toward the fortress. The three men watched him as he came to the gate, and the heavy iron door was partially opened. They could not see who was inside, but only that as Kainos dismounted and presented his order to release Kafar, the door began to close.

To their surprise, Kainos suddenly rushed forward and barged into it, sending two very large soldiers tumbling backward. As he drew his sword, Barah, Arak, and Pike spurred their mounts and galloped across the lawn, arriving to see Kainos in a standoff with the soldiers who had just gotten to their feet.

Marshal Sigao was there, but he was stunned at what had just happened. In the midst of the standoff, a squad of soldiers came rushing toward them, but Pike, who had dismounted and was headed toward Kainos, called out to him, "Get back!"

But Marshal Sigao held up his hand, commanding his soldiers to stand off and said to Kainos, "What is this? I will have no disturbances here!"

"You have a man in confinement here who must stand trial in my court. You must release him to me," said Kainos, holding out the written order.

But when Sigao saw Pike, he sneered, "You again! And with this ruse! I have had enough; take him!"

Kainos was about to spring forward to intervene, but Pike called out, "No! There are too many!"

Pike turned back to Sigao and said, "By what statute do you purport to detain me?"

"I do not answer to you!" yelled Sigao, enraged. Another squad of soldiers arrived and as they advanced on Pike, Kainos rushed zealously and heedlessly at them, but he was quickly subdued.

"Now, don't hurt the old man, fellows," mocked Sigao. "We would not want to dishonor his gray head."

There was nothing they could do to prevent Pike from being taken, and as the gate closed, the last thing they heard was Sigao saying, "Put him in the pit!"

They turned their horses around, but Kainos sat still. "I cannot accept this!"

"Well, you best!" said a voice from the guardhouse. It was a young soldier who was shaking in fear as he added, "They been *killin'* people. You got to go along with 'em or else! Lucky you weren't killed."

The three men quickly rode back to the city and down its crowded main street. Kainos was beside himself with anger. He abruptly checked his horse, exclaiming, "But what about my boy, Pike? I feel like I could take down that fortress with my bare hands!"

"Well, maybe that's what you should do then." Startled, the three men looked around to find out who had spoken.

"Fadzo!" exclaimed Arak as he spied the crippled old man sitting on the edge of a watering trough.

"Yep, it's me," he said. "And still alive too. That Rhaka fellow is turnin' real bad. If you go agin' 'im . . ."

He trailed off shaking his head. Then he slowly resumed, "And he's got a fair size army now in that fortress . . . and those giant men. They're none too smart, but they do what their told without asking questions."

He was about to continue when Kainos said impatiently, "Barah, Arak, we must do something!"

"But what *can* we do?" asked Arak.

Fadzo said, "Well, I'm sorry for your troubles, but I don't want to git caught talkin' to you because that Rhaka, he knows things . . ," and as he disappeared into the crowded street. He called back, "Don't go trustin' anybody!"

The three men looked at each other and spurred their mounts. "We had better get out of Makran," said Barah soberly. "There is nothing we can do for Pike or Kafar now and as for the Book, we must trust the Great One to make a way."

They were soon through the city and made their way back to Kainos's by evening.

— Eleven —

Within the fortress, Sigao commanded two huge soldiers who grabbed Pike, took his weapons, and roughly shoved him forward.

"You heard me, boys, into the pit!" bellowed Sigao as he left the soldiers and headed toward the citadel.

Pike kept his wits about him and observed everything that he could, but they quickly arrived at the prison building. Within, it was dimly lit with rows of barred cells on either side filled with prisoners jeering and sneering. At the end of the building, they descended some stairs that led to a very old, vaulted basement. It was dank, dim, and smelly; columns supported a low ceiling, and there were small arched windows above.

One of the soldiers unlocked the grated door at the foot of the stairs and shoved Pike through. As his eyes adjusted to the gloom, he saw that the dungeon was very large, and the far end receded into darkness. It looked like it had been used as a storage area, but now it was empty, except for a few stray barrels and crates. There were at least two dozen men there, huddled along the walls—some of them in poor shape. They eyed him suspiciously. Pike retreated to a corner and sat down on the well-worn stone floor. Soon, a clean-shaven man of very small stature with short brown hair approached Pike and sat down near him.

"So whajah do?" he asked. "I got throwed in here for arguin' about payin' an unfair tax! Just fer talkin', I say!"

Pike was cautious about answering and as he looked around at the others; the man continued, "Yeh, none of us done anything bad, but here we are. My name's Ruad."

Pike nodded to the man in acknowledgment but kept silent. From above, there was scuffling and yelling and then the door was heaved open and a big, burly man was thrown in. He hit the ground hard, but unexpectedly got right up, cursing and shaking his fist at the soldiers. After the soldiers had gone, the man turned to face the others, red-faced and breathing hard as if ready to fight.

Ruad jumped up and moved away saying, "We don't want no trouble, man. Got enough as it is."

The big man spun around and grabbed the iron bars of the door, shaking it violently and yelling, "You got no right! My farm is my own! You got no right!"

He kept yelling and pounding on the door until he wore himself out, and then slumped down on the floor. "They took my woman too," he said to no one in particular and then shocked everyone by beginning to cry like a baby.

"Now, mister," began Ruad, who was distressed at the man's outburst, "They can't keep doin' what they been doin'. It's got to get set to rights."

The big man looked up and wiped his face dry with his sleeve and said in a frustrated tone, "Yeah? Who's gonna set things to rights, heh? Who? You? You ain't even as big as my neighbor's little girl!"

He got up and started pacing around and muttering, "We'd have to get our own army, I say. . . , and those soldiers are brutes!"

After his rant died down, another man said, "And they been confiscatin' weapons. They come into my shop and took all the swords that I had made and then took over, thinkin' they could make swords—and that with *my* tools!"

Soon other men were telling their stories, and it became apparent that none of them were criminals at all. The day wore on and then near sunset another man, who was weak and in terrible shape, was thrust into the dungeon. Ruad, who was proving himself to be quite a compassion sort, went immediately to him and helped him to his feet. But the man cried out in pain, holding his side and trying not to straighten up. Ruad helped him over to the wall and put his own coat on the floor for the man to lie on. As evening approached, the men settled down to sleep, but Pike remained awake for much of the night.

In the morning, the man who had been brought in late was sitting up, though very uncomfortably and eating what the soldiers had brought. Ruad had given his own portion to the man as well, who received it gladly. Pike could see that he had been being beaten and fed very little for a long time.

After a few days, the man was feeling only marginally better, and Ruad asked him, "So, what happened that they beat you like this?"

The man was slow to answer and breathed painfully, but eventually he said, "Like you, I would not go along with them and asked that my goods be returned to me. I insisted that they uphold the law."

Ruad accepted his answer as did everyone else, who voiced their hearty approval, but Pike was suspicious. Over the next few days, unrest grew in the dungeon as more men were cast in, but there was a camaraderie in their desire for justice. One day, another man was thrown in, but his arm had been gashed and was bleeding. Ruad went to his aid and tore off part of his shirt to bind up the wound.

But he was inconsolable as he kept crying, "They killed 'im; they killed 'im!" Eventually, he told the story of how they had fought back against Rhaka's soldiers who tried to take a portion of their crops because they had no silver to pay the higher tax.

Ruad was incensed, "What can make a man so wicked?!"

There was no response until the man who had been beaten and starved said, "There is an evil in all of us to do such things."

But most of them immediately scoffed, and the big burly man, whose name was Bahr, said, "Now you take this Ruad here, there could not be a kinder man among us. You sayin' he could do what this Rhaka is doin'?"

The man only nodded.

"That's fools' talk!" said the big man and turned away abruptly.

The men began debating among themselves, and Pike moved next to the man and said in a muted tone, "What is this evil you speak of?"

The man smirked painfully and scrutinized Pike before answering, "You seek the truth?" but Pike only waited for the man to go on.

"Few will accept that they are cursed from birth."

Then Pike said, "This curse . . . is it called Kah-Taw?"

The man was surprised and looked cautiously about as Pike continued, "I am Pike, marshal of Agathon Outpost." But the man was hesitant to say any more.

"I believe you are Kafar," said Pike in a hushed tone.

The man did not indicate either way, so Pike continued, "I have met your companions and know that you are seeking to retrieve something that was stolen from you."

Pike waited for a reply, and after a few moments Kafar asked, "You have been helping them?"

"Yes, but you see where that has gotten me," said Pike with a slight grin.

"I am sorry, my friend. I know that this is not your fight," said Kafar putting a hand to Pike's shoulder, but he winced as he felt some sort of pain and then took a deep breath, which caused an even sharper pain. With difficulty, he settled back down onto the floor and closed his eyes.

A week passed, as more men were thrown in, and the dungeon began to get crowded. Fights broke out now and then, but Ruad always intervened and calmed the men down. The soldiers, who were all of the Meganthropos race, did not respond in any way to the men's objections or questions about how long they would be kept in the dungeon. Because of the damp, cool conditions and lack of food, Kafar was slow to improve and spent much of his time lying down. But he remained hopeful and of a good spirit, which puzzled Pike.

One day, Pike asked him about it, and he said, "There are opposing forces at work in this world greater than ourselves. Men are merely pawns in the theater of their battle, but my friends and I are on the side of good, so we do not fear death or lose hope because of adversity."

"You would sound as a fool to me, inventing these things if I had not seen the side of evil and the creature you call the Kahee-Nawb."

Kafar's eyes widened in alarm, and Pike went on to tell him of his experience. Soon, there were at least a hundred men in the dungeon, many getting pushed to the back where it was nearly pitch dark. One day, one of the men came forward and said that he had found a door, but that it was barred from the other side. Ruad and Bahr, who had become good friends, went to investigate and found it to be so. In the darkness Bahr found no latch or handle but felt that the door was made of wood.

"Maybe we could burn it," he said.

Ruad cautioned, "The soldiers . . . the smoke. We would be found out."

"How 'bout whittlin' it away somehow?" offered another man.

"Well, if any of us had a knife," began Bahr, "but there's nuthin' . . ."

"I have a knife," came a voice from the front of the dungeon.

They quickly returned, and Bahr said goadingly, "Ah, you want to talk to the rest of us now do ya?"

But Ruad admonished him and then asked, "Your name is Pike, is it not?"

He nodded and handed Ruad a small knife.

"Thank you, sir," he said.

And as they turned to go back, Kafar said, "I would counsel against trying to escape. If you are caught, you will remember the misery of this confinement as pleasant in comparison to the punishment they will inflict upon you."

Bahr and many of the other men ridiculed him, "Should we just wait here to die?"

"That's right! You speak of this Great One," said another man, "but he does not see us here!"

"We must make our own way!" said Bahr, and he snatched the knife from Ruad who remained there as the other men went back to the door.

Kafar winced as he lay back onto the cold stone floor.

Ruad came near and sat down saying, "Kafar, you are . . . different. How is it that you can be so hopeful? And this curse you speak of . . . I feel somehow that it is true. My father, he drank so much ale . . . I remember him lying there on his cot and his eyes streamed with water. He was sick and began to say how sorry he was, but then—"

Ruad broke down in tears and as Pike moved closer to the two, he said, "I am sorry for your loss." Ruad nodded and composed himself and then asked very solemnly, "Death is not the end, is it? I know it; there is more . . ."

He looked expectantly at Kafar, who still had his eyes closed and seemed very fatigued. He said, "Yes, my friend, there is more. Death is a portal into another life."

"And my father?" inquired Ruad, "What has happened to him?"

Kafar did not want to go on, but he said, "Those who die with the curse are doomed. I am sorry, my friend."

Ruad was horrified and hurriedly said, "What must I do? I do not want to be doomed!"

Kafar took a labored breath and urged, "You must seek the King."

Ruad was becoming anxious. He asked, "How? Where? I am trapped here!"

Although Kafar was nearly asleep from exhaustion, he said faintly, "The Great One will make a way."

"We had better leave him to rest," said Pike who moved over to an old crate and sat down. Ruad followed but he was pacing back and forth, very disturbed.

"I must get free," he said almost to himself and then turned to Pike, "Do you know where this King is?" But Pike could only shake his head.

For the next few days, the men took it in turns trying to carve a hole through the door, but it was difficult work, and the darkness did not help at all. Ruad spent much of his time sitting and thinking and wishing that he could get out since Kafar had told him where to seek the King. All the other men were bent on escape, and the anticipation of it was causing tempers to flare.

"Just burn it!" yelled Bahr. "We haven't even got through it yet!"

"Yeh, burn it!" called out someone else.

"We will be caught!" said Ruad who wanted to get out more than anyone else.

Soon, the men had fashioned a fire bow out of a small rope and a stick and had gathered bits of kindling.

"We'll just burn a bit of it at a time," said Bahr who was a woodsman and a hunter and had no difficulty starting a fire.

Unfortunately, the door was quite damp, and all that they accomplished was to create a lot of smoke. That set many of them to coughing, but the worst was for Kafar with his cracked ribs.

"Put it out! Put it out!" yelled Ruad and ran back, stamping on the small fire, which sent Bahr and some of the other men into a rage. They rushed at Ruad who ran toward the front of the dungeon screaming for help.

Bahr was brandishing the small blade, but Pike came between them and yelled, "Stop!" Do you wish worse for the lot of us than this?"

At that moment, a squad of the Meganthropos soldiers came down the stairs, led by a man who wore an officer's uniform.

"What is this disturbance?!" he bellowed, "And this smoke?"

All the men froze, and silence descended until Ruad said, "Having a disagreement, captain, and a bit of a fire to stay warm, but we are all settled now, aren't we?" he said looking at the men.

They all agreed and began to disperse and back away, as the captain commanded one of the soldiers, "Tode! Get in there and see what is going on!"

He was a Meganthropos, eight feet tall and as big as a house, and could barely squeeze through the door.

He took a few steps forward, peering into the gloom and said, "I don't see nuthin', captain; it's dark."

Suddenly, Bahr attacked him, stabbing him with the small knife. Tode panicked and shied away, dropping his spear as he fell to his knees and covered his head.

"We'll kill 'im if you don't let us out of here!" yelled Bahr holding the spear to Tode's neck. To the surprise of everyone, he did nothing but remain on his knees whimpering.

But the captain shrugged his shoulders and said, "As you will." With a look of disgust, the captain said, "He is not worth the bother." He turned with his squad and went back up the stairs, leaving all in a stunned silence. Bahr turned on the soldier and prodded him with the spear.

"You can get us out of here!"

But Ruad pulled him away saying, "He can't do nothin'! Look at 'im, he's not a soldier."

Then he said to him, "Your name is Tode?"

He nodded and after a pause, he said, "They came and told me and my brothers, we lived up in the mountain, that we had to come down and be soldiers."

He scowled and continued, "So we did, but I don't like it. I don't want to fight nobody; I just want to go home."

He moved back and sat down against the wall. Bahr's countenance suddenly softened as he said, "Your brothers, maybe they could help get us out of here."

"Yeh," answered Tode in a detached sort of way. "When they find out, they won't like me bein' locked up in here."

"Maybe we should just wait and see what happens," Ruad said to Bahr, who seemed agreeable.

Bahr said, "Well, I ain't just gonna do nothin'." Turning to Tode, he said, "Gimme that spear there. We been trying to whittle our way through a wooden door back there, but this'll do a lot better."

Tode held out the spear as Bahr continued, "Do you know where that door leads to?"

Tode, who had been lost in his own thoughts, suddenly came to; he said, "It comes up out back of the prison, on the outside. We could get out that way."

"Then what?" asked Ruad. "We're still inside the fortress."

Tode became more animated and said, "I could help. If we get out, we could wait until night; I could sneak to the barracks where my brothers are. They would help us; we could knock out the guards at the front gate and then open it."

But some of the other men grumbled and disagreed, saying that he didn't seem very smart and that they would all get caught.

This angered Bahr, who said, "You can all rot to death in here, but I'm getting out!"

With that he went to the back and began working on the door. Tode and most of the men joined him, but Ruad sat down near Pike and Kafar.

·--—— Twelve ——--·

Meanwhile, far to the south at the House of the
Book, Nikos was at peace for the first time in his life and felt as if he had a real
home and a real family. He was spending much time learning from Biyn and
had made close friends with two young men who were twin brothers, Zahab
and Barzel.

One day, while he was helping Chayel milk the goats, he said, "Biyn has
taught me much, and this place has come to feel like my home, but I have
been wondering about Kafar, Barah, and Arak, and the Book. I want to go
back north."

"I suppose you ought to talk to Biyn," she said. "But I would be sad to
have you go."

Nikos didn't see her blush with emotion as he continued, "And I want to
see my friend Makarios as well.

Barah had spoken of the Tsadaq to her, but she thought it all fairy tales.
The sacred Book is well named the Book of life and death, for indeed everything
depends upon it, and I wish for Makarios to understand."

Later that day, Nikos went up to the House to see Biyn, who according
to his custom, was at the table in the main hall with his books and writings.

"Ah, my son," he said as he arose and nodded in greeting. "Sit down."

As Nikos was about to speak, Biyn said, "You wish to leave, to go back
north?"

Nikos was surprised and nodded as Biyn continued, "Your mind has of
late, not been on your work, but you must not be hasty. There is much for you
to learn, though you have grown past many of the students here. There is more
for you to discover about what you have received from the Tsadaq. You must

truly know yourself and follow where you are led."

Nikos felt a bit subdued as he had expected Biyn's approval to go back north. Many things came to his mind to say, but in the end, he silently agreed.

Nikos began to spend more time in the House of the Book as he felt increasingly at odds with himself, questioning whether to stay and continue to learn or go back north. He spent time with Yasad, one of the other teachers, and kept his mind occupied with studying the teachings from the Book. Nikos learned that gaining knowledge of the Book made one grow strong and that memorizing the words of the Book was necessary.

Yasad was especially able to memorize and was a master at it, but one day as he and Nikos sat in the courtyard near the pool, he said, "Nikos, you have committed to memory in a few months what took me a year to do. Your ability is far beyond what I have seen before."

"But you are the master of memorizing," said Nikos.

"Yes, and although I began with a certain gift and have worked hard at it, your ability far surpasses mine. I have taught you all I have memorized of the Book. We can only wait for it to be returned."

"None of it has been copied or written down?" asked Nikos.

Yasad took on a more serious manner as he explained, "It is a singular book and cannot be copied. If one tries, the paper they begin writing on will burst into flame."

Nikos was incredulous. "How can that be?"

"There are many things we cannot know," answered Yasad. "But the truth is beyond question. That is why we commit so much to memory. The words of the Book are power, either for good or bad. If it could be copied . . ." but Yasad trailed off, shaking his head.

After a few moments he continued in a brighter mood and said, "But there is still much to be learned from the many other books and parchments that have been written about the Book over many centuries."

Over the next few weeks, Nikos's desire to go back north didn't leave him, but he began to have a strong desire to help find the Book. Its loss was being increasingly felt by all at the House, and a sense of unrest was taking hold of many of the people. There was discord as well, and it seemed there was thievery going on with the farm's resources. One day, as Nikos was coming out of the main barn, he heard loud, heated talking out in the field and looked to see his two friends, Zahab and Barzel, repairing part of the stone fence line.

"But it's been months!" said Barzel, who was a bit hot-headed and harsh. "We must have the Book back! *We* could find it; we must!"

"My brother!" said Zahab to Nikos as he approached. "We were just having a nice talk," and looked pointedly at his twin. Zahab was the more mature and of a gentler temper.

"But we are getting nowhere here!" continued Barzel, who threw down the stone that was in his hand. "We can't just keep waiting!"

At that moment, a horn sounded from high up on the mountain.

"We are called to assembly," Zahab said to Nikos who had not heard the horn before.

Everyone on the farm—only about one hundred people—headed up to the House, some talking quietly and others shaking their heads.

Chayel, who was distraught, joined Nikos and his friends. "Our unity is disintegrating," she said passionately. "Indeed it is difficult without the Book here, but we must not give in so easily!"

Nikos nodded as Zahab said, "Master Biyn will have good words for us."

As they entered the House, Biyn and the other teachers were at the head of the table. The people filled the seats at the table and sat on benches along the walls.

"My people," began Master Biyn, "we are all feeling the loss of the Book and are at odds with each other and are not in accord with the Code of Berahkaw, which promises goodness to us if we follow it. We must not allow this to continue, for our strength is only in adherence to the code."

He paused and shook his head, "The Book has taught us the consequences of yielding ourselves to the wicked way of Kawlal—that its deception will be our ruin. You see some of our faithful ones have chosen this way and have left us. We must search them out and bring them back, and we must immediately turn ourselves back from the easy way. I do not doubt that Kafar, Barah, and Arak will be successful in finding the Book, but we must be patient. Remember the words of the Book that you have memorized and draw strength. It is the only way."

He continued with more instruction and encouragement and then dismissed the people. Nikos, Chayel, Zahab, and Barzel left together.

As they went down the road back to the farm, Zahab said to Barzel, "You must make amends with Taavah—"

Before he could continue, Barzel interrupted, "It's all just talk! This getting along! We need to *do* something. We must get the Book!"

With a dismissive wave of his hand, he walked on ahead and passed quickly down the mountain. Zahab shook his head and said, "I fear for him . . . for us because our strength also lies in our unity. We must be strong and vigilant. There is an evil presence taking hold here, and we must fight it."

Master Biyn called another gathering early in the evening after supper to again encourage and instruct the people.

After a while, Zahab whispered to Nikos and Chayel, "I do not see Barzel here."

They each looked about but could not see him anywhere. The meeting was short, but Biyn again implored the people to be diligent to keep unity amongst themselves and to be faithful to the Code of Berahkaw.

Later that night, Nikos could not sleep and lay in his bunk thinking about the Book and whether Kafar and his friends had found it yet. Somehow, he knew they had not. The idea came to him to ask Barzel to go back north with him to search for the Book, but he immediately rejected it, knowing it was not the right thing to do. Suddenly, he heard a faint sound amidst the silence of the night, and he listened closely. He got up and pulled on his trousers and crept into the hallway where there were many rooms on either side. His pace quickened when the muffled sounds alarmed him, as if someone was in trouble. He came to a room and put his ear to the door and heard a woman in distress. It was Taavah's room, a beautiful young girl barely twenty years old. Nikos tried the door, but it was wedged from the inside. He called out and then banged on the door, and her cries grew louder. Nikos could hear her struggling and frantically bashed against the door, but it held fast. Taavah sounded hysterical, and suddenly Nikos stood back from the door and wished with all his might that it would open. People began emerging from adjacent rooms when he rammed against the door again and instantly, there was a violent tremor as the door came off its hinges and fell to the floor. Nikos rushed in and saw Barzel jumping out the window and running away into the darkness. Everyone was shocked by what had just happened, and Nikos most of all. Taavah, clothed in her night dress, flung herself upon him. He took her into his arms as she clung to him crying. Quickly, someone brought a lamp.

Nikos saw that it was Zahab, who asked, "What has happened?!"

"It was Barzel," began Nikos. "He was treating her shamefully."

Zahab was incredulous and visibly shaken; he said, "I cannot believe it!"

As people crowded around the doorway, a young boy exclaimed, "What happened to the door?!"

Zahab said to Nikos, "You . . . did this?"

Nikos only nodded in disbelief as Taavah continued to sob and hold tightly to him.

Soon, an older motherly sort of woman came bustling into the room and said to Taavah, "Oh, now, my dear, come with me," and led her gently out of the room.

The young boy looked in wonder at Nikos. "How did you do it?" he asked with his eyes wide in amazement.

But Nikos, still astonished himself, was speechless.

Zahab inspected the door and found it even more amazing that it was undamaged.

He picked up some objects from the floor and said, "Look at the hinge pins; it's as if they had been carefully removed!"

Nikos shook his head and said, "How can it be? I heard Taavah in trouble. I could not open the door, but I had to get in, and then it just happened."

Zahab, still astonished, said, "It is late. Let us set this door aright and in the morning; we must see Master Biyn."

Nikos went back to his room with a sense of foreboding. As he lay in his bunk looking out the window at the full moon, he thought about the many unusual things that had happened to him and felt great anxiety. He wondered what would happen in the days to come, and he thought of his days in prison and how life had been peaceful, simple, and constant. Even though the farm and the House of the Book and all the people felt like home and family, he still wished to go back north.

Nikos awoke early in the morning, feeling worn-out and had no desire to go see Master Biyn or talk about what had happened the night before. Still, he found himself heading over to the main house for breakfast and was joined by Zahab.

As they entered, they heard Chayel say in a very animated voice, "Yes, I said Chum is gone; someone has stolen him!"

Yasad was listening to her and looking disconcerted as she continued, "His saddle and bridle are gone from the barn and . . ."

As Nikos and Zahab joined them, she paused, seeing that Zahab was very upset. "What is it?" she asked.

He shook his head in disappointment and explained, "My brother is gone—as well, his belongings."

They looked at each other in silence as Zahab said, "I fear he has gone north. He has had the desire to look for the Book, but I believe that he has run away from what he tried to do last night."

As he explained it to her, she became subdued and said quietly, "How can all this be happening to us here?"

"Come," said Yasad, "Let us have some breakfast and then go up and see Master Biyn. We must seek his counsel."

Others joined them as they heard about the events of the night before and some shared about difficulties and unrest amongst themselves as well. As they went up to the House, more joined them until everyone had gathered there.

Biyn was grieved to hear of what had happened and took some time to ponder things before he spoke.

With a heavy sigh, he said, "Our adversary is gaining the upper hand. Our resolve to be true to the Book is waning. We have never had so few people at the House of the Book, and many of our countrymen have left the province, seeking to gain fame or fortune in the north."

He clasped his hands together and glanced around the hall, seeing that everyone looked as grim as he did. He said, "My people, we must unify ourselves against the influence of the Ra-Tsalem trying to turn us into the way of Kawlal. His wicked force is at work, and we must fight it. We must stand firm!"

He paused and then continued, "For the moment, we must find our brother Barzel and bring him home."

"I will search for him," said Zahab.

"And I will go with him," volunteered Nikos quickly.

As they went back to the farm, Chayel said, "I will come as well. I must find my Chum." She turned to Nikos and said, "I raised him from a foal."

"He seems really big for a mule . . ." suggested Nikos.

"It must be all the love he's received," said Chayel with a smirk. The farm had only a few horses and some mules.

Soon, the three were packed and ready to go. Zahab said, "Surely, if Barzel is going north, he will have gone through Yem and Yaam since there are no other sources of water."

As they headed out, Nikos asked, "But how will we find him? With this dry ground, there is no way to track him."

"Well, it will be nearly impossible," answered Zahab. "But we must hope someone has seen him or remembers that big black mule of yours, Chayel. It is all we can do."

They came to Yem by early evening and searched the village but found nothing. The next day they rode further west and north, inquiring of people they met, but their search was proving to be fruitless. After a few more days and a night spent on the unforgiving ground of the wilderness, they arrived in Yaam and went to the well in the center of the town.

As they watered their mounts, a man approached them. "My friend," he said to Nikos, "You remember me?"

Surprised, Nikos turned to him and said, "Oh, yes, you are . . . Esam?"

He nodded eagerly, and they shook hands as Nikos said to his companions, "Esam graciously allowed me to stay with him on my way through Yaam."

Zahab introduced himself and Chayel and then said, "We are looking for a young man. There is nothing you would have noticed about his appearance, but he would have been riding a black mule that is nearly the size of a horse."

Esam thought briefly and then said, "Oh yes, such a man was in Yaam yesterday evening. He quite made a fool of himself with too much drink at the tavern. He left on his mule going south."

Zahab sighed and shook his head. "Well, thank you . . ."

"It is late. I would be pleased to have you stay with me," Esam offered. They agreed and were appreciative of a comfortable night's sleep and a good meal. In the morning, Esam continued with his generosity by providing a plentiful breakfast.

"Thank you very much for your hospitality," said Chayel as they mounted their steeds.

Esam bowed and said, "Good fortune to you. May you find your brother and friend."

He turned and went into his shop, and the three rode to the outskirts of the town.

"There is not much more we can do," said Zahab looking south. "I wonder if Barzel did indeed ride off that way?"

"But why would he go that way?" asked Chayel.

Zahab, feeling dejected, only shrugged and said, "Let us ride down there a bit. Maybe good fortune will indeed shine on us."

But no good fortune was to be had as they searched in vain for any sign of Barzel. By midday they turned back east and headed to the oasis between Yaam and Yem, arriving by nightfall. They were tired, and Chayel broke down in tears, worried about Barzel and also her beloved mule.

The next day dawned very windy and made for a miserable, gritty ride back to the farm, which took most of the day. They arrived near suppertime, hungry, tired, and discouraged. Yasad greeted them and charged some young boys to care for their mounts.

"Come, we were just sitting down for supper," he said.

"We found nothing," said Zahab. "Only that Barzel was in Yaam but became drunk and rode off south."

He shook his head and began walking away saying, "I must see Master Biyn." They watched him go and then went in for supper. Yasad sat with a few other teachers as Nikos sat down with Chayel. Many others were also at the table, and there was a somberness overall, but as they ate, the mood lifted somewhat and conversations began amongst them. Nikos had been quiet, but he said to Chayel in a hushed tone, "I must go back north. I feel it stronger than ever."

She looked at him questioningly and said, "I do not know what you should do." She paused and then nodded ever so slightly, "But I am beginning to feel as you. I think we must do something. I would go with you."

Nikos glanced at her and said, "But your mother and father . . . your whole family is here."

"Yes, well I mean to return, just that we must go and find Kafar and the others and search for the Book."

Nikos took a deep breath and looked at her in a renewed way, but before he said any more, she continued, "Extraordinary things have happened to you—how you were spared in the collapse of the prison and saved from the Kahee-Nawb, how you actually saw the King face to face, and now what you did to the door of Taavah's room . . ."

"But I didn't do anything, I just wished it," said Nikos a bit anxiously.

But Chayel shook her head and said emphatically, "All these things have great meaning."

"No!" he whispered sharply as he arose and went out, walking swiftly in no definite direction.

Chayel quickly followed and as Nikos crossed the field, she caught his arm. "Nikos—"

He suddenly stopped and faced her shaking his head, "I am no one, just plain simple Nikos, and that is all!"

Emotion burned in Chayel, but finding no words, she reached out and took his hand, pulling him closer. Words failed Nikos, and they stood in an uncomfortable silence.

Soon the tension dissipated, and he said, "So much has happened to me .

. . I am afraid." He took hold of her other hand and looked into her eyes, "Do you fear nothing?"

She felt conflicted but resisted the urge to pull away from him. She said, "I fear what I feel . . . for you."

Nikos was overwhelmed and about to speak when Chayel suddenly looked past him to the west. "What is it?" he asked.

"An animal of some sort," she said, peering toward it in the dim light. "It looks like . . . my Chum!"

She broke into a run with Nikos right behind, but as she neared the mule, she saw that he was not well. He walked slowly with a limp, and his head hung down. He looked up in a labored way to see Chayel and brayed weakly.

"What has happened?!" cried Chayel. A rope tied tightly around his neck had caused severe abrasions, and there was a deep wound across his hindquarters that was crusted and matted with blood. Tears streamed down Chayel's face as she hugged him and led him to the barn. The mule went straight to the trough and drank more than it seemed he could hold.

"Oh, my Chum! My Chum!" she cried as she worked the rope free.

"This looks like a wound from some kind of a blade," said Nikos as he washed the mule's hindquarters, but at that moment the mule made a few odd sounds that startled Nikos.

Chayel glanced up to see that Nikos' face had gone pale. "What is it?" she asked quickly.

"He, Chum . . ." he began but shook his head.

"What?" insisted Chayel.

"I understood him."

"What do you mean?"

"Well, I heard him speak," said Nikos shaking his head and backing away.

Chayel went to him and took his arm and without a thought asked, "What did he say?"

"Barzel, um, harag . . . ish saw-deh. What does it mean?"

Chayel's eyes went wide in dismay. "They are wild people, the Ish-Sadeh, like beasts, and they killed Barzel," she said as if in a daze. "But how did you hear . . ."

"I do not know; he spoke it somehow," said Nikos who was very disturbed. "How is it that I understood him?"

"The Book speaks of such things, but it has been ages since . . ." Nikos felt a cold fear in his stomach about all the things that were happening to him that hadn't happened in generations. But sorrow quickly overcame him as he thought of Barzel.

"Why would they kill Barzel?"

"The Ish-Sadeh are a savage race," answered Chayel shaking her head. "They live to the west, along the foot of the mountains; they fiercely guard their territory. Maybe Barzel wandered into their lands after he left the tavern that night."

"I have heard of the Ish-Sadeh," said Nikos. "Two of them worked on Makarios's farm, but they seem civilized and kind."

"I suppose there are some who are not so brutal," answered Chayel as she finished caring for her mule and put him in his stall.

She kissed his nose and said, "You will be alright, Chum. I'm glad you got home," but tears flowed down her face as she turned to Nikos, "We must tell Zahab of his brother."

They went up to see Biyn and found Zahab still with him. Everyone at the House put aside their differences and came together to mourn for Barzel, which brought about a great sense of unity. After three or four days, things settled back into a normal routine, and Nikos again felt, more than ever, the desire to go back north. One day, feeling unsettled, he took a long walk down the road that led to the city of Zabach. He kicked at small stones and saw the occasional lizard or scorpion skittering away among the rocks and dry brush. It was hot and getting hotter as the sun peaked overhead. The arid, barren landscape was oppressive to Nikos and the further he walked, the worse he felt. Eventually, he turned around and headed back to the House, but at a much quicker pace. As he approached the outskirts of the farm, he saw Chayel coming toward him.

"Where have you been?" she called out. As they came closer, Nikos saw that she was furious.

"I have been looking for you!"

"Well, I —"

But she continued angrily, "It has been half the day! I could not find you anywhere and then . . ." but she trailed off and tears streamed down her face.

"I was frightened that something had happened to you."

She came near and hugged him as he said, "I am sorry, I was feeling restless . . ."

After a moment she pushed away and said, "Well, next time you wander off, tell me."

He nodded and said, "I have decided to go back north, whether Master Biyn counsels against it or not."

Unexpectedly, Chayel was in agreement. "I have great respect for Master Biyn, but we must also listen to our own hearts," she said.

That night, Nikos lay in his bed unable to sleep for a while as he thought about what he would say to Master Biyn in the morning. He awoke early, feeling very sober and went out to the fence-line to watch the sun rise.

He was eventually joined by Chayel who, when she saw his mood, said, "You will talk to Master Biyn today?"

Nikos nodded, and Chayel continued, "I must go to Qidmah today. I have had to delay going because of Chum's leg, but he is better now, and I have some goats to sell to a farmer there. I will be back by this evening."

After breakfast, Nikos went up to the House and found Biyn at his customary place in the main hall.

He rose to greet him and said, "Ah, sit down, my son . . ."

"You have told me that I must truly know myself and follow where I am led," began Nikos. "I continue to feel that I ought to go back north—"

"Yes, my son," said Biyn, "But there is much more for you to learn about yourself. You have received much from the Tsadaq—many abilities that you must come to know and understand. It is a great responsibility. You must not be hasty and stumble over what is under your feet by looking too far ahead."

Nikos felt at a loss and could only slowly nod in agreement. At that moment, Yasad came into the hall with a few other people. Biyn stood immediately, seeming to be glad of the interruption and gave an admonishing look to Nikos before he turned to address the others.

Nikos left feeling very unsettled and went back to the farm looking for Zahab, but one of the young boys informed him that Zahab had gone with Chayel to Qidmah. Nikos set to work on some chores and labored hard the rest of the day, trying to keep his mind off the increasing anxiety and unrest he was feeling. By suppertime he was tired and hot and very nearly feeling angry.

He went to the waterfall that cascaded off the mountain and had a dip in the pool beneath it. He began to feel very alone, but the constant splashing of the waterfall seemed to drown out the rest of the world—even his own thoughts. Suddenly, a voice shook him out of his peacefulness.

"Nikos!" It was Chayel. "Supper is almost over!"

He came quickly over to her and asked, "Was your trip to Qidmah successful?"

"Yes, yes. How did it go with Master Biyn?" Nikos immediately frowned and shook his head.

"He insisted that I need to learn more about myself, and about, well . . . about the abilities I seem to have—"

But Chayel interjected, "Nikos, you know that much has been given to you that none of us have. Surely, we have received gifts from the Tsadaq, but you . . . Master Biyn is right that you must know yourself better, but I feel that we cannot wait any longer. I do not think things are going well with Kafar, Barah, and Arak."

Nikos stood silent, and Chayel looked hard at him and said, "You are going to abide by Master Biyn's counsel. I see it in you. You will not go north."

"I am torn. Master Biyn is very wise and discerning. We are young and—"

"But we know what we ought to do," said Chayel heatedly. "In your heart you know it."

Nikos raised his eyes to hers and said, "I am not sure . . ."

But Chayel backed away and said, "Yesterday you were so set on going, no matter what, and now . . ." She looked at him so piercingly that he dropped his eyes to the ground. "Now that it comes to it, you fear to go," she said in a disappointed tone. "You must not let fear decide anything for you."

Nikos felt embarrassed and after a few moments said, "I did not ask for any of this, for these abilities."

"But you did, Nikos, when you saw the King. He gave you many things that you've always wished for."

Nikos was puzzled. "How do you know this?"

"Many times, I can see people's hearts. I know that you have always wished for a way to protect the helpless. You have felt powerless your whole life, and your heart has cried out for the power to turn wrong to right."

Nikos nodded as he hadn't even realized these things about himself.

"I suppose you are right," he said, but he was still hesitant as they went back to the main house for supper. There was little conversation, and Nikos retired early, feeling exhausted. He fell asleep quickly.

Just after midnight, as Nikos lay fast asleep, Chayel rushed in and shook him awake.

"Nikos!" she whispered fiercely, "wake up!" He sat up alarmed.

"What is it?"

"We must go!" demanded Chayel. "Gather your belongings!"

"To where?" said Nikos as he pulled his clothes on, groggy and confused.

"What is happening?"

"The Great One has sent a being called Tey-Rahk. We must go with him."

"What? To where?" repeated Nikos.

"He has commanded us to go with him!" Nikos rushed to get his things together, and Chayel gave him some food and provisions that he put in his pack.

She grabbed his arm and said, "Quickly!"

Nikos stumbled after her and stopped short, speechless as he came face to face with a giant white creature that was like a winged lion. It stood eight feet tall and crouched down to allow Nikos and Chayel to climb onto its back.

"I am Tey-Rahk," he said, "and I am sent by the Great One. Hold tightly to me."

As the creature raised its wings aloft, Nikos leaned forward and grasped handfuls of mane while Chayel held onto Nikos.

With a deafening rush of his wings, Tey-Rahk sprang into the air. Nikos was stunned, bewildered, and frightened, but Chayel seemed unafraid. She had read about these immortal beings in the Book and loved to read over and over the accounts of all the things they had done. She was awestruck but also felt delightful wonder at being part of such an adventure. Tey-Rahk swept high into the air and took up a definite direction rising higher and settling into a steady rhythm.

Chayel called out, "We are going north!"

Nikos suddenly remembered that this creature was like one of the two that were at the King's castle and began to feel calmer.

"Should we not have talked to Master Biyn first?" he called.

"Nikos, you have!" exclaimed Chayel. "And you have heard his counsel. Do you not see that we have delayed too long? You must not doubt but believe! And you must be strong. We do not know what lies ahead!"

Tey-Rahk turned his head slightly back toward them and said, "She speaks wisely."

Nikos was strangely compelled by Chayel's words and began to feel more at ease. Tey-Rahk flew very fast and after only a few hours had crossed the desert, but the darkness did not allow Nikos or Chayel to see where they were. Soon, they began to descend and landed in the foothills of a mountain range.

"Where are we?" asked Nikos as he and Chayel jumped to the ground.

"You must go to the town that is that way," said Tey-Rahk, pointing southward with his great white paw.

THE CURSE AND THE KING

"What are we to do?" asked Nikos.

Chayel said quickly, "Nikos! We must just do as he says. He is an emissary of the Tsadaq!"

She grabbed his arm and pulled him forward, setting off toward the town. After a moment, Nikos looked back and was alarmed to see the great white beast nowhere in sight. He faltered in his steps, but Chayel said, "Come! We must trust that we will be guided!"

·----Thirteen-----·

Barah and Arak had remained at Kainos's house but were becoming increasingly distressed with each passing day as they discussed what they could possibly do against Rhaka.

One evening, as they sat on the porch under the stars, Arak said, "I see no hope anymore. The Tsadaq gives no answer. How can it be that this wicked Rhaka should be allowed to continue to possess the Book and to rule so lawlessly? We can do nothing but wait for evil to overtake us!"

His despondency startled the other two men, and Kainos quickly patted his shoulder and said, "My boy, there is always hope." Abruptly, their attention was taken by a muffled sound away toward the barn.

"There is something over there!" said Arak in a hushed voice.

"I can see nothing," said Kainos peering hard into the dusk.

They listened intently for a moment as they took up their weapons and stepped down off the porch. Soon, two figures came from behind the barn, walking tentatively but then stopped, seemingly in disagreement.

Barah exclaimed quietly, "It is Nikos!"

"And Chayel?!" added Arak in amazement.

"How do you know them?" asked Kainos.

"I met Nikos in a town southwest of here," answered Barah, "soon after we came up from the south, and I worked with him in a camp. And Chayel, she is from our hometown, from the House of the Book."

"They are both people of the Great One?"

"Chayel is—"

Barah interrupted, "My brother! Nikos must have gone all the way to Zabach if he is with Chayel—something I surely did not expect!"

After a moment, Barah called out, "Nikos! Chayel! Come up. It is Barah and Arak!"

The two were startled, but they quickly made their way up to the house and as they neared, Chayel could be heard saying, "Did I not say that this is where we were to go?"

There were embraces all around and great gladness at seeing one another again, but Chayel quickly said, "Kafar . . . he is not here?"

Their joy dissipated as Arak said, "He has been imprisoned—"

"By whom?" interrupted Chayel heatedly.

"The overseer of this province—"

"What of the Book?" she continued, growing more animated.

"We have found it, but unfortunately this corrupt overseer has it in his fortress."

"And there is no way for us to get in," added Barah.

"There is always a way," said Chayel passionately. "How long has Kafar been imprisoned?"

"It has been a month and a half, and there is also a marshal who has been helping us—"

"You are just waiting, all this time?" burst out Chayel.

She turned to Nikos, and said fervently, "Do you see? It has been just that long! You knew you should have come back north . . ." She paced about, thinking furiously.

"But what can we do—" began Nikos.

Chayel went on, "What can *we* do? Nothing! But the Great One—do you not believe? Any of you?!"

She fumed a bit and then said in a calmer tone, "We *will* get Kafar out and also this marshal you speak of."

"How did you find us here?" asked Arak.

They were amazed as Chayel told them of Tey-Rahk and of flying across the desert, and she finished saying, "Then he left us, and we were guided to this place."

"Well, Chayel was," said Nikos sheepishly. "If it weren't for her, we would not be here."

They talked well into the night of all that had happened; but the unusual events of Nikos having actually met the King and the appearance of the Kahee-Nawb gave everyone a sense of foreboding.

In the morning, they made plans to go up to Makran and when they came out to the barn, they were surprised to see a huge white horse grazing near it.

"What is this?" asked Kainos. The horse looked at them intently as they approached and then came forward to Chayel.

"You know this beast?" asked Kainos. He was startled and unnerved when the horse spoke to him saying, "I am Tey-Rahk, an emissary of the Great One and will bear these two," gesturing toward Chayel and Nikos.

Kainos was speechless as Tey-Rahk's overwhelming presence and solemn countenance silenced any questions. Chayel smiled to herself and as Tey-Rahk bent down, she immediately climbed aboard. Soon, the five set out, but only a few of them had any real hope.

After some miles, Kainos, who had quickly become fond of Chayel and her fiery, confident personality, said to her, "My dear, we are riding toward a fortress that is locked and barred, guarded by an army of soldiers—many of gargantuan size—and ruled by an evil, heartless despot. Since you are leading us, you surely must have a plan."

She took some time to answer and then said, "Sometimes, plans have a way of making themselves."

By midday they were riding through Makran, but it was noticeably less busy, and there were soldiers along the main road, seemingly observing the goings on. As they arrived at the far side of the city, they looked out upon the fortress, and Chayel gazed up at the citadel, looking at it for a long time.

Eventually, she said, "A fortress is a false hope for victory, nor can it protect anyone by its strong towers."

Tey-Rahk quickly moved forward, and Chayel did not look back, but Nikos had little hope that they would not end up in the prison as well.

"What can she hope to do?" asked Kainos. "We should not let her go."

But Barah said, "She is not a foolish woman and can perceive things that we do not. But we must remain here since we are known by the soldiers."

Chayel and Nikos arrived at the guardhouse and as a soldier emerged, Chayel said in a forceful tone, "We must see the commander immediately!"

The soldier, after a moment's hesitation, quickly went to the small window in the gate and spoke through it.

"Why the commander?" asked Nikos quietly. But Chayel whispered sternly, "That is the way!"

After a few minutes, the gate opened, and a squad of soldiers stood there at attention as a Meganthropos soldier in a commander's uniform came forward. Nikos was stunned as a look of recognition came over the commander's face.

"Nikos?" he said, seeming to lose his composure.

His eyes darted to Chayel, "You . . . no . . . ," he trailed off.

Then he shook his head and took on an authoritative tone, "What do you wish?" he said to Nikos, but he kept looking at Chayel.

Nikos, who was quite taken aback, did not find any words, and Chayel quickly answered, "Commander, sir, there are two men in your prison whom I wish to be freed. One of them is my friend, whom I love."

The commander seemed mesmerized as he responded slowly, "He is your *friend?*"

He seemed confused and then continued, "What is his name?"

"Kafar, and the other is Marshal Pike."

The commander, who was visibly shaken, ordered that the two men be brought out, but the captain of the guard said, "But, commander—"

"Bring them!" yelled the commander in a sudden rage. He looked searchingly at Chayel and then glanced at Nikos before turning away.

As they stood there waiting, Chayel whispered to Nikos, "You knew him?"

"Yes, but . . . he is so different." Soon the two men were brought to the gate, and they passed through.

As it clanged shut, Kafar, who was holding his side in pain, exclaimed, "Chayel?"

"Oh, Kafar," she said as tears came to her eyes, and she carefully embraced him.

"How have you come here?" he asked.

At that moment, the guard came out of the guardhouse and said, "You all best be leaving. Lord Rhaka will not approve of you being freed."

They quickly went back to the city and passed through without incident. Once they were comfortably away from it, they all gathered in the lee of the mountain amidst some large boulders. There were tears and heartfelt greetings, and all were introduced to each other. Kainos, Barah, and Arak were incredulous that Chayel had been successful.

"I cannot believe . . ." began Arak, but Chayel looked sharply at him.

"Maybe that is the difficulty."

"What did you say to the soldier who was at the gate?" asked Barah.

"Well, it was strange. I felt compelled to ask to see the commander, but I do not know about soldiers and their ranks in the north. And then I said that Kafar was my friend whom I loved. It seemed odd to say it in such a way, but that is what came to me."

Nikos was looking at Chayel, and Barah asked, "Nikos, what is it?"

"Well, I know the commander; his name is Polus. Remember I told you about him—the one who lived by himself in the forest? He tried to kill the chief in Diaggello but got put in prison and then escaped."

He paused and then looked back at Chayel, "Your dark skin and black hair . . . I believe Polus momentarily mistook you for Makarios, or you reminded him of her. He loved her, though he had never loved anyone or anything before, and he was especially proud that Makarios called him her friend."

They all pondered that for a moment as Nikos continued, "But he is so different, he used to be like a child . . . and how he ever came to be the commander in Rhaka's army . . ."

"We had better get moving," said Arak.

With difficulty, Kafar got up behind Arak, while Pike shared Kainos's mount. They returned to Kainos's farm by early evening, but Chayel was ready to go right back to Makran.

"How do we not seek to retrieve the Book at once?" she asked them all.

But Pike said, "Now surely you cannot trust to chance again. Your fair words and the favorable mood of the commander gained our release, to which we are very grateful, but we must have more than luck."

Chayel suddenly turned on him, "Chance? Luck? Can you not *see?*" she said passionately, but then turned away and said, "Of course you can't; you are not one of us."

But Kainos took offense. "Now you hold on there! Pike risked his neck trying to get Kafar free and had no easy time of it in that dungeon as you can see. He is as much with us as we all are, though he does not believe the same as we."

"I am sorry," she said.

"And I as well," said Pike sincerely. "I have always believed that there is no more than what we can see and hold in our hands, but I really must concede that all that has happened is beyond chance and good fortune."

Soon Ella had prepared a hearty meal for them all, which was most appreciated by Kafar and Pike.

Chayel contended that they should go back to Makran in the morning, but Kafar said, "The Book is in the citadel, and Rhaka has been spending more and more time there. He has recently given this Polus fellow you speak of command of the fortress and army, though there is some dissention among the soldiers."

"There is no doubt," began Barah, "that Rhaka has become obsessed with learning the meaning of the Book. It has taken hold of him, and he will do all in his power to find someone who knows the language."

"Unless he already has," added Arak.

There followed an uncomfortable and ominous silence until Chayel said, "Whether he has or not, we must go back there, and then—"

Nikos interjected, "And then what? You saw the citadel, the fortress; what can we do?"

Chayel's passion burned again, "There is always a way! Did you not see that there are open windows in the citadel?"

"But they are mere slits, many stories above the ground and too narrow to pass through," said Barah.

"For a man, maybe," she countered—

Kainos interrupted, "My people, it is late, and we are tired. We will have clearer heads in the morning."

He said it with such authority that the conversation ended, and soon the meal was finished as well. With little room left in the house for sleeping, Chayel volunteered to sleep in the barn. "I am used to being near the animals," she said. "They bring me peace and help me to think."

Kainos gave her a few blankets, and Nikos went with her. As they went out, Chayel said, "I am having a bad feeling. I know Barah is right about there really being no way into the citadel even if we could get into the fortress."

A tear unexpectedly rolled down her cheek as she said in frustration, "We would need an army." Nikos looked at her with concern and felt similarly.

In the morning, they all gathered for breakfast, except for Kafar, who remained asleep.

"How are you, my boy?" asked Kainos of Pike.

"Glad to be free from that dungeon, but there are still at least a hundred men unjustly imprisoned in there. And the things this Rhaka is doing . . ." he continued, shaking his head. "I see no other way than to go to Silver City again and implore Lord Arkone to hold him to account."

"He rules over these provinces?" asked Chayel. Pike nodded as she continued, "He could bring a legion of soldiers?"

"Yes, but I do not think he will even lift a finger," answered Pike.

"I will convince him!" said Chayel fiercely. "Surely, he has not come to rule with no regard for what is right?"

"Remember that there are those who rule who deserve the slave's place," said

Barah. "And those who remain the servant but ought to rule."

That seemed to end the conversation and with breakfast over, Kainos went to Tachus Town to attend to his marshaling duties. It was nearly midday when a young man rode swiftly into the farm.

"I am looking for Marshal Pike," he said to Ella as she came to the door. "Marshal Kainos has a message for him."

Pike came through the door, and the man said, "You are Pike? There are soldiers from Makran seeking you and the man who was released with you. You must leave immediately. The soldiers have been going house to house through Tachus Town, and it will not be long before they come this way." He left as quickly as he had arrived.

"Where will you go?" asked Chayel.

"Well, I must go to Silver City, so I will head that way," said Pike.

"But Kafar, he is not well enough," said Chayel.

"I have a friend in a town west of here," offered Ella. "She lives in the lee of the Stone Mountains where you could easily elude the soldiers."

"We will all go," said Barah. "Since each of us has shown our face at the gate of the fortress, we must not take any chances."

They packed quickly and rode out, arriving in the village of Stone Hamlet by early evening. They soon found the house of Ella's friend, Eris, and after they explained themselves, she received them in. She had no children, and her husband had not yet come in from working, but she was very hospitable and prepared them a supper.

"I am sorry I have little room for you all to sleep," she said.

"Do not be concerned," said Barah. "We will go to the barn. In case Rhaka's soldiers come this far, it is best that we are out of sight."

The next day Kainos arrived almost before the sun had come up and found everyone still in the barn.

"My people!" he called in hushed tone, "Rhaka's men are still on the hunt, and they are especially looking for you, Kafar. I have awakened Eris, and she is making a meal for you all, but you will be found if you stay here."

"How many are there?" asked Chayel. "Could we not wait and ambush them?"

Kainos chuckled, which annoyed her and then he said, "Chayel, if ever I was in a battle, I would want you at my side, but this is not the time for fighting."

"Then what are we to do?"

"Eris says that they have a hunting cabin up in the mountains. It is an hour's ride, but you will be safe there."

Kafar, Barah, and Arak packed up to head out, but Chayel said, "Kafar, you will need time to heal, but I cannot just sit and wait—"

With a grin, Kafar held up his hand and said, "I would not expect you to. I know Nikos desires to see his friend Makarios. Go with him and fare well."

Soon, the three companions headed northwest up the mountain, while Pike, Chayel, and Nikos headed south.

"We can travel the same road for much of the way," said Pike as they followed the mine cart line that ran along the foot of the mountains on their right. Well after midday, they rounded a spur of the mountain, and the road turned sharply to the west.

"You must continue south and cross Stoney Creek," said Pike. "Then you will come to Brinestump Marsh. Be sure to stay west of it. By sunset you should reach Two Rivers and from there, you know the way?"

Nikos nodded as Tey-Rahk struck out across the meadow, moving swiftly with the cool breeze reminding them that autumn was coming on. Tey-Rahk seemed not to tire at all, and they came to Two Rivers well before evening. They crossed the bridge that spanned the swift flowing Tachus River and entered the city, immediately seeing a sizable army barracks.

"Why go all the way to Silver City when there is an army here?" Chayel asked. But as they came nearer, they saw that there were few soldiers there.

Suddenly, Nikos stiffened and Chayel said, "What is it?"

"Those soldiers there . . . ," he began. "That horse . . ." All of a sudden, Nikos jumped to the ground and approached the stable area of the barracks.

"Can I help ya my man?" asked one of the soldiers who was just removing his horse's saddle. Nikos leaned over the fence, looking hard at the horse, but he had no words.

"That there is a horse," said the soldier sarcastically. "His name is Sulky."

"Zeo?" said Nikos slowly.

"He ain't been owned before. He's wild caught."

But at the sound of Nikos's voice, the horse snorted and threw his head up, turning to look in his direction.

"Hey, now don't git him riled," said the soldier angrily. "He was hard enough to git all tamed down. Now, get along!" Nikos couldn't believe his eyes; but he surely was looking at his horse that he had lost so long ago.

"Nikos!" called Chayel. "We must be going." He was stunned and without thinking, he turned away and went to Chayel.

The soldier turned back to what he had been doing, and Chayel whispered, "You must not cause trouble. We can come back when it is dark."

They rode away, but Nikos kept looking back. "It truly is him," he said.

"That is surprising that he knew your voice after being apart for so long," she said.

They went to a tavern and had a meal, but Nikos could think of nothing else. After the sun set, they went back to the barracks, leaving Tey-Rahk in the tavern stable who continued to appear and behave like a regular horse.

The barracks, being situated on the outskirts of the city, had a large pasture area, which Nikos and Chayel quickly found. There were a fair number of horses in it, and Chayel warned Nikos, "We must not frighten them; let us wait until the moon comes up and we will better see if your Zeo is here." They sat in silence for a while peering at the horses, and then Chayel asked, "You certainly are not going to steal him, are you?"

Nikos only chuckled as she continued, "Well, of course I know you wouldn't, but how are you going to get him back?"

"It is enough that I have found him for now. But I will say as you would say of the Great One: he will make a way."

Chayel smiled warmly at him though, in the dark, he could not see it.

Nikos began to get impatient and called out in a loud whisper, "Zeo!" But none of the horses responded. He moved toward them, but they continued grazing, and as he looked among them from a distance, Zeo was not to be found.

"He must be in the stable," said Chayel as they left the pasture.

The next day, some kind of event seemed to be going on, as a fair number of people were all headed in the same direction.

"I wonder what is happening?" said Chayel as she and Nikos followed along, heading in the direction of the army barracks. Soon, they saw a small corral with twenty or so horses in it, and a crowd gathered around. A man on a podium was calling out numbers as another man led horses in front of the people one by one.

"An auction!" said Chayel as they worked their way to the front.

Suddenly, Nikos exclaimed quietly, "Zeo!"

"Where?" asked Chayel.

"There, in the back!" But as they listened to what the horses were being sold for, they realized that they had no means to even make a bid.

Nikos became discouraged, so Chayel said, "He is a beautiful horse."

Nikos nodded, "But look how unhappy he is."

As they brought Zeo up for bid, he threw his head and danced around, pulling his handler about.

"Nikos!" whispered Chayel, "Call his name, get him more stirred and unruly and maybe no one will want him!"

Nikos was slow to respond, and Chayel jabbed him with her elbow which caused him to suddenly call out, "Zeo! Zeo!"

This had an immediate effect as his horse turned and reared backward, causing his handler to lose his hold on the rope.

Chayel pulled Nikos back into the crowd as Zeo came toward them, "Quick! We do not want to be noticed!"

Indeed, the ruckus Zeo was causing allowed them to slip away, but the big black horse rushed about seeking some way out. Soon, they had a hold of him again, but he was led out, as no one was willing to bid for him. The auction ended with a few other horses that didn't sell being led away.

Chayel asked one of the soldiers, "Where are they taking them?"

He shrugged, "They ain't good for nuthin' anymore. You see the one is lame, and the others, they're worn out, and the black fellow, well, he's been trouble from the start. Now he's gone wild again. I guess they just take 'em for meat."

Nikos and Chayel followed at a distance and saw that the horses were put into a small pen out behind the barracks. They watched from behind some hay bales as a big black-haired man with heavy boots and an ill-tempered look approached the pen and gave the soldier a handful of coins.

"I'll send my boys later on to fetch these nags," said the man.

As soon as they both had gone, Chayel rushed up to the pen and called to Zeo, who responded immediately. He came toward her, and when he saw Nikos, neighed loudly. Nikos climbed into the pen and grabbed Zeo around the neck, burying his face in his mane, as Zeo nickered and pawed the ground. Nikos was flooded with emotion and tears streamed down his face as Zeo pushed into him.

After a few minutes Nikos said to Zeo, "I wish you could tell me all that has happened to you."

But Nikos was brought up short when Zeo said, "But I can now."

"You can understand him?" asked Chayel excitedly. "Like my Chum?"

Nikos nodded slowly and said, "You don't know what he is saying?"

"No, it is a gift you have from the Tsadaq."

Zeo pawed the ground and communicated more with Nikos, who then said to Chayel, "He says that since I spoke his name yesterday, he knows what all men are saying now. And from the look in his eyes, he truly knows."

"He is awakened somehow," marveled Chayel.

After a few moments, Nikos said, "But how can we get him back? That man did not seem like a charitable sort."

"He said he would send some men later. Maybe we could convince them of something," said Chayel.

They waited half of the day, and eventually two rough looking men rode up to the pen and began putting lead ropes on the horses. "Now this one here," said one of them pointing to Zeo. "Master says he's keeping for himself."

Nikos was about to approach them, when Chayel whispered, "Wait. these two will do nothing but what they have been ordered to. Let us follow them."

They watched which way the men went and then were soon following at a distance aboard Tey-Rahk. "Zeo is giving them nothing but trouble," began Chayel.

"He *knows* now," said Nikos incredulously. "I do not understand it."

"It is the way of the Tsadaq," she said. "There are many things we cannot fathom. And look, Zeo sees that we are following."

The two men rode through Two Rivers and then boarded the ferry to cross the Bradus River. "We had better take the next ferry," began Nikos, but there were few other people there, and the ferryman made them all get aboard. The two men quickly noticed Tey-Rahk, but also Chayel.

"Oh, that's a fine one," said one of them, to which the other replied, "The horse or the woman?" and they both guffawed.

Nikos began to get uncomfortable when suddenly, the uglier of the men addressed him, "You wouldn't want to sell your beauty there would 'ja, my boy?"

He elbowed the other man, and they laughed again. Before Nikos could respond, Tey-Rahk quickly whispered something to Chayel and after a moment she said, "Now, my fine fellows, I mean no insult, but do you really think you have enough money to buy *either* of us?"

They were chagrined for the moment, and Chayel continued, "We may do some bartering though. I would be willing to trade my fine white steed here for that black one."

The men were surprised and talked between themselves for a moment and responded a bit more respectfully, "He's a well-behaved one, is he?"

"As you can see," answered Chayel.

But the man became suspicious, "But now why wouldja trade such an excellent horse for this unruly beast?"

"My reasons are my own. Do as you will."

The man became agitated, feeling at a disadvantage, but the ferry had docked, and all were clattering off.

Chayel made as if she was going to ride away, but the man said, "Now hold up there!"

But the other man said to him, "Odus, we ought not do anything but what the master—"

"Now, shut up! We can think for ourselves. Master will love this one. You know he's always wantin' out of the ordinary."

As they all came up onto the road, Chayel and Nikos dismounted, and Odus signaled the other man to give the lead rope of Zeo to Chayel, but then he noticed that Tey-Rahk had no bridle or halter and began to question it when Chayel said, "Do not be concerned; he will follow with you."

Odus took another rope from his pack, but Chayel suggested that he would not need it, and the other man, whose name was Chawk, said, "How will he know to follow us?"

"Do not be concerned," said Chayel. "He will do as you ask."

The men looked at each other, and then Chawk said nervously, "This seems mighty irregular . . ."

"Now don't be worryin' about *irregular*," said Odus. "He's easily worth three times that one there. Master'll give us a handsome reward when we turn up with this fine creature."

Without waiting for a reply, he ordered Chawk to give Zeo's lead rope to Chayel. "Thank you, sir," she said as Nikos swung up onto Zeo.

"Now look!" exclaimed Chawk, "How is he riding that brute? He's all behavin' . . . this just ain't—"

"Shut up yer face!" yelled Odus as he looped a rope around Tey-Rahk's neck and turned east onto the road. They continued arguing as they rode off, leading Tey-Rahk and the other horses.

"But what about Tey-Rahk?" asked Nikos. "How will we get him back? We don't know where they are going."

"Do you forget who Tey-Rahk *is*?" she asked incredulously. But Nikos's attention quickly turned to Zeo, and he was overwhelmed with memories of riding him by the seashore and of how long he had been without him.

"I am so glad to have you back," he said, to which Zeo only threw his head about and pawed the ground in glee. Nikos was jarred from his memories by Chayel rapping him on his leg,

"Give me a hand up," she said. Zeo bore them both easily as they headed west down the Eastway Road.

By evening they had come to the lane that led down to Makarios's farm, and as they turned onto it, Nikos said, "We must not speak of the Great One. You remember Pike telling us how she stormed out of Marshal Kainos's house. And the day I left her farm as I went to seek the King, she was also infuriated."

"Some do not want to accept that there is something greater than themselves," said Chayel, "but that is to their own undoing." They arrived just as dusk was settling and saw light inside Makarios's house.

"Makarios!" called out Nikos as they started up the steps. "It is Nikos!"

The door opened quickly, and Makarios exclaimed, "Nikos!" and grabbed ahold of him in a bear hug. "Oh, I am so glad that you are alright!" she cried holding him tight.

Nikos was a bit too stunned to reply. Makarios, letting him go, continued, "My brother Steko found Dusko wandering the fields near his ferry just last week. She was very weak and had suffered an attack from some kind of animal. I feared you were dead."

As she finished, she embraced him again and said, "You must tell me what happened."

"Well, I have found my horse—" began Nikos.

Makarios, being unusually animated, peered at Zeo in the gathering dark and exclaimed, "Oh, I am so glad! Come, you must tell me everything!"

They turned Zeo out in the pasture and then came up to the house where Makarios prepared a meal for them.

"So, you have not introduced me to your friend here," she said.

Chayel quickly responded, "I am Chayel, from Zabach. Surely you are from the south?"

"Yes," said Makarios suddenly being defensive. Her terse response created an uncomfortable silence, and Nikos quickly asked, "Dusko, she is here?"

"Yes, in the barn," answered Makarios in a lighter mood. "She has just begun to eat again. I think she will fully recover, though she will have scars from whatever beast attacked her."

"Makarios," began Nikos a bit more seriously, "I have seen Polus."

"Where?" she asked quickly.

"Well, he has changed a lot and is the commander of Rhaka's army. He is in charge of the whole fortress in Makran."

"I cannot believe that. How can it be?"

"I do not know, but he is the one who commanded that Pike and Kafar be released. It was Chayel who spoke to him. I think he was agreeable because she reminded him of you."

They talked on past the end of their meal with Nikos telling Makarios all about what had happened to Kafar and Pike and of Rhaka's increasing lawlessness. But he did not speak of his journey south to the King.

Nikos awoke early and shivered in the brisk morning air as he went down to the barn to see Dusko. He found her standing quietly in one of the stalls and exclaimed, "Oh, Dusko!"

She was very thin, but nickered and raised her head, moving toward him as he entered the stall. He hugged her around the neck and rubbed her and said, "I am so glad you made it out of the desert, but the Kahee Nawb must have got you." The wounds on her left hindquarters had healed over but were still very visible.

"That must have been terrible," began Nikos as he took a soft brush and started brushing her.

"It was," she answered.

Nikos was startled and said, "You understand as well?"

"Not until you talked to me." Nikos began to wonder if all animals could understand him but continued grooming Dusko.

"You were lost in the desert for weeks then," said Nikos.

"A long time. I am happy to be here," she said.

Nikos opened the stall door and said, "I will take you out to the pasture. My horse is there, and he also understands me."

From the far end of the pasture, Zeo came galloping when he saw Nikos. Sar, Makarios's stallion who was in an adjacent pasture with his mares also came galloping over. He snorted and aggressively pawed the ground, wanting to get at Zeo and Dusko, who had entered the pasture with Nikos.

"Now how about calming down?" he said, but the stallion continued as if he had not heard. Nikos approached him and spoke some more, but it was apparent that he could not comprehend his words. Shrugging, Nikos admitted that he knew little about the new life that he had and turned back to Dusko and Zeo. They were getting on very well and soon fell to grazing, standing quite near each other. The sun had come up enough to begin warming the cool morning air as Nikos went back up to the house.

He found Makarios preparing breakfast and said, "I have been to see Dusko, poor girl, but she is very glad to be here."

Makarios looked at him quizzically and Nikos quickly said, "I mean . . .well surely, she is happy to have gotten out of the desert. I put her in the pasture with Zeo, and they seem to like each other."

Makarios nodded and after a long pause said, "I have thought much about you since you left. When Steko came here with Dusko, I thought surely you were gone, and I began to feel very remorseful for the harsh words I spoke the morning that you left."

Nikos was about to respond when Chayel came in. "I trust you have slept well?" asked Makarios, seeming to warm up to her a bit.

"Yes, quite," she answered. "Your home is a very comfortable place to be." Soon Makarios had a breakfast of bacon, eggs, and sourdough toast, with plenty of butter on the table.

"So, I have heard little about this new overseer you have talked about," said Makarios, "Only that many people had moved north because of favorable conditions for merchants and farmers."

"Well, it's all gone bad," said Nikos. "Rhaka is worse than lawless now; he's evil."

"No one is evil," replied Makarios. But she quickly added, "You said last night that Marshal Pike had gone to Silver City to report to Lord Arkone about his imprisonment and the way Overseer Rhaka has been governing."

"Yes," said Nikos. "And then he will be coming here to meet us, probably in three or four days."

"Well, I was going to Diaggello today to hire a few workers to help with barley and apple harvest, but I would much rather have you two help . . ."

"Certainly," said Chayel, "but what is apple?"

Makarios unexpectedly laughed out loud, but then composed herself, "I am sorry, Chayel; I did not know what an apple was either when we first came here."

The next few days were spent harvesting the barley and getting it dried and winnowed. One evening, as Nikos and Chayel walked up from the barn, Chayel said, "You have said nothing at all to Makarios about the curse of Kah-Taw, but is that not why we came?"

Nikos was slow to answer, "Yes, but she thinks it all fairy tales."

Chayel restrained a quick, heated response and then said, "Shall I speak to her? I am not as concerned with her response. Remember, the truth of Kah-Taw is to be valued more than life and feared more than death."

Nikos nodded and as they came into the house, they found Menka preparing supper and Makarios just coming in as well.

"Will you go back north with Pike when he returns?" she asked.

Chayel answered immediately, though the question seemed to have been addressed to Nikos, "Yes, I have joined my friends in seeking to recover what was stolen from us."

Makarios looked at Nikos, but before he could answer, she asked a bit stiffly, "What is this that was stolen? Barah spoke of it before you left."

There was an uneasy silence, and then she continued, "And you . . . you are not the same man that left here a few months ago. What has happened?"

Nikos was taken aback and had no words, but Chayel said, "He came to the King, and the terrible curse of Kah-Taw was taken from him."

Makarios became disturbed and stood up saying, "No. We will speak no more of this. I wish you a good evening." With that, she turned and went up the stairs.

"I am sorry for Makarios," said Chayel, suddenly very emotional. "She is very lonely. And you . . . I see the way you feel about her."

Nikos blushed but shook his head, "I care for her, but that is all it can be."

A few more days passed as they finished with the barley and brought in all the apples, but Pike still had not arrived, and they were becoming concerned. They considered going to Silver City but decided to wait another day or so.

At dinner the next day, Chayel said, "Makarios, you are from the south as am I, and I have been wondering where you grew up. My hometown is Zabach."

Makarios, who was feeling apologetic for her hasty departure the night before was a bit more amenable and said, "I was born in Maqom but grew up in Zabach. My father moved us there to get away from all the talk of that Tsadaq. They talked about being cursed and evil, and my father hated it. In Zabach it was no better, and it wasn't long before he moved to the north and learned the language, changing all our names." She paused becoming agitated and then continued, "It was my father's brother who drove him to it. After mother died in Maqom when I was seven, Yasad left us when we needed him most and went with those people . . ."

Makarios became very angry but was quickly distracted by Chayel who exclaimed, "Yasad? He . . . he is your uncle?"

"I do not think of him so," she answered sharply. "Only he is my father's brother."

Chayel turned to Nikos and said, "Yasad . . . he never spoke of having a brother."

"How do you know him?" demanded Makarios to Chayel and then to Nikos. "Do you know him?"

He was taken aback at her outburst and slow to answer, but then said, "Yes, he is a teacher in the House of the Book—"

"He is one of those people?" she asked heatedly.

But Chayel answered in a similar tone, "As am I, and so is Nikos!"

She revealed the red mark that showed her to be one of the People of the Great One, and Makarios turned quickly to Nikos, "Show me! You are one of them? Is that why you are so different now?"

He slowly uncovered his mark and said, "But it is true, all that they say. We did not make these marks ourselves."

Makarios scoffed, and Nikos, desperate to give more evidence said rashly, "My horse . . . now, I can understand what he says and Dusko too!"

She laughed out loud and was even more angry; she shouted, "You are mad!"

But at that moment, there was a rap on the door. A man's voice called from outside. Makarios quickly went to the door as a smile spread across her face.

"Pike," she said warmly, "we have been very concerned about you."

"I am sorry," said Pike. "I have been delayed because of the Bounties of the Sea Festival in Silver City. Lord Arkone was so merry and caught up with the whole affair that I could not even get a hearing with him. The whole city was on holiday, and I thought it best to wait until it was over."

"He will not help us," said Chayel quickly as Pike's countenance told the tale.

"Indeed, he is in his own world," said Pike frustrated and angry. "In years past, I have known him to be a firm and fair-minded man, but he has grown fat and apathetic. Although the commander of the barracks is sympathetic to us, he will do nothing without Arkone's command."

"Come," said Makarios, "we just sat down to supper; I will bring some for you."

"Thank you," said Pike, preoccupied with his frustration.

Chayel was incensed and said angrily, "How can one who has been given

THE CURSE AND THE KING

the privilege to rule over a people behave so? His indifference is no less lawless than this evil Rhaka is!"

"What can we do then?" asked Nikos.

Pike shook his head and said, "I do not know."

Makarios returned, and they all sat down to hot beef stew, which helped to soften the atmosphere.

They ate in silence for a few minutes and then Nikos said with an incredulous laugh, "We need our own army."

Pike chuckled at this, but Chayel was quick to say, "Then we shall get one!"

Makarios scoffed, and Pike glanced at her and then said earnestly to Chayel, "I was in that dungeon with a hundred men who were as unjustly imprisoned as I was. I do not doubt that they would fight Rhaka if given the chance."

"And how many more are there throughout the province who are also angry with Rhaka?" added Nikos.

As they began to consider this, Makarios fairly shouted, "This is foolishness! Are you all mad? An army! You cannot fight an overseer. That in itself is lawlessness!"

Nikos was indignant and said sharply, "Did you not wish for an army to get Polus free?"

"That does not mean that it ought to be done!"

"When the lawless rule," said Chayel, "the lawful must take up arms."

"That is from the Book?" asked Pike.

"Yes," answered Chayel glancing at Makarios as Pike added, "It seems there is much in the Book that is good."

"And evil," said Chayel gravely. "We must go back as soon as may be."

Pike nodded, "Yes, much is at stake."

"Indeed," said Chayel passionately. "I sense that Rhaka's dominion increases every day, and his evil thirst for power—"

"You *sense* it!" blurted out Makarios. "You are just a girl! What could you know? This Rhaka is not evil like you say. No one is! And you!" she continued, turning to Pike. "I see it, you are *with* them! How do you believe this foolishness?"

"It is not foolishness," said Chayel quickly. "Would a lawful ruler imprison Pike for weeks without cause?"

"Well, perhaps it was—"

But Chayel, who suddenly became furious, stood up, checked herself, and then said in a wooden tone, "Nikos and I are just going to . . . to take care of Pike's horse and check on the others, aren't we?"

She pulled Nikos up and walked quickly out of the house trying to control herself. She said, "I cannot understand! How does she make so light of things?"

Nikos had to trot to catch up and said, "Well, she hasn't seen how it is—"

"Seen how it is? Does she think Pike to be a liar? But of course, she is smitten with him and will only see what she wants to see."

They had reached the pasture and stopped at the fence as the sun was heading toward the horizon.

"She blinds herself to the truth!" finished Chayel leaning on the fence.

"She is *smitten* with him?" asked Nikos feeling a surge of emotion, but the approach of Zeo and Dusko interrupted them.

Chayel exclaimed, "She is so thin!" They hopped the fence, and Dusko, who was much less skittish than she used to be, came right to Nikos.

"Look at what that evil Nawb did to her," said Nikos as he pointed out the three long scars.

"Poor girl," said Chayel rubbing the young mare, "but she is healed from that, and soon she will be strong and well."

As the chill night air came on, they took the horses up to the barn, and Chayel gave Dusko a good feed of grain.

The next morning, Chayel joined Pike and Nikos late for breakfast and found them in an earnest conversation.

As she sat down, Pike said, "You must not speak to Makarios about your Great One, the Tsadaq. I could not change her mind one whit last night about any of it."

"Where is she?" asked Chayel.

Menka, who was bringing her a plate of griddle cakes and hash, said, "Sheh is out mendin' the fence and wishes you all fehwell." She went out.

"I will not leave her this way again," said Nikos, suddenly incensed. "Is she truly unable to show grace and so must avoid what she does not agree with?"

He got up and went out, leaving Pike and Chayel surprised at his sudden outburst. Nikos stopped on the porch, and as the house was on higher ground, he had a good view of the fields and soon saw Makarios far out down one of the fence lines. He started off toward her but began to feel regret over his anger and hard feelings.

He had gotten about halfway to her when he stopped and decided to let things go, but as he turned back, Makarios let out a horrified shriek, running madly away from something in the tall grass. Nikos bolted toward her, but she fell, disappearing into the grass and screaming in terror. Nikos was choked with fear, and everything went in slow motion as he came to her and found a huge wild boar attacking her. Nikos hardly knew what he was doing, but in seconds the boar was dead, and he turned to Makarios, who was groaning in agonizing pain.

She cried, "My leg, my leg!"

Nikos knelt beside her, but there was blood everywhere and before he knew what he was doing, he found himself with Makarios in his arms running toward the house calling for Pike and Chayel. He saw everything as if he were an onlooker and heard only silence.

"Nikos!" called Chayel. "Nikos!" He did not respond and only heard her as if she was far away and calling to someone else. But suddenly a strong hand gripped his shoulder and shook him.

"Pike!" exclaimed Nikos, his eyes focusing on him.

"You are alright?" asked Chayel, taking his hand.

"Yes, yes," he said quickly, "But Makarios—"

"She is taken care of, but you . . . ," said Chayel, "you have not been reacting to anything for quite a while."

Nikos took a deep breath, "I do not know what happened, but I am alright."

"Menka has sewn up the wound," said Pike "and given Makarios some strong tea made from the kathaylace plant. It will dull the pain and help her to rest."

Nikos nodded as Pike, who was quite disturbed, asked, "Was it a wild boar? Only the tusks of a massive hog could have caused that wound. Did you drive it off? What did you do?"

Without even a thought, Nikos said, "I . . . I killed it."

"Killed it? I must go see this beast," said Pike and without another word, he went out. Chayel and Nikos looked in on Makarios but found her to be asleep.

Pike returned sooner than they expected and approached Nikos with look of total astonishment. "Nikos," he said, "It is a huge boar, with tusks longer than my hand, and its neck though as thick as a bull, is broken." Pike sat down at the table, looking incredulously at Nikos.

"I do not remember even touching it," said Nikos as he joined him.

As Chayel sat down beside him, she said in an earnest tone, "It is the Great One. Nikos has abilities that seem to be much greater than most of us have."

Pike thought for a few moments and then said slowly, "It is hard not to believe all this. Kainos showed strength beyond that of a man at the fortress, and you, Chayel, you simply spoke and convinced the commander to release us. How?"

Chayel shrugged. "There are abilities, gifts from the Great One," but she said no more.

The day wore on and by evening, Makarios awoke, calling for Pike. The three of them went to the room and found her in better spirits than they expected.

Pike took her hand and sat down on the bed next to her, but she looked at Nikos. "I am sorry," she said. "I heard you talking, and I was quite harsh about this . . . about what you believe. My father, you know, he—"

But she suddenly winced in pain, and Menka came bustling in, "Now Miss Maka, you best get moh west."

Menka gave her more kathaylace tea and shooed the others out. Over the next few days, Pike spent much time with Makarios as she could do little else but lie in bed. They grew close, and Nikos felt a jealousy arising in him that he wished were not there.

One evening as the sun was setting and Chayel and Nikos were coming up from the barn, she said, "We can do nothing else here. We must go back. Do you not feel it?"

Nikos nodded. "I wonder if Pike will stay with Makarios?"

But Chayel seized his arm, pulling him to face her. "You would have him not go with us?" she asked heatedly. "Do not be foolish! He is a courageous man and is *with us*! You must abandon your feelings for Makarios. Jealousy is a cruel master and will only take you where you do not wish to go!"

She was so impassioned that Nikos was speechless for a moment, but then blurted out, "Have you never *loved*?!"

She took a quick breath as her dark eyes pierced through to his soul and then backed slowly away. "What do you know of love?" she asked rashly. "You cannot even see it when it is right before your eyes!"

A tear came down her face before she turned and ran up toward the house. Nikos stood stunned as she disappeared into the dusk and then felt ashamed about his resentment toward Pike. He retreated to the pond and sat down on the dock for a long while.

Fourteen

Chayel composed herself before she went into the house, feigning tiredness. She went to her room, quickly packed her belongings, and climbed silently out the window. Another tear came down her cheek as she paused in the gathering darkness and thought about Nikos. She wished that he had come after her, but for the moment, a bigger part of her was glad that he had not. She disappeared into the gloom down the cart path that led to the main road but had gone hardly any distance when she caught her breath and stopped in her tracks.

She spun around and was face to face with a gigantic creature, which seemed to have come out of nowhere. It moved toward her, and she exclaimed, "Oh, Tey-Rahk!"

"I will take you north," he said as he crouched down for Chayel to climb aboard. He was in his true form of a winged lion, and with a powerful leap and surge of his wings, he sprang into the air. As he soared higher, Chayel felt the bite of the cold night air and quickly snuggled down into Tey-Rahk's mane.

"Thank you for helping Nikos get Zeo back," she said and then, though she felt it presumptuous to ask any questions, her curiosity impelled her to ask, "What happened with those two fellows that you went with?"

Tey-Rahk made a sound that was most like a chuckle and said, "They have learned a lesson that they will not forget."

He said no more, and Chayel dared not to press. They flew on for a few minutes, and then he said, "Where is it that you are going?" She did not respond immediately as she had not quite decided, other than back toward Makran.

"Well, you know our Book is in the hands of our enemy, for he has made himself so by stealing the Book. But we are at a disadvantage and need an army to storm the fortress to get it back."

She suddenly felt foolish and that such a plan was unrealistic, but Tey-Rahk said, "There are many men who would join you to overthrow your enemy."

Chayel felt a surge of hope, and Tey-Rahk, after altering his course more to the northeast added, "But you must find them."

The moon had arisen and Chayel could see the Fragmoo Forest below them and the Stone Mountains in the distance. In only a short time, Tey-Rahk began to descend, landing in a vast field of green grass west of the village of Ekuus.

Chayel jumped to the ground, and Tey-Rahk gestured toward a farmhouse and said, "You will find an ally there."

He backed up and shook his great maned head as he prepared to rise into the air, but Chayel, who suddenly felt alone and a bit desperate, said boldly, "Will you not stay?"

He came near her, lowering his head, and Chayel rashly threw her arms around his neck as far as they would go, burying her face in his mane.

"You are strong, Chayel, and will find all that you need."

She held him tightly for a few moments and then stood back as he raised his great wings and sprang into the air. She watched him until he was lost to sight and then turned toward the farmhouse. Considering her weariness and the midnight hour, she snuck into the barn and found a cozy place up in the hayloft.

A very loud rooster awakened Chayel and as she came to, she heard the voices of two men arguing back and forth.

"Well, it ain't fair!" exclaimed one.

"Fair don't matter now," retorted the other. "What is, is what is! Now grab the other end there."

"Why should we take it? We're no better'n slaves now!"

"Slaves don't git right fair wages such like as we do, boneface!"

"But I'm still slavin', and for what? To pay master back? And all I did was tell the truth! You saw that beast fly away . . ."

"Yeah well, you ought not to have said so . . . what right-minded man would believe it?"

The other man scowled and then said in a resigned sort of way, "But it was the truth, and now the master brands us as crooks. It ain't fair, I say!"

"Well, there's no convincin' 'im different; now grab that there and come on!"

Chayel looked out from her hiding place and saw who she expected to see leaving the barn. She smiled to herself and quickly climbed down the ladder. The men were pulling a wagon loaded with hay out toward a corral and Chayel, feeling a bit mischievous and judging that the men were mostly harmless, followed. She stayed just behind them and when they were turned away, she jumped onto the top rail of the fence and sat there.

As one of the men turned around, he nearly jumped out of his skin when he saw Chayel. He went pale as death and stumbled backward falling over the wagon.

The other man was startled as well, but then laughed as the man on the ground pointed and stuttered, "Now, now there's go . . . ghosts!"

"Gird up, Chawk! It's just a girl!"

He turned to her and said, "Now you quite gave me a fright too. Where be you come from?"

But before she could answer, Chawk exclaimed, "You! You're the one as tricked us with that horse that ain't a horse!"

Chayel jumped down. "I recollect that you thought it was a very good deal," she said innocently. Chawk became red-faced.

But the other man, who was older and a bit gray-haired, introduced himself as Odus and said, "Now, miss, you knew about that horse?"

She only smiled and then Chawk, who had gotten to his feet and came near, still hot and angry, added, "And that 'e could talk?"

"He spoke to you, did he?" she said mysteriously.

Chawk was so infuriated that he only stumbled over his words, but Odus admonished him, "Now hush up! You can't pretend that brute didn't give you the chance to let him go before we got back here. And all we had to do was tell the master that the fair black horse broke away from us and we couldn't catch 'im."

Chawk was chagrined by this and without another word, set to work with the hay, his bald head steaming in the cool morning air.

"Now, what brings you here, miss?" asked Odus.

"My name is Chayel," she said. "And as a matter of fact, it was that brute you speak of who brought me here. His name is Tey-Rahk."

At this Chawk stopped his work and turned toward her, listening.

"Yes, he told us his name," replied Odus, "and that he was an emissary of the Great One, the Tsadaq."

Chawk began shaking his head, but Odus, seeing Chayel's response, said,

FOURTEEN

"Ah, you know of this Great One too?"

But Chawk could not contain himself and called out, "There ain't no such thing! And the bunkum that the beast was talkin' about . . . and how he changed like that . . . well it's all lies and tricks!" His face was beet red as he grabbed up the hay and fiercely threw it into the feeding box.

"Well, I believed what that Tey-Rahk had to say," said Odus. "Like I been waitin' my whole life to hear it. About the curse and the King, and . . . look," he said revealing a red symbol on his chest. "Do you know what it is?"

Chayel smiled broadly, "In my language it says, 'the People of the Great One.' You are one of us!"

She showed him her mark, and he was surprised, but Chayel added, "All of us who have received the remedy for Kaw-Taw have it."

Odus looked happier than he ever had in his life, but Chawk was furiously doing his work, not even caring that Odus wasn't helping.

"Well, that there is Chawk," he said and then lowering his voice, "but you see he don't believe."

Chawk was ignoring everything and, grabbing up the handle of the wagon, he stomped away.

"How he does not believe," said Odus shaking his head. "We both heard and saw the same miraculous things."

"That is the way of it," said Chayel. "It seems some are destined to believe, and others are not."

"So, what must I do?" asked Odus.

"What do you mean?"

"Well, I feel as if I have been chosen to . . . *do something.*"

Chayel responded, "Yes, we all have a destiny—"

But before she could finish, Odus continued, "Tey-Rahk told me of the Book."

Though Chayel looked at him with a shocked expression, he continued, "And I been hearing how Overseer Rhaka has been takin' advantage of the people in the towns near Makran. There's three brothers up in Karpone who been required to give half the crop of their pear trees to Rhaka. And now my neighbor—he runs a tavern here in Ekuus—he's had a few run-ins with soldiers thinkin' they don't have to pay the fair rate or even pay at all."

Chayel was quiet for a moment and then said, "Do you have a good sword?"

Odus nodded, "And I know how to use it; I've been in battle before, when I was a young 'un, but I been wonderin' about that weapon you got there."

205

"It's a tri-bow," answered Chayel. "It's smaller than most, but it suits me."

"Well, I ain't never seen anything like it."

"Say that post there is a bear coming at us," began Chayel and quick as a cat, she fit an arrow to the bow, took aim, and let it fly, hitting its mark before Odus even knew what was happening. He was incredulous and went to the post, pulling the arrow out with difficulty.

As he looked at it, he unexpectedly asked, "You ever kill a man with it? I mean that'd fair right do anyone in just like that."

For all her brashness and inner fortitude, Chayel was startled and was a bit shaken by his question.

He handed the arrow to her and said, "Well, now girl, I don't mean to get you all juddered, but you're the one as asked about a sword, like we might be fightin' someone, and where there's fightin', sometimes there's killin'."

Chayel looked back at him, not quite composed, and said, "I've never killed . . . but, then I've never had to." After a somber moment she added, "Bears though; I've killed a few. Sometimes, they get after the goats."

Odus paused for a bit and then said, "So, you haven't told me why you're here."

Chayel was hesitant to answer but then said, "Well, that wicked Rhaka has our Book, as you know, but it's in his fortress and guarded by his army. We need our own army to fight him. Tey-Rahk said I would find an ally here."

"Well, you have, my dear, and I am with you," he said in a warm, fatherly kind of way. "Too bad we haven't got any bows like you got there; that'd be a fair big advantage."

"Well, I made this myself," said Chayel. "My father taught me, but it takes time, at least a month to let the wood dry out."

"Well, what kind of wood?" asked Odus, becoming animated.

"Well, I do not know the trees in the north, but the wood must be very hard with a good straight grain," she said.

"Shagbark might do," he said. "We can check the woodshed; there's some that's stacked in the corner for fence posts."

Chawk returned and complained that there was more work to do and that he'd had enough of doing it all by himself. Odus motioned toward a building and said to Chayel, "See what you can find," and he headed off with Chawk who looked back at Chayel with a scowl.

Chayel quickly found the wood and looked through it, finding a few that were long enough and small enough in diameter. She picked them up and went out, but stopped short, suddenly questioning what she was doing.

"This will take most of the day, and what can I make arrows from or get sinew for the string?"

She thought of Nikos and then the Book and felt an urgency to get back to Barah and the others. Leaving the wood by the shed, she quickly found Odus pulling the small hay wagon back to the barn.

"Nothing suitable?" he questioned.

"Yes, but I must get back to my companions—"

Odus interrupted, "Now don't be hasty. There's no sense rushing and bringing naught but yourself."

His firm, fatherly manner slowed her down as he continued, "Remember that I said I am with you and surefire if there ain't lots of other folk who are fed to here with Rhaka and wantin' some justice brought to him."

Chayel considered his words as he added, "You got to look at trouble from all sides if you're wantin' a clear view. I figure time is on our side. There's plenty of discontent as it is, but the more time passes, the more heated folk will get, and that's more for our side."

Chayel saw the sense of it but also thought of how time was on Rhaka's side as well since he would delve deeper and deeper into the power of the Book.

Near the end of the day and after supper, Chayel began to have a strong sense that she was where she ought to be, doing what she ought to be doing. She had learned that the main business of the farm was raising racehorses, but also retraining unmanageable horses or nursing abused ones back to health. There were a good number of other men who worked on the farm, some with ill-favored appearances and others who seemed like vagrants.

She was glad that most of the men had gone into Ekuus for some ale and a good time, and she was happy to teach Odus how to make a tri-bow. As they worked, she told Odus much more about the Book and of Kafar, Barah, and Arak's efforts to retrieve it. They worked until late, carving the wood into staves and bringing them closer to the shape of a bow.

"This is not hard," said Odus, "Just hard work."

"No, the hard work will be learning how to use it," said Chayel smiling. "But you are right; it is simple, and you will be able to teach others."

Over the next few days, they made strings for the bows and collected river cane to make arrows. Odus learned to shoot and quickly became proficient, but Chawk wanted nothing to do with any of it and began working in a different part of the farm.

One morning, about a week after her arrival, Chayel said to Odus, "I feel that we must get up to Tachus Town."

Odus nodded, "Yes, and there are some here who would join us. Many have come down here from up north, having lost farms or businesses to Rhaka."

Odus went about the farm and quietly spoke to those he thought would go with them and by midday, he came to Chayel and said, "Well, there's six or eight of these boys who are riled enough to join us. We got to be careful though. Told 'em to go by ones or twos and meet us at Stoney Point Mine by tomorrow night."

Remembering that Chayel didn't know the lands round about, he added, "The Mine is right near Tachus Town and sittin' unused, so we won't be noticed."

Odus had a strategic way of thinking from his many years in the army, and Chayel quite admired him for it.

The next morning, they made ready to leave and though Odus only had one horse, he nonetheless brought a big gelding from the pasture for Chayel.

"This here is Chawk's horse," began Odus. "Or at least the one that the master lets him use, but Chawk, he won't go anywhere without me, so he won't—"

A disgruntled voice called out from behind them, "Where be you going, Odus?"

It was Chawk and though his face was hot and red, Odus responded nonchalantly, "For a ride."

"But that's *my* beast! And you can't go somewhere without me, and what business does the master got you on that I don't know nuthin' 'bout?"

But Chayel, who was easily angered by Chawk's uncouth manner said sharply, "He's leaving—"

Before she could continue, Chawk stiffened and without even a glance at Chayel said, "What do you mean you're leaving, Odus? You can't leave."

His whole demeanor changed to one of grave concern. "Now, Chawk, you ain't wanted anything to do with me all week—"

But Chawk bellowed, still with his eyes on Odus, "It's *her* ain't it? And that foolishness she believes!"

He began to look frightened, and Odus quickly said, "Now look, Chawk, you'll get on without me."

"You can't go!" he insisted. "I don't know no one else!" His eyes filled with tears, and even Chayel felt some compassion for him.

"I am sorry, Chawk," said Odus. "But this is real . . . realer than anything I ever knew. I got to follow, I—"

Suddenly, Chawk backed away, shaking his head with hot tears streaming down his face, "No! I see now; you're no different than the rest of 'em. Makin' me believe you was my friend!"

He ran madly away, leaving Odus nearly as surprised as Chayel. "Didn't know he felt quite like that," he said mystified.

"Ought you to go find him?" she asked.

"Don't think there's any makin' it right with him . . ." he trailed off and looked pained.

"I am sorry," offered Chayel. "I should not have exclaimed that you were leaving like that. And I suppose sometimes people are not at all what they seem."

"Yes indeed; I am sorry for him," said Odus softly, but then in a stronger tone he added, "But we must go. It will take us all day to get to the mine."

He paused and seemed to have second thoughts about Chawk, and so they did their best to find him but had no luck. They packed up, taking along the bows they had made and a bundle of shagbark staves and then headed out.

They kept to the main road and after some time, the village of Praho appeared in the distance.

"We'd be best off skirtin' around," said Odus. "But we got to get to the bridge and with the town right at the crossroads, there's no other way."

As they came nearer, Odus was shocked at what he saw. There was a new guardhouse and gate across the road, manned by many soldiers, some of whom were struggling with a man, trying to restrain him. Another man had jumped the gate and was running as fast as he could into the town with two soldiers chasing after him.

As they approached the gate, a soldier called out, "What's yer business?" Odus answered quickly, "Passin' through. We're going on to visit kinfolk in Stone Hamlet."

"*Whose* kinfolk?" asked the soldier, eyeing Chayel suspiciously.

"My old mum," said Odus in a pained way. "She's taken a bad turn and . . ." he trailed off shaking his head as Chayel added, "And I was hoping to meet her before she—"

The soldier hastily waved them through and said away from the others, "Forget the toll," and he turned to close the gate.

They rode quickly into town and Odus said, "Guess Rhaka's men ain't all bad."

But his attention was suddenly taken by the terrible state of the town. Many businesses were closed, and there were soldiers at almost every one that was open. The atmosphere was grim as shopkeepers looked frightened, angry, or dejected. The two passed quickly through town without incident.

As they crossed the bridge, they felt like they could breathe again, "How awful!" exclaimed Chayel outraged. "Why do they accept that?!"

Odus shrugged as they made their way across the bridge, but then said gravely, "Seems soon enough they won't be fightin' for what's fair, but for their lives."

·——— Fifteen ———·

At Makarios' farm, Nikos was awakened early in the morning by a rap on his door.

"Chayel is not here," said Pike.

"Not here?" queried Nikos pulling on his clothes and coming out. "You are sure?"

He thought about the night before, and Pike asked, "Something happened?"

"Well, yes . . . I suppose," said Nikos slowly.

"You need say no more. Makarios has bidden us to go quickly and find Chayel. There are no horses missing, so we ought to catch up with her quickly."

Nikos wondered at Makarios's apparent concern for Chayel as they prepared to leave. Soon they were ready, and Makarios met them at the barn.

"Nikos, I am sorry for my harshness to you and especially to Chayel," she said. "I wish you all good fortune, and please return here whenever you may."

They rode off and set a swift pace but did not see any sign of Chayel. They arrived at Steko's Ferry and questioned the ferrymen, but no one had seen anyone of her description. As they crossed the river, Nikos felt a cold fear in the pit of his stomach.

Pike, also full of concern, said, "This is the only crossing for thirty miles in either direction."

They rode slowly through Two Rivers looking for any trace of Chayel but found nothing. They rode the rest of the day with little conversation and arrived at Agathon Outpost by nightfall. They checked at the inn and the tavern and then went to the marshal's office, finding the young Dero on duty.

He jumped up and sputtered, "Marshal Pike, sir!"

Pike chuckled and shook his head. "Has Deputy Zuegos been training you again? Please sit down; you know there is no need for such formality here."

He asked him about Chayel and as Dero's eyes glittered at Pike's description of her, he lamented that he had not seen her. Nikos and Pike stayed at his cabin and made an early start of it the next day, stopping to see Deputy Zuegos. They were both on edge, being even more anxious about Chayel.

"Oh, Pike, I am glad to see you," Zuegos said as they came in. "Marshal Kainos has been quite concerned about your welfare and has asked me to send word—"

"Yes, I have been delayed," interrupted Pike. "But I must go up to Tachus Town myself, so I will see him. I cannot tell you how long I will be gone."

Zuegos was puzzled and about to speak, when Pike continued, "We are missing one of our friends. Her name is Chayel. She is a young, strong, beautiful southerner with short black hair. She carries a short sword in a dark red sheath banded with gold. You would not forget her if you had seen her."

"I suppose I would not," he answered and, for the second time since they had come to the Outpost, Nikos felt a twinge of jealousy.

"All has been well here?" asked Pike.

"Except for some folks coming down from up north," answered Zuegos. "Their overseer is makin' people none too happy these days."

"Well, we shall see about him," said Pike with a certain ferocity and clench of his jaw. Nikos silently seconded his sentiment as they went out and swung up onto their mounts, heading north.

Nikos spoke to his horse, but Pike asked, "What is that you say?"

"No, I was . . ." began Nikos but then stopped.

"Go on," said Pike.

"Well, Zeo, my horse here, well . . . he . . . I can understand him."

"He *talks* to you?" asked Pike incredulously.

Nikos nodded and continued, "But only after I came to be of the People of the Great One."

Pike was unbelieving, but in spite of that and feeling a bit foolish, he inquired, "What does he say?"

"He saw Tey-Rahk last night."

"That is Chayel's big white horse?" asked Pike and then continued, "I meant to ask you about that. When we parted ways coming down from Tachus Town at Brinestump Marsh, you two were riding her horse, and now you have this black one here."

"Well, yes, but Tey-Rahk is not *her* horse; in fact, . . ."

Nikos paused, feeling uncomfortable, but Pike looked at him, inviting him to say more.

"Well," began Nikos slowly and solemnly, "Tey-Rahk is not even a horse at all. Somehow, he changes from being an enormous white creature that is like a mountain tomcat, but with thick, massive fur around his head and neck and . . . well, he has wings too. He brought us up from the south, flew across the desert."

He felt foolish, but Pike said, "I am intrigued. I do not doubt you. I know you speak the truth—"

He suddenly stopped talking and became dazed. He began to fall forward; Nikos quickly moved Zeo toward him, but only managed to slow Pike's fall. They both hit the ground and immediately Pike cried out and then lost consciousness.

"Pike! Pike!" called Nikos, but there was no response. He pulled him to the side of the road and into the lee of a large oak tree. Nikos was a bit frantic but kept his wits about him and retrieved Pike's horse, tying him to a small tree. As he knelt next to Pike, he saw that he was very pale and recalled that he had looked so before when he was mystically attacked by the Kahee-Nawb. There was nothing he could do, so he just waited, trying to bring Pike to every so often. Less than an hour later, Pike regained consciousness and sat up with difficulty, feeling stunned.

"I saw it again," he said in a troubled tone. "That fearsome beast . . . ," but he shook off the feeling of fear and said angrily, "How do you fight something that you cannot touch?"

"The creature is real," began Nikos. "It came upon my friend and me in the Desert Wilderness and wounded him."

"Is it as large as it seemed to me?"

"About fifteen feet tall?" questioned Nikos.

Pike answered, "Yes, at least. And you *fought* it?"

"No, we tried hiding from it and then a bright white creature, I believe now that it was Tey-Rahk, swooped down and struck it dead. But its essence lived on and soon took bodily form again."

"What of your friend?"

"He died the next day."

"I am sorry," said Pike looking sincerely at Nikos.

"You need not lament; Nuwa is in a good place now."

"You believe there is more than this?" asked Pike gesturing at the things around him.

"I do not merely believe—I *know*."

Pike looked doubtful but said, "Well, I cannot deny the many things that have happened . . . and being somehow attacked by this evil creature . . . that is not imagination."

He seemed at odds with himself as he rose to his feet and said, "But come, we must get up to Tachus Town."

They got on their way again and passed into Fragmoo Forest, entering Smaragdos Province. The guardhouse at the border remained unused. After a few hours they emerged on the northern side of the forest to find a fully manned guardhouse at the entrance to the village of Palahos.

"What is your business?" bellowed one of the soldiers.

"It is my own!" retorted Pike, a bit agitated.

"Not in this province, it ain't! Now state your business or go back!"

Pike suddenly felt in a bit of a spot, when Nikos blurted out, "We are going up to Ekuus to race my horse."

One of the other soldiers came forward and said, "Ahh, he's a fine one. Ain't nothin' prettier than an Askonian, or faster. Good luck!"

He raised the gate and as they passed through, the first soldier began to argue with the other about the toll, but Pike moved his horse up to a trot and left them behind. They found Palahos to be quite a gloomy place with many soldiers about, and some of the shops closed up. On the other side of the village, Pike left the main road and headed west under the cover of some trees.

"I want to avoid the towns north and getting too near Makran," he said.

"I am with you," said Nikos. "There is an evil spreading out from there." They rode fast and soon came to the Old Bridge, passing cautiously over it.

On the other side, Pike suddenly chuckled, "I do not know what to think about your horse. Truly, he talks to you?"

"Yes. And as I said, he saw Tey-Rahk at the farm last night. Surely, he has taken Chayel up this way," said Nikos. "And that is why we found no trace of her."

"That makes me feel a bit easier, but we must hurry."

They soon arrived at Kainos's homestead and found Kafar there with Barah and Arak. Kainos bear-hugged Pike and said, "Ah, my boy! We have been worried about you all . . . but where is Chayel?"

"We hoped she would be here," said Nikos anxiously.

"What has happened?" asked Barah gruffly.

Nikos explained things, and Kainos said, "I would not worry about her. If there is one who can take care of herself, it is Chayel."

But Nikos, still quite concerned, said, "But where can she be?"

Pike chuckled, which seemed out of place to Nikos, and he felt a twinge of anger. "Remember how Chayel declared that we needed our own army?" asked Pike. "Maybe she is gathering one!"

But Nikos found no humor in that and scowled.

"I am sorry," said Pike. "We are all concerned about her, but if she is with Tey-Rahk, well how could anything happen to her?"

Nikos softened and said, "I suppose you are right."

"So, you were unsuccessful with Lord Arkone?" Kafar asked Pike who nodded.

Kainos invited them all to sit down and then brought out some blueberry malt. "Things are not going well here either," began Kainos. "Rhaka has taken over the towns south of Makran, and I have been wary of him trying to come into Tachus Town as well. But there is some good news. About a week ago, a man named Ruad found his way to me. He had been trying to find you and said that he knew you from the dungeon."

"He has escaped?" asked Pike.

"Well of a sort," answered Kainos. "The whole lot of them broke out of the dungeon. Some were killed, but most got out of the fortress. Ruad stayed behind and kept out of sight. In the confusion no one knew who had escaped and eventually, he took up being a cook in the fortress with no one realizing any different. He made friends with the other cook and is looking for an opportunity to help us."

"That is good news," said Nikos. "But why would he do such a thing?"

"Ruad has become one of us," said Kafar. "While in the dungeon, Ruad knew that Rhaka had stolen something from us, and now we have told him what it is. Rhaka has become intrigued with the Book, but without knowing the language, he can gain nothing from it."

"But inevitably, he will find someone who knows our language and then the Book will begin to be opened to him," began Barah gravely.

Kainos said, "Yes, and I fear he will continue extending his reach across the province. It is only a matter of time before he sends his soldiers to Tachus Town. We must be prepared."

The next day, Kainos and the men went out to the bridge that spanned a creek that cascaded down out of the mountains, flowing swiftly in a very deep channel. There was a narrow, but stoutly built bridge near the waterfall at the foot of the mountains.

"We ought to build a gate on the bridge," began Pike, "so that we can prevent Rhaka's men from coming across."

"But can they not just go downstream to cross?" asked Arak.

Kainos said, "It is at least ten miles to where the ravine becomes shallower—"

He paused as Kafar began shaking his head and said, "I do not believe Rhaka would march his men so far out of the way. He is ruthless and brutal and will meet our attempt at defense head-on."

"I will admit," said Kainos, "that barring this bridge seems a weak effort in the face of such a tyrant, but we must do whatever we can."

They all felt an urgency to complete their defenses and so immediately began to make plans, deciding to make a gate of wrought iron and determining that there needed to be a wall on their side of the ravine as well.

The next day, Kainos and Pike went to Stone Hamlet to employ the services of the blacksmith there to make a gate. Barah and Nikos accompanied them and then went on to High Peak Quarry just beyond the hamlet to see about some good square-cut stone for the wall. It took many days to plan and gather materials, but they made good progress and soon began digging foundation holes for the gate. Nikos and Barah managed that, having done similar work up at the prison.

About midday, their work was suddenly interrupted. A horse was coming from the east, galloping fast and ridden by a young boy. Barah quickly girded on his sword and took a position on the bridge as the boy approached.

As the boy neared, he called out, "I must see Marshal Kainos!" as he clattered to a halt on the bridge. He continued, "Soldiers! They are coming from Makran; I must tell the marshal!"

Barah looked beyond him and then stepped aside as the boy urgently spurred his horse forward. Nikos joined Barah on the bridge, and they both looked away to the east but saw no one.

Barah's hand went to his sword hilt and then in a tone that made Nikos's stomach knot up, he said, "You best go get your weapon."

As he turned and started toward Kainos's house, he was overwhelmed with fear and was in a cold sweat, flashing back to events of his childhood. Nikos's knees were weak as he ran, and his anxiety over Chayel's whereabouts only served to increase the dread he was feeling. As he neared the house, he met the others, who were headed for the bridge.

"My sword," said Nikos timidly. "It is in the barn—"

But the other men had passed by him quickly with very serious countenances, which raised Nikos's feelings to terror. He ran to the barn as if his life depended on it. Once inside, he barred the door and hid himself in the hayloft, not even thinking about his sword. Fear thundered in his head until all went silent. The next thing Nikos was aware of was someone calling his name. It was cold and dark, and he couldn't understand where he was, but suddenly everything came back to him, and he recognized Barah's voice.

"Here!" called out Nikos. "I am here!" as he scrambled down the ladder and ran out of the barn, running right into Barah.

"Nikos! We have been searching for you!" he exclaimed. Nikos still felt shaken and did not find anything to say.

"You are alright?" asked Barah. Nikos could only nod as they headed toward the house.

Then he said, "I am quite hungry."

"Well, we have been all day looking for you," said Barah, "and have not eaten either." Soon they were all at the table, and Nikos explained himself as best he could but with few words. He was feeling quite ashamed.

"You are not entirely to blame," began Barah. "The evil Ra-Tsalem can incite our feelings, driving us to do what we would not otherwise. We must stay strong and be vigilant."

"How can an intangible force goad us to do anything?" asked Pike. "We decide our own action, not—"

But Kainos quickly interjected, "Let us not contend about these things. We must keep our unity and prepare for Rhaka to come with an even larger force."

Nikos looked questioningly, and Barah answered, "Soldiers did come from Makran today, about twenty of them, but we stopped them on the bridge."

For the next few days, they worked on building a wall on the west side of the creek and were joined by many men from town.

As they worked, Barah said to Nikos, "You are worried much about Chayel?"

He only nodded as Barah continued, "She is strong and crafty. We must trust to that," but Barah was similarly concerned.

As the work went on, Kainos had decided to build a guardhouse into the wall so that he could set men to keep watch for any who approached from the east. So, the work continued, but tension mounted every day as they expected the arrival of a large force of Rhaka's men.

Soon the wall was finished, and they had only to set the iron gate in place, but it had not yet been completed. In the meantime, many of the men went downstream to where the ravine was passable and began building defenses there. The next day, Soot, the blacksmith arrived with the gate on a very large wooden wagon pulled by four burly draft horses.

"We'll need ever man you got to git this set up," he said to Kainos. "But once it's up, it'll swing easy as butter."

They all set to work getting the gate off the wagon. Suddenly, a small bird alighted on it chirping and clutching something with its foot.

Soot tried shooing it away, but Nikos said, "No, no! It's holding a small parchment. Look."

The bird, which was a white, puffy snow sparrow, fluttered to Nikos and landed on his shoulder, proffering what it was holding. Nikos, though startled at the bird's behavior, took it and unrolled the parchment.

He said uncomfortably, "I cannot read."

Pike took the rolled parchment and read: "Two hundred men by sunrise."

"But which day will it be?" asked Barah.

"And where does this bird come from?" asked another.

Soon, there was a general disturbance over such an odd occurrence, but the bird remained on Nikos's shoulder and chirped a bit, which brought a grin to Nikos.

He wondered if the bird could understand him and asked, "You are Meekrow?" The bird chirped an affirmative answer. Amid the uproar, no one noticed him talking to the bird, who told him that he had come from Ruad.

"Can Ruad understand you?" The bird nodded its head, and Nikos was incredulous.

"You are the only other who can," said Meekrow.

Nikos was enthralled, but was suddenly startled by one of the men saying in a loud scoffing voice, "He's *talking* to it!"

The sparrow flapped up into the air, frightened, but alighted again on Nikos. "That's because *he's* talking to *me!*" blurted out Nikos angrily.

The other man sneered, "It's a witless *bird!*"

This suddenly filled Nikos with rage and as he imagined attacking the man. Kainos yelled, "Now stop this!"

Nikos calmed down quickly, and the man retreated a bit, but remained silent.

"We must have unity!" insisted Kainos, "though we may believe differently or find things hard to believe."

"Nikos can understand the speech of some animals," said Barah. "It is an ability given him by the Great One—"

"Great one?" scoffed the man. "What is this, another figment? I suppose now you will tell me how evil I am, how cursed with Kah-Taw! I have heard of these daft ideas and this ridiculous *great* one!" Everyone was stunned into silence as he cackled and continued, "It ain't real, none of it! Curse this great one! Curse him—"

Suddenly, he reeled backward and fell to the ground, writhing in agony and then lay still. His friend rushed to him but recoiled in horror.

"He . . . he's dead!"

"What is this?" exclaimed Pike to Kafar, Barah, and Arak. "Who, indeed, is your Great One who will strike someone dead?"

But they were stunned into silence, and many of the men backed away and left them, until only a handful were left.

Soot, the blacksmith, stepped forward and said, "Mister Pike, sir, you heard that fool. Would you take kindly to havin' curses called down on you? Now, the Great One, he's more important than all of us and all the grand kings and stately rulers put into one and if he gets dishonored . . . well you see what can happen . . ." as he ran out of things to say and just nodded emphatically.

There followed a very somber silence as the men just looked at one another, but eventually another man said, "Well, we all are with you, though I don't know about believin' your way, but we got to stand against Rhaka, right fellows?"

The other men agreed. and after some time, a small wagon slowly approached. There was an old woman and two young men on it, and they went to the dead man's body and loaded it on the wagon. The woman began wailing in anguish, but the young men were silent as they drove away.

Everyone quietly got back to work, and Barah said, "The bird . . . it is gone." In all the commotion, no one had noticed that the snow sparrow had flown away.

"What did he tell you?" asked Barah.

"He came from Ruad, from the fortress," answered Nikos. "Ruad can understand him as I can. He said that Rhaka's men will be here by tomorrow morning . . . at sunrise."

But as he imagined meeting soldiers in battle, a shadow of the terror he had felt before passed over him, and he heard little else of what Barah was saying.

It was well into the evening, and they were all exhausted before they finally had the gate in place. It did indeed swing open very easily, but once it was closed and the bar slid into place, they all felt that it was a sure defense. Kainos set one of his deputies in the guardhouse to keep the first watch, and the rest dispersed to their homes.

Sixteen

The day was drawing to a close as Chayel and Odus drew near to Stoney Point Mine. Its entrance was up on a spur of the Stone Mountains near the bridge that crossed Stoney Creek into Tachus Town.

"Ought to be right up this way," said Odus as he picked his way through some underbrush and then amongst some trees.

They soon found the remnants of a cart path, and Chayel said quietly, "Someone is here ahead of us. See those stones have been kicked up there."

Odus smiled to himself as she endeared herself even more to him. Suddenly, a hushed but fierce voice called out in the dim surroundings, "Who be you?"

The two froze, but then Odus said, "Is that you, Eido?"

There was brief silence and then, "Yes, sir, Mister Odus," and a very young, slim man stepped out from behind a tree.

"Not all of us is here yet. Reo went up to Karpone to tell his brothers and his cousin 'bout what we're up to. Now, the mine is just up there, but I got to stay on lookout."

He ducked back behind the tree as Odus and Chayel continued on. The underbrush opened up a bit as they came to the mine, and they saw half a dozen horses tied on a line.

The other men had started a fire just inside the entrance and as Odus and Chayel approached, one of them came out, "We're glad you're here, Mister Odus."

As Chayel observed how young he was, she couldn't help saying to Odus, "I expected *men*." He only chuckled as they dismounted and untied their packs, including the gunny sack containing the bows and staves.

"I'll see to your horses," said the young man as Odus and Chayel headed toward the mine's entrance.

As they came into the light of the fire, one of the other young men blurted out, "A . . . a girl!"

"That's more than a girl," said another, getting to his feet, but Odus chastised him.

"Now, you all mind your business! For the time bein', we are *all* soldiers and got to keep clear heads."

At that moment a man in his late twenties came from the rear of the mine and said, "Oh, Mister Odus, sir" and then nodded at Chayel. "Ma'am." She nodded in return.

"Glad to see you got things well in order here, Kore," said Odus. "This is Chayel."

He nodded again and then helped them get settled. Only six men were there, but Kore told them that many more were expected to come the next day. As night fell, they put the fire out and closed an old wooden door that had been built across the entrance of the mine.

The next day dawned fair, but with an October chill in the air. Most of the leaves still clung to the trees, though some had descended to their winter resting places. Odus took charge of the men and began to instruct them in the use of a tri-bow, which most of them were very interested in, having never seen anything of the sort.

Chayel took up her bow to demonstrate how deadly it was, when one of the men said to Odus, "Now, what's she gonna do with nothin' but a *stick* like that?"

Chayel turned sharply toward him, but Odus put up his hand and said to Chayel, "Just you show him."

As she decided on a target, there was a rustling in the underbrush about twenty yards away, and she spied a large bird of some sort. Taking quick, but careful aim, she let her arrow fly and instantly there was an abbreviated squawk, and a few feathers flew up in the air. The men looked at one another incredulously as Odus commanded the man who had scoffed to go get the bird. He returned a bit humbled with a lifeless red-headed pheasant and dropped it in front of her.

"Sorry, ma'am——" he said.

Before he could continue, Odus fairly yelled, "Not sorry enough! Now that she's showed you how to *use* a bow, she's gonna show you how to *make* bows, and you'll spend the rest of the day carving them and whilst you're doing it, you best get your head in order about who we are and what we're doing here!"

By midday they were eating roasted pheasant, and some had begun to practice with bow and arrow, while Odus had others collecting river cane to make more arrows. The young Eido, who could not have been much more than sixteen, admired Chayel greatly and hung on her every word, taking in every detail about how to wield a bow.

Presently, the man on lookout came quickly to Odus, "Sir, there is band of horsemen approaching up the valley. It looks like Reo and about fifteen others."

"Be sure of it," Odus commanded, "and then lead them up."

Soon, they all came near to the camp, with the jingling of bridles, creaking of saddles, and the blowing and stamping of the horses. The man who led them, rode up to Odus and pulled his mount to a stop. He sat still and was very grave as was the rest of the men.

He clenched his jaw and said evenly, "Two of my brothers . . . they been killed, and the third, he's hurt real bad."

"I am sorry," said Odus.

"It was a few weeks ago," replied Reo, trying to maintain his composure. "They finally tried standing up to Rhaka's soldiers when they came to take their "tax.""

There was a very somber pause and then a big bear of a man said, "It's real bad up Makran way. That Rhaka don't give a fig for people's very lives anymore. Just takin' whoever and whatever he wants."

"He sure took a real bad turn," added another. "Like he ain't even human anymore. Well, we shall surely see that Rhaka gets what he deserves," he said and then led them into camp.

Seeing Chayel, he called out, "Maybe you can get us another bird or two?"

"Yes sir, Mister Odus!" she called back with a smile.

When Reo saw her, he did a double take and quickly said to Odus, "War is no place for a woman! Especially one so . . . beautiful."

He was taken aback and seemed not to hear Odus say, "I don't doubt she will surely show you different."

Chayel had started toward the woods with Eido right beside her. As they entered the trees, the land sloped up and the underbrush became denser. They went on for a little while and then Chayel said, "We are louder than a herd of camels in these leaves!"

"What . . . what is a camel?" asked Eido, but at that moment Chayel ducked down and motioned him to do the same.

"A deer!" she whispered as Eido followed her gaze. Chayel stealthily fit an arrow to her bow, but as she raised it, the deer became startled and sprang away. Chayel followed it but did not have a good shot.

As they returned to camp, Reo said to Odus, "Why is there a woman here? Women only beget children and strife!" Odus quickly held up his hand to Chayel, who had all she could do to contain herself.

"We are *all* soldiers here," said Odus. "We must respect each other as such!"

For the next few days, they worked on making bows and arrows and began to learn how to use them. Reo, however would have nothing to do with them and avoided having anything to do with Chayel. Early one morning, almost before dawn, one of the lookouts came running into camp and hurriedly woke up Odus.

"Mister Odus, Mister Odus! There's a couple hundred men comin' down the road from up north! They look like soldiers, sir!"

Odus got up quickly and was joined by Chayel as they followed the lookout back to his post. "See there!" he whispered, as Odus breathed a heavy sigh.

But Chayel said, "We must warn Marshal Kainos! Surely, they are headed to Tachus Town. No one will even be awake there!"

"It is too late," said a voice beside them. They quickly realized that it was Kore, the young man who was first to arrive at the mine.

"They are too near where the spur of the mountain comes down," he continued. "We could not get down there in time to get around it without being seen."

Odus had no immediate answer, but Chayel said, "Come! We can watch them from the cliff on the other side of the mine, where it overlooks the bridge! And then—"

She was interrupted by Reo who had just arrived. "Watch them?" he scoffed. "What good is watching? We have the advantage here and could attack them unawares!"

"We are less than fifty," began Odus, but Chayel turned and disappeared into the gloomy morning air as she quickly headed back toward the mine. Most of the men were astir, but she passed through and went into the mine and down to where Eido was sleeping. He was still groggy, but her fierce whisper woke him up.

"Quickly! Get your bow!" He hopped up, still not fully aware as they both went out and made their way up the hill and then through the trees to the cliff edge.

"We must get some brush and make cover here," said Chayel.

"What is it? What is happening?" he asked.

As she collected some tree branches, she said, "Two hundred of Rhaka's men are marching toward the town this very moment and will soon be at the bridge."

"But what are we going to do?"

"The bows!" said Chayel as she intertwined some branches and brush. Eido was just standing there uselessly, but soon Chayel had the underbrush arranged to form a screen.

"We can shoot them from here," she said excitedly. "They will never see us!"

"You mean shoot *people*?" he asked incredulously.

"They are the *enemy*, Eido!" she replied passionately. "They seek to rule all these lands and take everything for themselves. They will make us their slaves!"

Eido suddenly understood the seriousness of the situation and was about to speak when Chayel motioned him to get down. She pointed, and they both saw the soldiers coming around the end of the mountain and approaching the bridge.

The noise of the waterfall made it easy for them to speak without being heard, and Eido said, "Chayel! On the other side of the bridge, there's men down there. Look, some in the guardhouse and up on the wall!"

"They knew!" she exclaimed. "How did they know?"

"But look how big those soldiers are that are on the bridge," said Eido with amazement, "They will climb right over that gate!"

But Chayel had already fit an arrow to her bow and said very evenly and a bit savagely, "There are no creatures that are too big for a well-placed arrow."

Eido felt the tautness of the moment and watched intently, barely breathing. The biggest of the soldiers, over eight feet tall, went forward to the gate.

"They are Megan-something," said Chayel, taking aim with her bow, "not human, but a race from the north." Suddenly, the giant soldier brought his massive fists down on the gate and began to barge against it.

"Shoot!" whispered Eido, sounding a bit frightened. "They will break it down!"

Her arrow flew true to the mark, but straight into the Commander, who was standing just behind the massive soldier. This caused a great panic among all the soldiers. They began pushing and shoving to get off the bridge, some crying out in fear and looking around wildly as if there were invisible enemies.

"What is happening to them?" asked Eido.

"I suppose they have never seen an arrow before," answered Chayel. "It must seem to them to have come out of nowhere."

"They are all running away," began Eido. "But did you mean to leave him alive . . . the one you shot?"

"I meant only to wound him so that they will have to retreat to Makran to get help. Dead soldiers mean only that more come from behind to keep fighting. That commander will allow no one else to fight this battle in his place. He will return with a vengeance, but for now I suppose we have the victory."

A huge smile spread across her face, and Eido's great admiration for her brought a big grin to his. They watched the soldiers retreat in a panic carrying their commander, and then they returned to their camp. Only a few men were there, so they went down the path to the lookout post. Presently, they heard the men even farther down the path, arguing in heated whispers.

"But they are there! They are panicked and fleeing!" fumed Reo. "Their leader is badly wounded! We must strike now!"

"We cannot!" hissed Odus. "We are outnumbered four to one!"

Suddenly, Reo looked about and called out as loud as he dared, "Who is with me? How many more of us have to lose our homesteads, our goods, or our families?!"

No one moved, and Reo continued, "Did we not come to fight? Now is our chance; we must take our revenge!" Then a few of the men who had come with Reo came to his side, but the rest did not move.

"You are a fool to go out after them soldiers," said young Eido, which surprised everyone. "Now Chayel, she knows how to fight a battle."

"You are a stupid child!" yelled Reo, his passions erupting into a rage. "And all of you! As faint-hearted and timid as this woman here!"

"She's braver than you'll ever know how to be!" yelled Eido and rushed at him with his fists raised, but Reo cuffed him to the ground.

Chayel ran forward, but Reo shouted, "I'll show you courage!" as he drew his sword and picked up his shield.

He turned and rushed down the path toward the open field where the soldiers were fleeing down the mine cart line. Everyone was stunned and could do nothing but watch as Reo raced out of the cover of the trees and onto the road. The soldiers were quite a distance away, but he ran after them, calling out threats and violence as loud as he could. They seemed not to hear and were moving quite fast. While most of them had disappeared over a rise, a few in the rear turned back. They seemed unsure as to what they should do, but as Reo raced headlong at them, they came forward to meet him. They were average sized men, and Reo ran even faster toward them, but suddenly one of the Meganthropos appeared over the hill behind them. It was the one who had been trying to break the gate down. Reo faltered, but the gargantuan being moved alarmingly fast and was face to face with him before he could turn back. He grabbed Reo around the neck with one hand and lifted him off the ground. Odus and all the men looked on in horror as Reo struggled helplessly.

"We got to help him!" yelled Eido as he began to rush forward.

Suddenly, the giant soldier let out an agonizing cry and threw Reo to the ground. All the men skidded to a halt amongst the trees as they saw that an arrow was sticking through the soldier's forearm. The three soldiers again looked wildly about in fear and then in a panic raced away over the hill. After a minute or two, a figure appeared from the forest on the left and came across the field to Reo, who was not moving.

"It's Chayel!" cried Eido as they all suddenly realized that she was not with them.

As they went out to her, Eido exclaimed with great admiration, "You saved his life!"

But one of the other men said, "Not so fast there, he don't look too good."

Reo was unconscious, and his neck was inflamed and red and welted up, but worse was the nasty gash on his head. Odus sent a few of the men up the road to keep a lookout and then knelt down next to Reo. He tried reviving him but was unsuccessful.

Odus gave orders for the men to get Reo back to camp and one of them said, "We're sorry, sir, 'bout sidin' up with Reo, seein' how rash he's actin', but we're neighbor folk of his up in Karpone. We've all lost a lot."

He paused and was a bit hesitant as another said, "And runnin' out like that . . ." he trailed off, shaking his head.

"Losin' what you love can do bad things to a man," said Odus.

In the next moment, there was the sound of horses on the road, back toward Tachus town. The whole bunch of them were caught in the open and as Odus was about to give a command, Chayel said, "Wait! It is Marshal Kainos from Tachus Town and also Marshal Pike and the other three; they are from my homeland."

There was a collective exhale as they waited for the horsemen to reach them. When they were within earshot, Chayel called out, "You have had some trouble at the bridge?"

"Not as much as we could have," answered Kainos.

Reo began to regain consciousness, and they all turned to him. "You are alright?" asked one of his friends.

Reo nodded as he got up slowly rubbing his head and then said, "What happened?"

Odus was about to speak when Eido piped up, "Chayel, she saved you— shot that beast right in the arm!"

Reo scowled, partly because he was still in pain and then he looked at Odus, who said, "It was a right foolish thing you did, running after them like that. That brute was going to do you in and would have if it weren't for her."

All eyes turned to Chayel, except for Reo, who motioned toward Kainos and the others and asked, "Who are these?"

But Kainos, indignant at Reo's contempt for Chayel, rode forward and addressed him, "I believe you owe this fine lady a bit of gratitude."

A strained silence followed until Chayel said heatedly, "He does not owe me or any of us anything except not to do something so foolish again."

Reo immediately became so enraged that words eluded him, so he picked up his sword and shield and stomped off across the field toward the mine, stumbling a bit and putting his hand to his head. His friends looked at one another and seemed undecided about following him, until one set off, but not the other.

Kainos addressed Chayel, "Though you did not receive thanks from one less chivalrous than befits a man, we offer our sincere gratitude and are indeed indebted to you."

Eido beamed at her and as she nodded to Kainos, Kafar motioned in Reo's direction and asked, "What happened to him?"

"He ran out after those soldiers," exclaimed Eido, full of excitement. "Trying to show how brave he is, but instead showed what a fool he is, and the huge one got him around the neck, but then Chayel, she was hiding in the woods over there, she shot him with an arrow, dead in the arm!"

Everyone was quite surprised at his outburst and found nothing to say for a moment as Eido looked triumphantly at Chayel.

"We have been concerned about your welfare," said Barah.

"Tey-Rahk took me to a town east of here, where I met Odus," she answered gesturing to him, "and then we gathered some men . . ."

"And I know you," said Pike, motioning to a very large man.

"From Rhaka's dungeon," he answered. "Name's Bahr. There were quite a few of us who escaped from Rhaka, and it felt dang good bringin' a bit of justice to some of his soldiers on our way out."

They filled each other in on all that had happened and as they finished, two of the lookouts came back down the road, "Well, they are gone," said one.

"And as fast as they could go too," grinned the other

Kainos admonished them all, "This fight has only just begun. And now we must prepare for what is to come."

The sun had climbed into the sky, but the October air remained chilly as Odus sent his men back to camp, while he and Chayel joined Kainos and the others.

As they set off for Kainos's farm, Chayel said to Barah, "Nikos, where is he? He was not with you at the bridge either."

Barah took a moment to answer, and Chayel again asked, "You do not know? How is he not with us."

As Barah said, "He seemed not himself."

But Chayel shook her head indignantly, "Not himself? What do we even have to do with *ourselves*? We must do what is before us, and we must be as one!"

They arrived at Kainos's farm, and Chayel, feeling frustrated and disappointed with Nikos, offered to take care of their horses. She found Zeo in the pasture, and just as she was closing the gate after putting the other horses in, Nikos came slowly around the end of the barn.

"Chayel!" he exclaimed, but her demeanor and smoldering eyes cut him short. She took a few steps back and stood there looking intensely at him.

He looked to the ground and fumbled for words, "I . . . I have been worried. Where have you been?"

"Where have *I* been?" she said evenly with her eyes locked on him. He felt so ashamed of himself that he could say nothing and stood there helplessly.

"Where have *you* been, Nikos?" she asked. "Barah said that you were *not yourself*. What has happened? This is hard for all of us, and we need each other; we must be strong and unified!" Nikos could say nothing, and he stood there so long, that Chayel's anger began to subside.

"I am sorry," offered Nikos weakly, "The day when Rhaka's soldiers came,

I felt such fear, like that day when my foster father died on the beach and how I had been chased by some of the men from the town. That fear, I could not bear it . . . I hid in the barn."

He finished with an effort that seemed to physically pain him. Chayel let out a long sigh and looked out across the field, trying to manage her emotions. Eventually, Nikos said with some hesitancy, "This morning, it was the same fear, but even worse. I could not go out to the bridge . . ."

Chayel stood silent, but her emotions were still working furiously as she sought to understand, but at a loss, she said, "I do not know such fear." But her voice softened as she finished, "Still, our lives will depend on each other, when it comes to fighting the enemy. We must lay down our fears and thus they become the paving stones to victory."

She turned to go up to the house; Nikos was slow to follow, and Chayel's deep disappointment in him erupted, "Now you do not even have the courage to face your *friends*?! You indeed have let us down, but do not persist in it! You must overcome this fear, or the enemy will use it to great advantage and bring unexpected destruction!"

She stood waiting for a reply, but Nikos felt helpless, and his shame immobilized him. Feeling a violent anger suddenly arising within her, Chayel turned sharply away and headed up to the house.

As she joined the men, Kafar was saying, "Indeed, but we must believe that somehow we shall defeat them and regain what we have lost and protect what is still ours."

All eyes turned to Chayel, whose anger and disappointment were plain to see. "Nikos is down at the barn," she said stiffly, but to her surprise, Nikos appeared at the porch.

Before he could say anything, Kafar said, "It is a hard fight sometimes, to overcome fear. Our enemy can magnify it in us, so we must be vigilant and trust to the Great One."

"You are alright now?" asked Kainos.

Nikos nodded and slowly sat down, very grateful that they seemed to understand and required no explanation from him. There was a thoughtful silence amongst them for a few moments and then Kainos continued.

"Now, this Commander Polus, he will take personal revenge, and it will be upon the whole town, for he knows not who wounded him. We must make the most of the time that he will be recovering from his wound."

"But what do we do when he comes?" asked Arak. "Surely, he will come with far more than two hundred."

An uneasy silence fell over them until Kainos said, "We ought to take the bridge out, take the decking off it. There's little trade coming down from up Makran way these days, what with Rhaka commandeering everything."

"That certainly would stop them, no matter their number," added Pike.

"And then we ought to build a watchtower up on the mountain," added Odus, "so we can see 'em comin'."

They all agreed to the plans, and gathering the men from the mine camp, they quickly set about the work of carrying them out. Only Reo dissented, being visibly incensed; without a word of explanation, he packed up his gear and rode off.

"We are stronger now," said Chayel, and even Reo's two friends, who remained behind, agreed. Over the next few weeks, they built a watchtower on an outcropping of the mountain near the mine and constructed a path that zigzagged up the back of the mountain from Tachus Town so they could get to it without having to cross the bridge from which they had removed the decking. Odus set up men to take turns keeping watch and sent the young man, Kore, and a few others to the defenses that had been built downriver to also keep watch there. There was a small village near the defenses, and the people there were eager to help and give what was needed.

Chayel spent a lot of time at the camp, working hard at making bows and arrows and teaching the men how to use them. Eido was a natural, and it seemed his skill would soon surpass Chayel. The first snowfall of the season came much earlier than usual and with winter coming on, they expected no retaliation by Rhaka. Many of the men who had joined Chayel and Odus took up residence in Tachus Town or went back to their homes and farms.

"We'll keep sharp eyes out," said one as they were leaving. "We live near Makran and will gather everyone quick as may be if we see any soldiers comin' down this way." Pike also went back to his home and duties.

The beginning of winter in Tachus Town proved no different than usual as snowfall was infrequent, and the temperatures remained mild. Chayel and the other three from the south were, however, still finding it difficult, never having seen snow or felt such cold temperatures. Nor did they have the proper clothing, but the townsfolk were more than eager to help however they could and provided what was needed. It remained fairly temperate all through October and November, but then the snow came in December, and winter finally set in. Tachus Town remained very active with some of the folk cutting and gathering trees to sell for firewood and others trapping ermine and other small mammals for their fur.

One day, near evening, as Kainos and the rest were gathered in his great room, near the fireplace, they heard a clinking sound on one of the windows. They all listened carefully, but Nikos jumped up and went to investigate.

"It is Meekrow!" he exclaimed as he went out the door; he quickly returned with the little bird perched on his hand.

It was again grasping a piece of parchment, and Nikos handed it to Kainos, who read, "Man from south teaching language."

Silence fell upon them for a moment and then Barah said, "That is not good."

"A well-placed arrow would end his tutoring," said Chayel in a very serious tone.

"Indeed," said Kafar. "But we do not know who he is."

Nikos interjected, "Meekrow says that he could show us."

They all looked at one another, but Kainos said, "We would do better to turn him to our side. I am sure that Ruad is doing all he can."

Chayel's emotions began to rise and in frustration she exclaimed, "How do we continue to wait? Are we to trust so much to this man Ruad whom we do not really know? We must take this chance to stop Rhaka from learning the Book!"

Again, they looked at one another until Kainos said, "We *could* kill this southerner, surely you would not miss the mark, but it is not wise to risk so much. A matter of time and Rhaka would find another."

"Risk so much?" asked Chayel heatedly. "Would not each of us give our lives to do our duty?!"

"But we are the only ones who know where the Book is," ventured Nikos. "If we are caught or killed . . ."

This slowed Chayel down a bit as Arak said, "More than preventing Rhaka from learning from the Book, it is our greater duty to get the Book back."

Chayel acquiesced, but a scowl crossed her face as she said, "Then we must wait, *still*, and trust this Ruad."

"He indeed would give his life for this cause," said Kafar, "especially now that he is one of us."

December passed slowly and into January as they waited out the winter and for any news from Ruad. Eventually, spring drew near and one day, near the end of March, one of the lookout men came to Kainos and said, "There is a lone horseman at the bridge. He says his name is Ruad, and he is asking to speak to you."

"Have him come," said Kainos. Soon Ruad appeared, and Kafar spoke first, "Ah, Ruad, my friend; it is good to see you! I should like to properly thank you for your kindness to me in Rhaka's dungeon."

"Delighted to have been of service to you," he replied with a smile. "And Marshal Pike, he is well?"

"Yes. He is back at Agathon Outpost," answered Kafar.

"You have news for us?" asked Kainos as they entered his house, but they all could see that the news was not good.

Ruad took a long pause and then said heavily, "Koreb, he was the one teaching Rhaka the language, but he has become one of the People of the Great One. He has feigned being the unwholesome young scoundrel that he was, but it has been difficult, knowing Rhaka would eventually use his knowledge of the Book for evil. Koreb was afraid of being found out and was more and more anxious about the Book. I dissuaded him from just grabbing the Book and making a run for it, but Commander Polus has beaten him to it."

"Stolen it?" asked Nikos in disbelief as Ruad's expression answered the question.

"Where has he gone?" asked Chayel.

"He escaped north," said Ruad, "into Borrhas Province."

"This is good news," she continued. "The Book is free of the fortress. We must go after it immediately!"

But Ruad shook his head, "It is weeks ago, maybe even a month since Polus stole the Book. I did not know of it until two days ago."

"We cannot wait," said Chayel, "nor take time to think any longer. We must go!"

"There are great mountains in Borrhas," said Ruad a bit gloomily. "They are vast and uncharted."

"We must take careful thought to this," said Kainos.

Ruad continued, "Though Rhaka was still learning the language, I believe Polus had come to understand it. He seemed far above average of others of his kind, quite perceptive, and I think he was just bidding his time, waiting for the snowmelt so that he could not be followed."

"The worst danger now is the evil that knowledge of the Book will unleash through this Commander Polus," said Arak in a brooding sort of way.

As they made plans to head north into Borrhas Province, Kainos said, "I must stay behind and look after this town and lead the men who have come here to stand against Rhaka. Many of them have begun to make their homes here."

The next day dawned fair and mild; it was clear that spring was surely on its way. It brought a cheering feeling, but it didn't help Nikos, who was fighting fear again and sought for some reason that he should stay in Tachus Town. His fear was not wholly unfounded though as he had seen firsthand how unstable and violent Polus could be. A big part of Nikos wished not to find him, and he began to feel more and more ashamed.

As he stood on the porch awaiting the others, Chayel suddenly spoke from behind him, "Your heart is not in this," she said with a strong tone of condemnation.

Startled, Nikos spun around but could say nothing, and averted his eyes.

"How can you fear?" she asked fiercely. "Our lives are not our own, and if we must sacrifice them, death only brings us to our reward."

Nikos nodded as Chayel added, "Fear can change things in men's minds into something that they are not. You must *think*! What is your fear?"

Nikos became overwhelmed and exclaimed, "Stop!" A tear came to his eye, and Chayel took a step back as he said, "I am sorry . . . I cannot just will it away."

They stood in an uncomfortable silence as Nikos felt the sting of Chayel's disapproval and disbelief. "If you cannot control your thoughts and your feelings," she began, "you are a danger to us . . ." She trailed off not realizing how harsh her statement would sound until she had said it.

An apology formed in her mind but had no chance of expression as Nikos blurted out very angrily, "I will not go, then!"

He threw his pack nearly at Chayel, but then grabbed it up again, jumped off the porch, and ran toward the barn. She stood there in stunned silence as she watched him hop the fence into the pasture, jump aboard Zeo, and gallop away, jumping over the fence at the other end.

After a moment, she turned to go back into the house but was met by Kainos, Ruad, and her three countrymen, who were on their way out.

"Chayel, you are alright?" asked Barah, but she shook her head. "No, it is Nikos . . . but yes, I am alright."

She quickly composed herself and said, "He is gone."

"Gone?" asked Kainos. "Where?"

Chayel was feeling very hurt and disappointed with Nikos and so, trying to reign in her emotion, gave a curt answer. "On his horse, over the fence."

"Now, my dear," said Kainos. "What happened?"

Tears welled up in her eyes, and she stood like a statue, trying to compose herself.

"He is fighting his fear again?" asked Arak as Chayel nodded.

Then she shook her head, saying, "I told him he would be a danger to us . . ." she trailed off, expecting to be chastised.

No one said anything until Kafar said, "It is true. We must know we can depend on each other."

"I am sorry for him," lamented Arak. "He is fighting more than fear, though he may not understand; he is fighting the evil one as well."

"And the fight will only get fiercer," added Kafar.

A grave seriousness took hold of them as Kainos said, "I will try to find Nikos. And no doubt there is little chance of Rhaka or Polus coming against Tachus Town now that they are in great conflict with one another."

They packed quickly and rode out, with Chayel stopping up at the mine camp to talk to Odus.

She took him aside and spoke quickly and quietly, "Polus has stolen the Book, and we are going after him. The man who rode in yesterday, he is a spy inside the fortress at Makran and has only just learned of this, though it is some time ago that Polus got away with it."

"Such mutiny is welcome news for our side," said Odus.

Chayel nodded and continued, "Ruad has told us how to get to the crossroads at Praho; he will meet us there by midmorning tomorrow to help guide us, but I would have you come with us. You know some of the north lands."

"Well, I do not know much," he answered, "but I do know the ways of the mountains."

Odus was quick to pack and though he could not tell the men about his real reason for leaving them, he told them of Polus's rebellion against Rhaka and sent them back to Ekuus, instructing them to stay alert and draw more men together with them. He rejoined Chayel and as they headed down the path, another horseman galloped down from the camp. It was Eido.

"Mister Odus and Miss Chayel," he began, "where are you off to so sudden, and without us all?"

They were both surprised and pulled up short. "Now, my boy," began Odus, "you've got to go back with the others."

"Yes," added Chayel. "We must remain a small company."

"But I'm just one," he retorted and left the other two without a reply.

After a moment Odus said, "He *is* first-rate with that bow."

"And I'm real good at sneaking," added Eido hopefully.

Chayel was undecided, but after a moment, she said, "Well, six is little more than five, and you have proven yourself faithful and of a strong constitution."

Eido didn't know what she meant, but he thought it sounded good and besides, all he cared about was not being left behind.

They rode down to the others who agreed to have Eido come with them, but Odus said, "Now, Eido, you know there may be fightin' and maybe killin' where we're goin'?"

"Yes, sir, but what are we going for?" he asked a bit tentatively. "I heard Miss Chayel say that that Polus brute stole something. Are we chasing after *him*?"

Odus nodded, and Eido suddenly felt quite apprehensive, but he quickly overcame it, especially as he glanced at Chayel.

Seventeen

Nikos had galloped off to the west with his emotions stinging him more than the tears that streaked across his face. He clung tightly to Zeo's mane and rode as if he were being chased. Fear and flashbacks engulfed him so that he hardly knew where he was or what he was doing. Eventually, Zeo ran out of wind and slowed to a canter.

"Which way?" came a voice out of nowhere, which startled Nikos badly, but brought him back to some sort of sense. Soon, Zeo came to a stop and pawed the ground, seeming impatient.

"You . . . spoke," said Nikos in a very shaky voice. "But of course, I know you can."

"Which way?" he replied. Nikos slid to the ground and nearly right down to his knees as his legs were a bit wobbly. He began slowly walking, overwhelmed by emotion, and Zeo took up walking behind him and nibbling at grass as they went.

After a good long way of walking across a field, Zeo asked, "Will we go back to the others?"

The question startled Nikos and caused him to blurt out, "No! Why should we? It is not our fight! I would go home . . . if I had one, he finished forlornly."

He let go a big sigh and sat down in the grass. Zeo fell to grazing, and Nikos sat there for quite some time just thinking and feeling so many different things that afterward he could not recall much of it at all. The sun was nearly overhead when Nikos stood up, which brought Zeo, who had ranged across the field in search of sweeter grass, back to him.

"I cannot go back," said Nikos after struggling with himself for the last hour—knowing he ought to, but unable to overcome the fear of being in a battle.

He felt remorse and then anger as he thought, *"I am a danger to them anyway; Chayel said it herself."* He pulled his pack onto his shoulders and jumped up onto Zeo. With the sun overhead and being in open country, he had no idea which way to go. He looked around and remembered that he had been riding somewhat toward the mountains that were far off and decided to continue toward them.

The longer he rode, the more he began to think about Makarios and how amiable she had been when they left her farm right before winter and how she had bidden them to "return whenever you may." This brightened his mood a bit, but then he wondered how he would explain why he was alone, and this cast a shadow over what was otherwise a fair and breezy day. He rode on, but as the sun began to descend, Nikos realized that he had been going west for half of the day, not south. This deepened his sullen mood and almost made him not care at all which way he went. Soon, he came upon a track at the foot of the mountains that ran north-south, and he turned left onto it. By the evening, he could see a forest in the distance and decided to camp just within its border.

Nikos spent a very restless night and woke up far earlier than he wished. The sun was just rising, and the cool spring air kept him from leaving his bedroll. He lay there in the lee of a huge boulder and looked up through the trees at a dark blue sky beginning to streak with red. He thought of Chayel and felt ashamed of how he had run away. He wished he were stronger and more courageous, *"Like her,"* he thought, and then the words, *"You could go back,"* formed in his mind, to which he suddenly cried out, "No!" and threw his blanket off and got up.

"It is not my fight! I didn't ask for any of this!" He scowled and quickly packed up his things and called for Zeo, who came from the field north of the forest at once.

"You are not well?" he asked.

"No, I am not!" answered Nikos abruptly as he got aboard and prodded Zeo forward. Nikos hated how he felt. He nudged Zeo up to a gallop, as if to outrun his feelings. But the forest was still dim, and Zeo soon slowed, unable to see the way ahead.

Nikos hardly noticed as his thoughts had turned to Makarios, and all else faded away as he imagined seeing her again. The forest went on for quite a long way, but eventually he passed through it and came out into open fields. The track went on along the base of the mountains with the rails of a mine cart line running next to it. Soon, he came to a steep spur of the mountain that jutted out, and at its foot was a junction in the mine cart line. One set of tracks turned sharply to the right, going west, and the other turned to the left going south. Having been that way before, Nikos took the south track. They had not gone very far when a terrible smell came into their nostrils.

"Whew! What is that?" said Nikos, but it soon became apparent as the track had swung toward a marsh on their left.

"I hope this doesn't go on too long," he added, but he could see that the marsh was large and eventually, the track came quite close to it. The ground was becoming soft, and it looked as if the marsh had flooded recently.

Suddenly, Zeo stopped and pawed the ground and said, "We should not go forward."

"Why?" asked Nikos, but Zeo just threw up his head and shook his mane.

"We're going on," said Nikos and nudged Zeo forward, but he only danced sideways and would not move ahead, which suddenly made Nikos angry.

"Go!"

"We must not!"

"You will do as I direct you to!" insisted Nikos, but Zeo only skittered backward, half rearing. As he calmed down, Nikos again spurred him forward, but Zeo would not go.

Nikos leaped off and turned to face him, shaking his head, "Then I will go on without you!"

He turned and stomped down the path, hoping Zeo would follow, but the horse only neighed and pawed the ground. Nikos went on, not looking back and feeling very angry. It wasn't long though, before the path started getting soft and then muddy and soon there was ankle-deep water across it.

Nikos stopped, grimacing in the odious smell of the swamp. He nearly turned back to get away from it, but stubbornness drove him to take a few careful steps into the water, and then he saw that further on, it appeared to dry out. He slowly made his way, but it was only getting deeper. The bottom became spongier and the smell that was being stirred up as Nikos went along became overwhelming. It finally made him decide to go back, but he took one more step and suddenly, he was going down as if the bottom had fallen out of the marsh. He cried out, but only got a mouthful of muddy, repulsive water. He flailed about, and though an excellent swimmer, none of his efforts to stay above the water were successful. It felt like he was being pulled down, and as he went under, all went black and silent.

When Nikos was again aware of himself, he found that he was very hot and dry and lying on something extremely uncomfortable, like sharp chunks of rock, and it was almost pitch dark. As he sat up, a piece of it nearly pierced his palm and so he got up carefully, very thankful for the boots he was wearing. He kicked at the stuff he was now standing on, and it sounded like coal as it briefly clinked against other pieces. As he breathed in, he nearly gagged with how putrid and nauseating the air was, and with that shock, he suddenly wondered where in the world he was.

"I was drowning," he thought, *"but where in the world is this?"*

He felt a shock like nothing he had ever known, and he thought, *"Am I . . . did I die?"*

Terror gripped him, and he fell into a cold sweat in spite of the oppressive heat that surrounded him. It felt hotter than anything he thought he could survive.

Suddenly, something way off in the distance shrieked with such a sound of horror and pain that it made Nikos jump in fright and knocked him off his feet. He fell backward into the crushed coal and cried out in pain as he felt it driving into his flesh in many places. He got up trembling violently, not only in pain but in fear. The thing screeched again, but it seemed nearer to him, and he instinctively looked in that direction. He wobbled and bent forward with his hands on his knees to steady himself as he took big, heavy breaths.

He looked hard to see something in the darkness, though he wished with all his might to see nothing. Thankfully, he did see nothing, but he began to hear things—sounds so terrible that he immediately covered his ears. But he could still hear them and wished with all his heart that he couldn't. It made him feel profound grief and an overpowering terror.

As he tried to stop hearing, he began to notice a stuffiness like he was in an enclosed space. He stretched his hands out in every direction but did not contact anything. Suddenly, another terrible shriek, even closer, rent the air, and Nikos nearly fainted from fear, but he steadied himself. He took a step, but the coal made a disastrously loud crunching sound. Another screech from the creature rent the thick air and told him that it had passed by. With his hands out in front of him, Nikos took a few small steps in the darkness and came upon what seemed to be a brick wall. He put his hand on it, but immediately drew back from the heat of it. He began to move along it, touching it as lightly as he could and found he was inside some kind of small building.

Nikos was confused. He was nauseated from the heat and sickening odor and felt he would faint when, unexpectedly, his hand came upon a latch. He pulled it very slowly and carefully and found it to be a door, which he opened just a crack. As he did so, the horrible sounds became louder, and a dull red-orange glow faintly came into the room. He could see that the building was only about six feet square and made of rust-red bricks, although it could have been the color of the light that made them look so.

Nikos looked to see how bad the wounds were from where he had fallen; to his amazement there was not a single mark, and then he realized that the pain had gone as well. But then his attention was taken by hearing something wail pitifully in agony. He trembled in fear as he peered out and saw a massive city. All the buildings were made of the same brick as the one he was in. They were of different shapes and sizes, lit with the dull red-orange light, but all the windows were blackened.

Above the light, there was a blackness that canopied the whole city. The streets were made of loose shards of coal and were filled with dark shadowy shapes moving about that looked like people. Nikos then noticed how extreme-ly thirsty he was when the horrible shriek came again. Panicked, he slammed the door shut and to his absolute horror, he heard footsteps crunching through the coal and coming nearer. He nearly swooned when something banged against the door, and then he heard the latch turning. Nikos cowered in the corner, trembling violently as the door opened and was filled with a huge black shape. It seemed to have no substance, and yet a great power exuded from it. Then the thing spoke in a voice so lifeless and benumbed that it sent chills up and down Nikos's spine; his mind was spinning.

"You think to hide from your work?" The thing barged in with putrid foul air swirling into the room as it grabbed Nikos by the neck with a cruel, bony grip. It took him outside and held him aloft.

"Well? Answer!" it insisted, but all Nikos could do was gasp for air. He felt himself losing consciousness when he saw the black silhouette of a second beast approaching. It ripped Nikos out of the other creature's grasp and then croaked in a deathless way, as if it had never been alive.

"Go!" and then, it threw Nikos in the direction of all the people. He flew through the air and as he hit the ground, the sharp coal rent his flesh with such excruciating pain that he felt he would die from it. Worse than that though was the fear that enveloped him as the two creatures came toward him. Though there was light, they were still black shapes and of a hideous sort that he could not even describe. He scrambled to his feet and again saw that the coal shards had left no wounds.

"Back to work!" screamed the first beast and then let out the terrible shriek Nikos had heard before.

He covered his ears, but found himself yelling back in a tremulous voice, "I . . . I . . . don't belong here!"

"All belong here!" bellowed one of the creatures as it came up to him and struck him across the side of the head.

He reeled, but kept his feet as he added, "I . . . I . . . didn't do anything to deserve—"

But the other beast cried out, "Oh-ho! It's what you *didn't* do that sent you here! Now, back to work!"

Both the creatures came at Nikos, but he turned and quickly went toward the city. Soon, he was amongst the crowd of people, and the crying and moaning were worse than ever and pierced him to his very soul. The sense of pain and hopelessness he heard was beyond anything he had ever imagined. And the people looked strange, as if they were not as solid as real people. They seemed not to have any clothes on, but then they were not naked either. And every one of their faces was filled with different, but terrible levels of pain and anguish. They were all doing some kind of work, either carrying bricks in one direction or loads of broken bricks in the opposite direction. No one took any notice of Nikos, and he continued on through the city, desperate for water.

The terrible pain he heard all around him was overpowering, and the heat seemed to wrap around him like a heavy blanket. He made his way through the city and came to a place where the people were constructing a building and further on, he saw another one that was being knocked down. Eventually, Nikos stopped and sat down on a low brick wall, which was hot, but he was so overheated that he did not notice. People were carrying bricks to the new building and carrying away broken bricks from the demolished one. But they were doing so in great torment as they walked as gingerly as they could on the sharp chunks of coal. Cries of anguish and despair were constant. A tear rolled down Nikos's face, but his need for water was overwhelming him. He had seen nothing else but brick buildings and people. He saw some people mixing mortar and thought surely, they would have some water. He went nearer, but saw that they were using some vile smelling, thick black liquid and powdered coal.

Without any kind of forethought, Nikos blurted out, "Is there any water?"

There was a collective gasp as everyone froze and turned in his direction. Many of the groanings and expressions of misery increased and seemed to reverberate among the people.

"He . . . he said one of the words," moaned someone incredulously.

"No!" yelled a man, "there is nothing but this throbbing agony!"

"Can't you feel it?" called out another, who threw part of a brick at Nikos, which he was unready for, and it hit him square in the chest. He crashed back onto the road gasping for air and again feeling the sharp bite of the coal.

Another kicked him in the head and sneered, "Feel that?!"

"Always thirsty, never drinking!" cried a woman. "Always bleeding, never dying!"

Nikos staggered to his feet and suddenly locked eyes with a man in the midst of the throng.

"Kakos!" he said, "Is . . . is that really you?"

Nikos was so dry he could barely speak, and his head was throbbing. The man squinted at him and walked painfully across the coal, grimacing horribly with every step.

"Who are you?" he commanded in a voice with more pain in it than Nikos could imagine.

The man stood as lightly as he could, but his face was contorted and twisted in agony, as if it had been carved that way.

"I am Nikos . . ."

The man looked hard at him and then a look of recognition came over him. "You!" he yelled. "You're the one who sent me here! Years and years of this horrible misery! None of us deserves this . . . but you, you deserve it!"

He looked maniacally around at the people and screamed, "He murdered me!"

Kakos suddenly lunged at him, followed by many other people, though it cost them dearly to take such heavy steps on the coal. Nikos dodged them and wildly ran away, but to his surprise, no one followed except Kakos, who only made it a few steps before the intense agony of running brought him crashing to his knees. His cry of pain rent the air with such an acute rage that it sounded inhuman.

With a desperate gasp, he screamed, "I will find you!"

Nikos zigzagged his way among the buildings, but he hadn't gone far when he collapsed and dragged himself into a darkened doorway. He was weak and his head pounded terribly; he could do nothing but lie down.

Suddenly, he had a terrible thought: "There is no water here! She said, 'always thirsty, never drinking'"!

He cried out, "Oh, where am I? Is this even real?"

And then he nearly jumped out of his skin as a deathly voice wheezed, "Hiding again, are you?"

Then a black shape filled the doorway and grabbed Nikos around the neck, "Back you go!"

"No!" screamed Nikos. "Don't take me back there!" His absolute terror made his entire body quake, but he was helpless.

The beast had amazing strength and took him right back to the same people and shrieked, "Here he is! Now teach him what else you use bricks for!"

Then the beast threw him into the midst of the people, and they began throwing bricks at him from every side. Nikos had never known such pain. He closed his eyes tight and wrapped his arms around his head, screaming out in agony. Even though the people themselves were in great pain with every move they made, they were merciless. The moans, wailings, groans, and whimperings filled the air and increased in intensity until they reached a fevered pitch. Nikos couldn't comprehend such cold-bloodedness and as he cringed in a tight little ball, he peeked up at them, hoping for some kind of humanity, but there was only hate.

·——— *Eighteen* ———·

Kafar, *Barah, and the others arrived at the* crossroads in Praho, but Ruad had not arrived. They waited until well past midmorning; as the sun climbed higher, Odus said, "Looks like we're on our own. Of course, I know my way a bit from here. It's about twenty miles up to the pass, and the village of Keone is right there. Lots of those big Meganthropos, like that Commander Polus fellow, live up there."

They rode north, and the four southerners were awed by the sheer size of the mountains as they seemed to rise higher and higher the closer they came. As the road became steeper, it cut across at angles, and the land on either side began to rise into cliffs.

They went at a slow pace, and Eido rode up next to Chayel and said, "Miss Chayel—"

But she quickly interjected, "Eido," she began, a bit annoyed, "you've got to stop calling me 'miss' anything. It makes me feel like an old marm."

"Yes, ma'am—"

"And no 'ma'am' either! We're closer in age than we're not. Just call me Chayel, like an older sister."

"Well, I know how to do that, 'cause I got one," said Eido. "Lives up in Wildhorse Village with my uncle."

"You haven't spoken of her before."

"Well, I guess I shouldn't have talked about her now either." He paused until Chayel insisted that he continue.

"I kind of made up a story about my family before," he said. "My mother and father died when I was little, and we went to live with my uncle, but I ran away from there."

He suddenly stopped again and seemed to not want to say anymore, but then added apologetically, "Sorry I lied. That ain't being a man, is it . . . to lie?"

Chayel only looked at him thoughtfully as they rode on. It was evening by the time they reached the top of the pass and could see the lights of Keone twinkling in the distance. They turned off the road and made camp.

They all awoke early in the morning and as they packed up, Chayel asked Eido, "Where is this Wildhorse Village that you spoke of?"

"Well, I don't want to go there," answered Eido quickly. "But it is a fair bit past Keone. It's the last village in that part of the mountains; past that, it's just the wild."

They set off, but as they were passing the last mile up to the village, Odus slowly said with a bit of foreboding, "I don't recall there ever being a gate across the road . . . though I haven't been up here since way back."

As they approached it, Kafar said in a low voice, "It is Rhaka's men."

They could see that the gate was of new construction and that the soldiers who manned it were very much on their guard. There was a dozen at least, and the tension was high.

Before the travelers even reached the gate, one of the guards called out, "Who are you, and what is your business?"

They were quite unprepared to give an answer, but as they stopped at the gate, Eido bravely said, "We're goin' up to Wildhorse Village—"

"Where is that?" interrupted one of the guards, who along with the others, plainly hadn't heard of it before.

"Well, it's the last village on this road," answered Eido. "There aren't none past it."

The soldier, who was in charge seemed undecided about letting them pass, but then barked orders to four of the others, "See them well past Keone!"

After paying the toll, they were let in with two soldiers ahead and two behind escorting them. Chayel and Odus were especially chaffed at this, but their frequent glances at each other kept them calm. The town seemed sleepy and quiet, but right away all of them felt a tremendous sense of tension. Though there were some farms on the outskirts where men were busy with sheep or cows, the townsfolk watched them as they rode past, eyeing them with grim faces.

There were more soldiers than any of them had seen in the other villages, and they were keeping a very serious watch on things. As the travelers passed through, they began to see more and more of the Meganthropos, who seemed the most downcast of all. Eventually, they passed out of the village, but the soldiers continued escorting them, in front and behind. Chayel's frustration was rising, and Odus rode up next to her and squeezed her arm and gave her an admonishing look. They all felt angry at being treated so and just when Chayel felt she could contain her anger no longer, the soldiers reined their mounts around and headed back to Keone.

After they were well away, Arak said, "Something very bad has happened here."

"Worse than Rhaka just comin' in and taking over," added Odus.

"There was some fighting," said Kafar.

"And those buildings burned down," said Chayel.

"Maybe we should talk to some of the people," said Eido pulling his horse to a stop. "I mean there's nothin' up the way we're going."

But Chayel gave him an admonishing glance and asked, "Is that being a man, Eido?"

"What's she mean, boy?" asked Odus. "You said there's a village up this way, the last one on the road."

Eido was quite uncomfortable but after a few moments, forced out an answer, "Yes, it's where my uncle lives, where I lived until I ran away—"

"But you're from Ekuus," interrupted Odus, "where your mum and father live."

Then Eido gathered himself and set to explaining why he had made up a story about his family. He didn't say much about how his parents had died, but he described a lot about his uncle's temper.

"It didn't take much to set him ragin'," said Eido. "And when I got older and started needing to make decisions for myself, well, he couldn't abide that, and one day we came to blows. It wasn't smart to take him on, seein' he's a lot bigger than me and so, right in the thick of it, I just turned tail and ran. I've never been back."

Eido was still hesitant to continue, but the other four spurred their mounts, and he reluctantly went along.

"He's mostly right that there's nothing up this way," said Odus, "except for the village and after that, the mountains begin in earnest. I don't even know how far the road goes this way."

"We have few options," said Kafar, "but Ruad was convinced that Polus came up here. All we can do is search wherever we can."

They continued, and the road became steeper and narrower, with the mountains rising higher and higher. They eventually came up to another pass and were hemmed in by vertical cliffs on either side. As they began to descend, the cliffs on their left fell sharply and a bit further on, they dropped away altogether into a deep valley. Soon, there was a sheer drop on their left and cliffs that rose above them on their right.

The road was barely wide enough for two to go abreast, and so they went in single file. The view into the valley was stunning; beyond that, they could see range after range of gigantic mountains, many with jagged snow-covered peaks. Eventually, the road bent to the right and leveled out, passing into more even terrain but then, it quickly petered out. Beyond the field and the pine trees was all mountainous, wild and uninhabited.

"Where is the hope of finding *anything* here?" asked Arak a bit glumly.

They had all begun to have similar feelings, but Eido said, "Well, my uncle has lived up here his whole life. Wildhorse Village isn't far from here, though I sure don't want to be goin' there, but he could help us maybe." They continued and came into the pine trees and worked their way through them. After some time, they saw a small village in the distance.

As they neared it, Odus said, "I don't think they get folk comin' up here at all; they may not take kindly to strangers."

At that point, Eido suddenly felt quite useful and changed his mind about not wanting to go to the village.

"Well, I'm not a stranger," he said somewhat triumphantly. "Don't worry since you're with me!"

He took his horse to the front and took the lead, coming out into an open field, dotted with scrubby pine trees. But suddenly there appeared a dozen armed horsemen riding quickly to meet them.

"Stop!" yelled the man in the lead as the drew closer. "Who are you!" Eido saw that it was his uncle and suddenly wished that he had not put himself out in front.

"Answer!" commanded the man.

The group of horsemen had come close enough that a strong young blonde woman among them said, "Eido?"

His uncle's attention turned quickly to him, and dread of him had Eido wishing he could just disappear as Kafar rode forward.

"I am Kafar, and these are my companions," he said very formally. "We come in peace and seek only information—"

A young woman jumped from her horse, ran toward Eido, and pulled him down throwing him to the ground and pinning him down. She seemed quite angry, but tears ran down her face.

"Where have you been all this time?" she shouted heatedly.

Eido continued to be speechless as the woman got up, pulled him to his feet, and hugged him tightly. She said, "We have been so worried! And uncle was sick this winter. We needed you."

Eventually, Eido sputtered, "I . . . I'm sorry," as he kept an eye on his uncle, who had dismounted and was approaching him.

He expected to be clouted but was surprised by a rough and brief hug. "Glad you're still alive, boy," said his uncle, who then turned to Kafar and said, "I am Thumos, leader of this village. What do you seek?"

The tension had dissipated somewhat, and Kafar dismounted and came forward.

"Thank you for your favorable greeting," he said. "We seek a Meganthropos who has robbed us."

Thumos's brow knit together, and he considered Kafar's statement for a few minutes before speaking as he paced back and forth briefly. "A Meganthropos, you say?" he asked with skepticism. "I know them to be fiercely loyal and honest folk."

Kafar began, "We do not know them at all—"

Eido suddenly said, "Now uncle, I know the Meganthropos—*we* know them, up *here*, but I seen some of them do really bad things . . . down . . . down where I been, with these people."

Thumos relaxed ever so slightly, and the young woman who stood by him said, "Uncle, you remember—"

He seemed to know what she was going to say, and he relented even a bit more and said to Kafar and the others, "Tell me, what does this one who robbed you look like?"

"Well, they all look very much the same to me," answered Kafar.

"He is smaller than most," added Chayel, "and he would have an ugly scar on his chest."

"And I expect that his right-hand man would be another Megan," said Odus. "At least two feet taller, black hair that hangs down like ropes, and a terrible scar gashed down the side of his face."

Thumos could not hide a look of recognition and quickly said, "We must talk of this."

He swung up onto his horse and led them into the village, though it did not amount to much. But there were quite a few homesteads and farms and about fifty villagers in a very close-knit community.

"We get few people coming here," said Thumos as they rode, "and we rarely leave, so we have little knowledge of what goes on to the south."

He gave some kind of signal to the villagers that all was well and then led them to his homestead. He commanded Eido to take care of their horses and as he was about to object, Chayel quickly said, "I will help him."

Soon, they were gathered around a firepit, seated on logs.

"You came through Keone," began Thumos. "You see that there are soldiers there now." He paused and then spoke to the young woman, his niece, whose name was Keraia. "Tell them what you saw."

"Three days ago, I was in Keone, and all was as usual when suddenly this band of Meganthropos, about thirty of them, came in from the north and hid themselves all throughout the town. Then an army comes up to Keone from the south and tells the town leaders that they are going to rule the town now. Suddenly, it got very dangerous, and I climbed far up into a tree.

"Without warning, the band of Megans burst out and attacked the soldiers, and there was a bloody battle. Lots of the townsfolk joined in, but many were killed, and the army overcame all of them. The Meganthropos men fled north and then down into the valley to the west. The soldiers chased them to the edge of the valley, but it was too steep and rocky for the horses, so the Megans all got away. Their leader was what you described, and the bigger one, with long black hair, was right there with him."

There was a brief silence, and then she added, "But the way they were fighting was brutal. They weren't fighting just to defend the town, they were vicious, savage, not like any Megans I've ever known."

Thumos shook his head and said, "There is a city called Megalos to the west, in the mountains where the Meganthropos are from. They are a people who came from giants and humans and are rejected by the giants and by most people. We have had many dealings with them, and they are anything but what Keraia saw. They are kind and gentle, though they will fight to defend their own. It is unexplainable that any Meganthropos would do the things that Keraia saw them do."

They continued their conversation, and Thumos and Keraia learned of Polus's attack on Tachus Town and of all the evil that Rhaka had been doing and his dictatorship. Thumos sat very thoughtfully and then looked carefully and intently at the others, especially Kafar.

"There is much that you do not tell me," he said. "Indeed, your business is your own, just as mine is my own. Still, there is something unnatural in all this." He paused, plainly hopeful that Kafar would offer up more information.

Kafar looked at his companions and after a few moments said, "There is an evil that has been awakened in the world, and we are fighting against it. This unnatural wickedness will only increase so long as what was stolen from us is in the hands of the enemy."

Thumos looked intrigued and said, "Do you mean that this thing that was stolen is the explanation for the wickedness of those Meganthropos?"

Kafar nodded, "Well, it has aroused wickedness and empowers it."

They were all a bit surprised at Thumos's interest and openness as he continued, "I must know more. To know a race of people for my whole life and then to see some of them behave in ways that are in such conflict with their nature, I could not believe it and yet it is true. You must tell me what this is."

Kafar and his friends then went on to tell him and Keraia of Kah-Taw and how everyone is born with its curse. He listened intently and the more he heard, the more relieved he looked, and though the topic was serious, he suddenly laughed and gestured toward Eido and said, "So, you are not to blame for your disrespect of me! It is this curse that goads you to it!"

But even before he finished speaking, his face fell to a grave countenance, and he continued, "I do not make light of this Kah-Taw. You have made clear to me much that I have been perplexed by. I do not doubt a word of it. I have felt many of the things you have described, even this Great One you speak of. I have always sensed that there are more and greater things than what we see. But I must tell you, though I fear few things, I fear what the curse of Kah-Taw can become in people. If what Keraia saw those Meganthropos do in Keone is only the beginning, if this evil is growing, how do we fight such a thing?"

"We must disarm it," said Chayel unexpectedly. "The King can take away its power to do evil by turning people to the way that is right, so they must admit that they have the curse and are on the side of evil . . . but most—"

"Well, I believe it," said Thumos quickly. "I surely have felt this evil in myself." A look of recognition came over his face, and he added, "Indeed, I *do* believe! I've longed my whole life for something, and now I know it is this. Somehow, I now know what true, real life is and what a sense of freedom . . ."

Keraia wholeheartedly believed as well, and then Thumos looked at Eido and said, "Do you believe this?"

Eido was taken aback and did not know what to say, but Chayel said, "We all must come to our own conclusions and in our own time."

Thumos seemed like a new man and became very introspective for some time. He then said to Eido, "I am sorry; I regret treating you unfairly, sorry for making it so difficult for you to become the fine young man that I see you have become."

Eido was rendered quite speechless, and Keraia herself was stunned and said, "You . . . you have never apologized for anything; how can this be?"

Arak answered, "The curse also keeps people from doing the good they know they ought to do. Thumos is free now to do the good that his heart tells him to."

It is like the difference between life and death," she said.

"Because it is," said Arak.

She and Thumos wanted to know everything there was to know about the Great One and the curse, and they talked on and on. Soon evening was falling, and Thumos got a fire going while Chayel and Keraia worked together to butcher a pig and get a meal together. Because of their new bond as People of the Great One, they had quickly come to trust each other, and they shared about the Book and all about their homeland.

After dinner, Keraia said, "Eido, he is not here."

No one could remember when they saw him last, but Odus said, "Could be he's not liking this—you two suddenly believin' as you do. When I came to believed it, my friend Chawk seemed to start hatin' me."

The sun had gone down and with the fire burning brightly everything else around them was pitch black.

"I thought it such a good thing that Polus had stolen the Book out of the fortress," said Chayel. "At least we knew where it was then. Now . . ." she trailed off.

Arak said in quite a discouraged tone, "Yes, this country, it will be enough just to travel through it, but how can we hope to search for Polus here? Even if we find him, we cannot hope to wrest the Book from him."

No one responded for a few moments until Barah said, "We could make for the city of Megalos. If the Meganthropos people are as kind as Thumos says, they would help us."

"But they would be loyal their own," said Arak.

"Again, we have few options," said Kafar.

Odus cut in, "You know, I'm thinkin'. . . this Polus brute's got a lot of hate in him and also a lot of pride and if he got soundly defeated by Rhaka, he's going to want revenge. Maybe even dethrone Rhaka and take his place."

"But he only had a hundred of the Megans with him," said Barah. "He can do little to Rhaka with so few."

There was another silence, and then Odus said, "Maybe he's gone to Megalos himself to wrangle up a bunch more. As Thumos said, they are a loyal folk, and when they hear that Rhaka killed many of their own in Keone . . . well, who knows what they might do."

"Indeed," said Thumos, "They may be a gentle people, and they will take revenge for their own, but it is worrisome. I dearly wish to see no more Megans corrupted like some have been. We must fight to stop this evil from spreading."

In the end, they decided to head back south to Makran and wait for Polus; they believed he would inevitably return and mount an attack against Rhaka and the fortress. In the morning, they awoke to find Eido had returned and was preparing breakfast for them.

He was quite apologetic and said, "I am sorry that I ran off again last night. It felt like all of you were against me; all that you talked about, I don't . . . I can't believe as you do."

"Well, we are glad you are here now," said Chayel.

He looked at her sheepishly and then addressed his uncle, "I will stay here now. I know I am responsible to you and Keraia and all of us in Wildhorse Village. We must stay together and stay strong against these things that are happening."

After a breakfast as plentiful as Thumos could provide, they packed up and he said, "I hope you find the Book, but I must stay here and lead these people."

"And we must tell them of the curse and the Great One," added Keraia.

"That is the most you can do to overcome this evil," said Barah.

"Indeed," said Thumos. "We will keep a watchful eye for this Polus."

"Send word to Marshal Kainos in Tachus Town if there is any word to be sent," said Kafar.

"We are with you in our hearts," added Keraia.

They galloped off, and came down Wildhorse Pass into Keone, enduring the same ill treatment from Rhaka's soldiers as before.

After going five or six miles on the other side, Odus said, "I have a friend in Karpone who could be a great help to us. We could stay with him and keep watch for Polus and his lot. There is only one way down out of these mountains into Makran, and it passes right through Karpone."

"Unless Polus goes through the mountains," said Chayel, "and comes at Makran directly north of it."

"But the sheer cliffs that surround the whole city . . ." began Arak.

"We will just have to keep watch," said Kafar, "and hope for news from Ruad."

Barah nodded and said, "Indeed, he is our eyes and ears inside the fortress."

Nineteen

Meanwhile, after Polus's defeat at Keone, he and his men retreated to a stronghold in the mountains called the Rift. It was situated in a valley and was about eighty feet deep and one hundred feet long with sheer vertical walls. At the northern end, there was a series of caves where the valley closed up into the mountains beyond. There were old stone dwellings, and a freshwater creek ran through it; the entrance at the southern end was fortified with a wall and a gate.

"Uke is dead," said Polus in a very subdued tone. "And mum . . ."

The others stood about very solemnly and thought of some of their own whom they had also lost. "Rhaka will lose his life for this," seethed Polus. "Because I will take it from him!"

A yell of agreement went up from his men, and they began chanting something until Polus raised his hand. Though he was by far, the smallest among his men, he was the most intelligent and was greatly respected by all of them, especially Teras, whose loyalty was beyond question.

"Sir," he said, "we must go to Megalos. Many of our brothers were killed in Keone, and those in Megalos must be told."

Polus slowly nodded and said very coolly, "Yes, we must have justice, and they will join us."

"They will need to be trained to fight," said Megar, an older and distinguished Meganthropos who was Polus's second-in-command and very experienced in the strategies of war.

"Yes," said Polus after a pause, seeming to have been lost in thought. Then he said, "Yes, you must teach them."

"It will take some time," replied Megar.

"Revenge will be all the sweeter," sneered Teras.

"And you must teach them all you know of this Book," said Polus, patting a pack that was strapped to his belt.

"Indeed," said Megar with a fiendish smile. "Its deadly power can make even the least skilled soldier a lethal warrior."

"So, let us go," said Teras.

But Polus said, "I will leave that to Megar. My blood is hot for revenge, and it is long enough that I have not taken it upon one who thoroughly deserves it. All of you go to Megalos. Gather an army as large as you can and make a camp here at the Rift, and I will return in no more than two weeks' time."

Polus quickly turned to Teras and said, "You will go with me as well as Oxos and Onos." Polus quickly headed south with Teras and the two others, who were brothers and nearly as large as Teras.

"You know these mountains," Polus said to Teras. "Take us through them and so down past Makran, and then we must continue south."

Teras set off without a question and as they had great endurance, they went at a steady and relatively fast pace for hours and hours. As night fell, they were deep in the mountains when they stopped to make camp. In the morning, they set off again and by midday, they had come over another range of mountains to see the city of Makran below them.

"He will pay," said Polus rather to himself and full of hatred. "But first we must go west around the city and then continue south, keeping to the mountains."

But Teras's knowledge of the terrain did not go much past Makran and with the sun high overhead, they had to wait for it to begin going down to have a better sense of direction.

They traveled south for another day and then came down out of the mountains to the northern edge of Fragmoo Forest. They passed quickly through it and could see that the land beyond was fairly open country.

"We must wait for night," said Polus. As they waited, Polus talked to Teras, telling him where they were going as the others foraged for food. They brought back enough for all, including a small wild pig. After they had roasted it and finished eating, Teras apprised the others of the plan. Once darkness had fallen, they set out. They passed through a marsh and then followed a creek that flowed south out of it. In the distance they saw the moonlight dancing on a large lake and upon reaching it, they turned to the right and followed the river. The lands about were dark and silent, and the four men moved quietly through them. A forest loomed up on their right and after moving along it for a while, Polus suddenly threw up his hand, and they all stopped.

Until then, nothing had looked familiar, but right in front of him, he saw the place where, the summer before, he had crossed the Bradus River on his rampage to get the chief. He was immediately filled with many different emotions as he thought about how long ago that seemed and how different he was now. Disgust filled him as he realized how weak and childlike he had been. The years of loneliness came back to him, and then it was as if Makarios was standing right in front of him. Feelings of affection welled up in him and then a sense of abandonment by her as he remembered being left in the chief's jail and then carted away. Fury began to rise when he was jolted out of his memories.

"Commander?" said Teras.

Polus's anger turned into thoughts of revenge. He quickly calmed down and said, "We are close. We must cross the river and find a good vantage point where we can watch the town and then wait for daybreak."

Across the river they found enough vegetation and trees to conceal themselves and bedded down. But Polus lay awake late into the night, imagining the vengeance he would exact on the chief, and he savored every detail. When the sun had risen enough to give some light, Polus took the Book out, woke the others and read some. The effect was immediate, as the words filled them with wicked intent.

"We must watch the marshal's building to see who is there and when," said Polus very quietly. "We want to catch the deputy by himself." So, they watched and waited patiently for the next few days, and saw that Deputy Spoggos always arrived by midmorning, and the chief never arrived before noon.

As the sun set, Polus read certain parts of the Book to them again, as he had done each night. They seemed to live on those words as they had not eaten for the last few days, and they were filled with an energy for what they would do the next day.

Before sunrise, they all crept off toward the town. No one was yet stirring, though in some nearby farms there were a few roosters making themselves known. The four giant men went almost silently as their huge, bare feet padded every step. Polus quickly found his way to the building and went down an unused alleyway next to it and stopped at a high iron gate. They all crouched down in the dim light amongst old barrels and broken crates.

Polus said almost in a whisper, "Over this gate we get to the back door of this building. When we hear the deputy come in, we will knock on the door. He is proud but stupid and impatient and will come and unlock the door to see who is there."

Soon, they began to hear noises in the town and shops opening up, but they waited and waited for any sound from the marshal's building. They began to get agitated, and it was all Polus could do to remain calm and quiet as a seething anticipation simmered within. They felt the time moving quite slowly and after nearly an hour, Oxos and Onos, feeling the most cramped began shifting about and then into each other, which got them annoyed. One of them grabbed the other, but Polus cuffed both of them, and they immediately settled down. Suddenly, there was a noise of a key in a lock and then the slamming of a door. Polus checked to see that there was no one in the courtyard and then they went easily up and over the gate. Polus knocked on the door, grinning like a child playing a prank. The others were wickedly gleeful as well.

"Who is it this *early?*" yelled a man inside. "And at the *back* door! Go to the front!"

Polus nodded his head and whispered, "That is the deputy." He knocked again only a little louder.

"The *front* door!" yelled the man inside.

After another rap by Polus, they heard the man coming nearer and as he got to the door, he said, "If this is you same boys as last time, and since I'm in a good mood, if you all just—"

At that moment Polus banged on the door, and the man suddenly flung it open and was about to yell something when his jaw went slack, and he turned white as a ghost. The four men barged in, ducking through the door. Teras took the man by the throat while Polus went and locked the front door. The building was far too low for any of them except Polus to stand up in, so they had to squat down or go on one knee. Deputy Spoggos looked like he was going to pass out, and Polus signaled Teras to let him go. He fell in a heap on the floor gasping and sputtering and looking around wild-eyed at them all.

As his eyes fell on Polus, he squeaked, "You!" He shuffled backward until his back was against the desk, "You . . . you're dead! The chief said you got rightly killed trying to escape when you flipped the prison wagon into a ravine!"

"Death is justice for breaking a few bricks?" bristled Teras, which shut Spoggos's mouth like a trap as he wildly looked between them all.

Polus paced about and smacked his fist into his palm with a crack.

"I heard what he told the soldiers," began Polus with a sneer of the lip, "after they put me in the iron wagon! He told them that after they got halfway to the Outpost to strangle me to death and then drive the wagon into the Tachus ravine as if *I* did it trying to escape!"

"Now, now," sputtered Spoggos, scrambling up behind the desk to the chair. "I . . . I didn't say as I agreed with him. I mean I got to do what he says . . . you know he's the chief, but now I see he wasn't bein' fair . . . I mean *you're* fair, and now maybe it's the chief who ought to have something comin' to him?"

Spoggos's expression was still one of terror, but also a certain hopeful expectation. Polus suddenly grinned and then unexpectedly laughed and leaned over the desk at Spoggos, who clenched his eyes shut and flung his head to the side, expecting the worst. But all he felt was a heavy thump of Polus's thick finger against his chest.

"You are not so stupid as you seem," said Polus.

Spoggos peered out of one eye at him and spluttered, "Loyal I am, but now I see I been loyal to the wrong man—a man who is unjust and that ain't right, but you . . . you want justice and, and that's fair!"

Polus stood back, his frizzy hair just grazing the ceiling beams as he eyed Spoggos carefully. He sat up a bit straighter in the chair and after a few moments, straightened some papers on the desk.

He relaxed ever so slightly and said, "Now, I can help you with justice, Mister Polus, sir. What is it that the chief is—"

Suddenly, Polus's anger surged as if he had tired of Spoggos's little drama.

"He will die!" he thundered but then immediately lowered his voice. "Now we will wait for him, and then he will pay."

Polus went and sat against the front wall brooding in a very disturbing way.

Eventually, Spoggos said cautiously, "Mister Polus, sir. If you don't mind my askin' . . ." and then paused as Polus merely looked at him, though with quite a malicious expression.

Spoggos continued, "Well, you sure are different than before . . ."

But before Polus could reply, there was a sound outside, and the door began to open.

"Good morning, chief, sir," said Spoggos with amazing composure.

"You're quite early today!"

"Yes, yes," replied the chief slamming the door with his eyes on his satchel and grabbing at some papers that were falling out.

He went to the desk and bellowed, "Now, get out. I've got some special business to attend to and visitors coming by noon!"

Spoggos moved out from behind the desk and as the chief turned to sit, he fell back into the chair in shock as he beheld Polus standing at his full height in front of the door, which he had just barred, and the others stood behind him.

As the chief was fatter than ever, the chair tipped backward, and he fell heavily to the floor. His face turned red, and perspiration began beading on his forehead as he became hysterical with fear. He was in a lot of pain from the fall and couldn't seem to get up from floor. He heaved and grunted and became more desperate, looking wild-eyed at Polus, who hadn't moved but seemed to enjoy the chief's distress.

"Sp . . . Spoggos!" he suddenly squealed. "Do some . . . get him!"

But Spoggos, who had come to understand that Polus did have some code of justice and meant no harm to him said, "He came to see *you*, chief."

The chief's eyes darted to Polus and after managing to at least sit up, he said, "You . . . I saw to it myself that—"

Polus suddenly crossed the room and, leaning over the desk, said in a very quiet, but intense and deadly tone, "That I was put to death unjustly?"

The chief was now whimpering in mortal fear and seemed to be begging for his life, though his words made little sense.

"Enough!" hissed Polus in a disgusted tone as he flipped the desk out of the way. "You are repulsive, fat and helpless; you are hardly worth killing!"

He grabbed the chief by the throat and lifted him up as easy as a sack of potatoes and threw him down on a heavy wooden bench on the other side of the room. By now the chief was beside himself, moaning in pain and crying like a terrified child. Blood ran down the side of his face from a wound on his head. As he wiped his tears away, he smeared blood all over himself and as he saw it, his hysterics increased. Soon, he couldn't catch his breath, and he began gasping, becoming redder and redder in the face.

Suddenly, he clutched his chest and lurched to his feet, reaching out with his other hand and then fell quite hard face down. He was so still and silent that it was plain to see that he was dead.

"No!" thundered Polus. "This . . . this is not justice!"

Spoggos stood silently by, feeling a little bit in danger.

Polus turned on him, and he shrank back against the wall and stammered, "Now, Mister Polus, sir, remember . . . remember that you're the fair one, and I, well I ain't done—"

Polus suddenly turned away, still in a rage, but mainly one of frustration. He paced about for a few minutes and then looked down at the chief and shook his head.

Spoggos watched him carefully and then slowly said, "Well, now this might just work out, you know . . . I can say that the chief fell and hit his head, which is true enough and then—"

But Polus was clenching and unclenching his hands and then gave Spoggos such a deadly look that he immediately became silent. Polus shook his head and motioned to the others, and they went out the back of the building. They all quickly made their way out of town, down alleys and behind buildings until they came down to the Bradus River, over which they had crossed days before. There was a bridge a fair distance to their left, and many people were crossing back and forth as it was now almost noon. Polus came to a stop, strangely subdued and at a loss, feeling almost sad, but then as he felt how he had been robbed of the sweet satisfaction of killing the chief, rage filled him.

"Go back to the Rift," he said to Teras and the others. "I will see you there . . ."

Teras hesitated, but Polus shot him a look that quickly sent him and the other two on their way. Polus headed toward the bridge, lost in a world of his own. His appearance caused most to give him a wide berth, not only because he was so big and muscular, but also because he wore no shirt or shoes and carried a rather savage looking knife on his belt.

But he paid no attention to anyone and just continued down the road, which eventually entered Geroon Forest. He had lost enthusiasm for everything and felt quite alone as he walked along. After going a few miles, he realized that he was near to his old house, the place where he had lived by himself for so long. He soon arrived there and was filled with a sense of being home more than he had ever felt when he lived there. He had not felt such freedom and happiness in a long time. The sun blazed overhead in the clearing as he descended the bank down to his house and he found it just as he had left it. When his attention turned to the shed where he kept all the things that he carved, he stopped dead in his tracks. He remembered the scene when he had been standing there with Makarios, showing her the things he had made. And how, when Nikos asked for soap, he had got into a rage against those who had treated him so badly when he lived in Diaggello. The worst thought of all brought him to his knees and caused the tears to fall as he thought of how in his blind rage, he had almost brought his fist down upon Makarios. He was overwhelmed with remorse and felt exactly as he had that very day.

Unexpectedly, he heard himself saying, "Polus was bad . . . bad," and he felt a deep longing to see Makarios, and he felt that strange tugging in his chest.

He was wholly caught up in the flashback until he thought to himself, *"I will go find her,"* but as he referred to himself as "I," he was shaken out of his memories and overwhelmed with disgust at how he had been thinking and feeling.

Then he yelled, "I hated you! You accepted everything and were a fool, a child! You were so weak, uncontrolled as water, letting love consume you! And then she just left you, like everyone else! Indeed, I will find her . . ."

He took off down the path, yelling, "So weak you were! You never fought back! You just let them take you!"

His rage was at a fever pitch, hating who he used to be and all the ways he had felt. It was especially the love for Makarios that pained him because he remembered how good love had felt, but now he hated it. Still, he thought about her more and more, and though he tried to deny it and then ignore it, his love for her was still there. He began to feel such a great conflict between good and evil that his mind reeled, and he stumbled and fell.

He got to his hands and knees, breathing heavily, but felt the fight within beyond his grasp. One side cried out for good, to embrace love again, to feel the goodness of it and the safety and satisfaction, while the other side screamed for vengeance and insisted that hate was better than love. How long Polus struggled, he did not know, but eventually, he became exhausted and fell asleep right where he was, unaware of which side had won the fight.

When Polus awoke, he had no idea where he was or what had happened. It was dark, and he could see the moon overhead through the towering pine trees. He sat up and found that he had been sleeping on a dirt path. As his eyes adjusted to the light, he saw the forest around him as familiar and then suddenly everything came back to him. He got to his feet, but he felt wrung out and unsteady, as if he had fought wild beasts all night long. He turned toward his house with his body aching and his emotions so subdued that he hardly felt anything. He spent the night on his old, fur-covered bed, but awoke early the next morning still exhausted and also very, very hungry. As he looked around his house, he found that nothing edible had survived the winter months. He headed down the path toward the pond, remembering how peaceful it had been. But now it only reminded him of the person he used to be, and he hated it. He wanted to get back to his people, hoping to feel more like himself and leave his old self behind. He quickened his pace and soon arrived at the pond, taking a quick wash before going on. As he went, Polus thought of the chief and saw his bloody body lying there on the floor of the marshal's building. It stung him, that his revenge had been stolen. It was a disappointment that he could do nothing about, and it only served to increase his violent mood.

It was midmorning by the time Polus came out of Geroon Forest at the southern end near the Bradus River. Suddenly, he realized that he ought to have been going in the opposite direction if he was to Teras and the others at the Rift. He stood there for a while, still a bit disoriented. Without a real reason, he set off for Diaggello, but as he came into town, people stared, and some pointed at him; most gave him a wide berth.

Suddenly, someone yelled out, "That's him!" as another screamed,

"The one who kilt the chief!" People scrambled for doorways and ducked behind buildings, while others called out for the marshal. Polus was so surprised that he stopped and looked every which way, trying to see everyone at once.

"Now, what's all this commotion?" called a man who was coming Polus's way, but there was now little commotion as the main street had cleared. Polus's eyes locked on the man coming toward him. It was Spoggos, who was the new marshal, but as soon as he saw Polus, he froze in his tracks.

"You!" bellowed Polus, but Spoggos turned and ran faster than even he thought he could back to the marshal's building and got inside, barring the door just as Polus got there.

"Now Mister Polus, sir," sputtered Spoggos through the door, "I told 'em all that the Chief died by his temperament, that he 'bout frenzied himself to death—"

Suddenly, Polus pounded on the door and yelled in a rage, and then Spoggos did the last thing even he expected; he opened the door. Polus was so startled that he was speechless and didn't even move, but Spoggos grabbed his wrist and tugged on him to come inside. After ducking through the doorway, Polus looked incredulously at Spoggos, who was again locking the door.

"Now, Mister Polus," began Spoggos heading to his desk and sitting down, "you can kill me if it suits you, but you're a fair man, and you must believe that I told them the truth. I don't know who saw you comin' out of the building the other day, but when the town found out that the chief was dead, they all took to blaming you. Now I don't doubt that at this very moment, someone's gone to the barracks to get Captain Stagos—you just best get out of town."

Polus was so shaken and incredulous of Spoggos's actions that he did as he said, making his way through back alleys to the east side of the town.

As he came into open country, he suddenly heard galloping hooves behind him and a man yelling, "Get him!"

Polus bolted, running as fast as he could, which nearly matched the speed of the horses, of which there were at least two dozen mounted with the best soldiers that Captain Stagos had. Polus saw taller grass to his right, which turned into rougher country with bunches of green alder trees and birches further on. He made for these with all his might, but the horses were gaining on him. He dodged through the bushes and then got in amongst some trees, which slowed the horses down, but then uneven ground slowed them even more. Polus rushed on, but then without warning, he found himself hurtling over a very steep embankment. He tumbled some twenty feet, crashing at the bottom, but immediately jumped to his feet and looked to see the horsemen stopped at the top of the ridge.

"You *will* be brought to justice!" called Captain Stagos.

"You will regret trying to punish the innocent!" called Polus as he kept going.

He ran as if he were still being chased, not knowing whether the soldiers had found a way down. Eventually, he turned a bit to the east, hoping to circle around his pursuers and turn north, but it wasn't long before he got lost. With the sun climbing overhead, he had no sense of direction, but kept going, still fearing he would be caught. Soon, the land began to even out and open up into fields and then a few farms came into view. As the day wore on, he could see that he had been going mostly south.

He stopped and took cover and listened intently, but after many minutes he was convinced that he had eluded Stagos and his men. Now, his bruises and abrasions took his attention, but what was most evident to him was how hungry he was. After all his exertion, he was shaky and weak and began to feel forlorn and to wander somewhat aimlessly. After a good long while, he came near a farm, but kept out of sight, hunkered down flat on his stomach amongst some bushes near a corral. He saw a middle-aged man and woman doing chores and packing a wagon. Polus lay there, but his attention began to wander, and weariness overtook him.

Polus was suddenly jarred wide awake out of his slumber by a voice. The sun had nearly set as he peered carefully through the bushes.

"Yes, Miss Maka, weh will go soon in the mohnen, when the sun comes up," said the middle-aged woman.

"Very well then. I will see you in a week or so. Good night!"

Her voice electrified Polus to his very soul, and all he wanted to do was run to her and gather her up in his arms.

"Makarios . . ." he whispered in a soft voice that was very much like his old self.

He was mesmerized and took no thought to himself whatsoever as a love that he hadn't felt for a long time enveloped him. With the darkness, all he saw of her was her silhouette in the lighted doorway of her house. As she went inside and closed the door, Polus felt beside himself with longing and desperation to see her, to be near her. He quickly got up and moved silently around the edge of the farm and came up to the right side of the house. He paused, suddenly feeling anxiety and fear and uncertainty about what to do. As he stood there, his eyes naturally fell upon the warm square of lamplight on the ground and then up to the window from which it came. He stepped back to be sure the night shrouded him and looked in. His heart leaped within him as he saw Makarios sitting at a long wooden table next to an oil lamp writing on a parchment. He was transfixed and stood there for as long as she sat there. If he had thought of himself for even a moment, he would have realized how perfectly at peace and content he felt. When she got up and went out of sight, it felt like somebody clapped Polus on the back of his head. He shied away and spun around, but there was no one there.

Suddenly, an unearthly voice, which sent shivers down his spine, wheezed, "Remember who you are, fool!"

An icy, putrid wind seemed to pass right through him as he brandished his knife and called out, "Who are you?!"

A moment later, the door of the house opened and Makarios said, "Is there someone there?"

Polus breathed in sharply, and Makarios looked his way, though the darkness hid him. She listened carefully and was about to close the door when Polus, who was quite disoriented and now not even feeling like either of his selves, said, "Wait!"

His mind sought furiously for equilibrium and somehow in an instant, leveled back out to the man he had become. His first thought was vengeance, that she must pay for abandoning him. He stepped forward into the light of the doorway.

Makarios started back, but then said with astonishment, "P . . . Polus?"

"Polus is lost," he said plaintively and then held out his arm, "and hurt . . ."

He rolled his big eyes up at her and then came up the few stairs there were to the porch. She quickly came forward and took his hand.

"What happened? How have you come to be here? Nikos said—"

She suddenly doubted what Nikos had said, that Polus was a commander in Rhaka's army and thought he must have been mistaken.

"Please come in!" she said.

"And hungry. Polus is very hungry," he added with a cruel smile that she did not see.

"Now here," she said, "sit down, and I will clean those wounds."

As she when off to get soap and water, Polus felt a twinge of remorse, not only for having fooled her so far, but for the wicked intent he had. He began to have second thoughts, but suddenly there was again a chill foul air around him, and it felt like bony claws locked onto his neck. He tried spinning around, but he was overpowered and though he tried to call out, his wind was choked off.

"You *will* do justice to her, fool!" hissed the same voice as before, but this time with such rank maliciousness that it removed every trace of remorse or doubt in Polus. The grip on his neck was so tight that he could barely move, but he nodded in affirmation the best he could. Suddenly, he was released and as Makarios returned, he gasped mightily.

"Oh!" she exclaimed, "What . . . are you alright?"

Polus was bent over a bit, but once he got his wind back, he said very softly and sadly, "Polus got so afraid that you might leave him again that he couldn't breathe."

"Now, Polus, that will never happen. I couldn't help how things went before. I did all I could."

As she got to work cleaning him up and bandaging him, he said, "Polus is really hungry."

"Yes, but where have you come from? What happened last summer when they took you away?"

Suddenly, he was seeing the whole scene again, being paraded through town like a caged animal, with people laughing and jeering and then later on near the river, when the soldiers had tried to kill him by tightening the strangle chain.

He filled with so much rage that Makarios said, "Oh, you feel warm. Are you well?"

Their eyes met, and his expression caused her to cry out in fear and jump backward, spilling the bucket and falling over a chair. He stood up, and such a maniacal scowl had come across his face that she was rendered speechless. She struggled to her feet and tried to run, but the fear was so great that she had no strength.

She stared at Polus in wide-eyed disbelief and finally forced out a few words, "What . . . has happened to you?"

Polus relished the moment as she continued in great fear, collapsing into a chair near the wall. He grinned and sat down again at the table and looked across at her.

"Bring me some food," he said, but when she didn't move, he yelled, "*Now!*"

This jolted her out of her chair, and she stumbled into the kitchen, gathering some cheese and bread and a smoked ham. She looked wildly about and nearly ran right out the back door when Polus bellowed again, "*Now!*"

She rushed out with what she had and put it in front of him, backing away across the room to the chair. He ate like an animal and was finished in minutes.

"Now, how about a drink?" he said, almost sounding cordial. Makarios got to her feet and said, "I . . . I have mead . . ." as her eyes welled up with tears.

"Bring it!" he commanded, and she quickly brought a large jug full of strong mead.

As she set it before him, he suddenly grabbed her wrist and she instinctively pulled away, but his grip tightened like an iron vice. She cried out in pain and fell to one knee beside him and then he roughly pushed her away, causing her to sprawl on the floor. He then took up the jug and gulped down some of the mead.

"Oh, that is good!" he said as he eyed her getting to her feet. "And you . . . I thought the same about you until you abandoned me to that chief!"

"I couldn't—"

But Polus bellowed over her, "I thought you cared about me!" and then laughed maniacally shaking his head. "It's all meaningless! Pathetic! Love and forgiveness, faugh! It mocks the truth!"

He downed more mead as he continued, "It's contemptible . . . forgiveness! Forgiveness is unjust and only for fools!"

Makarios was on the far side of the room and fighting to keep her wits about her, but panic was clawing itself closer.

"And you!" he continued. "You said I should *forgive* the chief! Surely you jested! He deserved death and that is what he got!"

Makarios looked incredulous and said, "You . . . killed the chief?"

"I wished to," said Polus bitterly. "Every living part of me yearned for it, but he died right in front of me and robbed me of the pleasure!"

He stood up and looked sharply at Makarios, "I will not be robbed of justice again!"

She cringed against the wall as panic gagged her to silence, but suddenly Polus stopped short and asked quizzically, "But is death really justice . . . for you?"

He sat down on the bench with the table behind him, facing Makarios, and finished the jug of mead.

"You left me to die . . . that's what you did . . . in that hole" he said thoughtfully. "Should you not be left to die as well?"

Makarios, who was holding onto the chair beside her to keep from crumpling to the floor, began mechanically shaking her head and asked, "What has *happened* to you?"

"*Happened*?!" he roared springing to his feet and pounding his chest. "I'm not a *fool* anymore!"

"But you're so . . . different, so . . . *evil* . . ." she trailed off.

"Evil? That is wisdom!" he said with much condescension. "But to be good, to *love*, to be at the mercy of another . . . that is folly, madness!"

He scowled and suddenly crossed the room, grabbing Makarios by her shoulders.

"I will only do to you what you did to me," he began. "Since you meant for me to die—"

She was limp in his grasp and as he looked down at her, she said forlornly, "Polus, how . . . how can you be this way?"

"*Enough*!" he bellowed. "Do you see what mercy would do? Pervert justice . . . but now you will pay!"

Eventually, Polus emerged from the house, but found himself in great turmoil. He crossed the farmyard and started up the cart path, feeling that what he had just done was wrong, but also that it was justice. He was divided within himself and began to feel weak, unstable, and anxious. He walked faster, silently screaming in his mind that he was in the right, but his feelings intensified. He began to run until he was at full speed, but his emotions were like a tornado within. In the dark, he could barely see where he was going and in his furious attempt to escape himself, he stumbled headlong into a ditch, and all went black.

"Fella!" came a voice. "Hey! You alright?"

Polus felt himself being nudged and as the grogginess cleared, he suddenly came to full consciousness and leaped to his feet. It was early morning, and as he looked wildly about his eyes fixed onto an old farmer who had sprawled backward into the road.

"Guess you're OK there," he said as he got stiffly to his feet.

Polus scowled, but then feigned some civility. "I must go to Makran," he said. "Tell me the way."

The old man puzzled for a moment, "That's north," he said pointing. "That way. This here's the Eastway Road, follows right along the Bradus River and if you go east some, you'll come to a ferry and a river comin' down from—"

Polus listened to no more and set off at a quick pace. As the day was waking up, there were more and more people on the road and as he reached the ferry, he found it very busy. He continued down the road instead, still fighting opposing feelings and filled with hatred and anger.

As he came into a less populated area, he turned left off the road and plunged into the river. Halfway across, something seemed to grab his leg and pull him under. He struggled furiously, but the water closed over his head, and all went still and silent. He could see nothing, and the cool water suddenly went ice cold.

"You *have* done justice to her!" came a voice that was indescribably wicked. "Stop fighting yourself! You have done what is right! Listen only to *me!*"

The crushing hold on Polus's leg intensified, and all he could do was nod furiously in agreement. Moments later, he found himself gasping for air and thrust up onto the far side of the river. He pulled himself up the bank a bit and as he got to his feet, glared back at the river, feeling an intense hatred for whatever it was that had held him under. He continued north, but as he was in unfamiliar territory and his sense of direction was not good, he was many, many days trying to get back to the Rift.

He continued to struggle with remorse, but the evil force dogged him ruthlessly, assaulting him at times until he was exhausted. After more than a week of travel, he woke up one morning and felt that his evil tormentor was gone. He also felt a harmony within his heart and mind, though not understanding that it was because wickedness now reigned unchallenged.

Polus quickly got on his way and soon arrived at the Rift, greeted heartily by Megar, Teras, and the others. Megar led Polus into a building that they had fashioned into a headquarters.

"We have five hundred men," began Megar, "and the city of Megalos has supplied us with all the provisions we need. They send us with their blessing to execute justice."

"It is good," replied Polus. "We will attack Rhaka two days from now."

"How shall we breech the fortress?" asked Teras.

A maniacal grin spread slowly across Polus's face as he said, "There is a secret tunnel that comes out in the northeast tower. There is an entrance to it in these mountains just to the south of us. Gather a dozen men. Get digging tools. Megar, continue to train these men, keep them sharp!"

With that, Polus set out with his company and as they went, Teras asked, "How do you know of this tunnel?"

"While I was commanding the fortress, I looked for weaknesses in its defenses. When I was in the tower on the ground floor, I found a false wall. Behind it, stairs went down into a tunnel, which looked as if it hadn't been used in many years. I followed it out; the entrance was marked by a lone pine tree. Rhaka knows nothing of it."

·——— Twenty ———·

Nikos came to, and as he opened his eyes, he saw a beautifully tiled ceiling and found that he was lying on a perfectly smooth white marble floor. He sat up and saw an elegant hall, stone columns, and a throne upon a dais at the far end. He sprang to his feet, realizing he was in the King's castle. Suddenly, he remembered the horrid place he had just been in and couldn't believe he was alive. He looked down at himself and saw that he was wearing new clothes and boots.

He fell into a panic, wondering if this were real, until a voice spoke, "Fear not, Nikos." The voice was so captivating and persuasive that Nikos ceased to be aware of himself.

"Come and see," said the voice, but as soon as Nikos took a step, he realized how loud and jarring his footfall was, so he tried to walk as quietly as he could.

"Come freely!" commanded the voice. Nikos took another step and then saw two curved staircases on either side of the hall that went up to a balcony. As he looked up, he saw a figure standing and looking out the only window that was there. Nikos came up, but he earnestly felt he ought not look at him.

"What do you see?" asked the voice, but Nikos had been so taken by the presence of the King that he had not even looked out the window. When he did, the scene took his breath away. He saw a perfect world and when he recognized two of the people there, tears of joy streamed down his face filling him with happiness beyond description.

"This is the destiny of my people," said the King. "One day you will be among them and live forever in ever increasing happiness—more than you can even imagine."

Nikos was speechless as the King continued, "But you must go back, now that you know what life and death really are."

Without another moment passing, Nikos was in the green turfed valley, standing at the gate, with the same figures who had been there before. As he passed through, they nodded, and he went quickly along, remembering the place like it was yesterday. Then he thought of the terrible forest he had come through the first time, but he was surprised that he did not feel any fear.

Soon, he came to it, and his hand went to his sword hilt as he plunged in without a moment's hesitation. *"Fear has no place because death ushers you into perfect life,"* came to his mind, but he knew not from where.

Suddenly, a strange darkness seemed to materialize, and it became so dark that Nikos could not tell which direction he was going. He stopped and looked hard, but he could see nothing. He listened hard as well and didn't hear anything, but he began to imagine that he could hear some kind of creature breathing near at hand. At that moment a horrible vision of the evil Kahee Nawb erupted in front of him. The giant creature came at him, crashing through the trees. Nikos stood to meet him but was caught completely off guard because this time it was real. The Kahee Nawb swept over him, knocking him to the ground and wheeled about, screeching, "Fool!"

Nikos was dazed, but regained his footing and stood squarely at the beast and unexpectedly he heard himself calling out, "Fear is your weapon, but it is useless against me!"

The Nawb became enraged and rose to its full height, shrieking out incomprehensible words. It seemed to be trying to be more frightening, with its bloodcurdling cries.

"You are the fool!" yelled Nikos. "You are powerless!"

Then he rushed at the beast with his sword held high, but it squealed and shied away. It rose into the air, bashing through the tree branches. Once it was well above the forest, it cried out, "You will pay sevenfold!" and then it was gone, with a horrid shriek echoing across the sky.

It seemed to pull the darkness with it as sunlight flooded back into the forest. Nikos stood there catching his breath, shocked at his bravery, but then thought, "I wasn't brave at all. I just knew that there was nothing to fear . . . even if I should die."

Then he remembered what Chayel had said, "Fear can change things in men's minds into something that they are not."

He thought about the time at the oasis in the desert with Nuwa—how absolutely terrified he had been when the Nawb had attacked. He grinned and could hardly believe how different he was, incredulous at the change. When he came to the other side of the forest, he had expected to see a dry, arid plain and the city of Zabach off in the distance, but what was in front of him was the marsh he had fallen into. The forest behind him now seemed like the one he had come through on Zeo as he came down from Tachus Town. He was standing at the same junction in the mine cart line that he had been at before. He sat down on a nearby stump and took a deep breath, suddenly overwhelmed with all that had just happened. He shook his head as he looked around at the world, which seemed so small and tame by comparison.

"You have returned," said a voice behind him.

Nikos, startled, leaped up and spun around and exclaimed, "Zeo!"

"Yes, so you have named me," replied the horse.

"What day is it . . . ?" began Nikos, but trailed off, suddenly remembering the terrible place he had fallen into in the marsh. *And how did it happen anyway?* he thought. *How can you get there by sinking in a marsh?*

Nikos got up and said, "Let's go see Makarios." He jumped aboard Zeo who did not even wait to be signaled, but immediately started off down the right fork in the trail.

"I would not have disagreed this time," said Nikos patting Zeo, who broke into a gallop of his own accord. Nikos was happier than he had ever been in his life and reveled in the absolute freedom that he felt. They went west for a way down the mine cart line, but Nikos knew that Makarios's farm was to the south, and so turned left off the path.

They traveled most of the day and came to the northern shore of Huo Lake by evening. It was uninhabited, and Nikos quickly bedded down. The next morning, he decided to try to catch a fish for breakfast and found a creek that came into the lake from the north. He explored it, finding places where there were overhanging rocks. He knew that fish liked to take shelter there, and all he had to do was slowly reach under and grab. He was a little while at it, but eventually he caught a small fish and returned to camp. He was soon eating roasted catfish and smiled to himself, feeling satisfaction in having provided for himself.

Zeo was far afield but came quickly when Nikos summoned him. They came around the end of the lake to where the Tachus and Bradus rivers converged with the city of Two Rivers situated between them. They went without incident through Two Rivers to the ferry on the other side, and Nikos was reminded of when he and Chayel had been there. He felt regret at having deserted Chayel and the others at Kainos's and suddenly felt a very strong urge to return to them. But he felt an even greater prompting to continue to Makarios's farm.

Nikos arrived by midday and as he went down the lane , he realized that he no longer felt intimidated to speak the truth to her. His love for her was still there, but he was not at the mercy of his feelings anymore. He rode into her farmyard about midday, but everything was very quiet. He noticed that Samos was restless, neighing every now and then and running back and forth along the fence line.

Nikos jumped off Zeo and ran up to the house. He knocked on the door and called out Makarios's name, hardly waiting for a response as he went in. He was met by a bad smell and flies buzzing around a large ham bone with stale bread and moldy cheese littering the table. He saw an overturned chair and a broken oil lamp on the floor, and a terrible pang of fear struck him.

"Makarios!" he yelled as he raced through the house, but she was nowhere to be found. He ran down to the barn and looked across the fields, but all was still. Anxiousness knotted his stomach as he ran back up to the house and went in the back door to the kitchen. He called again, but there was only silence as he stood there at a loss and in tears. Eventually, his eyes fell upon the door to the cellar. He rushed to it, flung it open and went as quickly as he dared down into the dimness.

"Makarios?" he said in a quivering, soft voice. He saw baskets of potatoes and carrots strewn all over the floor and looked toward the root cellar. He could just make out that an iron bar was jammed through the latch and embedded in the door. He pulled at it, but it was immovable. A pitiful whimpering sound caught his ear and shot right through his heart.

"Makarios!" he called out and suddenly heaved on the bar with all his might, not only dislodging it, but also pulling the heavy wooden door from its hinges. He threw it from him and looked in, taking a step inside.

"You are here?" he asked gently into the pitch dark as he carefully made his way. He stooped down, feeling around and then his hand came upon something soft and warm. Nikos knelt down and gathered Makarios into his arms, bringing her up into the light of the kitchen. He was horrified at what he saw. She was filthy; her eyes were sunken and unable to focus. Her lips were swollen and cracked with dried blood on them, and her hair was dirty and tangled. He took her into the traveler's bedroom and laid her on the bed and quickly brought her some water, but she was not coherent. She felt very hot, and her eyes kept roving back and forth.

Nikos tried giving her some water, but she gagged on it. He knelt next to her, and tears came down as he whispered her name over and over. He took a cloth soaked in cool water from the well and squeezed some of it on her lips, but she did not respond. He soaked the cloth again and began rubbing it over her arms and face to help cool her. Soon, the water in the bucket had warmed and become dirty, so Nikos went quickly for more and filled a cup with water. When he returned, Makarios was very still, so still that Nikos's whole body shot through with terrible dread.

"No, Makarios, no!" he exclaimed as he put his ear to her chest. "Please!" he continued as he poured a bit of water into her mouth. She still did not respond, but as he continued to rub her with the cool cloth, she sputtered, and her eyes focused on him for a moment.

"Here," said Nikos and lifted her a bit, holding the cup to her lips. As he poured in a little bit, she coughed and sputtered, but swallowed. Soon, she took a little more and then Nikos let her back down on the bed. He sponged her forehead and gave her more water, which she took a little easier. Eventually, she seemed to fall asleep, and Nikos watched over her for the rest of the day, giving her more water when she stirred. As night fell, he put his bedroll on the floor next to her bed but slept very little.

Nikos awoke suddenly in the early morning and jumped up as Makarios said in a weary, weak voice,

"I am so thirsty . . ." He quickly brought water, and she gulped it down, but it was all that day and into the next before she was well enough to sit up.

She finally took some food and then Nikos asked the question that had been on his mind since he found her, "Who locked you in the cellar?"

Makarios sat on the edge of the bed and burst into tears, burying her face in her hands. Nikos moved next to her, and she leaned into him and sputtered, "It was Polus . . ."

"Polus?" he exclaimed, suddenly struck with an anger greater than he had ever felt, "How . . . why—?"

"Please," said Makarios. "I must take a bath."

"Of course," said Nikos. "Let me make it ready for you." Afterward, he went out and sat down on the top step of the porch. His mind began to race with questions about how in the world Polus had even come to be at the farm and why he would have done such a thing to Makarios.

The sun had climbed into the sky by the time the door behind him opened, and he turned to see Makarios looking more like herself. She joined him on the step and sat down, leaning into him.

"I am so glad that you are here," she said. "You saved me."

Nikos had no words for the moment, but looked straight ahead, feeling much less uncomfortable than he expected.

After a few minutes, Makarios said, "I don't know how Polus came to be here, but he said that I left him to die in the hands of the chief, so he would leave me to die. I couldn't believe that he would do such a thing. I tried to convince myself that he just wasn't in his right mind, that he had had too much mead. I sat there for a long time, trying to believe it, but eventually I became frightened that I would die in there. I felt an anger that erupted in a rage, and I began cursing Polus with terrible, ugly words. I swore that if I lived, I would take vengeance, and I imagined how."

She began to weep, feeling the same shame she had felt in the cellar. Nikos put his arm around her and after some time, she continued, "I remember shrieking, 'You will pay!' At that moment, I felt an evil in me that I could hardly believe. I saw that I would do worse to him than he had done to me. A weight of remorse overwhelmed me that I couldn't bear, and I cried out, 'I confess! This evil . . . it *is* in me! Forgive me!' I felt so helpless that I just began to cry and cry. I felt so lost, so desperate . . . but a light began to grow around me and then a voice, the strongest and most beautiful voice I have ever heard said, 'You have been given as you have believed.'"

Nikos turned toward her and looked searchingly into her eyes and was about to speak when she smiled and said, "I *do* believe now . . . I believe everything. Look!" She revealed the red symbol on her chest.

"I am so glad!" he exclaimed and quickly embraced her.

"I have never been so relieved of so much," she said, "and all in an instant!" But then she said with tears streaming down, "I am so sorry for how badly I treated you when you told me what you knew was the truth."

Nikos sat silent and slowly nodded his head. "We are all guilty of something," he said slowly, "but now forgiven."

They sat for some time, and Makarios eventually said, "You told me last fall that Polus had become the commander of a fortress, but I did not believe it."

Nikos remained thoughtful, but suddenly felt a raging desire for vengeance on Polus that filled his whole being.

"He will pay," said Nikos quietly, but vehemently and vowed to himself then and there to bring justice.

"No!" said Makarios unexpectedly. "He must be forgiven."

"Forgiven?!" exclaimed Nikos as he turned to face Makarios. "Such a thing cannot be forgiven. There must be justice!"

But she said, "What justice can pay for what he did to me? And is it really justice you want or vengeance?"

Nikos was brought up short and then hung his head as she continued, "I want Polus to know forgiveness, not just mine, but the forgiveness that comes when the curse is removed. We must find him. I know now that this evil is what makes men do what they ought not, what they want not. We are slaves to it, all of us, and Polus must be told the way to be free from it."

Nikos looked at her incredulously but was at a loss for words. They sat in silence for a while and then Makarios added, "It is not for us to mete out punishment," she said, "but for the Tsadaq in the Ayar Owlam-Mowth—"

Nikos looked at her sharply and asked, "What . . . what is that?"

But somehow, he knew that it was the place he had been in under the marsh, and he stuttered, "I . . . I was there."

"How?" she asked in amazement.

"I don't know, but the name you spoke . . . I know that . . . is it," he said in a labored voice. "How do you know of it?"

"All my growing up in Zabach, there were men who stood in the market and warned of it. It is difficult to say in the common tongue, but something like 'the place or city of those who are always dying', where the cursed go when they pass out of this world." She began to describe it, but Nikos had leaned forward and then held up his hand.

"Yes . . . I know. It is aptly named, "always dying but never dead . . . a living death . . . and the terrible heat and the pain they are in . . . the moaning and crying and shrieks of agony. It was horrible, and there is no relief . . .it never ends because time doesn't pass there. It is a never-ending now. I know because when I came back from there, it was the same moment that I had gone under."

"How did it happen?" asked Makarios.

"Well, there is marsh to the north, near the forest," he answered. "Zeo would not even pass by it on the path, so I went on foot. I was in up to my knees when I was suddenly pulled under. Everything went black, and then I came to . . . there."

Nikos stared straight ahead and then suddenly turned to Makarios, "I saw the chief there! He is dead?"

Her eyes widened and she nodded slowly, "Polus . . . when he was here . . . he said that he had gone to kill him, to take revenge, but that he died right in front of him."

They sat in stunned silence; eventually, Makarios said softly, "I am sorry for him . . . for the chief."

Nikos nodded, but inwardly he felt a sense of satisfaction—that the chief had gotten what he deserved, and he relished the idea of Polus ending up there too.

"And Kakos," said Nikos. "He was there. He tried to kill me . . . again."

"Kill you?"

"They all did. They just *hated* . . . like they weren't even human anymore."

Silence descended upon them again, and soon Makarios was feeling tired and went back inside to lie down.

After a week or so, Makarios was recovered and with Menka and Daggo back at the farm, she and Nikos headed north, but with very different purposes. As they came out to the main road, Nikos expected to head to Steko's Ferry, but Makarios said, "I wish not to see my brother. I do not want him to know of what happened."

Nikos nodded, and they headed west instead. As they rode Makarios said, "You seem a different man since I saw you last."

Nikos pondered for a few minutes and said, "I suppose. Being in that . . . in that place changed me. I had always feared death, not knowing what came after, but now I know it was the City of Dying that I feared."

After a few moments Makarios exclaimed, "Oh, how foolish I was, to deny the truth my whole life when indescribable happiness is offered! How can anyone not want to go to the City of Light?"

"I have seen that as well," said Nikos.

"You have been there too?" she asked, surprised.

"Well, no, but I have seen it from the King's castle," he answered, but came up short as tears of joy filled his eyes. "My mother and father are there."

"How did you know them?"

"I . . . I don't know. I just did," he said suddenly smiling. "And I will see them again."

Nikos and Makarios rode into Diaggello and as they passed through the square, they noticed that the statue of the chief was no longer there. They crossed the Bradus River and turned east, following the river on their right. Soon, Huo Lake appeared ahead, and they traveled along its shoreline until they came to the creek that flowed into it from the north.

"We can follow this up to the east-west mine cart line," said Nikos. "That marsh is to the northeast up there." He felt a twinge of fear, but quickly shook it off.

"It is called Brinestump," said Makarios with a bit of trepidation. "Many strange things have happened there."

"We will stay well to the west of it," said Nikos.

By day's end they arrived at the junction in the mine cart line, and Nikos pointed south to where the north-south line passed by the marsh.

"It was just down there where . . ." said Nikos shaking his head. "But how can it have happened?"

"I suppose there is much we do not know about how this world connects to the next," said Makarios.

They turned north into the forest and followed the line along the foot of the mountains to their left. As the day came to a close, they made camp and then arose early the next day, making it to Tachus Town by midmorning. They found Kainos in the marshal's building attending to his duties.

"My boy!" he exclaimed, "it is good to see you!" He bear-hugged Nikos and then turned to Makarios, "I am glad to see you as well. Come, both of you, and sit down."

He led them to a small back room, and they sat down at a small table. He looked curiously at Makarios and said, "There is a different air about you, Madame."

She smiled and revealed the red symbol on her chest, which caused Kainos to chuckle and give a clap of his hands.

"Hoorah!" he said, "How has this happened?"

But after glancing at Makarios and seeing her discomfort, Nikos said, "We may talk of it another time."

Kainos sobered a bit and then said, "Well, how about you, my boy? I see a difference in you as well!"

Nikos explained all about the City of Dying and the City of the Light and how it had changed his view of life and death.

"To die is better than to live," he said, "so there is nothing to fear."

"Indeed," said Kainos. "It is good to know what lies beyond the grave and is a great comfort."

"Meaning no affront to your hospitality, but I should like to continue on our way," said Makarios.

"Please take some food at least," said Kainos. "I was just about to sit down to the midday meal myself."

They agreed, and afterward Makarios was quick to want to get on their way. Seeing Kainos's questioning look, she said, "I must find Polus. I dearly want him to know about the curse and the King."

Kainos raised an eyebrow, "You sure you want to find that brute? He is as evil and vicious as I have ever seen."

"That is precisely why I must find him," she said. "He is on the path to destruction, and I long to save him from it."

Nikos felt his anger toward Polus well up, but he remained silent. At that moment, a messenger rushed in and exclaimed breathlessly, "Marshal Kainos, sir! There are one hundred soldiers approaching from the west. They appear to be from the garrison in Silver City. They are halfway between here and Stone Hamlet, sir."

"Show them the way here," commanded Kainos.

"Yes, sir!" he replied and quickly exited.

The three continued their conversation until the company of soldiers arrived and as they went out to meet them, Kainos addressed their leader, "What is your business?"

"I am Marshal Tauros from Silver City. We are on our way to Makran to take into custody a certain Commander Polus who is responsible for the death of Marshal Faggo of Diaggello, otherwise known as "the chief.""

"I am sorry to say," began Kainos, "that you will not find Commander Polus in Makran. He has risen up against Overseer Rhaka, and it is unknown where he is."

"Well, I still must see the Overseer of Smaragdos and obtain his assistance in this matter."

"I am afraid you will find him none too cooperative. He has become a tyrant, whose justice and authority originate from himself. He rules with fear and has ravaged the land by taking for himself all that he wants."

Marshal Tauros immediately dismissed Kainos's description, "Surely you are jesting. Lord Arkone would never allow such lawlessness to exist within the boundary of his authority!"

Kainos shrugged, "Nonetheless."

Marshal Tauros scowled, "You know not of what you speak!"

He turned abruptly away and commanded his men, and they moved out.

Nikos said, "Pike was right about Lord Arkone—"

Makarios interjected, "Yes, about being wholly unconcerned about matters outside his own fancy!"

She turned in a huff and climbed aboard Samos, looking expectantly at Nikos who quickly hopped aboard his steed.

As the last of the soldiers went past, one of them said, "You're right what yer sayin' about that Rhaka. My friend used to live up there, and it got real bad so he came down to live with me and my family."

"Might as well follow them to the fortress and see what happens," said Kainos with a grin. "I hope you find Kafar and the others. Good fortune to you both if you come across Polus."

With that, they swung in behind the soldiers and struck up a conversation with the one who had spoken to them.

"Most of us here," said the soldier, "know about how bad Overseer Rhaka has got. But Lord Arkone, he's a fool, livin' up in his big estate, like the world is a happy fairy tale!"

Then another soldier said, "And we don't feel none too good about goin' up to Makran with so few of us, but you heard Marshal Tauros; he is as dumb to it as Arkone is."

They rode on and came to Makran late in the day; Marshal Tauros commanded them to make camp just outside the city.

"Our best chance to find Polus is to stay with these soldiers," said Makarios. Nikos nodded in agreement.

Twenty One

Kafar, Barah, and the others had spent the last few weeks in Karpone, watching and waiting for any sign of Polus or news from Ruad. They had made trips into Makran and up to Keone, but they had found nothing. One day, they went up to Makran very early in the morning and observed that there were many more soldiers in the city and even more out at the fortress.

Arak said in a low voice, "If only there were a way to find out about Ruad . . . why he never met us."

Suddenly, a voice that Barah and Arak recognized spoke from the shadow of the building they were near, "It's good to see yer friend's out of that prison in the fortress."

"Fadzo!" exclaimed Barah quietly. "It is good to see you."

He nodded and continued, "So, if you all was supposed to be meetin' somebody somewhere in the last few weeks and they happened to be a cook in the fortress, they wouldn't a-been allowed out. No one was even allowed out of Makran when Rhaka sent whole bunches of soldiers out the gate. And that Megan commander . . . he ran off from the fortress with a bunch of his own kind."

Fadzo knew much more than it seemed like he ought to, which led Barah to say, "Rhaka sent his soldiers out to take over a town in the province to the north. There was a battle, and Commander Polus and his soldiers tried to defend the town, but they were defeated."

Fadzo was thoughtful for a few moments and then said, "Well, it was mighty unsettled in the fortress for a while I'll tell ya. I kin see why. This Polus fella, he's gonna want to rule . . . and, you still don't have that book yer after, else you'd a gone home with it by now."

There was an uncomfortable silence, and then Fadzo added, with a quizzical look, "Polus . . . he stole it from Rhaka, I'll bet. You been off lookin' for 'im?"

They all were surprised at how much Fadzo rightly guessed, which drew him into their confidence even further. As they were talking, a marshal and a group of about a hundred soldiers approached from the south side of the city and rode past them to the fortress.

"They ain't from this province," said Fadzo. "Somethin's afoot."

They watched as Marshal Tauros and his men approached the fortress, but as they neared the gate, it unexpectedly burst open. A mass of fighting men and Meganthropos spilled out, immediately embroiling them in the skirmish.

Nikos and Makarios were still amongst them and tried to retreat, but when Nikos suddenly saw Polus, a vengeful rage launched him forward. He drew his sword and with a warlike cry, he went straight at Polus, swinging with all his might. But he never reached Polus as a horse suddenly barged into him from the side and sent him flying off Zeo. Makarios tried to get to him, but the chaos parted them, and she found herself on the edge of the fighting. She wheeled Samos away and then turned back, seeing Polus and his men in disarray as they were outmatched by Rhaka's soldiers.

"There is Polus!" yelled Chayel over the roar and rumble of the battle.

As they looked where she was pointing, Barah called out incredulously, "And Makarios!" They were all stunned for a moment, but suddenly Chayel drew her sword and rushed forward, quickly followed by the others. The fighting was fierce and chaotic, and they lost sight of Makarios as they began fighting for their lives. They lost track of each other as well, but the Meganthropos were losing, and it wasn't long before they fled the battle, heading straight through the city.

The battlefield emptied quickly as Rhaka's soldiers pursued Polus and his men, but there were many dead and wounded from both sides. The carnage of the fight was gruesome with bloody, mangled bodies and moaning and cries of pain. Soon, other soldiers were emerging from the fortress to attend to the wounded. Odus and Chayel had come back together, and it wasn't long before they found Kafar, Barah, and Arak.

"We must find Makarios!" said Chayel, but they had barely begun to search when the sound of a neighing horse caught their attention.

"Zeo!" exclaimed Chayel and spurred her mount toward him. As she reached Zeo, she found Nikos on the ground at his feet.

"Quick!" she called as the others arrived, but at that moment, a hush fell over the whole place, and a voice called out that sent shivers down Chayel's spine. It seemed as if no one even dared to breathe, and even the wailing of the wounded quieted.

"Kill all these beasts that are left alive!" bellowed a voice that Kafar and the rest had never heard before but had no doubt who it was. A terrible oppression filled the air, and they felt like they could barely move as they slowly turned to see the Overseer Rhaka standing in the gate, head and shoulders above all the other men. He had long black hair that flowed down his back and a sharply trimmed beard and mustache. His features were very angular and his arms unusually long. Many more soldiers poured out of the fortress and formed ranks on either side.

"You see what happens when we are soft on the populace!" he bellowed as he began walking forward.

Every soldier called out some kind of affirmative answer in unison. All movement on the field had stopped as Rhaka continued yelling, becoming more and more enraged. He seemed headed straight toward Chayel and Nikos, but suddenly he turned around and finished his wrathful address to his men.

"Kill them all!" he shouted. "I will not waste resources on any of them!" He disappeared back into the fortress, and the soldiers who stood in rank began doing as they had been commanded, but some of the wounded fought back, and others tried to get away.

"Quick!" yelled Chayel.

But Arak stood there dumbfounded and said haltingly, "They . . . they're killing their *own* wounded?" Cries for mercy rang out here and there, but their attention turned to Nikos, who was alive but unconscious.

"He's not bleedin' anywhere," began Odus, but Barah stepped in and hefted Nikos up and set him on his own horse and then leaped up behind him, grabbing around Nikos like a sack of potatoes to steady him.

"But Makarios . . . ," said Kafar, "Where is she?"

As they looked around, Chayel quickly mounted her horse and cried out, "We must find her!"

They looked as long as they dared, avoiding the methodical advance of more than a hundred of Rhaka's soldiers who were killing all who still breathed. Then they fled through the city and went south into the foothills of the mountains and got far in amongst the trees. They were not being chased and so came to a stop, trying to get their bearings. They got Nikos to the ground, and it wasn't long before he came to.

"What . . . happened?" he asked slowly. Suddenly, his eyes went wide, "Where is Makarios?" He jumped to his feet and reeled forward into Chayel, but Barah caught them both.

Odus said, "Now, you best sit down."

"We couldn't find her," said Kafar. "But neither did we see her horse anywhere."

"We *must* find her!" said Nikos. "She is dead set on finding Polus, and I do not doubt she will pursue him alone if she must. She has become one of us and desperately wants Polus to be freed from the curse, even at the cost of her life! We must find her!"

— Twenty Two —

Polus and his men fled from Rhaka's soldiers and got away by quickly climbing into the mountains past Boulder Falls. They regrouped, but their defeat had cut their number in half, and many were wounded. They gathered around Polus, but he was only seeing Makarios, wholly mystified that she was alive.

"Commander!" called Megar, "You are alright?"

"Yes," he said haltingly.

"We must get back to the Rift," said Megar.

Polus motioned for him to order the men as Teras came next to Polus and asked, "Who was the woman? She saved you."

Polus madly shook his head and waved him off. They took the better part of the day to get back, but once they got to the Rift, Polus went into the headquarters by himself and sat brooding for some time, his emotions in turmoil. He couldn't believe Makarios had somehow survived and that she had risked her life to save his. He asked himself why until it nearly drove him mad, and the fight within began again. He feared that the evil being might come upon him, but it did not. Suddenly, he leaped up and burst out of the building, howling out in a frustrated rage. The desire for vengeance overwhelmed him, thinking that if Makarios were dead, the awful conflict within him would die as well.

"Teras!" he bellowed.

Teras came quickly, and Polus continued, "The woman you saw . . . we must find her!"

But at that moment, one of Polus's men came to him and said incredulously, "There is a *woman* at the gate. She is asking to see you."

"Is she alone?" demanded Teras.

"It appears so—"

Polus commanded Teras, "Detain the woman and take a squad of men out and make certain there is no one else; then bring her to me!"

He disappeared into the headquarters, having no doubt who the woman was, but feeling incredulous. With evening coming on, Polus started a fire in the stove and lit the lamp on the table. He sat down, nervously tapping his heavy thick fingers on it. A few moments later, there was a knock on the door, and then it was pushed inward by Teras with the woman in front of him. She came in of her own accord and stood there as Polus made clear to Teras to leave them. His desire to kill her was blunted by his disbelief that she was standing right in front of him.

"I am glad to see you, Polus," she said, looking him square in the eye. A firestorm of mixed emotions descended upon him and clouded his mind. Seemingly without realizing it, he stepped past Makarios and barred the door and then turned to face her. He shook his head as if to clear his mind but was completely disarmed.

"I no longer fear you," said Makarios, "because I no longer fear pain or even death."

Polus stared blankly in confusion, but after a few minutes, he looked sharply at Makarios and said, "How did you live?"

"Nikos . . . he found me, but only just in time."

Polus scowled, but then his countenance softened as he said, somewhat pensively, "Nikos . . . Nikos." Then he erupted in a rage, "It was him! He tried to kill me!"

His outburst sent a tremor of fear through her, but she did not move.

"*You!*" he yelled as if she were just as guilty, but then his anger evaporated, and he said, "You . . ."

A tear stung his eye, and he turned quickly away, wiping his hand across his face. Opposing feelings, which he now hated and feared, suddenly clashed within him again, and his rage returned. He stood facing the wall, seething with murderous intent.

Just as he was about to spin around, he felt Makarios take a hold of his hand from behind. "Polus," she said softly.

He froze and was overcome with a flashback to the time when Makarios and Nikos were at his house, and he had raised his fist in a rage to pummel her. He saw the forest around him, the shed where his carvings were, and Makarios in front of him, fearing for her life. Coherent thoughts whirled away into a tempest of feelings, and a sudden weakness brought him to his knees. His shoulders slumped forward, and his head hung down, and all he could hear in his mind was his own voice, *"Polus is bad. Polus is very, very bad."*

After a minute or two, he twisted around so Makarios was in front of him, but his eyes were on the floor. She stood silent, still with a hold of his hand. Polus's whole being was enveloped in guilt descending upon him like a wave of hot embers, burning him with regret and remorse like he had never known.

"You . . . ," he began in almost a whisper, "you . . . saved me." He raised his eyes, and they were filled with tears as he slowly shook his head and whispered, "Why?" But he gazed off and said to himself, *"How can it be?"*

"I want to save you from more than death," said Makarios, her eyes also brimming with tears. She stepped closer and took his other hand, and Polus burst into great sobs of remorse and shame, saying he was sorry. Eventually, he pulled away from Makarios and retreated to the other side of the room. He sat on the floor with his back against the wall and his face in his hands. After some time, Makarios went and knelt next to him and put her hand on his shoulder. He flinched and turned his head away from her.

"I forgive you, Polus," she said, but he vehemently shook his head and mumbled, "I . . . I am bad, evil."

"That is why you need forgiveness," she said. "Good people don't need forgiving."

Polus's crying suddenly ceased, and he looked up but still away from Makarios. His mind was working furiously as he kept blinking with his brow furrowed until he exclaimed, "I see!"

He lurched up to his knees and faced Makarios, "It will be like I wasn't bad. I remember!" He smiled broadly, but suddenly his countenance fell into a pit. "But what I did to you . . . how can you *forgive* . . .?"

He shook his head and slumped back against the wall. Tears filled his eyes again, and he was about to begin sobbing when Makarios grabbed his shoulders and gave him a shake, which caused him to look directly into her eyes.

"There is forgiveness for *everything*," she said passionately. "That is the way of the Tsadaq."

"Yes," he said, seemingly entranced, but suddenly an icy, sickly wave of air passed over them, and Polus was heaved up and thrown across the room by an unseen force. He crashed heavily into the wall, and Makarios jumped up but felt as if she had been struck on the side of her head with the words, "He is mine!"

She fell, but sprang up quickly as the sinister voice screeched, "You shall not have him!"

Makarios choked on the horrible fetid smell in the air, but managed to cry out, "In the name of the—"

But she was again knocked to the floor.

Polus was writhing in pain as the unseen evil attacked him.

"You are one of us!" screamed the being, but Polus was trying to fight back, yelling, "*No! No!*"

Makarios regained her feet and launched herself into the fray, grabbing around Polus and holding him tight. "In the name of the King, be gone!" she shouted and instantly, the thing let out an ear-splitting screech and disappeared into thin air.

Polus fell to the floor with Makarios on top of him, and before anything else could happen, there was a banging on the door.

"Commander, sir!" called Teras as he yanked on the door. "Commander!" But as the door was barred, it did not open.

Polus looked wildly about for a moment and then called back, "Return to your post!"

There was a pause and then a very uncertain, "Yes, sir!"

Polus scrambled to his feet and reached a hand to Makarios to help her up. He was still dazed as he exclaimed, "I saw him!" He reeled backward, and Makarios could do little but push him toward a chair on which he landed.

"I saw him!" he repeated.

"Who?"

"Him! The One . . . the King!" He shouted, pulling the Book from the case on his belt. "In here! I read all about him and hated him and everything he stood for, but now . . . I *see* that he is true!"

He smiled broadly and felt himself full of happiness; he looked at Makarios as she sat at the table. "And you . . . do you believe?"

She nodded slowly and said, "It is the only way I was able to forgive you."

Polus looked thoughtful as her eyes fell upon the Book, which he had put on the table. "It is smaller than I imagined," she said as she picked it up. As she held it, she was startled by feeling a warmth pass from it to her.

As she looked at the cover she said, as if to herself, "The Book of Chayaah-Mawveth. It is beautiful."

As she opened it, Polus said, "You can read it?"

"Yes, it is my birth-language, from my hometown."

"Where is that?"

"Far south, across the Desert Wilderness. The Book belongs there, in the Qodesh Bayith Sefar," she said, seeming to surprise herself by speaking the language.

She was even more surprised as Polus said, "The Sacred House of the Book."

"You know the language?" she asked and as he nodded, she added, "How?"

"Someone from your land, when I was commander in the fortress at Makran . . . we found him, and he taught it," he answered. Then his eyes fell to the floor as he continued, "But I have used it for much evil." He shook his head and teared up. "I was so blind to what was real. I thought I knew . . ." He trailed off and they sat again in thought.

Suddenly, Polus looked directly at Makarios and exclaimed, "I must tell them all! They must know this truth!"

But as he stood up, Makarios grabbed his arm and said, "No—!"

"Why?"

"Think where we are. All of them out there, every one of them is now your enemy!"

"No!" he exclaimed, pulling away from her. "They are loyal to me, to the death!"

She stood back and shook her head. Surprisingly, Polus calmed down quickly and then said, "What do you mean?"

Makarios picked up the Book and said, "It is this. There is the evil, and there is the good. To be on one side is to be the enemy of the other. Do you so quickly forget? You sought to enslave or kill any who would not join you," she added, motioning to the outside, "and will these do any less?"

Polus stared into the fire for quite some time, trying to make sense of it all.

"I thought I loved you," he began quietly, "but I only hated you. I tried to . . ."

He choked up, and Makarios quickly said, "You see then, the difference. You would give your life for me now."

He looked sharply at her, startled, but then slowly nodded.

"That is what love does," she added. "Teras and the others . . . they would violate me and then kill me. Do you see who you are to them now?"

His eyes widened in uncustomary fear; then he said, "Well, I am still their commander. They will obey what I tell them."

Makarios shook her head, "But you are different; they will know that."

"No, I—"

She came close and put her hand to his chest and said, "But you can't hide this."

In all the commotion he had not noticed the red marking until he looked down at it. "The People of the Great One," he said.

"It is upon all of us," she said and revealed her own.

Polus sat down and stared hard into the fire; after a while he said, "You said that you do not fear death. Why?"

She smiled and said, "Because there is true happiness beyond for me."

"How do you know this?"

"It is in here," she said, still holding the Book. "Have you not read of it?"

Polus shook his head, but then said, "I hated it. I see that I only believed what served my own purpose."

They sat in silence for a while until Polus said, "The Book must be returned to where it belongs. I will give it to you and command my men to let you go. Teras knows that you saved my life and has likely told the men, so they will expect me to honor you."

Makarios shook her head and asked, "But how will you get out?"

"That does not matter."

"Yes, it does! They will kill you."

Her earnestness caused him to pause and after a moment, Polus said, "Then it must be tonight, now when it is dark. I will take you to the gate. They will not see the mark on me. I will go with you out the gate as if to escort you."

"But the Book is not safe with me . . . alone," said Makarios. "And you are so different now that you will have to work hard to seem like your old self."

Polus was puzzled, but he stood up and secured the Book in the pack on his belt.

Makarios stood still and then said, "I am so glad to have found you and that you are now free from the curse."

He looked a bit pained and was about to speak when she looked him square in the eye and said passionately, "Do not say you are sorry again!" Her eyes smoldered with emotion. "I know your remorse and the guilt you still feel, but you must accept my forgiveness. You dishonor me if you do not."

"It is not easy," said Polus. They fell silent, but eventually Polus looked at Makarios and smiled.

"You see . . . the truth has made you free to accept that you are forgiven."

"It is good."

He went to the door, unbarred it, and pulled it open, but they found the moonlight a bit brighter than either of them liked. Polus yelled out in a voice that sounded just like he did before, "*Teras!*"

Teras appeared quickly and said, "Commander?"

"This woman must be honored for saving my life."

"Sir, but why—"

Polus silenced him with a very harsh and pointed glare.

"I will escort her up the mountain," he said and started toward the gate.

But halfway there, Megar came up and said, "Commander, sir, how can she go free? She knows this place now."

"No more!" shouted Polus as he kept walking. "She is harmless!"

He signaled for the gate to be opened and as they passed through, Megar called out, "Commander Polus, sir! You cannot—"

But Polus spun around and feigning rage, roared, "You dare to question me?! Teras, take him and put him in the trench!"

Teras hesitated and so Polus screamed, "*Do it!*"

A fog of uncertainty descended upon the men, and they all began to feel uneasy, but Polus walked with purpose and was soon lost to view in the gloom of the evening.

"Quickly," he whispered to Makarios, but considering the terrain, quickly was not at all possible, though she went as fast as she could. Soon, there was the sound of a ruckus behind them and then some indistinct yelling. The one thing Polus and Makarios both heard was, "I saw the mark!"

"Go!" said Polus to Makarios and then bolted off in another direction. She was startled and dismayed and immediately got in amongst some trees and boulders to hide. Darkness shrouded everything, and she could not make out the words of the shouting she heard, but the tenor brought tears to her. Soon, the commotion died away, and all was silent. She waited and listened, hoping Polus had evaded his men and would make his way back to her. Suddenly, she was shot through with a tremor of fear as she heard noise from the Rift and then the gate clanging.

"*No! That* way! yelled a voice. Makarios bolted, trembling as she ran low to the ground, staying hidden in the underbrush and boulders. She heard her pursuers gaining on her.

"There!" one of them yelled. Suddenly, heavy clouds rolled in, and rain began pelting down; thunder rumbled, and lightning split the sky. Darkness descended unnaturally fast and suddenly Makarios could not see her way at all, nor could she hear anything above the storm. A flash of lightning lit up a huge pine tree ahead of her and she dove in under its thick boughs and huddled up against its trunk. She tried listening for the sound of pursuers, but there was only the noise of the storm. She hoped with all her might that Polus had escaped, but she had a bad feeling that he hadn't. After a good, long while, she was convinced that she had evaded her pursuers, but with the storm and the darkness, she stayed where she was. The low, sloping branches of the tree kept her hidden and dry as she waited for dawn.

·────ꟷ Twenty Three ꟷ────·

The sun had nearly set as Kafar and the rest made their way north, finding the town of Keone unattended by any of Rhaka's men. As they approached Wildhorse Village, rain started coming down, and thunder boomed in the distance.

In the gathering dusk, Kafar called out, "Thumos, it is Kafar!"

As they drew nearer, someone holding a torch aloft came out and said, "Is Odus and Miss Chayel with you?"

"It is Eido," whispered Chayel.

"Yes—" began Kafar.

Barah interjected, "And Arak and Barah as well!"

"Come, come; you are most welcome!" said Eido, who seemed to be a very different young man as he led them right into Thumos's barn and then eagerly took care of their horses. Many of the villagers came and greeted them, but chief among them was Thumos, who bear-hugged them all.

"It is a delight to see you again!" exclaimed Thumos. "We have just finished supper, but I am sure we can gather some for you."

He led them into his house, and though it was cramped, they all sat down to a meal, which the villagers provided. As they ate, Thumos told them of how most of the village had accepted his word about the curse and the King and that they stood unified and stronger than ever as a community.

"And Eido as well?" asked Chayel.

A look of angst passed over Thumos's face. "No," he said slowly, "not him." After a pause, he continued, "We have not seen or heard anything of this Polus—"

"We have," said Kafar and went on to tell him of all that had happened.

"It is likely that Polus and his men came back to the valley up here, to the west," said Thumos. "They may have a camp or a hideout down there."

In the morning, they decided to go into the valley on foot, and Thumos and Eido went with them.

But as they were approaching the valley, Nikos called out, "There is Makarios's horse!"

He stood a fair piece down the road looking intently at them all. When Nikos called out his name, he neighed and came to him, nickering and pawing the ground. Suddenly, they were all startled as a woman appeared, coming up out of the valley.

"Makarios!" cried Nikos as she ran to him and threw her arms around him.

"I am sorry I left you," she began, but suddenly all the tension of the day before came forth in a flood of tears. After some time, she continued, "The Book . . . I had it in my hands, but . . ." and the tears came again as she thought of Polus and his fate.

"What happened?" asked Chayel stepping close to her.

"Oh, my dear, Chayel," said Makarios turning to her and unexpectedly hugging her. "I am so sorry for—"

"No, no," interjected Chayel holding her tight for a moment. "It is alright. What about Polus and the Book?"

"Polus . . . he has been freed from Kah-Taw!"

"That is good news!" exclaimed Barah.

"He has the Book?" asked Kafar.

"Yes, yes, but—" began Makarios.

Kafar interrupted, "Where is he?"

She shook her head, "I do not know. There is a hideout down there, walled and gated. Last night we, Polus and I, tried leaving, but his men became suspicious of him, and we fled. He ran a different way to lead his men from me. I don't know what happened or if he got away."

Tears came to her again, but she continued, "You saw the men who were with him yesterday; we cannot overcome them."

They all fell silent until Thumos said, "Let us go back to the village. We must make a plan."

They went to Thumos's house and sat down around the firepit, and Makarios told all she knew about the Rift and where it was.

"It would be wise to wait until nightfall," said Odus.

Makarios responded, "I cannot find my way in the dark. I have only been there once, as you know."

"You say the walls of this hideout are fifty feet high?" asked Thumos.

"Yes, and maybe more than that," said Makarios. "It is a deep fault, and the surrounding land slopes up a bit to the tops of the walls, but they are smooth and cannot be climbed."

"We could at least sneak up there and have a look inside," said Odus.

"And maybe find out what happened to Polus," added Chayel.

As they dispersed to make preparations, Makarios approached Nikos and said expectantly, "You have been very quiet . . ." He shook his head and looked at the ground as Chayel joined them.

After a few minutes he said, "I would have killed him if you hadn't stopped me. He would be in the City of Dying . . . forever . . ."

"He would have deserved it," said Chayel, "but vengeance, bringing justice is not for us."

Nikos slowly nodded, as guilt and shame weighed upon him like never before. Feelings of fear and anxiety overwhelmed him again, and his desire to run away from everything was strong, but it made him angry because there seemed to be no reason for it. He soon wandered off by himself and as he went farther from the village, he looked to the west, toward the valley. He scowled as he realized that his fear was in that direction. His remorse over trying to kill Polus also welled up, and he became overwhelmed with a need to atone for things somehow.

With a quick glance back at the village, he set off toward the valley, not feeling like himself at all. It was midday when he descended the slope and as he went, his fear gave way to a sense of injustice over all that had happened. He thought about Rhaka and all the evil he had done, about the Book being in the hands of evil men, and about what Polus had done to Makarios.

His pace quickened, but it took longer than he expected to get to the Rift, and his anger began to diminish. He saw one of the landmarks he was looking for, but doubt slowed his pace. He stopped and looked back and thought, "What am I doing here? What do I hope to—"

Suddenly, three huge men came out of nowhere.

"Yer lost in a bad place, boy!" exclaimed one of them gleefully. The biggest of them grabbed Nikos and put him in a choke hold, but his inherent tendency to yield to unwanted force took over.

"There ain't no fight in 'im!" said the soldier and threw Nikos to the ground in disgust.

Slamming into the ground with a thud, Nikos had the wind knocked out of him.

"He's harmless as a baby!" said another.

A third soldier said with a bit more seriousness, "We must take him to Megar." Nikos was dragged to his feet, gasping for air and thrown over a huge, muscled shoulder, making it even harder for him to breathe. He fought to stay conscious, but the next thing he knew, he felt a dull thudding in his side, and he heard a voice as if muffled by wads of cotton. The thudding sharply intensified, and Nikos was suddenly staring into the face of a giant man with a terrible scar down one side and ropelike hair swinging around his face.

Another blow brought Nikos to full consciousness, and he clearly heard the man ask, "Who are you? *Answer!*"

Nikos was flat on his back in the dirt and tried scrambling away, but the man pinned him down by his throat and with a curl of his lip again yelled, "*Answer me!*"

"*Enough, Teras!*" bellowed another one who stepped up to Nikos and peered down at him. Teras let him go and gave way to the other but not without a wicked sneer. Nikos was terrified and though commanded to get to his feet, he could not.

"See? Weak as a baby," said a soldier as Megar again addressed Nikos. "Who are you?"

"Nikos," he blurted out feebly. Teras shook his head in contempt.

Megar continued, "What are you doing here?"

Nikos sat up and, seemingly oblivious to all around him, got to his feet. He blinked a few times and then grimaced at the pain in his side. He saw that he was surrounded by a few hundred Meganthropos soldiers inside the Rift. His eyes focused on Megar, and he said in a sort of fog, "I got . . . lost."

"He is one of them!" exclaimed Teras. "Look!" He ripped open Nikos's shirt, snarling with hatred. Uncontrollably, he grabbed Nikos by the throat, lifting him in the air and sought to crush the life out of him.

Megar roared, "*No!* Do not kill him!" and rushed at Teras, knocking Nikos out of his hands. Teras stumbled back, but then came forward with a look of vicious disdain.

"You forget, I think," began Megar with a piercing look, "who is commander now."

Teras yielded as Megar feigned patience with Nikos and said, "Tell me now, what are you doing here?"

Nikos panicked and stood there trembling, unable to speak. Teras's anger flared, and Megar said to him, "Put him in the trench!"

Ripples of merriment could be heard among the soldiers as Teras shoved Nikos forward and across the compound to the north end. The walls of the Rift rose high on either side, but Nikos saw before him a deep trough in the ground, about twenty feet wide and thirty feet long, covered by very heavy iron grating. Teras unlatched a trap door in the grating and pushed Nikos into it. He fell ten feet to the bottom and landed so hard that all he could do was lie there, gasping and in pain.

After some raucous laughter, all became silent above and Nikos rolled over, grimacing in pain. The day was headed toward evening, and the far end of the trench was shrouded in shadow, so Nikos sought refuge there. As his eyes grew accustomed to the dim light, he was startled as he saw a huddled figure in the corner, unmoving and silent. Nikos wondered if the person was even alive but did not want to go any nearer. He sat down against the wall and shivered as the night descended in earnest.

Nikos awoke with a start early in the morning and immediately looked toward the figure near the opposite wall. He had seemingly not moved all night, which gave Nikos a bit of courage to venture closer, but the rising sun revealed who it was.

"Polus!" Nikos exclaimed and ran forward, but there was no response. His fear had vanished as he knelt and said much more quietly, "Polus, it is Nikos."

He groaned, but remained still, curled up in a ball and his breathing heavily labored. Nikos suddenly jerked back in horror as he saw blood all over him and that he had been mercilessly beaten.

"Polus, what happened?" Nikos put his hand on Polus's shoulder, and he winced.

"Nikos," he mumbled, but as he raised his head, Nikos saw that his face was swollen and bloodied. He suddenly thought of Polus the day he had met him, so innocent and eager to please, and Nikos's eyes welled with tears.

"Makarios . . . ," continued Polus, "Do you know where—"

"Yes, yes," cut in Nikos. "She is well. She told us what happened; she hoped that you had gotten away."

"The Book . . . ," began Polus but cried out in pain as he tried to adjust his position.

"I am so sorry," said Nikos. "Your own men did this?"

"Not my men anymore."

"It was the one called Teras," said Nikos. "The one with the scar, wasn't it?" Polus did not answer, but a fury arose in Nikos like he had never known.

Polus revived a bit and said, "Why they hate what we believe, I do not know." He grimaced in pain as he pointed to his chest. "He did this."

Nikos recoiled as he saw a horrible gash and torn flesh crusted with dirt and blackish red blood. "The mark of the Great One . . . ," he said shaking his head. "He gouged it off?"

"I taunted him," continued Polus, "saying that it's who I am and that no matter what he did to me, I would remain so."

At that point Nikos was surprised as Polus smirked a bit, but shuddered in pain as he added, "It is good to suffer for the Great One."

"We must get out of here," said Nikos.

But Polus said, "Even I cannot. This was built to confine men such as I."

Nikos looked up at the iron beams and bars and saw that they were even heavier than any bridge he had ever seen.

He sat back against the wall next to Polus, who turned painfully to look at him and said, "I wish you were not here, but I am glad you are. I have always feared dying, but more than that, I hated the thought of dying all alone." He heaved in a deep breath and groaned.

Nikos's face flushed hot with compassion, and tears stung him as he said, "You won't die here! I won't let it happen."

Polus grinned and said, "Only yesterday you tried to kill me."

Nikos was overwhelmed with shame and looked away, but Polus added, "I would have done the same, but I forgive it."

Nikos shook his head, but suddenly there were sounds overhead, and Megar peered down at them, with Teras and a few others right behind him.

Rage filled Nikos, and he sought to jump up, but Polus held him back.

"Ah, commander," said Megar sarcastically, "it is good to see you conscious. I don't expect that you are any more willing to tell us where the Book is?" Polus made no response and then Megar eyed Nikos and added, "Perhaps Teras could convince your friend to tell us?"

"He does not know," said Polus. "How could he?"

"Enough of this!" shouted Teras angrily. "We must continue to search for it ourselves, *Commander* Megar! Polus will never tell us. You know he would die first!" He finished with a huge scowl and then abruptly turned and walked away.

Megar stood for a moment and then said to Polus, "Then die you will." He turned away and called out orders to the soldiers, and it quickly became silent again.

"Will they find the Book?" asked Nikos anxiously.

"I do not think so," answered Polus, still looking downcast.

"You have hidden it?" Polus nodded as Nikos asked, "What will happen now?"

"They will let us die in here."

The day passed slowly and silently as the Rift contained only the wounded and those who were caring for them, while the rest were searching the valley. Nikos examined every inch of the trench but could find no weakness or way out. Dejected, he sat down next to Polus, who was looking worse as the day progressed. Not only were his face and lips swollen but they were also becoming dry and cracked with thirst.

Nightfall brought the sounds of soldiers returning, but to Nikos's relief, he and Polus continued to be left alone. Polus fell into a fitful sleep, but Nikos sat there, becoming more distraught with the thought that Polus would eventually die right where he was sitting. It repulsed him, and he got up and walked to where the door was overhead. He leaped as high as he could but was still well short. Anger welled mightily in him, and he leaped many more times, but it was no good. He had winded himself and gave one last mighty effort, but fell and found himself on his back, looking up through the bars at the sky to the stars beyond.

Discouragement filled him as he thought of Makarios and Chayel and the others. "*How can it end like this?*" he thought. "*How will they ever find the Book now?*" Questions raged through his mind, but it wasn't long before exhaustion ushered him to sleep.

⸺ Twenty Four ⸺

Meanwhile, back in Wildhorse Village, Kafar, Barah, and the rest were seated around the firepit, eating a late supper. The day before, they had found the Rift and snuck up to the edge of it at the north end away from the gate but saw very little activity. They had also searched for Nikos as much as they dared, but from their vantage point, they did not see Polus or Nikos in the trench. They turned in for the night not only still concerned for Polus, but now also for Nikos.

In the morning, a messenger pounded on Thumos's door and as he opened it, the messenger exclaimed, "Sir, there are many, many soldiers coming from Makran, a thousand maybe. They will be in Keone by midday!"

Thumos roused everyone, and they made their way to Keone and waited, staying out of sight, not knowing what to expect. The sun had climbed overhead when troops of soldiers arrived in the town, led by a man in kingly armor riding a stately, dapple-gray horse. A huge Meganthropos soldier walked at his right.

"It is Overseer Rhaka himself!" said Odus quietly.

"And the one next to him," whispered Chayel, "he was with Polus on the bridge when they attacked Tachus Town." There were, indeed, more than a thousand soldiers and as they passed through Keone, most of the populace had disappeared into houses or barns. They moved quickly and continued north, with Thumos and the gang following at a distance. The army arrived at the edge of the valley and Teras, for indeed it was he who was next to Rhaka, led them down, while a small percentage of them stayed behind with the horses.

From their vantage point, hidden among the pine trees, Chayel said to Odus, "How does Rhaka know of this place?"

"That big one with the long, black hair," answered Odus, "I think he betrayed them all down there."

Thumos signaled them to gather round and then said in a hushed tone, "Do you not think? Why is Rhaka here? What has he to gain?"

"Polus!" whispered Makarios. "They must have him then."

"Or the Book," added Arak.

"Or both," finished Barah.

"If we can do nothing else, we must at least see what happens," said Thumos and headed north through the trees with the rest following.

After some time, Rhaka and his troops along with Teras arrived at the Rift, and the soldier inside quickly opened the gate. Most of the soldiers though, were out looking for the Book and when they realized the force of arms that stood at the gate, they quickly disappeared into the mountains.

Megar came out of the headquarters and walked toward the gate yelling, "What is this? Why have you opened—"

When he saw Rhaka, he was overcome with dread and immediately feigned respect. "Overseer Rhaka, sir!" he said, "I am Commander Megar at your service!" His eyes darted to Teras and though he kept a smile on his face, his heart was for murder.

"Indeed, you are," said Rhaka in a very measured and sweet way. His manner was charming and captivating, and Megar at once found that he was at odds with himself, feeling agreeable to Rhaka.

"You have a certain prisoner here," continued Rhaka, "that you wish to turn over to me?"

"Yes," answered Megar though he wished to say the opposite. He commanded his men to bring up Polus and, in a few minutes, they returned but without him.

"Where is he?!" yelled Megar.

"Gone . . ." answered one of soldiers. Megar rushed to the trench, followed closely by Teras. They found the door open and saw a rope tied to a beam hanging down inside.

"Who has done this?!" boomed Megar, but Teras was enraged and fell upon him, and they began fighting. Megar's men yielded as the whole end of the Rift was filled with Rhaka's men.

"Enough!" said Rhaka, who stood near the trench.

Immediately, Teras flung Megar to the ground and said, "There is a traitor here."

"And it is you!" yelled Megar, coughing out dirt and getting to his feet. Rhaka was quite calm, almost serene as he turned to Teras.

"So, you have nothing for me?" he asked meekly, but a fire burned in his eyes that caused even Teras some trepidation. He was speechless and glanced about and was inexplicably overwhelmed with terrible fear as Rhaka's presence seemed to grow larger and to intensify.

"He, he—" began Teras, trembling. "Megar, he—"

"But my arrangement was with *you*, Teras," said Rhaka soothingly, "not with Megar." Then he smiled so warmly, almost affectionately that Teras began to feel more at ease.

Teras began, "Well, yes sir, that is true—"

Suddenly, in one fell swoop, Rhaka yelled out, "*You failed me!*" and struck Teras across the face with the back of his hand, causing him to crash to the ground. He quickly struggled to his feet, but he was quite shaken by how powerful Rhaka was, and his face was torn and bleeding from the armored gloves that Rhaka wore. He stood there shaking, in mortal fear and unwilling to even lift his eyes. Rhaka shook his head in disgust and said to the man next to him, "We must return to Makran. Polus will come to me. He cannot help himself. His desire to rule in my place obsesses him."

Rhaka turned to leave and as Megar and especially Teras were feeling relieved, he suddenly turned back and looked around and beyond them. Then his eyes focused on them, full of anger and vengeance, but his tone was compassionate as he said, "All your men have deserted you." He raised his eyebrows high and tucked his chin in a bit as he said, "So sorry for you." He pursed his lips and stood there a moment, seemingly undecided. Megar and Teras had never felt so helpless and at the mercy of another and could not explain why they were so terrified. Megar dropped to his knees, partly because he felt so weak, but also to beg for his life. He began to say something, but suddenly Rhaka bent forward toward him.

"Now, Megar," he said, as if he were talking to a child, "what can I do for you?" He smiled wickedly and lifted Megar's chin with his finger, but Megar began to shake in fear and kept his eyes anywhere but on Rhaka.

"Now, don't be afraid," he continued with a pout on his face. "You will only get what you deserve." And then again in one vicious act, he struck Megar mightily across the face and screamed, "*Death!*" Megar crashed to the earth, holding his face in his hands and crying out in pain. Rhaka paced around a bit and then returned to Megar, who began whimpering.

Rhaka knelt and gently turned him over. "Now, you see?" he began tenderly. "That wasn't so bad, was it?" But the whole side of Megar's face was a bloody mess, and he clutched at it in mortal pain. Suddenly, Rhaka rose up, dragging Megar by the arm as he strode toward the trench. His strength was astonishing as he threw Megar in like a rag doll. He turned on Teras, but he darted toward the trench and jumped in himself. Rhaka only rolled his eyes and shook his head and then commanded his men to secure the door.

"Leave no one else alive!" he commanded in a rage and then strode away.

High above, Thumos and the others watched from the top of the Rift, having only heard the words that Rhaka had yelled out. They were stunned by his power, and all of them felt a new level of fear but also an unexplainable admiration. Chayel shook her head and grimaced as she felt an attraction that she immediately hated.

"That there man is surely one to be reckoned with," said Odus with a sense of awe.

"We must fight this," breathed out Chayel through clenched teeth. Suddenly, their attention returned to the floor of the Rift as fighting broke out in and around the barracks. Rhaka's men were carrying out his orders, and it wasn't long before every one of Megar's men was dead.

"Killin' their own kind without mercy . . ." said Odus shaking his head.

"They are fiercely loyal to Rhaka," said Kafar.

Barah added, "Disturbingly so." They watched as Rhaka's men dragged all the dead bodies into the buildings, set them on fire, and then marched out of the Rift.

"He has left those two to die," said Makarios.

"They must have had Polus in there," said Barah, "but he got out somehow."

"We must learn all we can from them," said Thumos. After Rhaka and his men were gone, they made their way around to the gate. The buildings were still burning and the black smoke that rose was saturated with the choking smell of death. They stopped in the gate feeling a sense of respect for the dead and after a few moments, Makarios made straight for the trench, with the others following. As they approached, they could hear yelling.

"So, kill me!" yelled Megar. "But we will *both* die in here!"

"It would be a mercy to kill you," snarled Teras. "Better to see you die slowly!" They froze and looked up as Makarios appeared at the top, and then their eyes darted to the others behind her.

"*You!*" yelled Megar, jumping to his feet, but nearly falling as his head spun from the pain. "You corrupted Polus! You ruined him!" He spoke as one who had been bitterly betrayed and then sank to his knees, holding his bloodied face. But Teras, who was not as badly injured, came forward and looked carefully at each of them. His contempt and hatred of them was fierce.

"We must help them," said Makarios.

"Help them?" asked Odus in disbelief.

"We ought to put them out of their misery," said Thumos vehemently.

"Killing them would not do so," said Makarios passionately. "It would send them to a misery that cannot even be imagined!" She looked around at them and continued, "Would you execute them, injured and unarmed as they are? Or else leave them to die?"

"We should let them out then?" asked Thumos incredulously.

"They will try to kill us!" exclaimed Chayel. "They are evil to the core!" she finished, glaring at Teras.

He returned the stare and said through clenched teeth and a vicious scowl, "I know you," and then he held his arm up and said, "You . . . it was you that pierced me with that thing you have there." Suddenly, he lunged toward her like a caged tiger, leaping up and catching the bars of his prison, growling in a rage. Fear shot through her as she jumped back and felt her face flush hot in a momentary panic.

She quickly stepped back and in a rush of anger shouted, "I could have killed you that day! I wish I had!"

"You should have!" he sneered back. "Mercy is for fools!" He spun around and tramped to the other side of the trench and turned to face them and continued, "You ought to have killed us both by now! You are all fools! Your minds are corrupted and poisoned by the absurd things you believe!"

"It is you who—" began Chayel heatedly.

Odus put a hand on her arm, and she relented. Megar had sat down against the wall, more occupied with his wound than anything else, and was just staring at the ground.

Teras however continued in a rage. "Kill us or leave us to die!" he yelled and would have continued but when Makarios started to speak, he unexpectedly became silent.

"I do not wish for you to die," she began, "but to live and to live free of this curse that makes both of you such beasts." Teras was about to yell back but stopped in the midst of it.

After a moment, Megar looked up and spoke gingerly as his face had become very swollen, "What do you mean?" As Makarios's eyes fell upon him, she saw how similar he looked to Polus and was immediately filled with compassion.

"Can we not help him somehow?" she asked Thumos, but Megar asked, a bit more forcefully, "What is this curse?"

But Teras bellowed, "*Lies!* It is all deceit and foolishness!"

"You have heard of this?" asked Megar, wincing with pain, but Teras was enraged and began screaming incoherently and throwing dirt in the air.

Suddenly, he turned and advanced toward Megar, seething, "It is treachery. It is what destroyed Polus. You saw what it did to him, what he became!"

"And I saw what *you* did to him," said Megar. "Which is worse?" Such a look of fury came over Teras that it was truly frightening.

As he went for Megar, Chayel yelled, "*Stop!*" Teras jerked around to see her bow trained on him, an arrow fitted to the string. "Stop or you will die where you are!"

He paused and then slowly backed up a few paces, but his fury remained, and his eyes were fixed on Chayel.

Megar struggled to his feet and came forward, just below Makarios and looked up. "Tell me," he said, "what is this curse?"

Teras was beside himself and though Chayel had let her bow down, it was still at the ready, and her full attention remained on him so that he stayed where he was. Megar seemed truly contrite and remained expectant.

"Can't we let him out?" asked Makarios.

Kafar replied, "He could be playing us for fools."

Arak said, "I do not think so."

"What of the other one?" asked Thumos.

Barah stepped forward with his bow at the ready and said, "That one there will not move, because he does not wish to die."

"Well, it don't seem like a good idea to me," said Odus.

Teras was furious but remained silent, believing that Megar was only acting and that he would get them both out somehow. Barah trained his bow on Teras and pulled it back to full stretch as they opened the door and let down a rope. Teras stood still, watching like a ravenous animal as they pulled Megar up. With difficulty, they hauled him over the edge, and he just lay on the ground trembling in pain.

Teras licked his lips in anticipation of Megar leaping up and overpowering all of them, but his expectation sank into disbelief as Megar got to his knees and only knelt there hunched over. Teras's absolute fury rendered him speechless until it could not be contained and erupted in an ear-splitting screech. He rushed at them and leaped up at the door, but they had already latched it by the long bar that extended well back from the edge to a metal post.

If there was any doubt about the trench being secure enough to contain him, it was removed as he went wild, pulling and smashing and rushing madly about. It wasn't long before he was spent and collapsed in a sweaty, dirty heap against the far wall. His chest heaved mightily, and his rage and desire for vengeance still burned like a fire in his eyes. "I will kill every one of you," he seethed.

Thumos began speaking to Kafar and the others about what they ought to do about him, but Makarios had knelt in front of Megar. When she saw how torn and bloody his face was and the excruciating pain, her eyes filled with tears.

She looked up at Odus and Chayel and asked, "Can you find some clean water?" But Megar got slowly to his feet and said quietly, moving his lips as little as possible, "No, I will—"

But he reeled forward a bit and, though he was bulky and seven feet tall, Makarios instinctively moved forward to steady him. As she caught his hands, he looked down at her incredulously and said, "Why do you help me? I could kill you."

"I do not know that you will not," she answered, "but I will take the chance of it."

He staggered slightly as his head spun, and she said, "You must sit down." She steadied him as he slowly made his way to the guardhouse at the gate, the only building that had not been set on fire. The others followed, watching him warily, but his injury had him quite subdued as his head throbbed, and one eye was now tightly swollen shut. As he entered the guardhouse, he sat down on a heavy wooden bench, and Makarios came in behind him while the others stood outside. As Chayel came to the doorway, Megar glanced up, but groaned in pain.

He looked from her to Makarios and said in a questioning tone, "You risk your life to help me?" He grimaced and sat back against the wall and almost seemed angry.

"To tell you of the curse," she answered.

"It is worth your life?" he asked, scowling in disbelief. His condition was getting him agitated and when Barah and Odus appeared in the doorway behind Chayel, he tensed and looked around at them all.

Suddenly, he jumped up, grabbing an axe that was near the fireplace and seized Makarios, bringing the blade to her throat. Barah and Chayel instantly had their bows trained on him, but Makarios called out, "No!"

"You are all fools!" he bellowed. "Teras was—"

At that moment he began to lose consciousness and fell forward. Barah rushed toward him just in time to slow his fall and let him down to the floor. He lay there unmoving as Makarios knelt down and looked closer at his wound and arose shaking her head.

"It has gotten very bad," she said. "How could that happen so quickly? I do not understand."

"This Rhaka seems more than a man could be," added Thumos.

Odus shook his head, and Arak said gravely, "Evil is strong in him." Megar suddenly groaned and tried getting up but cried out and slumped back to the floor. Makarios immediately went to him but gasped in surprise.

Chayel stepped over, but recoiled exclaiming, "Oh! His . . . face!" Megar's face had never stopped bleeding, and now the torn flesh was turning black along the edges and proceeding at a rate that could be seen. One open eye was bleary and seemed to be unseeing, and his neck had swelled up alarmingly. He clutched at his chest as he wheezed and with his other hand, he reached toward Makarios and croaked, "Save me!"

His breathing became more labored and suddenly one eye bulged open. In terrible pain and mortal fear, he thrashed about clutching at whatever he could reach, as if he were falling off a cliff. His face and neck were engorged, and the blood ran freely as he began to convulse. He stared at Makarios with a final look of utter desperation and went limp. His head and neck seemed to deflate, and the blood around his wound quickly dried up.

Makarios cried out in horror as she covered her face and backed away. "I saw it!" she cried. "In his eye—the City of Dying; it was terrible!"

Chayel pulled her up and led her sobbing from the building. They were all silent as Makarios cried, held by Chayel. After a few minutes, Makarios looked toward the trench and said, "What about the other? Will his wound kill him too?"

She did not wait for a reply but ran to the trench. As she appeared at the top, Teras's eyes darted to her, but he remained sitting on the ground, leaning against the far wall. He had a look of resignation, but a vengeful fury still smoldered within. Makarios looked carefully at him, which angered him, and he rose up and came toward her, scowling murderously.

"Your friend," began Makarios, still upset over what she had witnessed, "is dead."

Teras's expression became somewhat quizzical. "Well, you *ought* to have killed him," he said almost triumphantly. "He was your enemy!"

"No . . . he—"

She burst into tears, which disgusted Teras. "He died from his wound," said Chayel angrily. Teras scoffed and turned away, still considering them all to be fools or liars.

The men took it to task to bury Megar, which took most of the rest of the day, considering his size. Makarios tried talking to Teras about the curse, but he quickly became infuriated and began to throw rocks at her.

Chayel pulled her away and said, "You know as well as anyone how futile it is when they refuse to listen." Makarios only nodded as she walked out of sight of Teras.

"Did you see though," said Chayel, "his wound did not look as bad as before?"

Makarios seemed lost in thought as she said, "We ought to get him some water." She went off to look for a bucket and left Chayel standing there.

She stood still for a moment and then went back to the trench, crossed her arms and called out passionately, "You are the fool! Your friend has passed into terrible misery, and you may soon go there yourself! Do you not fear?"

Teras looked at her but said nothing. "Surely you know," she continued, "Polus had the Book. Did he not teach you—"

At that, Teras leaped up and came at her. "*No!*" he snarled. "Not all of it is true!" He stood below her heaving and then said with a sneer, "What do you know of it?" But before she could respond he turned away, shaking his head and scoffing.

"I know the truth!" she called after him. He spun around and glared at her.

"Truth?!" he yelled. "What is truth?"

"The Book. It is truth! *All* of it!" she answered. "It must be all or none of it, and you know it!"

Teras was infuriated but found nothing more to say and then roared out incomprehensible words and stomped off toward the far end of the trench. At that point, Makarios came with a bucket of water and looked questioningly at Chayel. She went toward Teras who had disappeared into the shadow that was on one side. She looped a rope around the bucket handle and let it down and then pulled the rope back up.

Unexpectedly, Makarios smiled and said, "What was that you said about how futile it is when they will not listen?"

"It is so hard though," began Chayel sheepishly, "to know the truth and have him say that it is a lie."

"Yes," added Makarios.

The sun had begun to go down by the time the men joined Makarios and Chayel.

"We ought to return to the village," said Thumos.

"But what of him," said Makarios motioning toward the trench. "Are we to just leave him there? And for how long?"

"He has vowed to kill us," said Odus. "We cannot let him out."

"Yes," said Barah, "but though he has sworn himself as our enemy, we are not his."

"Our bows give us the advantage," said Kafar. "And he has a proper fear of them. It would not be just to leave him imprisoned as he has done us no wrong." The others agreed even though Odus was reluctant; Kafar stepped to the edge of the trench.

"You there!" he called.

There was no response and after a few moments, Odus said, "Well, leave him there then if he don't want to answer!"

But Kafar again addressed Teras. "We are not your enemy, nor do we have any ill-will toward you," he said, glancing at Odus. "We wish to set you free."

Again, there was no response, but eventually, Teras came out from the shadow and surprised them by chuckling as he crossed his arms and looked up at them. "You do not convince me," he said sounding almost amiable.

Kafar gestured for Arak to open the door, and Barah and Chayel stood back and readied their bows. For the first time since they had met him, Teras was uncertain. He looked at the open door and remained where he was but looked piercingly at Kafar.

"You are sincere," he said in disbelief. He turned and paced back and forth and then said, glancing at the open door again, "You would let me go free?"

"It is the honorable thing to do," said Kafar. "We are not your enemy and cannot just leave you to die."

Teras was in quite a quandary, but after a while, he leaped up and pulled himself through the door and then stood still, eyeing everyone carefully. He shook his head and muttered to himself, "Fools!" yet he remained still.

Suddenly, Odus blurted out, "Well, you're free! If I was you, I'd be on my way to give Rhaka what-for for splittin' your face open!"

Teras's countenance quickly changed, and a faraway look came into his eye as he snarled quietly, "Yes . . ."

"See, if you're Rhaka's enemy, you can't be ours," added Odus, "'cause we're agin' 'im too."

Teras scowled and looked murderously at Odus but had to agree with him. Still, he had not moved and was hesitant to take a step. Kafar signaled the others to move back so that the way toward the gate was clear. Finally, Teras moved forward, keeping his eyes mostly on Chayel and Barah, but as he passed by Makarios, she caught his eye and what he saw there seemed to confound him.

He came within arm's reach of her and suddenly, his face twisted into a rage, and he said through clenched teeth, "*No!* It is the same trickery you used on Polus!"

With one last look at all of them, he ran off toward the gate and was gone. They all breathed a sigh of relief and then Odus said, "Guess we got to watch our backs now that we unleashed that terror into the world." And indeed, they did watch their backs as they returned to the village, arriving there by nightfall.

In the morning, as they gathered for breakfast, they talked about what they ought to do about where Nikos and Polus might be.

"Why would Nikos not return here?" asked Makarios.

"I wonder if he is with Polus, added Chayel.

"And do they have the Book?" said Kafar. They had no answers and sat silent for a while, at a loss as to what to do. They spent the next few days looking for Nikos and Polus and hoped that they would turn up at the village, but all was fruitless.

One morning, Arak awoke very early and roused the others and said, "I had a dream last night. I saw a very old, dark, and forbidding forest, but deep within it was a clearing where the sun shone brightly down. There was a house, built into the side of a hill."

Makarios suddenly became animated, and Arak said, "You know this place?"

"Yes, I think so," she quickly answered. "What else did you see?"

"The door of the house was open," he continued, "and a large raven was squawking repeatedly up in the clearing."

Makarios waited expectantly for more, but Arak finished, "That is all I saw."

All eyes turned to Makarios, and she said, "That is where Polus used to live, in Geroon Forest, before Nikos came across him."

"What does it mean?" asked Odus intrigued.

"I do not know," answered Arak. "That is all I saw."

"We must go back down to Agathon Province," said Makarios urgently. "Maybe Nikos and Polus have gone there."

She stood up, followed by Chayel and Odus, but the others remained seated as Kafar said, "We do not know if Arak's dream has even happened yet, or if it is from sometime in the past."

"But we are accomplishing nothing here," exclaimed Chayel.

After a short silence, Barah said, "Arak's dream may be a pointer. It is at least something to go on."

"And it seems clear that Rhaka did not get what he wanted," added Kafar, "and that gives us hope." Another silence followed and eventually, they all agreed to go back south.

"At least we've got to see how much worse things have gotten," said Odus, "what with Rhaka running rampant as he is."

They prepared to leave, and Thumos bid them farewell. They covered the few miles between the village and Keone quickly, but as they approached, a soldier commanded them to stop and dismount and come forward on foot. Chayel and Odus remained with the horses, while Kafar, Barah, Arak, and Makarios came up to the soldiers. There was more than a dozen who had come from Keone; they stood in rank with a captain standing in front of them. Beyond the soldiers, they could see that a wall had been built across the road and for some distance down either side of the town.

"What is your business?" the captain asked Kafar, but before he could respond, Makarios said determinedly, "We are going through Keone." The captain turned to her and scowled.

"You dare speak, woman?" he asked with an unexpected viciousness, and a few of the soldiers behind him whooped and jeered, to which he paid no attention. The captain fixed his eyes upon her and softened his tone.

"Well, you are a fine one," he said smiling and then stepped very close to her. Instinctively, she stepped back, but he caught her wrist and pulled her toward him. With her other arm she sought to strike him, but suddenly Kafar leaped forward with his short sword drawn and knocked the captain to the ground. All were surprised, but none more than the captain himself. He quickly composed himself and though Kafar's sword was at his throat, he said, "I will make you wish that you had died right here." The conflict ended quickly as scores of soldiers surrounded them, and they were taken into custody.

"What of those two?" asked a soldier pointing to Odus and Chayel. The captain waved them off and said, "Leave them! What are they, an old man and a harmless girl!"

Odus and Chayel looked on in dismay as the squads of soldiers went into Keone, and the gate slammed behind them. Odus and Chayel turned to look at each other in dismay.

"We must get south to Marshal Kainos," she said.

"Don't think there is any way through these mountains," said Odus, "least not on horseback. There's nowhere to even make a start." Chayel glared at the unaccommodating mountains as Odus added, "We best go back and see Thumos."

They mounted up without another word, each leading two of the other horses and returned to the village.

Keraia came running out to meet them, exclaiming, "What has happened?"

They explained everything and then asked, "Is there any way south except through Keone?"

Keraia shook her head and said "Even on foot, it is very difficult." She explained that Thumos and some others had gone out again looking for Nikos and Polus, so they waited for them to return.

It was near evening when Thumos and Eido rushed into the house, "Your horses," said Eido when he saw Chayel and Odus, "Why are they here—"

He stopped short and asked, "Where are the others?" When it was explained to them, Thumos became very somber and just shook his head.

"Would that I had an army to overcome these evil men," he said. They had a very quiet supper and then turned in for the night. Chayel went to the barn and climbed into the loft and settled back into the hay. She took a few deep breaths and then suddenly the tears came.

"How can this happen?" she cried. "How can they all be taken by Rhaka's men like that? Are we not doing the good that we are meant to do?" She was overwhelmed with emotion and sought furiously for answers, but soon fell into a fitful sleep.

⸺ Twenty Five ⸺

Chayel was awakened a bit before sunrise and through her groggy thoughts, she heard a strange, muffled voice that kept saying the same thing. Suddenly, she was jolted wide awake by a sharp jab in her side as the voice spoke again, "Chayel, you must gather your belongings."

All at once, she jumped up and exclaimed, "Tey-Rahk! It is you!"

"Indeed," he said as he moved his huge maned head close to her. She could see his crystal blue eyes glittering in the faint light of dawn that made its way through a window. Though he stood on the floor of the barn, his size put his head level with Chayel in the loft.

"You must gather your belongings," he repeated, "and wake Odus. But see that you do not wake anyone else and then come to me out at the road." He slipped noiselessly out of the barn, just barely fitting through the big double doors.

Chayel quickly packed up and then stole quietly along toward the house. "He said do not wake anyone else," she whispered to herself. "But I do not know where Odus is sleeping." She crept up to the house and felt uncharacteristically nervous, being very concerned about carrying out Tey-Rahk's command. "*How will I even find him—*" she thought.

An unexpected sound behind caused her to freeze. "What are you doin' there, missy?" said a figure far too loudly, sitting by the firepit. Chayel spun around, recognizing the voice of Odus.

"Odus!" she hissed. "You must be quiet!"

"What is it?" he answered, barely audible.

"Tey-Rahk," she whispered. "He just woke me and said to gather my things and then come and get you. We must not wake anyone else and then meet him at the road."

Odus responded quickly, and soon they were on their way. "What were you doing up anyway?" asked Chayel.

"Woke up early and couldn't sleep," he answered. "Tryin' to think—"

Both of them were startled as Tey-Rahk seemed to appear out of nowhere.

"Oh!" exclaimed Chayel and then added, "Here, this is Odus."

"Yes, I know," he answered with the slightest tone of insult. "We must leave."

They climbed aboard and as Chayel began to tell Odus how best to hang on, Tey-Rahk's huge leap into the air and massive sweep of his wings drowned out her voice. They were high in the air before Chayel could be heard again, but Odus gave her a nudge, as if to be quiet. A strong sense of solemnity had fallen over him as he realized how truly powerful and majestic Tey-Rahk was. The flight did not take long as they flew south over the mountains and landed just north of Ekuus, near the horse farm that Odus was from.

As they slid to the ground, Tey-Rahk said, "You will find horses here. You must find Pike and be very careful about whom you trust."

Odus, still in awe of Tey-Rahk, said very formally, "Yes, sir, Master Tey-Rahk."

He was taken aback as Tey-Rahk glared at him with icy blue fire in his eyes and said, with a hint of a growl, "Do not call me that! But only Tey-Rahk." He shook his massive mane and then leaped away into the air. Odus stood stunned, watching him fly away, but he was soon lost to view in the dim light of dawn.

"Come on we've got to find Pike!" said Chayel quietly, yet forcefully. "We can get a couple of horses here?"

"Yeh, probably," he answered, looking toward the farm. "Wonder why he told us to find Pike."

"We must not question," said Chayel as she grabbed his arm and started toward the farm. As they came to an outbuilding, the sun had come up enough to show that there were a few new buildings.

As they looked around, Odus exclaimed very quietly, "No! Look, one of Rhaka's men!"

"And another," said Chayel pointing in a different direction. They got down in the long grass, suddenly feeling much more serious about the situation. The day's farm activities soon began, with some men hauling wheelbarrows and bales of hay, while others led horses out from the barns. Thankfully, there were only a few soldiers, and it seemed that they and the farm owner were in agreement with the situation.

"There sure are a lot more horses here than there used to be," said Chayel.

"And more workers too," said Odus. "I guess we could just kind of blend in once there's enough of them about." They made their way to the back of a big barn and snuck in, hiding in an empty stall.

"I wish Tey-Rahk had stayed," whispered Chayel. "Why could we not have ridden him, as a horse that is."

"Or he could have just flown us to where Pike is," added Odus. "Why would—"

But at that moment the barn door banged open. "Now just shut yer face and do wut I tell ya!" yelled a fat, red-faced man at a young boy who followed him, pushing a wheelbarrow. "They make us do the mucking out 'cause they're cruel," he added.

Chayel and Odus remained hidden, not having seen who had entered. Odus whispered, "It's Chawk!"

"The one who got so mad at you before you left here with me?" asked Chayel. Odus nodded, and then their attention returned to Chawk, who had not ceased yelling and complaining.

"Not like that, boy! Like this!" and then, "Now get that full; we don't want to make more trips than we have to!" And he went on and on, but eventually they went out.

"We better get out," said Odus.

"But what if we run into Chawk somewhere?" asked Chayel. "Surely, he will make a scene and call attention to us."

"Let's see where he went," said Odus, going to the front doors, but as he peeked out, he didn't see him anywhere. Seeing that there were more men about, Odus signaled Chayel, and they stepped out into the yard. Knowing how things operated, Odus joined in with the work, but almost immediately, a few of the young men approached and looked Chayel up and down.

One of them said, "Now, what do we have here?"

The other added, "Looks like a fine young woman!"

"But women ain't allowed," replied the first.

"Well, I say she is," said the other and reached out to grab her, but the next thing he knew he was knocked to the ground by a hard kick to his ribs from Chayel. He lay there gasping for breath, but anger quickly took him, and he jumped up screaming obscenities of what he would do to her. He lunged at her, but the other man grabbed him and held him back. Some others joined in, hooting and hollering, but when they saw soldiers approaching, all of them scurried off in different directions. Odus and Chayel stood there helplessly as three, rather unkempt soldiers, stopped in front of them.

"What's she doing here?" said one to Odus. "You know womenfolk aren't allowed!" The soldiers moved to take her into custody, but a voice came from behind Odus and Chayel; they immediately recognized that it was Chawk.

"Now, hold on there!" he yelled, brushing past Odus and holding up his hand at the soldiers, "That there is Odus's relative, so act decent!" The soldiers were less than professional but strangely had respect for Chawk.

"Now, she ain't here to work, you fools, but is lookin' to buy a horse, and Odus here was just showin' her around! Ain't that right?" he finished, looking at Odus, who was too stunned to say anything.

But Chayel quickly took his arm and said, "Yes, uncle, let's look at the horses now."

The soldiers were unsure about things, but one of them pointed at Chawk and said, "You owe us!"

"Don't be gettin' greedy now," said Chawk. "I been mighty fair with you so far." And then they walked away.

Then he turned to Odus, who was still shocked, and said, "Now, Odus, I right got to apologize for getting' so wrought up over you leavin' me like you did, but I learnt me a lesson! And got to say that I am glad to see you."

He stuck out his hand, and Odus shook it without realizing it and then Chawk bowed slightly to Chayel and said, "Sure am sorry for blamin' you like as I did."

Chayel, who was likewise amazed at the change in Chawk managed to say, "Thank you."

He turned back to Odus and said, "Now say somethin', or I'll think you gone off your compass."

Odus looked hard at Chawk and as he was about to speak, Chawk continued, "Now that's good to see, and it's the best thing that ever happened—you leavin' me, 'cause now I got some friends, and things are working out, except for all the slavin' I got to do, but that's just part of it you see—"

He took a breath to continue, but Odus cut in, "I am glad to see you bein' happy for once, and I sure thank you for savin' us from Rhaka's men, and you're not far off about us buying some horses, but we can't buy, we just need to borrow—"

Chawk's sudden change of expression cut him off. "Now you already done that," said Chawk crossing his arms. "Where's those two beasts you took out of here?"

Odus quickly explained the situation, and Chawk looked surprised and said, "You say Rhaka is takin' over everything and closin' off towns? Doesn't sound like what I know. He's been right fair with me . . . I mean with us here."

"Have you been beyond the borders of this town?" cut in Chayel.

His eyes darted to her, and he replied, "Well, no, but—"

"Look, Chawk," interjected Odus, "I sure appreciate you helpin' us, but we need some horses right quick."

He waited expectantly as Chawk looked thoughtful, though doubtful of what Odus had said about Rhaka. After a few moments he said, "Now look, I kinda got my own thing here, so I got some beasts, but you're *borrowing* them, and you got to promise to bring them back or at least make good on 'em."

Odus agreed, and Chawk led them off to a corral. It wasn't long before they were mounted up. Right before they headed off, Chawk said, "So, what exactly is the hurry? What is it that you got to do?"

Chayel and Odus glanced at each other and then he answered, "Well, like I said, that Rhaka is a bad man, and he's takin' over things, confiscatin' property, throwin' folks in prison, and we can't just sit by and watch it happen."

"Well, what are you gonna do?" he asked, seemingly taking things seriously. "I mean, just the two of you and all . . . , and is it really bad like you say?"

"Look, Chawk," said Odus, "we really got to go, but hopefully we will fare well and will see you again." He reined his horse around, followed by Chayel, and they rode south out of the farm to a road that ran east-west.

"Now, Tey-Rahk told us to be really sure about who we trust," began Odus, pulling his horse to a stop. "I think we've gone and muffed it already. We trusted Chawk." They both quickly looked back the way they had come, but there was no one to be seen.

"We better stay off the roads—" he began.

Suddenly, they heard yelling and the sound of galloping horses on their left. They just had time to rein their mounts away from the road when a man rode madly past followed by half a dozen soldiers, who were calling for him stop. As they were just about to round a bend down the road, one of the soldiers launched a spear, knocking the man off his horse. Odus and Chayel looked at each other in alarm and spurred their horses forward, setting a quick pace across the field.

"Those were Rhaka's men!" called Odus. "We got to get to Agathon Outpost right quick!"

"And hope we find Pike there," answered Chayel. It was more than forty miles to the Outpost, so they rode across country the whole day—thankfully without coming across anyone. The sun had nearly set when they finally came to the northern edge of Fragmoo Forest.

"Agathon Outpost is on the other side of these woods," said Odus. "It's about five miles, but we better lie low here for the night." They ate a cold supper and sheltered under a heavy old pine tree. In the morning, they were on their way early and had come down to the southern edge of the forest just as the sun was getting warm. Suddenly, a dog began barking and then another, and then, they heard men arguing. Odus and Chayel got off their horses and went slowly forward, still amidst the trees, but the ruckus was some distance away. The road directly in front of them ran parallel to the edge of the forest and open country beyond with a town in the distance.

"We got to go west down the road," said Odus. "But we best stay in the forest as long as we can." They were at the eastern end of the forest, where the trees were somewhat sparse, so it was easy going for some way, but eventually, it closed in around them, and they had to come out to the road. The early morning hour meant that the road was deserted, but as they rode on and the sun climbed higher, there were more travelers.

"Wonder why Rhaka's men were down here," said Odus. "Once we come out of the forest, we crossed into Agathon Province, and he's got no right overseein' anything down here!"

Chayel nodded as they continued on, being quite serious and watchful. The forest grew thicker and loomed higher on their right, but to their left was open land with vineyards dotted here and there. More soldiers approached, giving them a careful looking over, but they passed by without incident. Ahead, they could see a town and were surprised to see a gate across the road.

"A toll gate!" exclaimed Chayel quietly. "Like up north." Odus scowled and was suddenly very indignant, but Chayel calmed him.

"We must act as if we are just out for a ride," she said, "as if we have not a care. Now, look happy!" They arrived at the gate, which was manned by some of Rhaka's men, but they seemed less serious than those in the north.

"One silver damah to pass through," said a soldier, hardly looking at them. Odus paid, and they passed through. There were more soldiers in the town, some of whom were arguing with a merchant.

"We only take fifteen percent!" the soldier yelled.

The shop owner retorted, "But that's a whole barrel!"

"And besides, you got no right!" exclaimed another, but this only brought more soldiers and hastened Odus and Chayel's passage. Once through town, they spurred their mounts to a quicker pace.

"I got a bad feelin'," said Odus. "With the Outpost not real far from here, there's bound to be more soldiers." They rode out of the town and on for some time before more soldiers appeared in the distance. They were moving fast, and as they approached, Chayel and Odus slowed their pace. There were three soldiers and as they galloped up, one of them called out to Odus and Chayel, "Halt!"

They all came to a stop, with the soldiers looking like they had been in a scuffle of some sort and their mounts blowing and stamping and moving about nervously.

"What is your business?" demanded the one who was in charge. Neither Odus or Chayel had a ready answer, and the soldier continued, "Where are you coming from?"

"Down from Ekuus," answered Odus pointing to the north.

"There are no roads that way, captain," said one of the other soldiers. The captain looked hard at Chayel and then Odus.

"Do you not know that traveling in the open country is no longer permitted?"

"But we are on a road now," said Chayel, sounding a bit too animated, which drew the captain's attention sharply to her.

"You dare to speak, wench?!"

But she responded quickly, feigning respect and as she averted her eyes, she said, "Forgive me, my lord."

"You mock me?!" he yelled, incensed, and then commanded the two soldiers, "Take them into custody!"

But as they moved to do so, the captain said, "No, I will take the wench for myself!" He dismounted, and a sickly grin spread across his face as he approached Chayel.

"You will pay the fine alright; I can see you have more than enough." He took ahold of her horse's bridle to get him under control and then reached for her. But suddenly everything happened at once: Odus rushed the captain, Chayel kicked him, and her horse spooked and reared up, his hoof striking the captain in the head. He fell backward and hit the ground hard as the two other soldiers drew their swords and came at Odus and Chayel. In the blink of an eye, she launched an arrow, hitting her mark and knocking one soldier off his horse, which made the other pull up and veer away. Both the captain and the soldier lay unmoving as the other soldier circled his horse around, staring at them. He was shocked and got off his horse, looking carefully at the dead soldier and the arrow in his neck. He looked sharply up at Chayel, who had fitted another arrow to the string.

"Now . . . look, we're just—just doing what we're commanded," he stuttered, his eyes locked on Chayel's bow. "Now whatever that thing is there . . . I mean I don't even want to be a soldier. I—"

Odus cut him off. "Throw down your sword!" Immediately, the soldier dropped his sword and pulled a knife from his boot and threw that from him as well.

"Look, I don't want to die," he said. "I don't agree with none of this—"

"Where are you from?" demanded Odus.

"Kuon, just down this road a piece," he answered, pointing east, as his deportment as a soldier completely disappeared.

Odus motioned to the two dead men and said to Chayel, "We better get these out of sight. Keep a watch on this one. Now you there, give me a hand!" Odus dismounted, and he and the remaining soldier dragged the bodies into the forest and then took the bridles and saddles off their horses and let them go.

"What's your name?" Odus asked the man.

"Augie," he answered.

"We can't just let him go," said Chayel.

"He could help us," said Odus.

"I do not think we should trust him," said Chayel. "Remember what Tey-Rahk said."

"You promise you won't tell no one what happened?" said Odus, grabbing the man roughly by his uniform. He shook his head emphatically and cringed a bit.

"I just want to go home."

In the end, they decided to let him go, and he was profusely thankful and rode off east, not even remembering to get his sword. Odus and Chayel headed west down the road, but she suddenly burst into tears.

"It's . . . it's not like I thought it would be," she sputtered as Odus rode close and patted her shoulder.

"Killin' you mean?"

Chayel nodded, "He was coming for me though . . . I was just defending myself." It took some time, but she eventually composed herself, and when they saw Agathon Outpost in the distance, she was all business again.

"There's even more soldiers," said Odus. "Rhaka sure is spreadin' his evil around mighty fast. Let's just ride through and see what we see."

The soldier at the gate demanded the toll and then said, "What's your business?"

"Traveling," answered Odus.

"From where?" he said heatedly.

"Kuon—" began Odus.

Chayel added, "To the horse auctions in Two Rivers." The man scowled at her and then let them through. As the Outpost was a very small town, there were more soldiers than townsfolk, most of them congregated around the marshal's building. As Odus and Chayel neared it, they heard yelling inside. Suddenly the door was flung open, and a teenage boy was thrown out of it, falling headlong to the ground.

"Now, get out of this town," bellowed a large soldier in the doorway, "or you'll join the rest of them!"

The boy got to his feet and yelled back, "You can't just lock up anyone you please!"

The big soldier signaled to a few other soldiers, "Get him out!" They grabbed him and dragged him out of town and pitched him onto the road that came down from the north.

He had barely hit the ground before he was back on his feet and dusting himself off. "This won't stand!" he yelled, but the soldiers had already turned away and headed back to town. The boy stood there fuming, looking this way and that, but he was at a loss. There were other people around, but they were quietly going about their business.

"How do you accept this?!" he called out, raising his hands in the air, but no one paid any attention.

As Odus and Chayel approached, he called out at them angrily, "How do you just ignore this?!"

But Odus pulled his mount to a stop right in front of him and asked, "What's your name, kid?"

As Chayel stopped next to him, the boy gaped at her beauty. "Your name, boy!" insisted Odus, "What is it?"

"Uh, Dero," he said, turning back to him.

"What's going on? Who they got locked up?"

"Well, most of the good men from around here and especially Marshal Pike!" he answered, his anger flaring up. "A whole squad of them soldiers just rode in and took over, and I don't even know where they are from! Marshal Pike wouldn't stand for that of course, but there was just too many, and Marshal Pike surrendered rather than being killed, which I don't doubt they would have done!"

He took a second look at Odus and then at Chayel and said, "You aren't from here—"

Odus interrupted, "Look, I am Odus, and this here is Chayel. I think we're on the same side of this fight, but we ought to talk somewhere away from here. You got a horse?"

Dero nodded as Odus continued, "We're going to ride south down this road; you go get your horse and then catch up with us."

Dero nodded eagerly and ran off, skirting around the Outpost. About an hour later, he caught up with them, and they all continued riding along slowly. The road ran parallel and quite near to the Tachus River, which roared along in the ravine to their right.

"So, you know Marshal Pike, then?" asked Odus.

"Yes, sir. I'm his deputy," answered Dero.

Chayel snickered at this, which quickly angered him, but Odus continued, "Mighty young for that, ain't you?"

"Well, I'm not official yet," he answered, knitting his brow as he glanced at Chayel, and then he said, "But what are we gonna do about Marshal Pike?"

"That's a good question," answered Odus. "Sounds like the men we would need to help us are all locked up with him."

They rode on for a few minutes and then Dero said, "There is a spare set of keys in the building. They are in a secret place, so those soldiers won't even know about them!"

"What good are keys with all those soldiers there?" asked Chayel, but as Dero was about to respond with frustrated anger, Odus pulled his horse to a stop.

"Look, we got to figure this out," he said. "I got to know some more particulars."

Dero explained that about thirty soldiers had come into the Outpost two days before and had quickly locked up Pike and ten other men. "They aren't very careful though," he continued. "They're real arrogant, especially that one who threw me out of the building."

"What happens at night?" asked Odus.

"Well, I've been watching," answered Dero. "So far I've seen that two soldiers stay in the marshal's building, and the rest go to the tavern."

"We ought to watch 'em another night," said Odus, nodding his head and grinning. "And then, we'll have a plan." Dero led them to his family's farm. They waited until early evening and then went on foot through the forest to watch the marshal's building.

It went as Dero had described, and as they headed back to Dero's, he said, "If only we had a few more men, we could ambush those that are headed to the tavern."

"They'd be easy pickins, after they come out, yeh?" said Odus. Dero nodded as Odus continued, "You got a sword?"

"At the farm—"

"Well, we're gonna fight 'em aren't we?" asked Odus,

Chayel added somewhat lightheartedly, "And where there's fighting, sometimes there's killing," but immediately a grave look came over her.

"*Kill* them?" asked Dero incredulously. "Just *us*?"

"Well, you already tried asking nice about Pike, didn't you?" said Odus. "And is there anyone else round about who could help us?"

Dero slowly shook his head and said, "I don't even know where you are from. Why do you want to help? Do you know Marshal Pike?"

"We met him a while back," said Odus.

The next day, Odus helped Dero improve his sword fighting and found that he was fairly proficient with a sword but had never used it against anyone. By evening, they had returned to the same spot in the forest, waiting for the soldiers to leave.

Once they had gone, Odus said, "We'll try to get Pike and the others out first and then deal with the other soldiers. Now, we don't know if the door is locked, but we will knock if we have to, pretending to be lost or something. They won't be ready for us."

"Let me do it," said Chayel. "They will be quite a bit more off guard seeing just me." The sun had set, but there was just enough light to make their way across to the building. Odus and Dero crouched on either side of the door, and Chayel was just reaching for the handle when the door was jerked open, and a very large soldier, who was the captain, emerged, almost running into her.

Startled, he pulled back and said, "Well, well, what is this delicacy we have here? And right after supper too!"

Before Chayel could respond, Odus jumped up, followed by Dero, brandishing their swords, but the man scoffed and said, "What do you think you're going to do Grampaw? And you, again!" he added seeing Dero, "Do we have two more for the jail?" He backed up and gestured saying, "Well come right in!" and eyeing Chayel, he added, "I'll keep you for myself!"

Dero's youth and passion had him leap at the man with his sword pointed at his throat. But his inexperience landed him roughly on the floor, with his sword stripped from his hand.

The soldier quickly backed into the building, taking up a spear. "Now none of you want to die, do you?" Dero scrambled backward, his sword out of reach as Odus came through the doorway. They saw that there were no other soldiers there, and glancing toward the cells, they saw Pike and about fifteen other men, some of them looking the worse for wear.

"Well, kill 'im!" one of them called out.

"Yeah!" yelled another. "He beat me and then stole my horses!"

"As evil as they come!" added another.

Odus said to the captain, "Now, we can do this nice or not. You got these men unjustly imprisoned, and as citizens, we got the right to demand their release!"

"You got the right?" jeered the captain. "The only right you got is that you're *wrong!*" He laughed profusely, and Odus realized that though he had not gone to the tavern, it had not kept him from indulging in some kind of fermented drink.

"Since I'm a generous man," began the captain, "why don't I just let you and this young hooligan go free? And the young wom . . ."

He stopped in mid-sentence as they all realized that Chayel had not entered with Odus and Dero. Suddenly, the captain leaped forward, causing Odus to jump back in a defensive position, but Dero was frozen in fear.

Before Odus could do anything, the man had a spear at Dero's throat and was yelling in a rage, "Bring the girl, or he dies!"

"I am here!" called Chayel from outside in the darkness. "If you do not let the boy go, *you* will die!" She had her bow trained on the captain at an angle to the doorway and though she spoke strongly, her hand wavered as she thought back to the man she had killed.

"Bring her in, Grampaw!" exploded the captain, pressing the spear point against Dero's neck.

But Odus shook his head and yelled, "Let him go!"

"Bring her!" he called out in a frenzied tone as the spear pricked Dero's neck, drawing a spot of blood. Suddenly, an arrow whistled through the air, missing its mark, but striking the man in the shoulder. His utter surprise and the pain caused him to stumble backward as Dero leaped away from him and scooped up his sword. The captain's face was contorted in agony and perplexity as he grabbed at the arrow, but then he looked toward the doorway.

"You will pay with your flesh, woman!" he screamed and lunged toward the door, but Odus raised his sword and came at him. The captain's attention jerked toward him, and he reared back with his spear, but it was the last thing he ever did as another arrow sank deep into his chest. He fell dead, and all was silent.

After a moment, Odus went to the door. "You alright, missy?" he said into the night. She soon appeared in the light, tears on her face. Odus couldn't help but hug her, though she received it a bit stiffly. Meanwhile, Dero, though quite shaken, had got the keys and was letting everyone out.

"How has this come about . . . that you have come here?" asked Pike incredulously.

Chayel said, "Tey-Rahk sent us—"

Odus said, "Look, we got to deal with this situation here; we can explain everything later."

Some of the men removed the dead man, and they all took up their arms again as Pike took charge of the situation. They went out into the night and took up positions, waiting for the other soldiers to return. When they finally came, they were intoxicated and ready to fight, but Pike and the other men easily subdued them and locked them up. Odus and Chayel explained to Pike all that had happened since they had seen him last, finishing with how Kafar and the others had been taken prisoner by Rhaka's men in Keone.

"You said you were sent here," began Pike as Odus interjected.

"Well, we were sent to find you."

"By whom?"

"Tey-Rahk," answered Chayel.

"Who is Tey-Rahk?"

"An emissary of the Great One," continued Chayel. "You have seen him as that great white horse that I was riding, up at the fortress in Makran when you were released with Kafar. But Tey-Rahk appears in different forms; he is actually a huge, white, winged lion."

Pike had other questions, but he dismissed them and said, "Well, you indeed have found me, and the other men and I are quite grateful, but what were you to find me *for*?"

Chayel and Odus looked at each other for a moment; then Odus said, "Well, we don't rightly know, but we got at least to try to get Kafar and Makarios and the others free. And this Rhaka has got to be stopped too, especially with coming down into this province now and who knows where else."

"Indeed," said Pike.

Dero unexpectedly stood up and said, "Marshal Pike, sir, I got to go home."

"You alright?" answered Pike.

Dero nodded slowly and explained, "I just ain't never seen a dead man before, especially not one that got killed like . . . like that." He turned away quickly and went out, and the three sat silently as they heard the creak of saddle and harness followed by the sound of hooves fading into the distance.

"I know how he feels . . .," said Chayel slowly, "only worse because I did the killing." A tear rolled down her cheek, but she brushed it away.

"You saved Dero's life," said Odus. "If you'd seen the look in the captain's eye, you'd know that your arrow flew none too soon."

There was a sober silence, and then Pike said, "It will not take long for what happened to Rhaka's soldiers to become known. We cannot be sure that at least one of them didn't escape in the brief fight, and I am also concerned about the man you let go free."

He got up and barred the back door and began closing and latching the window shutters. "We will go to my cabin," he said, picking up the keys. "It is far outside of town and quite secluded." They went out into the night, and Pike locked the building securely.

Early the next morning, Pike roused Odus and said, "Chayel has been out by the barn, just sitting on the fence since I awoke."

Odus grumbled a bit, but when he had come fully to, he got up and went out. The day had dawned cool and cloudy, and a damp mist hung in the air. Odus squinted and scowled as he approached Chayel and then just stood next to her looking out at the world.

After a few minutes of silence, Odus said, "It doesn't get any easier, and you don't get used to it, but you learn how to live with it."

Chayel nodded and took a deep breath, "It's just, well, I know there was nothing else I could do. I suppose I did save Dero's life . . ."

"And those soldiers, down the road near Kuon," began Odus. "They'd a killed us too. We did what we had to."

"But killing them . . . ," said Chayel her eyes welling up, "you know where that sends them." Odus remained silent and she added, "It's terrible to think about . . ."

They fell silent and eventually, Odus said, "They made a choice. We all do, but if you pick the evil . . . if you pick the bad, there's bound to be a clash with the good, and both can't survive. And we didn't start this fight, but we got to fight it. How many good folk are there that can't fight for themselves? We got to fight and kill when it comes to it, or else evil will swallow up everything that's good."

Chayel jumped down from the fence and though she had a grave look on her face, the faintest smile appeared as she unexpectedly hugged him and said, "Thanks, Odus," and then headed toward the cabin.

As they entered, Pike said, "We will go up to Keone and do all we can to get Makarios and the others free."

They were soon on their way, heading northeast into Fragmoo Forest, staying off the roads and by midday, they were passing by Palahos well to the west of them. But they were close enough to make out that there were many, many soldiers and disturbances in and around the town. As evening neared, they passed by Praho and saw that the situation there was even worse.

"We're not far from Ekuus," said Odus. "We can spend the night at the horse far—"

Suddenly, a squad of soldiers thundered toward them, seeming to come out of nowhere.

"You there!" yelled their commander, "*Stop!*" The three were caught off guard and quickly surrounded.

"Travel is not permitted in the open country!" bellowed the commander. "Take them into custody!"

As the soldiers came near, Chayel suddenly called out, spurred her horse, and barged into one of their horses, knocking the soldier to the ground. Pike and Odus quickly followed suit, and they broke out and turned to face the soldiers with their weapons drawn.

"You have no ground to detain us!" yelled Pike.

The commander was enraged and roared, "Take them!" and rode full at them, sword raised.

Pike retreated and called out, "We want no fight!" But the commander did not slow and as he was almost upon them, Chayel's arrow flew true to its mark, and he fell from his horse . . . dead. The rest of the soldiers veered away bewildered by what had happened.

"What was it?" yelled one as another called out, "Some kind of witchery!"

One of the soldiers immediately took charge and reformed the men, but a few were white as ghosts as they looked at the dead commander.

Chayel said, "I am sorry, but he was going to kill one of us!" None of the soldiers were eager to come at them again, and their new commander seemed undecided.

"You cannot do whatever you wish," said Pike forcefully. "There are laws that govern these provinces!"

"Laws?!" exclaimed the new commander, "*We* are the law! Lay down your weapons!" But only Chayel moved as she fitted another arrow to her bow.

"You cannot take us," said Pike returning his sword to the sheath, "not without more dying."

The commander looked around at his men and shouted, "*Take them!*" But as the soldiers only shifted around and remained where they were, he yanked his horse's head around and eyed Chayel, seething with anger, and caused his horse to leap toward her. She started backward but Odus jumped forward, ramming his horse into the commander who crashed to the ground.

Winded and shaken, he jumped to his feet and screamed at Chayel in a rage, "You will pay!!" As he swung up onto his horse, he yelled, "Lord Rhaka will see to it!" He galloped madly off toward the north, heedless that only half his men followed him.

There followed a brief silence until one of the younger soldiers said, "We ought to bury him," motioning toward the dead commander.

An older one said in a louder voice, "Well, what do you think, boys? I ain't for this soldierin' anymore! It ain't worth dyin' for!"

Some agreed, but another said, "Rhaka will find out, and then . . ."

He trailed off, looking quite frightened, but Odus spurred his horse toward them all and stopped right in front of them. "Now, look," he began, "don't you remember those stories and legends your mums used to tell you when you was little? There was the good side and the bad side, and there was a fight in between. But in the end, who had the victory? You all better be dead sure whose side you want to be on!"

Suddenly, the older soldier jumped down off his horse, laid his shield and sword aside, and extended his hand to Odus. He said, "That's a right fair argument, old man! Name's Thurmin." He shook Odus's hand and turned to face the soldiers, "Well, whose side do you want to be on, boys?"

⸺ Twenty Six ⸺

Nikos awoke with a start and found himself shivering with cold and staring up into a star-filled sky. At first, he couldn't understand where he was, but as he scrambled to his feet, he had the feeling he ought to be very quiet. He crouched near a pine tree, listening and then felt his stomach gnawing at him in hunger. Then it all came back to him, how he and Polus had been let out of the trench late one night by a guard who was still loyal to Polus, how they had almost been caught by some of the other soldiers, but wound up escaping in different directions.

"Lost," said Nikos in a low voice, "for days I guess now." He had no idea what time it was as he looked for a more sheltered area to lie down in. But sleep was far from him as he heard every little sound and felt his hunger more than he could bear. He sat and waited for daybreak, and as soon as there was enough light, he ventured out.

"*But which way?*" he thought and remembered how hopeless he had been to ever get anywhere in the mountainous region he was in. "It all looks the same!" he said a bit too loudly. Suddenly, he was startled by a sound and spun around.

"Well, it *ain't* the same," said a very thin, old man who stood leaning on his walking stick. "Which way you lookin' to go?"

"Uh, . . ." sputtered Nikos, "Uh . . . Wildhorse Village."

The old man squinted and ran his hand over his long white beard. "It's that a way," he said and pointed to the southeast. "It's a fer piece though, and you look a might hungry, boy, so here, take what I got."

Nikos eagerly agreed, and the old man pointed up to the mountains and said sternly, "Now pay careful attention. See that one peak there and how there's two lower ones on either side? You just keep straight onto that middle peak, and you'll get where you're goin', and don't be diddlin' around, cause' it ain't always safe out here in these parts."

Nikos looked carefully to where the man was pointing, but when he turned back to him, he was gone. Nikos turned all the way around, but the old man was nowhere to be seen. Befuddled, but with the man's warning about it not being safe ringing in his ears, Nikos locked his eyes on the mountain peak and set off.

He walked all day but felt that he was getting no closer. Night fell, and he spent another cold night beneath a pine tree. The morning dawned misty and overcast and as Nikos looked for the mountain peak, he could see nothing but clouds. He shook his head and felt miserable with hunger and cold, and he had great doubt about which way he should go. But he set off and after a while felt hopeful as the ground began to rise. Soon, the clouds lifted, and Nikos scanned carefully for the three peaks and was overjoyed to see them much closer than he expected.

He tried to go quickly but became winded as the ground became even steeper; his progress slowed as the terrain became treacherous with loose rocks. He used his hands nearly as much as his feet and after a grueling climb, he came up on some flat ground. There was little vegetation and no cover, so he backed down the hill a bit to look around.

"*Keone can only be that way,*" he thought, "*And Wildhorse Village somewhere over there . . .*"

He set off in that direction, getting to a few scrub pines. To his surprise, he recognized the way and soon found the road.

"Nikos!" called out a woman's voice. It was Keraia coming from the village, and she ran to meet him.

She said, "We have looked everywhere for you!"

Suddenly, Nikos stumbled, overcome with exhaustion and hunger and fell to his knees.

Keraia helped him up and called for Eido, and soon Nikos was in a comfortable chair in Thumos's house with a meal before him. After eating his fill, Nikos related all that had happened and how he and Polus had been let out of the trench.

"So, I don't know if he got away," finished Nikos, "I have been lost this whole time. But tell me, what has happened here?

I saw Chayel's and Odus's horses and am glad to see Zeo, but no one else's?"

Thumos began, "Arak had a vision of what Makarios said was Polus's house in the forest. So, they set off to go there, but when they got to Keone, Rhaka's men took all of them except Odus and Chayel into custody. They returned here, but in the morning, they were gone, though their horses remained. It is like they grew wings . . ."

"That is strange," said Nikos. "And what of Makarios and the others?"

Keraia answered, "Eido and I went to Keone and spied things out. We saw how many soldiers there were though not as many as we expected; we also saw where we suspect your friends were imprisoned. Then we came back, and my father mustered the men of the village along with some of the Meganthropos who called on some of their kin from Megalos. We had the heart to fight Rhaka's men, not only to free your friends but also because it is wrong for Rhaka's men to be ruling over us like they've been doing."

Thumos continued, "So, we carefully planned an attack to remove the soldiers from Keone. We did not want to kill them; we wanted to reason with them to let justice reign, but they would not consent. We had concealed most of our forces, so when they sprang out of hiding, Rhaka's men were overcome. They foolishly fought anyway, and most were killed, but a few fled. That was two days ago now, and the retaliation I expected from Rhaka has not come. But the village is back in the hands of the people."

"And Makarios and the others were freed," added Keraia. "They went off at once to the place that Arak had seen."

"It is good," began Nikos. "I must follow after them."

"But not before you are rested," said Keraia.

Eido added, "You do look terrible."

"So, I feel . . ." replied Nikos.

As morning dawned, Nikos awoke more refreshed than he expected and was anxious to get going, but the smell of breakfast slowed him down.

"Come and eat!" said Keraia. As they sat down, she looked at Eido and said, "You are planning something."

Thumos looked at him, and Eido returned his gaze and said with more courage than he felt, "Yes. I will go with Nikos."

Thumos remained silent, so Eido tentatively continued, "It is ominous that Rhaka has not responded to our fight in Keone. I think his eyes are fixed on the lands to the south . . . He will try to take over everything, and we must fight."

Thumos took a deep breath and nodded.

"I would be glad to have him," said Nikos. Thumos provided them with provisions, and they were soon on their way.

As they neared Keone, Eido said, "It was terrible, how those soldiers attacked us . . . I never seen anyone killed before, but then it was happening all around me. I tried to get out of it, but then a soldier came at me and . . ."

"I know what you mean," said Nikos, "about being scared." They both rode on in silence, but suddenly fear knotted both their stomachs as they saw a group of Rhaka's soldiers on horseback in the village, near where the gate had been. But Nikos's fear was overwhelmed by an unexpected wave of courage as he called out, "Let us fight them!"

As they looked at each other, Eido was caught up in the moment and shouted, "Yes!"

They spurred their mounts forward, drawing their swords and bore down upon the soldiers, who unexpectedly yielded and swerved away. Suddenly, a rider wheeled around from among them and yelled, "Stop!"

The soldiers quickly closed in on them. Eido pulled up short and exclaimed, "Chayel?!"

"You are with these men?" asked Nikos, suddenly suspicious.

But Odus said, explained, "Now smolder on down. We *are* with them, but they *ain't* with Rhaka anymore."

"And you," Chayel said to Eido, "attacking these men three to one?!"

But his courage had left him, and he faltered, "Nikos . . . he—"

Nikos interjected, "How are these with you?"

At that moment, one of them rode closer and said, "Name's Thurmin. We came to help get these people's friends free, but it looks like they already are. What happened?"

Nikos sheathed his sword, and Eido told the tale. When he had finished, Thurmin said, "Well, that's good news. May you fare well in finding your friends!"

He nodded and galloped off with his men. Odus added, "Now, it's down to the real business—"

But Chayel said to Nikos and Eido, "I am shocked at both of you! To see you charging a squad of soldiers like that!"

Eido began, "Well, I got kind of caught up—"

Chayel turned to Nikos, "I would never have expected that . . ."

He was about to reply when Odus said, "Look, we got to get goin', I got a bad feelin' things are going to boil over like oil into a fire."

Pike added, "I do as well. We ought to get to Polus's house in the forest and hopefully find Makarios and the others somewhere along the way. You can lead us, Nikos?"

They set off at once, and Chayel rode next to Nikos and said, "You were fearless." But she lacked any more words.

Nikos pondered for a moment, "Well, I don't know; I guess for once I wasn't thinking about myself." They rode on for a while and as they came down the pass, Odus, who was in front, pulled up short.

"Now, we got some real problems," he said. "Look." There were many soldiers on the road, not moving but seeming to have a discussion.

"There's no other way down," said Nikos.

Odus added, "Must be at least a double dozen down there."

"What are we going to do?" shuddered Eido.

"We must meet them," said Pike.

"Yes," said Nikos as he rode up beside Pike. Chayel again wondered at him and felt a new admiration.

"How 'bout five to one?" Odus said to Eido and grinned, but he found no humor in it. They started off, and Chayel moved next to Eido.

"Remember your bow; it is a big advantage." He nodded stiffly but kept looking straight ahead. She moved closer and squeezed his arm, which turned his eyes upon her.

"Remember what it means to be a man!" she said.

Pike turned around and said to them, "We will greet these soldiers and just ride past."

But as they approached, a commander rode forward and yelled, "*Stop*! Where are you from?"

Pike reined his horse to a stop and replied, "I am Pike and am returning to Agathon Province. I am marshal at the Outpost."

The commander ordered, "Check them!"

As they rode forward, Eido rashly readied his bow and cried, "You . . . you stop!" The commander, who was a hardened and bitter man, erupted with curses and charged his horse straight at Eido, who veered to the side. Everything broke loose and suddenly, they were fighting for their lives. In the midst of it, Thurmin and his men emerged from among the soldiers and took out many of them. The rest fought fiercely—even savagely, but Chayel and Eido hung back, and their arrows took out many more. Pike and Odus joined following Thurmin's lead as he rallied his men and soon, they had defeated Rhaka's soldiers.

"Where is Eido?!" called Chayel.

"His horse is there!" shouted Nikos from some distance away.

They desperately looked around as Pike said to Thurmin, "All your men . . . they are alright?" He grinned, seeming to have enjoyed the fight and only nodded.

Suddenly, Odus called, "He is here!" Chayel rushed up and jumped from her horse, with tears in her eyes,

"You are alright?" she said kneeling beside him, but he sat up and winced in pain.

"Oh, your arm!" she exclaimed. It was indeed bleeding, but Thurmin quickly came alongside with some bandages and wrapped it up. Then he stood up, looked around and asked, "Anyone else got their innards spilling out?"

But Eido was the only one who had suffered an injury. Thurmin offered to accompany them with his men, and they all quickly got on their way. After some time, they could hear Boulder falls rumbling in the distance; the village of Karpone just beyond.

"Don't see too much goin' on," said Odus. "But maybe it'd be best to go east some and go around the village and then come down to Ekuus; otherwise, we could be riding right into a whole bunch of trouble we don't want."

"That is a wise plan, old man," said Thurmin grinning. "But me and my boys are going to ride on; maybe we'll find some more soldiers and convince them they're on the wrong side of this fight!" He spiritedly spurred his mount, and they all leaped away at a gallop. Pike and the others turned off the road, skirting the foothills of the mountains on their left.

"What did that commander mean when he said, 'check them'?" asked Odus.

No one had an answer, but after a while Nikos said, "I hate to think it, but it could be these red marks we have, the People of the Great One."

"Why would they do that?" asked Chayel incredulously.

Nikos took a deep breath and said, "When I was locked in the trench with Polus . . . well, he had been beaten mercilessly by Teras . . . first because he would not tell where he hid the Book, but also because he believes in the Great One. Teras gouged off Polus's red mark with his bare hand."

Chayel shook her head in disbelief as Pike said, "They would check us also?"

"And probably kill us," added Odus.

"I don't understand such hatred," said Pike.

"Me neither," said Odus, "but it's real . . . dang real."

They picked up the pace, staying well east of Karpone and then headed south. A farm appeared in the distance, and soon they heard cries and the sound of fighting. Nikos moved Zeo to a gallop, and the rest followed with Eido coming last, though he had fit an arrow to his bow. As they neared, they could see a good number of Rhaka's soldiers on horseback fighting some townsfolk who only had pitchforks and scythes.

Odus called out directions, telling Chayel to go to one side with Pike and to use her bow while he and Eido would flank them on the other. But Nikos rode hard right into the midst and knocked two soldiers from their horses before he wheeled around and came at them again taking down another.

The soldiers were in confusion and as Nikos charged them again, he called out, "Get back from these men! We do not want to fight!"

The farmer and his men, though startled, gathered behind Nikos, and the soldiers gathered in the middle as Chayel and Pike closed in from one side and Odus and Eido on the other.

Suddenly, one of the soldiers, whom Nikos had knocked from his horse yelled out, "This ain't your business! Who do you think you are?"

Nikos rode forward, pointing his sword at him and said, "I know the difference between right and wrong."

Another soldier called out, "You don't know nothin' 'cause this is the *master's* business!"

The farmer stepped forward and said, "It ain't! This is *my* farm!"

Suddenly, one of the soldiers charged him, raising his sword and yelling, "You will give the tax!" But as he descended upon the farmer, an arrow pierced his throat. The others shrank back and looked wildly around, not knowing what they were seeing.

Odus rode forward and said, "You all best put down your weapons; there's more where that—"

But suddenly, the soldiers sprang back into action, with another yelling, "The master *will* have his due!" They fought harder and more ruthlessly than any of the other soldiers they had come across. But in the end, most paid with their lives, and some galloped away. When it was over, only one of the farmer's men had been seriously injured.

"Why, I can't thank you enough, kind sirs!" said the farmer, and then as he saw Chayel, he flushed red and quickly added, "And lovely madame!" He was quite portly and not suited for fighting at all.

As he turned to help with the injured, a very large man with a dark, thick beard came forward and said to Pike and the others, "It is good to meet again!"

"Would that the circumstances were better," answered Pike. "You are Bahr, are you not?"

He nodded and continued, "And this ain't the worst of it. Not only is that Rhaka tyrant takin' high taxes and stealing, but now he's killin'! But it seems only certain folk . . . and it's worse to the west. We sure got a fight on our hands. Thanks again!"

He turned to the farmer and his men as Pike and the others gathered together. "We must go to Tachus Town," said Pike.

But Chayel quickly said,

"The Book, we *must* find it! We will be much stronger with it."

"And we can't get ourselves killed," added Odus. "We don't know what's happened to Kafar and the others. Nikos here, well . . . he's the only one as knows how to get to Polus's house, and that's our only clue."

Then Eido said to Pike, "And we *got* to get through, and we're way better off if you're with us, Mister Pike, sir."

"Then let us go," he replied, and they set off at once, heading south through the open country toward Fragmoo Forest.

Twenty Seven

It was a cold, wet night as Kafar, Barah, Arak, and Makarios took shelter under the Old Bridge near Palahos. They had narrowly evaded many squads of Rhaka's men as they came down from Keone but felt safe enough where they were for the time being.

"I cannot believe they will kill for what a person *believes*," said Makarios shaking her head. "But I hated it myself . . ."

"Yes," said Kafar. "It has gotten to be very dangerous very quickly."

"We must get to Polus's house as soon as we can," said Arak.

Barah countered, "But what of these lands? These people? They're fighting for their lives—"

"No!" whispered Arak fiercely. "This is not our fight! We *must* get the Book! The vision did not come to me for no reason!"

"Any fight against evil is our fight, Arak!" said Barah.

Suddenly, they heard the sound of many horses approaching the bridge overhead from the east. The company went slowly and then came to a stop.

"No, this has got to be the way," whispered a man, as another said, "Well, we dare not go north toward Makran."

"Besides," said a third, "we got to be well south of Tachus Town to get across Stoney Creek."

"Well, let's go then and fast as we can," said the first man. They moved out and began crossing the bridge; it was a larger company than Kafar and the others expected.

As they quickly disappeared into the night, a man at the tail end of the line could be heard saying, "I hope we make it."

"How do we not join them and Kainos?" said Barah.

"We must remember," said Kafar, "that finding the Book may depend only on us, since we do not know what has happened to Nikos or Polus."

"And Makarios is the only one among us here who knows the way to Polus's house," said Arak. "Does not the Book say, 'All fight in the war, but not in every battle.' The best way we can fight this evil is to find the Book."

There was a long silence and then Barah, who seemed to be the only one on his side, said, "My heart is to fight with these people, but it is the wise choice to go for the Book."

In the end, they decided to make for Polus's house and then took a few hours' sleep, awaking before dawn. They quickly got on their way as Makarios led them. They went directly west and by the time the sun had risen, they came to Stoney Creek where it flowed south into the Fragmoo forest.

Makarios reined her horse to a stop and said, "It would be safer to follow the creek down through there than continue in open country."

They turned in but hadn't gone far when Barah said, "We are not the only ones to think so." Though there was no road, there was a clear path beside the stream with the hoofprints of many horses.

"What do you think it means?" asked Arak as an uneasiness settled upon them.

"This is no place to fight or even flee from Rhaka's men," said Kafar. "It is too closed in. And I fear they may be guarding this way." They all looked downstream, but with the sun still low on the horizon, they could not see very far.

"We ought to go back," said Arak; Barah agreed, and they turned around and came out heading west, close to the forest on their left. The Stone Mountains rose in front of them, and the peaks glowed with the rising sun. By midday they had come to the foothills and soon reached the mine cart line that ran at the base of the mountains. They quickened their pace and soon saw a few horsemen on the road ahead.

"They are not Rhaka's men," said Barah as they neared them and then called out, "Ho there!" The riders quickly faced them with swords drawn, but it was plain to see they were in no condition to fight.

"We are not your enemies." said Kafar.

"And we would have none if Rhaka had not made us his," said one of the men with much effort.

They were both wounded, and the other, who was worse off said, "We must continue south . . ."

"We will ride with you," said Kafar. They had gone some distance and were approaching a spur of the mountain when a troop of soldiers rushed around it and came right at them.

"Like rats in a trap!" yelled one of them. With the mountains on their right and Fragmoo Forest thick on their left, they wheeled about and raced back up the road but were met by another group of soldiers. Kafar led the way. The fierceness of their attack took the soldiers by surprise, and they broke through their ranks.

They galloped north at full speed and Kafar called, "Go east of the creek! We cannot lead them into Tachus Town!"

The soldiers began to lose ground and broke off the pursuit. But as they neared Stoney Creek, more soldiers rushed out of the forest, nearly crashing into them. There were too many to fight, and Kafar signaled them to keep fleeing. After going some distance, the soldiers turned back, letting them go.

Kafar guided them into a stand of trees and as their horses stood blowing and stamping, he said, "They are guarding the way south. There is no way through."

"We must go back to the Old Bridge," said Makarios, "and cross the river at Palahos." Without warning, a small band of soldiers came over a hill some distance away.

"Do we fight?" asked Barah.

Kafar held up his hand, but as the horsemen neared them, they could see that they were not Rhaka's men.

After a few minutes Kafar rode out toward them, and they quickly took up their arms, but he said, "We are not your enemies. Rhaka's soldiers are guarding the way south. Even together, we are not enough to overcome them."

As they approached, Kafar saw a few women and children behind them and added, "Come this way."

Soon they were in the cover of the trees, and one of the men said, "The whole north and east . . . Rhaka's taken it over."

"We're just trying to get away," said another.

"And they're *killin'* folk," added a young boy, "just for havin' some kind of mark on their chest."

"They checked all of us," said a forlorn older woman.

"We don't want nuthin' to do with the folk they are lookin' for," said the first man. "We just want to get away and make a home somewhere."

A somber silence descended on the group as they seemed to look to Kafar for an answer. They seemed about to ride away when a young woman ventured forward and said, "We've heard folks are going to a place called Tachus Town—"

"That it's still safe there—," interrupted the young boy.

"But we don't know where it is," finished the woman. Kafar and the others looked at each other, and he said, "It is on that creek twenty miles to the north."

"Should we not go with them?" Makarios asked Kafar.

"We cannot get south," said Barah. "We may be better prepared to learn what we can at Tachus Town."

Kafar pondered for a moment and turned to the group and said, "We will take you there." They set out, having to ride through open country and staying west of Stoney Creek. They saw no one else as they traveled, and by evening, they were close to Tachus Town.

Suddenly, a strong voice called out, "Who goes there?!" startling them all.

Kafar replied immediately, "I am Kafar! We are friends of Marshal Kainos!"

"Stay where you are!" called another voice from a different direction.

They remained still, but looked around and could see no one. A bowshot away they could see a tall stone that had not been there before. After some minutes, six horsemen, fully armed, came quickly through the gate and approached them. One of them rode ahead of the others and stopped, looking over Kafar and the others carefully.

"You are two companies," he said. "What do you say for yourselves?"

"I am Kafar, friend of Marshal Kainos," answered Kafar. "And these are Barah and Arak and a friend, Makarios, and these—"

"And we're escaping from that evil Rhaka!" blurted out a man from the others. "And we heard about Tachus Town—"

"That it is safe—" interjected the boy.

But the leader of the six men held up his hand, "Please keep silent!" he commanded. "Many have come here, and we cannot sustain any more."

One of the six rode forward to the other and said, "Marshal Kore, sir, I can vouch for Kafar."

Barah said, "Ruad! It is good to see you!"

Marshal Kore looked between them and spoke to Ruad, "You know these men?"

Ruad nodded and said, "They are the ones who brought the word of the Great One to Kainos and indeed to all these lands."

"And she is with us," said Kafar motioning to Makarios.

"She is of the Great One?" asked the marshal as he signaled one of the men forward to confirm, but a commotion erupted among the other group of people.

"They're checking for the mark!" cried the older woman.

"We'll be killed!" shrieked the boy as one of the men yelled, "They're all, they . . . they are the marked ones!"

A general panic set in, and the man wheeled his horse around followed by the rest of them, and they all galloped back the way they had come.

The marshal let them go and said to Kafar and the others, "Come with us," and he rode back toward the gate. As they entered and the gate clanged shut behind them, the marshal signaled his men, and they rode off.

"Ruad, stay with us," said Marshal Kore

By the time they reached Tachus Town, the sun had set, and the light of many candles and lanterns began to appear in the houses and barns. Despite the peaceful appearance of things, Kafar and the others sensed much tension. As they rode, they heard cries of pain and moaning here and there, and a deep solemnity hung over the town.

They arrived at the marshal's building, and Marshal Kore said, "Forgive my sternness and formality. Much has happened here in these last days . . . we cannot be too careful. Please come in."

The deputy who was attending said, "I will be at the bridge," and he went out.

Kore had them all sit down and then said, "We are glad to have such men as you, and also you, ma'am, on this side of the fight, but tell me Ruad, how do you know them?"

Ruad glanced at Kafar, who gave a slight nod. Ruad said, "I met Kafar last summer in Rhaka's dungeon. He told me of the curse, and I came to believe. Then after the winter, I came to Kainos's from the fortress to tell Kafar and his companions about, the—"

But he stopped and glanced at Kafar as Marshal Kore said, "There is much you have not told me," and he looked at Ruad for an answer.

Kafar spoke, "He has not told you because he is a faithful friend to you, but also to us."

Kore took a deep breath and said, "Well, your business is your own."

"But we are brothers in this fight," said Kafar, "are we not?"

Kore unexpectedly smiled and with a look of relief, said, "Indeed, I am free from the curse as well—"

But Barah interjected, "I believe we have much to tell each other, but where is Kainos?"

At this, the countenances of Kore and Ruad fell, and a somber silence descended. After a few moments Kore said, "Rhaka's men attacked us yesterday. There were a thousand men, and more than half were Meganthropos. They could not get through at the bridge and so attacked our southern wall. The fighting went all day, but eventually they broke through, and Kainos led the charge against them, but there were so many, and those Megans . . ." He trailed off shaking his head.

"It is hard news to bear," said Barah and a reverent silence followed.

Eventually, Kafar said, "But the town has not been taken . . ."

Ruad glanced at Kore and then said, "One of the Megans, kind of small , suddenly turned against them all, and out of nowhere, he called out to his fellow Megans to fight with him against Rhaka's men. One of them responded and then another and then more. There was much confusion, but we pulled back as they fought each other. Soon Rhaka's men were beaten, and those who were not killed fled; even some of the Megans remained loyal to Rhaka and also ran away with the other men."

Suddenly, Makarios said, "This Meganthropos, he is here, in the town?"

Kore looked between them all and said, "You know this one?"

Makarios could not hide her emotion as Ruad continued, "If you mean Commander Polus, he is indeed, though he is no longer commander, but now is one of us."

"Was there anyone with him?" asked Barah.

"I don't know," answered Ruad. "I never even saw where he came from." He paused and then looked at Makarios and said, "You *know* him?"

"Yes," she said still full of emotion.

"How?"

"It is a long story, but I told him of the curse, and he believed."

Ruad was incredulous, "How? Where?"

"After he attacked Rhaka's fortress, I tracked him and his men to his hideout and demanded to see him."

Ruad was astonished, "*Alone*?"

"He *had* to know of the curse," she answered, "and how to be saved from it—"

"He could have killed you," said Kore, full of wonder.

Makarios became very sober and said, "He had already tried that, but that is past." Kore could only look at her in continued amazement. "I . . . we must see Polus," said Makarios.

Ruad said, "After yesterday's victory, the whole town has taken him as their new leader, even though Kore became the marshal, since . . ."

He trailed off, and Kore, who had not ceased to look at Makarios, said, "It may be best to wait until the morning. I would not even know where to find him."

"And you all could do with a meal?" asked Ruad.

They agreed, and Barah said, "How is Ella? Kainos's housekeeper."

"And her two boys?" added Arak.

"She is well," answered Ruad, "as are her two boys. Kainos left his farm to her, and she is there. I don't doubt they would be glad to have you, especially her two boys; they asked about you for quite a while after you left at the end of summer last year, especially you, Arak. They called you the King's men."

Ruad took them to the farm, and they were warmly welcomed.

Makarios awoke very early the next morning, having had less than good sleep. She slipped quietly out of the house into the cool, gray morning. Fog hung in the air as did the somberness of the day before. No one else was stirring as she started walking toward town. As she came up to the main road, she thought she heard something and stopped to listen. A groaning, whimpering sound came faintly to her, and she continued, bearing toward it into a field. The fog was low and obscured her view and as she neared, the sound suddenly stopped.

"Is there someone there?" she asked.

There was a sudden intake of breath, and a very large voice said timidly, "Who is it?"

"I am Makarios. Are you alright?" She moved forward and then came face to face with a huge Meganthropos sitting behind a tree. He jumped up and away but then bent forward and peered at her.

"You said your name . . ." he stated in an odd way and took a step toward her. He was nearly eight feet tall with huge arms and a large, knotted forehead, and his face was streaked with tears.

"Makarios," she said stopping in front of him. "That is my name."

"You? Makarios . . . *you* are Makarios?"

She nodded and said, "You look very sad."

He looked away, and tears rolled down as he again sat against the tree.

"Yes," he said, "My brother, he died in the fighting."

Makarios sat next to him and said, "I am sorry for you and for your brother."

He nodded and then turned to her, "*You* are Makarios? Polus will be so happy! He told me all about . . . He . . . He doesn't know you are alive!" He jumped up and said, "You must come! He will be so happy!" He paused abruptly and added, "My name . . . my name is Tode."

She began to reply, but he grabbed her hand and started off across the field saying, "He will love to see you!"

But Makarios could not keep up with his pace and nearly fell. Tode caught her and pulled up short saying, "Tode is sor . . . *I* am sorry."

He let go of her hand and continued on more slowly, but soon came to a homestead and headed toward a big barn. As they neared, Makarios took Tode's hand and pulled him to a stop.

"Just tell him *someone* is here to see him," she said with a trembling voice. Tode suddenly became very quiet and moved more slowly as he went in. Makarios could barely hear him as he seemed to be whispering,

"*Someone* is outside and wants to see you, and she . . . she is alive!"

"What do you mean, Tode?" asked Polus sounding annoyed. After a few minutes, the door opened. Polus appeared groggy and tired, but when he saw Makarios, he stopped and stared at her unbelievingly. His lip quivered as she came to him and tears rolled down her face as he took her up into his arms.

"I didn't think you had got away from Megar," she cried.

After quite a few minutes of embracing, they let each other go, and Polus said, "I didn't. They caught me, but not before I hid the Book."

"But how—"

Polus said, "Tell me, do you know of Nikos . . . is he well?"

"I do not know where he is," she said. "We were in Wildhorse Village ten days ago—Nikos and I and some of my countrymen and a man named Thumos who was helping us. But Nikos went off somewhere, and we couldn't find him. We looked for you too." She looked at him searchingly and added, "But they caught you; how are you free? They did not get the Book?"

Polus shook his head with a look of great pain and said, "Teras beat me, but I would not tell where the Book was. They locked me in the trench, and the next day, they threw Nikos in."

Makarios was incredulous as Polus continued, "One loyal to me let us out, but the others were alerted and came after us. We ran in different directions."

Makarios teared up, but Polus said, "We must trust to the Great One .
. ."

Makarios looked at him sharply and then smiled and said, "Yes, yes, of
course." She shook her head and said, "I forget. It is so good you are saved
from the curse."

But a look of anguish came over him, "I learned so much from the Book .
. . when I was with Rhaka, so much evil . . . I lost all sense of right and wrong
. . ." He looked at Makarios and burst into tears.

But she said, "No! Do you forget forgiveness? To still feel guilt for what
you did dishonors what it cost for me to forgive you. Cast it from you as far as
you can to the west and then look to the east and never look back."

Polus sat down on a bench near the barn leaning forward with his elbows
on his knees and his chin in his hands. The rest of the world seemed to recede
behind the gray dampness and stillness of the air. After some time, Polus said
quietly, "It is so strange . . . how different we are now. How does it happen? To
love instead of hate . . ."

"It is a power far beyond us," said Makarios, sitting next to him. "It is the
only hope for these times."

Polus suddenly stood up and exclaimed, "Yes!"

He turned to face her, and she said, "I know . . ."

Polus continued, "If only Rhaka could be turned from this evil!"

"He would not be hard to find," she said with a grin, but then sobered a
bit. "But if he is hardened against it?"

Polus sighed, "We must trust to the power of the Great One."

The day began to lighten, and soon there were people about; Polus said,
"We ought to go see Kore and Ruad and your countrymen. They are with
you?"

She nodded, and they set off toward the marshal's building and were soon
met by Ruad coming from the other direction.

"Ah, just the two I was hoping to find! Breakfast is ready, and there is
much to discuss."

They entered the marshal's building and after introductions, Polus said to
Kafar, "I have met you before."

"Yes, I was a prisoner in Rhaka's dungeon last fall, and you let me out,
along with another man."

Polus thought hard and finally said, "Yes, and Nikos was there at the gate, and
a woman—" He looked quickly at Makarios, "Like you . . ."

"That was Chayel," answered Kafar.

"Do you know . . . is Nikos alright?"

"We were separated about ten days ago," said Barah. "We do not know any more."

They all sat down to the meal, and Kafar said to Polus and Makarios, "We have talked to Kore about the Book. We must go as soon as we can. Arak had a dream that it was somewhere near your house in the forest. Is it so?" Polus nodded.

"It is hidden there, but I . . . we," he began, motioning to Makarios. "We must go to Rhaka, to free him from the curse—"

But Arak suddenly stood up and exclaimed, "*No!* The Book is fairly in our hands!"

"Does not the Book command to love those who would kill us?" asked Makarios.

Polus continued, "The Book is well hidden. But I know Rhaka's anguish, the horrible wrenching between good and evil, as if your very flesh were being pulled from your bones."

"Yes . . . ," added Barah.

"Surely, there are others who could reach him," said Arak. "We cannot risk being killed. We *must* get the Book!"

Tensions began to rise as a division occurred among them until Polus called out, "I must go to Rhaka! I would gladly give my life to see him freed from this evil."

"And I will go with you," added Makarios with a note of finality that brought a brief and somber silence.

"So let it be," said Kafar, "but the three of us, we will go for the Book." Barah and Arak nodded as Kafar added, "We are all of one heart in this?"

They all agreed, and Polus told them where to find the Book. He said, "When you have it, you must immediately return to the House it belongs in."

"We shall," answered Kafar. "Our people will be mightily strengthened to fight this evil with the return of the Book."

They soon had prepared themselves, and Makarios came to her three countrymen and said, "I bid you farewell. I do not doubt we will see each other again before this is over."

·——— *Twenty Eight* ———·

Nikos, Pike, and the others made their way south finding fewer of Rhaka's men to avoid, but they had to go through Two Rivers to get across the Tachus river. As they rode into the city, there was little activity and no sign of any of Rhaka's soldiers. Some of the shopkeepers eyed them warily as they rode by, but others were just going about their business.

They came to the far side of the city and were approaching the bridge when Nikos said, "There was no gate here before."

Chayel added, "And that guardhouse either."

"Don't see no soldiers though," said Odus. As they came to the bridge, a portly bald man came out of the guardhouse, holding a spear that did not suit him very well.

"Ho there!" he commanded, holding the spear like a staff and rapping the end of it down on the wooden decking, "That'll be one silver damah each to cross!"

They looked at each other. Chayel suppressed a grin as Pike rode forward and addressed the man, "By what authority do you command a toll?"

The man took a step back and said, "I am the . . . the city clerk and . . . by order of the marshal . . ."

"This here gate looks more like Rhaka's business," said Odus.

"Open the gate!" commanded Pike.

The man fumbled with the spear and dropped it and said, "You got to pay!"

"And like one of Rhaka's spears too," added Odus.

Pike dismounted and opened the gate as the man retrieved the spear and pointed it at him. "You fool no one," said Pike. The man dropped his pretense and said, "Well, his soldiers were here and chargin' tolls, but three days ago, they all up and left, going north, so I just took up doing their work . . ."

They all passed over the bridge, and Eido said, "Doesn't sound good. Wonder where they went in such as hurry?"

They rode on, skirting the north side of Huo Lake and were approaching Geroon Forest by nightfall.

"There is an old unused road somewhere here," said Nikos. Soon, they had found it and turned in, going some way up the track. They camped for the night and, in the morning, made their way to Polus's house, finding it neat and put in order. But the door was open.

"It's like in Arak's dream," said Odus. Nikos and Chayel went in and carefully searched everywhere, but they emerged not having found anything.

"We should check Polus's shed down the path," said Nikos. "Maybe he left a clue . . ." But after carefully looking through all the tools and things Polus had carved, they came up empty.

"Maybe we should go up in the clearing," said Odus. "Arak said he saw a raven there, squawking." They went up, but Eido stayed behind and went into the shed, impressed and intrigued with all the carved statues. He looked through them all and was about to go out when one caught his eye. He noticed that it looked very different from the others. He took it and went up to the clearing, finding the three men standing there at a loss.

"I found this," he said. "It looks really different from everything else and looks almost new." They all looked it over, and Odus said, "Looks kind of like a pool of water."

"Maybe Polus left a clue," said Nikos.

"Yeah, and it's different from all the bird and animal carvings," said Eido.

Nikos took it and looked carefully at it as Odus said, "And it looks like a fish there."

"As if it's under the water," added Eido. Suddenly, a raven descended from seemingly nowhere, squawking and startling them all. It landed about thirty feet away and took a few hops in a northwest direction and squawked again.

"This happened to you before, didn't it?" asked Odus.

Nikos answered, "Yes, on my way through the desert to see the King. A black bird led me the right way out of the desert."

They started toward it, and it hopped away again and went into the forest. As they followed, it stopped cawing, but kept looking back and then flew some distance ahead and landed near a creek and hopped into it. It gave three distinct calls and then flew away.

When they arrived at the creek, Chayel asked, "What does it mean?" After searching and looking and thinking, they came up with nothing.

Eventually, Eido said, "Well, what about this carving? It's like a pond or a pool, but this is a stream."

"But the fish," said Nikos, "It's under the water . . ."

"Should we dig?" asked Odus.

But Nikos continued, almost to himself, "Under the water." And he looked north up the stream, repeating, "Under . . ." and immediately set off.

The others followed and caught up to him standing at a big, smooth rock in the middle of the stream, with the water flowing off the edge onto a flat rock and then down the slope. Two rocks stood vertically upstream, through which the creek flowed.

"What is it?" asked Odus as Chayel bent to look closer.

"And this," she said. "It's all carved . . ."

"Polus made this," said Nikos. "The Book is under this rock."

"Under the water . . .," said Eido.

"How can we move it?" asked Odus.

"It may be under the smaller flat one," interjected Pike. "It seems Polus meant for us to find it, and he would not put it where we could not get it." They heaved up the rock and amidst all the splashing water and straining, found a small square hole lined with large flat stones.

Chayel bent down, reached in, and quickly stood up with the Book in her hand. They all looked at it in wonder, hardly believing it was real and that they actually had it.

"It is smaller than I expected," said Pike, "and it's a wonder to me that it is not even wet."

They were all somewhat transfixed as Nikos carefully took the book from Chayel and opened it. As he scanned its pages, his eyes widened, and he said to Chayel, "I can *read* it."

"That . . . that's amazing," she said. "How can it be?"

Odus moved closer and exclaimed, "Well, dang, I can too! Them are some peculiar lookin' letters though. Don't know how this can be."

Pike and Eido crowded around, but neither of them could read it.

"That's strange then," said Odus.

Pike replied, "Not so strange; Eido and I are not of this Great One."

There followed a brief silence as Chayel gently took the Book from Nikos and said, "It is hard to believe that it is right here in our hands."

They all looked at each other and a soberness came over them.

"Well, we got a decision to make," said Odus.

"Indeed," said Pike.

"How do we not just leave for Zabach immediately?" asked Chayel quickly.

"What about Kafar and the others?" asked Nikos.

"It is difficult," said Pike. "We do not know where they are or what may have happened to them—"

"But we have the Book . . . here . . . now," cut in Chayel. "And the way south to Zabach is clear; Rhaka's men are in the north. Surely, the Great One has made the way for us."

Silence fell again, and after some time, Odus said, "It sure seems like we ought to just go, but what about puttin' the Book back in there and we go try to find Kafar and the others?"

Chayel shook her head as Nikos said, "It would be safe enough, and Polus would still know where it is if . . . if we got caught up in fighting."

"But then what?" asked Chayel. "He does not know the way to the House of the Book. And how could Kafar and the others find it here?" She crossed her arms and paced about.

Pike suddenly spoke to her with a bit of an edge, "I do not doubt we were led here by this Great One that you believe in. And do you not believe he can lead the others here as well if we do not find them or fail to return here?!"

Chayel stopped dead and said, "I *do* believe!"

"Is it truly belief if you do not *trust* the one you believe?" added Pike. She looked sharply at him with fire in her eyes.

Odus put a hand on her shoulder and said to Pike, "Now, we don't need to be doubtin' anyone's belief right now; just let's decide what we ought to do."

"What do you say, Nikos?" asked Pike.

"We ought to find the others," he began. "The Book will be well hidden here, but Makarios does not know of this stream and what the carving would mean."

Odus said, "Well, what about leavin' a message in that hidey hole for Polus, and then hide the Book somewhere else with a clue where the others could find it, in case we cannot get back?"

"We would all know where it is then," said Pike.

Chayel burst out, "No! We cannot take these chances. We *have* the Book;

it must go back home now!"

Suddenly, Eido held up his hand, eyes wide and whispered, "Did you hear that?" They all froze and listened carefully. They could hear voices back the way they had come.

Then one called out and they were coming through the forest and still some distance away, "Ho there! You who these horses belong to, show yourselves!"

Pike held up his hand for them to remain quiet, and they could hear orders being given by the one who had called out.

"Should we put the Book back?" whispered Odus.

As Pike shook his head, "Our horses are there," he said. "We will feign having lost one of our company. Chayel, hide up there over that rise, and we shall see who these men are."

Nikos added, "There is a road about a mile directly west of here that runs north-south. It comes out at the town of Diaggello. If we get separated, we must find you there!"

"We should not separate even now!" Chayel whispered fiercely, but they heard some men drawing nearer.

"Quickly then," said Pike. "They do not sound like a large troop."

"Or like Rhaka's men," added Odus. As Chayel disappeared into the forest, the others went warily toward the clearing, but were met by a few dozen soldiers who quickly surrounded them.

"Lay down your weapons!" called out one brandishing his sword and calling behind him, "We've got them, captain!"

Pike, Odus, Nikos, and Eido remained still but kept their weapons girded on themselves.

A man approached and said, "I am Captain Stagos, commander of the barracks in Diaggello. What is your business here?"

"Our business is our own," said Odus quickly.

"Not now, it isn't!" he barked. "Not with this menace from the north making its way into these parts! Explain yourselves! Where is the fifth member of your party?"

"Lost sir!" said Eido as he snapped to attention. "We came to visit our friend here, but didn't see him, and now we do not know where either of them is, sir!" Stagos had just enough pride to be taken in by Eido's feigned respect, but still commanded some of his men to search the forest.

"We will see if your story proves true," he said.

After quite some time, the soldiers returned, and one of them said, "We found something sir, a stream with some odd rock carvings and the footprints of these here, plus the one who is supposedly missing—a woman by the size of the tracks."

Another soldier, who came from the clearing said, "Sir, the house in the hill over there . . . no one has lived there for a long time."

"Take them into custody!" commanded Captain Stagos. "And find the woman!"

Pike suddenly held up his hand and said, "We will not resist you, and we do not want a fight, but if you attempt to disarm us, we will defend ourselves."

Stagos hesitated and then commanded his men, "Escort them out to the clearing!" They went peacefully and remained patient as Stagos's men searched the forest.

After quite a while, the men returned and reported, "Captain Stagos, sir, the forest is nearly impassable further in. We tracked the woman only a short way until the terrain made it impossible."

Stagos became angry and looked fiercely at Pike, who stood resolute to fight if need be.

Then Odus said, "Captain Stagos, sir, we're on the same side of this fight, so it's no good fightin' each other. We got our business, and you best let us get to it."

Stagos scowled and hesitated, seemingly at odds with himself. He waved his men off and then turned abruptly and followed them over the hill. After they had galloped away, Pike and the others made their way back to the stream, but even he who was an expert tracker could not follow Chayel's trail for very long. They called out, but there was no reply and after searching as far into the forest as they dared, they returned to the clearing.

"It's a might distressing," said Odus. "I wouldn't think it'd be like her to leave like that."

"Indeed," said Pike.

Nikos added, "We ought to stay here tonight to see if she returns. If we go farther into the trees, we will likely get lost ourselves."

"Agreed," said Pike looking up at the heavy canopy of leaves.

With no sign of Chayel by morning, Nikos, Pike, and the others made their way down from Polus's house to the southern edge of Geroon Forest.

"Well, Chayel has got to be *somewhere*," said Odus.

"We must see if she has come to Diaggello," said Pike.

Nikos added, "Yes, if she found the road, that's where it leads."

"Maybe we best split up," said Odus, "and two of us go east and up around the end of the forest; maybe she made her way out up that way."

"Let us meet at Steko's Ferry in two days," said Pike, and they all agreed.

Then he and Eido headed toward Diaggello, while Nikos and Odus followed the river down to the end of the forest and turned north. They skirted the edge of the forest and scanned the open lands to the east. They were alert for any of Rhaka's soldiers as they approached the northern side of Geroon Forest. Suddenly, three horsemen were riding hard toward them, coming down from a spur of the Stone Mountains.

But when they neared, Nikos called out, "Barah! Kafar!"

As they came together, Barah said, "It is so good to see you! Alive and well!"

"And you as well!" replied Nikos. "You escaped Rhaka's soldiers in Keone?"

"Yes, the townsfolk and some Megans from up north defeated the soldiers, and then we—"

Nikos interrupted, "Makarios, she escaped with you? Is she well?"

"Yes," answered Kafar. "We all came to Tachus Town and found there had been a battle with Rhaka's forces the day before. They defended the town, but I'm sorry . . . Marshal Kainos was killed."

"He was a good man," said Odus, "and he is in a better place now."

After a somber silence, Arak said, "Polus was there too. He came alone, in the midst of the battle, and rallied many of the Meganthropos soldiers to fight against the others. It turned the tide."

"He is there now?" asked Nikos.

"No," answered Barah. "He and Makarios went to Makran to try to reach Rhaka to free him from Kah-Taw."

Odus's eyes widened, as he said, "Now, that's some bravery!"

"Indeed," said Kafar. "But where is Chayel? Do you know of her welfare?"

"Well, that's just what we're doin'," said Odus. "We're trying to find her."

"We have just come from Polus's house," said Nikos. "Chayel was with us there and also Eido and Marshal Pike. We found the Book, but just as we did, some soldiers from Diaggello came upon us, and Chayel rushed into the forest with the Book to hide. Some of the soldiers went in to find her but did not go far. I believe they feared getting lost. We haven't seen her since."

"We're up this way hoping to find her," added Odus.

"Pike and Eido went to the bridge at Diaggello," said Nikos. "If she made it out that way, they will meet us at the ferry in Two Rivers in a few days."

"It is an ominous forest," said Arak.

Kafar added, "Let us hope to find her." They all scouted west along the northern edge of the forest and searched within it as far as they dared but found nothing. As evening neared, they made camp just within the forest.

"Tomorrow, we must chance going further in," said Kafar.

— Twenty Nine —

Polus and Makarios left Tachus Town, she aboard Samos and Polus on foot. They went silently for a few miles as they traveled along the mine cart line that skirted the foothills of the Stone Mountains.

"It seems a lifetime ago," said Makarios, "when we met . . ."

Polus continued on seeming to have not heard, but after a while his pace slowed and then he stopped. "Yes," he said, "a lifetime wasted and nearly ruined, until you saved me." He began walking again and continued, "I hope Rhaka will be turned from the deadly path he is on. The Book says that the day will come when all evil is judged, and those who are on the side of it are doomed."

"But there is a point of no return," she said, "from which one cannot be saved. We must hurry."

They left the mine cart line and headed across open country and had come halfway up to Makran when they saw many soldiers in the distance. As they neared, one of the soldiers yelled, "*Stop!*"

Polus and Makarios were quickly surrounded by more than a hundred men, and their captain approached them. "Commander Polus . . . sir?" he said unbelievingly.

But a large Meganthropos called out, "Fool, Polus!"

Another said, "Traitor! You will die!"

"And what is this delicacy you have brought for us?" asked the captain, looking at Makarios. He then commanded the soldiers to stand down, especially the Megans, but none obeyed him.

Another Megan called out to Polus, "Now you will pay with your life, but not before you have suffered the justice of betrayal!" The Meganthropos soon became very dangerous, having no regard at all for the captain or the other men.

"And who will get the prize for bringing this one to Lord Rhaka?"

"We *all* will be honored!" bellowed another.

"Now, get moving!" called one as they prodded at Polus with their spears. As they got closer to Makran, more Megan soldiers joined them, mocking and yelling, some throwing stones and sticks at Polus. The Meganthropos among the soldiers became so agitated and provoked by Polus that the captain sent them on ahead while he came behind with a small squad of soldiers and Makarios in his custody.

Soon, he came to a halt and commanded, "Bring the woman!" She was still aboard Samos, but dismounted and came to the captain willingly, though he was agitated and very angry.

"Who are you? What do you have to do with Polus?" he bellowed, waving his arms. "Why has he come here without any defense?! What is the meaning of it? Does he think he—"

But suddenly, he stopped and looked directly at Makarios, "Do you make no answer, wench?!"

Makarios calmly returned his gaze and was about to speak when the captain yelled again, "You will answer me! Do you not see that I have the authority to do to you anything I wish?!"

"You are mistaken," she said, "but you may believe as you will." Her measured, calm response seemed to stun him, and he became somewhat rattled.

"Tell me," he began more calmly, "what goes on here? Polus has walked into his death by coming here like this, and you, whoever you are, will suffer the same fate!"

"We are willing for that," said Makarios, "if only you would hear the truth from us." He shook his head in frustration and glared at her.

One of his men said, "She's one of *them*."

"Check her!" commanded the captain. The soldier roughly pulled her shirt aside to reveal the mark.

"We got to kill her on the spot," said the soldier. "Lord Rhaka's command."

"Not until we get some use out of her," said another.

"And fine, high-quality use too, looks like!" called a soldier from within the ranks.

"Shut up, all of you!" yelled the captain and turned to Makarios. "You will tell me why Polus has given away his life like this! And you with him . . . who are you?!"

"We have come to tell Rhaka and any who will listen about the curse that all men are born with—"

One of the soldiers called out, "Ha! The only curse is that I haven't got my hands on you yet!"

The soldiers began jeering and yelling, and the captain, thoroughly frustrated and beside himself, commanded them to move out. They arrived in Makran by midday and passed quickly through, finding a mob of Meganthropos soldiers in front of the fortress yelling about betrayal and mocking and chanting something in their own language. They were all circled around Polus, who stood in the middle, bearing the blood and bruises of their abuse.

The captain tried to get control of the situation and began commanding his men, but Makarios leaped from her horse and ran through the throng of Megans. She burst out into the middle of them and up to Polus. A dead silence fell, and everything came to a halt as she stood looking at them all with fire in her eyes.

She took a deep breath and cried out, "You speak of betrayal and justice and honor, but you are *wrong*! You are the ones who are the betrayers! You have forsaken your own people who live peaceably and are loyal to each other! They do justice, while *you* are unjust! Condemning Polus for turning from this evil, for doing what is right—"

They began to shout again, but the captain rushed into the center with a squadron of his men and yelled, "Stop this! Lord Rhaka will have my head and some of yours if you keep this up!"

Suddenly, one of the Meganthropos, named Gamal, stepped forward and called out, "Yes! Let them alone! We must do nothing rash! Polus will be dealt justice and who better to do it than our Lord Rhaka himself!"

Some of them shuddered at this as the captain added, "And you all will be credited with Polus's capture!"

They settled down but were surprised when Makarios said, "Well, take us to your lord then, so that you may receive your due for such a miraculous capture!" She looked around at them in anger and set off herself, quickly followed by Polus. The captain stumbled over some words and hurriedly brought his men into formation around them. They reached the fortress and passed through the gate but stopped well short of the citadel.

"*Halt!*" yelled the captain. "Bring the prisoners forward!"

But Makarios had already made her way past the soldiers, which caused the captain to rush toward her. As he grabbed for her arm, Polus suddenly swung his granite fist, knocking him senseless.

"*No one* will touch her!" he yelled, looking around with chilling ferocity. Many of the Meganthropos, having had Polus as their commander, remembered their respect for him, but others scorned him. At that moment, Marshal Sigao came rushing up but stopped dead in his tracks when he saw Polus.

"You!" he exclaimed, but Gamal, seeing his opportunity, said, "We have captured him, sir!"

"What is this that you want me to believe?" scoffed Sigao. "And who is this woman?!"

"She insisted on being taken captive with Polus, Marshal Sigao, sir!" answered Gamal.

Sigao scowled at them all and then went to the citadel, a stone's throw away and talked to the guard. He returned, facing squarely up to Polus.

"You are a fool!" he whispered fiercely. "Do you so easily forget the terrible power and malice of Lord Rhaka? You *will* die!"

"We are willing for that," said Makarios, "if only you will hear—"

But one of the Megans stepped nearer and asked incredulously, "Willing to die for *what*?"

Another Megan, inexplicably intrigued said, "You will *die* just to tell us something?"

"What is it?" asked a third.

A murmuring began among them until it was suddenly silenced by the opening of the citadel door. All stood as still as statues, and as Lord Rhaka emerged, a wave of dread fell upon them. Some shook for fear, feeling anew his powerful presence. Even Polus was dismayed at the effect Rhaka had. Makarios reached for Polus and steadied herself on his arm, trembling in fear. They looked into each other's eyes and thought that they may well die but did not speak.

Rhaka walked slowly, almost casually as if he were just out for a stroll. As he neared them and his eyes fell upon Polus, he was taken aback, but concealed it, save for the slightest little sneer. He looked about and bellowed, "Who dares to summon me?!"

Sigao was nowhere to be seen, but Gamal stood there trembling and fumbled for words. As Rhaka turned to him, he stuttered, "Lord Rhaka, our master, I . . . we . . . all of us have captured Polus, and . . . brought him to you."

He bowed. As he looked up, he cringed as Rhaka stepped toward him and looked at him so piercingly that he could barely stand.

"Now, tell me," began Rhaka bending toward him, "what is your name?"

"Ga . . . ga . . . Gamal, my lord."

"Why so frightened, hmm?" asked Rhaka as if he were talking to a child. "Now, there is nothing to fear, dear one, if you have spoken the truth to me." Rhaka gently patted Gamal's shoulder, and he flinched as if he had been struck.

"Oh, poor little one," cajoled Rhaka. "You *have* told me the truth, *haven't* you?"

Gamal was so overwhelmed with an unexplainable terror that he fell to his knees with tears streaming down. As he covered his face with his hands, he mumbled, "Ye . . . yes . . . the truth . . . I have told you."

Rhaka drew a deep breath and slowly shook his head and then bent down and said sweetly into Gamal's ear, "Another lie? You lie *again* to me?"

He straightened up and continued, "Do you think this one comes here unbound and stands here willingly? This is the *truth* you want me to believe?" An inhuman rage welled up in him and as his face contorted and he raised his arm, Makarios suddenly remembered what he had done to Megar at the Rift and how horribly he had died.

She lunged forward with all her strength in front of Gamal and screamed, "*No!* Stop this!"

Rhaka was shocked and momentarily froze, his eyes fixed on her, but his rage melted into a wicked smile.

He stepped back a pace and adjusted himself to properly face her, "My dear madame," he said sweetly, "your ill manners surprise me. You seem such a woman of quality. It is too bad you will not live to make amends for your rude interruption." He leaned toward her and added, "Have you anything to say that might save you from your fate, my *dear?*"

A surge of courage filled Makarios, and she said, "My fate, Lord Rhaka is not in your hands, so I need say nothing."

Rhaka was taken aback but did not show it as he said, almost to himself, "So foolish, these mere . . . *people.*" As he glanced at Polus and then back to Makarios, he said, "The fate of the *world* will soon be in my hands—"

But Makarios cut in, "No! You are the foolish one! You think yourself to be something you are not, but you will die the death of all men!"

"Die?" he said incredulously, as if he truly couldn't understand it. "Now, my dear lady, you begin to intrigue me, but my midday meal awaits."

Suddenly, he turned and began striding away and with a wave of his hand, he called out, "Put them in the pit!"

But after a few strides, he turned back, "No! Put *him* in the pit and that one there . . ."

He gestured toward Gamal, and said as sweetly as a loving father, "Come here to me, my son."

All were breathless as Gamal slowly approached and stood trembling before him. Rhaka was silent for a few minutes, seeming to enjoy the terror he created. Then he asked quietly, "Does not a son honor his father?"

Gamal was so overcome with fear that he could only nod, and as Rhaka stepped closer, he collapsed to his knees.

"Now ,my dear boy," he continued, "have I not been as a father to you?" Suddenly, Rhaka grabbed him by the throat and as he raised him up off his feet, screamed, "*Then where is my respect?!*" and struck him across the face with his armored glove slashing deep into his flesh. All the soldiers drew back as Rhaka flung him to the ground.

He shook his head in disgust and began striding away and then with a wave of his hand, called out, "Bring the woman to me!"

All remained rooted in their places until he had gone into the citadel and closed the door. Makarios stood trembling, feeling as weak as water and as one of the soldiers grabbed her arm, she nearly fell.

"I need no help or urging to go to the citadel!" she exclaimed angrily. "That is what I came for!" She twisted away from the soldier and went toward the citadel but felt faint as a wave of fear washed over her. Immediately, a gentle but strong arm was around her shoulders, and she turned to see a thick, hefty man with piercing green eyes and long braided red hair that fell to his waist, clad in ornate golden armor over a purple linen shirt and kilt.

"Be strong and courageous," he said smiling and then added with a somber tone, "Remember what you *know*."

She was about to speak when she suddenly found herself at the door, surrounded by guards. The captain came out of the citadel and motioned for her to go in. The citadel was dimly lit, about fifty feet across with a flagstone floor and paneled walls of cedar wood. At the far side was an elaborately carved table made of a rich dark wood, strewn with many books, and above it hung a chandelier filled with dozens of candles. There was a large chair, very much like a throne with its back to the door. The room was eerily quiet, and as the door closed behind Makarios, she jumped in fright, her hand instinctively going to her sword hilt. Suddenly, an overwhelming dread gripped her as she heard a deep, brief laugh.

"You will find that useless, my dear lady . . ." came a voice that sounded like nothing she had ever heard before. "And how is it that you think you would even need it here?"

She felt dazed and disoriented and then found herself walking toward the chair.

"You are welcome, my dear one," said the voice, which was oddly comforting. As she came around the end of the table, she saw an elaborate meal laid out.

"Come and sit down," said Rhaka, who sat in the large chair and motioned to a small chair across from him. She collapsed into the chair, as if in a dream world and unable to speak.

"Now, you think I am the foolish one?" he said sweetly and chuckled, shaking his head and then gesturing at his surroundings. "Does this look like the house of a fool?" He chuckled again and picked up a piece of bread and as he began to eat, he added, "Please, eat."

But Makarios felt hardly able to move or even remember why she was there. Rhaka looked up at her and paused, "Please, eat," he said smiling. "It will be your last meal. I am happy to provide such a fine one for you."

Suddenly, the words, "Remember what you *know*," came into her mind, and she began to fight to recall anything familiar. It was as if she was underwater and struggling to get to the surface. Gasping and taking in a big breath she said, "I *know*."

Rhaka looked at her quizzically, and he seemed to her to be much less frightening as he said, "Know? What do you *know*, my dear madame?"

"The truth," she answered with great effort.

"The truth? Why, what *is* truth?" he asked with an endearing smile. A definite edge came into his voice as he added, "Now will you continue to be such a rude guest and not eat what I have provided?"

With difficulty, Makarios said, "You know of the curse—"

Rhaka clenched his jaw and put his food down. He was about to speak when Makarios said,

"You are ruled by it."

Rhaka's eyes suddenly blazed with fury; his whole body became taut as he nearly leaped up, but he controlled himself and said, "Ah, you are one of those who believe the *lie.*"

She had come to herself again and said, "You know the words of the Book—"

"*No!*" he screamed, slamming his fist on the table and knocking his chair backward.

Makarios jumped up and backed away as he stood there enraged, in a moment of uncertainty. Then he glared at her and came around the table toward her. She stood there in great fear, but with a strength and courage not her own, she faced him. He bore down on her but pulled up short.

"You do not *fear?!*" he shrieked. "*I will kill you!*"

"You will gain nothing by it," she said trembling. "I only wish for you to be free—"

"*Free?!*" he yelled and then turned and gestured around the room. "I *am* free! This world . . . it's all mine! I rule these lands!

"But there is one you do not rule," said Makarios. "The one you wish to rule the most— *yourself.*" He spun around seething and lunged at her, but again pulled up short and stood heaving with clenched fists.

"You deserve death," he seethed, "and—"

"What will it accomplish? So, I die," she said and pointed toward the floor at Rhaka's feet. "There my dead body will be, but after that, there is no more you can do." Rhaka stared at the floor and then slowly looked up and glared hard into her eyes.

She felt a stab of fear as she saw how strange his eyes were—neither brown nor green nor blue, but black and white in stark contrast. For the briefest of moments, Makarios saw a helplessness in him and quickly said, "You *know* the curse; you *know* you are enslaved to the Ra-Tsalem, but you can—"

But Rhaka squeezed his eyes shut, grabbed his head and screamed, "*Silence!!* I rule! I am the lord and master!!"

He suddenly grabbed her by the throat and bellowed, "You repulsive wench! You spit upon my hospitality; you speak lies at my table, and you deny my lordship. But look around you; I am the king, this is *my* palace, *my* kingdom and what *I* say is the truth."

Makarios frantically gasped for air, but Rhaka held his grip, and his demeanor suddenly changed.

"Oh, my dear, do you wish to speak?" he said softly. "Would you like to tell me more *truth?*" She felt herself losing consciousness as he said, "My poor little one, I cannot hear you. Speak up." He leaned very near to her, tightened his grip and hissed, "What, nothing to say?"

Makarios fell limp, and Rhaka strode to the door and threw her out, calling to the captain who had been at the ready with a few soldiers. "Into the pit with her!" he bellowed in a rage and disappeared back into the citadel.

Marshal Sigao approached Makarios as two of the soldiers took hold of her, and one of them said, "She's . . . dead, sir."

·——— Thirty ———·

In Geroon Forest, Chayel came to herself, lying at the bottom of a deep gully. She remained still, listening, but hearing nothing, she got up slowly and brushed herself off. She climbed up out of the gully but had no idea of the direction she ought to go. Suddenly, a low growl wafted through the air, and she looked sharply toward the sound. She peered through the dim light, but all she could see was the jumbled ground of boulders and logs. Something was moving toward her, and she herself growled, drawing her sword and rapping it on the underbrush.

Suddenly, a great gray wolf leaped over a big log toward her, and she stumbled backward, yelling, "No!" which unexpectedly made the wolf stop in its tracks. Chayel scrambled to her feet and saw that the wolf was looking at her inquisitively and seemingly not dangerous at all.

"You won't eat me, will you?" she said lightheartedly. The wolf seemed to relax, and Chayel sheathed her sword and knelt down.

"You're not a wild one, are you?" He came warily toward her and stopped, but as Chayel remained still, he came within arm's reach. She held her hand out, and he came closer yet and she stroked his fur.

"You are *someone's*," she said, "but you're all bones . . ." The wolf seemed glad of the attention and affection and as Chayel stood up, he remained near her.

"Well, I've got no food to give you," she said, "and I'm about as lost as you seem to be."

She started off, directly away from the gully, hoping to find her way back to the clearing. The going was rough, but she soon came upon a sort of a path and stopped. "*This can't be the way then,*" she thought, "*Because—*"

But the wolf suddenly trotted past, startling her and then some way ahead, he turned back toward her and waited. She reasoned that the path might lead somewhere and that at least it made the going easier. She continued for a while but was getting a bad feeling that it wasn't anywhere near the right direction. Soon, the path disappeared, and the forest closed in a bit; she thought that at least the wolf would go in a straight direction, but suddenly realized he was nowhere to be seen. Chayel went on and began to get hungry and thirsty, but she saw only strange looking mushrooms and dark greasy pools of water. The grey-green canopy of leaves was lower, and she was overtaken with a feeling of doom as she sensed that the sun was beginning to set in the outside world. She found a few pine trees and some dry ground beneath them and as she put her small pack down, the wolf suddenly appeared behind her.

"Oh!" she exclaimed and spun around, but then breathed a sigh of relief. She sat down against the tree and was surprised when the wolf snuggled down next to her.

As she stroked his fur, she said, "I wonder . . . Lukos?" The wolf's head popped up with his ears pitched forward, and he looked into her face for a moment. "Of course! Makarios said you were missing . . ."

Chayel awoke with the wolf pawing at her, and she exclaimed, "What is it?"

But Lukos bounded away and up onto a log, surveying the area. The sun had risen, and the rain had cleared off. Chayel saw a part of the forest that was much brighter than the rest, so she headed toward it and was joined by Lukos, who stayed close to her. Soon, the trees began to thin out, and the ground became more open and even and she came upon a stream, which she found good to drink. She kept on toward the lighter part of the forest and eventually saw an opening, beyond which was an open field. She made for it, but suddenly became very wary, wondering if there would be any soldiers about.

Lukos put his nose to the air and let out a low growl and slipped away into the underbrush, but Chayel's attention was fixed ahead of her. She went slowly and came to the edge of the forest, which ended abruptly as if the lands beyond had, at one time, been cleared. She quickly realized by the position of the sun that she had been going north, "*Exactly the wrong direction,*" she thought angrily, "*but at least I'm clear of this miserable forest!*"

There were mountains ahead and what looked like some kind of road, but she stayed within the forest and skirted along the edge of it, heading east and hoping to find some way south. Suddenly, she smelled wood smoke and thought she heard voices in the direction she was going, and went even more cautiously. As she drew closer, she looked for a way around, but it was all open country or back into the forest.

Suddenly, she was grabbed from behind and easily overpowered. "Oh-ho! What have we here?" said a burly, bearded young man. "Now, don't go strugglin' or you'll hurt yourself, wench! And we don't want no damaged goods!"

"You will regret this!" said Chayel fiercely.

But the man paid no attention as he began walking and called out, "Hey fellers! Look what I caught!" He came into a camp just within the forest where there were three other men, and they gathered around.

"Ain't this sweet!" said one.

Another said, "You are a fine one!"

The third man took her bow and added, "Now, what here is this thing?"

"I would love to show you!" said Chayel angrily.

Then the man who had a hold of her said, "If you'll be nice, I'll put you down." But he laughed and suddenly just let her go and shoved her so that she fell into the midst of them all. Before any of them could react, she had a small knife in her hand and slashed the arm of the first man who reached for her. He recoiled in surprise and clutched his arm, but his face turned to murder.

He was thin and scrawny with a scraggly beard, so when he leaped at Chayel, the bigger man, whose name was Sehpo, easily stopped him, saying, "Now, Stawk, you'll get yer turn! Don't go hurtin' 'er!"

"Now, let's have that knife," said one of the others. Chayel gave it up, seeing that she really had no chance to fight her way out. They took everything from her and rummaged through her pack.

When the Book was pulled out, Sehpo said, "Now, what's this? Looks mighty fine," but then he tossed it amid the other things strewn on the ground and added, "That's mine, boys! Could get a fair mite at the traders fer it, but in the meanwhile . . ."

He grabbed Chayel by the arm and started toward the forest as the others sat down around the fire again. Chayel knew what was about to happen and never felt so helpless in all her life. The tears came as Sehpo pulled her along, and after he had gone a good way into the forest, he threw her to the ground.

She scrambled backward, but he grabbed her ankle and growled, "Lay still, you worthless wench!" She furiously kicked at him and tried to get up, but as he came down toward her, a silent streak of gray fur barged him over and ripped into his arm and then clamped his jaws down on Sehpo's throat. The man struggled mightily, but, Lukos held on until the man lay lifeless.

Chayel was shocked, but suddenly the thought of the Book laying there on the ground crowded every other emotion and thought out of her. She got up and listened and then made her way back toward the camp, followed closely by Lukos. The men remained around the campfire, talking and laughing, and she could see her belongings where they had been thrown—the Book among them. Her tri-bow and arrows were nearer to hand, but she could not reach them without coming into the open. She settled herself down, well hidden, and waited.

After quite some time, the man who was called Stawk got up, stretched, took a swig of some kind of drink, and said, "Now ain't he getting' on a bit?"

Another said with a bit of an edge, "Well, yeah! There'll be nothin' good left fer us!"

"Maybe he made off with 'er," suggested Stawk. "Wouldn't it be just like 'im? Always keepin' the good stuff for himself!"

The other two looked at each other and jumped up. "Wonder how far 'ee could have got by now?" added Stawk slyly. "You best go see!"

The two lost no time making off into the forest and after waiting for a minute or so, Chayel went straight for her sword and her bow, startling Stawk and veering away just as he spun around.

"Hoi!" he exclaimed as Chayel stood between him and their weapons. Her belongings and the Book were beyond where Stawk stood, and she knew her time was short.

"If you want to live," she began, sheathing her sword and readying her bow, "Let me get my things, and I'll be on my way."

But Stawk scoffed, "Yer not goin' anywhere, wench!"

He came at her, and she backed away saying, "Stop!" But as he kept coming, Lukos leaped out from the forest and came straight at him. Stawk screeched and dove to the ground, covering his head.

Chayel called out, "Lukos, no!" He landed on Stawk, but then yielded and retreated behind her. She quickly ran and grabbed her pack and gathered up her things as Stawk scrambled to his feet. Suddenly, cries rang out in the forest, and Chayel took to her heels, with Lukos next to her. She dared not go back into the forest and so ran east across open country.

"He's dead! He's dead!" she heard behind her as another called, "Get her!

Get her!"

They were all after her now, with swords and spears. The one called Stawk was gaining on her, and she looked for any kind of cover, but all she saw was a stony ridge and a few large boulders amid the tall grass. She leaped behind one and spun around, her bow at the ready.

"*Stop!*" she yelled as the men neared. "I wish not to kill you," but they came on until she let fly an arrow into the leg of one of the men.

As he careened to the ground screaming, Stawk skidded to a halt, and the other man turned and cried out, "My brother! My brother!" and turned on Chayel in a rage, coming straight at her, but he never made it. Suddenly, a huge white beast swooped down from above and knocked him down. Stawk screeched and dove to the ground, but Chayel ran forward, as the beast folded its wings and turned toward them all.

"Oh, Tey-Rahk!" she called and was received by him as he bent toward her and lifted his great paw to embrace her. The tears came as emotions overwhelmed her, but she soon stood back from him, about to speak. But he rose to his full height and padded toward the three men who stood together, frozen in fear. Tey-Rahk stood looking so fiercely at them that one fell to the ground, and Stawk covered his head, trembling.

"What is your name?" asked Tey-Rahk in a voice that even sent fear through Chayel.

"Sss . . . sss . . . Ssstaw . . . tawk," he sputtered, his eyes on the ground.

"How do you dare to threaten a daughter of the King?" he asked loudly.

Stawk fell to his knees and tried to respond, "Pl . . . please, sire . . . I . . . . I . . .," but no more words came. Tey-Rahk approached the man with the arrow in his leg as he lay there whimpering and hysterical with fear. As the great lion lowered his head toward the man, he screamed and tried to leap up, but Tey-Rahk pinned him to the ground with his huge paw.

"And you," he said, lowering his face to within inches of the man's face, "There is murder in your heart."

"No, no, no!!" he wailed and closed his eyes and waited to be crushed in the lion's jaws. But Tey-Rahk only plucked the arrow out of his leg and stood back from him. No wound remained, and he looked incredulously at Tey-Rahk. Suddenly, a look of awe came over his face, and he got up far enough to go down on one knee in front of Chayel.

"Forgive me, woman," he said, "for the wrong done to you." He laid down his sword, and the other men were shocked.

"Dune! What are you doing?!" shouted Stawk, who had retreated to what he thought was a safe distance.

"He does what is wise," said Tey-Rahk. "You would do well to do the same."

Stawk sneered and backed further away, pulling the other man with him, who called out, "My brother! What is wrong with you?!"

But Dune rose to his feet and looked straight into Tey-Rahk's crystal blue eyes and asked, "What must I do?"

Tey-Rahk answered, "It has been done for you, as you have believed."

Dunamis was overwhelmed and not knowing what to say, he said, "I will go with you . . ."

But Tey-Rahk answered, "Go and bury your dead and tell of the great things that you now know."

He stood still, unsure what he should do and then turned to Chayel. "You believe too?"

She reached toward him, and he shied away, but she caught his shirt collar and pulled it aside.

"You must be careful," she said. "Some will kill you for this." As he looked down, she added, "It shows that you belong to the Tsadaq, the Great One." She showed her own mark.

Stawk again angrily called out, "Dune! Come with us!"

Tey-Rahk lashed his tail and looked toward them, letting out a low growl.

"*Who* would kill me?" asked Dune nervously.

"Rhaka's soldiers," answered Chayel. "But there are many others who hate this name."

Stawk was about to call out again but was cut short as Tey-Rahk leaped forward in their direction with another growl. Stawk shrieked and disappeared into the forest with the other man.

As Tey-Rahk turned back, Dune said, "Please sire, I have nowhere to go . . ."

Tey-Rahk said, "Do not call me 'sire'; I am a fellow servant," and then unexpectedly said to Chayel, "You must go. Do you wish him to come with you?"

Quite surprised, she had no ready answer and after a moment or two, Tey-Rahk said to Dune, "Make yourself ready." Dune ran to the camp and gathered his things and saddled two of the horses, letting the others go free.

Meanwhile, Tey-Rahk said to Chayel, "You must go to Two Rivers; there you will find someone that you can trust."

But she said, "Will you not come?"

He chuckled, as much as a lion can, and answered, "Go with this man; it is the best way."

Knowing Tey-Rahk, she accepted his word, hugged him, and said with a smirk, "I will miss you, *again*!"

He bent close to her face and said with affection, "One day, when this is all over, we will see each other as often as we wish." He leaped into the air with a great rush of his wings and rose high into the sky.

As she watched him go, Dune approached, leading both horses and asked nervously, "You *know* that one?"

"Rather, he knows me," she answered.

"Who . . . what *is* he?"

"Mostly just what you see, but he would say that he is an emissary of the Great One."

"I am glad . . . glad he is on our side . . . now that I have chosen a side." Dune was young, near Chayel's age with long dark hair and a short thin beard. He had few belongings and seemed not the sort to have been with Stawk and the others.

They mounted up, and Dune said, "Again, I am sorry—"

Chayel interrupted, saying, "You need be sorry only once; my forgiveness has been given. Now, tell me, do you know the way to Two Rivers from here?"

He nodded and turned his horse more to the south. "Please . . ." he began, "I don't understand all that has happened. I don't even know your name."

"I am Chayel," she said.

Dune continued, "Tell me . . . I feel so different, like I have a different life, a new one . . ."

"The Great One abides in you now. You are free from the curse of Kah-Taw."

"Yes . . . I had felt the weight of it more and more of late, though I did not know what it was until I met Sehpo. He was one of Rhaka's soldiers, a commander I think, but he left the fortress. He told me about a book that Rhaka had, a very sacred book, one in a strange language . . . he is from the same country as you? He talked the same way."

"I suppose he was," she answered.

"That is where the Book came from?" Before she could answer, Dune continued, "I wonder why the Book is in this land. Where is your country?"

"It is far south, down past the Desert Wilderness."

Dune paused and then said, "That beast, that creature . . . that—"

"His name is Tey-Rahk."

"Are there many more like him?"

"There is one other—"

"Why would *he* have been here to save you at just that moment?" Suddenly, Chayel pulled her horse to a stop, and Dune exclaimed, "What is it?" and looked around nervously.

She sat for a moment and then said with a bit of an edge, "Please, it has been hard today . . ."

Dune became quiet, and they rode along for a good long while in silence. Soon, they came over a rise in the land and saw a large body of water in the distance.

"That is Huo Lake," said Dune. "We will get to Two Rivers by nightfall."

After a few moments, Chayel said, "You wish to say that you are sorry again, for speaking so much, asking so many questions." He nodded, afraid to say anymore.

"Think no more of it," she said, "Indeed, there is much to learn . . . the ways of the Tsadaq and from the Book—"

Dune interjected, "But . . ." He stopped, but she nodded for him to continue, "The Book, there is only one. But how shall we learn from it . . . Rhaka, he has it."

Chayel did not respond, and Dune was thoughtful for a moment and then looked down at Lukos who was following along with them and asked, "He is yours?"

"No, a friend's," she answered. "She said he was missing, lost I suppose, but now he is found."

"I feel like that," said Dune more to himself than to Chayel. The sun began to go down behind them, but they rode on and sometime after the moon had risen, they came to the north side of Huo Lake.

Thirty One

Rhaka's soldiers took Polus to the prison and locked him securely within. He found himself amongst mostly townsfolk.

Suddenly, a scrawny old man called out, "You! You stole my boys' horses! You ordered them to do it!"

As Polus turned to look at him, another called out, "Yeh! Why you in here? Didn't steal and kill enough for that old Rhaka?"

"Now, you'll get yer due and suffer the same fate as the rest of us!" taunted a third.

Many more began to jeer, but suddenly a very large Meganthropos came forward and addressed him, "Commander Polus, sir?"

Polus replied, "Onos? It is good to see that you escaped Rhaka's massacre at the Rift."

"Yes, and my brother Oxos escaped; we're the ones as let you out of the trench. It is good to see you alive, but how did Rhaka capture you?"

"He did not—," answered Polus, sitting down on a crate.

Before he could finish, the old man called out, "He's one of *them*! Look, you can just see some of that mark!"

"*That's* why he's in here!" said another. "Rhaka's killin' them as has the mark!"

"Stop!" yelled Onos, "if you want to keep livin'!"

They all shrank back as he came forward, nearer to Polus and said, "And the Book?"

Polus shook his head, wondering if he could trust Onos and said, "The Book, yes . . . we must get out of here."

"But—" began Onos.

At that moment soldiers were heard on the stairs. The door was unlocked, and a soldier came through carrying Makarios. He glared at Polus and fairly threw her upon him and went out. A hush fell over everyone as Polus held her to himself and stood stock-still for a few moments and then began to tremble in fear. He moved toward the wall and slowly set Makarios down on an old blanket on the floor.

The old man whispered, "Is she . . ." but trailed off as Polus sank to his knees and cried like he never had before. He knelt there as weak as if his own life had gone out of him. After a while, Onos knelt beside him and put his hand on Polus's shoulder.

Eventually, a clean-shaven young man came forward and said hesitantly, "Please, sir . . ."

Polus slowly looked toward him, and the man approached and said, "I am as you, of the Great One."

Polus nodded, his face puffy and streaked with tears. "Please, if I may," he continued and reached for Makarios; Polus suddenly exploded into action and caught the man in a choke hold.

"No one touches her!" he yelled seemingly in a daze, but Onos grabbed Polus, trying to loosen his grip on the man.

"You'll kill him!" he screamed. Others jumped into the fray and soon had the young man free as Polus fell against the wall.

"I can help her," the young man said from across the dungeon, but someone near the back laughed as did a few others.

Then one said, "She's *dead*!"

Polus snapped out of his daze and sprang to his feet, but Onos jumped in front of him, "Polus, no!" he called. "Leave them!" Polus eased off and looked back at Makarios.

"Let me help her," said the man, bravely coming closer. He looked carefully at Polus, who tipped his head toward him and then knelt beside her. He took her hands into his own and put his forehead against hers and then sat back.

"She will live," he said looking up at Polus.

"Live?" he replied incredulously.

There were some stifled laughs, but Polus seemed not to hear as the man added, "If the Great One wills." He again took her hands into his own and put his forehead against hers. After some time, he sat back, but Makarios did not stir.

"Make her live, ha!" yelled someone from the dark end of the dungeon.

"Yer a fake!" called another as many more began to call out and hurl insults. Polus became enraged and sought to take on the whole lot of them when suddenly Makarios gasped and drew in a deep breath. She sat up, looking wildly around and as she struggled to get up, Polus scooped her up into his arms.

"He . . . he killed me . . ." sputtered Makarios frantically. "I . . . I saw him throw me out of the citadel." She began sobbing as Polus held her tight.

It seemed that time stopped, and the room was dead silent until the old man whispered, "How can it be?"

Many were astonished, but others scoffed, saying she hadn't really been dead. "You are alright?" asked Polus, letting go of her.

"Yes, yes, but I am alive. How—"

"This one here . . . he made you live!" said the old man and turned to point but saw that the man was no longer there.

"What in blue blazes?!" he exclaimed. "Where's he got to?" But no one could find him, and a division occurred among them as to what had happened and whether any of it was real.

"Well, I for one believe!" yelled the old man at them all. "And you, *you* said she was dead . . . *dead*! Want to change your story now? What do you think . . . that she was just sleeping? And what about the man who brought her to life? You all saw it! Now where is he? Want to say *he* didn't exist?"

"Shut up yer face!" yelled a rather large man coming forward. "It's all lies and tricks!"

"I can't stop saying what I just seen with my own eyes!" retorted the old man, facing up to the other.

"Stop this!" called Makarios, stepping between them, which quite surprised them all. "The truth is not truth because we say it is, but because truth just *is*. What is real cannot be denied, though you are free to disbelieve it."

They calmed down, and Makarios tried to teach them about the curse of Kah-Taw, but they would not listen and began to debate among themselves and then with the old man. Polus, Makarios, and Onos retreated to a place near the front, away from the others, where the light of the moon came in through a small window.

"How long have you been in here?" asked Polus in a hushed tone. "And your brother, where is he?"

"When we escaped the massacre," answered Onos, "we came right down to Makran and went into Rhaka's army, to spy things out and look for an advantage . . . and revenge. Oxos is still free in the fortress. I have only been in here a day."

"We must trust the Great One," said Makarios.

Onos nodded, and they all settled down. Deep into the night, Onos suddenly awoke and found the old man right next to him, "Your, brother," he whispered. "He is at the window!"

Onos went silently to it, and Oxos whispered fiercely, "Can you believe . . . Polus in our hands! And the Book . . . I will come in one hour's time and get you out!"

"Wait!" said Onos. "There is a woman; she must have a horse, so we will not be slowed down!"

"The woman? She is dead!"

"No, she . . . Polus will not leave her! She must have a horse! Bring that big bay; he will be the fastest!" Oxos began to get incensed, but Onos cut him off and went back to Polus, awakening him.

"Oxos, he will come in one hour for us. We must be ready!"

Soon, Oxos appeared at the door, and the three of them stole up the stairs and past two guards whose throats had been slit. They made for the front gate where there were more dead soldiers, and they slipped unseen into the city. With Makarios aboard her horse, they moved very quickly and came out into open country under the light of the moon.

"We must get all the way to the forest!" said Oxos as they moved directly south. They kept a steady pace and with more than thirty miles to go, they didn't arrive until nearly daybreak, but they passed safely within. As the forest grew thicker, they slowed their pace with Oxos continuing to lead them. They had passed almost halfway through to the southern border of the forest when Polus stopped.

"Wait! . . ." he said.

Oxos cut him off, "No! We must keep going!"

"To where?" asked Makarios. "Are we not free now? And we are very grateful that you have rescued us, but—"

"No, we must move!" insisted Oxos.

But Onos asked suspiciously, "To where, my brother?"

Oxos drew his sword and turned on Polus, "You will take me to the Book!"

Polus was unfazed, and Oxos screamed, "Where is it? You will show me! We must move!"

At that moment, a half a dozen Meganthropos suddenly came upon them from behind with swords drawn. Teras was leading them.

"Well now," he began, addressing Oxos, "what is this you have done?!"

A few of the Megans disarmed him as Teras continued, "Betrayal? Is your mind so small that you could not remember to bring him to me? Or did you never intend to?"

Onos looked sharply at his brother, who had no reply.

"Fool! Such disloyalty shall be paid for!" Teras drew his sword as they restrained Oxos, but Onos ran at him, yelling, "No!" only to be stopped by the other Megans.

Teras unceremoniously ran Oxos through with his sword and then turned to Onos. "Would you be next, or is there honor and loyalty in you?"

Onos stared in disbelief at his brother's lifeless body and said slowly, "I . . . I am with you, Teras."

Teras looked hard at Onos and said to one of his men, "Give him his brother's sword!" As Onos joined the others, Teras turned to Polus, but Makarios caught his attention.

"You! You were dead!" he began and turned to one of his men, who replied, "Yes sir, she was—"

"It is a deception!" Teras cried. "You lie!" and held his sword to the man's throat.

The man dropped to one knee and said, "By my honor, sir, she was dead. I cannot lie; do with me as seems good to you."

Teras relented and turned sharply back to Makarios, "How can this be?"

He stepped closer to her, and she said, "By the truth that you deny, I live."

He scowled and shook his head, becoming angrier and bellowing at Polus, "You will take me to the Book!"

But Makarios said, "The Book belongs to no man and must be returned to the place where it belongs."

Teras turned on her in a fury, "You will *die!*"

"It will gain you nothing," she answered fearlessly, which amazed and disarmed him. He turned on Polus and grabbed him by the throat, screaming, "Give me the Book!" and threw him to the ground.

"It is out of my hands," answered Polus as he got up and stood with his arms crossed.

"You will tell me who has it!" Teras seethed, but they remained silent.

He was beside himself with frustration and anger when one of his men said, "I've seen this kind . . . with the mark. They will not betray their allegiance. They would die first. Let them go. We will follow them."

But this further enraged Teras. "Like *dogs* following their master?!" He stood heaving and looked at Polus with a deadly stare and after some time, he waved his hand, releasing them.

·——— *Thirty Two* ———·

On the north side of Geroon Forest, Nikos woke
up just after dawn and got a fire going and was soon joined by the others.

"Well, seems we done all the searching that can be done up this way," said Odus.

Nikos said, "Maybe we ought to look into the forest a bit farther."

"No," interjected Arak, "we must go back east."

The men looked at each other and, knowing Arak's intuition, silently agreed. As the sun rose, they packed up and headed out, with Arak leading the way.

They had come nearly to the eastern edge of the forest when Odus said, "Now, how did we miss this?"

Just inside the forest, they had found a campsite and as they looked around, Arak said, "There were four men here, but also some smaller prints . . ."

"Chayel's?" asked Odus.

"Let us hope so," said Kafar.

"But these saddles . . ." said Barah. "It appears that two horses were let go."

"And two have gone this way," said Arak, pointing east across the open field. They set off and soon approached a rocky ridge.

"Well, somethin' happened here," said Odus as he quickly hopped off his horse. "An arrow! And there's blood on it."

"Surely, it is Chayel!" said Barah.

"But who did she shoot?" added Odus.

"And look at these huge tracks," said Arak.

"Well, that's heartening," said Odus. "No doubt that was Tey-Rahk."

"Chayel could be anywhere then," said Nikos.

"Unless she is on one of the horses that went this way," said Odus.

"Well, the tracks are headed southeast," said Arak. "Is that not the way we must go to meet Pike and Eido?"

They quickly set off, and though they soon lost the tracks in the tall grass, they kept on toward Two Rivers. They rode most of the day and eventually came down to the north side of Huo Lake. As they came over a rise, they saw a band of horsemen some distance away.

One of them called, "You there! By the command of the Lord Rhaka, stop!"

As the soldiers approached them, Kafar said, "Let us meet them but be at the ready."

Soon, they were surrounded by twenty or more soldiers. "You must be accounted!" yelled the captain. "Get off your horses!"

When they hesitated, the captain again bellowed, "Get down!" and his men moved closer, wielding their spears.

"What do you charge us with?" called Kafar.

Immediately enraged, the captain screamed, "You do not submit, so you will die!" And they suddenly found themselves under attack and at a disadvantage to the soldiers' spears. They fought only to defend themselves, but after some minutes of furious fighting, Arak was impaled by a spear and when Barah suffered a serious injury, Kafar signaled for them to flee. Their sudden retreat caught the soldiers off guard and so gained them a slight advantage. They galloped hard and came to the Bradus river, following it toward the west. They soon came to the bridge at Diaggello and amidst some townsfolk, charged up onto it and wheeled around to face their attackers.

Suddenly, one of the soldiers fell from his horse with an arrow in his chest and then another as two horsemen came bearing down on them from the north. "Stop!" yelled one of the riders as the other cried, "Or another will die!"

The soldiers regrouped and as they did, some of the townsfolk, seeing that they were Rhaka's men, turned on them, some brandishing weapons. Drawn to the commotion, others joined the fray, and the soldiers were soon outnumbered.

As they were driven off, the captain yelled out a promise of retribution from Rhaka, but the townsfolk jeered and threw rocks at them. The people of Diaggello felt that they had won a great victory and went off into town cheering for themselves, leaving Kafar, Barah, and the others still on the bridge.

"Pike! Eido!" shouted Nikos.

Kafar called out, "Arak! He has fallen!" They turned to see Arak on the deck of the bridge, bleeding profusely and groaning loudly.

"Quickly!" said Kafar.

A man from the town jumped down from his wagon saying, "I am Rawfah. I can help." They got Arak into the wagon, and the man took him into town, bringing him into a building and quickly cleansing his wound.

"I am a healer," he said. "Hold this! Press it here!" He tried to stop the bleeding, but minutes later, Arak lost consciousness. Rawfah worked furiously to revive him, but there was no response.

"No! No! Let it not be!" he cried as he continued.

Soon Kafar stepped next to him, and Rawfah looked quickly to him with tears in his eyes and said, "I am sorry." He was as distressed as they all were. "So sorry . . ."

He stepped back, and they all stood in stunned silence as Rawfah covered Arak with a cloth.

Somberness came upon them as he said to Barah, "Let me see to your wound."

After Barah was bandaged up, Eido said in a disbelieving tone, "What . . .what are we going to do?"

They looked at each other and then Nikos said, "We are not far from Makarios's farm. We could . . ." but he trailed off.

Barah added, "Bury him there?"

Nikos nodded as Kafar said, "It is a grievous loss, but we must go quickly." Rawfah offered his wagon, and they were soon on their way.

"You did not find Chayel?" asked Eido.

Odus shook his head and said, "But we did find one of her arrows . . ."

"With blood on it," added Nikos. "We think she's headed to Two Rivers."

"With someone else," added Odus. "But Tey-Rahk was there too, so maybe she's with him or a prisoner of the other rider or what, we don't know."

As they passed out of Diaggello, there was quite a ruckus between the townspeople and Deputy Spoggos who was saying, "Now you can't go fightin' with Rhaka's men! It's best to just go along with them. We can't beat them—"

But some of the people booed, and one called out, "But we *did* beat them!" To which the crowd agreed, but they soon fell out of earshot. Within an hour, Nikos and the others along with Rawfah in his wagon turned onto the track leading to Makarios's farm.

Halfway to the farm, Nikos held up his hand. "Wait!" he exclaimed. "I see tracks here . . . many men and wagons."

"Looks like Rhaka's men," said Odus.

Nikos continued, "If we go west across the fields and then south, we can come up to the farm behind the barn."

"Lead the way!" said Kafar. Leaving Rawfah and the wagon, they galloped off. Soon, they had come around and into some cover south of the farm. They left their horses and crept along, keeping low and under cover until they reached the edge of the barnyard. The pasture had more than two dozen horses in it and there were soldiers drinking and laughing.

"This is bad," whispered Nikos. "And I don't see Menka or Daggo or their mules."

"I say fight the enemy where they are," said Barah.

Odus added, "Yeah, there's only about twenty of 'em."

"And I could get a bunch with my bow before they even knew what was happening," whispered Eido, which surprised them.

Odus said, "Seems a might unfair . . ."

"Unfair?!" hissed Eido. "*This* is unfair! All of—"

Suddenly a few of the men turned and looked in their direction. They all froze, but the soldiers quickly resumed their drinking. Pike signaled them all, and they retreated to their horses.

"They should be arrested for trespassing and illegal possession of property," Pike said.

"We ought to go back to Rawfah," said Barah. "Let us take care of Arak, and then we will return here."

"Seems they'll be easy pickin's," said Odus, "what with the progress they're making with that mead."

As they got on their way, Nikos said, "Makarios's father has a farm not far from here. He is a strong man. I expect that he has not allowed soldiers on his property. He would probably allow us to bury Arak there."

They soon came to Rawfah and headed to Baros's farm. As they came down the road, they saw a lone man far out past the barns along a fence line and Nikos said, "That is Baros. Let me ride out to him. He will be more favorable without all of us coming upon him."

There was much activity on the farm and as Nikos rode past the men who were working, he nodded to them, feeling much different than the last time he had been there. Coming across the field, Baros approached him and called out, "Ah, Nikos!" but looked past him to the others.

"Yes, sir—" began Nikos.

Baros continued, "Makarios, she is not with you?"

Nikos shook his head and said, "No—"

"She has been away," interrupted Baros. "I have not seen her for some time."

His face showed a concern that had aged him. Nikos dismounted and came toward him and as Baros began to speak, Nikos held up his hand and said, "Baros, sir, much has changed."

"Well, you sure have," he said.

Nikos continued, "I am of the Great One now, but I shall speak no more of it knowing your feelings."

"So, who are these," asked Baros gesturing to Kafar and the others.

"Friends, though one has just been killed."

"Killed?! By whom?"

"Rhaka's soldiers—"

"Where?"

"On the north of Diaggello."

Baros paused and then said, "So, he has his evil hands down this far now, does he?"

Nikos looked back at the others and then said, "I am here to bury our fallen comrade. We have no—"

"Here?" interrupted Baros. "Why not where these friends of yours are from?"

"They are from the south, down past the Desert Wilderness . . ."

"Why do you not then take him to my daughter's farm?"

At this Nikos paused, and Baros, becoming agitated said, "Tell me, boy! What is it?"

After some moments, Nikos said, "We have just come from there. Rhaka's men have taken it over—"

Suddenly, Baros erupted in fury, calling out curses and death threats as he started off quickly toward his barnyard.

"They will *pay*!" he fumed.

Nikos called out roughly, "Baros! Sir!" Surprised, Baros spun around to face him, and Nikos continued, "There is a marshal with us who can bring justice to these soldiers."

"Oh, they will taste justice!" bellowed Baros as he mounted his horse, spurring him into a gallop. As he neared his men in the field, he called out to them, and they quickly followed.

Nikos knew well enough to do no more, so he returned to Kafar and the others. As he approached, Odus said, "Now, you done told him about the soldiers over there?"

"He looks a furious man," said Kafar.

Barah added, "Indeed."

"Well, it came to it," said Nikos, "and I could not deceive him."

Eido said to Pike, "You won't stop them? He can't just be killin' people, even if they are doing wrong."

Pike sighed and shook his head, saying, "These are difficult times. We must rightly judge who the enemy is and even if this man is on the wrong side of the law, he is not our enemy."

They stood silent as their thoughts turned to Arak. "You may use my land," said Rawfah.

"That is kind of you," said Kafar. "We will return for his bones in the future. It is our custom." They set off to the west and soon arrived at Rawfah's farm.

After they had buried Arak, Rawfah led them to his small cabin and said, "Please, it is past the midday meal. Sit here while I prepare." He quickly went inside, and they sat on the porch, somber and thoughtful.

After some time, Barah said, "I remember the one who pierced Arak through . . . his face . . . he is one I know from Zabach and now one who twice deserves to die." They silently agreed and sat silent until Rawfah invited them in for the meal.

"I am sorry there is little room . . ." he said as he served them.

They ate with no conversation and as they finished, Rawfah said, "You are good men; I know you will wish to offer me something, but please, it is my honor. You have lost enough today."

They thanked him and as they came outside, Eido pointed and said, "Look!" Across the land to the east, a column of smoke was rising.

"I guess Baros and his fellows made a complete end of Rhaka's men," said Odus. "Burned the whole lot of them!"

"We must make for Two Rivers," said Pike, "and hope to find Chayel."

As they got on their way, Odus said, "We're headin' into it now." They went straight north until they came to the Eastway Road and then turned onto it, heading east. There were many travelers and tradesmen going about their business as Pike led the way through them.

By late afternoon they were nearing Steko's Ferry and Odus said, "Looks like a bunch more of Rhaka's men."

"And they're operating the ferries," added Nikos. "I hope Makarios's brother is alright. He owns these."

Pike signaled them to stop. "We must not go together," he said. "Let us go in pairs and hope we are not recognized, but we must all be aboard the same ferry. If there is a fight, flee to that big oak in the field behind those barns to regroup."

Pike called Eido to go with him and as they approached the ferry, Eido said quietly, "They're checkin' them for the mark . . . and ain't lettin' 'em get on." Pike led the way but rode past the ferry and immediately headed for the oak tree. Odus and Nikos came next, following them to the tree.

Just as they arrived, there was a commotion at the docks, and a soldier yelled out, "That's one of them!" motioning to Barah, who recognized the man who had killed Arak.

They wheeled their horses around and made for the tree as a captain suddenly commanded his men, "Get them! Dead or alive!"

As the company of soldiers came at them, Pike called out, "I am Pike, marshal of Agathon Outpost. You have no right or authority here!" The soldiers came on, but Pike and the others made a united front; Barah and Eido ready with their bows. The captain slowed his men and brought them to a stop some distance away, joined by more soldiers who had come across the river making for a very large company.

"I do not care who you are!" bellowed the captain. "You have broken Lord Rhaka's law and will be executed!" The dock had come to a standstill, but some men had begun to gather, picking up whatever was at hand for makeshift weapons.

A tension-filled silence ensued, until someone in the midst of the crowd cried out, "Well, we don't care who *you* are!"

"Yeh! We're sick of you chargin' tolls," called another while yet someone else yelled, "And takin' our goods!"

"And me most of all!" yelled another who was mounted on a horse armed with a sword and shield. "These are *my* ferries and no one else's!"

Pike spurred his horse forward, followed by the others; everything was about to let loose when a large group of horsemen approached from the west.

"You've outstayed your welcome!" yelled the leader. It was Baros and his farmhands and many more who had joined him on the way from Makarios's farm. He brazenly rode right up to the captain, still furious, "Get out of our land, or you'll suffer the same fate as those who tried takin' my daughter's farm."

"Every one of 'em dead!" called another from his gang.

"And rightly so!" yelled someone in the crowd on the other side. The captain and his soldiers were caught in the middle. An old man stepped forward with a pitchfork in his hand and tears in his eyes as he said,

"I oughta run you all through, killin' my boy as you did!" The crowd suddenly became riotous, and the captain and his soldiers, well outnumbered, lost no time in retreating, galloping off to the east.

"They'll only come back with more!" said one.

Another added, "Shoulda killed 'em all!"

Suddenly, Baros bellowed, "After 'em boys!" as he and his men spurred their mounts.

Soon, the ferries began running again, but the fervor of the crowd had spread across the river. Fury at Rhaka's men unleashed itself as the whole city rose up against the remaining soldiers. Many were killed as the rest were fleeing whichever way they could. Pike and the others gathered on the outskirts of the city.

"Rhaka won't stand for none of this," said Odus.

"I think I better get home," said Eido. "I fear it's real bad up there . . ."

"And my heart pulls me to the Outpost . . . ," said Pike looking pained.

Before he could continue, Kafar said, "It is your place . . ."

"I do not doubt we will see each other again," said Barah.

——— *Thirty Three* ———

Deep within Fragmoo Forest, Makarios mounted her horse and with Polus next to her, they headed south. Teras and his men followed some distance behind.

"Rhaka will presume that Teras is dead," said Makarios quietly, "having left him in the trench . . ."

"And he is well known by all of Rhaka's forces," said Polus. "He will want to avoid being seen." They soon came upon Stoney Creek and picked up the pace, approaching the southern reaches of the forest by midday. Beyond lay Brinestump Marsh to the west and open country.

"You will stop!" commanded Teras.

But Makarios brashly called back, "Or what?"

Teras immediately flew into a rage and came at her, but Polus intervened, and they became embroiled in a fistfight.

Polus was getting the worst of it when one of the Meganthropos called out, "Teras, sir! Sir! Soldiers are approaching!" He signaled two of the others to break up the fight and eventually got Teras's attention.

"They have not seen us!" he said as he dropped to the ground and signaled his men to do the same. It was a very large battalion that Makarios and Polus did not wish to meet either, so they all withdrew into the forest.

After the soldiers had passed, Makarios said, "Some of them look to have been in a fight."

Polus added, "And why are they heading north? We must hurry."

Teras approached them and was about to speak when Makarios looked sharply at him and said, "It is vain to follow us. We will not lead you to the Book and indeed, it is likely out of our hands by now."

Teras was vexed and stood seething in rage until an evil smile spread across his face, and he said, "Then you are of no use to me. So, I shall be pleased to kill you both, slowly and justly."

He signaled his men, but suddenly Makarios spurred her horse and leaped away, followed by Polus. They burst out into the field and veered away to the right, heading straight into Brinestump Marsh. Teras and his men rushed upon them but as they were crossing the marsh, some of them suddenly sank under the water and were gone. Makarios reached the other side, but Teras caught hold of Polus, and they both went down in a splash and flurry of water. They fought furiously, but Polus was wholly outmatched by Teras's size and was only trying to get away.

Makarios came back toward them, but cried out as she saw Onos, suddenly coming at them with his sword raised high. Polus had just got free and stumbled backward when he saw the sword coming down upon Teras.

"No!" screamed Polus and lunged forward, startling Onos, but the blow fell, missing Teras as Polus came between them. The sword glanced off Polus's head but cut into his shoulder as he fell unconscious into the water.

Teras rose up, unsheathing his own sword and came at Onos screeching, "Fool!" He was in such a fury that Onos turned and ran with such a fearful speed that he outran Teras. Meanwhile, Makarios jumped from her horse and tried to pull Polus out of the water but could not. She sat there and cradled his head above the water as tears flooded her face.

"No, no, no . . ." she sobbed as the world around her faded out. Polus groaned but remained unconscious as blood poured from his shoulder. Suddenly, Teras approached, bent down and grabbed Polus and dragged him out of the marsh and all the way into the forest. Makarios hardly knew what she was doing as she followed and took care of Polus's wound. As the bleeding slowed, she soon became aware that Teras had gone back into the marsh and was stomping around, kneeling down and feeling under the water. Eventually, he came back toward Makarios, unexpectedly sullen and vexed, shaking his head; he sat on a fallen tree some distance away. He soon got up and began pacing around, his anger growing.

With Polus as comfortable as she could make him, Makarios approached Teras, who quickly spun around with a rage smoldering in him. "It is *enough!*" he yelled sounding confused.

Makarios, who was strangely calm, said, "You are wondering about your men, what happened to them." His only response was to cross his huge arms and glare at her.

"Strange things have happened in that marsh," she said, adding ominously. "Your men have gone down . . . to destruction. It is fortunate that you did not suffer the same fate."

"Fate?! What fate?" he bellowed. "There is no—"

"It is the destiny of all men to die," retorted Makarios, "and after that, judgment!"

"You lie!" he screamed. "There is nothing beyond!" He took a step toward her, but she stood her ground and crossed her arms as well. Teras stood fuming, but silent.

"Tell me, where are they then?" she asked.

He clenched his jaw and turned away, returning to the log he had been sitting on. Polus stirred, and Makarios quickly went to him as he groaned and caught his breath, his shoulder stinging him. He slowly sat up and struggled to lean back against a tree, his head throbbing as he looked around.

Seeing Teras, he asked, "He is well?"

"Yes," she answered, "but strangely fixed on his own thoughts."

"Where are the other men? And Onos?" he asked and after she had explained, she added, "When I saw his sword come down, I thought surely you would be killed, but somehow the blade turned, and you were struck with the flat of it."

Polus reached up and felt his head and winced. "It is bruised," she said and smiled, "but you will live."

Polus reached out and squeezed her hand and then looked toward Teras again, but he was gone. "I am sure there will be a sword or two in that swamp," said Makarios and set off, quickly returning with one.

The afternoon was wearing on toward evening as Polus and Makarios moved further to the west and deeper into the forest. They found a rocky outcropping that afforded some shelter, and as Makarios got a fire going, she said with a smirk, "Well, if Teras still wishes to kill us, he will have no trouble finding us."

They sat near the fire talking for quite some time and eventually the sun began to go down. Then they heard someone approaching, though none too quietly. Suddenly, Teras emerged from the trees and threw down a small feral pig.

"You will prepare this!" he commanded angrily and then dumped a pile of wild potatoes near the fire, "and these!" He handed a small knife to Makarios and then sat down roughly on the ground across from Polus, glaring at him.

"You will not kill us then?" she quipped, but quickly went outside the camp to butcher the pig. Teras sat staring into the fire for a few minutes and then looked sharply at Polus.

"Why?!" he thundered and then got to his feet. "Why?!" He paced about with anger and frustration mounting. "You had no defense! No defense against Onos! Why would you throw away your life?"

"Seeking to save yours—"

Teras cried out, "*Fool!* You go against all that is right! It is unjust!"

He stomped around fuming, but Polus said, "To die in your place? If I choose it, is it unjust?"

Teras stopped dead still and looked at Polus. "It is senseless!" he exclaimed. "You still believe this . . . about a curse—"

As Makarios returned, she interrupted and said, "We not only believe it, but we *know* it, because it is truth. It is just what *is*, whether you believe or not."

He shook his head and fairly growled as she finished preparing the meal. They ate with little conversation and soon afterward, Polus settled down and fell asleep. Teras moved some distance away, but as Makarios approached, he quickly turned around, getting angry and shaking his head.

"There is nothing to believe!" he sneered. "There is no 'truth' . . . and such fools, not leaving me to die in the trench!" He stepped toward her and roughly grabbed her arm, looking piercingly into her eyes, "Even now, you would not fight for your life!"

He pushed her away in disgust, but she said, "Because the truth is more important than life."

Teras became even angrier and grabbed his sword and his other belongings and turned away. "I will listen to no more of this!" he raged. "Or I will kill you!"

But Makarios, overwhelmed with courage, called out, "The Book *is* the truth, *all* of it! But do not think you will ever find it with such an evil heart!"

Teras stopped in his tracks, his shoulders heaving in anger. He spun around, throwing everything down and roared, "You lie!" He came back toward her and grabbed her by the throat and hissed in a whisper, "I *know* the Book; I have had it in my hands . . ."

His face was inches from hers as he seethed, "And I *will* have it again, and I will teach *you* what truth is, slowly and painfully."

He threw her down so hard that it stunned her, but she slowly got to her feet and stood trembling.

As he began to walk away again, Makarios said, "Is that why you will not kill me now?"

Teras was as angry as when she saw him locked in the trench and yet she continued, "Indeed, you *cannot* because something restrains you."

He stood stiff and glared at her with such a monstrous look of murder in his eyes that she faltered and nearly buckled to her knees.

He clenched his fists, but she continued, "It is the truth you deny, the *One* you deny who stands in your way. You can do *nothing* unless the Great One allows it!"

Teras was in such a frenzy of rage, but somehow unable to act against Makarios, that he began to tremble. With a great effort, he grabbed his belongings and crashed off into the forest, letting out an ear-splitting scream of frustration.

Makarios immediately collapsed to her knees and burst into tears as Polus rushed to her. "What happened?!" He exclaimed "I heard Teras scream. Where is he?"

Makarios was overcome, and Polus helped her back to the fire, even as he himself had some difficulty getting there. He sat against a tree with his arm around her and after some time, she began to tell him what had happened.

Night had fallen, and the fire began to die down when suddenly a sharp whisper came from the forest, "Polus!" He jumped up with the sword in his hand and turned toward the voice.

"Polus! It's Onos!" came the voice again.

Makarios put some more wood on the fire and asked, "You are with us?"

"Yes, yes," he stammered. "I . . . I saw all of it! What you did . . . I couldn't believe it!"

"Well, then you are safe here," she replied.

He came out of the trees immediately saying to Polus, "Sir, Commander, sir, I was never with Oxos, with his plan . . . I didn't even know of it." He knelt on one knee before Polus and laid his sword down. "I am in your service."

Polus bid him to stand, and Onos, seeing Polus's wound continued, "I am so sorry."

But Polus held up his hand and said, "Please sit and eat; there is some left over."

But Onos had barely got started when he said to Makarios, "And I saw . . . I saw a man standing in front of Teras when you were telling him that he could do nothing to you!"

"What did he look like?" she asked.

"He . . . he was tall, not like a giant, but tall; he wore shiny armor and purple clothing and had a red beard. His hair was braided like a woman is wont to do. And he just stood there and then when Teras ran off, the man turned and looked right at me, like he could *see* in the dark, and then he disappeared!"

Onos shook his head and looked at Makarios, who said, "It was one of the Elyone, servants of the Great One. But they are not men. I had heard of them as a child, but never believed—"

"Well, I believe," insisted Onos. "I *saw* him! Teras could do *nothing* and that's just what you said! And that, well, that Elyone, that's why!"

"You believe in the Great One?" asked Makarios.

Onos paused and then a look of doom came across his face and then shame as he said, "But I am evil. I see it now . . . how was I so blind?" Tears welled up in him as he thought of the past. "I never knew there was One so great, so far above . . . and the Book. It contains his edicts of good and evil . . . I *know* now. Those who do evil, they are untethered, guided only by their own knowledge and can only do the evil that is their nature. And Teras . . . that Elyone saved him from committing a great evil . . . and yet he does not even know it."

He fell silent and bowed his head and after some time, looked up at them with a look in his eyes brighter than the sun.

"I am free of the curse," he said softly, "and I truly am with you now."

The night drew on, and so they each got as comfortable as they could and went to sleep. Polus awoke late in the morning and groaned as he sat up, his shoulder aching. Makarios quickly came to him as he got to his feet.

She said, "Onos, he has gone after Teras, to try to save him. He is fearless, believing that the Elyone are all around him, to protect him."

Polus looked at her dubiously, "Do you believe in them?"

"They are described in the Book," she began, "and before I went into the Citadel, there was one beside me, holding me steady. They appear as Onos described; he would not know unless he had truly seen one."

Polus pondered that for a moment and then said, "I learned much more about beings called the Taw-Kath. They are purely wicked. When I was with Rhaka, we sought to summon them, an army that man cannot defeat, but we could not."

"Maybe they are not real," she said.

"But the Book speaks of them," said Polus, "and if the Elyone are real, surely the Taw-Kath are as well. I believed in them when I wanted it to be true, but now I would not wish it."

"We must get on our way," said Makarios. "Surely, Rhaka has sent his soldiers out after us."

They set out, heading northwest and soon came upon Stoney Creek and followed it until it intersected a mine cart line. They went on the narrow road next to it and by afternoon, saw Two Rivers ahead of them.

"I wonder about Kafar and the others and the Book," said Makarios, "and I worry about Nikos . . ."

"We must get through the city," said Polus, "and then across the river—"

"Yes," she said. "My brother runs the ferry; maybe he will know something."

"We ought to go separately," added Polus. "I must not be seen by any of Rhaka's men. I will go around the city and meet you on the other side of the river."

"At my brother's cabin," said Makarios, "a bit west of the ferries on the north side of the road."

Makarios rode into the city and sensed that something had happened because there were no soldiers to be seen, and the people seemed to be celebrating. She passed through quickly and soon came to the ferries on the other side.

"Ah, my sister!" a man called out. "It is a good day and doubly so!"

"It is indeed a good day, brother," she said as she got down and hugged him. "It is good to see that you are well. What has happened in the city?"

"Father was here and riled us all up, and to a man, *everyone* turned on the soldiers—"

"Father was *here*?" she asked.

"Yes, a day ago. He found that soldiers had taken over your farm—"

"Daggo and Menka!" she exclaimed. "Are they alright?"

"Father said that their wagon and mules were gone, so they must have left, but he is very worried about you."

"I must see to their welfare," she said.

Steko added, "It is almost dark and time to shut down the ferries. I will see you at my cabin?"

"And maybe find a meal waiting for you!" she called out as she spurred Samos onto the road. It was only a short way, and she soon arrived and quickly put up Samos in the barn. As she emerged into the gathering dusk, she was

THE CURSE AND THE KING

surprised by Polus stepping out from behind the barn.

"Oh! It is good that you got through safely," she said. "My brother will be here in a while."

They both went into the cabin with the cool night air coming on and Polus, being wet from his swim across the river, started a fire in the hearth. Makarios began preparing a meal.

After some time, Steko walked in saying, "It is good to see a light in the window!" But when he saw Polus, he was startled, and his hand went to his sword hilt.

Polus remained seated on the floor by the fire, but said, "I am Polus; it is good to meet you."

"I know who you are," said Steko eyeing him with suspicion, but Makarios came and put her hand upon her brother's shoulder saying, "He is not who he was, and you need not fear him."

"What do you mean, 'he is not who he was'?" he asked. "And how is he with *you*?"

"It is a long story," she replied, "but come, let us eat while it is still hot."

After supper, Makarios cleaned up, and Steko took his seat in a big chair while Polus again sat by the fire, opposite him.

"If I did not know you by sight," began Steko, "I would not know you at all. You do not seem capable of the things I have heard about you."

As Makarios joined them, he said to her with a questioning tone, "And you, dear sister, seem not like the same woman that I've always known." She began to tell him all about her experience of being trapped in the root cellar and of meeting the King and coming to believe in evil, especially in herself.

He was silent for a moment and then said, "So, it is true then—everything that we heard growing up in Zabach, those men standing in the squares warning about Kah-taw and proclaiming about the great Tsadaq."

His brow furrowed, and he continued, "But what of the one who locked you in the cellar . . . why? Did he seek to rob you? Who is he? Has he been brought to justice?"

Makarios glanced at Polus and said, "I have forgiven him."

"What?!" exclaimed Steko, becoming angry, "*Forgiven*? You do not want justice?!"

She shook her head saying, "I am as guilty of killing, though I only wished it in my heart."

Steko rose to his feet exclaiming, "Who is the man?!" and paced to the other side of the cabin and turned around. "I will bring justice! I could fairly kill him with my bare hands were he before me!"

Polus said, "*I* am the man."

"You?" said Steko incredulously. "What is this?" and looked at Makarios.

"It is true," she answered, "and it is the way of the Tsadaq."

"But it is unjust!" he exclaimed glaring at Polus. "Who pays for the crime?!"

"The King," began Makarios, "he has paid—"

But Steko interrupted, "No! no! How does he have anything to do with this?! He is a ghost, a phantom; real blood must be shed to pay for this!"

"But he *is* real, I saw him—"

"What?! A vision? A dream? Maybe an imagination?!" retorted Steko, who looked hard at Polus. "Blood must be shed!"

"I am worthy of death," he said, "and do not refuse to die."

Steko took up his sword, but as Polus stood motionless, Makarios cried out, "It will change nothing!"

She came between them, wresting the sword from Steko and saying, "My brother, you know the teachings from the Book and about the final judgment, what we heard our whole lives growing up . . . when all things will be reconciled." Steko relented, frowning and returned to his chair as Makarios continued, "You know how the King became a real man and was executed to pay for the crimes all of us have committed—"

"No!" he exclaimed. "How does it even make sense?" Makarios remained silent and sat down as Steko stared into the fire. He sat silent for quite some time and then looked between Polus and Makarios.

"This forgiveness . . . it is real. And you . . .," he said looking at Polus, "you are not one who could kill. How can this be?" He sat, again looking into the fire and then said to Makarios, "I know you will tell me . . . the curse, it has been removed, that the King has forgiven him . . . I saw it in Zabach. My friend . . . when we were just boys, one day he became like a whole different person and refused to do so many things that we had always done . . . and I hated that . . . because Father said that it was all lies. He said, 'You see how your friend has deserted you,' but he never did; it was I who left him, and I would curse him to his face, but he . . . he always forgave . . . ."

Steko looked down at the floor and took a deep breath, letting it out slowly. After some time, he said, "So, Father said that you have been gone from the farm . . . ."

"Yes," she began. "I must tell you, the Book, the sacred Ciphrah Chayaah-

Mawveth was stolen from the Qodesh Bayith Sefar—"

"Stolen?" exclaimed Steko, belying a certain reverence. "How?"

"Through terrible deceit—"

"Where is it?"

"We do not know," she continued, "but we are looking for it. Rhaka had it and as you see, has used it for great evil, but while Polus was commander, he stole the Book and hid it. Three of our countrymen came from the House well before winter, and we are hoping that they have retrieved it from its hiding place."

"Can you describe them?" asked Steko, but at that moment, there came a light knock on the door.

"Makarios!" came a loud whisper.

She immediately went to the door and opened it, saying, "Nikos!" He quickly came inside followed by Odus.

"You live!" she exclaimed and grabbed hold of him.

When he saw Polus, Nikos said, "And you as well!"

The three embraced and as they let go, Makarios asked, "What of the Book? And Kafar and the others?"

Nikos face fell as he said, "There was a fight with Rhaka's men . . . Arak was killed."

Sadness filled her, and she sat down, but after a bit, she looked up and said, "Well, now he is where we all want to be, but we are left here to do what we must. What of the Book?"

"We found it where it was hidden, but some soldiers from Diaggello came upon us. Chayel had the Book in her hands but was separated from us while hiding in the forest."

"And we been lookin' for her ever since," added Odus. "But we saw Polus come across the river near the lake, and here we are."

"Kafar and Barah are watching out on the north side of Two Rivers," said Nikos. "They will meet us at the ferry tomorrow."

"And what with all the townsfolk having driven out the soldiers," said Odus, "there's goin' to be real trouble now from Rhaka."

Makarios and Polus glanced at each other and then told the story of how they had been imprisoned by Rhaka and then escaped and all about their encounter with Teras.

"We may have less time than we think," said Odus.

Thirty Four

Chayel awoke to see a man reaching for her, and she leaped up with her sword in hand, but it was Dune.

He stumbled backward stuttering, "It . . . it's me!"

"What is it?" she asked, scowling.

"I am sorry—"

She exclaimed, "Can you *not* be sorry? Tell me, what *is* it?"

"Well, I woke up real early, even before dawn and so I snuck down the lakeshore toward Two Rivers, just to scout things out, and for one, there's no soldiers anywhere to be seen, but I also found where there are two men camped. And then I came back here. I thought you should know because we won't get past them once the sun—"

"Only two, you say?" interrupted Chayel.

Dune nodded as Chayel continued, "Well, now that I am awake . . ." She saddled her horse, and Dune followed suit; soon they were on their way.

After a few minutes she said, "I am sorry for being harsh—"

"Already forgiven!" said Dune quickly and smiled at her.

Smiling back, she said, "So, these men . . . where are they?"

They rode on for a bit and then Dune said, "Well, they were there . . ."

He looked around nervously as Chayel added, "And no soldiers anywhere? That is strange."

The sun had just peeked over the horizon as they came to the bridge that crossed the Tachus River into the city. Chayel pulled her horse to a stop as she saw that the toll gates had been uprooted and burned.

"Something sure happened," said Dune.

They continued across the bridge as Chayel said, "Tey-Rahk said that I will find someone that I can trust, but I do not know anyone here."

The city was very quiet, but as the sun climbed into the sky, shops began to open. As they made their way through, the business of the day began, and there were many friendly "good mornings," and some children were playing in the street. But Chayel and Dune remained sober and soon came to the other side of the city.

"Well, I am famished," said Chayel. "There was a tavern—"

Suddenly, a man approached from the ferry docks. "Excuse me, miss," he said as he glanced at Dune. "You are together?"

Chayel paused and said, "Tell me, what has happened here?"

But the man went on, "You are from the south?"

"As you are," she answered cautiously.

"Do you know Makarios?"

Chayel could not help her reaction, and the man said, "Then you must come with me." He started toward the ferry, but as Chayel hesitated, he turned back and called out, "Quickly!"

She moved forward, but Dune said, "Can you trust him?"

"We shall see," she answered.

The man trotted to the ferry and signaled them to come aboard, allowing no one else. The river, already very wide, though shallow and slow moving, was even wider with all the spring snowmelt from the mountains.

Once they were well away from the northern shore, the man came to them and said, "I do not doubt that you are Chayel. They have been looking for you." She remained cautious and silent, so the man continued, "I am Steko, Makarios's brother. She is at my house with some of our countrymen and a Megan named Polus and an old man. You need not fear—"

Glancing at Dune, he finished, "I know . . . everything."

"There is a man named Nikos. Is he there as well?" she asked.

"Yes," he replied.

"And a young man named Eido?"

"He and marshal Pike went back north. The danger of Rhaka has never been greater." And then he continued, telling her of all that had happened in the preceding days. As they reached the other side, Steko said, "My house is just down there, on the shore of Huo Lake."

"Thank you," said Chayel as they both spurred their mounts and quickly arrived . Just as they came to the barn, Kafar and Barah emerged from it, immediately going for their swords. But recognizing Chayel as she jumped from her horse, they came toward her as she ran to them, and they all embraced.

Chayel said, "Arak, he—"

Kafar answered, "He has fallen."

Chayel's jaw tightened, and a tear glistened in her eye as she said, "Rhaka's evil is mounting to the skies, and he *will* pay."

Her anger grew, and Kafar said, "But that is for the Great One. Now tell us, how have you come here?"

"Makarios's brother at the ferry . . . he has told me all that has happened here . . . and this is Dune. He is with us." Dune nodded and showed the mark.

"Welcome, brother!" said Barah. "But let us go to the house; our time may be shorter than we know."

"I will see to the horses," said Dune as the others went to the house.

Kafar knocked on the door saying, "It is Kafar and Barah" and went in.

Immediately, Odus exclaimed, "Oh! My girl—" and grabbed Chayel in a big bear hug with tears of joy.

"Yes, yes, I am alive," she said as Makarios and Nikos also hugged her, and then she turned to Polus, who stood unsure of how he would be received.

The whole room became silent as Chayel slowly said, "You have done much evil . . ." He slowly nodded, and Chayel added, "It is fortunate that I am not your judge."

After a long pause, Barah said, "It is so good we have all found each other again."

"The Great One will accomplish all his will," said Makarios. Chayel took her pack off and reached inside, pulling out the Book and laying it on the table.

"So, what happened up in the forest," asked Odus, "that you got lost?"

She grinned and answered, "I meant only to hide behind a big fallen tree, but when I jumped over it, there was a deep gully, and I fell into it. When I came to, I couldn't tell which way was which . . ."

She recounted all that had happened and told about Tey-Rahk and how Lukos had come to her. Then there was a knock at the door, and Dune came in.

After some greetings, Kafar said, "We must quickly make plans to return home."

"We will go to my farm and get provisions," said Makarios. "I must also see about Menka and Daggo's welfare. I hope my father has returned from chasing after Rhaka's soldiers."

Chayel said, "We must immediately go from here."

"And leave your father and the others in the care of the Great One," added Barah.

"I agree," said Kafar. "Your brother, he can provide what we need." Makarios was unsettled but she nodded in agreement.

Polus said, "I will head north and do all I can against Rhaka."

Odus added, "And I think I'm best off headin' back up to Ekuus to do what I can as well."

·——— *Thirty Five* ———·

Pike and Eido rode north and arrived at the Outpost by nightfall. It was unusually quiet; no one was about, but as they came up to the marshal's building, Dero burst out, "Marshal Pike, sir, it is so good that you are here! Well, it would have been better a few days ago—"

"Now hold on," he said, getting off his horse, "Slow down. What is it?"

"All Rhaka's soldiers . . . well, sometime after you left, more came back here and took over again. Then day before yesterday, they all up and left, going back up north, and then Deputy Zuegos decided he should follow them to see what is happening up that way, and a few other men went with him, and he left me to do the marshaling—"

"And you're doing a fine job of it," interrupted Pike, "but I'll get these horses put up. You two go in, and get some supper started."

"Yes sir!" exclaimed Dero, and as they headed toward the marshal's building, Eido introduced himself.

"So, you are a deputy?" he asked.

"Well, no, not officially, but someday . . . ," he answered and then added, "But I seen a dead man, killed right before my eyes . . ."

He trailed off, and Eido nodded saying, "I know how you feel."

Soon, Pike came in and after supper and much conversation, Dero said, "Well, I got to get home, but it is good you are here."

"Yes," replied Pike. "Eido and I will remain here tonight."

The next morning dawned gray and windy, and Eido found himself awake very early. It was still dark, but he saw a lamp flickering in the other room. He approached, and Pike looked up from his writing, "Ah, you are uneasy as well?" he asked, putting down his quill. Eido nodded and sat down opposite Pike.

They sat in silence for a few minutes, and then Pike said, gesturing toward the outside, "I feel an evil howling in that wind." Eido swallowed hard and looked up at Pike, who returned his gaze and then said, "I will make breakfast."

"Do you have any black tea?" asked Eido. "What with all that's gone on, I've been missing it."

"Over there," said Pike. "There is a well out back." Eido took the kettle and went out and found the wind stronger than it had sounded from inside. He filled the kettle quickly, but then stood listening for a moment. He almost thought he could hear strange voices in the wind, ghastly ones that made his hair stand up.

He quickly retreated inside, and Pike said, "You are alright?" Eido looked so grave that Pike put a hand on his shoulder. "It's just . . . ," but he trailed off taking a deep breath.

Soon, they sat down to breakfast and after a few minutes, Eido said, "I am glad for the tea."

"It is my favorite as well," answered Pike. "A bit more like home."

"Yes," said Eido. "I do want to get home, but it feels like riding straight into the jaws of a bear—or worse."

"I will go with you," said Pike. "We must see what is happening to the north. I hope to the Great One that the Book is already headed home."

Eido glanced quickly at him and asked, "You believe?"

Pike paused and then said thoughtfully, "I believe that there is something."

"Like something . . . beyond?" interrupted Eido. "When I was outside, I thought I heard voices on the wind, evil ones, like screaming terrible things, being driven along . . ."

Pike's gaze fell to the floor; he nodded absent-mindedly and said, "I believe now that there is more than just what we see in this world."

They finished breakfast and talked for some time over tea. Soon, the wind began to die down, and the morning dawned. Eido volunteered to clean up and Pike stood gazing out the window.

Eventually, he said, "It is good to see the sun."

"And the wind is gone," added Eido.

Suddenly, Dero came in, "Good morning, sir!"

"Ah, it *is* good," said Pike turning around. "I must accompany Eido to his home in the north."

"Deputy Zuegos said he should return today," replied Dero. "Maybe you will see him."

"Yes," said Pike smiling. "So, you are again in charge. I will return as soon as I can, but the times are increasingly evil. Be alert and do not be ashamed to flee if any of Rhaka's men come here."

Dero became very solemn and said, "Yes, sir. I'll make sure my family is ready too."

Pike and Eido packed up and were soon on their way, heading north up the road through Fragmoo Forest. As the day warmed up, their mood lightened even more, but after some hours and nearing the northern edge of the forest, Eido suddenly pulled his horse to a stop.

"What is it?" Pike asked quietly.

Eido sat listening and then shook his head. "Like the voices in the wind . . ." he muttered. "There is a danger near." He spurred his horse a good distance into the forest and dismounted.

"You hear something?" asked Pike. Eido nodded and took up his bow.

"We must go farther." They crept slowly among the trees until they could see beyond the forest. What they saw brought great fear upon them. Spread out in the grasslands at least a half mile away was an encampment, a great host of men and Meganthropos soldiers.

"How did you hear?" asked Pike, but Eido shook his head, "It was not human . . . the voices . . . maybe only in my mind, but unearthly, wicked."

Suddenly, movement to their right and much nearer caught their attention, and they dropped to the ground. A squad of mounted soldiers, much closer to hand, was moving west across the field, but then came to a stop. They were approached from the north by some kind of horrifying creature. It had the body of a bull but also the torso of a man, and its head was like a skull, but with eyes and horns and upswept pointed ears. The skin was black, leathery and somewhat oily, and soon a putrid smell wafted over Pike and Eido, who had all they could do to stifle coughing.

"What *is* it?" whispered Eido.

Pike only stammered, "It . . . it's like . . ."

Suddenly, he screamed out, "*No! No!*" and clutched his head. His face was deathly pale as he leaped to his feet and lurched out into the open as if he were fighting something. Immediately, the soldiers turned in his direction, and Pike ran toward them and then fell to the ground and lay unmoving.

Eido was frozen in fear as he watched them surround Pike and when one of the soldiers waved in his direction and called out a command to the others, he turned and ran. He crashed through the underbrush and leaped onto his horse, riding for his life down the road. After some miles, he turned into the forest and paused to listen and was convinced he had gotten away. Back on the road, Eido set a quick pace, going south, but suddenly heard a lone rider catching up with him. Reining his horse around, he drew out his bow and fit an arrow to the string.

"Do not fear!" called the rider as he drew near.

"Who are you?!" yelled Eido. The man pulled his horse to a stop. He wore a dark hooded cloak and had a long, braided beard.

"Who are you?" demanded Eido.

"I am one sent to help," he answered. "I serve the Great One."

"Help what?" he said, wrangling his horse, which had become nervous. "Your friends—"

"How do you know them?" retorted Eido. "Why should I believe you?"

"It is at your friends' peril if you do not."

Eido wavered and said, "You came from up north too, did you see—"

The man interrupted saying, "The marshal is out of your hands; we must go south. Come, we must go quickly!" He spurred his horse to a gallop, and Eido followed immediately, though reluctantly. After some time, they came down to the southern boundary of the forest and back into Agathon Outpost.

Dero came out of the marshal's building and ran toward them, "You are back?!" he called. "Where is Marshal Pike?"

Eido jumped down from his horse and came to him, "They, he . . . Rhaka's forces, they took him!"

"Why?! How did you get away?" asked Dero, looking past to the man behind him.

"I just ran through the forest—but you must warn all the folks around here. It looks like Rhaka is going to march down here soon with all his troops!"

The man rode forward, and Dero said to him, "But what about Marshal Pike?"

"He is out of your hands," said the man. "You must go quickly now and warn your family and everyone else that you can about the evil coming from the north."

"Yes, sir!" he said and turned and ran back to the marshal's building and quickly rode for home.

"Come," said the man. "We must get as far south as we can before nightfall."

They headed down the road at a fast pace, passing through Batou and coming to Two Rivers as the sun was setting.

"Let us go across the river," said the man as they came up to the ferry.

"Last run!" called the operator. They were soon across the river and then continued south into open country. As the sun finally disappeared behind the Stone Mountains, they came into an area of very old, large trees, and they found their way to a ramshackle cabin.

"Gather some firewood," said the man and went inside. It was plain that no one had lived there for a long time; as Eido returned with an armload of wood, there was already a light in the window. He cautiously entered and saw that the man also had a small fire going.

"Thank you," he said as Eido dropped the wood nearby. "You have many questions."

Eido remained silent and sat down on a chair. "You seem to know a lot. . . ," he began slowly, "about everything, but I don't even know your name." The man had got the fire burning bright and as there was another chair, he sat down.

"My name would be hard for you to understand. So let us use our time to speak of what is important. First, you must be hungry?"

"Yes, sir," answered Eido. "You said that you serve the Great One, but I don't know if I believe that there even is a Great One."

The man brought out some bread, cheese, and a flask from a pack and offered them. "Thank you," said Eido and dug in, suddenly realizing how hungry he was.

"If you do not believe in the Great One," began the man, "what is your hope against this rising evil in the north?"

"I . . . I don't know," he said. "I guess I do not have much hope."

"Do not fear; the Great One is real and will eventually overcome all evil, but for now, you must be strong and take your place in this battle."

"But I don't think that I believe," said Eido. "What if I don't believe?"

"I can only tell you the truth," replied the man, "and what you must do."

Eido suddenly felt fearful and looked into the fire, taking a deep breath. The man remained silent until Eido looked at him.

"Your friends have all found each other," he began. "They have what they sought and are headed home, but in two days, the overseer in the north will begin moving his soldiers south, and they will sweep through the land. He will soon know where your friends are."

"How do you know this?" asked Eido becoming agitated and fearful. "How can you know about . . . about my friends? And . . . and how can you know the future?"

"I cannot make you believe," he said. "I can only tell you the truth."

Eido scowled and again stared into the fire, but said, "You said that if I didn't believe, my friends would be in danger. I just can't *decide* to believe in this Great One!"

"Can you choose to do what I tell you?" he asked. Eido held back anger and remained silent for some time as many things raced through his mind.

"Truly, you are a servant of this supposed Great One?" he asked, looking hard at the man.

"I am of the Elyone and stand in his presence," he replied. "And you will see the truth of my words if you obey them."

Eido felt a resolve come over him and said, "Then I will test your words. Tell me what I must do."

"It is good that you have freely consented, for indeed, you have been chosen for this," said the man. "You must find your friends and tell them that they must turn aside to a hermit who lives in the mountains until those who are chasing after them pass by."

"How can I find them?" asked Eido standing up and feeling more agitated than before. "I don't even know my *own* way in these lands!"

"Will you *indeed* test my words?" questioned the man. He remained quiet until Eido sat back down.

"You must continue south, and then into the wilderness."

He said no more and after a few minutes, Eido asked, "What then? How will I know the way?"

"You will be shown," he said, "because you *must* find it. Your friends depend on it, though they do not know it."

The next day, Eido jumped up, as wide awake as if cold water had been poured on him. He looked wildly around and quickly went outside finding the sun high in the sky and a pack full of provisions by the door. Suddenly, the night before flooded his mind, and he looked for the man, but he was nowhere to be seen.

"*Guess it wasn't just a bad dream last night,*" he thought as he slung the pack on and saddled up his horse. "*Wish it had been.*" Suddenly, an image of Chayel came vividly to his mind. "*The Book!*" he thought. "*The man said they had it and were going home!*"

His mind flashed to the north, to Rhaka and his army, and he saw himself between the two, sparking a resolve like nothing he had ever felt before. Eido quickly set out, but with his way hemmed in by trees and unsure of the direction, he made his way back out the way they had come. Though the sun was directly overhead, he knew south by keeping the town of Steko's Ferry and the river directly behind him. He rode on through grassland, but the longer he rode and the farther he went, the more he started to doubt.

He pulled his horse to a stop and looked back. "*Where am I even going?*" he thought, "*It all looks the same! And who knows where they even are!*" Anger rose in him, and he turned his horse around, "*Besides, my place is at home!*" He was about to spur his mount forward when the words of the man echoed in his mind, "*You must be strong and take your place in this battle.*" What did he mean by "my place" scowled Eido? But he again thought about Chayel and turned his horse back to the south. "*But where are they? Ahead of me or behind? Or not even going this way?*"

He sat still, his doubts even stronger but was startled when his horse started walking forward. Eido let him go and shook his head thinking maybe it was a sign from something or some*one* he didn't even believe in. Soon, the land began to rise, and he continued for some time even as the sun was descending. Eventually, Eido came to a ridge and saw a mountain range beyond.

"The hermit!" he exclaimed out loud, startling himself and suddenly realizing how very quiet it had been all day. He glanced about, but there was nothing but the silent grasslands, so his gaze returned to the mountains. They ran north to south and where they sloped down toward the west, they ended abruptly at the desert. Eido headed down the ridge and was soon on dry, rocky ground. "*How will I find the hermit?*" he thought, followed very quickly with, "*But of course, the man said I had to find Chayel and the others, not the hermit, and only that I had to tell them to turn aside.*"

He spurred his horse to a trot, wanting to get off the sandy ground and into the green foothills. Eido looked to his right at the unending expanse of the desert and rode closer to the mountains, imagining for a moment what it would be like to be lost in endless dunes. With the sun near the horizon, he made camp in a narrow ravine with a small stream.

Eido awoke, stiff and sore, wondering about Chayel and the others. "*How will I find them?*" he thought as anger mounted and he again doubted and began to feel foolish for having believed the word of a stranger. "*He wouldn't even tell me his name,*" thought Eido. "*Why should I believe anything that he said?*"

He looked up into an empty blue sky and called out, "If you are real, show me!" He waited a moment, but all he heard was the trickling of the stream and a few birds. Eido scowled, "Go south he said, so I have been going south!"

He was soon on his way, but something his father used to tell him came into his mind; "Sometimes, the only way to get where you're going is to wait." Eido yelled, as if talking to his father, "Well, I don't *know* where I am going!" He continued riding, but the phrase kept coming back to him. He tried to ignore it and moved his horse to a trot. After some time, he looked up at the sky and gruffly said, "You want me to wait? Then I will wait!"

He had come to a place where the foothills flattened out into a grassy field, and he stopped, unsaddling his horse and letting him go free to graze. The sun was climbing higher in the sky as he sat down in the field and looked west across the desert. He looked north and south, but there was not a thing to be seen in any direction. He laid back in the grass and stared up into an endless sky, wondering and thinking about many things.

The next thing Eido knew, someone had ahold of him and was saying his name, "Eido, wake up!"

He snapped to and found himself face to face with Chayel. "Get up!" she insisted, pulling at him. "What are you doing here?" He jumped up and though the sun had sunk low in the sky, he saw Kafar, Barah, Makarios, and Nikos behind her—all on their horses.

"How is this possible?" continued Chayel. "How—"

Eido suddenly fixed his eyes on her and cried out, "Chayel! You must, you all must—"

"No!" she said. "Come, we must get as far as we can before the sun goes down!"

"His horse is there," called out Nikos as Barah went and brought him near.

"Quickly!" commanded Chayel as Eido saddled him, and they all got on their way.

"We don't want to be in the desert at night," said Nikos.

Chayel added, "Eido, tell us how have you come here? Why?"

He had finally collected his thoughts and said, "You have the Book, and Rhaka will soon know where you are—"

Kafar cut in, "Wait! We must make for that spur of the mountains and get up into the valley. Then we must hear all you have to say."

They moved up to a slow gallop and with just enough light left, they came into the valley and found shelter among some tall rock formations. Each of them got to work making camp and after a quick meal, they sat down around the fire.

"Now, tell us all you know," said Kafar.

"Well, this man, he came to me," began Eido, "and told me that you had found each other and had the Book and were returning home and that—"

"What man?" asked Chayel.

"Well, after—" began Eido and then exclaimed, "Rhaka! He took Pike! I barely got away!"

"From where?!" asked Makarios. Eido explained everything about seeing Rhaka's forces and how Pike had staggered out into the field from the forest.

"Attacked again," said Barah.

"By the evil Kahee Nawb," finished Nikos.

"Well, whatever happened," continued Eido, "they have Pike, and I got away riding as fast as I could. Then after—"

"Who is this man you talked about?" asked Chayel.

"Well, after I got away and slowed down, he just seemed to come out of nowhere behind me on the road."

"What did he look like?" asked Nikos.

"Nothing out of the ordinary, except for the big black cloak and that he said I wouldn't understand his name." They glanced at each other with a sense of foreboding.

"When did you meet this man?" asked Chayel.

"Yesterday, and then we rode down and stayed in an old cabin some ways north of here, but when I got up in the morning, he was gone. He left this big pack of provisions."

Barah shook his head. "It does not bode well," he said. "Who can he be?"

"Well, I don't know," continued Eido, "but he told me that I had to find you all and tell you that Rhaka will soon know where you are and that you have the Book and that in two days, he will begin moving all his forces south."

"It is good that we have such a head start," said Nikos.

"But how can Rhaka know where we are?" Chayel wondered.

411

"And how does this man know that Eido knows us?" added Makarios.

Barah asked, "Who is he that he would warn us?

And how can he know that Rhaka will move south in two days?" asked Kafar.

"If any of that is even true," said Chayel.

"Well, I don't know," said Eido, "but he sure didn't seem bad. He said, 'I can only tell you the truth' and then left it up to me to believe or not and to do what he said."

"What else did he tell you?" asked Makarios.

"That I had to find you and tell you—let me remember his exact words. He said that you all 'must turn aside to a hermit who lives in the mountains until those who are chasing after you pass by.'"

They looked at each other, and Chayel shook her head and said, "That is foolish! We *must* get to the House of the Book as soon as we can, where no force of arms can assail it!"

"It does appear to be bad counsel," said Kafar, "but what if this man *was* sent by the Great One?"

"Yes," said Makarios. "What else could explain how Eido is here?"

"And that we are passing this way as well?" added Nikos.

A silence descended for some time, and then Kafar addressed Eido, "Is there anything else you can tell us about the man? Did he even speak of the Great One?"

Eido thought for a few moments and said, "Yes, he said that he was one who stood in his presence."

"Of the Elyone?" asked Nikos.

"Oh, yes," answered Eido." Now that you say it, I remember, he did call himself that."

"But he looked like any other man?"

"Yes, but the black cloak; he never took down the hood, not even once, and he said, 'you will see the truth of my words if you obey them.' And, well, so far, they have come true."

Another silence followed, and then Kafar said, "Let us think on these things, and tomorrow we will decide what we ought to do."

The day dawned bright and fair. After a quick meal, they packed up and gathered together.

"We are at a crossroads," began Kafar. "Much of what has happened and has been said rings true, but we know that the evil one can disguise his servants to seem good and right."

"It indeed seems like evil counsel to turn aside and *wait*," added Chayel.

"And we know of no hermit who lives in the Eastern Mountains," said Barah.

They looked at each other and came to a consensus, but as Kafar was about to speak, Eido said, "Well, I believe the man. I told him that I would test his words and, so far, it has happened as he said that it must."

"It may seem so," said Chayel, "but we *must* continue with no delay."

"I agree," added Barah; Makarios and Nikos also nodded.

Kafar paused and after a few moments said, "Let us continue on and if this man's words are truly of the Great One, may he show us this hermit."

They set out at a quick pace and rode most of the day along the foothills of the mountains. As evening approached, they again sought shelter in the lower reaches of the mountains.

The next day dawned with a crimson sky, seeming to frown at them over the mountains. As they got on their way, Kafar said, "When we get to a spur of the mountains that juts far out into the desert, we must turn south away from the mountains. They veer too far to the east to continue following them."

They were all agreed, except for Eido, who remained silent, earnestly looking for any signs of the hermit. As the sun rose higher, the red sky gave way to dark clouds and an uncustomary coolness. They rode on and then Eido, who had been feeling an increasing sense of foreboding, rode up next to Nikos.

"Do you believe in . . . uh, well, *omens?*" he asked.

Nikos suddenly thought back to the day that he had met Makarios, right after the prison had been destroyed by a strange storm and how she had talked of omens. He looked into the sky and a chill passed over him followed by a sense of fear.

Looking sharply at Eido, he replied, "I . . . I don't know . . . why?"

"Well, the sky," said Eido shaking his head. "I don't think it seems right, somehow."

"Yeah—" began Nikos.

But Kafar called out from up ahead, "We are nearly there!" They soon arrived at an arm of the mountains that crossed their path and extended far into the desert where it petered out.

"We must rest our horses," continued Kafar, "and let them graze and get some water." They ascended the shallow arm of the mountain and came down the other side, finding a field of grass. They let their horses go free under the gloomy skies as Barah made a fire in the lee of the mountain.

"Do you see that pillar of rock out there?" asked Kafar as they took a meal. "We must begin from there and go directly south, keeping in line with that other pillar of rock to the north."

He pointed toward it, and as Eido looked, he felt a great heaviness and looked back to the south along the edge of the mountains.

"It is well that we have two days head start on Rhaka," said Barah, but Eido's mind wandered, and he arose and took a walk to the south.

After a few minutes, Chayel caught up with him. "You look for some sign of the hermit?" she asked.

Eido remained silent and kept walking, scanning the landscape. "Well, we know these lands," continued Chayel, "And—"

"You don't believe me!" exclaimed Eido, turning to face her. "I wish I were home. I've done all that I was told to!" He turned and continued south at a faster pace and added, "You will see!"

Chayel found nothing to say and walked with him, but after some time, she felt that they ought to get back to the others.

Suddenly, Eido stopped and pointed. "Look!" he said.

"What is it?" Chayel followed his gaze but did not see what he was pointing at.

Eido ran forward over some distance toward the mountains and then stopped. "It's gone," he said, looking around.

"What was it?" asked Chayel.

"It was right here," answered Eido, looking this way and that, and then up into the mountain. "There, we must go that way. It is that way!"

He turned to Chayel, and she asked, "What did you see?"

But Eido shook his head, "It is gone now, but this is the way! Look!"

Chayel looked where he was pointing and said, "I don't see—"

"We *must* go this way!" he insisted. "Can't you *see*?"

But she saw nothing out of the ordinary as Eido added heatedly, "Don't you *believe*?!" He went some distance up the slope and then up onto a massive four-sided stone and looked further into the mountains. "It is here!" he called, but Chayel had not followed him and remained silent.

As Eido returned to her, his eyes glistened with tears, and his face was hot, "How do you not believe?!"

Chayel began, "I—"

"Aren't you one of the believing ones? The ones who believe what they cannot see?!" Exasperated, Eido started back to the others.

Chayel said, "I believe that you believe what you are—"

"What good?!" he yelled. "If you do not act!"

He would say no more and as they came to the others, he went a stone's throw beyond them, but Chayel said to them all, "He says he found the way to this hermit, but I saw nothing."

"Did not Eido say that *he* would be shown the way?" asked Kafar.

"But to turn aside and just wait," she answered. "How can it make sense?"

They talked at length and then gathered their horses, preparing to set out. Eido came back to them but remained silent as he climbed aboard his horse.

"Take us to the place you saw," said Kafar.

Eido, still wrought up, said, "Will you indeed follow?" and roughly reined his horse around. As they neared, he again saw the sign from a distance, but not when they drew near to it.

"It is that way," he pointed, "Past that square stone." He sat resolutely, seeming much older than his years.

After some minutes, Kafar said, "Let us go some distance that way."

"Will it not use time that we ought not to?" asked Chayel.

Makarios added, "Yes, it seems unwise . . ."

Kafar said, "Barah, what is your counsel?"

After a few thoughtful moments and a glance at Eido, he replied, "To continue south."

Turning to Nikos he asked, "And you?"

"Well," he began slowly, "maybe we could go a short way up there."

"But who knows how far it is," said Chayel. "If it is indeed the way at all."

Kafar sat thoughtful and then with some heaviness said, "We must continue south."

Eido gave no response, but as they turned their horses around, he said, "I will not go with you. I cannot."

"Eido—" began Chayel.

"No! It would betray the truth! You will all see!" he exclaimed and spurred his horse up past the stone. The rest of them remained still.

Then Nikos said, "Let us follow him for now; surely the Great One will show us the way."

They agreed and caught up to Eido, where there seemed to be a clear path, but after some time, the way became more difficult. It remained so, and then Barah said, "This is too hard on our beasts."

They all came to a stop as Kafar said, "It looks not to get any easier."

Eido had ridden ahead and said, "But I see the way!"

"We should go back," said Makarios.

Kafar rode up to Eido, looking at the way ahead and said to him, "I am sorry. We must go back, or we will not have time to get to the oasis before nightfall."

He remained where he was as Kafar went back to the others.

Chayel quickly went to Eido and said, "Please come—"

"No!" he shouted with tears in his eyes, "I cannot betray what I believe is the truth!"

"But—" she began.

"I must do as I believe."

"Please," she said as her emotions began to spill out, "come with us."

He shook his head. "And you must do as you believe."

Her tears flowed as Eido added, "I *must* seek the hermit! I must see if he is there . . . if he is real. I must *know* if I have believed the truth or not."

He spurred his horse forward, and Chayel returned to the others, feeling heartbroken. They made their way back to the desert and to the column of stone. Kafar led the way as Nikos rode up next to Chayel and said, "Eido, he is alright?"

She nodded. "He has gone to find the hermit. He says that he must know if it is the truth or not— I have never seen him more certain of anything."

They continued on under a gray and cloudy sky, but after some hours, it became darker and began to feel like some kind of presence overhead. Kafar called them all to a stop, and Nikos immediately said, "I am beginning to feel a real fear."

They looked up and noticed the sound of strong wind above the clouds. "Will we make it to the oasis before dark?" asked Makarios.

"From what I know," said Barah, "it is somewhat more than a half a day's journey."

"And with this cool weather, we can go more quickly," added Chayel.

They set off and went for an hour or so, but when it began to get even darker and the wind picked up, Nikos called out, "There is an evil in this wind."

Makarios added, "Yes, it is ominous; we must get back to the mountains."

"And we cannot see the stone column anymore in this gloom," added Chayel.

Suddenly, from far away there was a faint screeching sound, and it turned Nikos's stomach to knots. They turned their mounts and rode furiously toward the edge of the desert, but the screeching only grew louder. A shadow seemed to pass overhead and then came to the ground some distance in front of them.

"Stop! Stop!" yelled Kafar. "It is there!" Their horses were almost mad with fear, but they were able to stay astride them.

"The Kahee-Nawb," said Nikos, reeling a bit, but then he said, "We must be strong!" Courage came over him, and he rode toward the beast who stood heaving and steaming some distance away.

"Ssss, the one I have come for," it wheezed standing to its full height.

It lifted its wings aloft and then violently swept them forward, causing a putrid and nauseating wind to rush over everyone. The horses screamed as they reared and bolted, but Nikos held onto his steed, drew his sword and rode straight at the Nawb, who hissed and leaped into the air. Barah had fallen from his horse, and the others were scattered as the Kahee-Nawb swooped down upon Nikos, who slashed at it, hitting his mark. The beast screamed in rage and swung back around as Barah ran at it with sword drawn.

Nikos and Kafar rallied to him, but the Nawb swung low, seeking to barge them to the ground. Kafar rode toward it and swung his sword but was dashed to the ground as the creature lost its balance and tumbled headlong. Its putrid stench and altogether wicked and malicious presence disoriented them all, yet Barah yelled a warlike cry and ran toward it. The beast scrambled back and at the last moment swung its tail, whipping into Barah with one of its spikes. Nikos and Kafar jumped from their horses onto the beast and hacked at it, but it rose up, screaming in pain and swept them off with its wing. As it righted itself, it again lashed with its tail, knocking Kafar to the ground. With a triumphant shriek, it lunged at Nikos and grabbed ahold of him, driving its claws into his flesh and rose into the air.

"No!" yelled Kafar, but it rose higher into the gloom and was gone.

Barah lay on the ground some distance away, and Kafar ran to him. "My brother!" he called and knelt beside him as Chayel and Makarios came swiftly to them.

"I am alright," said Barah; he groaned as he struggled to sit up.

"It took him," said Kafar as he whistled for his horse.

"Yes," said Makarios in tears. "May it be that he is alive."

"Yes," said Barah, "but what does it want with him?"

"It is well that he was not carrying the Book," said Chayel.

Soon, they were all mounted up, but Barah did so with some difficulty as his wounds pained him. Still, they set off at a fast pace and after some time came to the edge of the desert and found Nikos's horse there. The unnatural gloom lifted only to show that the sun had already begun to go down.

"We must get well up away from the desert," said Kafar.

Chayel added, "If we could get up the mountain, I see a clear path over that way." They agreed to follow the path and passed on. But it wasn't long before Barah began to feel worse as his wounds became more painful, and Nikos's horse began to slow down.

"Poor Zeo," said Chayel. "I hadn't seen that he was injured."

Makarios looked at Barah's injuries and said, "We have seen wounds do this before, ones which Rhaka himself inflicted."

"Yes," added Chayel. "And remember Nikos telling us about Nuwa who was injured by the Kahee Nawb—that it didn't seem enough to die from . . ."

"Let us get to the top of this rise," said Kafar, "and see if there is some flat ground and a place to camp." As they came to the top, they found a very tall stone wall across the path with a simple wooden gate in the middle. It was closed and too high to see over, even on horseback, but Chayel jumped to the ground and approached the door.

She peered through the crack along the edge and said, "There is a valley and a lake, but it is much in shadow with the sun behind the mountain now." Before anyone responded, she lifted the latch, swung the door in and took a few steps inside.

Makarios dismounted and quickly came to the door. "It is so quiet in here," said Chayel to her in a whisper.

Makarios pulled her out as Kafar said, "We must go in. There is no place for us among these rocks and trees."

He and Barah dismounted, and they all led their horses through the gate, finding that the path ended there. A field of short green grass dropped away from them down into the valley, but with dusk settling, they could see little else.

"Let us get to the lake at least," said Makarios, "and wash Barah's wounds."

The lake was quite some distance away, and they went as quietly and quickly as they dared. About halfway down the slope, Chayel pointed and whispered, "A light!"

It was well past the lake and up some distance on the mountainside. "I did feel like we were entering someone's house unbidden when we came through the gate," said Makarios softly.

They continued on and finally came to the lake, and Makarios immediately tended to Barah.

"It is indeed someone's dwelling," said Kafar.

Chayel added, "The hermit! Do you think it is?"

"I do not doubt it now," said Barah, wincing in pain.

"Perhaps he could help us," said Makarios. "Barah's injuries need more than we can do for him."

"Should we wait until morn—" began Chayel.

But suddenly Kafar went down on one knee, grasping at his side in pain.

"You are hurt as well!" exclaimed Makarios, coming to him.

"Yes, it is—" but she helped him down to the ground.

"I will go," said Chayel. "Perhaps it is best if there is just one of us." They agreed, and she set off at a brisk pace and after some minutes, rounded the end of the lake. A path and some stone steps led up to a log house built into the mountain. She stood uncertain and as the moon showed its face, she saw a low barn off to her right and some fences and a lone horse in a corral.

Suddenly, someone came out of the barn, hopped the fence and headed toward the house. Chayel, already still, froze like a statue, hoping that the dark and the distance would hide her. The man had nearly got to the steps when he stopped and looked toward the lake, but as his eyes passed Chayel, she knew she had been seen.

"Who is it?" he said, pulling his sword from its scabbard.

She drew in a deep breath and said, "Eido?"

"Chayel?" he replied incredulously and sheathed his sword.

She quickly went to him, "We need help. Barah and Kafar . . . they are injured."

"Where are they?"

"Down by the lake," she said. "But is this the hermit?"

"Yes," said Eido. "I suppose you came the same way I did . . . through that gate? There is no other way in. You see these mountains on either side . . . I just knew this was where the hermit was, but he seemed to be expecting me, and well, expecting *all* of us. He said, "Are there no more?" and then I explained things, and he seemed genuinely grieved and then—"

"Eido, I am so sorry," cut in Chayel.

"But we must get help quickly, especially for Barah; he has been badly injured by the Kahee-Nawb."

Eido stiffened in fear. "I have heard of it. It is real?"

Chayel just looked at him and then said, "And it took Nikos. We do not know if he is alive." She held back tears and prompted Eido toward the house.

As they came to the foot of the steps, he stopped and said, "He is . . . well, he doesn't seem, uh—"

"Just go!" whispered Chayel with a push. They ascended and came to a very tall wooden door with ornate iron hinges. There was a metal knocker in the middle with the likeness of a bull's head and a ring through its nose. Eido banged it firmly and immediately a deep voice boomed from inside,

"Is that you Eido?"

Chayel was startled, not only from the loudness of the knocking, but more so that she couldn't even imagine what sort of a person the voice belonged to.

"Yes, sir!" called out Eido.

"Enter!"

But Eido remained still and said, "There is one with me . . ."

He looked at Chayel and then back at the door as there was no immediate reply. Chayel heard heavy footsteps and then the latch lift.

The door was opened quickly. "Who is this?" demanded the man, who towered above them, wearing a robe and with flowing gray hair and beard.

"My friend, Chayel," said Eido.

"Just this one?" he asked, raising his bushy eyebrows.

"Well, no sir," he replied. "Three more are down by the lake."

"*Three?*" he said in a louder tone.

Chayel had never felt more intimidated in her life and remained behind Eido, hardly even looking at the old man. He seemed to her almost a giant and seeing his hands, gnarled and old, but still looking very strong.

"Speak, woman!" bellowed the man, which shook Chayel and caused her to grab hold of Eido's arm.

She timidly looked up at him and said, "There are only three, sir."

The man roughly crossed his arms and just looked down at them.

"There is a fourth," ventured Chayel, "but the Kahee Nawb took him."

The man scowled, "Alive?"

"We don't know."

"And the others?" he demanded. Chayel looked up into the man's eyes and said, "They are hurt; we need your help."

"*My* help? Bring them!" he again scowled and looked out across the valley and added, as if to himself, "So slow to believe . . ." and then stepped back inside and closed the door.

Chayel and Eido turned and quickly got down to the others. "Oh Eido!" exclaimed Makarios, "it is good to see you. I am so sorry that we did not believe you. We know that this is the hermit you spoke of."

"How is Barah?" asked Chayel kneeling next to him, but Makarios shook her head.

"And Kafar, he is slowly being taken too . . ."

Makarios burst into tears, and Chayel hugged her, but Eido said, "Hurry, Malak said to bring them up to him! Come!"

With difficulty and much pain, they helped the men onto their horses and went slowly toward the house. As they approached, they saw a lamp lit in the barn and then were hailed by the hermit. They came to the barn, and the hermit quickly lifted Barah down and took him in. A bunkhouse was built into the front of the barn, and the hermit laid him on one of the beds.

As he looked at Barah's wounds, he shook his head and looked compassionately at them all. Kafar came in, but fell and then clutched at his side, and Malak said, "This wound, it is deep and your friend . . . there is more to this than the physical, there is an evil in it that you both must fight against with all your heart and soul. Nothing that I do will save you if you do not overcome this evil. But I will do what I can."

He quickly went out and soon returned with poultices and bound up their wounds. Then he turned to Eido and said, "Boy, come and help me prepare a meal for them!"

Then he went out, with Eido right behind him. Barah was groggy and soon fell asleep.

But Kafar said, "It is hard. I feel the evil seeping through me from this wound."

"We are surely with you," said Chayel.

Makarios sat thoughtful and then said, "If only we had believed Eido; this wouldn't have happened."

"And still, here we are," replied Chayel, "and now we *must* wait."

Kafar sat on the bed and said, "And we can do nothing for Nikos but trust him to the Great One . . ."

After some time, Eido returned with a large kettle of stew and said, "Malak says to make yourself at home here in the barn, and to assure you that you are quite safe and welcome to stay as long as you need."

After a hearty meal, Makarios sat with Kafar as Chayel and Eido took care of the horses.

"I am sorry we didn't believe you," Chayel said to Eido.

He replied, "I doubted too."

They came to Zeo and began to clean his wounds. "Poor Zeo," said Chayel.

"But not too bad," added Eido. "At least not like Barah."

"Yes," she replied soberly.

The morning dawned gray and rainy, and they were awakened by Malak who had started a fire in a wood stove near them.

Chayel quickly came to him and said, "We are very grateful, sir."

Malak turned and faced her, "And I'd be grateful if you would stop calling me, 'sir.' My name is Malak or nothing."

He then went and knelt by Barah, but turned to them and said, "I cannot rouse him. What of the other?"

Makarios quickly went to Kafar and with difficulty woke him up, but he was weak and confused. Malak redressed Kafar's wound as well as Barah's, but he shook his head and said to them, "I do not believe that he will recover."

As Makarios and Chayel looked at him in desperation, he held up his hand and said, "The Great One does not make mistakes, and even though you have, this is what must be."

He started toward the door and called Eido, "Come with me!"

Makarios sat down on the bed next to Kafar and took his hand and again broke into tears. "What are we to do?" she cried. "How can this be the way?"

Chayel sat next to her but found nothing to say. After quite some time, Malak and Eido returned with some porridge and roasted meat, but Makarios waved him off.

Without a word Malak went to Barah again and then said to Makarios and Chayel, "Come, he is passing . . ."

"No!" exclaimed Makarios and knelt next to the bed.

Chayel followed and said, "He is so cold . . ." She laid her head on his chest, but moments later looked up with tears. "He is gone," she said.

Malak stood silent as they cried; Eido knelt with his arm around Chayel. Soon, she stood up and pulled Makarios to her feet and hugged her.

Malak pulled a blanket over Barah and said to the women, "I will bury him."

They turned away to Kafar, who was a bit more alert, and he said, "Barah? He has—"

Makarios's tears told the tale as she sat down on the bed. Kafar managed to sit up, with much groaning, and put his arms around her as they both wept.

Chayel and Eido stood a bit away from them, and he looked at her keenly and said, "You have no doubt that Barah still lives . . . in this other place."

She only nodded and after some moments said with the slightest of smiles, "And I will see him again, only with all of this evil . . . gone."

She turned to Eido and said, "I am glad you are here."

She hugged him, but he became flustered and blurted out, "Yes, yes, it is a hard time, but come, we . . . we must eat."

Chayel smiled to herself and then said, "Indeed. I fear much more will be required of us now . . ."

But Makarios sat with Kafar, neither of whom had any appetite for food.

Chayel spent most of the morning tending to the horses, giving them a good grooming and cleaning their hooves. When she came to Zeo, he nickered and shoved his nose into her.

"You are a fine one," she said, pushing his head aside, "but let me see your wounds." Zeo turned about in the stall with her as she said, "These gashes look better already." Zeo pressed into her and then pawed the ground.

"You miss Nikos," she said, stroking him, and he threw his head and nickered again.

"And I as well," she said tearing up.

By afternoon, the sun was shining, and Eido came to Chayel and said, "Malak says that we will have fish for dinner," and then he smirked adding, "but only if we catch some from the lake."

As they walked down, Eido said, "I am sorry for Barah and for Kafar too, but remember that the man said you only had two days ahead of Rhaka . . ."

"Yes," she replied, "But Kafar . . . he is not well enough."

"Should you wait? It seems it will be many days yet," he replied, "I think you must go."

"You will not go with us?" she asked.

He shook his head saying, "I must go home, but I will stay here with Kafar until he is well."

They arrived at the lake and found a wooden pier and a fishing pole on the shore. "How do you get fish out of a lake?" asked Chayel.

"You have never fished?" he asked and picked up the pole. "Watch and you will see." But an hour later, he had caught nothing, though they could see some big fish out in the water.

"We just keep waiting?" asked Chayel. "Could we not shoot them with an arrow instead?" Without waiting for an answer, she quickly went and got her bow and when she returned, Eido asked, "How will you retrieve the fish?"

She thought for a moment and said, "Tie the line to my arrow."

Soon, they had it fitted and Chayel took a shot but missed and pulled her arrow back through the water. "There is something strange; the fish isn't where it looks like it is."

After a few more tries, she hit her mark and soon had caught four big fish. "How much easier!" she said as Eido agreed.

"Indeed. It is good to have enough for Malak as well." It was nearly evening when they returned to the barn. Eido set to work on preparing the fish as Chayel went to Makarios who was still with Kafar.

"He has been asleep most of the day," she said, "and he is feeling a bit better, but still so weak."

As she teared up, Chayel put a hand on her shoulder and said, "What is it?"

"He said we must leave tomorrow without him if we are to get safely back to the House of the Book."

Chayel nodded and said, "Yes—"

At that moment, Malak came in with a bushel basket of vegetables and some spices and set them down near Eido.

As he came toward Kafar, Makarios stood up and was about to speak, but Malak grabbed a hold of Kafar and shook him, "You must wake up!"

All were startled, and most of all Kafar, who quickly awoke and was more alert than he had even been that morning. "And you must eat," continued Malak.

"Ye . . .yes," sputtered Kafar.

"Good." As he turned to go out, he said to Chayel, "See to it!" But Makarios was quite angered and would have gone after Malak if Chayel hadn't stopped her.

"He means well," she began.

Kafar said weakly, "Indeed, he does. Makarios, you must not condemn his way . . . he has done everything for us."

"You feel well enough to eat?" she asked.

"No," he replied, "but I will."

Eido finished cooking the meal on the wood stove, and the aroma filled the barn. The meal went quickly, especially for Kafar, who ate little and groaned deeply as he lay back down.

Malak came in early the next morning and found only Makarios awake. He approached Kafar to redress his wound, but as he touched him, he pulled back.

"What is it?" asked Makarios anxiously, but Malak shook his head and pulled the blanket over Kafar's face.

He looked piercingly at Makarios and said, "You must be strong, and the other one, she too. I am sorry . . ."

He lifted Kafar's body and went out as Makarios stood in utter disbelief and then collapsed to her knees in tears.

Chayel awoke and seeing the empty bed, quickly came to her, saying, "How can this be? When—"

Makarios shook her head and said, "During the night . . ."

After some time, Malak came back in and commanded, "Prepare! You two must leave immediately!" Then he went out.

Makarios suddenly filled with great anger, went after him and cried out, "Do you have no heart?!" She grabbed hold of him and raised her fist to strike, and he allowed the blow to fall.

Chayel was speechless and expected the worst, but Malak said quietly, "My dear one, I know the grief, the sorrow . . . my own son went to the grave as well."

Makarios welled up in tears and remorse as Malak unexpectedly drew her to himself, consoling her. After some moments, he continued on his way, and the women stood somewhat at a loss. As they slowly began to pack up, Eido came in and went to Chayel, hugging her stiffly, his face flushing red as he said, "I didn't expect this . . ."

Makarios nodded sadly as they went out to the corral. Malak came from behind the barn leading Barah's horse, packed with all that they would need.

"*Come!*" he called out and handed the lead rope to Chayel and started across the expanse of grass.

As the women mounted up, Eido said to Chayel, "I never met anyone like you, and am so glad to have known you—"

At that moment, Zeo neighed, leaped over the corral fence and galloped to Chayel, nearly running into her as he neighed again and pawed the ground.

"He will not be left behind, that one!" called out Malak who was already halfway to the lake. His pace was tremendously fast, so the two women spurred their mounts after him, with Zeo following close beside. Malak led them up to the gate and then down into the desert.

"I will lead you to the Bah-maw," he said, "and then you will see your way from there." They went on for an hour and a half and Malak never slowed nor seemed to tire. Soon, the sand began to slope up and eventually, they reached the top of a ridge.

Malak turned to them and said, "You see that to the west and south? It is the Ammuwd Eben." They both looked and saw a massive pillar of some sort, and Malak continued, "You *must* reach it by midday and from there, you will see your way to the oasis. And you know that you must *not* be in the open desert at night."

Makarios was about to speak, but Malak held up his hand and looked keenly at her, "All is well and as for these provisions, I know that you are women of gratitude, but I have more than enough. You will fare well and need know no more, but you my dear, may need this."

He produced a small leather bag and handed it to Chayel. "It is ground charcoal shale. Prepare your arrows by coating the tips and when you shoot," he chuckled, "Well, you will see . . ."

He turned abruptly and started back the way they had come. Chayel and Makarios watched him for a moment, looked at one another and then began descending the ridge.

As the sand leveled out, Chayel said, "Well, there is hardly anything you *dare* say to him, he is so . . . so—"

"*Himself,*" finished Makarios, shaking her head. "He knows so much more, it seems, than he ought to."

They rode on and it seemed that the pillar never drew nearer, but eventually it began to look bigger. "It seems we are moving after all," said Makarios.

Soon, they had ascended a rise to the column, which was much larger and taller than they expected. It looked to be made of a single piece of stone, carved with intricate designs, ten feet square at the base, and rising nearly eighty feet above them.

"What did Malak call this?" asked Chayel, looking up at it.

"The Ammuwd Eben," she answered. "It looks like it has stood here for centuries." They dismounted and watered their horses and gave them grain.

"Malak *is* a strange one . . . ," said Chayel, "to be so brusque and yet so generous to provide all this."

Makarios had to agree and then said, "It is just about midday; we had better get going."

But at that moment, a rush of wind began, growing stronger and stronger.

As it increased in intensity, they looked toward it and saw a darkness being driven along by a violent wind. The women scrambled to the lee side of the pillar and covered their faces, holding their horses tightly. The storm came on with howling ferocity as a wall of sand slammed into the pillar behind them. It swept past with a deafening roar, and the women lost all sense of reality. They huddled close together as it went on and on, but soon the worst of it passed, and it swirled up into the sky and was gone. They shook themselves off and got on their way as the sun shone brightly down upon them again. They spent the rest of the day getting to the oasis and came into it, finding a narrow path, which quickly became soft, damp dirt. The huge tamar trees towered above them with their broad leaves blocking much of the fading heat of the day. The lush undergrowth did not allow for much of a view of what was ahead, so they dismounted and went carefully.

They approached a clearing, and Chayel said, "There is no one here."

"But see, there have recently been many," said Makarios.

"Maybe twenty or more, from the north," replied Chayel. "It is unusual for that many to travel through the desert together. It is well that we were delayed."

"I wonder," said Makarios. "Could it have been some of Rhaka's men?"

Chayel shook her head. "Eido said that Rhaka was coming with *all* his forces."

They set to work making camp at a small log lean-to and eventually sat down at a campfire.

"I hope for Nikos . . ." said Makarios somberly.

Chayel only looked at her and then back into the fire with a slight nod of her head. Makarios was about to say more, but Chayel said, with tears welling up, "It hardly seems that he could still be alive, in the claws of that beast, but remember that it said, 'the one I have come for.' Rhaka must have believed that Nikos had the Book, but how would he even know . . ."

"We ought to put this fire out," said Makarios suddenly and without waiting for a reply, did so.

"Yes," said Chayel, "we dare not think that we are safe from that creature even here." She took a brief hold of Makarios's hand and added, sounding brave, "We must not fear—"

"Though we *do* fear; we *both* do," said Makarios squeezing her hand before letting go.

Makarios awoke early, just at sunrise and went to her horse, giving him another good brushing. "Oh, Samos," she said, holding him around his thick muscular neck and leaning on him. He nickered and turned his head into her as she added, "You are indeed a comfort."

After some time, she went to Chayel and woke her, and they were soon on their way. Coming out of the oasis, Chayel said, "I wish we could follow the tracks of the horsemen that were here, but look, they are lost to the sand already."

They continued for several hours and as the sun reached its peak, they approached a steep dune. As they neared the top, Chayel said, "I think we will be within sight of the border. I will go and see . . ." She hopped down from her horse and crept up to the edge, but then waved Makarios up to her.

"There are yet more dunes," she said, "but need we really be so careful?"

Makarios replied, "If it were not for that band of horsemen, we would go with all speed . . ."

As they descended the dune and continued, Makarios added, "Maybe we should go directly south and come down to Emeq Gorge. No one would travel that way, and there is nothing else there."

"I think you worry too much," replied Chayel. "Rhaka is far behind, and we are almost home! But we will go your way."

By midafternoon, they came to the border and pulled their mounts to a stop near the edge of the gorge. They looked carefully in both directions but saw no one and not even a thing moving, so they headed west along the rim. The land was flat and open and as they rode, the gorge became shallower, and soon they could see the town of Yem in the distance.

"Almost there," said Chayel.

But at that moment, two men on horseback rode up out of the end of the gorge and came at them, spears drawn.

"*Stop!*" yelled one of them.

But Chayel had an arrow to the string and called, "Do not come nearer!"

And Makarios, though shaken, but with sword drawn said, "You have no right here!" But they advanced and the women could see that they were northerners.

"Do not come closer!" yelled Chayel.

But they scoffed, and one said, "Or else what, wench?!"

"Or you will die!" They came on, and an arrow flew, piercing through one of the men, who fell from his horse.

The other pulled up exclaiming, "What is this?!" looking incredulously at the lifeless body of the other man.

Chayel had fit another arrow and said, "You will let us pass!"

The man retreated, and then suddenly wheeled his horse around and galloped off toward the town. Without a thought, Chayel was after him.

"Surely, there are more!" she called to Makarios. They were catching up to him and nearing Yem, when suddenly more than a dozen horsemen came at them from behind some outbuildings and an old brick wall.

"Get them!" yelled the man ahead of them. The women were quickly surrounded, disarmed, and their horses taken from them. Then they were held at spearpoint.

Soon a man approached, and as he saw Makarios, he exclaimed, "You?! You were dead!"

She faced toward him and said, "Sigao?! You are a long way from home."

"My Lord Rhaka threw you out of his citadel! I *saw* you dead my*self*!"

He roughly grabbed her arm, and Chayel suddenly lunged at him, throwing her elbow into the side of his head. He fell to the ground dazed as some of the other men grabbed her, but Sigao was enraged and quickly got to his feet. His eyes were blazing as he came at her sword drawn, but suddenly a huge Meganthropos came between them. He grabbed Sigao like a rag doll and slammed him to the ground, this time rendered unconscious. The women did not even need to see the face of the Megan, for there was no doubt who he was.

Chayel grabbed hold of Makarios to steady herself as he bellowed, "What is this?! Who are these wenches? These women are *nothing*!"

"Commander Teras, sir!" called out one of the men, "they came from the north, out of the desert, sir!"

"Then you have searched them?" The man faltered in fear.

Another said, "No sir! Marshal Sigao—"

"*Enough*!" yelled Teras. "I will search them myself and then you may do as you wish with them!" He roughly grabbed Makarios and finding that she possessed nothing, turned to Chayel, who was restrained by the men. She struggled and started to say something, but Teras took hold of her neck with his huge hand and squeezed down.

"You will not speak!" he shouted and then tore off the small pack she had on. He rummaged through it and suddenly froze. An evil grin spread across his face as he pulled out the Book and held it aloft.

"It will be this easy?" he exclaimed. The men knew of the Book, and some had seen it before, and a cheer went up.

Sigao had regained consciousness and came toward Teras saying, "Our Lord Rhaka will reward us richly! We will soon meet him triumphantly."

But Sigao shrank back as Teras stepped toward him and said seething, "You forget your place!" He turned to the women and said, "You *fools*! Now you see what your "justice" and "mercy" bring to you!"

He guffawed and looked piercingly at Chayel, "And you! Telling me you know what truth is! *This* is truth!" He growled and backhanded her across the face knocking her to the ground. As Makarios reached for her, Teras caught her by the arm and wrenched her around to face him.

He seemed to be filled with a power not his own, and his eyes were like fire as he sneered at her, "I remember your words that day at the Rift, when Megar ought to have killed you. You said that you would 'take the chance of it.' Now you will, and you *will* pay!"

He threw her to the ground and ordered his men to lock them up in a small building not far away. It was dimly lit, with a dark fireplace and one small window, barred with iron.

Chayel was very angry and paced around and then whispered fiercely, "How can this be?! We were *home*! How does the Great One allow it?!

But she stopped short as she saw that Makarios had sat down against the wall, holding her arm gingerly against her side. "Oh! Are you alright?"

Makarios nodded, but then said quietly, "It is sad . . . Teras, he knows the truth. He *saw* it and *felt* it that day in the forest when he sought to kill me and could do nothing against me." After some moments she continued, "But you . . . how do you question the Great One? You know the truth, that he allows *only* what is good for us, for *all* of us, even this . . . Do not let your passions make you forget that."

Chayel became thoughtful and sat down on the floor next to her, a tear glinting in her eye. "I am sorry. We have lost so much." Her emotions overwhelmed her, and she broke into tears, and they both wept.

After some time, Makarios added, "And Nikos . . . we must believe that he still lives." Suddenly, they heard a ruckus outside and jumped up, listening at the window.

"We should wait for Rhaka?!" called one. "The Book is in our hands! Should *we* not rule?"

"How do you *dare*?!" said another.

Makarios whispered, "That is Marshal Sigao . . ."

"Such a coward," added Chayel.

The arguing went back and forth until Teras bellowed, "*Enough!* Sigao! Do you welcome all who stand with Lord Rhaka?" A silence descended, and the women sensed much doubt and confusion among the men.

After some moments, Sigao answered, but with little conviction, "I am loyal to my Lord Rhaka!"

Soon about half the men agreed and moved over to Sigao, but then a Megan called out, "Are we loyal to a man or the Book?!"

"You speak well," replied Teras.

There was another long silence until another man spoke, "I am loyal to the Book, commander, sir and to the man who possesses it!"

Teras laughed in a maniacal way as a new and sinister presence seemed to come upon him. The rest of the men quickly gathered to him and stood at odds with Sigao and his men.

Teras looked piercingly at them, as if to give them one last chance and said, "Do you still stand with Sigao, foolishly loyal to one who will soon lose all his power?"

They all stood uncertain and until Teras screamed with an evil ferocity, "*Choose!*" Almost as one man, they scrambled over to Teras, leaving Sigao standing alone.

"Now—" he began.

But Teras lunged at him, grabbing him by the throat. "You have sealed your fate!" he said and threw him into the desert. "Start walking!"

He hesitated, but Teras lunged at him, and Sigao began running.

"Two of you, follow him," commanded Teras, "and continue until nightfall and then return." He turned to the rest of the men and said, "We will leave at dawn and return north by another way! Now, bring the women to me!"

They were quickly brought out and thrown roughly to the ground as Teras continued, "You will show us the way!"

"We will show you *nothing!*" yelled Chayel as she got up. "You have no right—"

At that moment, one of the men struck her and hissed, "Show the commander respect, or you will die!"

"I will show the way," said Makarios quietly.

Teras came near to her and bent forward. "You disgust me," he said. "You said you would die for the truth; now you will not even fight for it!" She was about to reply when he grabbed her by both arms and drew her to his face, snarling, "You will speak no more!"

She cried out in pain as he wrenched her off the ground and threw her into the men, yelling, "Lock them up! Now, let us celebrate!" yelled Teras. "Surely, there is ale or mead in the town!"

The rest of the day passed slowly for Makarios and Chayel as they sat in the small building, dirty, hot, thirsty, and in pain. They spoke little and as the sun began to go down, they fell asleep even with the revelry of the men going on outside.

The moon had risen, and it was hours before dawn when Chayel was awakened by the door latch being lifted. She quickly roused Makarios, and they both remained still but as ready as they could. The door opened very slowly and a huge Meganthropos ducked low and came in and then pushed the door almost to. He came near and knelt down, remaining silent.

"What do you want?!" whispered Chayel fiercely as they scrambled up and backed away, terrified to see that it was Teras.

"Do not fear . . . ," he said as tears streamed down his face.

The women were shocked as he continued, "I am so sorry for hurting you, but I had to . . . to fool the men. You have saved me. You see, I am of the Great One now."

He revealed the mark, and Makarios exclaimed, "Oh! In the dark, you can see the red letters . . ."

"Yes," answered Teras, "and the brightness hurts me when they glimmer like this."

Makarios rashly came forward and pressed her hand against them but pulled back sharply. "It is hot too!" she said as Teras breathed a sigh and got to his feet.

"We must go," he said and held the Book out to Chayel. "You know the way to the House of the Book?"

"Ye . . . yes," she sputtered, nearly speechless, "You are . . . truly you are one of us . . . how—"

But Teras held up his hand, suddenly becoming agitated.

"We must go," he whispered urgently, "while we have the chance!" He went out silently and the women followed him as he went around the building away from the men.

"Here are your belongings," he said. "Prepare your horses!" He was becoming more impatient, but they were soon ready and set off toward Yem. The moon was bright, and they were going quickly, when they heard a commotion from the camp.

"He is gone!" yelled one, while another called out, "Betrayed!"

"Come!" called Teras and began running, "Show the way!" Chayel took the lead and galloped ahead, around the west side of Yem and then turned south, but the men were hot after them.

·———— *Thirty Six* ————·

Nikos came to and cried out in agonizing pain as he tried to sit up. The moon shone down brightly, and a putrefying smell surrounded him. He lay stiff in the sand as it felt like swords were piercing into his body. He saw a huge black shape next to him and suddenly remembered how the Kahee Nawb had carried him into the sky. The pain was immense, even as he looked to see that he was still in the grip of the Nawb, though it was dead. Nikos was covered in blood, and the sand beneath him was wet and sticky. It was dead silent, and he could barely breathe as a terrible fear came over him.

"*Oh, let me not die!*" he thought as he reached down to feel where the Nawb's claws were. Trembling, he took hold and tried to pull, but pain like searing lightning shot through him. Taking a breath, he set himself and got a better hold on the clawed hand and pulling with all his might, he wrenched it out. He rolled away and reeled in pain, face down, clinging to consciousness. He was bleeding profusely from the wounds in his back and abdomen. He again rolled over in excruciating pain and looked up into the sky, trying to breathe.

"Don't let me die . . . ," he whispered through clenched teeth and squeezed his eyes shut.

His thoughts began to spin and swirl when suddenly a voice said, "Give me your hand!"

Nikos twisted around and saw a figure standing above him saying, "Give me your hand!"

With great effort, Nikos gutted out, "I . . . I can't—"

Still, he bent all his thought on trying to move, and then the man seized his hand and raised him up. Immediately, Nikos felt within himself that his wounds were healed and in one moment, all the pain was gone.

He stood shocked and astonished and stumbled forward, but the man steadied him and said, "Your life is granted you. Go in this strength, and you will prevail."

Nikos did not ask, "Who are you?" knowing who it was, but before another thought had crossed his mind, the man had vanished.

Nikos turned to see the dead hulk of the Kahee-Nawb laying there with his sword buried in its neck. He couldn't remember the fight, but when he took hold of the hilt and pulled out the sword, the whole scene flashed through his mind. Fear again gripped him, but in the midst of it, the words "*go in this strength*" came to his mind.

"What strength?" he asked, but immediately he understood that it was the strength of the power that had just saved his life. He thought of Makarios and Chayel and the others and wondered what day it was. He quickly set off south, with the mountains near at hand to his left and continued on through the night, feeling an urgency that seemed to keep him from tiring at all.

When the sun began to rise, he saw the stone column that was the guidepost to the oasis. He looked for any signs of the others as he went but saw nothing. It was drawing toward midday, and he was only halfway to the oasis when a wind started blowing, and soon sand began to kick up. Nikos looked behind him and saw a wall of clouds approaching and noticed that the wind was increasing, so he began to run. The wind seemed to push him forward and just as he was engulfed, he came over a dune and fell down the other side. He lost all sense of reality as he struggled to breathe while shielding his face, coughing, and getting pelted with sand. Blinded and desperate, he got up and stumbled on as the wind howled around him. Over another dune, he went steeply downhill and seemed to get under the worst of the wind and sand as it roared above him. Nikos went on at a furious pace, hardly even thinking, but as suddenly as the storm had come upon him, it passed by and dissipated up into the sky. He fell to his knees, coughing, trying to catch his breath, as his eyes stung and watered. After some time, he got to his feet, but when he looked around, there was nothing to see but endless sand.

With the sun overhead, he had no idea of north or south and so set out for the highest point of land, hoping for a view of something that would help. Arriving at the high point, he saw land far away to his left that he thought looked like the Eastern Mountains. He set out and as the sun began descending to his right, he took comfort, knowing that at least he was going in the right direction.

Evening came, and soon darkness fell, followed by the moon rising. Nikos stopped, feeling a familiar fear, but shrugged it off, feeling safe in the fact that his life had been spared and believing that there was yet a greater purpose for him.

As morning dawned, he came over a dune and saw mountains ahead, but still very distant. He knew that it was the mountain range south of Zabach, where the House of the Book was. He picked up his pace and went all day, his thoughts fixed on the others and finding them. As evening descended, he came to the top of a very large dune and unexpectedly found himself almost at the border of the province, marked by a deep gorge. He descended toward it. As he approached, he saw a black shape in the sand, but pulled up suddenly, realizing that it was the body of a man wearing the uniform of Rhaka's army. Nikos moved closer and saw that he had not been dead too long and took what he could find on him. He went toward the gorge and found it precipitous and far too deep to traverse, but he saw a bridge to the east. It spanned the gorge—at least a hundred feet across and made of heavy timbers and iron.

Suddenly, a movement on the other side caught Nikos's eye, and he immediately dropped to the sand. Peering through the dusk, he saw that it was only a horse, though it was saddled and had some bags on it. He watched it for a few moments as it was moving about picking at whatever vegetation it could find. Nikos started across the bridge, watching carefully for any other movements. On the other side, he approached the horse, and its head came up slowly and Nikos thought that it must be a war horse that had belonged to the dead man. It came toward him, and he saw that it was not well.

"You need water," said Nikos and then realized that he had not had water for days and was mystified as to how he had walked so far. But his thoughts were interrupted as the horse suddenly became very uneasy and eyed him warily.

"Easy now," said Nikos.

"I know your voice," answered the horse, quite startling Nikos. "But you are a man."

"Uh, I am not the same as others," Nikos said. "I can understand what they do not."

"I know all your words," the horse said. "There is only one word from men that I have heard. They feed me hay and grain and say, 'Trogo,' but I don't know it."

The horse pawed at the ground, and Nikos answered, "It is a different language. It means to eat. Maybe it is your name. But come, you need water—"

"You will give me water?" asked the horse.

"Yes," he replied. "If we go toward the mountains into the forest, we can find a stream." He started off, but the horse stood still.

"Well, come with me," said Nikos turning back. "You are free to do as you will."

The horse was uncertain, but eventually came to Nikos and followed him as they walked. "You will not ride me?" asked the horse, but before he could answer, the horse continued, "What is 'free'?"

"That you choose what you will do," he answered. The horse lowered its head and remained silent as they went. After some time and as they neared the mountains, Nikos said, "My name is Nikos . . . all people have names."

"Nikos," said the horse, looking at him, "*You*."

He nodded and replied, "And you are Trogo."

They had come into a field of grass, and the horse's ears pitched forward as he said, "I hear water," but he stood still waiting for Nikos.

"That's what I mean by 'free,'," he said. "Free means that you can do what you wish to do."

"I've done that before," said Trogo, "and was lashed for it."

He again stood uncertain, and Nikos added, "You are free. Go."

The horse remained still, but then started slowly and after glancing back at Nikos, took up a trot and soon came to a small waterfall cascading over a rock face into a pool below. The horse drank for a long time and then stood watching Nikos, who was taking a long drink. The sun had gone down and for the first time in many days, Nikos felt tired.

But he looked at Trogo and said, "I will take off the saddle and the other things." The horse stood still as Nikos came to him, unbuckling and unstrapping everything. "You are truly free now," said Nikos. "No one will make you do anything anymore."

Trogo walked some distance away into a patch of green grass and began to graze as Nikos looked through the saddle bags. He found a bedroll and some food and after taking a dip in the pool, had a small supper and went to sleep.

Nikos awoke early as the sun was just coming up over the Eastern Mountains. Suddenly, he had a dreadful feeling and looked to the west, listening with all his might. There was faint rumbling and immediately he thought, "*Quickly!*" He jumped to his feet, grabbed up his pack and set out, but a whinny from behind turned him around.

Trogo trotted toward him and said, "You are going."

"Yes, I must!" said Nikos as he continued.

Trogo fell in beside him, saying, "You must go fast?"

Nikos nodded. "I will carry you," said the horse.

Nikos paused, and Trogo added, "I am free."

Nikos grinned and said, "Then I agree, but I will ride without any of the things that you are used to."

He hopped aboard, and they set out, with Nikos teaching Trogo how to take direction as they went. They were still at least a day's ride from Zabach, but with Trogo still somewhat weakened after being lost in the desert, they only made it halfway. They stayed well to the north and bypassed two villages. Then by nightfall, they turned south, avoiding a sizable town and headed for the forest at the foot of the mountains.

The moon had risen. Feeling tired, Nikos said, "I will go into the forest a bit to sleep, and you see there is much grass here," but Trogo was already hard at grazing.

Nikos was awakened suddenly and found Trogo standing above him. "There is trouble," said the horse, raising his head with his ears pitched forward and looking north toward the town.

Nikos quickly got to his feet and crept up to the edge of the forest. The sun was well up in the sky, and he saw many men—some on mules, camels, or on foot leaving the town and quickly going west. Without a word, Nikos took up his belongings and got aboard Trogo, who set off of his own accord in the direction all the men were going. They went along the edge of the forest, and after some hours came abreast of another, larger town to the north. They saw all the men meet up with what seemed like most of the townsfolk. There was much tension and wrangling, with voices raised and many pointing to the west.

"We must go faster," said Nikos, and Trogo immediately took up a slow gallop. They began up a rise in the land and as it began to level out, he slowed the horse and then jumped off, getting behind a rocky area to survey the land. The city of Zabach was in the distance, but fear gripped Nikos as he saw the plain filled with Rhaka's army. They were arrayed in ranks, facing the cliff where the House of the Book was, but they were hundreds of feet back from it.

Around the army stood the peoples of the land and from them Nikos could faintly hear sounds of moaning and grief. There was a pavilion of sorts in the middle of the army, but as Nikos watched for quite some time, nothing was happening. He was about to turn away and wondering what he ought to do, when a man came out of the pavilion and began walking toward the mountain. Nikos couldn't see the road that zigzagged up the cliff face to the House of the Book, but that seemed to be where the man was going. Nikos suddenly thought of Kafar and the others and felt a surge of hope, "*Surely they have returned the Book!*" After quite some time, the man came back across the plain to the Pavilion, and Rhaka came out. He bent near to the man, seeming to say a few words and then straightened up. The man fell to his knees and raised his hands as if in surrender, but Rhaka struck him mightily across the face. The people cried out in great fear and loud mourning as the man lay dead. After an hour or so, another man was sent across the plain and when he returned, the same thing happened. Nikos was enraged and as he thought furiously about what he could do, he saw men coming from the towns he had passed.

He leaped aboard Trogo and raced off toward them, getting down the slope and out of view of the plain. There were fewer than a thousand, just gathering behind the ruins of an ancient castle. As Nikos came near, he called Trogo to a halt as many men on mules came quickly toward him. He raised his hands as they surrounded him, and one of them spoke, but Nikos could only answer in the common tongue. They became agitated, but Nikos remained with his hands up.

"You must listen!" he yelled, but this only incited them. More men closed around him, but they began to get angry at one another as well.

"Stop!" called Nikos, but as he jumped down from Trogo, the horse suddenly reared up, pawing the air and neighing. He came down and lunged at the men, spooking the mules and causing some of the camels to bolt. In all the confusion, a man rushed through the crowd shouting at them all in the language of the land. He turned about, gesturing with his hands and unexpectedly got them calmed down.

"Esam?" said Nikos.

"Yes, yes, it is me!" he answered enthusiastically. "I remember you . . .Nikos!"

They gave each other a rough hug, and Esam quickly continued, "We must stop the invaders!"

"They are too many for you," said Nikos, "and these tools you have . . . pitchforks and hoes . . . you cannot fight those soldiers with these!"

Esam spoke to the men, and they became even quieter; then he said to Nikos, "We are a peaceful people and do not know how to fight. What can we do?"

Nikos was surprised at how passive they became, and then he explained who Rhaka was and what he wanted. Suddenly, a young man brandishing a sword came forward and exclaimed something, and a shout went up from the men.

Esam said, "He says we must give the Book."

Nikos shook his head, and all the men became riled up. He said, "It is not ours to give! It is of the Great One and belongs in the House of the Book!"

"No!" yelled the young man, "it must be given!"

He spoke loudly again to all the men and held his sword aloft, and an angry chant began.

Esam signaled Nikos to follow him into a doorway of the old castle away from the din and said, "They are calling down curses and insisting that the Great One is how you would say a "fairy tale" and that it is his people who are causing all of this."

"But it is *Rhaka* who is sending the people of this land up to the House!" said Nikos. "And *he* is the one executing them when they return without it!"

"Yes," answered Esam, "I don't know why the people believe—"

But at that moment a battalion of soldiers rushed around the side of the castle and engaged the men. While some tried to fight and others were fleeing, Esam and Nikos retreated further back into the castle.

When one of the soldiers fell dead near the doorway, Nikos suddenly went forward. "Help me!" he called to Esam, and they pulled the man inside. "I will disguise myself!" Nikos put on the tunic and helmet and took up the shield and sword.

"I will get among them and see what can be done!" He quickly found a horse without a rider and leaped aboard. But the fight had moved well east as all the men of the land were fleeing. Many lay dead and as Nikos caught up, those who had not gotten away had surrendered. There were about three hundred captives on foot, and the soldiers had surrounded them and were driving them back to the plain. Nikos felt a certain hopelessness as he followed behind, realizing how unable the people of the land were to defend themselves.

The soldiers arrived back on the plain and headed to the pavilion with their prisoners, but Nikos fell back and went unnoticed into the camp. Many of the soldiers were sitting around drinking and joking with each other, but there was a great sense of restlessness, and Nikos wondered how long they had been there. He dismounted and put the horse where the others were and then began scouting out the camp.

After he had gone some distance, he could see the cliff and where the road crossed back and forth up to the House of the Book. Some soldiers were stationed at the bottom while many others occupied the farmhouse and the surrounding land. The sun was heading down as yet another man was forced to walk across the plain and up to the House. Nikos scowled with anger as he continued down the rows of tents and came upon some wagons loaded with provisions. Suddenly, a ruckus broke out, and he turned to see a horse coming up behind him with soldiers calling out and running after it.

"No! No!" called Nikos. "He is mine!" as he ran forward. Trogo, for it was indeed him, stopped and lowered his head as Nikos came to him.

A man in command approached and said, "Get him out of here! Take him across to where the other beasts are!"

He gestured toward the fenced fields near the mountain and then added, "Take those two beasts there as well and get them out of the sun! They are about good for nothing now!"

Nikos quickly complied and went to a wagon where two large draft horses were tied. As he came near, he was startled by someone chained to the wagon who was eyeing him warily. Nikos kept his head down and pretended to have trouble untying the horses.

"Polus!" he whispered, "It is Nikos!"

Polus acted as if he hadn't heard, but then he gave a quick glance and grinned, "I got caught trying to follow them since I did not know the way," he said. "But Onos is among the soldiers. He will get me free at an opportune time. Nikos slipped in between the two large horses and continued working at the knot.

"I will try to get up to the House," said Nikos and then led the horses away.

Trogo went next to him and said, "I will carry you?"

Nikos gave him a rub on the neck and jumped aboard saying, "We must go across the plain to the forest there."

He directed Trogo to the north, going around the army, and soon they came to the fenced farmland, which he remembered from when he had been there in the spring. Many officers and commanders had taken over the farmhouse, making the people of the land to be their servants. Nikos brought the horses through a gate into the field where there were many others grazing, and he led the two draft horses toward a grove of trees. He let them go free near a stream and then went to the barn. No one paid any attention as he gathered some grooming tools and went back to the horses. But Nikos was carefully observing everything and trying to come up with some kind of plan. As he was brushing one of the horses, a wailing came across the land, and he knew that another man had just been executed.

"He will pay!" seethed Nikos, and was startled by a voice calling, "Nikos!" but he saw no one.

He glanced at Trogo who was grazing some distance away and then the voice again, "Nikos! Here!"

He turned quickly and then saw a man behind a tree near the waterfall. He led the horse that way and then slipped into the forest. There were about half a dozen men behind the man, still with their shovels and rakes, though a few now held swords.

"Esam!" exclaimed Nikos, "I am glad to see that you got away!"

"Yes, yes," he said with some anguish, "yet many of my countrymen were not so fortunate."

"And I saw hundreds captured," said Nikos.

Esam shook his head and said, "He will kill them all. The fear among the people is great."

A few of the men called out, exclaiming things and Esam explained, "They said, 'You must help us,' and 'You know how to fight.'"

Nikos paused and then said, "Tell me—"

But Esam interrupted, "We should get away from here, away from the danger for now. We will go to Qidmah, to the east. You have a mule?"

"A horse—" he began.

"Good, good!" said Esam as they went off into the gloom. Nikos got Trogo's attention, and he came to him quickly.

"We must go!" whispered Nikos and hopped aboard, leaving the fields, thankful for the cover of the setting sun. As he came along the edge of the forest, he saw some mules and a few horses tied to a line ahead. After some minutes, Esam and the rest came and mounted up and headed east. They rode on and after the sun set, they saw a few lights in the distance.

Arriving at a large farm, they were expectantly welcomed by many other men, who began all at once to ask questions, speaking in the language of the land. They gathered around and became even more anxious until Esam held up his hand and spoke. Nikos sensed that he was giving them some directions as some of them dispersed, while others set about taking care of the mules and horses. In a small outbuilding Nikos and Esam sat down to a meal with a few others.

"I told them to eat and rest," said Esam, "and in the morning, you will tell us what we can do."

As Nikos was about to speak, Esam held up his hand. "Yes, you are not knowing yourself what can be done," he said, "but I try to give them hope for now."

They finished the meal, and the others who were there soon went out. Esam went to the door and glanced about and then said in a hushed tone, "I must show you . . ." and revealed the mark of the Great One.

He grinned broadly as did Nikos, but he quickly said, "But these people, they blame this way for the intruder."

Nikos nodded and said, "When did he come?"

"With the sunrise yesterday," answered Esam. "I was in my hometown of Yaam when this horde came from the desert. Such a thing I have never seen, and great was my fear. They swept across the land, but I came ahead of them to warn my countrymen; unfortunately, there were few who believed."

He paused and took a deep breath and then continued in a hushed tone, full of awe, "This man, Rhaka, he is indeed powerful and very fearsome. When he came, he went up to the gates of the House of the Book as if he would walk right in. I thought he would, but though he exerted all his might and rent the side of the mountain and the ground shook below, the gates stood fast. He became furious and struck some of his own men, throwing them down the cliff. I couldn't believe, but of course, my belief that the curse and the King were a fairy tale was gone after I saw how such a great power as Rhaka was unable to do anything against the House or the Book . . . I saw it in my mind, bloodred leather and gold binding at the corners. It is beautiful . . . Ciphrah Chayaah-Mawveth . . . It is indeed *real* . . ."

Esam was shaken and looked earnestly at Nikos as he continued, "I have heard the stories from the Book shouted in the marketplace my whole life," he whispered, "and now I *know* they are true! But the people—they stand helpless in fear. You saw, even our stoutest ones were easily defeated. And this Rhaka is plundering all our goods . . . his men are taking everything . . ."

Nikos remained silent and thoughtful, but then said, "I must get up to the House. With this uniform I can go among the soldiers that guard the road. They are careless and are not paying attention to anything. You must try to get the people to take their flocks and herds far away to the east or into Zabach and then bar the gates. They cannot just continue to accept this as they are! Remember, the Great One is greater than all!"

Nikos went out and quickly returned to the forest near the House. He could hear laughing and jesting in the farmhouse, and the encampment at the foot of the road had many fires and general revelry going on. Nikos waited for hours until things quieted down and then went across the field and past the barn, passing unnoticed into the crowd of soldiers.

He came to the foot of the road and walked on past and as he looked around, he saw an opportunity and headed up the road. But he had hardly taken a step when an overwhelming fear attacked him. He grimaced and stumbled, as if he were being attacked and then cried out. Suddenly, there were many soldiers surrounding him.

"What are you doing?!" yelled one, but Nikos only mumbled and tried to get to his feet. The fear was paralyzing, and he struggled mightily.

Another soldier came forward. "Leave him be!" he demanded. "He's about as drunk as the rest of us!"

"Yeah, what's it to you?!" said the other.

A third soldier added, "And what's 'e doin' goin' up the road?"

"Well, he ain't going' up it now, is he?" said the second man and helped Nikos away from them. The ruckus quickly died down, and soon most of the soldiers had gone to sleep. The dark of night had descended.

And Nikos felt like himself again as the man whispered, "Come this way!"

Nikos followed, and they passed beyond the tents and came to a small landslide and got behind it.

"I know you," said Nikos.

The man quickly responded, "Yes! and you are Nikos."

"You are . . . Ruad."

"Yes!" he whispered. "There are many of us in Rhaka's army, hoping to be able to do something."

At this Nikos sighed and said, "Indeed, we all hope . . ."

"You were going up to the House?" said Ruad as a little bird suddenly alighted on his shoulder.

"Oh," exclaimed Nikos softly, "Meekrow, he has come with you?"

Ruad grinned, "He would not be left behind. But tell me, what are we to do? Rhaka will not stop sending men for the Book, only to kill them. And the people of this land—"

"Yes" replied Nikos shaking his head. "They cannot fight it seems . . ." After a pause he added, "I will go up to the House."

They waited for some time and then Nikos headed up the road. When he arrived at the gate, he suddenly thought of the many men whom Rhaka had sent there. He felt grief and a powerful resolve to stop any more from dying. As he stared off across the plain, he saw the many lights in the encampment of Rhaka's forces and saw that there were far more soldiers than he had realized. Suddenly, he was jarred from his thoughts by a voice.

"Who is it?" said someone from behind the gate.

"Nikos," he answered quickly. The door swung open, and Chayel emerged, immediately grabbing Nikos in a great bear hug. She was speechless and cried and began to tremble, holding him even tighter.

After some time, she sputtered, "I sought the Great One so much for you," she said. "It is miraculous that you are alive!"

Nikos took some moments and then said, "You have been watching at the gate . . ."

Chayel was caught off guard and nodded as she stepped back in, securing the gate. The moon had risen, and Nikos could see the courtyard and that no one else was there. They went to the pool and sat down on the low stone wall that surrounded it.

"Kafar . . . Barah, they are gone . . . the wounds from that beast overcame both of them . . ."

Nikos sat next to her and took her hand and after some time, said, "Makarios, she is here?"

Chayel nodded before saying, "And Teras—"

Nikos stiffened, but she said, "Were it not for him—"

"He is of the Great One now?" he asked in amazement.

"Yes, he feigned allegiance to Rhaka who foolishly made him his commander again and sent him and twenty men with all speed to try to seize the Book before it was returned to the House. We narrowly escaped the men who had been with Teras."

Tears came again as she shook her head. "It is so hard though, all of us here . . . safe, but the people down there . . . and when the men come to the gate . . . I cannot bear to see them, knowing they will go back to Rhaka empty-handed."

She suddenly grew angry and shook her head. "How can one be so evil?! He will kill all my people and devour our land!"

Nikos leaned forward with his elbows on his knees and said, "He will keep on with this—"

"What can we do?" interrupted Chayel and stood up. "We are so few .

. ."

"But the Great One, he is with us," said Nikos, "and some of our people are down there. Do you remember Ruad? He was a cook in Rhaka's fortress. He kept us informed about things that were happening there, and he has secretly come with Rhaka's army. He said there are many more with him wearing Rhaka's uniform. I have seen Polus too. He has been taken prisoner by Rhaka, but Onos is among the soldiers to get him free."

"And there is Teras," said Chayel. "He is as good as four men." She crossed her arms and paced back and forth and said, "Come, it is late. We will see what the morning brings."

Nikos awoke to a commotion and the sound of yelling. He dressed quickly and went out, finding Teras, Chayel, and some others at the gate and a man on the other side.

"Give the Book!" he screamed. "Your fairy tale is killing us!!" He was hysterically furious and pounded on the gate. He called down curses on the Book and demanded that it be given.

But Yasad, one of the men inside the gate, said, "The Book belongs to no man; it is not ours to give—"

"I won't go back to be killed by that madman!!" yelled the man. As he stood heaving and steaming, he saw some soldiers start up the road. He became frantic.

Yasad tried calming him, but he screamed again, "*I won't go back!!*" and he suddenly bolted, running straight toward the cliff. As he went over, his screech rent the air and quickly faded.

Yasad looked at Chayel and the others in disbelief and said, "How do we stop this?"

Teras shook his head and said, "Rhaka will not cease . . . ; it is like a game to him. He will consume them as he consumes bread."

"And why they will not fight?" asked Nikos. "How do they not blame Rhaka?"

They stood at a loss and then Yasad said, "We must see master Biyn." They started toward the Great Hall, but Chayel and Teras hung back.

Nikos came to them and Teras said in a low voice, "Why must we talk? We must fight!"

"Yes," said Chayel.

Teras added, "And the people of the land, they have bows like yours, a great advantage."

Chayel added, "And they may be a greater advantage than we know." She set off at once toward the small house that she shared with some others and took up her bow and the pouch Malak had given her.

"Let us see what this is," she said and went out into one of the fields, getting away from the great hall and the other dwellings.

"Malak called it charcoal shale," she explained as she dipped her arrowhead into it and fit it to the string. She let it fly into a distant fence post, and it exploded into flame. They rushed at it, and Teras knocked it down, stamping out the flame. An evil grin spread across his face that belied his previous nature, and Nikos whooped in excitement.

"We must find those who will fight!" exclaimed Teras.

"Indeed," added Nikos as Chayel retrieved her arrow.

"It is not burned!" she said as they started back toward the House.

"I saw your mule down at the farm," said Nikos, "Is Zeo—"

"Yes, yes," answered Chayel, "he is here, up in the fields behind the stables!"

As they approached the House, Makarios came toward them and called out, "Nikos!"

They came together in a hug, and she held him tight, saying, "Chayel and I beseeched the Great One so much for your welfare!"

"I am well, indeed," he answered.

"You must tell me what happened," she continued. "How is it that are you unhurt?"

Nikos felt a rush of emotion and then a heavy feeling of solemnity and said in a low tone, "The King . . . he saved my life. The Kahee-Nawb's claws pierced through my whole body when it grabbed me. Somehow, I cut its head off, but I came to still in its grip. My blood soaked the ground around me . . . I would have died but the King appeared and healed me."

Makarios shook her head in amazement and then said slowly, "Do you . . . . are there . . . scars?" Nikos hadn't even thought of that but lifted his shirt to see massive scars.

"Oh!" exclaimed Makarios, overwhelmed.

"I've never felt more pain," he replied, "except when I was in the City of Dying . . . there can be nothing worse than that."

Makarios became quiet and looked at him with increased gratitude that he was right in front of her, well and whole.

They went to the house where Chayel was staying, and Makarios asked them, "Why are you not speaking to Biyn with the others?"

But at that moment a small sparrow alighted on Nikos's shoulder, which startled them all. It chirped for a bit, and then Nikos said to them, "Ruad is down below, disguised as a soldier; Meekrow says that some of the people are saying that we threw the man off the cliff."

"We must not delay," began Chayel. "We must get down there and away before the people gather as a riotous crowd. We can do no good from here."

Makarios doubted, saying, "But what does master Biyn say? We should be with the others, speaking to him."

"No!" exclaimed Teras. "The time is past for words!" They stood at odds.

Then Nikos said, "He is right and Chayel too; we must go immediately!"

But Makarios would not go and went back to the Great Hall. Teras armed himself with a sword, and they went quickly to the gate.

"But I will be seen," said Teras. "The soldiers will know me," he scowled.

Chayel replied, "Yes, Rhaka would have all his forces after you. We will go down before dawn tomorrow. We can use this time for you both to learn to use a bow."

They went off to the fields again, but Teras would have nothing to do with using a bow. A few hours later, they came to the Great Hall and met Yasad as he was coming out. He was quite upset, and Chayel said, "What has happened?"

He scowled, "We are blamed again for throwing another man off the cliff. Rhaka has been sending a soldier up with his victims and then feigning that they are trying to save them from being pushed by one of us while the soldiers are pushing them over."

"What does Biyn say?" asked Nikos.

"He says we can do nothing . . . ," replied Yasad, "that the only solution is to do what we cannot and that is to give the Book." Yasad stiffly crossed his arms and added, "But I cannot bear for another of my people to be killed by Rhaka."

Makarios joined them as Nikos shook his head and said, "I know the people of this land are not fighters, but why do they not run away from Rhaka? Instead, they stand out on the plain like sheep—"

"Waiting for slaughter," finished Chayel.

"Rhaka's presence has overwhelmed them," said Makarios gravely. "They are helpless. Even we can barely stand before him."

"But we *can* stand," said Chayel a bit angrily.

"I am going down to the gate," said Yasad. "We must at least try to change the destiny of those who are sent by telling them of the curse and the King." Stepping out onto the road, they saw even greater crowds gathered on the plain and more coming from the east and also out of Zabach.

"What are they doing?" asked Chayel.

"Look," said Yasad. "Rhaka's soldiers are handing things out to them, as if giving them gifts!"

"It is their own goods!" exclaimed Chayel. "And yet they bow down!"

Suddenly, a shout went up from some who were nearer at hand, and they pointed up at the cliff, rushing toward it. But the soldiers down below barred them from going up. The crowd screamed at them, cursing and chanting, and throwing dust in the air. They were in a fury as more joined them.

"We must go back in," said Makarios.

The sun was high overhead when another person was sent across the plain. When they reached the bottom of the cliff, the crowd could be heard chanting something.

"What are they saying?" asked Nikos.

"They are *praising* this one who has been sent!" answered Chayel incredulously. Soon, the man reached the top, followed by a soldier holding a spear at his back. The man fell down at the gate begging for his life, and Yasad said, "Be saved from the fate of this accursed tyrant and believe in the King!"

But the man was hysterical with fear and heard nothing. The soldier kicked the man, telling him to get up, but he only fell flat on his face screaming.

"We must do something!" exclaimed Nikos.

"We cannot open the gate!" said Yasad as the soldier hauled the man to his feet. He stood there trembling on the edge, and the soldier got back out of sight of the crowd. He was about to jab him in the back with his spear when Chayel let fly an arrow. It hit its mark, and the soldier fell dead, but the man still stood there.

"Turn!" called Yasad, but the man was frozen in fear.

"Look here!" said Chayel. This got his attention, and he turned toward them. Yasad began speaking to him, but the man stared at the dead soldier in disbelief.

"You . . . you dared to kill him? Lord Rhaka will be very angry—"

He quickly looked toward the pavilion as if he himself would suddenly be struck dead. "You need not fear him," said Yasad, but the man was filled with terror and stepped over the dead soldier, slowly heading back down the road.

Chayel retrieved her arrow and Nikos said, "What do we do with him?"

But it wasn't long before a few soldiers started up the road.

They arrived with weapons drawn, and one of them bellowed, "What have you done?!"

"We sought only to save the man's life," said Yasad.

"He will die anyway, you fool!"

"They all will!" added the other soldier, "and for what? Your mindless belief in a book that is worth less than camels' dung?"

They hefted the dead man as Yasad called out after them with the message of the curse and the King, but they only scoffed. As the day passed, another was sent up, but this time with two soldiers, one carrying a tall shield. The man was old, gray haired and grizzled, screaming in the language of the land as he came. No one could get a word in and after a few minutes, he turned and pushed past the soldiers, heading down, but still yelling and waving his hands in the air. They watched him go all the way across the plain and come before Rhaka, but then the old man turned his back on him. Yasad caught his breath, and Chayel's eyes widened.

"What does it mean?" asked Nikos.

"It is the greatest action of disrespect that one can show to another," answered Makarios. "In this land, a son would be executed by the family if he were to do that to his father."

They could see that Rhaka was infuriated as he commanded the man to turn around, but he would not. Two soldiers then came and forced him to turn.

"He *will* pay!" seethed Chayel as Rhaka struck the old man dead.

"Or be freed from this curse," said Makarios.

Chayel turned sharply and yelled, "No!" shaking her head. "It is too much! How can there be forgiveness enough?!"

But her rage suddenly dissolved into tears, and Makarios put her arm around her as Yasad said, "Even a single crime against the Great One needs a forgiveness as vast as himself."

"Or a punishment as big," added Teras with a murderous look on his face. As the day drew to a close, another person could be seen trudging across the plain, and Yasad said, "I can bear no more. They can't even hear." He turned and started up to the House.

After quite a long time, an old woman and two Meganthropos soldiers arrived at the gate. She stood unsteady and trying to catch her breath. Makarios shook her head and tears filled her eyes as she said quietly, "How is Rhaka even human that he can do this?"

THE CURSE AND THE KING

One of the soldiers pushed the woman toward the gate, commanding, "Ask for it!"

She fell, and Chayel almost let an arrow fly, but Makarios stayed her hand. The woman crawled to the gate and helped herself up by it and looked at Makarios for a moment and then turned to the soldiers.

Taking a labored breath, she said, "You will return to your master without me."

The soldier guffawed and reached for her again, but the other blocked his way and then shook his head saying, "Do not!" But he tried pushing past, and they scuffled.

The first soldier threw the other down, who then called out, "No!"

But as the huge soldier reached for the woman, she said, "You shall not touch me!"

Suddenly, his hand cramped into a fist, and he fell to his knees, crying out in agony. His hand and forearm shriveled before their eyes as bones could be heard breaking.

Tears of anguish flowed down his face, and he could do no more than whisper desperately, "Help me . . ."

But the woman said, "Who am I that I could help you? I am no more than the dust of the earth."

He knelt, trembling and groaning in pain and then looked at her in great anger. "You," he seethed . . . , "you did this . . ."

"Do you not yet fear?" she asked, but he struggled to his feet and with difficulty drew his sword with his other hand.

The woman stood trembling, but said, "Do not do this thing. There is yet hope for you." She glanced at those behind the gate and held up her hand.

He raised his sword as the woman gazed steadily at him and said, "The curse you are under, it rules you. Do you not feel it?"

The other soldier stood transfixed, but then said, "It is real! This—" and then lunged at the other, just barely deflecting the sword as he brought it down upon the woman. It struck the ground and flew out of his hand as he stumbled backward and fell, clutching at his shriveled arm.

He screamed at the old woman in rage and pain, "*You!* You are the wicked one!" He was mad with fury and barely able to stand, yet he came at the woman again.

But the other soldier yelled, "You *fool!*" and lunged, hitting him hard in the face. "We are all under the same doom! Would you gather more for yourself?"

He ran at the soldier and swung again, sending him stumbling off down the road, screaming and swearing to take vengeance on all of them. Suddenly, the old woman tottered and began to fall, but the soldier gently caught her.

"You must help her!" he said to those behind the gate. She steadied herself and took hold of the soldier's hand and looked up into his face and asked, "Do you know the danger you are in?"

He looked around and then back at the woman. "I . . . I do not know," he said fearfully, "but somehow, there must be a final justice . . ."

He knelt on one knee to look the woman in the eyes and a tear rolled down his face. "You said there was yet hope for him," he said gesturing backward. "Is there? Is there for me?"

The woman sighed and looked down and then back up, "The Great One chooses whom he will and makes them servants of the King."

"Please," said the man with his tears increasing. "I wish to serve this king. I have been so wicked serving this . . . this tyrant!" He looked out to the plain and then back.

"He promises so much," he said angrily, "but he only keeps taking!" His eyes smoldered black, and he stood up turning back toward the plain and added, "I should kill him right now!"

The woman came around in front of him and said, "Would that be justice?"

The soldier was surprised and became agitated and said, "He deserves death!"

"Do you deserve it less?" she asked. "Does not your own honor require life for life?" He stood towering above her and then took a few steps away down the road shaking his head, "He deserves death!

Suddenly, the woman went at him and roughly grabbed his tunic and exclaimed, "No! It is not your place! And you cannot face him! You know his power; you will die!"

He was taken aback, and his anger faded. She pulled on him and turned him back and said, "You must serve a new master. Come, you must choose the one who has chosen you."

Immediately, he saw his lifetime of wickedness pass before him, and he was overwhelmed with guilt and shame. He fell to his knees and cried out as if he had been struck and then fell on his face, clutching his chest. He became so still that he seemed dead. Makarios opened the gate and rushed over as the old woman knelt by the man.

The others also came out, and Teras turned the man over and he groaned, still grabbing at his chest. With the sun nearly down, they could see a brightness beneath the tunic, which then began to fade.

"Aghh, it burns!" he exclaimed as he struggled to sit up, but when he saw Teras, he screamed out in fear, "*You!* No!" and he scrambled up and away as Teras also jumped up.

But the old woman grabbed hold of him and commanded, "Show him!"

Teras quickly revealed the mark of the Great One, and the woman ordered the soldier, "Come closer!"

He came tentatively and saw the mark, though barely visible in the fading light. "What is it?" he asked also looking down at himself.

"It is who we are," answered the woman, "The People of the Great One."

"I . . . I feel so different," he said, "Free . . . washed somehow . . ." He looked at Teras again and asked, "And you, you have chosen this Way?"

"Rather, I was chosen," Teras answered. "I was in a rage wanting to kill some who followed this Way when . . . ," but he stopped short. Then he finished, "But yes, I have chosen to follow the Great One."

The soldier shook his head and then laughed unexpectedly, "It is like a dream, and my whole life has been the nightmare . . ."

"Come," said the old woman. "We must get inside the gate."

As she approached, Chayel stepped into her path. "I am sorry," she said, "but you must show the mark, though I do not doubt—"

The woman suddenly took Chayel's hands into her own and said, "My dear child, do not be sorry; we cannot be too careful." She showed the mark and pressed Chayel's hand against it.

They all went up to the House where the lamps were already lit and went inside, but the old woman took hold of Makarios and pulled her aside. "My daughter," she said, "sit down here," and went to a stone bench against the wall.

She looked steadily at Makarios for a few moments and then tears came to her eyes. Makarios leaned closer, and the woman asked, "Your father, he is well?"

Makarios nodded slowly as the woman continued, "And your brothers?"

"Yes . . ." began Makarios, looking hard at the old woman, who took hold of her hand and said, "May I tell you my name?"

Again, Makarios nodded, barely even breathing, feeling an overwhelming sense of wonder. The woman took her other hand and briefly closed her eyes, taking a deep breath and then said, "Minnith . . ."

Makarios suddenly had memories of a lifetime ago, and her eyes widened, "Ma—*mother*?"

The old woman burst into tears and threw her arms around her, but Makarios felt frozen.

"Oh, my child, my child," Minnith cried and hung onto her for so long that she began to hug her back and then a lifetime of tears began to flow as she dimly recognized her mother.

After a long time, Makarios said, "You are so different, but of course you would be, since you know the Great One now."

"Oh, my child," she said cupping Makarios's face in her hands. "I have sought from the Tsadaq, all these years for you and your brothers to be freed from the curse . . . and that I would see you again."

Makarios hugged her again and held on saying, "I remember you . . . now . . ."

"My dear, dear one . . ." said Minnith.

After some time, Makarios sat back and said, "I wish also for my brothers to be freed from the curse . . . and Father as well. But tell me how . . . Father told us that you had died?"

A stern look came across her face and then sadness as she said, "His hatred of the people of the Book . . . I would not leave this land. I was hard and stubborn. He took me to Maqom, many days east of here and left me. I had nothing but the clothes I was wearing. I was heartbroken to be away from you and your brothers . . . it took many weeks for me to get back to Zabach, but there were strangers living on our land, and I knew that your father had taken you all and gone north. I went back to Maqom, trying to forget my life in Zabach.

"I was so young, I never doubted Father's word about you . . ." said Makarios tearfully. "When we arrived in the north, he changed our names, and we had to learn the language. He never spoke of you again."

They sat silent for quite some time until Makarios asked, "How is it that you were sent up here? You must have stood before Rhaka . . ."

Minnith unexpectedly smiled and then laughed, "Oh, I was before him, but I did not stand, I could not. His presence is terrifying."

"Yes," replied Makarios thoughtfully. "But how were you chosen?"

"I offered myself. I sought to come up here to see Biyn because we must *do* something. The people are murderous toward us. No one makes themselves known; we are all scattered and hiding. Is not now the time to be telling of the curse? This tyrant is the very picture of it."

"Yes, indeed," replied Makarios as they saw Chayel coming toward them.

She approached and nodded, saying, "I am—"

The old woman held up her hand. "Do not say again that you are sorry for stopping me at the gate. It cannot be needed a second time, when it was not needed the first." She held out her hand in the customary greeting of the land and said, "I am Minnith, and you are Chayel."

She blushed and took the woman's hand, wondering how she knew her name.

"You are admired by many," said Minnith, "though also looked down upon by those who value what is worthless."

Chayel was taken aback and quickly said, "You . . . you were so brave out there, facing that soldier . . ."

"My child, *brave*?" she replied. "Does not the Tsadaq guide the hand of every living thing? And if our life should be taken that another be saved, should we not give it?"

Makarios looked adoringly at her mother as Chayel answered, "Yes—"

Minnith continued, "Do you know well the Book?"

Chayel paused and said tentatively, "Not as I ought."

"You will do well to memorize more of it," she said with a scolding tone, "especially this: 'Strive for love within to surpass fear of the cursed without.'"

Chayel stood there like a chastised child as Makarios quickly stood up and said, "I hope that you have come to call us for supper."

"Yes," she answered, and they started off across the hall.

Thirty Seven

Nikos was suddenly awakened and found the sparrow Meekrow furiously chirping and hopping around on him.

"Go down to Ruad!" he chirped and then flew madly about. Nikos leaped up and rushed out, grabbing his sword. It was still dark, and he had no idea what time it was as he came down to the gate.

He stopped and listened intently and was startled as he heard someone outside. "Nikos? It is Ruad," he said and then came up to the gate. "Rhaka is in a fury about the old woman he sent up who never returned. He assumes she is of the Great One and, with the morning light, he will have his soldiers seeking us. I do not doubt that he will begin executions to force us to return her. Gather all the people you can and come down; we must warn all we can find."

Nikos ran back up to where Chayel was staying and quickly knocked, "Chayel!" he called and slowly opened the door.

"Nikos?" said Makarios who was also there.

"Yes, it is me," he replied. "We must go now!"

Minnith lit a lamp and said, "I will go up into the tower and beseech the Tsadaq for us all."

Nikos went out and quickly returned with Teras and the other Megan, whose name was Taku. Nikos said, "We must take horses from the corral down at the farmhouse."

They went out the gate and stole silently down the road. There were a few smoldering campfires, but they saw no movement among the soldiers. They passed into the forest at the base of the cliff and came out near the farmhouse.

It was dark and silent as they went into the corral. Nikos whispered to Chayel, "Your mule is in the barn." She and Makarios went in as Nikos went into the field and called out, "Trogo!" as quietly as he could. After a few tries, the huge horse came lumbering toward him.

"You!" exclaimed the horse, but Nikos grabbed his muzzle and whispered, "Be silent! Come with me!"

He moved quickly toward the barn with the horse right behind him. Chayel and Makarios were ready, and Nikos found some tack for his mount while explaining to Trogo why it was needed. The horse gladly accepted whatever Nikos commanded.

"I am free," said Trogo as quietly as he could. They mounted up and with Ruad in the lead, they went across the field and out of the pasture.

"We will go to the old castle and wait until sunrise," Ruad said. "There are many others gathered inside and though some still wear Rhaka's uniform, they are one with us."

The old castle lay in ruins on the east side of a rise in the land, out of sight from the plain where Rhaka was camped. After some time, they drew near the castle, and Ruad sent Meekrow up and over the wall. A few moments later, a heavy iron gate swung open, and they went inside and found many lamps lit and all the windows shuttered from the inside.

They dismounted, and a man came forward. "Esam!" exclaimed Nikos. "You have done much to fortify this place!"

"Yes. It is good to see you!" he answered.

Makarios rushed past, saying, "Polus!" and they embraced.

But as Teras came into the light, Onos, who stood near to Polus drew his sword and nearly rushed at him, but Teras held up his hands and backed away.

Polus advanced on Teras and looked at him piercingly. "I am as you," said Teras, and they saw the mark, which was plain to see even in the dim light.

Polus let out a long breath and said, "It is good."

Teras went down on one knee. "Forgive me," he said, "for what I did to you."

Polus took a deep breath and said, "I forgive it," and held out his hand.

Teras took his hand and rose up as Polus added, "It is healed," pulling his shirt aside to show that the words of the mark had reformed.

Teras was astonished and said, "As it was before . . ."

"It is who we are," said Makarios, "and that can never change. No matter what we do, the mark will remain."

Teras shook his head, a tear in his eye and said, "It is such a gift . . . this new life."

He again felt great remorse and looked at Polus who said, "Do not be sorry any longer. I have done worse than you."

He glanced at Makarios, adding, "And have been forgiven for it."

Onos came forward and held out his hand to Teras, saying, "I am glad that you have been saved from the curse."

Teras grasped his hand and said, "I am sorry for your brother Oxos —"

Onos stiffened, tears welling up as he turned away. Esam approached with Ruad, and Nikos and said, "We are all of one mind—to try to get the people to move away from Rhaka?"

They all agreed as Nikos added, "We must. They are so deceived, but we must warn the people of the Great One as well. Ruad says that Rhaka is furious about the old woman he sent up to the House who did not return."

"At sunrise," said Ruad, "he will command that our people reveal who they are, but many of them seem to be under Rhaka's spell like the rest."

"We must be strong," said Chayel, "and make it known what Rhaka intends to do."

"He will fill these towns with his army," said Teras, "and massacre if needed, just for this one old woman."

They continued to make plans as Makarios called Chayel to join her at a small table. Makarios burst into tears, and Chayel leaned close and took her hand asking, "What it is?"

After some moments, Makarios said, "The old woman—" she began.

But she lost her composure and started crying again. Chayel put an arm around her and said, "She is a strong one—"

Makarios took a deep breath and said, "She is my mother."

Chayel was stunned and knelt down, looking her in the face. "How? I thought your mother—" began Chayel.

"Yes. My father . . . he hated the people pf the Book so much, and my mother . . . she did not believe then, but she still refused to leave these lands. He left her and took us all north. He told us that while she was out tending the goats, a wolf had killed her."

"It must be so difficult . . . ," said Chayel, "And in the midst of all this."

Nikos came to them, and Makarios arose and grabbed onto him, crying again. Polus and Teras approached and stood with them.

"It is the old woman . . . ," began Chayel, looking at Makarios, who stood back from Nikos and added, "Minnith is my mother."

They looked at each other gravely, and Nikos said, "She is fearless—"

"Her courage would take her straight to Rhaka," said Chayel, "if she knew what he will do to the people of the Book."

"We *must* get them away from here," said Teras suddenly and full of emotion. "It is good that she is safe in the House."

As the morning dawned, they rode into the courtyard near to a part of the wall that was still standing. Chayel came near and looked through some of the crumbled masonry and saw the people already heading toward the plain.

"Why?!" she shouted fiercely. "Why do they go out to him?"

Teras shook his head. "They are bewitched."

As the sun came up over the Eastern Mountains, Esam said, "Let us go by twos and not all at once."

"I will remain here," said Teras, "and keep watch to the west."

He went up on the rampart while each of them paired up with one who knew the language and went out among the people. Chayel and Nikos went together and found the people very subdued, trudging along, barely even noticing them. Chayel dismounted and walked along as Nikos followed behind. She tried speaking to someone, but they ignored her, as did many others.

She turned back to Nikos but saw an old man, whose eyes were sharp and focused coming toward her. She recognized him and called his name. He came to her and looked at her knowingly and then moved her aside from the throng of people. He spoke in the language of the land. Nikos sat aboard Trogo and waited, keeping a lookout on the people as they passed.

After a few minutes, the old man rejoined the crowd, and Chayel shook her head and said to Nikos, "That was Isram. He is a hard man . . . and he is rich. He says he goes to see the 'ro'iy,' the spectacle of what Rhaka is doing. But he is unconcerned about it all and says that this tyrant will soon tire of what he is doing and return to his own land. He knows that we are of the Great One but does not care. He sees most of the people as weak fools."

"I would agree," replied Nikos as a young woman approached Chayel and cried out, "*You!* You are one of them!!"

Nikos jumped down and came between them, holding the woman back, but her eyes never left Chayel as she continued screaming, trying to get at her.

A crowd began to gather and a big, brawny young man called out, "And *he* must be one of them too!"

"Stop this! We have done nothing!" exclaimed Chayel.

But the young man pointed toward the plain and said, "You've stolen his book! He has only come to take back what is his own!"

"That is what he told you?" retorted Chayel angrily. "He lies!"

"No! You lie!" yelled someone in the crowd, and then others began jeering and calling out, "They must pay . . . and give the book!"

Chayel and Nikos quickly got on their steeds, but the crowd had gotten very large and closed around them. Some began throwing stones at them when suddenly, there was a ruckus behind them toward the east. At least thirty horsemen were approaching and caused the crowd to turn toward them.

The leader was a big, dark-skinned man with a full black beard and long flowing hair who look directly at Chayel and called out, "I am Moosar!"

Those who were with him circled around the people. There were as many women as men, and they were all tall and dark-skinned; they wore armor, carried swords and bows, and were mounted on large, black horses. Moosar rode into the center, and the terrified crowd fell back. He reined his horse about, and it half reared up and came down, pawing the ground.

"Do not go out to that oppressor!" he commanded. "Why do you submit?" More and more people were arriving, and Moosar directed his people to surround them.

"Is there one who will answer me?" yelled Moosar. "This oppressor is the wicked one! Has he not taken your goods and your flocks for himself? Does he give you little of what is even your own?! He will leave you with nothing! Who will answer to this?!"

One of his captains repeated his words to the people in their language, but no one said a word. Moosar looked at the young man who had accused Chayel and had been the first to throw a stone at her.

"You!" yelled Moosar. "Come forward!"

But he did not move until someone pushed him from behind. He stumbled out into the circle, shaking in fear as Moosar rode toward him.

"Not so brave now," he said as the young man sputtered an apology and then backed away, disappearing into the crowd.

Moosar looked at Chayel and said, "There is more that you wish to say to these people?"

She was startled by his directness but rode out and addressed them. "I am indeed of the Great One, the Tsadaq!" she said and revealed the mark. "We all bear this and would give our lives for this belief! We have done nothing wrong; we have not stolen this Book from that evil man! It was stolen from *us*, but now it is in the House where it belongs! It was written by the Tsadaq, and no man can make a claim upon it. If you try, you will find yourself fighting against the Great One himself!"

She paused and looked around at the people and then added, "Who will deny this?"

They remained silent until the old man Isram, emerged from the crowd and spoke loudly, gesturing and pointing at the people and then, with some final words, he laughed them to scorn and went out of their midst.

"He says he denies the truth I speak," said Chayel. "But he also says that you are fools for believing this evil despot who has made himself your ruler, that *he* is the one killing you and not the People of the House! He says that you have foolishly closed your eyes and stopped up your ears to the truth."

She looked around at them all in anger and after some moments, someone called out, "Isram is right!" While others said, "Lies!" and "The man is feeding us!" A dispute arose, and some of the people turned and continued to the plain, but most remained and began talking among themselves.

"Go home to your towns!" commanded Moosar. "Tell the people this truth! Take your herds and your flocks away to the east, out of reach of this madman!"

But one of the young men said, "Can't we stay and fight?!" A cheer of sorts went up as many other young men gathered around, but most of the people dispersed, quickly going back the way they had come and convincing others to turn back and join them.

Teras came out of the castle, and all Moosar's people immediately had their bows in hand, trained on him.

"No!" yelled Chayel. "He is with us!"

Makarios, Polus, and the others came and stood between Moosar and Teras. There was a tense standoff until Moosar relented.

"Who are these?" he asked pointing to Teras, Polus, and the other Megans. "I do not know your kind. Why do they wear the uniform of the enemy if they are with you?"

Chayel explained it to him and then asked, "Who are you?"

"We are the Leb-Abbiyr people," he answered, "from Deleth in the mountains. We have seen what has been happening and that these people will not fight, even for their own lives."

He shook his head as Chayel said, "I do not understand it though I am one of them."

"We must fight," said Moosar, "or be enslaved to this tyrant!"

"It is good that you will use bows," said Chayel. "They have only swords and spears."

"This is a great advantage to us," said Moosar with a grin.

Chayel said, "And even more so . . . come this way!" She led them into the courtyard of the castle and showed them what her charcoal shale could do.

Moosar was amazed and looked at Chayel in wonder, but she said, "This is a gift from the Great One, given by a wise man—"

"I do not believe in what these people call Tsadaq," cut in Moosar.

"Then you will tell me how that can be!" exclaimed Chayel pointing at the smoking stump.

She crossed her arms and looked straight at him, but Makarios came next to her and said to Moosar, "I am Makarios. We are very grateful to you and your people—"

But at that moment, Esam came and said, "This Rhaka is holding many people of the Book prisoner. We must get them free."

Moosar looked out at the plain, squinting as Esam continued, "The people are only contained by the soldiers around them, in the northern part of the army."

Moosar grinned and a glint came into his eye. "We shall set your people free," he said with great assurance. "We must come from the north, where the land slopes up to the plain . . ."

He grinned again as Nikos said, "I will go with Ruad into the army and get word to our people that once the soldiers are attacked, they should flee into Zabach and bar the gate. Wait until you see us there."

As he turned to go, Chayel took his hand and looked meaningfully into his eyes, but she hesitated and turned away. She took the charcoal shale and shared it with Moosar's people, pouring it into their bags and pouches until they were all supplied.

"How is such a small bag not used up?" asked Moosar.

"By the goodness of the One whom you do not believe in," said Chayel. "Now come, let us go!"

Moosar mustered his people, and they set out going north, out of sight of the plain.

Thirty Eight

Nikos and Ruad mounted up and went with Polus, Teras, and the other Megans who had come out of the army up to the ridgeline above the plain.

"We will wait and watch," said Polus. "This Moosar has much confidence—"

"Too much," said Teras, "but we will join the fight when it is least expected."

Nikos and Ruad made their way back out to the army, and as they went, they saw yet another lone figure walking toward the House.

Nikos shook his head, "He is merciless."

"And resolute," added Ruad, "to the death."

They came into the camp and found there was much more tension, and the captain began yelling at them, "You two! What are you doing there?"

"Headed to the prisoners, sire!" exclaimed Ruad.

"Well, hoof it!" he commanded as Nikos grinned at Ruad, and they spurred their mounts. They came to where the prisoners were and found them quietly sitting on the ground in small groups talking amongst themselves. Nikos and Ruad dismounted and went to the nearest group.

"Do you speak the common tongue?" asked Nikos, but none of them even looked at him.

They came to the next group and before he could speak, one of them looked up and said, "I do, what do you . . . ," but when he saw Nikos, he sputtered, "You are—"

He looked quickly around and then back at the ground, adding almost in a whisper, "I know you from the House!"

Nikos quickly explained what was going to happen and finished with, "Spread the word. When you see us arrive at the city gate, be ready!"

He and Ruad sauntered out to their horses and off into the camp. After allowing the prisoners some time, they went to the city and found that there was very little happening.

"This is good," said Ruad, "but we ought to get one of these gates closed and bring the other one nearly to."

They did so and at just that moment, they saw that Moosar and his people had come up and formed a line within bowshot of the soldiers.

"You will free the prisoners!" yelled Moosar, which caused the soldiers to scramble for weapons, and a few were quickly astride their horses. They waited for no commands but rode rashly forward.

"Stop or you will die!" called Moosar, but this was met with jeering and more soldiers rushing at them. He tried one more time, but then signaled his people, who let their arrows fly. Every soldier fell dead and was on fire, which stopped all those who were coming behind them dead in their tracks.

"Charge them!!" commanded a captain who was well out of range, but the soldiers hesitated. Moosar and his people came forward and launched arrows into the camp, lighting things on fire and causing many of the soldiers to scatter. The prisoners saw their chance and bolted toward the city. Some soldiers went after them, but they were all taken down with flaming arrows.

The people ran across the plain, and more soldiers from farther away sprang into action, but they were too late. The prisoners got into the city and closed the gate while Nikos and Ruad joined Moosar's people. Their horses were swift and sure-footed in the sand and easily outmaneuvered the soldiers.

They launched arrows and caused fires all over the camp as Rhaka's forces were mobilized. But even as Polus, Teras, and the many Megans with them had joined the fighting, they were soon losing the battle as soldiers came at them recklessly, more afraid of Rhaka than of dying.

"*To the castle!! To the castle!*" yelled Moosar. They turned and outpaced their enemy, getting safely into the castle. Up on the battlements, they let their arrows fly repelling the soldiers, who retreated quite some distance. Some among Rhaka's troops called down curses upon Moosar and his people roaring thunderously as more and more joined in. Becoming angry, Moosar fit an arrow to his bow and pulled back with all his might. It went far, ending one man's reveling and silencing the rest of them.

"You will all die!" yelled one vehemently.

And another yelled, "You will answer to the master!"

The soldiers went back to the plain where fires still burned and smoke ascended. Moosar scoffed, but Nikos was sober as he came down to Chayel and Makarios who were in the courtyard.

"So, we have freed our people," he said, "and they are safe in the city as we are, but we can do nothing from here."

As the sun climbed into the sky, Polus and Teras came to them, saying that another person was being sent across the plain. Tears burned in Makarios's eyes, and Nikos was filled with furious indignation.

Teras stood resolute as Polus said, "If only these people would fight!"

They stood at a loss and after some time, Moosar came to them, quite subdued and said, "Our victory was great, but this tyrant . . . he is relentless. And out there on the plain, I feel a power I do not understand; he seems more than a man can be . . ."

"It is the Ra-Tsalem," said Chayel, "the evil one. It possesses him."

Moosar scowled but had no reply as Makarios added, "What you believe doesn't change what is."

The day wore on, and their anger and frustration grew as Rhaka continued sending people up to the House. Their executions caused the people of the land to come against the castle, infuriated and again cursing them.

"These people are as brute beasts!" yelled Moosar angrily. "Did they not see how we liberated—"

But at that moment, one of Moosar's men came to him saying, "Sir, there is a young man at the back gate with hundreds behind him, saying that they will fight!"

"I will believe it when I see it!" he replied and went down to the gate at the back of the castle. He found it as he had been told. There were mostly young men and some women, on foot or on mules; many were on horses from Rhaka's army that had run free after their riders had been killed.

"I am Esek!" exclaimed the young man. "We will fight! And use our bows!" They were all armed with many arrows; some had weapons scavenged from dead soldiers.

"You have finally come to your senses!" laughed Moosar.

At this, the young man became very sober and said, "Indeed . . . there is something that being near to that tyrant does . . . I have been to the east, away from there speaking to the people, and we've come to see the truth."

"You must be strong," said Chayel who had come through the gate next to Moosar.

She tossed a small bag to Esek and added, "Share this with all your people. It will not run out. Dip your arrows in it, and they will bring fire to anything that they pierce."

Moosar was again in a jovial mood, anticipating another battle, when Makarios rushed through the gate and grabbed Chayel, exclaiming, "My mother! She is going back across the plain, back to that wicked one!"

She jumped aboard her horse with Nikos not far behind. Chayel grabbed up her bow and was hot after them as they thundered toward the plain.

Esek, caught up in the excitement, tried to follow, but Moosar stopped him. "No!" he yelled. "We must plan how we will fight! We cannot just rush out! We must enter in with the greater hand as we have already!"

At that moment, Teras and Polus charged out intending to follow Makarios, but Moosar grabbed a hold of Polus, nearly being dragged down by him and exclaimed, "You will be taken captive!"

But Teras spun around and bore down on him, grabbing him by the throat, "Even if we must die with them, we go!" Moosar held his hands up in disbelief as they both raced off.

Makarios, Chayel, and Nikos rode straight toward Minnith, but only halfway there, more than a hundred soldiers came at them from the north.

Chayel slowed and fit an arrow to her string, as did Makarios and Nikos. Three soldiers fell dead, but the rest kept coming. Chayel and the others wheeled around to face them, letting arrows fly into their midst, lighting many on fire. They broke ranks and veered away and in the midst of that, Teras and Polus crashed into the fight, barging horses to the ground and killing men with their swords.

But more and more soldiers were mustered and rode swiftly, bearing down on them until they began to be surrounded. Makarios, Chayel, and the others were with their backs to each other, when a cry went up, and a melee broke out to the east.

Moosar and his people had come upon the soldiers from behind with a rain of arrows coming down like lightning among them. The young man, Esek, also led many hundreds on horses and mules into the fray, remaining out of reach of the soldiers while shooting arrow after arrow. Soon, all Rhaka's men were engaged in the fight, which was drawing closer and closer to the pavilion.

Makarios broke away and rode straight to her mother, followed closely by Nikos and Chayel. Suddenly, there was an ear-splitting screech, and their hearts paled in fear. A shadow seemed to pass over the sun as the Kahee-Nawb swooped down upon the mass of fighting men. It cut a swath through them and then wheeled up into the sky, screaming with a wicked rage. It sought to come down upon the fight again, but all had scattered, and the Nawb swept low over the plain.

Suddenly, Rhaka emerged from his pavilion, and all seemed to go into slow motion. He walked out and held his hands up, standing with his eyes closed and smiling as though he were basking in the sun. The Kahee-Nawb landed behind him, holding its wings aloft and gave a triumphant cry. All Rhaka's forces rallied around him as Makarios reached her mother, with Nikos and Chayel behind them. Somehow, they all gathered before Rhaka and could do nothing but wait, not even daring to raise their eyes. Rhaka crossed his arms and then stroked his perfectly trimmed beard as he surveyed the people. He looked especially upon Teras and Polus and then to the commander of his troops.

Suddenly, he bellowed, "*You!*" and then pointed to the ground in front of him. The commander fell to his hands and knees, shaking in fear and struggled mightily to get up.

"*Bring him!*" commanded Rhaka to some others. "Set him on his feet here!"

But the man could not stand; he was trembling and crying like an old woman. The soldiers held him up as Rhaka said in a soft voice, "Now, now, why do you fear? If you do well, will you not hold your head up?"

He bent down and looked into the man's face, but his eyes were squeezed shut as he stammered hysterically. Suddenly, Rhaka grabbed him by the throat and demanded, "You will look upon me!"

The man forced his eyes open as though he were trying to look at the sun and Rhaka let him down. "Now, isn't that better?" he asked in a soothing tone. The man nodded frantically as the tears streamed down his face.

"But why all this fighting?" asked Rhaka as though he spoke to a child, "The camp burns . . . and all these dead . . . this is how you would command my great army?"

Rhaka heaved a dramatic sigh and stepped into his pavilion and came out with an armored glove in his hand. When the commander saw it, he froze as his breath left him.

Suddenly, he went stiff and clutched at his chest, screeching in mortal agony, and he died where he stood, falling flat on his back.

Rhaka shook his head, muttering to himself, and waved his hand commanding the soldiers to carry the man away. He then turned toward the old woman, and as he did, his eyes fell upon Makarios, who stood with her. He momentarily froze in disbelief as he remembered throwing her lifeless body out of the citadel.

He quickly composed himself and commanded them to come to him. Both of them struggled in great fear, unsteadily holding onto each other, but Makarios seemed to hear a voice saying, "Remember what you *know,*" and strength came upon her.

She held her mother up as they stopped in front of Rhaka who looked directly at her and said in disbelief, "You . . ."

"That is right!" exclaimed Makarios for all to hear. "You killed me, but now by the Tsadaq, I live!"

At the sound of the name, Rhaka quaked in fury, but then calmly closed his eyes and took a deep breath to speak, but Makarios cried out, "No! You will not hide the truth!"

His eyes flew open, but he again calmed himself and bent toward her. "And what truth is it," he said with a sneer, "that you accuse me of trying to hide, my dear?"

She looked at Polus and Onos and continued, "They saw me dead; they know it! And that one there," she said, pointing at Marshal Sigao, "he knows it too!"

"Ah," said Rhaka sweetly, "Does he now?" Sigao immediately came trembling and falling down before him, but Rhaka was disgusted and kicked him, commanding him to get up.

"Now tell me," began Rhaka softly, "you don't believe this silly story, that she was dead and is now alive, do you?"

Sigao shook his head furiously as Rhaka turned to Makarios and said, "There, you see? And now you will wait your turn to pay for your lie."

He looked at Minnith who stood as straight as she could and fixed her gaze on him. She was shaking in fear but said firmly, "No . . . you will pay."

Rhaka blinked in surprise and then laughed at her scornfully, looking down upon her with murderous contempt. He pulled his glove on as his soldiers surrounded them as a solid wall with their spears pointed out.

Rhaka stepped toward Minnith, but she suddenly turned her back to him.

He stopped short and roared, "*You will look upon me!*"

All felt a terror come over them from the dread of Rhaka's presence as he bellowed at Minnith, "*You will turn to me!*" When she didn't move, Rhaka added, "Or this one dies right now!"

He grabbed Makarios and drew her to his face, fiercely whispering, "And this time I will cut you in *pieces*!"

He flung her to the ground, stunning her, and Minnith spun around and cried out, lunging at Rhaka, landing a blow on his chest. He laughed loudly and caught her as she stumbled, setting her upright.

He then dramatically knelt on one knee and said, "Now my dear little maw-maw—"

But she was furious and looked him squarely in the eyes and said angrily, "You will surely die for this unless the Tsadaq is merciful and you entreat his forgiveness for the intent of your heart!"

She wrenched herself away and suddenly struck him across the face, falling backward.

Nikos caught her as Rhaka exploded to his feet in a rage that sent a new shockwave of terror and dismay across the land. He screamed out in a fury of incomprehensible words until his eyes fell upon Minnith again. He stood heaving and clenching his hands and then suddenly leaped forward, descending upon her with his gloved hand raised high.

Immediately everything seemed to come alive again as Polus and Teras rushed forward trying to get through the soldiers. Moosar and his people attacked them, and many of the townsfolk began launching arrows into the army. At the same time, the Kahee-Nawb flew up into the air, and as Rhaka's gloved hand was coming down on the old woman, Nikos jumped forward, blocking Rhaka's blow.

He crashed to the ground as Nikos drew back uninjured and in stunned amazement. Everything suddenly came to a stop as every eye looked at Nikos, and wonder and astonishment gripped them all.

Rhaka slowly got to his feet and seemed in a daze, but as he focused on Nikos, his eyes sharpened, and his expression twisted into a ghastly wickedness. He breathed in deeply and let out a beastly roar and then stood heaving and clenching his hands once again. His whole body quaked in fury, but Nikos stood firm and with all his might said, "Be saved from this curse! It will doom you to—"

Rhaka threw his head back and laughed maniacally. "You *fool*!" he screamed. "*You* are the cursed one, because I decree that *you* are doomed and will indeed die this day!"

He shook his head in disgust and gestured at Nikos's bow, "Look at you! You come at me with sticks? And you think me a mere man that you challenge me?!"

There was silence as all seemed to hold their breath, still bound under the dread of Rhaka. He took off his armored glove and commanded, "Bring me a sword!"

Nikos gathered all his strength and called out, "I will not fight you!"

Rhaka threw his hands up in disgust and laughed incredulously. His whole demeanor lightened, and he walked up to Nikos and dropped the sword point down in the sand. He leaned close to Nikos's face and said seething, "As if you *could* contend with me, you *worm*!" His anger began to mount again as he turned back toward the pavilion.

"You are defeated already," said Nikos, "if you do not seek the King!"

Rhaka instantly became enraged and screamed, "*Enough!*"

He spun around and was about to rush at Nikos when his mind suddenly filled with an image of how he had already been struck to the ground. Then a sickly, sweet smile spread across his face, and he came slowly to Nikos, who had begun trembling in fear.

"Oh, my dear boy," said Rhaka bending toward him, "do you now understand who the master is?"

"I . . . I wish for you not to die and go to—"

"*Die*?! I cannot die!" exclaimed Rhaka, throwing his head back and roaring with laughter. But just as suddenly, he snapped forward with murderous black eyes fixed on Nikos and said, "I am done with this game!"

For a moment, Nikos saw fear in Rhaka's eyes and exclaimed, "Do not turn away from the calling of the King!"

But Rhaka ignored him and called out to the Kahee-Nawb, "Come, my majestic one! Your claws have been in him once, now they will finish him!"

The Nawb screeched with delight and rose up into the air, with all eyes on it as many screamed and fled or fell face down in terror. Nikos felt weak and could hardly even think as he took up the sword that stood in the sand next to him. The Nawb wheeled high up into the sky and screamed straight toward him.

As the beast was nearly upon him, things went into slow motion, and Nikos spun out of the way and swung the sword, gashing the Nawb's wing. It viciously squealed in pain and rose up, quickly turning back, but it faltered and as it swooped down, Nikos swung again, slashing open its underbelly. It screeched and crashed, rolling across the sand as Nikos rushed to it, jumping up onto its heaving torso.

The beast twisted to face him and scrambled to regain its footing, but Nikos cried out, "You shall never rise again!" and drove his sword in up to the hilt, piercing its heart.

At the same moment, Rhaka screamed and came toward them in a fury, dropping to his knees at the Nawb's head. "No! No! No!" he cried and held its face near to his own as tears flowed.

Blood soaked the sand as the Nawb feebly gurgled, "Mas-ss-ter . . ." It reached up to him but then convulsed and went limp. Time seemed to stand still as Rhaka knelt with his head bowed in disbelief.

Eventually, he got to his feet and pulled the sword out of the Kahee-Nawb and then breathed in deeply before he turned around. He stood woodenly but then threw his head back and his arms out, screaming like a beast. A great surge of energy went forth from him that knocked many off their feet, causing some to cry out in pain. He seethed in a rage and came slowly toward Nikos, who was barely able to stand.

"*You!*" yelled Rhaka, pointing at him. "How will you atone for this?" He threw the sword at Nikos's feet and stood breathing heavily with clenched fists. Again, he screamed furiously, "There is *no* recompense! But *you will pay!*"

He took a sword from one of the soldiers and faced Nikos. An overwhelming fear rooted everyone where they stood, but Nikos said, "I will not fight you!"

Makarios suddenly was filled with courage and called out, "We only wish for you to be saved from the curse!"

Rhaka's eyes jerked toward her and then back to Nikos, "Ah," he said in a very calm tone. "Ah yes, of course, you would waste your own life, fool! But surely you will fight for this fine wench, hmm?"

"Nikos, no!" she called.

But Rhaka continued, "Or maybe you will redeem the old woman there. She owes her life to me."

Someone in the midst of the townsfolk called out, "She owes you *nothing!*"

Rhaka turned sharply, "Who dares speak! Bring them to me!"

His soldiers pushed through the crowd, but the man willingly ran out into the open right up to Rhaka, stumbling in terror. He cried out with all his strength, "And *you* are nothing! You must believe the Tsadaq —"

But Rhaka grabbed him by the throat and lifted him off his feet. The man gasped and managed to say, "You will kill me, but after that there is no more you can do—"

Rhaka suddenly thought back to when Makarios had said the same thing before he had killed her. Doubts filled his mind, and he wavered, feeling at odds with himself.

A storm of emotions erupted into fear, "If he should rise up, I would look the fool," he said to himself, but immediately an icy, deadly voice in his mind screeched, "*Kill him!*"

Rhaka hesitated and then felt bony hands closing around his heart and again, the wicked voice screamed, "*Kill!*" As the hands tightened their grip, Rhaka's eyes flew open in desperation, and he twisted the man's neck with such wrenching force that he died instantly.

Rhaka gasped for air and collapsed to his knees, clutching at his chest. The hands loosened their grip, and Rhaka breathed deeply. When he looked up, all the people were leaning in at him, staring. He felt overwhelmingly humiliated but met it with a fury greater than he had ever known. His eyes fell upon the man whom he had killed, and he jumped up, hacking him to pieces with his sword. He shook his head and cried out in triumphant victory. When he saw the carcass of the Kahee-Nawb, a demoralizing sadness struck him, and he spun around, glaring at Nikos, his eyes filled with inhuman wrath. Rhaka rushed at Nikos screaming incomprehensible words and leaped into the air, swinging the sword with both hands.

Nikos jumped forward and ducked just under the sword as Rhaka went over him and crashed to the ground. He was in such a frenzy that he was on his feet instantly.

Nikos felt everything in slow motion and had no fear as he called out, "I will not fight you!"

Rhaka was like an animal and howled as he came at Nikos in a fury. He avoided Rhaka's sword, and barreled into him with such power, that he launched him backward, and Rhaka crashed into the pavilion, bringing it down in a tangled mess. All the people exclaimed in amazement and stood breathless, looking at Nikos in wonder.

Suddenly, a crashing commotion began in the wrecked pavilion, and Rhaka came forth in a rage. The people were shocked, as he bellowed out his anger and annoyance, "You *dare* to challenge—"

But someone laughed, and then a few others snickered. Rhaka stomped forward and screamed, "You will all *bow!*" But he drew back when he suddenly didn't recognize his own voice. It was higher pitched, sounding more like an old woman.

The people pressed forward, and Rhaka quickly looked around at them all. Someone asked, "What happened to him?"

Another said, "He is *nothing!*"

Rhaka felt a cold fear and trembled violently, even afraid to speak. He looked at his hands and arms and then toward Nikos, who was now taller than he.

"Your authority has been removed from you," said Nikos, hardly realizing that he was speaking.

Rhaka blinked in surprise and mumbled, "No . . . no . . ." He grimaced as he felt unbearably weak and looked around helplessly, screeching, "*No!*"

He felt in himself an ordinariness that shocked him, and the eyes of all peering at him seemed to bore through to his soul. The people pressed even closer as Makarios suddenly came forward and began to speak to him, but he shied away.

"No! No!" he cried and could bear no more. He grabbed up his armored glove, which was now far too large, and with difficulty got aboard a horse and galloped madly off to the north, screaming in fear and fury.

A tension seemed to break, and all the people of the land came together, seeing Rhaka's army as the enemy. The soldiers drew back and scrambled together, forming a line.

Nikos ran between them. "No!" he cried. "The enemy is gone!"

Moosar and his people ranked up, but stayed back as the young man, Esek, rode out and yelled toward Rhaka's forces.

"You will leave our land!" There was much indecision among the soldiers, and a tense standoff began as Esek added, "You have no claim here!"

Suddenly, the gate of Zabach was opened, and it seemed that the whole city assembled, and they poured out, roaring with one voice. They rushed across the plain, coming at the soldiers from the side, who instinctively turned toward them to fight. Esek and all the people with him let out a thunderous shout and attacked from behind.

With their fear gone, the people's anger erupted in a fury that overwhelmed Rhaka's army. They were driven northward, and though the soldiers were fleeing for their lives, the people kept chasing them. They went over the ridge in the land and drove them toward the desert. The people who remained, older folk, young women with their children, and some older boys gathered close around Nikos in awe.

"How did you do that?!" asked one as others shook their heads in amazement.

"You have saved us!" called a young woman.

Another said, "This is the one!" A murmur and more exclamations rippled throughout the crowd until they began chanting something. Nikos was dumbfounded as Chayel and Makarios came to him.

"What are they saying?" he asked anxiously.

"It is a myth from their folklore," said Chayel. "They think that you are the Great Shepherd who, it is said, will lead them to a land of rivers and streams."

Makarios added, "The legend says that a powerful man, not born of them, would first defeat a mighty and evil enemy who had oppressed them."

The people were joyous and began to dance around Nikos even ignoring Polus and Teras as they came through.

Suddenly, Moosar rode out into the center, waving his hand and yelling, "You fools! This one is an ordinary man! He cannot be this Shepherd that you uselessly believe in!"

They stopped chanting, with many getting angry and disagreeing, while others stood still and looked sad. They began to argue back and forth until Moosar shouted, "*But . . .!*" and held his arm up, pointing his finger to the sky.

A hush fell on the crowd as he continued, "But what he did to that tyrant *is* beyond any man—" The people again looked at Nikos in wonder and came closer, some even kneeling.

"No!" called Moosar and wheeled his horse around scattering the people. "It was the power of the Tsadaq! This Great One that he believes in!"

The people quickly erupted in a rage and suddenly eyed Nikos with contempt. Someone yelled, "He is one of *them*!"

Others called out threats; Moosar signaled his people, who quickly surrounded Nikos and the others. The people were yelling, tossing sand into the air and throwing rocks at them as Moosar moved them away through the crowd. The people trailed along after them, but when Nikos, Moosar, and the rest went back into the old castle, their anger quickly cooled.

Chayel was angry and said, "The people believe in nothing!"

"Or everything," added Makarios.

"Indeed," said Moosar. "They are so weak and changeable."

"Why then did you risk your lives for them?" asked Teras incredulously. "They deserve nothing!"

"In their welfare, my people have welfare," replied Moosar. "Though we live far up in the mountains, we come down to trade with the people in Maqom and Omed—it would not do for us if a tyrant should rule these lands."

Chayel said, "You claimed the power of the Tsadaq over what happened to Rhaka. Do you now believe?"

"It is hard not to," said Moosar thoughtfully. "But I cannot say that I do . . ." He said to them all, "You are most welcome in my homeland if ever you should come there. We are south around the great spur of the mountain near Omed."

He led his people out the gate and thundered away to the east. At that moment, the old man, Isram, rushed up and asked for Chayel, but when he saw Nikos, he exclaimed, "You! I must talk to you!"

He came in and asked earnestly, "Tell me, how did you withstand that Rhaka? How did you make him helpless?"

Nikos was still shaken, but said, "The Great One—"

"No!" exclaimed Isram, "You! What is this power you have?"

"It is the Tsada—"

"No!" he said getting exasperated, "*You* did this thing—"

Chayel cut in, "None of us can do anything; it is the Tsadaq! He accomplishes all things for us!"

But Isram scowled and shook his head and said heatedly, "I saw *him* do this thing!"

He turned back to Nikos and fairly yelled, "Tell me how!"

But Nikos said, "You must believe—"

Isram flung up his hands yelling, "In what?! These fairy tales?!"

"You have seen the truth for yourself!" said Chayel, but Isram ignored her.

He said to Nikos in a much calmer voice, "I am a rich man . . . this power you have . . ."

He nodded, and Nikos said, "I possess nothing—"

Isram suddenly became enraged and reached for Nikos, but Teras quickly came between them, and Chayel cried out, "You *fool!* The gifts of the Tsadaq cannot be bought with silver or gold!"

Isram relented and stepped back. "You are the fools," he said sullenly. "Imagine what could be done with this power, but you will not!" He shook his head and walked out of the gate roughly pushing his way through the crowd who had gathered.

As Chayel attempted to close the gate, some of the people called out, "Wait! We believe! Tell us, what must we do!"

They pressed forward, but others mocked them and tried to pull them away.

"Stop this!" cried Makarios. "Are they not free to choose to as they wish?"

Teras quickly went out and bellowed, "You will allow them their freedom!"

Polus also came, and many of the other Megans with him so that those who were sneering backed away.

But some kept calling out, "Lies!" or "Now he will rule us with this strange power!"

In the midst of this, Esek and all the men who had gone after Rhaka's army were coming across the plain in great triumph. All the people suddenly ran to meet them, even those who had said that they believed, and there was much rejoicing, and quite a procession passed by the castle. The people were now proclaiming Esek to be the Great Shepherd. They went some distance east, drawing more and more people until all had joined the throng. Esek led them back toward Zabach, and the whole city came out to greet them and erupted with thunderous approval. They entered the city, and the gates closed after them.

"How can it be that *no one* believed in what they saw?" said Chayel angrily. "The Kahee-Nawb killed? Rhaka defeated? Only the Tsadaq could have done those things, and yet this Esek is their hero! He doesn't even fulfill the prophecy of the legend."

Suddenly, Minnith swooned and fell, but Teras caught her as Makarios rushed over.

"What is it?!" she cried.

"I am so tired," answered Minnith, "and thirsty . . ."

"Yes, yes!" replied Makarios. "Quickly!"

Chayel brought some water and after some time, Minnith had revived a bit.

"Let us go up to the House," said Makarios.

"I will carry you," said Teras. "It is too much for you to walk." But Minnith resisted, insisting on walking herself. They went out of the castle and headed toward the House and were soon joined by a crowd of people coming from Zabach, led by Makarios's uncle Yasad.

"We thank you," he said to Nikos and Ruad, "and to all of you who set us free from Rhaka's men. We saw his defeat and when he went past the city gate, we could hardly believe it was the same man." They continued on and were met by many coming down from the House, rejoicing and welcoming them. As they started up the road, Minnith faltered, and Teras, who had walked close beside her, swept her up.

"Now, I will carry you," he said with a wide smile as she finally and gladly accepted.

It was late afternoon when they went into the Great Hall, and many began preparing a feast. But amidst this, Chayel drew to the side, followed by Nikos and Makarios.

"Kafar, Barah, and Arak deserve this," she said sadly as they stood somberly by, and then added, "but I know that they have received their reward in full." A tear rolled down as Makarios took her hand.

"Come," she said, "they are rejoicing in the presence of the King, so let us!" They joined the throng as the feasting began. Evening fell, lamps were lit, and soon mead was served, and minstrels began a new song. Many began dancing, but Chayel went out into the moonlight and walked across the courtyard looking up at the moon and into the sky. She came to the pool and sat down on the low wall that surrounded it and stared at the water, as still as a mirror. Suddenly, an image appeared, and she started back, but then peered more closely.

"Tey-Rahk?"

She turned around as he said, "Yes, it is I." He stood, as tall and majestic as ever. Chayel jumped up, and he received her as she threw her arms around him, burying herself in his mane.

"Oh, Tey-Rahk!" she cried and held on for quite a few moments as he clasped her with much affection.

"You said that we would see each other again," she continued, "when this was all over. Is it—"

He released her and stood back, saying, "My dear one, for your part, for this time—yes, it is over." He sat down, drawing his tail around his paws as she looked into his crystal blue eyes.

"I am so glad to see you," she said. "It is a sad and glad time . . ." She looked into the pool again and put in a finger, causing a ripple to spread across it.

"All we did . . . it cost so much," she said. And as the water became still again, she added, "But now, peace . . ."

Tey-Rahk stood and looked into the pool with her as she leaned against him. "You have all done well, but you must tell the people to beware of this young Esek. He has foolishly claimed the victory and the glory for himself, though it was a host of the Elyone who drove your enemy far into the desert."

Chayel pondered for a few moments and then said, "Yes, he should not accept the acclaim as the Great Shepherd that the people—"

But Tey-Rahk lashed his tail and rumbled within, "You must warn him to turn from this path he is on, or his life is forfeit."

Chayel only nodded as Tey-Rahk took a deep breath and looked up to the House. He then stood and leaned his great furry head down next to Chayel. "Nikos will go back north," he said softly. "You must let him go."

She quickly stood up and turned toward Tey-Rahk but found no words. After some moments, tears welled up, and she looked down at the ground, seeing Tey-Rahk's huge white paws upon the flagstones.

"I will," she whispered and then came a flood of tears as Tey-Rahk drew her to himself. She cried as she never had, feeling so much all she had been through with Nikos, Makarios, and the others and lamenting the loss of Kafar, Barah, and Arak. After quite some time, she stepped back, wiped her eyes dry and took a deep breath, looking up at Tey-Rahk. "I know that you will go now," she said.

He added, "But I will see you again." He went a few paces and then with a powerful leap, swept up into the air and disappeared into the night sky.

About the Author

Charlene Ralph is a born-again Christian, artist, and author, with a talent for drawing and writing. Her greatest passion is Jesus Christ, to love him, know him, obey him, proclaim him, and be more like him. "He is the driving force in my life and the heartbeat of all that I do," proclaims Ralph. Raised in Rochester, New York, in a Christian home with an older brother and twin sister, author Charlene Ralph was married at twenty-three, moved west to a small town and gave birth to her daughter at twenty-six. She serves in the band at her church, Journey Christian, playing bass, lead electric or acoustic rhythm guitar.

www.ingramcontent.com/pod-product-compliance
Lightning Source LLC
Chambersburg PA
CBHW050120030726
47505CB00007B/1961